ALIUM

GRADY LYNCH

Milton, Ontario

Brain Lag
Milton, Ontario
http://www.brain-lag.com/

Cover artwork "Among the Sierra Nevada Mountains" by Albert Bierstadt, 1868

Title page illustration © Elizabeth Lowry

Library and Archives Canada Cataloguing in Publication

Title: Alium / Grady Lynch.
Names: Lynch, Grady, author.
Identifiers: Canadiana (print) 20220243468 | Canadiana (ebook) 20220243506 | ISBN 9781928011798
(softcover) | ISBN 9781928011804 (ebook)
Classification: LCC PS3612.Y535 A75 2022 | DDC 813/.6—dc23

Content warning: Violence

For Liz. With special thanks to Catherine, Dillon, Will, Mom and Dad, Joe, Andrew, and Jason.

CHAPTER I
TO DREAM

The poison sea billowed in a great fabric. Winds out-shook the waves as bedclothes, unfolding while they fell. Low through their collapsing lace swept gulls like shining needles, drawing the robes of the world together on gossamer threads departing. Yet even stitches so fine burst as they were sewn, new shapes swelling in relief against an always different tapestry of ocean.

Only meters below the surface, but for a distant rumble, the dimensionless vault of open water was a vast cosmos of ageless silence. So gradual were the transitions between its many colours that the eye moving deeper could not know where one gave to another. Rich purple layered with magenta filtered into turquoise, now indigo chasms opening on solid navy firmament. Here there was little light or motion at all, yet still more nameless shades mingled into featureless abyss.

Save the dark green pillars of seaweed, life was scarce and subtle in the deep. But here, all alone, was a dweller not so native, and easily spotted. Just above those titanic listing stalks this curious object drifted out of place. It was no rocky fish, nor even a great sunken log, though it looked as much. Here was a young ogre called Ogwold, far from his home on the shore.

Long roots of hair wreathed his rocky shoulders in knotted black. Grey skin reflected the remote light no brighter than along the chiselled hook of his nose. Yet upon the stone slabs of his eyelids played only darkness. They were shut, black overhung caves in a craggy brow. Ogwold was lost in that activity which brought him the greatest joy in life, an emergent property of these deep waters, far from the land, his people, his work. He was dreaming.

Or so he had been. Groaning doors of rock lifted; pale grey eyes flickered out into the open. Balling up, now stretching his bony toes, the ogre flung back his head, twisted his bulky trunk, and wrung the sleep from his cracking bones—a stone statue crumbling to life. Even in this stiff state, his movements through the water were true and natural. He was unnaturally quick and slender for his kind. Flat feet locked together, powerful legs whipped the water in terrific bursts. Apish arms streamlined, blocky shoulders tight to his ears, three thunderous kicks might bear him any distance. On such inertia he soared, rotating slowly, reflecting on his reverie.

Ogwold loved dreams as much for their going as their coming. He found the empty spaces between waves beautiful as their cresting boundaries, and loved the sea dearly for this reason. It seemed here that all things drifted through the bottomless deep like schools of fish shimmering against a changeless, infinite substrate. This medium—to him—was consciousness, equal in beauty with any thought, however grand, to emerge thereof and carry out its life.

He was quite alone, however, in his affection. His people, the Nogofod, despised the sea in every way: its turbulent voice, corrosive touch, the purple-sick taint of the sluggish, humped surf-fingers ever groping the beach, sucking steaming insectoid corpses from beneath the sand. Many were the terrifying tales of that ocean. Shunned were those said to linger near to it; awful disfigurement would plague their offspring. Whatever the stories said, this ogre had not suffered the slightest impairment.

When he was little, Ogwold had leaned curiously from the edge of an ancient stone dock. Insatiable even atop this feature—jutting far out into the slurping water—his knees slipped, and hands out-flung to break the fall met no resistance. The sudden silence which enveloped him beneath the surface became his fondest memory. His father Ogdof lumbering, then rushing from the deck of a docked ship had pulled him desperately out of the water. But his son was unchanged, grinning rather with the welcoming touch of the sea, the plunge into something grander, while his rescuer's arms smoked and blistered.

Returning in the secrecy of dusk—lowering his huge face into the surf— Ogwold found no difficulty breathing underwater. Rather than dissolve, his stony jowls trembled with new vigour. His big heart swelling with the undertow pulled him into the cool waves diving. Lanky arms parted and drew back the water naturally for the first time. Legs bound together kicked as in a tail effortlessly realized. Gravity was lost with the known world. Somewhere in his rocky spine nameless cores long unnoticed began to stir. Ogwold was at peace.

Each day, when the last galleon had been loaded, when the traders had departed in their cracked wagons back up into the heavy-shouldered hills, when the last ogres, hunched with sweat, gathered to smoke their pipes in musty salt-rotted cabins, Ogwold lurched stealthily down the bare shore by a secret inlet, far from the village. He would walk out slowly into those purple folds which clothed him not in capture but embrace, drew him out into the swaddling open ocean when none could know to spiral over the kelp canopy and dream of places long hidden from such folk as the Nogofod.

Ogwold slowed gradually in his swimming. That time came, aestheticize as he might the beauty of absence, when he wished for inspiration. Letting his limbs drift apart, he lowered his gaze into the depths for some new cue. The stunning complexity of the kelp canopy always inspired his greatest visions. But lately he wondered if such reveries were merely the echoes of a secret more wonderful, obscured beneath the inmost forest.

If the sea were a great garment, the land was its wearer, and somewhere within must persist its vital organs. Ogwold had weaved dreams from such clothing many times, but never had he dared to seek flesh. Now, coasting on the world's swelling pulse, he envisioned a booming heart nestled in the ocean floor, ribbed in the leviathan kelp. There was no throb, though, or sound at all, or warmth, save the pumping in his ears. Still, there needn't be a real organ in the dark. All he desired was a possibility, a germ for the mind. With a kick he streamed down into the forest. Dark blue water filtered into black.

Upon the monolithic kelp stalks phantasmagoric slime moulds clung, ever morphing in hue and shape. In their sickly glow other creatures were revealed. Globular organisms squeezed the water between their many tentacles, floating slowly thereafter as in contemplation. Scuttling, translucent feather-dusters twirled in place. Tiny mushrooms dragged lazy tendrils through the black water, but they seemed agenda-bound, one snaring in its evil hairs a new creature—misshapen, bug-eyed, covered in whips—which seized horribly, shuddered, and was drawn into the undulating maw of its capturer.

In contrast to these motions flowed varicoloured streams of particles, wherein Ogwold discovered a greater majesty still. Tiny bioluminescent histories fizzled in furious prismatic currents, generations sparking and searing, now quiet and still, at once clamorous and vain. He felt in his mind a soft chattering, some ancient language spoken beyond the threshold of consciousness.

Ogwold wondered if even these relationships were a foreground to some greater mystery, the source of sea life itself. The sound even—or was a dream beginning—of an immense, thudding heart vibrated in his skull. To behold it, he dove further into growing darkness. The luminous slime moulds thinned with depth. Now only pale violet striations shed soft, grainy light, and with time even these strains faded. For a long while there was only black void, pure and empty. Endless were all directions. The young ogre could envision his own body only through each slow, forceful kick.

At last there appeared distant, bright points, like stars on a moonless night. Yet in their light, as he drew nearer, no abyssal world-heart was revealed. Instead, these star-points became the brilliant apices of colossal spires, the dizziest reaches of a many-towered, crystal city, swathed in a light all its own. Entwined were its many structures with shimmering, argent avenues, where a strange and silent people streamed about its emerald industry. They were like in countenance to the Novare men and women Ogwold knew well, the traders, the Lords and Ladies, the Knights, with flowing hair and noble features, that race which ruled over his kind—yet, they were different.

Long green, blue, opalescent manes rushed behind smooth bodies shining in cold-jewelled mail. Upon lambent skin, mingling with the sea-shadows, there gleamed in chance ripples coruscating layers of scales, some blue, others green, nacreous, violet. It seemed that each entity showed forth an underlying hue all its own. Most dazzling of all were the long, iridescent membranes spilling from their shoulders. They were like wings whose long, bony structures—spanned with voluminous chutes of webbing—worked the water as strong fins.

One gaunt woman of long jade hair landed, crouching in elegant gargoyle vigilance atop a lone steeple set apart. Great wings glorying in her wake, now shaken, drawn tight to the body, she turned her head up and away from the city, and looked to high-hovering Ogwold with radiant white eyes. But there was something else.

A subtle tremor connected the waters of dream and reality. The dazzling city foundered in a surging bright glare white as the woman's eyes, suddenly retreating into black. Darkness as behind closed eyelids swelled crushing and total. There was an unnatural silence in the sea. Perhaps it had wrinkled in the back of Ogwold's mind, turned overmuch upon the dream, but now an unmistakable shadow menaced upon his senses.

He opened his eyes slowly, turning upwards. Here was a true native of the abyss. High above in the distant slime-light of the kelp trunks, a great diamond head filtered out of the shadows, each of its dull scales a boulder. One sunken eye from the side of the skull plastered Ogwold in a sick, yellow desire. Attached was an endless serpent, thick as the immense trees around which wound each coil into unseeable shadow, and perhaps as long. Here in the darkest fathoms of the kelp were not magical cities but unknowable, ancient monstrosities. Feeling all too well understood, he thought even he could smell the exhaust of numberless dead carrying forth on the water, as if a storm of lost souls went with the serpent always.

It seemed suddenly that the forest and sea retreated beyond the creature. The yellow eye-globe vanished. All kelp between it and the ogre were blown asunder. High above, a patch of pure open ocean became visible, so rent aside were the sea plants up to the very canopy. Out of this strange, brief peace Ogwold in a frenzy kicked out his legs like stout whips to escape. Water and seaweed around him were consumed. Cavernous jaws—all but detectable in their massive breadth—closed upon his arm. Scaly lips froze his neck and ribs. There was an awful severance. Dark blood plumed.

Blinded and wracked with adrenaline, Ogwold completed the kicking motion and spiralled into the shadows of the kelp—now swaying massively back into position—while the beast, having ripped tearing away, now chewed, bones crunching mutedly through the water. The great vacant eye staring at nothing.

In the blood-choked darkness came the pain, like viscous molten metal even in the bone-chilling water, slugging through the veins. Each heartbeat stoked the fire. The sea narrowed into one suffocating black point as the bitter heat grew in searing reality. The raging river of blood gushing from his shoulder socket left behind arid channels in the soul, glaring visions of enormous white and sterile deserts, everything dry and dead. Dreams were impossible. There was only the uncompromising sterility of heat and death.

Then the faintest touch of cool water licked the ogre's undermind. Ogwold was beneath the sea, cradled in the bedclothes of that place where he was most free. A chorus of voices sang for valour and life, calling up from the silver towers, from the shining streets. These were unmistakably the spirits of the sea people far below. Were they dreamt or not? Was this monster, this wound as real? Ogwold would escape with his life regardless. A rage to persist bubbled and broke, a geyser in his heart flooding the oppressive deserts of death with new life.

He set his jaw, squatted against the broad trunk of the stalk to which he clung, black blood globing him, coursing away in webs, and erupted towards the shore—toes pointed, left hand pressed firmly over empty shoulder, lower body scourging the water. The swiftest silver fish were left in his wake as he built speed with enormous thrusts. Beginning in his stomach, rolling through the hips, thighs, whipping with loose ankles, his broad feet carried each dire impulse from the heart, catching and flinging the water like great stone paddles.

From the still, dark deeps below then came a sweet, bodiless voice: "Cease your animal swimming, and fly!"

At once Ogwold felt them. He was familiar with the notion of these secret cores, like joints that he could never quite crack. Now like ribs unclasping the lungs and heart, they unspooled from his vertebrae. Loose, elastic skin, at first slowly, sluggishly poured into the water, dazed then alerted. Great membranous chutes exploded from beneath his shoulder blades, catching the smooth current. Yet now the shocked organs breathed, meeting water as wings the sky. Exhausting their tremendous volumes they flattened into thin, tough fins, and Ogwold flew.

The shadow of the beast melded with the inky deeps between the kelp trees. Ogwold looked everywhere for the source of the voice, but he was alone, rushing through darkness. The fins extending from his spine worked it seemed of their own accord, and expertly. But when he willed that they strain harder still, their motions became more deep and grand, and his speed was increased. Nevertheless, his blood, winding through the forest, led the way. Even now the great serpent closed, its vast nostril-slits filled with the smoky liquid, the once sluggish eye now calm and alert as if woken from a long, tedious sleep.

The pain in Ogwold's shredded shoulder shrieked and groaned, his bones trembling. He was all but drowned in the noxious stench of death. Now came the horrible double-edge of an active imagination—or was it as real as his wing-fins, as the voice which called them forth, as silver cities—for he heard even the thousandfold wailing of souls damned to haunt the stinking maw which now yawned behind him.

Suddenly, his waist was encircled in gentleness unbreakable as it was graceful.

Green-blue tapestries unfurled above and angled like slicing blades, filled like mighty sails. Off he shot now by no thought of his own, and it seemed that the monster struggled to follow. Its retreating eye grew awesomely desperate for so small an object of prey. Ogwold's fledgling fins retracted sleepily into the spine once more, capped with bone as the pain consumed him. The wound was too much, the loss of blood too great, and dry darkness—visions of expansive nighted deserts rising from beneath the sea—choked his throat and eyes.

The last he saw was a high blue cheek, long green hair, one brilliant white eye trained on the horizon, and lips, moving it seemed, communicating some secret knowledge, he felt, drifting off, of great importance.

Ogwold awoke beached under the early evening sky. Deep pain hollowed his shoulder, but no blood muddied the surf sucking at his back. Groaning and rolling like a boulder onto his side, he reluctantly inspected the limbless stump which was his right shoulder. The mangled mound was bound tightly in what appeared to be seaweed. Just seeing this makeshift bandage, the pain dulled, and he was able to sit up and inspect it more closely.

The sheen of it was strangely iridescent, and it was far too solid—he noticed, rapping upon the plant-matter with his big knuckles—to be a gauze of kelp. Now he saw, gawking, that strong, gnarled roots wrapped around his shoulder and neck, holding the bandage firmly in place. Following these his hand discovered where thick cords split into countless veins and plunged deep into the flesh of his back and ribs. There they pulsed, tugged, gulped as in feeding. It was impossible to know how far into the body they wormed.

But this powerful digging, this metal-hard, grasping foreign vegetation so tenaciously invasive did not weaken him at all. Rather, bone-deep, it lifted and supported him. With every powerful squeeze the plant imbued only greater vigour into its host. Ogwold might have stood right up were it not that the swelling and pumping of the thing suddenly reminded him of the storm of blood having escaped him in the first place. The thought so deathlike made him dizzy and hot; slab-like he thumped back onto the cold sand.

Once before he had seen a Nogofod man's leg hacked away in many sloppy axe-strokes. Such were the favoured punishments of Lucetalian knights wasting away on this desolate shore: disabling those whose livelihoods depend upon the integrity of their bodies. The blood, which had burbled and flowed dark and viscous at first, suddenly gushed—when the thigh-bone at last split—in bright liquid torrents. The ogre died before Gurgof could cauterize the wound, let alone bandage it.

Ogwold's stomach felt unnaturally airy at the memory. But more troubling was the notion that, even had the poor ogre survived, he would not have found work. Ogwold still had his legs, but a one-armed Nogofod would scarce find the trust of a trader. To be a greater burden on his father, first as a blaspheming sealover, and now a cripple, a lowly dufwod, as the Nogofod call the useless, weighed most heavily of all.

The cold, ripping wind drank the seawater from his skin. He sat up once more on his left arm and, turning his head from the shore, looked over the rocky foothills, rising in the distance as they interlaced and built their bulks up into the full features of the Mardes, the mighty mountain range ensconcing the beach and stony desert. So far as Ogwold knew, it went on forever. Higher still, above the dizziest peaks, he beheld the tallest mountain of all, which rose sharp and featureless, encircled, then vanishing in an immortal canopy of gloom.

It was Zenidow, the Place Without Peak. Nowhere in the vapour always surrounding it could the eye detect some termination of its height. Altogether different from the other mountains, it shone always, even upon a moonless night, an immense argent gemstone fitted into the crust of the world, as if some great chunk of heavenly citadel had fallen to the realm of mortals, making everything around it seem all the less glorious. The setting sun sweltered beyond, a bloody hemisphere partly eclipsed by the great mountain, its corona spraying fiery filigree. Ogwold sat long watching the light recede, streams of flame slowly thinning into dusk.

Behind him, over the sea, the first moons began to show their different faces. Tonight it was Somnam and Vitalem that appeared. The first was Ogwold's personal favourite, for it was known as the Vault of Dreams. It was just beginning to wane in its phase, but he could only tell as it was early in the evening, and a fading touch of sun still painted the firmament. Enormous and gibbous as it was, the dim navy complexion of Somnam would soon be nearly indistinguishable from the full darkness of night. Vitalem was the Heart of Growth, jonquil lord over that which is becoming. Far smaller and blindingly bright in transit across the vast, dull face of the other, it was an orb of pure yellow light.

Rising, Ogwold tracked down and donned his rough, aged tunic, striding reluctantly homeward now along the surf, sea foam sloshing between his toes. Dragging his huge feet through the springy sand, he thought less of dreams and magic. Deep water was the place for such things. Now the cold air of his Nogofod truth stripped away all moisture. Every loafing step towards his village was a step towards dry reason and law. Thoughts of luck and survival were supplanted with uncompromising shame. He had thrown away his precious fitness in a place long forbidden. Now he would not be able to work. His father would take on extra loads. The other Nogofod would sigh like sliding gravel and shake their great manes resignedly.

As images of disapproving elders orbited Ogwold trudging, far along the rocky sand up-rose the leaning shacks of Epherem. The Nogofod settlement studded the beach along and away from the water beside a row of ancient stone docks. Three tall galleons from Lucetal—the royal city across the sea—rocked in the slapping tide. In the morning, the traders from Occultash would arrive with their bursting carts, and the ogres would begin their long-designated task, loading everything aboard.

In the beginning, the Nogofod were something like the Novare. Tens of thousands of years under the yoke of Lucetal had made them culturally subservient. Due to the physical nature of their work and the radiation of the omnipresent, mutant sea, their figures had become hulking and grey, their arms long ropes of muscle, their hair invariably black and impossible to maintain, and their legs far too stout to be called Novare. Eternally hunched, these immense, benign shapes roamed the shore with jarring footfalls, the smallest adult five times the mass of the largest Novare man. Those knights of Lucetal who kept them from leaving the coast had grown to loathe their image, calling them ogres. None knew whether the class or vocation came first.

On the outskirts of Epherem was Ogdof's cabin, Ogwold's home, constructed of dark tutum logs, with an angled, thatched roof, a cracked, stone chimney, and one arched window enshrining the sea. Even thirty strides from the place, Ogwold could smell the potent fumes of the normgrass, Lucetal's gift to ogres. Embedded long ago in the rocky ground, the hardy, invasive weed grew now in shaggy profusion all down the coast. Most densely it choked the tutum groves, yet some tough though less potent strains survived even in the hilly upland, and it was said that the norm had adapted to and populated even the northern deserts.

Dark green, hung with sap, norm stank powerfully of the sea. While the Nogofod had among them a great love for this dank stench, only Ogwold's nose could perceive that the taint of the purple water was its chief ingredient. He imagined that all the gnarled tufts and dense patches twined their roots beneath the crust, and in a bundled nerve led to the ocean, the source of their power over the mind. It was this dream more than any which had tempted him to smoke in the past. But even if Nogofod minds could be changed, he would not spoil the tranquility of his kind. If the sea was most hated by ogres, norm was most loved.

For his many idiosyncrasies, Ogwold's father was a typical ogre when it came to the norm. He smoked always after the day's work in traditional Nogofod fashion. Milky tongues of stinking vapour eked from beneath the cabin-door, crawling curiously about its frame. Pulling open the salt-rotted wooden plane, Ogwold quickened them into a white cloud.

"Dad," he said, stepping through the veil of smoke, rocky shoulder replaced by hanging head, preparing for the worst. "I've lost an arm." He turned, saying this, to reveal the bandaged wound.

Ogdof was seated by the hearth with a long wooden pipe, carefully carved and seasoned over many years. He was large even for his kind, with dark-grey skin and the long, sharp nose of his son. A jet black, knotted beard spilled into his lap, though his great, scarred head was completely bald. Ogdof was normally one whose heavy eyelids masked all emotion, but they rose right up at the sight of Ogwold's bandage, metallic irises catching the firelight, and a half-eaten tutum skin fell softly from his free hand, brushing the wooden floor dryly.

Ogwold stood in the door silently. He might have looked brooding if the wind didn't blow the hair out of his anxious eyes. His father rose, lumbered over and hugged him tightly. At last he stepped away, shaggy arms folded, inscrutable woolly eyebrows bearing down. "You were in the water."

"Yes, but..." Ogwold struggled to look forward, ground his teeth. "I was attacked! By a monster that could have swallowed a Euphran!"

The old furrows in Ogdof's face darkened to their full depth. "The water has eroded your flesh and bone. You might have lost your life." He sighed, turning to the window.

"About the threat to my life you're not wrong," said Ogwold, recalling the serpent's awful yellow eye. "But I promise this was not the work of water itself. I was very far out, and deeper than I've ever been. The creature came upon me out of ancient waters." His left hand found and gripped the shoulder-stump as he spoke, as if seeking comfort there. "It was an awesome thing really... Dad, there are many creatures which call that place their home. Like me, they prosper in the water... Just as there are—as you say—monsters in the desert and the high mountains, I should have known that the ocean has its predators."

Ogdof had returned to his seat, and now took up his pipe. Though his eyes were still shaded, it seemed by the tilt of his great head that he weighed his son's words carefully. "You seem hearty for one to suffer such a tale. And there is no blood anywhere I can see." He sipped on the piece for a moment, and white smoke curled from his nostrils. "What is this bandage? I've never seen Gurgof use such material."

Ogwold winced. If speaking about sea monsters was strange, he now risked seeming completely mad. Loosening his grip upon the shoulder-dressing, he engendered his breath to come evenly. "I woke up on the beach with my wound already bound," he began. "I wouldn't have escaped but for the help of another. There was a woman in the water. She saved me." Ogwold pulled his tunic back, revealing the pulsing roots that dug into his flesh. For the insanity of his son's words, and the alien nature of the bandage, Ogdof seemed strangely aloof. Though the other was partly relieved by this, for inexplicable things were adamantly shunned in Epherem, he sensed that something was deeply amiss with his father. "I doubt we'd have an easy time removing it," he laughed, trailing off.

But Ogdof's silence continued. His weighty eyelids closed in thought, disclosing nothing. White tendrils of smoke coiled about his arms, snaking along the floor as he rocked, listening to the crashing waves. He looked out through the window over the dark sea beneath the twilit sky blossoming with white flowers. Noting the fullness of bright Vitalem in the growing darkness, he thought of a time before Ogwold had come into the world, when these old boards were younger and stronger, when this chair didn't creak so much. He had built the immense seat himself, and it was a fine thing. It was a modest, one-room home that they lived in, with two ancient, yellowed pads along the far wall for sleeping, an expertly crafted table and set of chairs, also his own work, and a wide crate laden with dried tutum fruit. Long before Ogwold was born had the old ogre lived here by the sea.

"I am sorry for going to the water," Ogwold broke the silence. "The call of it is ceaseless. When I am there... everything makes sense. But I wish no shame on us. I won't go back. I'll work hard." He balled up his left fist like a lumpy stone. "I can still help the traders with this arm; it's the stronger anyways."

Ogdof at last set his coveted pipe aside, folded his hands. The deep furrows in his forehead, and about his oft-tightened lips, now soft and full, seemed to melt and vanish. A great tension was released, and his eyebrows rose, suddenly lighter. He began to speak, not looking at his son but gazing out the window into the great endless roar of the sea.

"When I was very young, I too was transfixed with the ocean." One of his gnarled hands made, reflexively, to reclaim the pipe, but he stopped, held it wavering there, and returned it to his lap. "I liked to watch the waves." His lips quivered and he closed his great grey eyes. "One day, she sought me out. She understood my curious heart, she said. She was interested in what I might have to say about the land. We spoke. For what little time she could we walked upon the sand together. We fell in love. For many seasons she was my reason."

He looked up at Ogwold and there was a warmth in his old grey eyes. "Where she is pure, you are partial. Ogwold, the sea people are your ancestors." He returned his gaze to the window, as if it had been difficult to look so honestly into a face he had deceived. "The stories about them are accurate for the most part, though they fall short in telling of their beauty. In my time, I've learned that most stories are, in fact, somewhat true."

Ogwold was so shocked he forgot entirely about his missing arm. His mouth moved aimlessly, unable to form words. Ogdof went on, for it was all coming to the surface now. "Partly I believed that you could resist the ocean. Though, she told me this would never hold. Fear—I thought—was enough. But I knew you were in love, natural as anything. I forbade it all the same, and that was cruel."

With this word he forced himself to look back and into Ogwold's eyes. "I promised to reveal the truth of your blood if I found you again in the water. And yet, I know you've been going there for years. I cannot hold you back, Ogwold. Your mother's name was Autlos-lo. She was born of the poison sea."

The waves crashed, rocking-chair creaked, fire crackled. Ogdof's pipe went unnoticed.

At last Ogwold spoke. "The poison is not poison for me."

Ogdof stroked the deep scars that striated his old arms, where the seawater had scorched him to the bone. "To hide such a thing from you was of course impossible. And you are quite lean for a Nogofod. The bones in your face, too, and your shoulder blades resemble that of the Flosleao."

"Flosleao. What a pretty thing... Where is she now?"

"I do not know. She was an ancient being, and may have passed. The last I knew of her was in finding you, wrapped in seaweed on this very doorstep. It was stark night when she came to deliver you; somehow I knew you were there. That morning I knew she had gone. I always felt she would return for you." Ogdof's old cheeks were drawn into a rare smile. "She was a loving woman, and cared deeply for the life growing within her. She trusted me to raise you well and care for you always."

"And you have, Dad." Ogwold turned to the window too now, and looked out into the gleaming face of Vitalem riding along the water. "I am sure that it was Autlos-lo who saved me. But... I think she wanted me to leave the sea behind. I'll not be saved again."

"You may swim, Ogwold. I will not stop you any longer. I only ask that you not allow the sight of it to any of our kind. We are simple people, as you well know; many will not understand." The pipe had found its way back into Ogdof's callused hands. Already he was packing fresh norm into the bowl with his chipped thumbnail.

"You are ashamed of me."

"I am not! But I wish to have peace here." He struck a match. "This is my homeland, and yours. We will be ostracized by this knowledge..." Ogdof took a long, satisfying pull from the stem. The next words fell out of his mouth in a cataract of hoarse smoke. "And there is no place for a Nogofod thrown out than to stick upon the spears of Novare." He fell at the word 'Novare' into a fit of deep, throaty coughs.

Ogwold went and sat beside his father at the hearth. The anxiety seemed to have melted from his features; he moved across the room slowly and surely. "I will not return to the sea. You are as much my blood as Autlos-lo, who is gone. I love you Dad," he said softly, looking into the fire. "I will live like the Nogofod from now on, though with one arm I will surely be a burden on you." He looked up into Ogdof's face expecting worry but finding only a simple kindness. Ogdof clapped one hand onto his son's massive thigh and sighed.

The warmth of the fire bathed Ogwold and seemed to dry the moisture from his eyes. As ever, the roar of the sea called to him through the window. Like music did the cool sound of the surf fill his ears, taking shape, forming words, and he recalled there looking at his beaming father the face of his mother, her softly moving lips, the song which she sang to him both carefully and urgently while she pulled him from the deathly sea. Now her words came clearly upon the waves in solemn salutation:

> *Back upon this cradle resolve never*
> *To release your heart. Fix instead fated*
> *Vision—above all things—on Zenidow*
> *Yet higher still. Dive, swim rather in the*
> *Seas of night above immortal; dream with,*
> *Know rather the spaces between the stars.*
>
> *Take this elder of the sea, and through it*
> *Drink the other waters of the world. Love*
> *And light it needs in teaching you to speak.*
> *Deep into the blood and bones now reach its*
> *Careful roots, and always hereon will you*
> *Have in common the memory of peace.*
>
> *At the peak of the peakless find kinship*
> *With godly things in plain sight incarnate.*

Ogwold sat in the chair beside his father, and gazed into the fire, massaging the strange plant which seemed now altogether friendly, nestled in his destroyed shoulder. It was a gift, he was certain, of far greater magnitude than he could know. A gift, and the beginning of a quest. To Zenidow, he thought, the greatest mountain in the land. She would have me go to Zenidow.

CHAPTER II
LAND LEGS

As if summoned, Wog—who came often at this hour just past the evening meal—charged through the door bellowing. He was smaller than Ogdof but in every way more stout. His snub nose had been shattered many times over, looking quite shapeless. Frizzing, stringy hair mingled such with his prodigious but ratty beard that one could not be told from the other. His whole mangy head was a cohesive ball of hair.

"Ogdof, it is time!" he roared. "Ah!" He stared horrified at the kelp-wrapped stump of Ogwold's arm, big reddish eyes beaming out from a hirsute mass.

"Damad caught me trying to cross the boundary, and lopped it off." Ogwold waggled the poor mound, doing his best to obscure within his tunic the more glaring eccentricity of the roots sunken into his flesh. "Gurgof mended it for me."

"Gurgof indeed. He is known for strange practices, but I've never seen such a bandage. It is unnatural and reeks of black magic."

"It is a new technique, but quite effective in the healing," said Ogdof dismissively, tapping the charred contents of his pipe into the hearth. "A medicine from Lucetal actually."

Wog, seeming to accept this for now, rumpled his face into a foul assembly of trenches and canyons of wrath. He was always ready to enforce the laws of Novare; more interesting to him was Ogwold's transgression than the impropriety of his dressing.

"Why would you even think to cross the boundary, fool. You are just like your father when he was a little nogwof, selfish and stubborn, always sullying the noble work of our kind with his silly whims and false hopes."

Ogwold looked in wonder at Ogdof, who had always seemed to him a paragon of the Nogofod. His father had donned once again the stoic frown and impenetrably heavy eyelids more familiar to his son. "Do not speak to Ogwold this way," he said out from the shade of his enormous eyebrows.

"Well." Wog pretended to ignore him. "A consequence well earned, that." He grunted at Ogwold's bandage. "Perhaps the norm will ease your pain." Wog loathed any who abstained from the grass, and judged viciously those who rarely partook in its smoking. The custom in Epherem was, especially upon being punished by the guards, to alleviate one's pain by smoking the grass. It was considered a way of honouring the Kingdom and paying remembrance to the boundary.

A silence passed. The surf roared its timeless voice. Ogwold would not return to the sea. He would play the part of Nogofod. "I will smoke," he said confidently.

"Ah! We shall see about that." Wog chuckled, producing a leather sack from his tattered cloak. "I've cut and rolled this norm just today. It is a fine strand, lighter than most. I suspect that its coloration belies... extreme vitality." Eyes flaring with these last words, he brought out of the sack a long, slender cone of tutum leaf, wrapped expertly to encompass perhaps two ounces of fine green grounds, peeping brightly from a slender mouthpiece. He sniffed its length hungrily. "It is magnificent," he murmured, as if he were alone in the room, his bleary eyes expanding.

"You have a talent," said Ogdof, taking the wrap gently. He leant and dipped the wide end of the cone into the tallest flames that licked from the hearth, and precisely it burned. A thin river of opaque smoke coiled down the leaf, up and along Ogdof's arm, and pooled in wide, white ripples.

"That too is a talent. Give it here!" Ogdof handed the smoking cone to Wog, who at once set the thin apex to his lips and pulled deeply, his eyes passionately sealed, great chest expanding joyfully. Just as the cone was gigantic, Nogofod lungs are capacious. For a moment it seemed that he would never release the stuff, but long and smooth he finally exhaled an immense fog into the room. Straight away his eyes moistened, reddened, matted cheeks blossomed. He smiled serenely, and it was—despite his usual temperament—a beautiful smile to behold. "By Chalem my King! This is fine as a bout over in one throw!"

He handed the leaf to Ogdof and leaned back feeling the warm fire all over him, humming an ancient tune. Ogwold knew it well, the story of Gravog, who won every match of wrestling—the favourite sport of their people—in moments. Ogwold much preferred Wog in this state, for he was greatly pacified and seemed to have forgotten his distaste. He imagined that Wog's mind was held tight in a barbed mesh at all times, a rusty cage of rules and traditions whose coarse bars could only be bent or melted by the weight and heat of the smoke. But then, smoking norm was one of these traditions.

Ogdof drawing from the smoking cone produced a thin, wandering caravan of clouds amidst the vast desert of smoke. "Here, son," he said, watching his creations trundle on with red eyes, just peeping from beneath his massive eyelids, all but closed now. He held out the wrap. "How long has it been since you've been weighted?"

"Oh, years, I think," said Ogwold, taking it. "I stopped feeling that I needed the stuff."

"Ah; yes, to need is a burden," Ogdof intellectualized, looking exceedingly weighted himself. "But our people find it necessary to smoke norm, and ever have. It soothes our labour, and brings a merry gloss to the evening." Ogdof always became very philosophical when he smoked, and being so inwardly fixed, struggled to comprehend the feelings of others, such as—even now—his son's obvious consternation.

"And it doesn't impair the mind," Wog cut in, "unlike the filth the Novare guzzle. Have you ever seen a drunken tradesman?" Ogwold certainly had. Like all Nogofod he never envied a draft.

"Well, I don't know about that. But yes, we walk in straight lines, if that's what you mean," said Ogdof haughtily. "I would not say that it enhances the senses. Though it makes for a restful night."

"I myself work all the harder with the norm in me," Wog pressed. "It immerses me in what I do, fuses me to the task at hand. Everything is ten times denser on norm. I feel heavier and heavier. Heaviness is happiness for a Nogofod!"

"I feel quite the opposite, though I agree about the sensation of weight," mused Ogdof. "It is preferable, I think, as an end to the day, like a weighty blanket. I too enjoy the leadenness. But, it is much easier to carry the tradesmens' treasures when I am light on my feet."

While they argued, Ogwold stared at the smoking cone in his hand, and his heart quailed. Now he remembered why he had quit the norm. The grass was well known for its silencing of dreams. Dark and artless were the nights of the norm-user. Ogwold had felt many times before that even those wonderful reveries of the day became at most foggy suggestions of something greater, easily dispersed, when he smoked regularly. However, he thought solemnly, perhaps he could do without a dream or two. More often than not they involved the ocean. His mother's clear wish to send him far from the water was not enough to quell its call. Even now the waves beckoned, and he wondered what visions waited in the kelp, whether the silver city was truly there, far more accessible than the mountains.

He drew the wrap to his thick lips carefully and sipped the white smoke. Heat spilled into baking lungs so easily that he did not think to stop. Yet upon exhaling, instantly there arose as from nowhere, a raw, burning pain. At once his booming cough erased the debate between Ogdof and Wog. Thoughts of the song of Autlos-lo evaporated. The sound of the ocean became as white noise through the window, evoking nothing.

"Ha! He is like a child," Wog sneered. "How do you call yourself Nogofod when you cannot hold your smoke?"

"Leave him be, Wog. It has been a while, and this norm is very powerful. Already my eyes are like stones. Here, Ogwold, take this coin to the purifier and draw yourself some water."

Ogwold, still coughing, lurched through the door with a waterskin, appearing in the world as a cloud. Other grey clouds too, though far more vast, had come out from over the sea, shrouding the sky so that he could no longer see the moons or stars.

Loping round the cabin wall, he stopped to lean against the wood, wet with sea-air. His breathing was shallow, but soon waves of warmth cheered through his chest, and he was taken by a delicious sluggishness. It was nice to move slowly, methodically. And so he lumbered with a kind of mundane enthusiasm towards the waterhouse at the centre of Epherem, forgetting his troubles.

The knight there was a Novare man with braided red hair called Larclos. He wore the white armour of Lucetal, and a royal blue cape was drawn over his shoulder. He stood just inside a great, silver-poled tent, which swelled softly in the sea wind. The purifier beside him was an impossibly simple thing, a metallic pillar, and a bronze gate fixed over one metal spigot. Ogwold slowly placed his father's silver onto a low table. Through the sweltering gravity of the norm, the man seemed almost happy to see him.

"Sir Larclos," Ogwold slurred. Larclos was far from the worst of his kind. Though it was not common for Nogofod to speak directly with Novare, this was a lonely knight who rather detested his compatriots. Of all these violent and surly soldiers, he spent more time than any in the company of Ogwold's people. He gazed up into the Nogofod's distant, rocky face.

"Ogre," he said, in a kind of greeting, taking the waterskin and—lifting away the gate—holding it beneath the stream of gleaming water which poured from the spigot. No one knew or could explain why this water was safe to drink. As with the planting of norm along the coast, the Lucetalians had long ago built the purifiers for the venomous sea, ground and rain water. Even Ogwold would vomit if he ingested fluid from one of these sources straight, though he suspected it wouldn't kill him.

Gazing into the divine stream of pure water, he suddenly recalled the events of the day as if coming out of a fog of smoke. Now he had all kinds of curious questions, but the seriousness of his earlier sobriety was absent, and he approached the issue of his mother playfully. How did he make his wing-fins appear again? Did he really see the silver city? How did the Flosleao breathe underwater? He pawed at his throat with a kind of lethargic wonder, imagining that somewhere were arranged invisible fine gills like those of the little silver fish.

He realized he was grinning stupidly as Larclos held out the engorged waterskin. Ogwold laughed aloud, and the booming made the knight visibly uneasy. His stiff, autumnal moustache twitched and he seemed instinctively to handle his scabbard. Taking the skin, Ogwold limply but exuberantly waved his hand, as in goodbye, and stumbled away.

Lumbering woozily onward, he looked out over the turbulent water. Even though all of the day's passions were now recalled, the initial daze of norm broken, the voice of the sea was increasingly less painful to his heart. Though it could not take his memories, the norm could certainly strip them of emotional vitality. It had stopped up all channels of love and loss. Now he could look with purely intellectual, aesthetic interest on this place which had been before so personally significant.

Indeed the sea was uncommonly beautiful; but so were the gunmetal clouds oiled with twilight, and the stony beach painted in long shadows. He turned slowly, absorbing every norm-enriched detail as the moon-touched ocean gave way to parched white land rearing a tumble of loose stone studded with dark hardy tutum groves. Even the tilted, weather-beaten shanties of Epherem were suffused with new interest. Beyond the sleepy village his eyes wandered into the barren, rocky hills, along the stately mountains red-eaved with the setting sun, larger now, taller yet, beyond even these to the enormous, snow-streaked peaks which circumscribed the bulk of distant Zenidow. Ogwold stared in wonder, as if seeing the mountain for the first time. Through the rosy veil of the norm the dazzling landform became only more captivating; its brilliance blotted out the world.

The Nogofod told many tales of Zenidow. Yet only now did Ogwold truly understand why, for nothing before had seemed so majestic to him as the sea. Ogdof called it the dorsal fin of the Rock Lord, chthonic Pistris, plowing inexorably through eons to shape and shepherd the lesser mountains, the small hills even, every mineral manifestation taking shape between it and the coast, urging the crust ever onward, too gradual for mortal eyes. Wog called it a tower to damnation. There was no apex, he said. Those who sought the heights of any mountain chose madness, an endless climb to nowhere, but Zenidow especially was a reminder that flesh and blood know its place.

"Yes," Wog would drawl, blue smoke filtering from his gnarled locks, "it is true that Novare prosper while we shoulder the weight of their gold. But the Novare mind is too like the flame, set on glory, to be so sturdy as our own. He requires some kind to look down upon lest he fall to doubt. We stone-minded bear this sacred burden graciously." Saying this with honeyed self-assurance, he would take a long draw from his pipe. "And Zenidow," he would laugh odiously, "is not even for the Novare."

In defiance of such eloquent complacency echoing out of memory, Ogwold scanned the sheer face of the unachievable mountain far off with new vigour. Rising behind the red-orange snowy crowns of the highest crags, it was a pale silver tower stretching into a high whorl of black clouds. When the impossible task of finding some peak hidden in that dark spiral of nebula failed, he found himself looking for any sign of greater detail, as he did in the forests of kelp, among the folds and rolling creases of cloud. So it was that from that omnipresent canopy obscuring the highest reaches of Zenidow, a single line of vapour descended against the silver-white rockface and kindled in the final light of evening.

Atop that terrace of cloud Ogwold beheld the woman from the silver city, Autlos-lo, his mother. She held her many-braceleted hand over steady white eyes to block the light, though her hair flamed red as the sinking sun. Great dark wings folded along her back. If the woman had not looked so like his mother, he would have said he had seen Caelare herself, Goddess of Altum, which is the world. All mortals know her, if they know any gods of the pantheon. She is the Creator of Altum, Sky Queen, mother to all Euphran, Lady in the Sun. The one thing a Novare child might have in common with a young Nogofod, if ever they should meet, might be this timeless knowledge, that she can be seen in the setting day star looking for her long lost kin.

Ogwold turned forcefully away. No Nogofod had ever seen Caelare. And Autlos-lo—she belonged to the sea. Perhaps the near encounter with death had dragged the stuff of dreams into the light of wakefulness. He could not forget that Somnam itself was bearing down on its most devout student. But how could reverie pierce the bliss of norm? Even the sea, loudest summoner of his heart, had grown meaningless in its majesty. Looking out over the water now he was relieved to find that still it was simply a beautiful expanse of billowing purple fabric, evoking nothing.

Then the norm took over completely. As in a fat egg of lava crushed over the scalp, viscous waves of searing inexorable gravity rolled through Ogwold's skin, pulling his blood to the centre of the world. His mouth sagged, jaw fell open, eyes drooped, back bowed, and his long left arm struck the ground like dead weight. Sitting seemed that it would be truly righteous, and immediately he fell flat on his rear end with a boom that cracked the rock all around.

He imagined that the roots growing through his shoulder from the strange bandage had worked their way down through his skeleton, helixing the spine. Bundling and now poking out from its base he envisioned now that they rummaged in the earth, pierced the crust, and wormed out to the sea, tightening his fusion with the rock as they went. He was a fixture, a grey, immovable obelisk on the beach.

It just so happened that he faced the mountains in this ossified position. He could see far off the clouds that clung to Zenidow, the red-black relief of his mother interposed with the white face of the mountain bright and clear as her eyes, which met his at last. She lowered her elegant hand, having found the object of her search.

But with one shift of the wind, one subtle transition in the shaded complexities of that echelon, she dissolved into ghostly wisps. In this moment the disk of the sun at last retreated beyond the world, and night fell. Though the yellow glow of Vitalem played upon the clouds, it was clear that she had gone. As the sea was now voiceless, so was the mountain tenantless. The lids of Ogwold's eyes groaned shut like the doors of stone tombs.

CHAPTER III
FAIRIES AND FUNGUS

The young witch Sylna buried her chin amid folded arms. Ringed fingers tapped rhythmically, still charged from their work, while impatient heels rose alternately from the floorboards. From this highest windowsill in the tower, her large brown eyes peeking out over spilling blue sleeves reflected the immense snowy crags that fenced the frosted tree-tips of Pivwood. An evening zephyr drew her brunette locks to frame the view, flipping and twisting with the long cobalt sash tied round the cocked cone of her wide-brimmed grey hat. Beside her leant a slender, white bow against the cobbled wall.

Sighing loudly, all at once she backpedalled and collapsed into an aged crimson armchair, long legs flying up, flopping down, toes wiggling in woollen stockings. The burnished legs of the chair were carved into the likenesses of wise, if somewhat daft turtles. As she stroked their heads with her feet, tall candles flickered to life throughout the great room, contending with the shadows.

The capacious dome was equal parts library and observatory. Its rich wooden flooring blistered as much as the sagging desks with her master's indecipherable papers. Diagrams and maps similarly esoteric plastered the stone walls as in some grand conspiracy. Along the curving sequence of windows, the oblong, rickety bookshelves with their cobwebbed, forgotten ladders were completely void of literature. Instead, their cryptic tomes stood throughout the room in precarious stacks looking in relation to one another like the ruins of a lost architecture. Thrown nonsensically into musty corners, or twinkling in the gloom under the desks and other red velvet seats were mysterious artifacts of intricate metal.

The wizard Nubes was not known for neatness or lucidity of thought. He had, however, given Sylna one clear assignment before leaving. "You must stir up a very special storm," he had said, holding her hand and—for a man who is often about to laugh—looking quite serious. The yellowed map he produced with perfunctory flourish and equal sobriety still was pinned up beside the window. Smudged charcoal encircled the arid foothill city of Occultash, at the distant feet of the Mardes, that range of ranges whose highest, iciest peaks surrounded this forest, Sylna's tower, and of course Zenidow the Great.

"The wakener will pass through this city hostile to his kind, and he is not easy to miss. He'll need cover on the night of his arrival. Sylna, you must perform this task here; do not leave the forest." Beside the sooty ring the witch in neat blue ink had written the date her storm was due. "Everything depends upon the Fabric." Nubes had squeezed her in a warm hug. Then he was off with only the lunion Videre for company, a strange wooden chest strapped to her sloping shoulders. The wizard and his great cat had their own task in far away Lucetal, down through the mountains, out over the sea. Such a journey even from these highest to the lower ranges of the Mardes alone would make for mythology; Nubes and Sylna were the only Novare ever to stand so close to Zenidow. Sailing over the toxic sea was another journey in itself.

She stared at the ominous charcoal, now the little blue numbers. Few months remained to learn this art of storm-casting. Nubes' infuriating guidance had been—as always—to meditate. Yet her practice sunup to sundown for nearly one year now had not yielded a single raindrop since his departure. She sighed again, more solemnly this time, retracting her feet from the turtle-heads and wrapping thin arms about her bony knees. One last option had become particularly salient among her thoughts over the last few days.

She might seek the Piv. They were the elder spirits of the forest, little verdant faeries she had never seen but whom Nubes had visited and described many times before. Elegant mushroom people they were, akin to butterflies, with large eyes and soft green faces easily mistaken for foliage. They were an ancient race, old as Altum he had told her, the first forms of life to comprehend the Fabric. Nubes many times had spoken of their bond with the ecosystem of Pivwood, including its climate and weather. But any friend of Nubes was sure to be enigmatic. She could not help but think that they might offer the same advice—you must meditate, Sylna!

Yet, it had become impossible to think that another day in the tower would expire any differently. Each day she exhausted herself at the window, and each night stared at the looming map, sulked at her master's riddles, considered again and again the totality of her incompetence—and thought at last of the Piv. She would make up her mind, pace around determinedly, and prepare a hiker's lunch. But always the gnawing suspicion that just one more stand in the tower would finish the task deterred her.

Sylna closed her eyes and let out a low, whistling sigh. She hummed a tritone. Some time to clear the head was essential. The hard task of communing with weather quite failed and over with for the day, she could finally focus on some astronomical work. At the thought alone a warm smile melted her anxious complexion, and she looked again out of the window.

Night had begun to lower its gauze curtain. The stars and moons of Altum like shining actors took their stage as from coulisses in the cosmic backdrop. Lucifella and Amorcem had soliloquies this evening. The first was the brightest object in the night sky, and though the Second Sun was quite a small moon, even its crescent state was a blinding sliver against the dark, as if the fabric of the night had been gently sliced, pushed just barely inward against endless radiant deeps. Amorcem, the other, was the emblem of Love. Dun, rufous, covered in craters big and small, Nubes said often that this moon was the most important of all, for it balances the others, harmonizing their orbits, and reminds all weavers of the Fabric in so doing that each subtlest thread is essential to the grand design.

The sky was clear enough that Sylna with naked eye could observe the Reach, which appeared now as a vast varicoloured surge of cosmic dust arching over the treetops and across the sky so ineffably far beyond the Moons of Light and Love. This galactic spiral arm was visible often on nights such as these atop the highest mountains of the world. It was in describing this billion-fold river of white stars and roiling blue, red, purple nebulae that Nubes' lessons in cosmology began to differ greatly from those of the non-magical folk. The astronomers of far away Lucetal believed that the features of the Reach represent the very extremity of the Cosmos, that Penulouir itself—the Citadel of the High Gods—can sometimes be glimpsed as a composite light in the constellation of Chalprim Kingfather.

"Alas," Nubes would say. "The scholars see only so far as their telescopes allow."

With a swoop of the hand, Sylna drew her master's own grand instrument down from the high ceiling on magical threading; its kidney-shaped body swung groaning round to where she sat. It was a long, brass tuba, extending up through the conical roof where it encompassed a vast lens ultrasensitive to the remotest of light. Etched with arcane glyphs, the enchanted machine had not only special precision, but also the ability to see as though unperturbed by Altum's atmosphere. Sylna fixed the scope upon that bright spot which is said by Lucetalians to be Penulouir, and with some fine adjustments revealed the flowering nebula to be none other than one of many stellar nurseries common to the night sky.

Though the structure of the Reach does appear to be a single arm, Nubes had told her that the true nature of Semoteus—the full galaxy of which the Reach is but a part—is hidden even from magic users. "It is not a matter of power," he would say, "but of being quite stuck inside the thing. Only by examining other galaxies can the good witch or wizard come to any sound conclusions about the structure of our own." Sylna made another adjustment more coarse, and the telescope whirred with energy, extending its vision beyond the familiar stars of Semoteus.

Now appeared to her thousands of dissimilar bright points cast about a dark oblivion, yet each of these small blurs were entire galaxies. Most were elliptical in shape, but many too took the spiral form, spread at varying angles in different ages of development. Some seemed totally eccentric, but Sylna herself had theorized that these were merely standard systems in the midst of chaotic fusion, clashing and orbiting their enormous wells of attraction. She chose one spiral galaxy of like age to Semoteus, angled so as to clearly reveal its manifold sweeping arms and glowing core. This perhaps was how Semoteus might appear to some distant mage of another galaxy.

The limited technologies and astronomers of Lucetal were unable to detect or even infer these countless billions of other small universes. Understandable was their belief that the Reach itself was everything. Looking out into these awesome spaces, it was always funny to Sylna knowing that the real Penulouir, which neither she nor Nubes had ever found in all their work, must exceed even the intergalactic horizon. The Seat of Scelgeorat, Usurper of Primexcitum, was unknowably more grand and beautiful than anything she could imagine. Perhaps it existed in higher dimensions fundamentally inaccessible to mortal faculty.

Even so, she thought, recalling the lens' lucid look to the closer structure of the Reach, no work at the scope was more satisfying to her than in studying the different worlds, like Altum, that had their home in Semoteus. Unfortunately, there were no other planets in the System of Caelare, but Nubes' telescope allowed for vividly close inspection of distant planetary bodies in their orbits about alien home-stars. She wished more than anything to visit them.

She and Nubes together had discovered and tracked hundreds of worlds from this vantage. Many of the charts and books all about the room in leaning stacks and windmilled sheafs detailed the subtleties of exoplanetary law in Nubes' flowery scrawl or sometimes her own narrow hand. There were gigantic gas worlds pockmarked with immortal storms, ice worlds with enormous orbits incredibly far from their suns, and terrestrial planets like Altum, though bone-dry and without atmosphere. There were often rings about both types; Nubes held that some such structures had even ranges of mountains upon them.

Her personal favourite world was Kellod, which she had named. The predicted—and, pending cosmic catastrophe, always accurate—location of Kellod in its orbit was pre-set as a command in the enchanted panel of silver dials at her master's desk. Noting that this part of the surface of the turtle-footed wooden table had grown strangely tidy in his absence, she thumbed the dial for Kellod, so weathered compared with the others, and zoomed back to the scope.

Really, Kellod was one of sixty-odd moons orbiting an enormous gaseous planet, but Nubes told her that the neighbourly heat of this host world should maintain liquid oceans beneath Kellod's encasing crust of ice, even so deadly far as it was from its sun. Sylna was quick to speculate that luminescent life might exist in these seas. She could hear Nubes now. "To postulate that the presence of water alone might indicate life is a woefully Altumian perspective."

Despite him, for many hours she looked on that distant, limpid sphere, taking neat little notes on a fold of parchment until she could no longer keep her eyes open. As she lay back in the enormous crimson chair, sleep coming over her in a shadowy velvet blanket collecting out of the spaces between flickering candle flames, a powerful knowledge rose out of the relaxed mind—clear as the crystal surface of Kellod. She thought to herself: Sylna, you must seek the Piv.

The boisterous chimfrees woke Sylna with their rampant chattering and squabbling. Their graceless voices caromed through the tall, narrow windows with the dawn breeze that chilled the tip of her nose upturned. Yawning in the awkward chair as the first rays of light struck the dark wooden floor in dusty shafts, she stood clumsily, stretched, wobbled back and forth on her heels, and hung touching her woollen toes for fully twenty minutes, listening to the wildlife and rushing leaves mingle with the blood in her ears.

Hanging there, her back loose, swaying softly at the base of the spine like a pendulum, the resolution of the evening returned to her. There was no conjuring this storm without the aid of something greater than herself. There was no more standing at these tower windows praying for a miracle. She would find the Piv—somehow.

Standing, she shook out her blue cloak, snatched her pointed hat from the table, and made for the spiral steps. But she returned immediately to reclaim her white bow from its place beside the window, fitting it about her shoulder with a silver string. Now down the tower she wound, running her hand along the humpy, shining banister, passing with candour all of the strange rooms and oblong doors, many of which she was forbidden to enter.

She had learned to trust Nubes when he said that some magic was beyond her. In a woeful reminder, up loomed the triangular orangish door behind which she'd suffered the horrible burns upon her back. Clear and jarring as ever, she remembered the bright, neon blue light which had erupted from that space when she had fitted in the stolen key. She listened intently, but there was nothing. Off she scurried.

In the sixth floor dining hall she breakfasted on the strange but undeniably hearty mushrooms that could be found all throughout the forest, and sipped a fuming black drink which made her skin tingle and her eyes leap to wakefulness. As with most mornings the first rush made everything seem much more exciting and manageable. What was last desperation the night before became a virtuous quest in the wide day. By the last dregs of the drink and morsels of dried fungi she was quite resolute.

Outside, the wind was fresh, sky pure and blue, trees radiant in the clear light. She sucked up the alpine air and listened to the rumours of the different avian creatures. An aborjay covered in teal feathers fluttered noiselessly on its leather wings. High above circled the bladed shadows of gold-eyed fontus hawks. Now sped by the little red pucks with their bright yellow beaks, swirling and stirring up the grasses as they flew low, spying for insects. There upon the ground trundled inexorably a great armoured flundle, the common beetle of the wood. It was an enormous thing of nearly metallic carapace, but still the smallest of the pucks handled it with easy joy and the others tittered along as they all went off together into the brush, for there was plenty to go around.

Watching them go, Sylna marvelled at the trees. She loved them most of all. The massive, elder trees, each seeming to mark some unique species in its own right. The greatest of these was a tall and noble kind, though old as any and of the darkest, deepest green. An ancient sentinel, it would have stood far statelier than Nubes' tower were it not for its stooping age and immortal weariness. It reached its weeping boughs about the stone and embraced the whole of the structure with care and solitude.

Growing straight up along the opposite side of the tower was a younger tree of leaves whose colours often changed. At present they showed luminous, bright greens and yellows, the occasional flash of red, but in a month who could tell?

This tree looked proud in the presence of its compatriot, though it was thin and wiry, and its more numerous, spindly branches far shorter. It too was nearly as tall as the tower. The only object which surpassed the trees of Pivwood in height was the brassy gleam of Nubes' telescope, protruding like a great eye from the shingled dome.

But the equal height of the old and the young tree-wards—just above average throughout the forest—was more than enough to stratify three clear ecosystems: a canopy, too thick for snow to penetrate, bursting with flying creatures; a humid middle tier loud with the jostling, smacking and cheering of fruit-eating chimfrees; and a loamy, shaded floor where the ground-born and infinitude of insects made their burrows, hills, paths, playgrounds.

Lastly, though not lowest, for many grew large and high-roofed, and others sprouted from or climbed even the different kinds of bark, were the mushrooms. They burst all over the rotting logs, craned leaning and swaying over the high grasses and springy turf, swelled like growths from the hanging vines, or clustered patiently in the eaves of branches. In limitless kinds and colours they represented species primordial and new, so useful in brewing, eating, treating maladies, some even possessing, according to her master, spiritual knowledge. Nubes loved them all—even the poisonous ones—dearly, and in the days before he left long hours were spent collecting them in the deeper wood. Always he spoke to them in the funniest little whispers and giggles, sometimes sitting at length beneath a large awning of fungus, hugging his knees and grinning stupidly, rocking back and forth.

Reminded again of her master, Sylna looked high up and out over the snow-touched treetops. Above all things loomed Zenidow, that enormous silver spire which seemed to shoot from the very centre of Pivwood, as close to mortal eyes as ever it has been. The tremendous shining monolith rose seemingly quite close to her position, but who can say how far one travels, infinitely approaching such a massive thing never changing in its size, always seeming near no matter how long one walks. All she could be certain of was that the base of the strange mountain was indeed contained by the forest. Nubes alone had gone to it, and only once.

Perhaps one day Sylna would as well, but today she was for the wood. Though the trees were dearest to her, she loved everything about the forest of the high mountains. Each and every creature, plant, and fungal body, even the otherworldly bacteria and viruses which Nubes displayed on sterile slides of glass under his golden microscopes. She loved the rich loamy soil and the big mossy boulders, the way the sky seemed so pure and deep in the high spaces of the vibrant canopy.

Here the world danced and sang, bursting with life, death, joy, despair. And all led back to the Piv. They were an ancient race, having no relation to Novare, Xol, witches or wizards, for no mortal but they had even set foot in this place before Nubes first came to study Zenidow. They were, he told her long ago, the manifest consciousness of the forest itself. And so he named the place Pivwood.

As it was any young morning, Sylna strolled off into the trees. She followed no particular path, though there were many which Nubes had drawn or taken in her memory. Yet he never left to see the Piv in the same manner, and had told her many times that one does not find the Piv but who deserves to be found. The old rhymester, she thought, always speaking in verse. Though he had excluded Sylna from these ventures, he had not exactly forbidden her seeking the fey folk. The dangers of the wood were intimidating enough, if it was his design to prevent her wandering off alone. But today her mind was made up. Taking her bow and holding it low before her with string slightly drawn she walked, and held her heart open, casting her aura whispering among the trees and out to the wildlife.

Dense was the forest unmolested by Novare or Xol. The many-eyed chimfrees above her kept their distance, and as a rule seemed never to leave the thick network of branches they loved. Though many animals here were small, curious and kind, some were very dangerous. One of the most deadly was an enormous cat, with the long snout of a wolf, she called the Moon Tiger. Videre had been one of only two such lunions she or Nubes had ever encountered. How the beast was tamed she had no knowledge, but Nubes and Videre had seemed as ancient friends reunited when she was introduced.

Gentle and understanding as was Videre, to encounter one of her kind in the wild was a treacherous thing, and Sylna had not the way with animals of her master. Despite her skill with the bow, she doubted she possessed the power or strength of mind to subdue or repel such a beast, or any fearsome predator of which there were many. All this is not to speak of the poisonous plants that appeared so beautiful, translucent and prismatic, covered in lethal dews, or the horrific ambulatory carnivorous weeds, which pretend to be humble old ferns as you sally by.

She came in time nevertheless unscathed to a river, and decided to walk along its bank, for its voice was cool and soothing, and as she listened her mind was returned to thoughts of peace. It giggled and rushed beside her, and the trees seemed to lean over them both, dappling the variously twinkling and shaded wavelets which parted around some smooth boulder, now rejoined and flowed in one motionless band of continuous water. Just as the streamlets fed into this singularity, Sylna calmed herself with the great truth that even the killers of Pivwood were essential voices in the intricate harmony so beautiful to her.

The river went on, meandering, widening, narrowing, splitting, joining, until it opened suddenly upon an expansive, glassy lake. Over this gleaming surface the trees could not quite reach, and so the sun spilled here in a sheet of golden light. Out in the water were small islands, and drifting pads of vegetation whose stringy vines snaked out into the water. The liquid was supremely clear, so that Sylna saw all shapes of fish streaming about as she walked along a slight bar of sand. There were many other creatures too. Amphibious little hopping things with hundreds of white eyes slapped the water with long swishing tails. Buoyant white birds with huge belly-like beaks cocked their heads and assessed her through big black orbs in the sides of their oblong skulls. The scaled snout of an unseen reptile sailed along the bank like a periscope, but descending quite suddenly never returned. Of course, there were also the turtles, turtles everywhere, big ones, small ones, two headed ones. She laughed watching them go about their careful business. Before meeting Nubes she had never thought twice about turtles, but now she found them quite charming.

At the far shore the land sloped gradually downward. The river appeared out from a tremendous roaring waterfall cascading from the bouldered edge of the lake. Clambering down the slick rocks through the spray of crashing water, Sylna found herself in a low, gloomy land full of thicker and darker trunks that seemed more tall and ancient than any. They were hung with ropy, fuzzy vines, and all seemed wet with the mist that now permeated the forest floor, and floated over the water of the river—which she continued to follow—in milky clouds. Everywhere there was sodden moss and the smell of dew.

"Why hello!" A tiny voice came up out of the vapour, and Sylna stopped, looking about. "I'm down here!" The voice rose from the grasses at her feet, and seemed to have come directly from a small plant. Though, there was something odd about this plant that Sylna could not quite comprehend, until it moved in a way plants simply do not. Awakening to some subtle cue she beheld a diminutive creature of astonishingly sudden salience. About six inches in height, with short, translucent wings, clad in leaves, it had soft green hair and greener eyes. Even something about the wings had the hue of the forest, though it seemed that all the colours of Pivwood were contained in them as well. "A witch!" The creature beamed.

"A witch someday, just Sylna for now." Sylna smiled. "Hello to you too! At first I couldn't see you among the ferns."

The little man bowed stoically. "Wanuev I am," he said, standing rigidly straight all at once and jabbing a thin little thumb into his chest.

"Wanuev, that's a wonderful name."

"Thank you!" Wanuev beamed so hugely that Sylna could not help but join him.

She said, "Wanuev, have you heard of a people known as the Piv? At least, my master Nubes calls them by that name."

"The turtle man!"

"Yes! You know him?"

Wanuev became queerly skeptical, almost as if he was doing an impression. "These... Piv you say." Speaking in an intellectual drawl, he pulled at an imaginary beard in a way profoundly reminiscent of Nubes. "I've heard of them perhap."

Sylna had her own impression to give now, one of exaggerated seriousness. "Well I'm on a very important quest to find them." Wanuev raised an eyebrow like a little arching stem over one impenetrable emerald iris. It was an expression that said: I see that you also like to play. "Tell me Wanuev," said Sylna more sincerely though, dropping her act. "What is this place?" She looked around the misted hollow, decked in vegetation wholly novel to her eyes. She could hear the river rushing, but it was now fully obscured in fog.

"Oh, it is a special place to my village. But I had just left..." Wanuev eyed her coyly, nictitating. "Would you help me with something?"

"Help you how?"

"I'm becoming an adult today!" he burst out as if he'd been holding this reality in for far too long.

Sylna laughed high and clear. "Well, isn't that a task for you alone?"

Boyishly Wanuev sulked, jutting out his lower lip. "At least come with me. Lonely is this solemn deed. If you keep me company, to the Piv I'll lead."

Sylna could not stop smiling at the little fellow. "Well all right then. But I'm rather in a hurry."

Wanuev fluttered up and grabbed her forefinger with his tiny hands. Then he really flew, suddenly pulling her at first leaning, now stumbling, then dashing farther into the mist with surprising force. His iridescent wings formed a thin vitreous sheet in motion, so quick and luminous they were. And his flight was perfect. He did not bob or float whatsoever, but sustained one constant plane above the ground as they rushed through the trees and thick fog. Sylna was now running, for he pulled her very quickly. Yet at length he released her hand, and she ran beside him.

"Don't you have some spell for flying?" Wanuev asked, spinning in place. He folded his arms casually behind his head, reclining as he zipped along.

"I suppose there is some way of doing it, but that seems a waste to me. Besides, aren't you flying as fast as you can?"

Wanuev stuck out his tongue and vanished in a stream of green light. Sylna laughed as she avoided the trees that loomed suddenly out of the mist, skipping over great gnarled roots, maintaining her stride against the wet turf only with carefully coordinated footfalls. She could hear Wanuev giggling madly up ahead. He let her catch up soon enough.

They ran for so long, and through mist so endless, that Sylna grew silent, and felt unsure of herself. It was impossible to know the time, as the sun was smothered by the canopy here, and the light that did eke through, maintained as well by luminescent moss and grasses which now began to crop up in greater heaps, was eerily homogeneous everywhere they went. Eventually they seemed to have arrived at Wanuev's destination, for he had stopped ahead of her. She joined him and looked down into a circular blanket, a veritable bowl of mist so purely white as to be perfectly opaque, though she could tell from the way it hugged and clung to itself that there was a body of water beneath it all.

"Okay, Sylna. Here I go." Wanuev seemed suddenly sober, chipper as he'd since been. His wings became still, and his smile sank into a solemn grace so thorough she could not tell if he was making a joke of it or preparing to die. Then he walked boldly out into the mist until it was impossible to see him at all.

Sylna seated herself at the foot of a great, grey tree to wait. This part of the forest was certainly a place of power. She could practically hear and see the threads of the Fabric which normally could only be sensed through meditation. She took up her long, white bow, and drew back the dew-glinting string with perfect form, aiming between the spaces of the wet trees. Closing her eyes, she reached out to the forest, aligning her spirit as in an arrow fitted to the taut string.

She felt that the trees embraced her, spoke to her in languages she might never comprehend, but with soothing voices, toneless, loving, ancient symbols woven into her consciousness by the most gradual processes of growth. If time were difficult to track already, now Sylna lost her sense of its passing altogether.

Suddenly she was quite startled back into her body by the noisy arrival of Wanuev, little as he was. She lowered her bow, slowly loosening the string. The little plant person was like a flower wilting from too much water.

"You're back! Are you an adult now?"

"My elders will be very proud." Wanuev nodded gravely, seeming indeed many years older.

"And you certainly seem more serious these days. Is that what adults are?"

Wanuev's face brightened suddenly. "Ha! You should go in and become one yourself, Sylna!"

She peered out into the fog. "There is something very odd about this place. I would be lying to say I'm not curious."

"There is nothing to fear but the self. I was afraid that I might forget one day how to fly." He looked up again solemnly, the expression seeming so peculiar on his fey face. "But I cannot tell you what I really learned."

"I'll go in," Sylna said. "If you can do it then why shouldn't I?" She smiled. "Perhaps I'll learn something about my task. I'm in a sore spot for answers, Wanuev."

Wanuev raised his twiggy little eyebrows and smiled. "Seek the isle of pale blue fungus," he said with the didactic air of an old scholar. "Just take a seat right on top, and you might find more answers than you're looking for."

CHAPTER IV
A VISION OF FLAME

S ylna rose with the careful nervousness of her resolve. Slowly she bedded her bow in the spongy moss, turned to face the cryptic mist, and assured herself of its safety being that a little fellow like Wanuev had entered easily enough.

She stepped into the fog. Even as it swam up her legs, circling them, clinging or passing on, she was convinced of her growing closeness to the alien source she had sensed all along. Soon she was wrapped in mist, cold, wet folds of it weighting and leaking through her clothes. Droplets of clear liquid fell from the tip of her nose. For perhaps two minutes she steadily walked through pure fog, seeing nothing else. Yet as from nowhere she came upon the water, surprised by how clearly it was revealed, for the mist rolled away as in a layer peeled back from the edge of a crystal clear pond. The surface was impossibly still. All around it was impossibly white.

Carefully removing her boots, Sylna stepped into the water. Its temperature was perhaps the same as her own, for she felt only its moisture, and the heaviness of her cloak which plastered to her as she descended. Now up to her waist, her sharp chin, blowing bubbles from her nose she paddled out into the white deeps of roiling fume until there appeared a shrouded blue mound. Pulling herself soaked up onto this springy surface she stumbled among a host of scrawny, winding mushrooms the colour of the sky, dusted with white speckling. Softly they glowed, like little lanterns. A dust of azure spores hung around their shrivelled heads, mingling with the mist.

In the light of the mushrooms, tracing their long stalks curiously, she gasped softly, seeing that they did not disappear into the ground, but were extensions of it. There was no difference in colour, luminosity or texture when she touched and pressed against the material which was her seat. Tough and porous, she could not help but think that it was more fungus. But what a strange fungal body it was, so complex and ridged with sulci and—now she realized—ever so slightly pulsing. Here was a beat, then for a minute there was silence; another beat came, fleshy and warm.

How large was this brainish mass, she thought, looking out over the water seeming so endless in the abyss of mist. Slowly, she became transfixed anew with this wall of vapour. She watched the surging, billowing folds, like intricate falling blankets flung and rippled by an infinitude of tiny, invisible hands. Even as they fell and swelled, shrank, turned and inverted, their subtle movements seemed in time to coalesce to some greater end.

Then she saw him. As in a chance motion, the cumulative motions of fog were realized, and each smallest detail became an essential aspect in a greater design. Massively, Sylna beheld the impression of a face turning towards her. The closer she looked, the greater detail leapt from this vision, and she saw the fullness of the man. Colour came to the fog with her attention, red and ferocious, tearing through the soft white mist. The figure was chained by ropes of pure fire, his arms and legs outstretched to their extreme as in a cruel star, and everywhere around him immense flames chugged and burned. His body smoked and sweltered, covered in scars and blistering lesions. Unknowable pains were in his eyes, which somehow remained open and calm as his complexion, bespeaking immortal endurance.

Now Sylna saw that he was suspended over a lake of lava, that this place extended leagues in all directions. It was in looking down along these horrifying distances that she realized—as if recalling some distant dream—she was no longer in the forest. She was here with the flame-chained man in this burning awful world. All was fire. Even above them there were only flames to see; the horizon was a tremendous conflagration stretching like mountains that warped and leaned out over them to form a great blazing dome. She could not, though, feel the heat at all. The only remnant of the forest was the cold wet touch of the omnipresent mist, the spongy give of the island against her feet, like a medium from which her experience actuated.

She floated up now as if carried by the very motions of this fog, suspended just beneath the man's hanging place, and he looked down upon her with sorrowful eyes. He was completely hairless, the fire having burned away all but his most blunt features, even his eyelashes, even the cilia in his throat she imagined. His skin was a continuous open sore, a singular charred wound, so that it had no natural colour. But the eyes retained an unmistakable glory. They were not Novare, she felt, she knew. She had never seen one of the gods before, but she understood intrinsically that this entity was not mortal. Then he was gone, and the flames with him.

Sylna stood arms outstretched, tears rolling down her cheeks. Only mist in a white wall replied. She could feel the porous fungal brain pumping beneath her feet. The hot liquid dripping from her eyes fell upon the grooved, throbbing matter, shimmering in the glow of its fruit. For a long while she stood looking down at those droplets of water against the strange blue cerebrum of the island.

When she came out of the mist as from a battlefield, Sylna found Wanuev playing a tiny wooden flute. Many strange birds with long orange tail-feathers, which had been hopping around him in a kind of dance, suddenly flew off at the coming of the big person. She took up her bow from its place beside the tree and thrummed the string once. Water left her clothes in a cloud of droplets, and she was quite dry, sighing with relief.

"Was that not a waste too?" Wanuev's lips were poised at the mouth of the flute. He played a shrill melody, then pocketed the instrument mysteriously. It seemed as though he imitated Sylna's grace in his movements, though she would not have noticed.

"I saw a horrible thing," she said, ignoring the attempt at humour. There was no enthusiasm now in her dialogue with the fairy.

"Well don't unload it on little old me."

Sylna frowned, still shaking from the experience. "I may seem angry with you but I promise I am not. It is just that I will need some time to recover." Staring at the green imp she could not help but add: "And a warning might have sufficed! Only the self to fear?"

Wanuev grinned sheepishly. "How could I have known you would have such an intense maturation?"

"Maturation? Of course," she huffed, slinging the bow over her shoulder.

"I am proud of you, Sylna," he said, now sounding very sincere. "Well, let us see about these Piv then..." He trailed off, visibly perplexed at her grief.

Quickly Wanuev guided her away from the misted place, and they came back into the land of the dark old trees by the river, walking in awkward silence for some time. The lambent moss and verdure faded away; more familiar mushrooms appeared in the clearing air. The land rose again, fell again, and the river meandered off in its own direction. Slowly Sylna began to centre herself, taking in the beauty of Pivwood as it returned, but still the horrible flames and ageless eyes scalded her every thought. At a seemingly random point Wanuev paused, lighted atop a low fern, and swept out his thin arm grandly.

Sylna saw only more forest, and out of frustration with the fairy she said none too kindly: "The Piv are here?"

Wanuev with one large eye looked at her sidelong from his bent position. "What do you mean? They're everywhere!"

Sylna shook the images of fire and haunting godly eyes as best she could from the present. Recalling how Wanuev had once been invisible to her, she was reminded just how charming the little creature was, and for a moment she was ready to think him harmless and merely a prankster for sending her into the horrible fog. She returned her gaze more closely to the wood. At first there were only red and blue mushrooms, swaying ferns glittering with dew, humped mosses, but again as with some subtle change in dimension she began to differentiate from the vegetation first one slender winged shape, there two more, here three, now a diverse community of exquisitely discreet creatures looking very much like Wanuev.

Once she saw them they seemed clear as day: lounging on branches, hanging from vines, sleeping in little pea-pod hammocks, wandering about through the tall grasses, crouching inside of warm hollow logs bursting with luscious rot. Their green coloration in combination with their lithe and easy movements made them appear like plants waving in the breeze, rippling along in harmony with all other parts of the forest. Sylna felt a fool for expecting buildings, or really any recognizable form of living here. But there was one guess she had made correctly.

"So you are a Piv then?" She smiled weakly at Wanuev.

"Ah, now that she's got what she wanted she's all smiles. Yes, good witch." He bowed several times in quick succession. "A noble Piv I am." Several nearby fairies giggled at this display; when Sylna looked to them they smiled warmly.

Wanuev led on, and soon they had quite the promenade of little green entities flying and scrabbling and hopping toadstool to toadstool after them. The company came to a tall mushroom, slender and white-stalked, capped with a flowing mauve dome whose long weeping tresses of azure silk drizzled into the grass below.

Atop this majestic fungus sat a single and seemingly important Piv. Her hair was thick and silvery green as her gown. She had bright emerald eyes, and rosy little cheeks touched with mint. Not one but two pairs of wings draped about her seemed to swell and softly contract as if breathing. Atop her head was a crown of twigs and tiny red berries, though they seemed enormous against her wee yet stately brow.

Sylna knelt before this Piv. "My Lady," she said, removing her broad, pointed hat.

"Oh relax," came the reply in a soft chirp. "You are Sylna, aren't you, Nubes' little apprentice?"

The witch could not help but smile more fully now. "Nubes spoke of me?"

"Oh, all the time." The green lady smiled in return such that her eyes were drawn nearly shut. A light was in her face so pure yet so alien as to reflect a different age of life upon the face of Altum. "I am Muewa," said the Piv, standing upon her toadstool and extending her tiny hand. "How do you do?"

Sylna reached gently out and took the impossibly thin fingers in her own, seeming so immense against this delicate assembly of fine muscle and bone there rested. "To be frank with you, Muewa," she said, releasing the Piv's faint touch, "I am wholly spooked. Apparently," she looked askance at Wanuev, "I've become an adult today. But if the experience was any indication I doubt I am ready. Wanuev took me to a very powerful and doomful place full of mists and blue fungus. I've had a vision most terrible which I'll never forget. Yet it was so vivid and real that I cannot but think it was some omen."

"Wanuev!" Muewa rose in fury. "You abominable creature!" The Piv boy, who had become gravely silent as Sylna spoke, zipped suddenly away and hid himself behind a large leaf. Muewa sat and kneaded her forehead. "Firstly, if adulthood were a convention among us, Wanuev—young as he is—would have reached that milestone several hundred years ago. Secondly. You've been to a mycelial upwelling of Oerbanuem." She glared at the leaf which obscured Wanuev. "It is one of very few places most profoundly sacred to our people, loved as they are feared."

"Mycelial... as in the vegetative body of a fungus? Nubes used that word to describe the filamentous networks beneath the forest floor." Sylna had thought aloud at first, favouring a distraction from memories of raging flame, but continued with vigour now as she saw the joy in Muewa's listening. "The little filaments, he called them hyphae; they navigate the soil looking for nutrients or places to spore. Mushrooms are really just the fruit of their hidden branches; even where you do not see them, mycelia exist below. And Pivwood rests on a very dense concentration of different mycelia, having their unique digestive processes to thank for its diverse ecology... as well as its profusion of mushrooms."

Muewa laughed like a silver bell. "Nubes could not have concealed his favourite topic next to turtle kind; but, he withholds part of the story. Oerbanuem is the ego of one organism. It is the emergent soul of a cohesive interspecies network of fungal interconnections which covers the entire continental plate of Efvla." As she spoke she became no less gay in demeanour, though it seemed a serenity beyond emotion was opened in her bottomless green eyes. "Animals, plants, microorganisms, the soil and its composite elements large and small, all that filters below, all that is bound to the cycle of birth and decay must interface in some way with this network. Through endless unseen channels, countless millions of mycelia in dynamic hyphal congress locked, impulses of thought and feeling travel leagues in an instant. What Oerbanuem senses in the southern deserts it processes only moments later in these very mountains and under the northern elz forests."

Sylna was mystified, and so thankfully entranced with Muewa's way of teaching that she forgot her commitment to posture and sat fully down, cross-legged in the soft grass. "Nubes certainly didn't speak of this. I thought that each fungus explored in solitude." Her eye followed the sinewy stalk of Muewa's toadstool down into the loam, where she imagined endless fractal veins of thought venturing and splitting until they wound along an even greater network of mats stitched together on neural threads all throughout the forest. "But..." She looked up out of these dizzy labyrinths of hyphae. "I did not doubt their complexity. He often said that the individual mycelium of most any fungus rivals the mortal mind in capacity for thought."

"Oh easily." Muewa laughed again. "And imagine if you and I could fuse our perspectives perfectly without speaking; together we would surely make a greater mind. But why must a fungus accomplish such enormous intelligence?"

Sylna had considered something like this in younger years, but never in the context of plants, fungi, or even other animals. Why—she had often wondered—was the Novare mind so full of understanding in a world doomed to expire? Embarrassed by the cynicism of her past, she hastened to reply. "I have only known that they consume detritus and enrich the soil."

"You are correct, but to call these their primary roles is to say the Novare exist merely to feed and breathe." Muewa patted the silky top of her seat and sighed reverently. "Oerbanuem constantly touches the ecology of Efvla. It studies and loves as much the microscopic fission of single-celled bacteria upon a blade of grass as it does all the vast histories and technologies left behind by the ages of mortal races. From what it learns out of boundless compassion it returns to the environment in its manifest Will through impressions too subtle to know or gradual to understand. Over millions of years these influences take shape in the transformation of ecosystems, giving rise to new life, extinguishing what must fade, uniting what seeks the other.

"Even the creations of the Novare arise from these processes, for the engineering of their minds was in primordial days begun. To us Piv, Oerbanuem is God, not as world-maker, for that gift was Caelare's, but as world-shaper, the sentient, deterministic force of Nature on Efvla. We recognize ourselves as the Will of Oerbanuem incarnate, possessed of flesh and bone, for a brief moment fruited and uprooted from the mycelium to be blessed with individual consciousness. We have lived here for as long as the oldest trees, listening for the Will, ensuring that the forest above as it is ordained from below will come into being."

Sylna looked up with awe in her face. "Then this place of white mists... the blue island and mushrooms; what are they?"

"That blue fungus we call trypteanu, the only aspect of the mycelial universe not only which breaches naked above the surface, but also which represents the eldest and wisest structure in all Oerbanuem. As Nubes would say, an exposed body of trypteanu is like the pure, beating cortex of Nature unfleshed. Such bare nodes are our direct line of communication. When we draw near, the raw emanations of mycelial thought are so powerful as to become physically real, for there our consciousness is abstracted into pure psychic energy. In such places, we practice communion with the Will."

"Muewa. I hope that it is not a great disrespect to your people that I have so wantonly sat upon this thing. If it is any condolence, I have never been so moved by terror as I was in that place."

"I am not at all offended." Muewa smirked. "Rather I am quite impressed. Even Nubes never dared approach a bare node of trypteanu. Lover of psychedelia such as he was, the true might of all fungal consciousness unleashed was far too intimidating."

Sylna suddenly laughed, as if sneezing; quickly, however, solemnity returned. "It is hard to imagine a fearful Nubes, but this place was surely not to be entered without the utmost caution. I feel lucky not to have been driven completely mad. My experience for all its impossibility was as real as anything I've ever seen or felt. I knew even as I recalled myself and the forest that it could not have been meaningless. Yet what I saw was worth rejecting. All around me was a raging lake of fire, and looking down upon me with endless pain was a prisoner whose eyes were a god's."

"Strange. That is a horrible sight, but Oerbanuem is Eldest and has always moved through love. It does not err and has prescience of many things. Come."

Sylna bowed her head towards the small lady's outstretched hand, which rested like a grazing leaf upon her brow. The wind rushed through the trees, and the surrounding Piv sat silent.

"I see your prison and prisoner, and know them well." Muewa took her hand away and sat calmly for a moment, thinking. "This is a dire thing. To think that out of the most ancient past such doom could complicate the quest of a young mage. The god you saw was the Old King, True Lord of Secundom, which is the universe. Primexcitum he was called, and he once ruled the Cosmos from his seat at Penulouir."

Sylna was stunned by so simple and clear an interpretation of what had seemed utter chaos before. "Nubes told me this story," she murmured as if recalling it for the first time in many years.

"It is one of the oldest and most fundamental. But few are the rational recollections of a single mind thrown defenceless into the abysses of fungal wisdom." Muewa teased a silken green lock of hair which springing back curled like a stiff leaf around her chin. "I wonder if Nubes knew that you held some relationship with it."

"What do you mean?"

Slowly the curl unwound into its former flow. "The hyphae of Oerbanuem remember the First Age of Altum, before the departure of Caelare, before the sundering, when Efvla and its sister plates were one continent. The mind they actuate is more ancient and intelligent than we can know, and shows forth only the deepest and most true secrets of the world and its hearts." The Piv looked long into Sylna's eyes before continuing. "My dear, you have some connection with Primexcitum."

Wanuev came out of the grass and fluttered up to rest on the toadstool. "I'm sorry, Sylna. I didn't know you would have such a scary dream."

"It was no dream, imbecile," Muewa scoffed, "and I see now that there is no reality in which you yourself made communion. Still, perhaps you've shown something very important not only to her but all of us. The girl has brought about the first notion of Primexcitum in ten million years." A twinkle in Wanuev's eye belied his returning pride, though apology was still written into his features.

"It's odd," Sylna said. "Now that I hear it from you, I am surprised I did not recognize the scene earlier. The story of Scelgeorat and Primexcitum has been at the centre of my relationship with Nubes. Do you know why he came to this forest?"

"To study the Alium of course," said Muewa.

Sylna nodded. The Alium. It was that word which had brought Nubes so far into the mountains in the first place. Whatever it was—divine technology, a sleeping angel, the shard of a fallen star—it was an artifact of great power, hidden somewhere deep within the bowels of Zenidow. It seemed to Sylna that all Nubes' work was bent upon its discovery. "Perhaps that is why he came to visit you so often?"

"We Piv know little of the Alium, but we did help your master reach the place he calls Zenidow."

"He believes that the Alium was meant for Primexcitum."

"So I've heard."

"But what it is—who can know?" Wanuev added, seeming more bold as the conversation had come to compliment his mischief. "We all sense its presence, and ever have. But it is Oerbanuem's Will that we leave it be."

"Yes, I can always feel it..." Sylna smiled awkwardly at Wanuev's ability to vacillate so smoothly between silliness and sobriety. Yet now understanding the terrible but awesome gift the little green man had given her, she addressed him not as a trickster, but as though he were an extension of Muewa. "I don't pretend to know what it is either, but I've seen it, or at least part of it. Nubes was able to extract its herald."

Wanuev quickly replied: "And what needs heralding?"

"After many months within the mountain Nubes achieved a prophecy. The Alium sleeps until it meets a certain person. Now he has gone to find them. The only instruction he gave me, apart from continuing my training, was to cast a storm over the city of Occultash and through it shelter this wakener on their journey. I owe Nubes this one deed if I owe him anything." Sylna saying this sounded much older than she looked, now addressing Muewa directly. "I may not ever see him again. Lucetal is very far away. He did not tell me to come here, but now—as my craft fails me and I find myself yet blind to the nature of weather—I feel that this is the only way. I know that you bring rain to the forest."

Muewa closed her eyes and sighed. She sat silently for a long time before speaking again, still without looking. "I can help you Sylna, but you must promise me two things."

"Anything!" Sylna's eyes lit with youth returned.

Muewa's solemnity did not look strange as it had before on Wanuev's elfish face. Rather her features resumed an ancient and natural countenance. Now her own, timeless age showed. She said, "What do you know of the Xol?"

"There is a word I know well. I've not met a member of that race, but Nubes spoke often of their mythologies, and with great reverence. They are the purple folk, the prescient people of the black forests of Efvla, much older than the Novare but I suppose they are still young compared to the Piv. Nubes said that they are the very reason the trees north of the mountains are stiff and black, but he would not say whether this was a good or a bad thing."

"That wizard plays ally to all." Muewa sighed, the ghost of a smile flitting through her gravity. "Both Novare and Xol are older than you can know, Sylna. And like the Novare, there are some due reverence, but others who must be feared." She closed her large eyes.

"The Xol threaten you? But their homeland is as far from this place as the great sea, and the Euphran are their mortal enemy. There are few places as dangerous to the Xol as these mountains."

Muewa nodded. "Yet a powerful group of their sorcerers makes its way to us even now. The mycelium shudders most terribly in its connections with the trees, who sense no entity more acutely than one of that race. The people of the black forests fail to recognize the delicate position of any one organism as an essential aspect of the Fabric. Therein they abominate their native lands and sever their connection with Oerbanuem. Still, Nubes would say that there are many Xol who scorn their ancestors and pray for the return of mortal wood to the north. Even these sorcerers who approach Pivwood do not change what they touch; they are most eccentric for their kind, both in power and wisdom. Yet whether their intentions may once have been innocent, one of their number has fallen under the shadow of a great evil. The one called Zelor has dominated the spirits of his company, and turned them to his will. He desires the Alium, and will burn all Pivwood to find it. But we shall show our power before all is over. Perhaps it was Oerbanuem's Will that we stand not as mere gardeners, but defenders."

Sylna bowed her head gravely. "If there is an evil one with them, then they must not have the Alium. Besides, I would protect these old trees any day. I will stand with you, Muewa."

"Very well," said Muewa, and she smiled. Her eyes opened again on bottomless gulfs of understanding. "You are a kind soul, Sylna."

It was in this recognition of character that the final subtlety of Pivwood became apparent to the witch. As if she had always felt its immortal gaze, Sylna realized the eminence of an elder spirit which hung over and embraced the being of Muewa. It was the image of an immense bird whose white and grey feathers glowed softly against the foliage. Six seraphic wings out-stretched and brightly shining were in this moment brought together and settled against the great body of the creature which seemed to arise out of space itself. Ethereal was the bird all through, down to its silver talons hanging like mild blades just over the tips of grass, so that it shimmered into being, exchanging presence with the wind and air, and Sylna could not tell where precisely it bled away into nothingness.

"I shall do what I can," she said in awe. "But I see now that already you are in the care of godly beings. What is a witch when you are defended by such spirits?"

"You have noticed my partner Faltion," Muewa said, bowing her head. The bird preened itself majestically. Its white, brilliant eyes flamed and turned like drifting stars. "That is not so simple a feat, even for the most powerful mages. Yes, most all Piv carry with them a spirit of Altum. We are born many of us already with our partner in the world, while others come into life alone and must seek theirs out. Wanuev is one of these."

"Faltion is your sibling?"

"In a way. But Faltion is far older than I. More is she my mother, yet too she is the ancestor of all the eastern march of Pivwood."

Sylna rose up upon her knee as when she had first approached Muewa's toadstool. "I am honoured Faltion, Lord of Birds, to fight beside you."

Faltion nodded solemnly, and withdrew her equine face into the fold of one great wing as in sleep. The corporeality of her feathers kindled and dissolved in ribbons of light conflowing with the sunbeams that pierced the canopy of the forest.

"We need your help all the same," Muewa went on. "Zelor has brought a power not of Altum to his aid. Any pupil of Nubes will surely grant us greater strength, and I see already that you are a skilled mage. The bow you carry is light with a sewer's awareness. But therein arises my second need: we know nothing of your true relationship with the Fabric. There is a dark road ahead of you if it is sights of the Old King that come to you among the naked neurons of Oerbanuem. Come and sleep the night among us. Tomorrow we will hear your tale."

Muewa floating up and away led Sylna through the trees to a dry, shaded bower, where the dews of the forest seemed not to trespass. There the tired witch fell back in the loam, listening to the endless dripping water against the broad fronds that made a roof above her. Each drop, she imagined, fell from the very top of the tallest trees, sliding down, leaf by leaf, now with this tree, there another, here gliding along a hanging vine, plunking down upon a broad frond, dripping onto a mossy branch, sliding back onto the eaves of a fern last of all to patter above her resting place. Listening to the endless flow she imagined that sleep was the moment when one bead of moisture could no longer cling to its leaf, and she let go.

CHAPTER V
NOVARE AND XOL

The mercenary Byron sat alone beneath a weeping tree. His thin, scarred arms were tightly crossed. Shadow was in his face. Swathes of stars filled the spaces between the streaming grey-green leaves, which sighed each to their own in the soft night, though the cratered battlefield beyond lay silent.

Metallic Bellumroth, the Moon of War, plowed boldly through gaseous Pacemn, the changeful Moon of Peace dispersing in nebulae of colour. Looking up at the gold-red vapour breaking like waves against that intractable silver hull, Byron envisioned the enemy, across the vast, torn plain scattered with bloodied armour, twisted arrows, waiting for morning.

The Xol army lurked amid the steely elz trees, black as jet, motionless in the wind, much taller compared with those that sheltered the Novare. Byron alone among his kind knew that the Moons of War and Peace went by different names in the Xol tongue. In the land of the black trees they were Zedoras and Fextol. But he would call them by their Novare names, lest his employers suspect treachery. Already he had come to them out of wilderness bearing no sign of affiliation with Lucetal. But such a notion was pointless to the mercenary; other Novare were not his enemy.

Now the last oils of twilight bled through the dusky treeline. But for the smouldering fires of the Novare encampment, light came to the battlefield only of the clashing moons. Having waited many hours for dark, Byron returned his gaze to the sad metal which lay across his lap. It was a sickly blade, poorly made and everywhere notched, all King Chalem's Host might spare for a titleless wanderer. It would not do.

Noiseless he rose, stealing into the somnolent grounds of men, gliding past smoking fire-pits and tents rippling in the night-wind. The grass whispered, flacmor trees soughed. Most had retired, horses standing stoically by, while captains whispered dutifully through the night in a long, lambent tent at the centre of it all. Commander Leostoph was there, tracing his finger along the war table. Around his crowned shadow brooded four dark generals, capes at rest as they listened. The frost had only just thawed; in the morning naked battle would flourish anew with the sweet grasses and blue flowers of the country.

Passing this meeting and many more of less import, the rushing shade that was Byron came upon a broad, white tent. Beside it in the dirt was staked a lone spear, tied off with the rippling blue and gold flag of arms, just visible in the yellow light flickering from the restless flaps of the entryway.

Within, the old armourer took great pains over his writing. He clung to a low, splintery desk beside a molten candle. Its light washed over and escaped the inky wrinkles in his face. He squinted up at the empty entrance. From the dark pits in his brow twinkled a kind of wishfulness. "Well come on in then," he said dismissively, dipping his quill in a vial of ink, and turning dutifully back to his crinkling pages.

Byron stepped out of the dark, a sudden wind pulling his ragged cloak slantwise against his lean frame so that he was all black fluttering cloth. The high collar blew over his mouth and nose, so that only his single green eye could be seen under rippling short brown hair. The old man continued scribbling scrupulously.

"I need a sword," said Byron.

"Oh? And what's wrong with the one you have?" Tenderly placing aside his quill, the old man pushed up his wire glasses, bushy eyebrows knitting together, and mournfully turned from the writing desk.

In one swift motion Byron knocked a rusted shield spinning from the nearby table, and with his other hand swung down upon it almost too fast to see, striking it as it fell through the air. There was a ringing crack. A shaft of metal wheeled and stuck vibrating powerfully in one of the wooden beams supporting the tent, while the shield thumped mutedly into the grass. Byron threw the crippled hilt of the old sword, still bearing about one foot of metal, to the ground beside it and folded his arms.

Down slipped the dirty spectacles as the armourer leaned back in the rickety chair. "Well!" He said. "Well. My days! Well... Well." He continued, rising hunched in the flickering shadows. He was exceedingly frail, but Byron could tell by his poise that the man had once been an accomplished swordsman. Raising one caterpillar eyebrow the armourer said, "You deserve a stouter weapon!" He rocked on his heels and murmured, wheezing. Then a keenness took him all at once; his old eyes were clear. Out from his whiskers issued a wheezing, tittering laugh, surprisingly high pitched for a man his age.

The armourer shambled over to a broad trunk in the corner of the tent, and burst its old locks each in a cloud of sediment. Heaving up the great lid he dragged out from the rising dust a leather bundle, some four feet in length, and thick. He had to wrestle the thing from its place, and only levering it over the edge did he manage to cast it heavily into the grass. Huffing, he slammed the trunk closed and promptly sat on it.

"By Bellumroth I can't even lift the thing." He gasped, clutching his ribs. The enormous package ruminated darkly under Byron's eye. "Used to be Rishpard's sword," said the armourer still breathing heavily. "Bloody beast of a man. Long gone now, but it's not like his weapon was anything sacred. Ugly slab of a thing really. A crude bludgeon for a crude warrior. The blade is mostly duravium— unbreakable stuff but mighty dense." He chuckled throatily. "It's impractical; couldn't possibly sell the thing. But it'd be a tough one to break." Winking, it seemed that the old man even kicked his legs gaily at the thought of someone actually wielding the thing.

Byron walked over to the bundle, stooped, and drew it from the grass by its tightly wrapped hilt, which was long enough to grip comfortably in two hands. He held it there angled against the ground and a sneer seemed to flicker across his face. "I'll take it," he said.

"Easy, boy. Show me you can swing it and it's yours." The man fell awkwardly from the trunk into a dancing stagger and pulled at the canvas wrap passing by. Coming away with a sheet of dust it revealed a rugged, leather scabbard. Lengthwise a series of lunar phases—invoking Bellumroth it seemed—were etched into the material. Byron unsheathed the blade deftly for its weight. The metal was dull and dirty, and the edge essentially blunt, but it was thick, long, and immensely heavy. It was his kind of weapon.

He raised the hilt to eye level slowly. With sudden speed he swung the length of the blade straight down alongside the table. Holding the weapon perfectly level, a blast of wind filled the canvas walls, and the grass thrilled beneath him. It appeared to the old man that not a muscle but those of Byron's arms and shoulders had participated in the motion, for throughout his wiry body had remained still as stone.

The gigantic sword returned to its sheath, and Byron strapped the leather scabbard to his back, for the weapon was too long to wear at the hip. Gaping, the old armourer could do little but laugh weakly as the gangly mercenary said, "Thank you, old man," and departed.

Now there was only the rushing night-wind and the sound of the tent rippling. The armourer slowly closed his mouth, chuckled, shook his head, and returned to the seat at the table. Dipping his quill into the inkwell thoughtfully, his eyes wandering fell on the chunk of metal protruding from the wooden support. As the egg finds its inexplicable moment to hatch, he suddenly began writing with furious energy.

With the rising sun filtering through the leaves, horns brayed and metal clanged all throughout the camp. Long tables laden with meats, rugged grasses, bread, and bowls of clear water were besieged by shouldering lines of hungry knights, while scraps of dried viands and gruel were handed out to a mangy line of hired soldiers.

In the raw morning light armouries bustled with warriors exchanging equipment, buckling, fastening, duelling grimly in the tall grass, sharpening their edges afterwards, speaking anxiously or over-proudly of their thirst for combat. Medical tents were staked fresh and ready, billowing cream cloth canvassing tools clean and shining in orderly rows on metal surfaces. Engineers stood in thought or made fine adjustments to their great machines of war while conscripts rolled forward carts of ammunition. When the last preparations had been made, a grand silence fell upon the army.

Rank upon rank they stood, the thousandfold soldiers of Lucetal clad in white mail and girt with longswords, blue shields at their backs inscribed with the Crest of Lucetal: a white panther biting the throat of a golden snake. The burly carried morning stars, long halberds, hefty spears, war-hammers slender and crude, while the stout-hearted slung longswords over their backs, and the fleet-footed wore rapiers or short swords. Still more precise warriors of slighter build carried javelins for throwing, or sturdy longbows seated across the shoulders to string up in the initial charge. Many rode beautiful well-armoured horses with cannons for legs and flaring nostrils. From all of their silver helmets spouted plumage of gold kindling in the dawn.

Among these regal warriors, mercenaries of manifold histories and all ragged or prodigious shapes fulfilled their assignments, armed—if they came not bearing their own equipment—with what could be spared. With them came the peasants and the forced conscripts, the prisoners of Lucetal doomed to fling their hopeless vessels into the maw of the fray. If Byron were upset with the sword he had broken, these hopeless bodies had much to complain about, for many of them were outfitted only with bludgeons.

At last the bright crescendo of the True Horn sounded. Leostoph, riding out among the knights on his great white horse, smote his shield with a bright gauntlet, and galloped along their ranks. "Stout are the hearts of Novare!" He shouted over the steady assault of hoofbeats. There was a great roar from the knights and many mercenaries who despised the Xol. A clamorous clanging of weapon and gauntlet against shield rent the still morning air. "Out there," called the Commander, "the Demons plot their foul advance. The Witch hungers for blood! Protect your country! Their hope shall break upon this field! For Chalem! For Caelare!" He unsheathed his brilliant lucidium blade, shining in the now-risen sun. "For Lucetal!"

Calling out these last words, Leostoph lowered his sword parallel to the ground, implicating the vast clearing. Along this motion the legions of Novare raged surging from the protection of the forest to meet their opponent. Five enormous and proud hosts thronged into the open field so ordered by their captains and lieutenants, and a sixth—the greatest—followed with the Commander himself at its head, readying his storied spear. Outfits of archers spilled out and formed up just beyond the shade of the trees, wherein engineers stood beside trebuchets and catapults cloaked in brush. Two hundred of the finest cavalry waited with them in silent reserve, pawing the turf.

Across the war-plain, the Xol issued forth from their dark, metallic stretch of the forest. In a tight phalanx of thousands they wrapped and regrouped around and out from the immense black elz trees which mark the beginning of their territory. Never employing the metal of Novare, their equipment as much as their Empire was wrought entirely from the strange hard bark of these titanic trunks. Girt in such jet black armour, backward-arching, gleaming talons flowing over the left shoulder, hefting black shields—each embossed with the emblem of a sharp leaf—behind which they prepared deadly bark lances for lunging, the purple folk bore down in inseparable assembly. Their twin tails swished behind them as they approached, high-pointed purple ears jutted wing-like from the claw-like helms which all but covered their pupilless white eyes.

Though the Xol, silent in their advance, seemed so unlike the bellowing Novare so mad for glory, when the first waves of either side slammed one against the other the clamour was universal. Shields rang out; swords sparked. Blood both red and white arced through the clear sky.

*

Byron went at the army's will with Captain Athbrast, who rode high-seated among three hundred Knights, shouting commands. With a thrust of his greatshield he bid two lieutenants take their parties to flank one small group of Xol infantry now driven away from the greater phalanx. Fleet horsemen reacted as a muscle in their captain's body to isolate them. The sheer mass of his infantry plummeted forward to finish the work. Byron went with them, though he did not arrive before the battle was won. His one eye was not for this small victory, as it scanned the full theatre of conflict closely for a more particular breed of enemy.

Even as Athbrast's men slew the last of their prey cornered, a jarring boom wrenched the land. Blue meteors arched from the far forest and thundered through the battle-locked hosts of Xol and Novare. Fresh craters bloomed in the war-scarred earth. Mangled, boiling bodies and shattered armaments flew into the air smoking. Horses screamed and shook their manes ferociously as they dissolved into dust and blood. One bold captain shouting the name of his people was obliterated in a hurtling gob of solid, blue lava. Ezfled had come. Leostoph's nemesis; Novare called her the Demon Witch.

She glided into the clearing unarmed but for a trailing black robe, suspended in her azure aura. Long, deadly tails writhed and switched like scythes as she scanned the knights of Lucetal with cold hunger, insane locks of white hair spiralling and foundering. Her hands ejected thick slugs of magma which melted the infantry and carried on inexorably to the wooded encampment, sucking down the trebuchets and catapults that lurked too close, but passing by the trees as a river unto stones. High amoebic flames stayed behind to form a barrier around the witch and any Xol soldiers in her vicinity. She willed the movement of each flame as they were extensions of her body, drawing them close, sending them forth, detonating them with hateful grimace or slicing tails.

Only the hardened troops regained their posture in the battle. Yet even the most valiant of these struggled to evade the damning barrage of flames, and only with the time-honoured skill of one who faces death each day. Still, fearless captains emerged proud-hearted from the smoke and gathered what men persisted into new squadrons bound by love of country. War-hardened knights rallied their allies' hearts. Horses were turned round. The heroes of the field rose from anonymity and cried the name of Lucetal anew. Forth resumed the charge.

But the new arrivals, which nightly came, many of which had never clashed with true magic, were stunned by Ezfled's destructive power, and fleeing they became her favourite prey. Laughing, she drew the most cowardly up from the grass by some unseen force of will, and burned them too from within, with the shuddering squeezing of her bony hands. One hopeless lieutenant she drew high into the air before her on invisible hooks; in a dramatic flourish of her tails, psychic tides ripped him asunder, his entrails spilling into and somehow feeding the conflagration of her strange magic.

So long had Ezfled's power been fixed upon this front that the Xol legion had fortified a towering black elz tree fortress great as any Novare citadel. Looking up at the spiralling metallic mountain of mutant wood, leaf, orbiting cloud, Byron saw that the purple folk would hold their position here indefinitely, if not support an assault of their own. He was one of few Novare who knew that the Xol had not started this conflict of nations. The war, he thought, was senseless. Lucetal would never take the old forest. But, at last, he had spotted his personal reason for participating.

"Where are you going, soldier!" Athbrast reined in his horse, shouting at Byron, who flew in a lean rush—one hand gripping over the shoulder the hilt of his greatsword—straight for the heart of the main body of contest; but meeting grinding blades with a Xol general in his own right, the Captain forgot his wayward mercenary.

"Archers! Pierce her heart!" Leostoph roared from the rear guard through the clearing smoke. Athbrast hewed his opponent with the blade of his shield and took from his back a sturdy bow, nocking a silver-headed arrow and bellowing for his knights to do the same. Other distant captains, banners ripping in the wind that surged with Ezfled's power, conveyed similar words to their soldiers, and the hosts of ranged warriors posted behind the battle lines took aim. A storm of glittering darts arced from the edge of the clearing and rushed for the witch. But the stabbing metal rain turned to ashes in the air, and Ezfled laughed a cold and wicked laugh heard all along the ranks of Novare.

By the third volley to dissolve at Ezfled's gaze, Byron had nearly reached the greater mass of battle. Even under the weight of his huge sword he was swift. Many Xol that broke from the fight to accost him were evaded by his long strides. He ran straight through, ignoring Novare and Xol, streaking alone and obvious through the cratered field towards Ezfled. Perhaps it was the lack of mount or rank that obscured him from her bloodlust, as now it seemed that the more stately the man, the more gruesome his death at her hands. Though even the clothes beneath Byron's pitiful leather armour were ragged and dirty, if she had caught the glare of his hard green eye she may have thought twice.

Now drawing near to the most torrid flames of her vantage, he met with ten royal knights who also had come this way. Before them hard and tall stood a mass of black shields and stabbing lances, a thick, advancing wall of Xol warriors circumscribing the high blue flames of Ezfled. Forward rushed the brave men to battle. With a bright clash the two companies met. Black spears impaled the chests of brave Novare, but compatriots rushing forward avenged their absence, cutting down the slayers exposed.

Byron arriving at the line of contact pulled powerfully forward his enormous sword. Down it slammed from shoulder-scabbard to the earth, cleaving the nearest Xol soldier in two. The huge blade passed straight through shield, armour and flesh, white blood erupting in its path. Rushing through the messy gate of bleeding body-halves, turning, dislodging and heaving round the weapon, driving forward he gored the next opponent through the gut. Sunk down to the hilt in armoured flesh, the blade was now outfitted with a broad shield.

Bowling forward so armed, Byron routed the crowd. Well surrounded as he slowed, swinging the enormous sword in a wide arc—the dead soldier flying from it and smashing into another—he chopped one Xol in half at the waist, eviscerated the next, and had still enough momentum in the movement to crush the ribs of a third beside him. Breaking free as the other Xol cowered and stumbled back, many hewn down in their distraction by the other knights of Lucetal, he made straight for the evil blue fire that burned all around Ezfled.

In one motion, he leapt over the wall of flame, landing poised within. All around, Novare soldiers burned in various stages of disintegration. One monstrous captain and scarce Xol guards—the witch's pride was immense—stood relatively at ease, none of them noticing the shadow which had fallen among their number.

Byron threw his hilt mightily into the exposed throat of one tall warrior, and bearing down sheared his head like a woodcutter. The downward strokes of two others oncoming he parried equally along the length of his sword quickly upraised. As they staggered from the clash he spun with the force of their blows and swept their heads away. Another nearly cut him, swinging a jagged black scimitar, but falling to one knee beneath the slash Byron heaved his own weapon clean through the fiend. The soldier fell flat on his back, white blood spurting skyward in gouts around the monolith planted in his torso.

The hulking captain of these few now slain rushed forward with a savage spear, triple pointed and serrated all along each edge. This Xol was broad-chested as the beastliest Novare, and his gauntlets were studded with wicked talons. Still, the mercenary listed aside smooth as shade. The lunging brute nearly fell over himself, and—pulling his sword from the still profusely bleeding other—Byron hewed his stumbling head in one arching slash, trailing white fluid.

Flinging out his blade so that blood slid from it in sheets of fine white mist, he sheathed the weapon now somewhat cleaned, stooped, and plucked the awful spear from the stiff grip of its fallen wielder. Hoisting the haft onto his shoulder, Byron thrust the weapon—whistling through the air—headlong into the witch's heart, some twenty paces away.

Ezfled never saw it coming. She wailed horribly. Awful white ichor spewed from the fatal wound. Her pale hands remained for a moment in the air, as if they still had power. In a heartbeat her body struck the ground, and all was silent. Her queerly small and mortal corpse twitched once, and then all knew—for all had seen her fall—that she had passed from the world. The blue fire sank into the ground and withered. Five hundred surviving Xol retreated madly into the far forest.

"Stop them," shouted a nearby Captain. Groups of cavalry swept through the retreating army, leaving some several hundred to achieve the safety of the black elz forest beyond, where thousands more surely waited to protect them in the immense tree-fortress.

"Soldier! To me!" Byron turned to the deep thrum of black-bearded Leostoph, who galloped out into the field. "Show me your face," he said, when Byron met him covered in shining white blood.

Leostoph gazed down from his huffing stallion. For a moment his eyebrow flickered as if noticing the size of the weapon on the skinny boy's back. "That was valiant, soldier. What is your name, and who is your captain?"

"Byron... Athbrast."

"Athbrast!" Leostoph called.

The captain arrived in a flurry of sod, and slid from his grey horse. "My Lord."

"Why is your knight clothed in rags?"

Athbrast, lifting his blooded visor, peered at Byron. "He's no knight, my Lord. Most likely a beggar, or a prisoner. Wait," he muttered, catching Byron's jade gaze. "He is a mercenary. I remember now. Joined our convoy on the road."

Leostoph looked long at the young man before him. At first glance, Byron was quite average by all accounts, though slim and tall. Looking closely, one saw that he was latticed in deep, dark scars, and that his posture was one of a caged animal waiting for its moment. His one green eye squinted sharp and hawklike. Greasy brown hair stuck out in odd patterns from the gaps in his simple leather helmet. A scraggly beard betrayed his youth, and his face was quite pale. But he did not at all look to Leostoph the way his soldiers did after a battle with the Xol. There was no fear in that eye.

"What made you so bold as to attack the witch head on?"

"It was the only way."

"Speak clearly, boy," growled Athbrast, spitting into the dirt. "Lord Leostoph is your Commander."

"Be calm, Captain. But yes, what do you mean?"

Byron squinted up into the sun-halo of Leostoph, all black flowing hair and bright armour. "She was everything to them."

Harshly, a grieved wailing split the stillness. Throughout the metallic forest on the far side of the clearing countless birds of all shapes, sizes and hues burst screaming for the sky. Then a great rumbling sounded as if the very crust of Altum was shaken at its core. A numberless force of Xol burst through the trees in a solid black wave. Some rode scaled serpents with bright eyes that writhed through the field, devouring Novare whole and spitting horrible acid that dissolved and fused armour and body in one stinking pool. Twelve high-helmed Xol knights of storied dread rode muscled, reptilian tetrapods, great leathery wings flapping soundlessly. They dove and swept and ripped entire horses apart with steely talons.

Leostoph ordered Byron to his side, and made with the rear guard for the woods. Companies of brave men and women closed in behind their retreating commander to face the fresh legions, and they held the line fiercely. Leostoph threw up a dazzling blue powder, and the cavalry hidden among the trees came rampaging among the bout, driving their lances and spears through the enemies that thronged everywhere. The remaining trebuchets were wheeled forth, and a great barrage thundered upon the field. Massive boulders felled the winged lizards in single blows, crushing their brittle spines so that their papery wings flapped helplessly, shivered and died. Stray shots seeming without target rebounded and rolled through phalanxes of Xol charging, leaving twitching, flat corpses in deep furrows and troughs in the grass and dirt.

Through still more valour here untold, a divide took shape, and the routed knights became as a clear, radiant wave crashing against the darker. Archers impaled the flying creatures, stitching their tough necks with shining shafts. Infantry gathered into shielded, advancing walls, diverting the rain of spears and slashing out in deadly concert. Cavalry rushed like silver winds through the battle purifying the messiest conflicts. Swords swept; lances leapt; halberds cleaved and stabbed.

Huge Vonodan with broad axe separated the head of one serpent from its trunk when it struck out to find purchase among his soldiers. Lunging he unsaddled the rider, slamming the blunt end of his weapon straight into the black chest plate; flipping the haft round he split the fallen with a killing blow. Viscera erupted against his bearded, hard face. Another great serpent fell when lithe Racolox flayed its belly with her twin swords out-sweeping. Ageless Dradliroth danced back and forth with exquisite technique, carving dexterous paintings of white blood with the fine point of her rapier. Down rained the black-helmeted heads of her opponents. Boiling, white blood scalded all around, melting not only the armour of men, but burning their mounts so that they yelped and quailed.

Still, more legions of Xol poured from the wood. Monsters even more bizarre raked powerfully over the tops of the stiff, black trees. The mightiest of these was a true Euphran, enormous in size, decked in duravium-hard purple scales which shone in the sun. Its neck alone was the length of the greatest serpent in the field below, and its head was like a vast trebuchet armed with elegantly savage white teeth big as swords. Bright and burning were its yellow eyes. Like the clouds of a dark sunset were its enormous lilac wings. Along its limbs and flowing from its ears were long, gossamer tassels of silvery, diaphanous webbing.

Astride this great gleaming creature in black saddle, thin arms proudly crossed, robe billowing, came a sorcerer of awful might. A terrible fear went with him. The Euphran shook the world beside Ezfled's corpse, and its dark rider, sliding like a bead of oil down its scaly side, knelt there, a humped black cloak shaking with fury. He appeared defenceless, but few were brave enough to come near. The Euphran keened loudly at the sky rather than bother with the knights whose swords and spears clanged hopelessly against its diamond hide. The mere sweeping of its tremendous tail painted a blood-soaked berth for its grieving master, who placed one withering, purple hand over Ezfled's young, lifeless chest. He knelt there listening carefully, but rose wrathfully as he looked directly over the plain into Byron's eye, that green beacon where the mercenary stood amid the fray.

He had not followed Leostoph one step, already advancing, brandishing his massive sword. "Where is Zelor!" he shouted in a ragged voice over the clamour of death. But an invisible force flattened him suddenly to the ground, suffocating his speech, squeezing his lungs and ribs, and the more he fought, the stronger its pull became like a noose tightening around his throat, dragging him hatefully through the razed field and through the charred and broken bodies strewn all over until he lay gasping for breath at the feet of his summoner, still, somehow, grasping the hilt of his blade with both bloody hands.

"Death is too sweet for you," said the sorcerer, lifting Byron up into the air, sword and all, with the same invisible force, studying him while his face flushed and he fought to speak. He drew the mercenary—struggling, spitting, cursing—below the Euphran, and plastered him against its freezing stomach, binding him with psychic cords. So small did he look tethered to the beast's body that his fury quite amused the old sorcerer. But it was a fleeting emotion.

The old Xol, for Byron could see now deep lines of age in his countenance, knelt once more over the corpse of Ezfled, and a tender blue flame—such as her own—consumed her flesh while he closed solemn eyes. Slow did she burn at first, but in the quickening of a sudden flash she was vaporized, and little remained there in the grass. The sorcerer listened to the sounds of war as they made a melody to guide her spirit. At last, he floated up and took his place again at the saddle. The Euphran spread its vast, mauve wings. In a gentle breath they soared high above the battlefield, for which the sorcerer seemed to have little care now. They arced widely, and swung out over the strange black elz trees that follow the Xol everywhere, leaving behind the world of Novare.

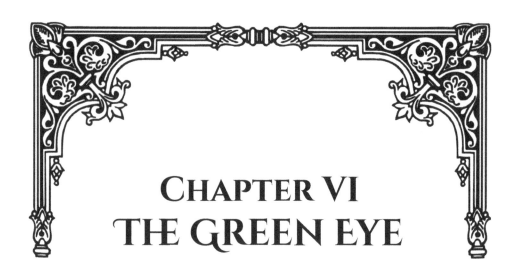

CHAPTER VI
THE GREEN EYE

reezing mists washed the land as the Euphran interposed a purple streak against the changeless grey sky. An endless obsidian forest opened beneath them in ranges of towering elz trees, more black and tall as they went. Soon the metallic trunks rose taller even than the trajectory of their flight, and angling steeply upward they came to a supremely mighty elz tree, mountain-broad. The monster lighted upon one of its massive branches, large enough to host many such beasts. The yawning heights of the tree extended far above into dense, gunmetal clouds.

Byron was lifted again by the same magic that had held him perfectly immobilized during the journey, and cast floating into a tall archway carved in the black bark. He was pushed and held against a broad wall within. The sorcerer, darkening the entry, raising his hands, conjured four searing rings of blue flame and sent them to bind the mercenary's wrists and ankles tightly. There he was left alone, limbs outstretched to their extreme.

The pain that came from the blue rings possessed him as a malefic soul incarnating. It burned and tore and seemed to evaporate his blood, melt his flesh, and dissolve his very bones. Even he could envision this gruesome loss in vivid detail as he seized. Yet somehow were his quaking limbs yet whole and uncorroded when he dared open his eye and look. Endless as was the pain, so was his capacity to survive and experience it. Never did this unfire waver; never was there any respite from its dominion physical or mental.

Awful hunger gnawed the gut. Vicious parched discs lacerated his arid throat. The sensation of liberty in his muscles, the notion of peace, the feel of fresh wind—though it mocked him just beyond the open arch—became as dreams distorted beyond memory. Horrible visions of sixfold blood-red eyes shining, of clutching, unfurling tentacles of shadow loomed over him in nightmare abysses. He gnashed his teeth terribly. Eldritch glossolalia echoed in the pit of his mind.

In one of these visions he beheld Zelor, leering out of the dark, lit up in the hideous red light of the pitiless six eyes which in two evil columns ensconced him. Enraged Byron called out to his old friend, clawing at the black deeps. In streams of hateful laughter the enormous visage dissolved and ran through his fingers, but he closed them at once, seeing how lost he had become. There it was—the Will. Now clarity came to the mercenary even through this powerful curse, and already the darkness faded. Now he felt the presence of the room and fire brands; now he saw the archway opening on the misted sky. The pain so deathlike before had become a dull echo, as mundane to him as blood flowing in the veins. Now, he waited.

On the seventh day, the sorcerer returned. He came and sat cross-legged in the centre of the room. His cowl was drawn back, and Byron saw that his skin once purple had paled into a kind of sickly blue. White veins stood out against his gaunt cheeks; his jaundiced eyes were milky and distant. Yellowish grey, stringy hair fell in clotted masses down his shoulders and into his lap, where he folded his gnarled hands. Byron spat dryly, but even this small effort wracked his body with pain.

The sorcerer said, "You are the Green Eye."

Byron scowled back unblinking.

"Fool. Do you go into such a war thinking even the common Xol would not recognize you?" The old sorcerer laughed a dry, empty laugh which trailed off and died. "Wait until they see. Have you ever heard of the vodox?"

Silence.

"Of course. It is a thing, you see, which exists within all Novare, but never a member of the Xol. A spiritual, an abstract thing it is, and it can only be plucked from the very innermost vault of the psychic body." As he spoke, the sorcerer had placed a wrapping of linen upon the floor; now he unrolled it. Revealed were four gemstones each of stunning eccentricity. "This here," he said, selecting one deep blue stone, faintly luminous, "is the vodox of Lexanrud—Ah! You know the name," he sneered. Byron had become stiff and the sound of his teeth grinding was as rock against rock. "Yes, he too was a knight of Molavor. These others are Lucetalian but... oh, to add another Molavorian to my collection. You're the very last, aren't you?" Dropping all pretense of amusement, the sorcerer raised his wrinkled hand.

A blind but intelligent prodding sputtered to life and dug vigorously into the back of Byron's mind. It was not a foreign sensation, this invisible worm forcing itself between the hemispheres of the brain. He knew well the ways of the Xol, and he knew just as well that a vodox was but a crude approximation of any being's vitality. No soul of his fallen comrade lived in that sick rock. Yet looking at it and remembering valiant Lexanrud he grew far more enraged than even he had been by his being bound and tortured for so long. He drew upon this pain, hardening his spirit in the way he had learned in dealing with Xol magic for many years. He envisioned a Molavorian shield, a dull, dun colour, raw and unbreakable, bearing the sylvan crest of his home. All means of force were turned aside by such resolve. Into its integrity he poured all of his hate.

The invasive waves of the sorcerer's will seethed, welled and slammed against him only more powerfully with remorseless prying clutches. Encapsulating Byron, now welded together on all sides the Molavorian shield-image bore the brunt of the crushing flow and fused with his being, so that he was all metal and will. Still harder did the black waters crash and smother him like an unbreakable marble at sea. But such oceans of might that challenged to dominate the soul brought only greater hope to Byron's heart, for he pursued chiefly the most high-ranking Xol on this quest. Surely a magic user of this magnitude was close to the Empress. And so he guessed—as he had before on the battlefield—that this sorcerer must know something of Zelor's whereabouts.

Steeped in hubris was the old fool to think he could easily subdue this mind which he had so clearly feared as to starve and torture for seven days. He is just like the witch, thought Byron; he is just like all of them—full of pride. Rage burned and grew there in the heart of this metal-soul that was Byron tossed in the waves of the sorcerer's magic. Now the stirrer of the storm seemed distant and weak, exhausted, flailing to maintain the pressure of its will against the bottomless resolution of this mere Novare. Letting out a sharp cry the sorcerer bore down desperately with one final flood of energy, but it was not enough, and too costly a feat. The worker of the great psychic tide fell from his godly vantage and collapsed on the shore of consciousness.

There Byron sailing in metal shield-ship mastery found him helpless and alone. The metal of Molavor about him dissolved into the psychic background as he strode ashore gravely. "In this world of thought," he said, walking slowly towards the splayed, terrified sorcerer, gesturing to the seething mindscape of sea and sky part-formed, part-oblivion all around them, "all are vulnerable. I do not know how to come here as you Xol do so easily, but now that you have brought me..." He looked at his hand smiling. "Interrogation will be much more simple."

He knelt then solemnly, and reached out this time with his own thoughts prying into the other. At once the enervated mind of the sorcerer was his to hold, and he looked deep into its contents for his enemy Zelor. Perhaps hours expired, or minutes, seconds, a breath, a year, centuries back in the great elz tree while the wizard's eyes were whites endlessly straining to roll further back into his head, his slobber spattering the floor, the droning of his throat unable to cease. There Byron's furious eyelid was tightly sealed, but beneath it the one green eye worked back and forth, scouring the dark halls of the sorcerer's memory.

No longer was he in a vast ocean. Instead, along gloomy passageways were high, austere doorways, and through each he beheld some new alien experience. Here he was as a young boy studying the arts, raised in the community of magic from birth, now he hunted high in the elz trees, now he wept in a dank cellar with bleeding lashes across his shoulders, and now he was a man dressed full in glorious black robes, and he went about with an immense power and wisdom. He was called Elleon of the Blue Flame, and he lorded over a school of fire. The Empress even, Fozlest herself, would listen to him, and now at last Byron beheld her dark council in a memory.

Elleon stood beside her throne. His cloak was hemmed in gold, such as he wore now, cowering on the floor, but in the vision he stood tall and noble with a crystal circlet atop his brow. Fozlest had summoned the Six, the Zefloz as they are called by their people, the most powerful mages in the kingdom and personal servants of the Empress. Byron could feel the old sorcerer's fear at their coming, for he was nothing to them in might, though his cunning had earned him this place beside the Empress.

They manifested before the seat of Fozlest one after the other. Some were detained, but the urgency of her call was not one to ignore. They appeared as quickly as they could and bowed before their master. "At ease, my children," Fozlest said, standing and going to the window. "I have a great task for you. Elts, Zelor, Xelv, Feox, Fexest, Xirell, I send you to Zenidow."

Suddenly, the dark vision was sundered by an echoing, wet crack, and Byron fell to the floor, freed of the fire bands. Elleon's head had burst, and its contents sloshed onto the floor behind him. He sat still cross-legged, hands folded, his open cranium hanging back.

Byron leaned against the wall, breathing heavily. Outside the wind howled, and he could hear the monstrous Euphran restless at its post. Zenidow, he thought. He had heard the name. It was said to be the tallest and most unreachable place in the world, a tower to Caelare herself. But Byron had never been to the mountains. His life had ever been shaded by the trees and washed by the sea. Calmed by this memory, he stood and went to explore the spacious rooms of Elleon's tree. Room to room he went, finding thankfully a great parlour, and in it stores of black meat. The food had a strange acrid smell, and he had never tasted the like, but it fulfilled his searing hunger. There was also water to drink in great tankards. He washed his face in a basin, and sat beside it hanging his dripping head for some time, simply resting.

A winding staircase took him to a grand library. Here he spent many hours sifting through dusty, leather-bound tomes. When he was young, he had known and worked with many Xol, for they and his kinsmen at Molavor had been peaceable before the coming of Lucetal over the water into Efvla. He had learned their lettering, and many of the books were to him legible. They described intricate histories, philosophies on magic and science, and many too contained beautiful poetry or stories of valiant heroes from ancient days, when the trees were green. It was true that many Xol, especially those closest with the flow of energy that grants them their power, mourn the petrification of the forest, permanently blackened at their hands. Byron had known such citizens of Xoldra before the rift.

He became particularly enthralled with a beautifully maintained copy of *The Xoloi*. Its scriptures told of a Cosmos he had heard described in pieces, but never in the original lyric as it was sung in ancient days, and he was deeply moved, reading each line with purpose.

> *Out of All and into dazed being came the*
> *Spirits of Thought with breath seizing. Many*
> *In awe fell at once, moved, raising altars*
> *To their maker that hallowed memory.*
> *The hearts of others took at first sight to*
> *The Void, festooning with lanterns of fire*
> *That which darkness coveted. In this light*
> *By a third group, desiring solace, were*
> *Made proliferous moons and globéd worlds.*
>
> *Threefold among the Cosmos this choir sang*
> *Carving into spheres godly histories.*

From the hot cores, out of rock, into skies
Rose vast houses for their society.
Yet, out of the substrate too came souls with
Purpose undesigned, dying as in birth:
Mortality was known in Secundom.

From all ways communed they at Penulouir
The Centre, and it was Primexcitum,
Among them mightiest and King, who laid
Upon immortals this decree: Recede
Into the stars, and abide the children
Who bud and flower of their own virtue
In these havens we leave them unauthored.

Many years had passed since Byron had thought of his own mortality, for he feared little in his pursuit of Zelor. Now humbled and saddened by the great works of the Xol, he missed his enemy dearly, for once they had been inseparable, bound up in their acceptance of ephemerality and love for combat. But a curtain of shadow fell upon these images, each a memory from their youth, Byron and Zelor duelling, travelling, teaching, working the land, and in all reflections this cold, black fog separated them Novare and Xol, born adversaries. He slammed the book closed. A diaphanous sheet of dust rose and fell, spreading and trickling through the half-light.

Looking up, he saw at last that there had been all this time a wide map of the world spread and weighted at its corners upon a circular table in the corner of the room, and he hastened for it. Many were the masses of land that seemed strange and new to him etched in fine ink on the yellowed paper. But here was the body of land home to the Kingdom of Lucetal, called by the Xol Petrampis, and across the sea to the East was the continent of Efvla. Holding his finger to this sprawling shadow of dark forest, occupying the entire northern hemisphere of the continent, he wondered where Elleon's tree might be.

He scanned southeast over the endless woods, until the trees gave way to desert. This land was hilly and dry, and intolerably hot—it was noted in a stylish scrawl. Up the hills went until they gathered and rose into great mountains, and these mountains carried on to the sea, rising ever higher. They were called the Xosfir, in large, bold scroll of another hand, though he imagined the range had another name in Lucetal. At their uncharted centre, in tiny lettering, was the word Zenidow and a question mark. He only realized then that the word was the same across languages.

Byron rolled the map and folded it twice in half before stuffing it indelicately into his cloak. Then he begrudgingly returned to the room where Elleon's corpse sat still in its position of deep meditation. Ignoring the horrific sight at first, he took his sword from the table and strapped it again to his back. He sighed long, listening to the wind outside for a moment, and finally turned to face the sorcerer.

A hard light was in Byron's eye. Back was his unshakable resolve. He gripped Elleon's cloak and dragged him out into the pale grey light. The cold wind rushed against his face, and he could not help but relax in the ecstasy of his liberty from the labyrinthine tree. The monstrous Euphran, still roosted, at once perceived the situation, and its wings shivered.

"I've slain your master!" Byron shouted, and he threw the sorcerer's body down upon the gigantic branch where he stood. The empty cranium rebounded off of the metallic bark, and bits of brain scudded along its surface.

So broad was this place for footing that it was practically flat here by the entry-arch. The Euphran was perched on a thinner bough of the tree further out in the open air. As if sighing now it opened its wings and hopped massively—though deftly—to the greater branch, enormous, wicked talons slamming into the metallic bark, and snaked its long purple neck over Elleon's body. "So you have," it grumbled. "What does it matter?"

Byron grinned. "It matters everything to a Euphran."

The long gossamer tassels stiffened, great yellow eyes widened, vertical black pupils stretching and opening unto chasms of dark shock. "How can you know this thing?"

"I am no Lucetalian. I know a Euphran when it looks me in the eye. You are bound to me, Gryshnam."

The Euphran snorted at its name. "Slay me then, and be done with it."

Byron scowled. "Take me to the Xosfir. Then I release you."

"That is the proudest home of my kind." The deep pupils dilated even further with the strain to disobey. "I shall be devoured for the scar of Elleon's saddle."

Though Gryshnam said nothing to justify its forbidden partnership with Elleon, Byron was impressed with the creature's ability to speak against its new master. The pain of its treachery was nearly deeper than blood loyalty. He sympathized with the Euphran. For whatever reason it had come to serve the sorcerer, he could not fathom that Elleon had been a kind master. He took out his map again. "Right," he said, furrowing his brow over its esoteric features. "Occultash may be close enough."

"Occultash... yes; the Xol spare no sacred words for the cities of Novare." The yellow eye flitted to the map and back out along the empty horizon. "But I must leave you there hastily. Even the lowlands are not unknown to them, though they prefer the desolate peaks."

"Your freedom is promised." Byron held out his hand.

"So be it," the Euphran snorted, hot wind blasting the mercenary. Then he lowered his neck and huge shoulder so that Byron grabbed the edge of the saddle. With one leap he was fitting his boots into the leather catches of the black saddle and leaning forward to grab the elzbark pommel that jutted from the front of the rig. As soon as he was settled, Gryshnam leapt from the branch, flung out his wings like long violet clouds, and fell banking into the grey sky.

CHAPTER VII
MASTERLESS

Elts could not say what leagues wrote the fissures in her frozen feet. Dumb to the passage of time, up steep, choking woods, over ice and crag, blindly in white flurries, she held behind the trudging black cloaks and swishing tails of her company as it was her nature to do so. Numberless months had waxed and waned with the neon-blue phases of Xeléd, yet even if the Moon of the Change was divine for other Xol, she thought no blessing could come of it.

Deathless winds swept jagged claws along naked bones. Hidden drifts of snow swallowed legs whole. The wet of the eyes and nose froze like thorns turned back upon the defenceless flower of the face. Out of stillest silence came the explosive, tearing storms layered with stabbing hail. Sheer escarpments and open chasms yawned suddenly underfoot, spanning miles of detour. Save the appearance of some blood-boltered predator, scarce were the opportunities to sate their wretched stomachs.

The rare settlements of Novare even along these remotest peaks were indignant as any towards the purple folk. Zelor was quick to anger and overzealous in vengeance, yet many gracious nights were spent thereof in the cabins of the dead. They made their choice, Elts would assure herself, curled against the gelid boards. Outside the corpses froze into a mass. But such memories were warped by distance.

It seemed now they travelled at last through wilds uncharted by Novare as much as Xol. Three cycles of Xeléd had shone unhindered by adopted shelter upon their weary camps. Each coming darkness they huddled around the blaze of Feox's flaming greataxe sunken into the rock, holding alternate watch at the shimmering perimeter of Xelv's defensive conjurations, scouting ahead through the nighteyes of Xirell's familiars.

Worst of all were those abyssal, sleepless nights. Slithering bush-creatures made covenant with foul hissing things that crawled out of rocks under the different moons. In the pit of dark, a race of tittering eyeless troglodytes had its day. Yet there was something familiar to Elts lying far from civilization in the total pitilessness of these moments. The peerless mountains dissolved her new prestige, that grandiose status uniting her company so awkward and—she often felt—unearned. Far from the rigid hierarchy of the black city Xoldra, here was the true, indifferent world where she had first found her way. After so many years she remembered almost fondly the squalid, ungoverned Hollow of Wyx, and a life of orphan vigilance.

But to say that the others of her party did not consider themselves paragons of rank would be a gross error. Feox's unassailable pride came purely from battle, while Xelv, ever since that myth-shrouded arrival, had known the Empress' side better than any. Xirell, Fexest, and Zelor ascended more naturally, through pedigrees of storied blood. Trained from birth, despite what humility they might cultivate, the highborn Xol were innately accustomed to privilege. Yet these five and Elts the unproven were as one to their race. Together they were the Zefloz, elite in the Empire's highest, and few in number.

As any morning, Elts' thoughts could not stray long from the wrenching torment in her toes and heels. The daily numbness of pain long endured would not comfort her for many more hours of walking. With each grinding frozen step now accentuated came as well a presence of mind, disrupting thoughts of Xoldra and Wyx, of her ill-fitting title—the White Zefloz. Now she realized that the strangely massive, dark objects leaning into her periphery were not trees, but the hulking stone ruins of an old sylvan settlement. No close look was prerequisite in seeing that these structures had nothing to do with the Novare.

Typically far behind the others, she had little time to explore, but could not contain her fascination—here were staggering signs of elder life! Her personal interest as a member of the company was in seeing what no Xol before her had done. At last the Zefloz were sent into true wilderness; at last they stumbled upon things to which countless, if not all generations had been ignorant.

She lingered under the shadowed, leaning Cyclopean structures whose alien proportions confounded all known bodies, stepped slowly over cracked, moss-choked courtyards and cloven tabernacles, raised ancient stone chalices carefully in her freezing hands to study their rings of senseless alphabet. Between friable pillars she snaked, hands clasped behind her back, leaning around wind-eroded obelisks erected, she figured, following their trajectories into the sky, as in alignment with stars in heaven. Rather abruptly the structures grew rare, and the strangling hold of the stony alpine forest began to loosen. Gnarled, frozen branches enshrined her egress in a ceremonial tunnel hung with dazzling icicles.

Out from under the dead, snow-decked branches she appeared behind the waiting Zefloz, small and dark in their black robes before an immense open expanse. The tails of Zelor formed signs of impatience. In the clear light what was grey and dense became pure and clean. Rolling on and away in blinding glory was a great unfolding blanket of white. The huge slope was interposed by a wide river descending out of the frozen trees farther along the ridge where they stood. Rushing with great chunks of ice, seething over awesome rapids, it ran vanishing into an ocean of fog that roiled in the valley below. Above all, Elts could see their goal: Zenidow, shooting high as ever into its canopy of clouds.

Rising like sentinels in front of the Great Mountain, a final range obstructed the Zefloz. Huddled together were the implacable titan shoulders of three snowy peaks, larger and more treacherous than any before encountered. The middle and rightmost mountains were broad-based and jagged-toothed, thrusting the cloud-wrapped multiple points of their serrated apices like the crude battlements of giants. But the leftmost was quite different. As though a flat, clean cross-section of land had long ago been pulled straight up from some mantle-deep slot, this ten thousand foot vertical formation was sheer-faced down to the mist obscuring its connection with Altum, and would have been completely vertical, and taller than its companions were it not leaning only slightly against the middle. Yet even more stunning was that part of its composition which was clearly unnatural.

Embedded in the upper reaches of the smooth sun-drenched face was a spiny clustering of tall, leaning black towers and crumbling castle walls dark as pitch. Though it was unclear how such magnificent structures could be affixed to the featureless wall of rock, it was obvious to Elts that this was no work of the ancient architects of the forest. Perhaps, she thought, it was the mark of a race even older and wiser. It might have been once a citadel of the gods themselves, forgotten in their retreat to the stars. Though, any Xol might compare the looks of it to the cities of Novare.

Seeming to take no notice of the awesome vision afforded them after months of suffocating forest, Zelor descended busily down and out into the open snow. One by one the others silently succumbed to some invisible dominion in their hearts and followed his long, beckoning tails as if, like hateful leashes, they drew the Zefloz forth. Indeed, they did not follow him out of free will, for by some black art he had dominated their minds. None but Elts and Fexest seemed still to think for their own.

The coloured hemming of the black robes of the Zefloz bespoke their different titles, and Zelor's was silver as the blades of the Novare, for though he was the greatest swordsman in the Empire, he abhorred the use of elz bark. An argent scabbard swept from his waist into the folds of that cloak, and he wore another, smaller but finer weapon along his back. Tall and broad-shouldered, with deep purple skin, long straight white hair, and black eyes, the Silver Zefloz fought with the legendary technique, and used only the metals and weapons of the Knights of Molavor with whom he had spent his greatest years.

Yet long ago he had betrayed and destroyed with their own lessons that single race of Novare to which the Xol were long allied. In the name of the Empire, he had sown the first seeds of distrust long before the war with Lucetal, whose kingship was ignorant of Molavor. Therein he was important to Fozlest, the Empress of Xoldra. But though the might of Zelor was plain, she would never trust him. If not for his treachery against those who took him in and so kindly blessed forth the art he loved, she detested him for his temper, his hate of sorcery, and for the many years he spent too close to the Molavorians she had always feared.

Therefore she placed in command of the expedition to Zenidow that sorcerer who was closest to her: sexless Xelv. Hairless, white-eyed, and cat-bodied, the bearded tails and fair skin of Xelv showed forth a brilliant blue as out from ancient myth. Scripture told that the ancestors of the Xol were sky-skinned; many legends surrounded Xelv who alone bore that pigment. Those twisting cobalt tails spoke a dead language unrecognized in Xoldra, and the crafts of summoning and knowledge of Xeléd especially with Xelv far surpassed what was known. One hundred years ago the Blue Zefloz came out of the untamed West pledging fealty to Fozlest for reasons unspoken. Xelv was above all things the most loyal in her court. Yet even that wisest sorcerer, the Hand of Fozlest itself, had surrendered seemingly without conflict the reins of this quest so important to her, going always in Zelor's shadow, the first to do his bidding.

Close behind Xelv in following at the tail-commands of Zelor, and second to become like a silent thrall to silver was Feox. Born a slave, tails shorn off by merciless drivers, brain misshapen and teeth destroyed by contest in the fighting pits of Zentref, Feox of the Fire rose through the brackets of death to become the most famous gladiator in all Xoldra. He won his freedom in a bout against the Red Zefloz of old, whom he broke before Fozlest over the head of that warrior's own axe. He claimed the flamed weapon thereafter, and was never seen without it. Simple minded, brutal, ursine in form with torso tree-thick, he was the Empire's most powerful physical force. Patchworked with dark purple hide, the stringy clumps of his violet hair swung back and forth with affected masculine swagger as he lurched after Xelv. Yet when he turned, in profile one noticed the strange, feminine dignity of his features. Perhaps for this reason he detested women, obeying Fozlest's commands only with dangerous surliness. Loud and hateful was his belief that Elts and Fexest should not have come on the journey; he spoke to them only out of what condescension he deemed necessary. But he was not so conservative with the men. Often he would mock the androgyny of Xelv, the old body of Xirell, and though he had perhaps most in common spiritually with Zelor, to him he was the most bitter and resentful. All the more surreal and contradictory was it to watch Feox pad after his enemy like a trained animal.

Third to fall in line in descent of the snowy slope, and only this morning to have changed, was Xirell. The spry codger was normally full of song and story, always delineating new plants and animals, cooing in melodic susurrus to some animal companion. It was nigh impossible to shut him up when his intellect was stimulated. Yet lost as Elts had been in her thoughts and the ruins out of time, only now—seeing him drift ahead as a mirthless spectre, head bowed, gnarled fingers limp—did she realize his transformation. Even the day prior he had spoken about the subordination of Xelv and Feox only as it was an unfortunate quagmire, assuring her that Zelor could not control them all. But his silence and abjection during these early hours when he was usually most gay made an omen most fell. Grassy eyes before intelligent and curious were barren and cracked. Ancient smile-marks sagged with stiff death. A sick pallor of grey cursed his wispy cheeks, and his long flowing moustache—that source of wit—went untwisted, forgotten by hands now thoughtless.

As Xirell shuffled on into the open, the noble septry which he'd befriended long ago in the valley before the forest winged out from over the wood and perched upon his shoulder. Its jet feathers folded back, vigilant eyes taking in every slightest detail around them. The wizened sorcerer at such a time should have tossed the creature some new morsel from within his voluminous pockets, spoken rapturously into its bristling feathers, sent it eagerly off on errands both essential to their progress and silly as his fancy often was. Many meals had found them in this way, or seemingly useless artifacts which Xirell would add to some hidden trove, smiling knowingly. Yet now he said nothing. The great raptor shifted foot from foot anxiously. Then it flew away, perhaps forever. Black-cowled Fexest, still of clear eyes and seeming independence, glanced back at Elts as if to say "him too," before plodding out after the others.

It was this horrible absence so sudden and total in the Green Zefloz which forced Elts that morning to recognize the evil of Zelor. Old Xirell was the only reason she walked alongside these elite members of the Empire she had always loathed.

As she lastly joined the procession down the great slope into the distant river valley, she let an old and special memory seep up from unconscious vaults, growing clear as the white snow. Supplanting the vacant eyes of her master with remembered vitality, she fell into a vision of younger years, when all Xol sorcerers were patently malefic.

It was ten years before she ever heard the word Zenidow, deep in the less travelled southern forests of Efvla.

Slanted sheets of rain lacquered the metallic elz trees; ceaseless smattering against densely woven branches roofed the night. The passionate moon Svel pressed its broad orange hemisphere through the dripping, petrified leaves, a rising halo for the batlike silhouette of Elts, hanging from a high bough.

Looking down along the pale paths at the tramping imperial raiders, she pulled a mask of elz bark over her eyes, now blue points piercing through angled slits. Steely dark wings hugged and lifted jutting behind her temples. Only her short ivory hair could betray her in the night, for her slender gauntlets, plated shoulders, tunic and greaves were all perfectly black. Silently she dropped, falling free for a thunderclap, then swinging by a fine cord of rope. Against the ripping wind and rain she touched deftly down, rolling through the high, muddy weeds. Dashing forward on the momentum of her landing, with a flick the line loosened lithely from the branch above and leapt spooling to her hip. Clipping the tight coil to her belt alongside her different knives of bark, she stole through the sprawling, high-walled labyrinth of roots.

If those ranging black masses were mountains, the Hollow of Wyx among them was a secret valley. One enormous elz tree ensconced the village with protective arms thick as many trees are tall, clasping at their point of embrace in a great gate, spreading their interlacing fingers to split seams of entry. Yet bored in the rootwalls all about the perimeter were cracks and tunnels more subtle; through this dark dimension Elts streamed, coming into the lanes of Wyx unnoticed. The lights flashing by—eclipsed each in a breath by her swift shadow—were the cave-like entryways of hovels carved in the countless smaller roots which wound, knotted, and diverged in a terraced network wall to wall. The glow of their open mouths bathed the raiders as they passed the corpses of defiant mothers and fathers contorted in the slush, or the occasional sibling, too old to recruit, slumped upright and gutted. Black blades flashed with stains of fresh white blood. A giant figure showed his unique tails by their rain-sheen; the one was surgically outfitted with sickle, long and wicked, the other artificially engorged.

The nearest raider to the low, rushing Elts might have felt the shifting gale even through the rain. But there was no time to think it unnatural. She tackled him in a suffocating grip, rolling with one hand firmly over his mouth, vacuuming air from his body. Cocooning wind muffled the struggle, as with— one by one—the metamorphoses of four others, falling from her hands like motionless chrysalides in the dark. For the next group more distant she shaped air-darts, dense and fine. Out she flung these invisible points; twelve hearts they impaled. Unhanded weapons slapped against the rain-soaked soil.

The brute with the mutant tails ripped at his chest, white blood spurting into the light, sunken purple eyes like deep cups scouring the lane for their adversary. Elts' spiky white hair and bright glare, suffused with the hovel-light, floated spectral in the black. Three more darts came even as he noticed her, but with dexterity the scythe tail parried. He stood pridefully at ease while this appendage did the work. Elts flung and followed swiftly a mass of dense air down the lane. This time the raider held up his arms and thicker tail to deafen the blast, but already a blade of pure wind and rain condensed in Elts' left hand; now she swung out with deadly precision. The curved edge passed through the front of the raider's cloak, splitting his belly. Clean, exuberant blood cascaded to the ground, that cataract followed by one knee, planted there defeated.

"Rolv!" the raider shouted, clutching his draining gut. "The Wind is here!" Barely had these words formed when Elts removed the air behind them. He crumpled into the mud. She took her hand away from the cold lips.

"The Wind of Wyx." A Xol man appeared in the entry of a nearby hovel. He was tall and lean, clad in the black robes of a sorcerer. Atop his tilted head was a crown of elz bark, as if he thought himself a ruler. Long magenta hair curled in all directions over his shoulders. White eyes cold and raw stared through the rain. His hands at rest twitched almost nervously with horrible power.

Elts' short tails bunched like serpents behind her in a sign of threat. "It amazes me how straight-backed you murderers stand," she growled.

Rolv laughed, folding his hands into the crooks of his arms, as if they'd grown hot under her attention. "It takes a solemn heart to make the hard decisions. You must know that the most powerful sorcerers are those raised from birth. Imagine the feats you could accomplish if you too had the opportunity for such thorough education." He smiled vacantly, but already his face began to stale with apathy. "You're late, anyhow. I've had my prizes transported."

Elts spat into the sodden earth. "Don't think that your small success in a sty like Wyx is any sign of greatness."

"So you admit the children have no future here." Rolv's eyes pulsed with new attention. "Why do you defend the place if it is so... worthless."

Elts thrust her hands forward, palms open, releasing all that she had drained from the lungs of the raiders. First as a monstrous blossoming gale the wind burst forth, but as it wailed down the lane all was consolidated into a raindrop point heavy as an anvil. Still Rolv was faster. The near-invisible cannonshot stopped before his eyes. He turned it away with a casual hand, closed his fingers into a fist—the form dispersed in a rush of water vapour.

"No. Even if we had captured you young..." He looked disdainfully into his empty palm slowly opening. "Your way with Xeléd is too weak. There is no thread-sense in you at all." He smirked.

Elts ground her teeth, rain streaming from her mask. If this was the place, so be it. From the short scabbards strapped to her belt she drew two curved elz knives. Though she charged forward with all force, Rolv laughing held out his hand merely as if to pluck a ripe fruit, and stopped her in motion, limbs frozen in their approach. Blue eyes shone with bleary rage as she struggled.

"How is it you've earned a name among my men?" Compressing his fist, so too did the force around her from all sides crush more powerfully. She could not utter a sound or breathe at all. The inevitable had come. Out of unbearable pain somehow she calmed herself, ready to join her parents. In that moment she was closer than ever to accepting that the holiest moon Xeléd was truly the gate of heaven, that Xol scripture was the Word, that the shadowy forms of her family would be reunited in the blue eye of the Cosmos. Let the people of Wyx defend themselves for once.

Suddenly, the night swallowed Rolv. Elts in the moment of his vanishing fell from the air. She landed on the balls of her feet, driving her stout tails back through the mud, though still she staggered some. Looking up she beheld in place of the sorcerer a great root mighty as the wall of Wyx. So natural was its appearance wedded to the soil, that were it not for the gouts of displaced water still showering and splattering all around, it would seem as though the knuckled black mass had always been there.

More surprising was the moustached stranger striding out from behind it. Posing with the disorienting manner of one who addresses an old friend, he manipulated his thin but very long tails in ungilded greeting, popped his bloated top hat up and down, and called out over the bluster: "The Wind of Wyx I presume?"

Elts had never seen a Xol like this man. His robes were fine and hemmed in lustrous emerald. His hat was bound in a dark green scarf, and a gemstone of like colour nested in its folds. At his shoulder was perched a leathery black and blue aborjay with bright red eyes which squeaked tentatively when she peered.

"I'll take your silence as a yes, Miss Wind! Would you kindly lend your conversation?" He said this turning and walking across the lane. "We might go into this hovel here... I'm afraid our friend has already sent its occupants away." His voice faded as he disappeared under the archway, smoothly as he'd come.

Elts stood soaking and still shaking from the psychic vise of Rolv. Rain pelted her face and clattered against her shoulder plates as she stared up at orange Selv and considered her options. Despite his obvious nobility and allegiance to Fozlest, she decided to follow the man. His assistance could not go without thanks. He had slain a royal sorcerer anyhow—and with evident satisfaction! She had never considered that there might be dissent among the ranks of Fozlest. The thought alone stoked in her a fire long smouldering.

Above the entryway to the hovel hung the twiggy emblem of a merchant, but inside, bathed by the white light of three listing, half-expired glowlets, there was little of value to behold. A simple table had been overturned. Awful white blood stains raked out from the corner. Three squalid sleeping mats, composed mostly of tough grasses, seemed heavily damaged, as if their occupants had been attacked unawares. The aborjay was nestled into one of these, eyes closed, beak tucked into its blue feathery stomach, wrapped in the naked leathery wings. There were no bodies.

The old man took out a slender wand of a glossy brown material Elts had never seen. Sweeping it, he righted the table and simple stone stools, and took a seat, looking over at her curiously, pulling at the ends of his wispy moustache. His hair was long and black frizzing out from beneath the hat, which she saw now in the light was quite old. His skin was pureblood purple. His eyes, though, were deep green, a colour she had never before seen in the Xol complexion.

"I mean you no harm," he drawled. "Really, I don't often take credit from the trees, but that root was my doing."

Elts sat down still cautiously, nervous tails against the ground. "You saved my life."

"You certainly seemed to be having some trouble. Why and, one needn't take a long look to see that you have no connection with Xeléd." He smiled warmly for acknowledging so base a thing in their culture. "The miraculous source of your aerial powers aside, I'm more surprised by your choice to defend the Hollow of Wyx. Of all places!"

Elts sensed only kindly curiosity in these words, but still she was guarded. "What are your intentions, warlock? How do I know you're not a more subtle slaver?"

"Xeléd down!" The old man was appalled, pulling off his hat and holding it to his heart. "Pardon me, Miss Wind, for I am called Xirell." He stood and bowed solemnly, his tails poised in a tableau of formality and reverence. "Personal mage to the Empress Fozlest and self-proclaimed explorer-naturalist at your service." He sat once more, returned his hat carefully to its seat atop his wiry hair.

"Fozlest... She is the worst of all." A shadow fell over Elts' face. "You ask why I defend the Hollow? Because no one else will, especially the Empire. It's a forgotten place where Xol fend like beasts and starve alone. Here, raiders stalk the lanes in plain sight. The child or children taken from this hovel will grow up learning to kill and take like any rightful student of her craft. Fozlest doesn't know or care where her sorcerers and sorceresses come from. She has eyes only for power."

Xirell leaned back in his chair, twirling the seemingly longer tail of his moustache with methodical dexterity. "Perhaps you see that I abhor the vile practice of men like Rolv. Honestly I haven't a heart for the academies either, even those that are imperially sanctioned. Yet, you should know it is not Fozlest's intention that children be taken from their homes."

"Then why doesn't she do something about it?"

Xirell harrumphed grimly and attended to the other end of his moustache. "Alas. You are right to say that she does not care for or even know the names of such places as the Hollow of Wyx, or rather any of the southern dells."

Elts sighed. The rain outside fell in hissing sheets. "Tell me," she said suddenly, for she'd been wanting to ask, "what is your wand made of?"

Xirell laughed loud and clear, sounding much younger than he appeared. The aborjay opened one eye restlessly, annoyed but intrigued nonetheless. "Why, the Novare know it as wood. To the Xol it was once called xel."

"Wood? You mean like a forest? I've not heard of xel."

"Ha! 'Wood' has come to mean such a thing to our people, a forest, yes, an expanse of elz trees which haven't wood at all even in their innermost cores; but always and first it names the true flesh of the trees. Before elz bark," Xirell swept out his hand as if indicating the petrified black metal trees all around them, "there was xel," he brought his hand back to the wand, and lifted it towards Elts, who took it cautiously. "We Xol rarely come upon such a thing unmolested."

"Elz are not trees then?" Elts muttered, now looking with even greater awe at the wooden wand, trying to imagine a tree made of the substance.

"They are the memories of trees. Yet real living forests exist all over Altum, waiting to be explored. Say; I'll tell you all about them if you take off that mask." Xirell smiled. The aborjay behind him sat up suddenly in a strangely Xoloid posture, its wings spread out for support, globular eyes trained on Elts. She hesitated; still, though the mask had a special purpose other than keeping the raiders from recognizing her, she removed it.

"Ah," said Xirell. "You are young, as I thought. Some stories speak about an old woman with lassos of wind. And I dare say, the colour of your skin is..."

"I am Elts," she said, cutting his thought short.

Xirell nodded. "Well then, Elts." The aborjay closed its eyes and snuggled again down into the thatched sleeping mat. "When the Empire was young, the forests were green and brown, yellow and red. Trees of all ages existed, of different sizes and shapes and species. The Xol and Novare were in love. Yet the Novare were wise in those days, and let nature be, while our ancestors—more deeply moved, we tell ourselves—could not abide that the trees might be burned or lost to the ages. Those ancient Xol drew upon powers of Xeléd long lost to us, and froze the trees so that they might never decay. To ensure that what was done might forever persist, they infused their children with that blessing, now a curse. Wood near to us slowly becomes hard and black, unbreakable, yet the life therein immortalized is rather undead. Everywhere we linger overlong the trees transform to elz. Fozlest too wishes for the return of wood and leaf, but no Xol for many thousands of years can tell the secret of our effect on nature. It is a thing most sad, for I myself am a great lover of life as it grows naturally in the world. I travel far to see it, and find with happy heart that the Novare continue to care for the forests as they were in elder days." Xirell sighed. "Of course, there are benefits to the elz trees," he went on, as if he had to, no longer interested in his moustache. "They are mouldable, and make for excellent armour and equipment. In the great city Xoldra the trees are worked into intricate towers of great majesty."

Elts was silent, processing all of these things so new to her. She had before seen the elz trees only as stoic, changeless guardians abiding the little folk who nested in their roots. "Then how does your wand remain as it is? Unless you only just found it."

Xirell smiled and rolled the piece hand to hand. "It has been with me for nine seasons, and I am yet to see the taint. Many years of study and adventure have taught me a ward of protection, but I can only extend it so far as this twig; and who knows how long it will last." He gazed fondly at the wand.

Looking down at this small and feeble object which stood to defy eons of elder power, Elts began to see Xirell not—like all sorcerers—as an extension of Fozlest, but as an independent manifestation of nature. "You can't have come all this way for knowledge if you're already undoing fate..." She looked slowly up from the wand. "And I've heard that these southern woods are the blackest. I doubt you'll find xel here."

"And so we get to the heart of it." Xirell chuckled. "Word of the masked Xol vigilante, bane of the raiders, the Wind of Wyx, has reached much farther than you can know. Not to Xoldra itself, but to me at least. I've come precisely to find you, Elts. Actually, I found you out seven days ago. I've been watching you carry on among the branches like a regular flying losv. I would have observed a little longer, but this Rolv was quite another thing entirely."

Elts placed one hand gently over her mask lying on the table. "I always knew I'd run into a real sorcerer."

"Ah but you are quite something yourself, Elts. You may have no natural bond with Xeléd, but your sense of its influence is such that few behold. Even the greatest mages fail to comprehend the flow of the world as I see in your... wind magic." He gestured ambiguously. "With the proper guidance you will go far. You may have to work on your feelings for the Empress, however."

Elts raised one silvery eyebrow. "How do you mean?"

"You might stand beside her yet." Xirell smiled as she frowned. "Right, you are not so easily persuaded. And you have no reason to respect the Empress. But then, how about this: travel the forests with me and see Efvla. See wood! The trees as they are! I only very rarely go to Xoldra. And I would quite appreciate a student. It is so very difficult to find Xol unblinded by the rhetoric of elz aesthetes."

"And if I refuse?"

Xirell smiled, and there was age in his eyes. "I've merely offered you an apprenticeship."

Elts regarded him still with incredulity, but she was beginning to warm in her cold blood. A life of solitude had not been kind to her nature. Her eyes fell again to the beautiful wand lying so simply upon the table, this artifact from a lost world protected by the art of the new. "It is tempting, but I cannot leave the people of Wyx undefended," she said at last.

Xirell gazed at her with wonder, twinkling green marbles sunk beneath flaring eyebrows of jet. "Hrm. Well, with Rolv gone I'm sure other raider-sorcerers will come snooping about. How will you defeat them?" Sparks traced the penumbras of his eyes; Elts stared into them with cold determination. "I see you have made up your mind. Another proposition then. It's about time this business of raiding be stopped. I would like to linger here and teach you more, but I cannot stay in Wyx; I am hunting a mysterious creature and can ill afford to leave its trail unfollowed any longer lest it fade. Come with me on this quest—it shouldn't take longer than the Spring—and when we return, I will help you free this land from all villains." Xirell held out his gnarled hand.

Elts smiled, the first that she had worn in many years. "I would be a fool to spurn your assistance. It has been my goal for many long years to rid the Hollow of evil, and clearly my current power is insufficient," she said slowly. "But if I'm to leave the children of Wyx unguarded for a full season, I'll have one condition. Gladly I'll adhere to your lessons Xirell, for it is clear to me that you are as good natured as you are wise and powerful, but your aid must only come in that: lessons. It will be the Wind alone, and not an imperial sorcerer which blows the demons away. And if I'm successful... if there are truly no more raiders in the Hollow, then I would love to see Efvla. You touch a lonely chord in me with your designs. I wish to see this wood where it is abundant, if it is so common a thing to the Novare."

Xirell laughed, and when he was finished smiled broadly as one who after earnest entreaty is quite understood. And he said: "Then we must begin at once."

As in a chance beam, sudden sunlight refracted into and exploded the rainy darkness of memory. Frigid day reflected in massive expanding vision off of the glittering white slope leading down into the river-valley. Yet clear as the snow blazing, as the shining face of distant Zenidow, as the black towers of the sheer city affixed to the mountain before it, as the rich, true wood all around her in the mortal trees of the mountains, Elts remembered that night. But there was no more Wind of Wyx. There was no more Xirell, though the suggestion of his form like a husk drifted twenty yards ahead in the shadow of Zelor.

While the glaring snow had ripped away the final blanket of reverie, deep in the dark inner fabrics of memory a different kind of interruption had wormed, and it was this unwelcome bedfellow which originally awoke her senses. That unmistakable notion which forces consciousness to its utmost surface: the incessant probing of another mind into her own. Did Zelor at last move to enslave her spirit? But when looking around, sliding her eyes down the slope and over the trudging Zefloz, Elts recognized a far different urgency. What rapped upon the mind's door furtively but not invasively was rather a psychic inflection from the only other woman in their party.

Fexest—the Black Zefloz—was the longest standing member of their rank after Xirell. Out of the mane of her jagged, sable hair slunk a dreadlocked whip from nape to knee; shadowy bangs like dark claws overhung her onyx eyes. Pale violet in complexion, ropy, restless tails barbed with mauve hooks, it was unclear with what race of Xol her family had mixed to diverge from the pureblood. Yet most things about Fexest were unclear. Her past was a mystery to all but Fozlest, and she spoke little at all with anyone. Apart from a light satchel of black leather, and her uniquely studded gloves, she carried only a short dagger. It was clear enough, however, that she was gifted in strange arts. Light was often distorted in her presence, subtly turned away from her figure. In the same way was sound warped so that when she strode it seemed brusquely in absolute silence. Even her mass seemed to fluctuate. She could leap like a floating leaf to impossible heights, or sink into immovable solidity amid a river which only a golem of stone might ford.

If anything is known of the Xol, it is that they communicate mind to mind, for even those born outside of the light of Xeléd are natural telepaths. So it was that Elts returned the silent call of Fexest in this secretive language. "You and I are alone."

There was no need for physical acknowledgement. It was the back of her black cloak that Elts watched, and even in so doing she looked askance lest the others turn round and suspect treachery. Fexest replied in turn through the channels of the mind: "Yes. All but Zelor have ceased to be."

"He controls them. I've never heard of such an art."

"The flow of Xeléd does not go with him. This is something else."

"I thought he detested all but armed power. Could he really be the same Zelor?"

The roar of the now invisible river reached their pointed ears. It peppered their faces and clothes, wedding with thick droplets of moisture their persons to the fog. The other figures of the company bled into hazy shadows; Elts walked among a mirage host, not knowing from which suggestion of embodiment came the voice of the Black Zefloz in her mind.

"I knew Zelor when he was young," Fexest began. "When he left Xoldra and trained with the Novare of Molavor. But for his unshakable determination he was weak and frail, a petulant runt. He demanded that the captains teach him their sword art, and one day they took him in for whatever reason, be it political or—perhaps he found real companionship. There was always something in the Novare that Zelor admired. He has abhorred the Xol and all users of the subtle arts of war and science. Even his born connection with Xeléd through rock and stone he ignored; I have never seen him turn a pebble. And now this sorcery: more profound than any we know." They slushed through the sodden grass. All was white mist now, even the bleary shapes of the other Zefloz fading. Fexest had never spoken so much in the presence of Elts. Still, she went on. "This new power cannot be his own," her disembodied voice bloomed anew. "I have dreamt many nights now, of black tentacles and a shining beak, of red eyes remorseless and undying. They watch him, from where I know not. Perhaps there is no more Zelor and only this thing."

"I've not dreamt since we entered the mountains," said Elts. "Yet I know one thing without a sign from the gods: he desires the Alium for himself."

"Whatever wears that dead flesh so poorly; indeed, it must seek the Alium."

"If we challenged him when the others were of their minds, we might have stood a chance in carrying on our mission. But..." Elts trailed off. She looked up into the blind fog to where Zenidow must loom above all things. Despite the likelihood of death and subjugation to Zelor, she realized then that she wanted to reach the mountain more than ever before. Even if Xirell could not be saved, was such a journey to the top of the world not the very reason she followed the Green Zefloz out of Wyx?

"The mission cannot be abandoned," Fexest's tone cut in, mistaking the anticipation in Elts' aura for fear. "He may have power, but he is yet mortal. I'll freeze his heart, and leave him a statue in the woods. If you care for Xoldra and your Empress, Elts, you care for the Alium. And if you do not, I'll finish the job alone."

Elts swallowed her anger at this ardour for Fozlest. She could never understand how such high-minded and educated Xol could truly love their so evidently selfish ruler. Xirell most of all surprised her by his faith in Fozlest. Though he would never undermine her feelings on the subject, no story of abandonment and negligence could change him. "I do not care for Xoldra; Fozlest even less," she said, grimacing through the waves of confusion from her interlocutor. "But I do care for Xirell. He was my true master and dearest friend. I will not flee before I can learn if there is a way to recall his mind."

She prepared herself for wrath, but felt only pain. Fexest was hurt, and though she did not speak for some time, it was not out of frustration; rather, she seemed solemn and resigned. Like Xirell, she knew well that Fozlest was unloved; but for one of the Zefloz to call up such maledictions was a new and exquisite sadness.

At last she said, "And what if there is no way? You run?"

"No. If Xirell is gone forever, then I will do everything in my power to slay Zelor. And... even if he can be saved, he will feel the same as you."

Fexest exuded cold concession. "Then you are all right, Elts. I will not ask why Fozlest is your enemy. But I will not wait to attack. Xirell is gone, I am sure of it."

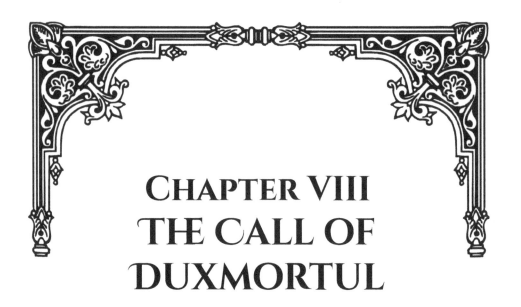

CHAPTER VIII
THE CALL OF
DUXMORTUL

They came by midday to the foot of the great slope. The river rushed powerfully near, infinitely eminent. The curling mist took to the shapes of looming structures, clinging to and hovering in milky nebulae about cracked, stony walls festooned with lichen. Natural tables, spires, and humps of rock reared everywhere from moving pools of fog. They were ancient buildings, hewn of a milk-white stone, looking very much like the confounding structures Elts had studied in the forest above. The only difference was in their clear veins of rich blue ore, softly glowing. Several monolithic slabs leaned stuck in the earth, caked with ice, covered in hieroglyphs which only she recognized.

Through this field of alien relics, full of eerie breezes and deep silences, mist frothing up like a ceaseless chemical reaction, they came quite abruptly into a village which smacked certainly of the Novare. Perspiring, wooden cabins and some larger barnish buildings for storage and livestock replaced the ruins. Hardy mountain goats bleated in stalls there, and many others grazed on the sparse tufts of yellow grass, sometimes which forced their way up through dark crevices in the rock. Paths long used—and freshly trod, cleared painstakingly of snow—wound through the village in no particular order, though there were some more central, roughly cobbled areas where living quarters were clustered. Then Elts saw the men. Novare sat with their boots flopped out in exhaustion, smoking pipes, their faces smothered in dirt and tar, long wiry beards soaked with water vapour. From the low-glowing windows came the clatter of dishes, which carried over their slumped shoulders into the silent streets.

Established Novare life astounded Elts in this unfathomably desolate part of the world; she figured its population wholly ignorant of even other montane civilization, let alone the Xol. As she joined the hooded, black-robed figures of the Zefloz in plain sight of the villagers, one man became particularly alert, though he continued to lean, arms crossed, against the shadowed boards of a seemingly deserted cabin. He wore high black boots, a long, tattered scarf, an equally dishevelled coat, and a wide-brimmed hat with one brass buckle. Grizzled and grey was his shapeless beard, though the vigour of his piercing hazel eyes was clear. That glare was the first that Elts saw when she came out of the fog.

Zelor stopped some yards from the first house, ahead of the company. Voluminous hood thrown away, wet, white hair streamed in the cold wind. His high purple forehead was smooth, but the muscles around his black eyes were tight and knotted with impatience. He drew one long finger out from his robes, and held it up above the roofs of the shacks. Now Elts saw that here the fog above had parted, and the sky was revealed in a clear blue vault. Zelor indicated the high face of Zenidow, rising more massive than ever beyond the three final great snowy peaks in their journey. He made no expression when he spoke, yet his voice carried easily through the silent village, over the roar of the river. "We seek the mountain."

There was a building commotion among the people. Many women and children came from out of their homes, and other red-eyed delvers crowded at the windows or stumbled into the streets, pulling high-collared coats shakily around thin shoulders. When the talking subsided and no one yet had answered, a screaming and wailing burst suddenly out of the people, and a young man was dragged by invisible jaw and talon from their midst through the rocky ice. He writhed from the ground until the crown of his head snapped snug into the sorcerer's lowered palm, legs scrabbling, unable to find purchase on the frosted grass. Upon that suctive contact he wilted, still and silent as those who watched.

An older man in tattered clothes ran wildly from the crowd brandishing a wood-axe, but his yell died in the throat, and he was lifted from the road as Zelor's free hand rose in a fist. With that hand sudden-opened, bent fingers spread like claws, there was a wet crack, and the attacker's body was perfectly bifurcated. So clean was the sundering as to be for a moment bloodless; two clean halves of a man drifted apart, but even as they fell to the ground one, then the other, they began to spew bright red fluid, and their organs toppled out like sick bags. The watcher with the scarf and buckled hat left flying down the street into the haze.

Zelor returned his eyes to the younger man, limp as a carcass hung from the meat-hook of his grip. Yet even as those black pits swung round they turned also up, back into the skull, as if scanning some different world therein. A soggy crunch summoned Zelor to his senses, and he shook his head blearily. A fractal crevice had split in the man's cranium; as the sorcerer—seeming almost surprised—released his grasp, the head separated into triangular and rhomboid shards which littered the snow noiselessly. The corpse followed in a heap, a river of blood gushing over the rocks, staining the river brown.

There was weeping in the crowd, and a woman ran out to hold the dead shaking. Zelor examined his empty palm as if it held something before known only to the man, and turned to look up at the distant black city situated on the sheer face of the nearest mountain. The impression of shock gone, determination rippled his stiff features. Only Elts looked to react when the man died, but she quickly joined Fexest in stifling her feelings, an art at which the Xol are skilled. The other Zefloz stood vacantly by.

A cacophony of hoofbeats tore the shrouds of mist into archways through which rode a host of men mounted upon many-horned goats. The studly animals halted with aplomb, followed by shreds of turf and flat rocks leaping and rolling, and lowered their solemn faces. Their intelligent eyes were trained upon the Zefloz. The riders wore rough armour smithed out of the same blue ore which latticed the stones in the area. They wore as well dark blue capes, torn and weathered. Their leader was a man of great dignity, though his mount was no different from the rest. He wore dull armour as well, though his cape was white, and upon his breast was the golden image of a sickle.

At the sight of the slain, the men were roused into hoarse shouting and the clamorous drawing of blue-bladed swords. They dropped from their shaggy mounts and strode towards Zelor, who stood still over the corpses, looking thoughtfully out at the ruined black towers of the city on the mountain. The only figure to dismount slowly was the hazel-eyed man in the scarf from before; he stood off to the side now with the people. Fexest again surprised Elts with speech, going swiftly to Zelor's side. "Please be wary! Swords mean nothing here!"

The man with the badge held up his hand and passed through the soldiers to stand before the Zefloz. He looked at each of them, Zelor longest, Fexest last whom he addressed. "I am Iglon, Lord of the Mine. What is your purpose here, and why have you killed these men?"

"They refused to show us the path to Zenidow," said Fexest plainly. Elts could hardly contain her disgust, but seeing the narrowed eyes of Zelor soften with

Fexest's subservience she guessed at the subtlety of this lie.

Iglon turned to look at the cowering people, his enraged men. "No path could be so precious. I cannot believe this violence was justly provoked." Many boots clomped forward, but turning, Iglon with one look bade his men sheath their blades. "What is Zenidow?"

"It is there," said Zelor gravely, and he pointed to the far-off tower in the sky, above all things, just—it seemed—beyond the strange mountain whose sheer face somehow supported the black ruins.

"Ah." There was no fear in the man's eyes, but it was clear now to Elts that he was aware of his helplessness in standing against Zelor. "Perhaps there is a way I can speed you on your way. I know nothing of that mountain, but there is one among us who might. He is deep in the mines, however, and will not return until the next sunrise. If your haste abides, I will bring him to you."

Zelor looked long into Iglon's rugged features before speaking. "I shall wait," he said. "If your men raise their swords I will destroy them." Suddenly he went away.

Iglon motioned at the soldiers who with great resentment mounted their beasts or turned walking back into the ethereal mist. "Citizens, please, to your homes. Stay indoors for the rest of the night and do not come out until the bell is rung."

When the villagers had gathered up the bodies of the slain and taken them away, and the streets were cleared and awfully still, Iglon finally rode off after his troops. He did not look back. The sun began to set. The Zefloz had long ago dispersed as a breeze among the monoliths on the outskirts of the village, Fexest disappearing into the shadow of a tall slab.

Elts alone who had stayed to watch the mourning went slowly to the riverbank. The brown blood had washed away, for the river was swift. It was beautiful to her, the way the mountain wind sculpted the crystal water, the way it misted her face. The sumptuous flow reminded her of her inability to work with any medium except for the wind. Always she envied water workers the most, for she found the nature of that medium most akin to the subtleties of her own, which she loved. Despite this ineffable knowledge, she could do no more than impose upon the latter with the former. Waves could be shaped from the surface, curtains of liquid could be drawn forth and altered in the air, expressing complex patterns, the different droplets weaving and compounding as they fell back to the river.

She was, however, distracting herself, and soon her hands lay quietly in the snow. With the water growing still, great gleaming chunks of motionless moonlight assembled between the chance blocks of ice rushing by. This night the heathen moon Ozfled the Godless had risen partly waxing, and it seemed fitting, for Elts—no matter how many of Xirell's impassioned lessons she endured— could not bring herself to believe in the spiritual traditions of her kind. And godless as she was, so too was she without the power all Xol associate with scripture. Her gift of wind was only that—a gift.

The reflection of Ozfled was incredibly clear in the cold water, white but faintly blue, latticed in seemingly organized networks, like roads or canals, though surely these were merely the impressions of geological activity long ended, for the godless moon was a dead moon. Beside it she looked down at her glassy reflection superimposed against the innumerable stars that faded into being with the night. Her icy blue eyes looked back. Above her short white hair, two forked tails stirred the air, but she at once withdrew and wrapped them again around her waist.

She rolled away from the river into the soft grass of the bank, looking up to the stars. Now she saw that two other moons had begun to appear from bulging echelons of dark clouds. There was Xos, the Moon of Death, and Lofos, the dreamt moon visiting only those asleep. Lofos was gigantic and dim, nearly the colour of the night sky, and perhaps only apparent to Elts in the bright white light of Ozfled and the red, immaculate surface of Xos. Dreams, she thought; they were important to Fexest. Somewhere, out there, in the spaces between the points of light, she imagined the horrible tentacled thing from Fexest's nightmares—lurking with endless patience. It was upon this strange and unsettling meditation that she drifted off to sleep.

Zelor sat cross legged atop a high, tilted slab, haloed in the dull yellow light of a fourth moon which had risen long after Elts retired. It was the distantly waning, dim yet somehow simmering Foz, the Moon of Power. He watched Elts by the river, but soon his eyes too were drawn to the stars. Attentive yet burdened as with great sash-weights, he fixed his gaze there deep into the night, and even an expression of awe appeared to cross his face. At last he laid along the ridge of the structure, one arm hanging down into the cool air.

Fexest slipped between and attracted the shadows of the monoliths like a bead of dark liquid. Her knife now naked was black and curved, small and slight. Bare feet worked without sound through icy weeds that should have cracked and rustled, but silent as the stone itself she crouched now at the base of Zelor's high bed.

She willed a weightlessness that lifted her like a dark fog from the ground, and each her fingertips and toes she connected as with magnets to the rock; she drifted along its length to her target like a black spider. As she could reduce the sway of mass, so she could amplify it. The blade of her knife would weigh a thousand tons at the moment it was raised above Zelor's chest. It would impale him to the core of the world, but even if this blow was not sufficient, the curse of petrification long ago etched into her weapon would be upon him from the moment his blood was tapped. He would become like an elz tree, an effigy to the birthright he abominated.

She drew up at last behind the sleeping sorcerer and set the fine point above his sternum, granting it gravity enough to drag buildings beneath ground. Yet nothing moved. The knife felt light as ever in her hands, both of them bearing down, twisting at its hilt. Then it began to turn, turn towards her, no matter the force of will with which she quaked to force it away. Now it levelled at her heart, and the eyes beneath her trembling hands opened coldly and slowly. "Fool," said Zelor. The knife sank inexorably into flesh. Fexest's blood ceased to flow, and she ossified there atop the rock, bent over him.

When he awoke with the raw dawn, Zelor looked firstly into Fexest's vitreous eyes. Almost he scrambled back, having forgotten entirely her assault, but as the vision of her looming over him with black blade crystallized in his memory, he slowly remembered how he had rebutted her, how he had forgotten so easily his promise to the puppet eyes of Xirell—I cannot destroy another. Yet here another stood even more wholly ruined. A Zefloz wasted; and how could he have slept so soundly in the shade of a corpse? He was changing, and quickly. Nights especially became fugues of drowsy wrath. Calming himself with steady breaths, he thought of Elts. Only she remained.

He must not lose her. But the only protection he could offer, as always it seemed to be, was fear. Yes: let this rebellion squashed be a reminder of his power. And if she could not be demoralized, so be it. Next time he would control himself. He leapt down from the rock and stood poised in the grass, tails snaking there about him. "White Zefloz," he called. She stood from her place by the river, face shaded in her hood. He gestured to the frozen treachery of Fexest above, but if Elts struggled to remain stoic upon noticing her, he could not see. "If you've the same design, your fate looks dead upon you from that rock. But you are powerless as she." Zelor felt then a tremor of submission in her, and so without another word he went away to seek Iglon.

Elts sat alone in the quickening morning with the memory of Fexest and her words of honour. Her hatred for Fozlest and the Empire was unchanged, but the pain she'd seen the day before in Fexest's eyes had affected her in the uncanny way of Xirell's passion; now that it too had been silenced, she felt a bitter anguish for the Black Zefloz.

If even Xirell loved Fozlest, perhaps Fexest—so moved to sacrifice without question—might as well have been pure and good. Now more than ever Elts needed to know why such valour could be owed that cruel Empress. Yet even if Xirell was revived to his senses, she knew that he could not help her understand, as many times before he had tried. The Empire had done her too much harm. Still, she saw beauty in Fexest's faith as much as his, and it lifted her heart from despair. She would find a way to awaken her master; and if all failed, she would kill Zelor.

At last she could bear to turn from the soothing flow of ice-water. Avoiding the direct sight of the statue of Fexest, she saw below it that Zelor had left his equipment and pack at the foot of the rock. Something was there among the bags and shadows, an undeniable presence, a black, cold stare. Looking quickly around, Elts stole over to the shaded luggage and carefully leant the largest pack on its side. Beneath it in the cool dark seemed the source of the energy, a small sack tightly cinched. It emanated awareness, as if a godly eyeball were stowed there. Perhaps Zelor had taken it out in the night and forgotten to pack it away. Whatever it was, it was sure to be important. She opened it without hesitating, drawing out a hard bundle bound in leather, about the size and shape of a large egg. Slowly she removed its husky wrappings.

Revealed was the metallic idol of a horrible monster. Purely black but for its six red eyes, aligned in threefold columns on either side of its shining beak, seven tentacles hung down from the bulbous ellipse in petrified coils together echoing the posture of a grasping hand. Even beginning to follow the roiling tendrils Elts' attention was recalled to the red orbits as if she had never looked away. Like bloody gates into mad, forbidden abysses they pulled at her face. Completing the impression of alienness was the ineffable material out of which the idol was composed. It looked at first to be elz bark, being shiny and black. But such bark is incapable of storing warmth, while this material was hot to the touch, and grew hotter the longer she held it. Now too a torrid grip settled into the back of her skull, and her legs shook, but her hand only tightened around the odious thing. She could not release it, sank to her knees now, felt that the bones in her hand would explode from the pressure. She slumped over the image of the blinding eyes enraptured. The sunlight dampened, vanished; dying colours bled into that reddest red which seared and grew. Then all was black.

*

She floated in an infinite expanse of affectless ether, enthroned in oblivion. It was impossible to know if days, years, epochs had passed. There was nothing like time or space here. Yet there was thought; long she had thought. Eternal plans groped in the dead dark like dense weeds. So tireless was their gradual growth that final flowers even more slow to form were long blossomed, long withered. But they would return from the dust. Fully petalled they would burst alive to her purpose should it arise, whatever it had once been, she was sure of it.

There was a notion: a light in the void. It came from within. Eyes opened. Below: a smooth black floor. Ahead: a featureless room, but for the translucent dome which made its ceiling. Through the crystal glass there flickered countless stars, and a soft, blue world, a shaded sphere, thrice ringed in hurtling belts of frost. Hanging beside it was a small white moon.

"You have slept long during our voyage." A being materialized. It was perfectly black, shining, many tentacled; along its oval body, between the stacks of red eyes, a sharp fin jutted out. Massive as it seemed, the entity was slender and in ways elegant. The six organs of vision pulsed softly, seeming each to have their own thoughts. The polished hide gleamed like armour, though whatever wore that sumptuous metal was similarly shaped, for the creature's appendages wandered with the unconscious nature of hands at rest. Its voice, however, was the most peculiar trait of all, for it sounded both like nothing ever Elts had heard—neither male nor female, deep nor high—yet at once uncannily familiar. It was as all voices. She understood it perfectly. The tone it used now was one of profound respect. "Great Duxmortul," said the voice, coming from all directions. The tentacles arranged themselves in a cryptic gesture. "You are risen."

At the sound of these words, a great cognizance large as the abyss enveloped Elts. Her own tentacles stirred with power. She slipped, it seemed, into a sunken part of the mind, as another ego had taken over the processes of the body. Still she saw through strange eyes, felt with strange skin. In this strangeness she remembered her own self at last, looking about the incredible vessel with new awe. When she studied again the being which had addressed her as Duxmortul, it was the very likeness of Zelor's idol.

"Vok," came a deep voice, and it was both her own voice and another. "I am awake." The other being's tentacles worked quickly in response. Though their meaning was lost on Elts she sensed an enormous tension. Unable to control the movements of her vessel, she found herself floating near to the clear glass, looking down at the blue world thereout.

Vok's speech filtered into meaning. "...A primitive race, alone on their planet. They are composed of frozen water almost completely, though they are suffused with light and awareness. We all recognize it, and can feel it even from orbit. They are stubborn and have detested our presence from the start."

"They are weak," said Elts.

"They have little technology, though they construct magnificent artifacts. It would be wrong, perhaps, to call these expressions architecture. I am not sure whether the creatures require shelter, or respite even from their work."

Another voice somehow distinct arose as from nowhere. "Master, it is a profound honour to sense once more your wakeful eminence. As Vok has perhaps not mentioned, these are ferocious and barbaric entities. They fail to understand their fate." Only then did Elts realize that the new voice had come from the surface of the blue world which floated outside the wide window. Now she understood the familiarity in their speech—the shining black creatures were telepaths. But even the Xol struggled to communicate over distances greater than a few miles. These beings were capable of having conversations across worlds.

Elts unfurled her tentacles with a body disconnected from these thoughts, still looking through the glass dome. Before her eyes, as if it were an extension of her unwilling soul, one long black limb swollen and glistening, far more vast than any which sprouted from Vok, was raised before the planet's little moon. Her eyes fixed upon that lone satellite. It swallowed itself, collapsing inward easily as breath. The once solid globe now swept round the planet in a fine dust, accreting into the rings.

"I suspect these creatures are not driven by fear, Great Duxmortul," said Vok softly.

The vision of space dust vanished. Infinitesimally later Elts floated high above a great field of brilliant frost. Xirell had taught her long ago all Xol astronomy that he knew, but Elts could not have expected the true awesome wonder of a different world. This planet was covered in ice, great shifting sheets extending for hundreds of miles, clashing together to throw up immense ranges of blue-white peaks that stretched to the stars. There were no suns, and now no moon to blind the vision of the greater Cosmos.

Yet there was much light, and as Vok had said, it came from the people. They were everywhere, and looked as pieces of the world itself. Like spiders were some of them, others more centipedes, but most all of shapes incomparable to Altumian forms of life. The amount of their legs and shapes of their bodies varied one to the other, and none seemed precisely alike.

Vok appeared in the air beside Elts soundlessly, making no show of it. "Their bodies are everywhere supremely sharp," she said, "and shave and shape the ice easily. They can also produce a seemingly sourceless warmth from within themselves and work the ice into a mouldable state. Retracting that warmth the ice at once regains its solidity. That is how they build their great structures."

Elts now saw tall, leaning towers, arches, domes all around, yet these glittering cities of alien art smoked and melted. Gigantic black vessels, shaped also like the body of Vok and—she inferred—Duxmortul, were everywhere deathly poised upon vast tentacles worming hungrily into the ice. The great parasites threw up the insidious red glare of their lights upon the ornate, gleaming walls and spires.

"They do not appear to have any organs whatsoever, but their light does concentrate in a fine point on some part of their surface, usually the trunk, sometimes at the tips of their limbs (though it appears movable); through this point they perceive the world—we think." Watching the ice creatures as she listened, Elts now understood the true magnitude of Vok's telepathy. Not only could she communicate from planet to ship, but Vok's mere mental projections could also influence the minds of species completely alien to her own. Clearly the ice creatures had heard Vok well, and found her words in a way soothing.

Then Elts spoke: "God is among you. Behold: I raze the heavenly bodies." She held up a great tentacle to the space where once the moon had reflected the light of the world. "And I raze worlds," she said, slowly drawing that long limb away from the sky to threaten the surface of the planet. "Surrender or die, mortals."

The ice people rumbled and clacked. They emitted harmonic aural bursts that vibrated in Elts' mind like the strumming of immense harps. They had no weapons but their bodies, which were yet formidable, no technology but their ways with ice, which were yet many. No flora or fauna had ever kept them company in this barren waste. If Vok had spoken longer she might have explained that the very crust of their world was formed of ancestral flesh. They were, in fact, the planet, and the planet was composed of their history. Now they charged over the plains of their maker to destroy the fire-breathing machines from the sky.

Elts, wracked with unwelcome pleasure, was sickened by Duxmortul's feelings as her own. The other tentacled creators began to disappear in bursts and flashes. Vok stood silently by. The great black ships withdrew their sharp pincers from the high structures, dripping with ice-blood, the heat of their engines ravaging and warping the surface as they departed. Undulating her tentacles, Elts cast an aura of heat that sweltered round her body, and watched as the icy denizens melted and distorted in approach, dying in helpless horrifying mounds and seeping into, rejoining the world. She flew high above the attackers' heads and clawing limbs, where they could just dream of reaching their destroyer. "So it is done," she boomed. "You do not exist."

She beheld her seven tentacles splayed over the world looking like the hand of the void. Below, the ice and its people went dreadfully still. Deep in the heart of the planet a lone tremor shivered. Then the rumbling began, and long it continued. Plumes of the planet's cold core erupted from the crust. Freezing lava frothed and bubbled everywhere. Elts felt the life of the planet in her grasp, but now it began to pull back. Long had Duxmortul slept; Elts' strength was depleted. But she bore down with all her might, feeling intimately how madly she desired the death of the world, and the planet broke. Everywhere the ice people felt the heart of their collectivity distant burst. Brilliant white streams of life flew from the cryovolcanoes that now pocked the surface, and in conjoining rivers of light arched for Elts' shuddering tentacles, pouring into them. She drank and drank, while the black ships waited in orbit.

Then the planet cracked. The crust shifted, mountains fell within themselves, and titanic chunks split. An immense explosion rocked the sky, but throwing up great red energy shields, Duxmortul's ships absorbed the impact, and fell out of orbit smoothly. Elts remained at the core of it all, still drinking. Tentacles spreading somehow wider, tighter, absorbing with abandon all of the planet's life and blood. Even as the dust and ashes began to reform and accrete into a dense dwarf body, she sucked them up so that nothing was left. When at last that sector of dull rock and asteroids was lit only by the distant stars and the evil glow of the black ships, Elts finally lowered her limbs. With vile satiation came a deep sadness which, somehow, reminded her of Zelor.

Loudly the roar of the river returned. The idol had fallen from Elts' hands into the snow, where it steamed, the cruel eyes facing upwards. Prodding which had dulled now became probing as she looked on it, and she knelt again in sudden total pain. It was almost impossible to tear her eyes away from the figurine. Even being able to fling herself away from it, still she saw the two columns of red diamond eyes inscribed in her consciousness.

Gripping the elz-bark mask at her waist, she drew the wind about her for protection, and though it did little to mute the call, she was able to lift the figurine on a gust and force it back into its leather pouch. Then she ran from the place and plunged her face into the river for a long cold while. She lay afterwards gasping for breath beside the water. She shivered, realizing that Fexest's lifeless frozen body had been looking down at her all the while she was enthralled to the awful idol. But now she could think only of Xirell. More than ever she wished to save him from Zelor, from Duxmortul. At least she could kill him and end the misery that no Xol—not even Fozlest—deserved.

When the sun was high in the sky, covered by dark clouds though it was, the telepathic summons of Zelor brought her down into the village. Not a soul was there, but the call had come up from the sloping lowest reaches of the place. And so she walked through a different part of town away and down from the river where the houses were more like huts and shanties. Around a bend of rock and twisted, dead trees appeared a great and ancient mine shaft leading into pitch darkness ensconced in a proscenium of three massive slabs. Before the entrance was a clearing studded with hitching posts; to the far side was a surprisingly well maintained wooden cabin with a slightly smoking chimney of blue stone.

Beside it Zelor sat, eyes closed, on a tall, rotting log. Xirell, Feox, and Xelv slouched shade-faced at an awkward distance from him. Iglon stood in the middle of the clearing with many more soldiers than before, some mounted, others standing with stiff spears planted in the ground, some of them armed with bows which they held ready. More of these archers Elts noticed were posted above the cavern on outcroppings, and along the trail down. A group of villagers and soot-streaked miners gathered at a safe distance. Few women or children had come but those who had gone against the will of their families. An old man kneeled quaking before Zelor's seat. He was covered in fine black dust and dirt, and a bag full up with rocks lay beside him.

"Ardua," said Zelor, turning to Elts but looking high beyond the reach of the mist. Following his gaze she looked to the distant, icy towers and crumbling walls of black ruin affixed to the sheer mountain-face high above. It was the strange city they had seen first coming out of the endless wood.

The old man coughed and spoke in a hoarse whisper. "Ardua, yes. It was our true home. Not long ago it was a great kingdom. Our mines wound so deep into the mountain that there is one passage even which leads to the other side. From there one might see the Great One unoccluded." He drew in a rattling breath, smacked his chapped lips. "But the city was beset by a great sickness. We fled the walls and moved here to Quiflum. The only survivors but for the Queen herself are here now."

"Have you seen this passage?" Zelor asked without inflection.

The old man spoke very cautiously. "I have been as deep as it runs, but... I have not been to the other side of the mountain. No one has."

"This sickness," said Elts. "Will it not kill us too?"

The old man shut his eyes. "If you wish to avoid the sickness, the mines are far more dangerous than the city, for they are its source."

"Are you afraid to return?" Zelor said.

"Aye, sir. I am."

"Then take us there in confidence," said Zelor. He placed his hand over the man's trembling skull. In a tortured moment the lifeless body fell bleeding from the head, and Zelor rolled it away with his naked purple foot. He looked pitilessly into the palm of his hand, where the man's every memory had entered into his consciousness. Elts was reminded instantly of Duxmortul's insatiable thirst for power. The look upon Zelor's face was that of utter void, yet in it there was the same deep sadness, a sadness that almost reached Elts' heart were it not for the horrific deed worked thereof.

There was a staggered twanging of bows, and long iron arrows flew for Zelor. In a blinding swathe of flame Feox was compelled by the instinct of his master to uplift his burning axe. The ashes of the shafts trickled in the wind. Zelor looked up to the guards who stared wide-eyed in horror. He raised his hand.

"Stop!" Elts running forward grabbed his wrist, feeling in a surge—as if tapping some discreet network—his fury at her interference. Swiftly she released him and stepped away. "There is no reason for taking more lives, or any at all. Zelor, this is not the way of our people."

He grimaced, as if remembering something detestable. "The old man would not have kept up. It is more efficient this way."

"And what about the men before?"

Zelor set his thin mouth in stone. "Fear is a great persuader."

"And these soldiers who have no chance of even touching you? You'll waste them for the sake of fear though we are done here? You enjoy it." Zelor lowered his hand, balled it into a fist. There was a shadow over his face. One of the guards audibly exhaled. Elts pressed him. "What will you do with the Alium, Zelor? Will you offer it up to Fozlest as is our task?"

"I will not," he roared suddenly. "Fozlest would use it to rule the world." Elts had never seen such fire in his eyes. "The Alium must be destroyed," he said solemnly, smouldering now. "Now, do you wish to carry on like Fexest, or will you keep your wits?" He held out the quaking fist before Elts. An awful chill emanated from it, invisible silken strands of gluttonous propriety snaking, itching to latch and sink and tear and drink.

"I am all that remains, Zelor. Kill me and you are alone at last. If that is your wish then hasten its passing."

The Silver Zefloz seemed to stand down, and a shadow passed from his place. "If you oppose me I will not hesitate. But I admit the others are not what they used to be. Fexest especially is a sore loss. We will need more strength than my own for this task. Little that we know of the Alium—that it rests within Zenidow, that it has at least some physical form, that its song is heard only in the minds of the prescient—it can be no mortal tool."

"And how then should mortals mar it?"

"There is a way," he soliloquized. "At great cost, power lends itself." He was silent then, eyes far away. High above brooded the black icy towers of Ardua.

CHAPTER IX
SMOKE CLEARS

ut of senseless dark, Ogwold stirred to some notion of the sea. Booming surf on the windowsill echoed the deaf roar of dreamless sleep. Smacking morning lips tasted salt air curling redolent in his big nostrils; their corners turned up. The backs of his sealed eyelids began to ripple, at first with seeping sunlight, then with flowing hangings of water evoked. He rolled over on his lumpy mat to nurture the incipient dream. The fugue of norm had blotted out the light of reverie overlong.

The liquid curtains drew together, swept forth as a yawning wave. Blackened purple at its genesis, rolling from wine-dark base to diaphanous lilac crest, the enormous swirl arched, hung, crashed down unfolding in explosions and geysers of whitewater. Just before the point of greatest violence, Ogwold fell back as unto a seam in the undertow, slipped within the sucking continuum of water kicking streamlined, letting out the long, flowing membranes from their secret sockets in his shoulders. A matrix of timeless currents converged upon, blew out and filled those wing-fins, and there arose from the open water a great music harmonizing as through many voices. Among them was his mother.

Pleading as she was out of care and understanding, Autlos-lo sang only the word Zenidow. In a cadence those three commanding syllables rippled and repeated through the hidden choirs of Flosleao, compounding in volume and profundity as they went. So changed was the song by this word that the very medium of water shifted to fit its instruction. The sea turned massive and slow as a great body, gradually hastening, now exponentially faster, shifting downward, angling all ways inward, becoming somehow shallow and limited despite its former endlessness, sucked too soon from Ogwold's desiccating skin and dragged—clinging in mockery to his ribs and helpless fins—far beneath the world.

Back upon this cradle resolve never
To release your heart. Fix instead fated
Vision—above all things—on Zenidow
Yet higher still. Dive, swim rather in the
Seas of night above immortal; dream with,
Know rather the spaces between the stars.

The spout of final drainage evaporated before it fell. In place of it all was a vast desert, a changeless plane of white-hot infinity sculpted with skeletal dunes petrified in eternal rise and fall like the fossils of waves long extinct. Far, far away stood one shining, cloud-girded feature too tall to tell.

Ogwold leapt blindly out of bed, cracking his elbow on the wooden floor. Blossoming pain crystallized the reality of the cabin in a lucid shard. Suffocating sands dissolved like a veil, opening on yellow half-light, widening the frame of perspective. The edge of the handmade table in the centre of the room rose in definition. There was his father's pipe, lying on its side, charred bowl beckoning, a tail of ash winding about its carefully hewn body. Even as he recognized this portal back to dreamlessness—that void seeming now so sweet and safe—the sound of the ocean outside became again like a great music dragging his senses back to nightmare. Again the water touched him, left him; the doomful desert loomed torrid and portentous.

He lurched for the pipe too hastily and slammed his leg into the table, spilling the leather pouch of norm beside it everywhere. When he reached to resolve the mess, no arm followed his impulse; but here was his left. Now he remembered. Despite the strange, healthful vigour in the pit of the wound, which had felt at first like the phantom energy of the limb now gone, it was a special kind of madness to realize that he could not perform this simple task of holding the pouch and guiding the normgrass back inside.

For now, the absence of his arm was nothing compared to the still loudening call of the water. Ogdof could help him clean up the grounds later. With some fumbling Ogwold was able to messily prepare the pipe. Shaking, he jammed the stem between his broad teeth, and struck a match against the table, breaking three before a flame arose. Hand trembling, pipe bobbing up and down under his awkward bite, he lit the curling tips of the snug grass, thirstily sipping from the curved mouthpiece. Streams of white smoke billowed from his thick, grey lips and hairy nostrils, disrupted and chased away by raucous coughing as the pipe clattered to the table and spilled black-green nuggets.

Even as he finished exhaling, Ogwold's eyes reddened, bulged, sagged. Warm spectral arms reached out from some invisible but intimately near dimension, embraced and massaged the soft tissues of his mind with angel fingers. Moments from a crescendo of total unbearable purpose, the song of the sea foundered into a dumb, mindless noise, evoking nothing. He laughed and sighed at the routine crashing of the waves, familiar and comforting now as the cawing seabirds, the creak of his chair, and the sounds of Nogofod feet crushing rocky sand. What was so awful about the desert anyhow; like the sea, it was beautiful in its own way. Even Epherem had its charm. He threw himself back onto the sleeping mat, reflecting on his mother's singing not as a dire omen, but as a serendipitous window into a secret past too grand for immediate concern. Zenidow—it was just a place. Why shouldn't he go to it? Perhaps one day, he thought, lazily watching the smoke drift and pool over the table.

The first shaft of sunlight cut through a chink in the rough leather curtains over the window. "Smoking in the morning? So you side with Wog." The peripheral dark mass of Ogdof sat up and snorted the pungent air.

His son lay grinning goofily through tombstone teeth, misty eyes placidly roving about the room, falling upon and gazing in childlike wonder at the luxuriant bandage around his right shoulder. Its faint iridescence kindled in a brassy outline with the dawn light. "Wog was right about one thing," Ogwold murmured. "Norm makes everything feel so sturdy and vital. Right now I feel like I'll be just fine if I never swim again. Pretty as the ocean is, it's nice enough to just listen and remember. Besides, there are all sorts of other pretty things in the world."

"Well that's something." Ogdof smirked. "Though I suspect with age alone the subtleties of life grow more beautiful, norm may hasten that process. It has indeed many medicinal properties physical and spiritual. Certainly, it has helped me to see things from perspectives I would call essential. But remember, it is all right with me if you must swim, so long as you are discreet," he went on, rising and touching the ceiling with his long, rough arms; the scars long ago eroded by seawater looked natural as the rocky musculature they canyoned. "You needn't turn to the grass over-heartily if it is only to soothe your loss. One puff goes a long way. I had to carry you home last night, you know. You'd collapsed in the middle of town." A long rattling groan tumbled from his grizzled face while he stretched. Drawing open the curtains so that the single beam of light expanded and washed the cabin in pale sun, he lumbered to the food crate sleepily and began collecting tutum skins, bringing them to the table. His heavy-lidded eyes turned impassively over the spilled norm.

"It's better if I don't swim," mused Ogwold from his mat. "I was too fixated on one part of the world, when there are so many other things to explore and understand. Besides, I've drawn enough attention to your house. The norm has opened my eyes! It might help me enjoy real Nogofod business as much as I did swimming." Saying 'Nogofod business' as though he were some stuffy scholar, he folded his arm behind his head and looked out through the window, over the seething, dawn-touched waves, and thought of the previous day's events. Though the norm still could not push her from his mind entirely, with the smoke thick in his system, the plea of Autlos-lo still seemed so harmless and distant. "Perhaps one day, I'll leave Epherem…"

"And go where?" Ogdof grunted from the table, eyes sunken like caves in his furrowed brow. "Last I checked the business of Nogofod was to stay put."

"Once I've truly understood that business, I mean, this life I've shunned, then I might go out and try to understand other things too." Ogwold was fascinated by the ease with which he could speak of things before so stressful, and so he went on. "I think I'll go to the mountains, to Zenidow actually." The idea seemed so abstract and surreal that he smiled as it was a thing merely of fancy.

"Zenidow," said Ogdof gravely; but turning up one corner of his low mouth he added, "Of course, the next logical business to master." Unable to enjoy his own joke, he fell, however, to brooding silently under his enormous eyebrows, slowly chewing the tough tutum skin in wide circles.

Not quite hearing his father, Ogwold rolled out of bed as if the blankets were too heavy to lift, crawled playfully a ways, slowly boosted forward from his knee, and slouched with wide, careful movements to the table. His eyes were bleary, and each step was conducted like the setting down of a heavy, stone coffer, but a smile spread over his face. It was a nice and good thing to move so slowly, as if there were enough time for anything in the world, ambling like a newborn across this new floor in this new world, treating the commands of his mother like a story to be played with, taken seriously some other time. So it was that he became gradually theatrical in his disposition, stopping beside the table and looking out through the window over the horizon with the parodically burdened brow of a hero. "Autlos-lo sends me there."

"Ah, now I see. I should have known more dire circumstances than sea-monsters must summon her." Ogdof was taking things very seriously despite his son's dramatics, though Ogwold immersed in the pomp of his act did not notice. "But what will you do about the guards?"

"I'll quit the coast at night," Ogwold quickly announced, assuming the stance of a great tactician. "The watch is only vigilant near the village. I know places by the water where neither Novare nor Nogofod dare go."

"They are not even so watchful near the boundary," Ogdof added thoughtfully, brushing his salt-knotted beard. Crumbs of springy tutum skin rolled out and bounced along the table. "Most nights they would rather drink, not to say they don't love a good chase. But a Nogofod simply does not run away. Our culture holds us here more than Novare with swords." He looked to his son almost wistfully. "Still, if you are seen in Occultash you'll be slain straight away. Even if you can survive the leagues of desert ahead, how will you disguise your ogredom there?"

Ogdof's insistent intellectualizing finally reached Ogwold, for he had not considered the journey any further than the act of leaving itself. Occultash was the only Novare city anywhere close to Epherem. Governed as well by the oversea authority of Lucetal, it was a vast trade settlement built along the face of Shadith, the nearest true mountain to the sea. Traders and delvers from the range came exclusively through that hub in their long journey to offload in Epherem. It was said that the road into the Mardes, otherwise shielded by sheer walls, began only in the heart of Occultash, in a great tunnel carved out of Shadith. Immersed in such logistics as Ogdof had raised, Ogwold reflexively took up the pipe once more, and struck a match, this time very successfully. As he spoke now, watching the outward billowing smoke as if reading therein a secret lettering, the last traces of theatrics left his voice, and his heart spoke sincerely for all its former jocularity.

"It would have to be at night as well then. I hear that the journey from the coast to the city is more subject to delay, and that the gates are left open for caravans that arrive after dark. Maybe I could slip through them and find a good place to hide, look for a vantage on the tunnel into the mountains or a place to stow away during the day. But there would be guards at the entrance into Shadith. If the traders tell us anything it's that the government of Occultash thinks it owns the road into the Mardes..." As the last trail of milky smoke dissipated into raw sunlight, Ogwold suddenly suspected that he sounded quite stupid, and the inertia of this anxiety shifted his thoughts to the comforts and consistencies of life in Epherem. Only a fool would abandon this place where every necessity was near.

"It is possible," said Ogdof, chewing powerfully. He had listened with intensity. "I myself considered it many times when I was younger."

Ogwold was appalled enough that the norm-weight behind his shame swung its momentum to surprise instead. "You? How many secrets have you left to reveal?"

"Not many." He chuckled. "I used to hate Epherem, the idleness of our race, and Novare more than anything. I thought the norm was planted here to control us, that once long ago our ancestors roamed Altum freely. But hate... it was never a powerful enough drive. I am proud of you for finding your own way to love Epherem, even if it happened to be in doing the thing all Nogofod and Novare jointly despise." Now it was Ogdof's turn to look out at the purple waves. "Though, I suppose your loving the water is the fault of my own pursuit of meaning. The love that changed Epherem for me was for your mother, and now you, Ogwold. When I first beheld you and saw the cheeks of Autlos-lo etched into your little face, I knew I could never leave you. Taking you beyond the boundary was quite out of the question, and now I am too old for such business anyhow."

Ogwold smiled, grey-red eyes big and misty. He had never felt so proud of Ogdof as he was then, imagining his father as a young adventurer, glossy-haired, surly to his elders, unconcerned by work or pay. "I love you too, Dad. I won't leave you either."

"Autlos-lo is not to be ignored, Ogwold. Now, I don't know a single Nogofod that's made the journey, but the King's arm is only so long. If somehow you were to make it into the deep mountains, I think you would be all right."

"Well, let's not be hasty," said Ogwold, laughing nervously. "One day I'll go. You're right, I should listen to her." His hand rested near the pipe of norm. "But for now... I feel like I've never embraced our kind. I want to love Epherem as a Nogofod, not a Flosleao."

Ogdof gave his son a stare cryptic as any, nearly closing his slabby eyelids, bearded eyebrows like a furry awning shadowing all meaning. "There is not much to it, son." Then his face softened, and there was a twinkle in the dark like the first star of the night. "But do as you will. Be careful of that grass now. It is good therapy in doses, yet in large quantities over time it drains a mind. For an old ogre like me with nothing left to seek, it is ever a great source of calm, but for a young man like you, Ogwold," Ogdof clapped his great mitt down on his son's hand, pinning it to the table before it could reach the pipe. "Perhaps there is such a thing as being too calm."

*

Ogdof soon finished his breakfast and went to fetch water from the purifier. His son sat unmoving in the musiclessness of the ocean. Like a circular, self-affirming truth repeated on the surf as in his mind was the surety that he could stop smoking whenever he wanted. For the time being, he thought, it was quite sensible to plug up his ears until, perhaps in a week or two, the song of the ocean and the threat of the desert became more bearable. While the norm had earlier quieted her song, only a truly prodigious amount of smoke would really take his mind off his mother. That was what he needed though, a full disconnect. Nodding as if communicating this to the empty room, he took an enormous, almost desperate pull from the pipe, coughing as burdened by lungfuls of sand for several minutes.

Thick layers of heavy heat packed against his streaming eyes, and his breathing grew awfully shallow; but when the intense weight settled he slumped back under a leaden blanket of total contentment, forgetting all his ails. So powerful now was the trance of norm that his mother's song and notions of an adventurous young Ogdof faded into meaningless, lovely colours and incoherent sounds, unable to mark his consciousness. Chewing a tutum skin with a beautifully empty mind, he watched daybreak slowly gather far over the simple, elegant waves beyond the window.

As if it were determined to reawaken the deeper meaning of those waters, his left hand wandered to the whorl of vegetation where his right shoulder should have been. Not particularly reminded of the plant's source, Ogwold did, however, notice something very strange. He could feel the callused palm of his left hand where it rested on the solid bandage. Though it was a dull feeling, as through the buzzing roil of a bloodless extremity, there it was, skin against skin. He reached all along, following the thick roots to the places where they sank beneath his hide, under the ribs, around the shoulder blades. Everywhere was that same intimate and uncanny sensation felt. Everywhere too did he sense that the bandage had slightly grown.

Suddenly he saw in the reflection of the glossy material the angry, spittle-flecked face of Wog, and all sense of wonder left him. Rude and oppressive as he was, that ogre was at least a friend of his father's. Far worse reactions would follow him in Epherem should his greener shoulder be even partly glimpsed by a stranger. Fear and worry now intensified as pleasure and satisfaction had moments before. Rummaging through the clothes at the foot of his sleeping mat, Ogwold tore away from his oldest tunic a long scrap of cloth, and quickly wrapped the wound, obscuring its alien colour and texture. Looking at the snug stump, he remembered too clearly that he was now simply a burden on Ogdof.

He would never be able to lift the traders' chests. Absolutely inundated in norm as he was, still some begrudging, forcibly sunken self forced him to recall the bestower of the bandage and her command.

Perhaps he really should leave Epherem. With this thought a pulse of clarity quickened his blood, and his heart seemed to beat as before danger. He sat envisioning now in vivid detail his second vision of Autlos-lo, looking so much like Caelare riding her chariot of cloud, scanning the world, waiting at the top of the Peakless Place for her son to answer fate. But he must be absolutely certain, said a creeping paranoia in his buzzing breast. He noticed the smoke drifting through the room, how it swirled all around as if to comfort him in a sunny blanket, and the pungent, baking smell calmed him slightly. If this quest was so important, he thought, another vision would surely come. One more vision; just one more, a third and final sign from beyond—so seemed threeness to him mystical. If he saw his mother again in the face of the mountain, he would leave Epherem at once!

Plowing through the dew-soaked door he turned and shielded his glassy eyes against the white glare of distant Zenidow. With grey-red stare he sifted the echelons of its dense crown, hunting every shadow in the billowing fog for the suggestion of some figure, the blazing hair unmistakable in his memory, the graceful recline, the searching, radiant eyes, the velvety dark wings. But there was no sign of her. Not one swirling cloud bore any form but that, a nebulous fluff, such that he began to tell himself the striking vision from the night before was only dream. Yet, what was a dream so powerful that even norm could not hold it back?

Ogdof came stomping up from town with a full skin of water. "What a radiant sight is Zenidow at sunrise!" he declared sonorously, following his son's gaze. "Folk are wrong to say such a place is evil. Wog would probably tell me now that the most damned things show themselves as angels of light." He handed the wasterskin to Ogwold, who drank deeply, dousing the smoky cotton in his throat. "Well! Unless you're off to see it for yourself," said Ogdof from the shadowed caverns of his brow, "Caelare summons our labour. Come! There is far less shame in the one-armed Nogofod who works than in the one-armed Nogofod who hides in his father's house!"

With day pouring over the desert and rushing up along the feet of the mountains, a drowsy caravan crested the arid hills bubbling in rocky humps down to the sea. Rickety covered wagons wobbled and rattled over the rough, winding path, drawn by stout, horned cornibets, who huffed and drove their wide hooves into the shifting ground. Reins loose in their raw hands, somnolent tradesmen swayed and bobbed, dreaming of the treasures betrayed at chance wobbles twinkling in the dusty deeps of their shaded storage.

Nogofod of all hulking shapes, bent and stately, lurked about the docks, awaiting hire. Rugog and Dur—two ash-skinned ogres around Ogwold's age—pushed to the front of the group, shaggy arms proudly crossed, cleft chins bare of scruff and bulbous heads closely shaven. Swarthy Wodfud, largest and strongest in Epherem, arrived latest but more noisily than any, clapping her huge hands down upon wincing brutish shoulders dwarfed as she stomped by. Youngest of the group and lightest in countenance was Ogrud the orphan, a frail pole somewhere in the midst of Nogofod like big rocks tumbled together. Wise Gurgof the village healer stood off to the side watching the bright orb of Caelare's Palace rise fully above the sea, his heavy braids pulled back and bound with Lucetalian twine. It was he, Ogdof's only other friend, who would agree soon to the conspiracy of having bandaged Ogwold's arm.

The first wagon to reach the broad, flat stretch of rocky land before the docks ground on its slow wooden wheels to a snorting halt. Its largest cornibet shook from haunch to great head grumbling while the others of the team stirred the gravel and panted loudly. Already the next cart was settling in, the horned beasts being calmed, presented shallow bowls of water; beside it another arrived. "Ten brutes!" the first driver shouted, sliding down from his seat, sending up a plume of rock dust, through which he stepped, hands stuffed into the deep pockets of his fine coat. "We're putting it all on the *Celeritas*!" He nodded towards the smallest of the three great galleons from Lucetal, already anchored.

There was no contest for the job. Ten giant figures lumbered forward. They reached their grey, rock-muscled arms into the dark tent of his cart, and one after another drew away with immense black chests, quaking from the weight. With slow, thunderous footfalls, shattering the thinnish plates of rock that scattered the beach, they made for the docks. If one guessed that the slumped posture of these trollish creatures indicated lethargy, the inexorable labour which followed would silence them. The Nogofod are powerful and endlessly durable creatures, their strength marvellous. So long as the load fits between their massive arms, even the smallest hoists three hundred pounds smoothly as they harvest the norm or pick tutum. Yet more impressive than strength or stamina is their unflinching integrity. Questions were not asked. Orders were received with dignity. Great respect was given to the Novare and their prized possessions. Even wrathful Wog passing by with a high, bound stack of jewelled caskets looked as though he carried the most precious and venerable objects in all the world.

Despite the honour and reliability of the Nogofod race, the traders were greatly covetous of their goods, and there were always some ogres, shunned for whatever reason—the light in their eye, the way of their stride, the stink of their sweat— who went often without coin. So it was that even those such Nogofod received tasks and payment before one-armed Ogwold, who found himself quite alone, seated on a wide, sun-baked boulder, looking up into the mountains, his back to the sea.

"Ogwold! Ogwold!" It was broad-shouldered Fodfof, daughter of Fodwush and Gorfof.

Ogwold stood slowly up laughing. "Fodfof! Where are your friends?" He wobbled slightly, dizzy from the heat of the sun.

"I should ask the same of your right arm!" She skidded in a cloud of sand and gravel, rooted bulky arms to her hips.

He looked down at her, though just barely, for she stood nearly the size of an adult Novare. Fodfof had long black hair like all Nogofod, yet in place of the common dull grey her eyes were a rare, rich silver. Like all female ogres she had a low, tough chin, large ears, and a stately nose. As with all children, Ogwold was perhaps too honest with her. "I tried to leave Epherem," he said. "It was severed as punishment."

"Leave? But why?" She squinted up into Ogwold's norm-fogged eyes. "You look... different, Ogwold."

"I'm not sure. It just came over me."

Fodfof folded down the corners of her wide mouth. "You've been swimming, haven't you? Mokod saw you go into the water yesterday after the traders went."

Ogwold sighed. If it was difficult to sneak away from the villagers, it was impossible to be free of Fodfof and her friends. Partly it was his own fault, for he spent much of his time telling them stories, pointing out the Nogofod constellations, teaching them to track the ripest tutum in the grove or plant its seeds where they could best tap the groundwater. They had known for almost one year that he went into the ocean, but they kept his secret, for they loved him. He was unlike the other adult Nogofod, and had no issue talking about magic or things at all, really, that mightn't exist.

"Well you can tell Mokod that I'm never going to swim ever again." Ogwold placed his hand over his heart. "I've promised that to myself."

"Really?" Fodfof smirked, disbelieving. "We'll see about that."

Ogwold smiled and went to cross his other arm over the first, but there was of course no limb to accomplish that impulse. A shadow passed over his face.

"So you leave the ocean, and then you leave me! What's the matter with you?"

"I'm not going anywhere. It was a silly idea."

She grinned, showing a mouthful of dun, flat teeth. "Good! I don't think Mokod could go on without your stories."

"Oh, Mokod speaks much better than I. Even the Novare are entertained by him." Ogwold began to smile, thinking of the little myth-maker, but already the expression wilted. "I enjoy it here with you all... But now I'm without hire. No one will entrust their treasure to a one-armed fool." He slumped back onto the wide rock, chin in his palm. His long black hair shaded his face in windy locks and spilled twisting round the cloth-wrapped stump at his right shoulder.

Fodfof frowned and watched him sulk. All at once she said, "I'll find you a job, Ogwold!" When he looked up he saw only a cloud of rock dust that was the exhaust of her departure.

The norm was still heavy on him and it was easy to sit there drinking the heat, melting into the rock, becoming like a morose wax statue. He felt even that he was in the perfect state for a fine dream, right in the liminal space between waking and sleeping, but there was only red darkness behind his eyes. Eventually he took to listening then, to the sounds of the Nogofod tramping through the sand, the meaningless majesty of the sea ever crashing and booming, the shouts of traders and grumbling of cornibets. He felt supremely left out. The sun passed its apex in the sky, and headed slowly over the Mardes, paring away the shadows in their eaves, so that the furthest, snowy peaks lit up brilliant and blinding white as always-radiant Zenidow.

From the folding rows of the endlessly arriving caravan by the docks, one dishevelled vehicle turned and rolled Ogwold's way. At the reins of but one weary, gaunt cornibet was no trader, but a true delver in ragged clothes, covered in dirt, captaining his own haul. Alongside his eminently collapsing cart stampeded a crowd of young Nogofod, Fodfof at the lead. With her was Mokod, Yongog, Shug, Gorfol, Oduk, and Wugor, all charging powerfully forward, rock and dust flying up from their great naked heels, calling his name. Ogwold stood and smiled as the children swarmed. Struck as by many careening boulders, he let himself fall backward into the gravel—though he needn't help them much—and they piled all over him laughing and tumbling. "Ogwold, are you really never going to swim again?" Mokod sat painfully on his chest, cross legged.

"Yes," Ogwold managed. "Now get off of me, ogres!" He rose with sudden strength and shook them overboard. Roaring he chased Mokod down to the beach, but he stopped even as he began, looking out to the ocean which had been at his back all morning. As before it was simply a vast purple turbulence of water, seething and flowing one wave against the other. Coming back to the other children, who had gathered around the arriving wagon, he addressed the delver warmly, promising that he could still help even with only one arm.

"He's got a strong constitution, this one," barked Gorfol, and she punched Ogwold hard in the ribs. The blow sounded like a boulder dropped onto wet sand. "He could outwork any Nogofod!" The other children laughed and snorted as Ogwold doubled over comically and wheezed with only partly dramatized pain.

The delver smiled and chuckled like he had seen such a display many times before. Unaccustomed, however, to riding, he clambered awkwardly down from his mount, leapt tentatively into the gravel, and nearly fell flat on his face. He had on black leather boots, a disgusting, patchwork cloak, and a tattered, dusty cap wreathed with frayed tawny hair full of sweat and dirt. Smiling brown eyes peered out from the mass of hair over teeth that were stained nearly the same hue as his nut-brown skin. "I'm sure he can help," he said warmly.

"Thank you, sir," Ogwold said, carefully sitting cross-legged on the ground so that he was eye level with the delver. "I haven't found work all day."

"So I heard." The delver watched Fodfof and her friends already charging off. Even among the hardy Nogofod, children are not fond of work, and so they went to play elsewhere. He turned back to Ogwold. "I'm leaving the mountains for good," he said proudly, stroking the bony back of his exhausted cornibet. "I've enough rare ores here to settle down in Lucetal." The beast looked at him anxiously, as if pleading that their journey be over.

"I will be most cautious with their transport," Ogwold recited dutifully.

The delver laughed. "Of course. There are six crates in the back. At your own pace, friend."

Rising and lumbering round to the side of the wagon, pulling up the canvas, Ogwold found in the stuffy shade a filthy pack, a dirt clodded pickaxe, several battered oil lanterns, and two rugged metal helmets. Beside the miner's tools were several wooden chests dully latched. If they had been aligned or stacked in rows before, the jostling journey had knocked them all over. He wrapped his long arm around the closest, righting it, sliding it nearer. The splintery sides dug into his ribs where he tucked it firmly, and chafed his skin, but his left arm was strong and held it fairly tight. It seemed he would at least be able to help with loads of this size, but this was not much of a test; whatever ores this delver had found, they were uncommonly light. "To the *Celeritas*, please," said the delver peeking round the side of the wagon; he smiled so wide his eyes were drawn shut.

Ogwold found the norm in his work. Peace, solidity, safety, all those encouraging effects which like blades of grass themselves had wilted since his last smoke, now quickened, curled, stiffened hearty and green as though the weight of each package under his arm were a beam of sunlight or a drop of crystal water. Back was the heaviness and understanding of the morning; back was that chugging inertia to amplify all feelings. Simply and clearly as came the empowerment of his tasks, going wagon to deck, wagon to deck, one package following another, that Ogwold became enraptured with belonging. Indeed, the shapes of Nogofod trudging alongside seemed to share with him an unspoken burden, this timeless privilege of humble service. The weight not only of chests but of this secret honour too settled into his being like the natural, vital tug of flesh upon bone. Even as he placed one package aboard the *Celeritas* he craved the next; yet those moments were so outside of time, so touched with meaning that he would stand senses alive and relish the heat and sweat and weight of his labour as it caught up to him. It was truly as immersive a practice as Wog had so reverently described the night before.

So the day passed, and the next, and another. For weeks, months, one season, Ogwold dismissed all that ailed him. Each morning, when the alarum of the sea broke his slumber, he dissolved the song of his mother in norm. For many days after breakfast he stood weighted beside the cabin scanning the highest reaches of distant Zenidow, as if Autlos-lo might yet send a new vision. But always the sterile mountain was desolate. As dreamless nights and visionless mornings gave way one to the other, he eventually stopped looking for her, and the mountains became like a backdrop, a non-place, unattainable as the sky itself. Now he was a true Nogofod man, whose eyes never strayed from his work, whose blood rushed for the transfer of precious things too weighty for Novare. At last he embraced the ways of his father's people, and placed his faith in custom.

Unnatural as it was to see him so agreeable and content, Ogwold had never wanted to spend so much time with Ogdof, and now with all those great secrets finally undressed, there was a closeness between them which he treasured dearly. Even as water and good tutum became a luxury, Ogdof did not press his son to recall the words of Autlos-lo, or confront the subject of their poverty. Though many were the days from which Ogwold returned with an empty purse, such were the nights when Ogdof ensured him that all was well, that tales would be told in Occultash one day of the Nogofod with but one arm who carries yet any load. Then they would smoke together by the fire and be merry and tell stories, for norm was free, and merriment was never before so abundant between father and son. Oftentimes Wog would visit after dinner, and Ogwold found even that obnoxious brute to have his charms so long as you joined him in smoking, for he was quite a raconteur once you were used to him, and loved few things more than a powerful laugh.

For this one gilded season Ogwold's life was a pleasant, unsurprising routine, and there is little else to say of those days, each like the other, but that he became much closer to his father. Yet as if their relationship had at last reached some threshold of love and trust such that could carry on forever, as if there were some internal clockwork in his animal heart which reached its goal, sprang, broke and undermined the mechanism of its routine, on one morning, at first like any other, sitting at the table watching the waves through the window as their meaning foundered in the norm-state, Ogwold smoked right through their stock. It was not for the sake of being more greatly weighted that he filled the wooden pipe many more times than usual, but for the sweet act itself of drawing in the hot smoke, letting it spill out in liquid blue coils overlapping in the sunlight, blanketing the table, falling from its fine edge in milky cataracts, rising and venturing out of the window, investing that great sea which was no threat at all to the imagination they protected. Bustling through the door heavy-eyed and giddy to audaciously carry something far too heavy for a one-armed man, he forgot all about the need to go and cut some more.

Never before had the norm run out. Whenever even the wooden bottom of their norm-crate was partially revealed, Ogwold was quick to visit the tutum groves and gather the finest, greenest tufts from the gnarled shrubs that grew most profusely at the bases of the weird trees. But that night, when all the work was done, when he had shared a wrap with Ogdof and Wog by the hearth and curled up warm and heavy, it slowly occurred to him what he had forgotten to do. Blearily he realized that no grass would drown out the sea-song of dawn, but he was so tired, and still so exceedingly weighted that going into the groves after dark seemed preposterous.

When the golden light of sunrise cut anew through the leather curtain, and, as if propagated through this swath of light, the sound-waves of the ocean became like the purposeful singing of numberless Flosleao, Ogwold leapt from his sleeping mat, as always, with the urgency of one in crisis. Even as he began to breathe more evenly and allowed the suddenly taut muscles in his big back to uncoil, looking to the table, now the empty norm-crate, with finality he remembered the dearth of his medicine. Ogdof was already up, sitting at the table nibbling tutum and sipping carefully from the waterskin. Even the sudden crisis of Ogwold's awakening was mundane enough, but as his son careened by, Ogdof's eyes raised high as they were able, gunmetal irids nearly half exposed. "Ogwold! Your bandage has grown!"

And so it had. Hung with the linens of its destroyed dressing, a dense whip of tightly wound, verdant nerves stretched about one foot from a massy cerebrum of vegetative musculature. The roots which tethered this bulb to his empty socket had grown more numerous overnight, digging into the neck, back, chest and ribs so thoroughly that in places—surrounding the trunk like vines—they met and fastened together. While this evolved embrace seemed to creep and pulse even now deeper and tighter against him, more astounding were the fine movements of the living appendage they fed. The hard, slender shoot-bundle moved as unconsciously as Ogwold gawked, joining his other hand in feeling the exuberant green coils tapping into his flesh. Through the nest of freely flowing tendrils at its narrowing terminus, he could feel everything thereby touched, and even—if less powerfully—through the root-flesh so palpated.

"It is a gift from Autlos-lo," said Ogdof coming over and placing his huge hand upon the swollen green shoulder-bulb. Ogwold jumped with the intensity of the sensation rippling through his new extremity. "A magical thing," his father went on. "Perhaps it is ancient Flosleao technology, or something she found on her travels through the wide sea. One day it will become an entirely new right arm, son. Why, you're better off for going into the water!"

> Take this elder of the sea, and through it
> Drink the other waters of the world. Love
> And light it needs in teaching you to speak.
> Deep into the blood and bones now reach its
> Careful roots, and always hereon will you
> Have in common the memory of peace.

Assaulted by the increasingly clear voice of Autlos-lo, as it had risen from the sea-roar so long clouded by norm, Ogwold forcefully ignored the sensations that surged through the plant growing in his shoulder, and attacked his father's surprise. "It is a sore sight if I'm to find work!" he shouted, staring into Ogdof's eyes, seething at the sound of undying surf. Closing them tightly and clenching his jaw, he contained his frustration. "Dad... I'm sorry. I can't start the day without a smoke." He spoke now low and gravely as one in need. "Help me obscure this thing and we'll deal with it later." He turned madly to his mat and began throwing clothes and blankets every which way.

Cutting an old tunic down the seam, they made a sling which Ogdof knotted around the plant from shoulder to opposite hip. Ogwold was able to draw in the greenery so as to be surprisingly compact inside. For now, the others might believe they had merely changed for a thicker, more comfortable dressing, but Ogdof could only think that the plant would certainly outgrow its new container. Clear as this doom revealed itself as well to Ogwold, as soon as the new bandage was snug, he rushed out to the groves breakfastless, in search of something, anything to smoke.

Yet even barrelling through the door at full speed, even as his first stomping strides split the thin plates of rock, Ogwold felt that something else had changed. It had been many months since he had gone so long without norm in the morning. In these unheard hours the music of the ocean had shifted in tone, calming of its own accord. Now reached his ears not demanding notes of dire purpose, but sweet melodies of compassion and truth. Sprinting, then jogging, plodding, tramping, he eventually stopped, at the outer rim of the tutum groves, listening intently. His head was clear, his posture easy and tall. Slowly his spine straightened and his good shoulder rotated back behind it, allowing his chest to open and breathe the salt air. The wind ripped through his clothes cool and exhilarating. Far off a bird of prey called to the goddess. At last he turned to see the water, not as taboo or tragedy, nor purely as a thing of beauty, but as a place where once he belonged.

The purple waves boiled on the horizon where day poured through its bright circular gate, now rising in the cobalt sky. One thin, radiant cloud shot atop that close star, and upon it rode the winged form of Autlos-lo. As before, Ogwold was reminded of Caelare, so enshrined by the sun was his mother as that deity in her mythic palace. She raised her long arm, sheathed in an arrowhead of gulls, ringed in golden vapour, and turning to its direction Ogwold's eyes found the upper reaches of Zenidow. He stood long, looking up to that mountain. Had thoughts of norm returned they would have departed unrecognized. The fibres of his sapling arm strained to grow. Turning back in some timeless moment he found the sun riderless. Still, he had had his vision.

CHAPTER X
FAREWELL TO EPHEREM

Ignoring the din of the tradesmen, Ogwold wandered into the shaded grove, going beneath the broad leaves on their spindled, black branches, so that for Ogdof's sake he would not be seen avoiding the work.

He plucked one of the sky-blue tutum fruits, testing its fleshy weight, turning it in his hand, peering between the wide boughs ensconcing far away Zenidow, thinking of Autlos-lo, of Caelare herself even, awaiting him at the summit unseeable. So uplifting was the light of her hair, the breeze which she rode. How could he have stayed in Epherem after even once perceiving such glory and its command? Hanging his head in shame, his gaze fell low on the weeds of norm growing densely about the tutum trunks as was their nature, dark green, caked with sap, stinking of the sea. He saw them now as once his father had: invaders on the shore, brought by Lucetal to numb the minds of its servants.

"Young master," came a soft voice quite close. "Are you available?" Nearly jumping, Ogwold turned and beheld a dizzy shadow eclipsing the sun, slowly coming into focus as he adjusted from the shade of the grove. It was a noble codger, evidently quite wealthy, cloaked and cowled in dark rose, lacing his ringed hands atop a gnarled, black staff. Coruscating light through the wind-rustled boughs and broad leaves dappled his merry complexion, and his fog-white beard blazed along its jagged edge.

His deep blue eyes gestured to a stunning beast as it followed behind. It hadn't hooves, but four paws, and thick, curved claws which sank into the loose rock it traversed, carrying its package—a medium sized wooden chest—strapped between high triangular shoulders. The creature was lean, long and lithe for its enormous size. Two sets of tall pointed ears flicked and tucked as in the motions of some subtle language. In a similar manner its sinuous triplet tails swished and undulated independently, from each tip a sable tuft darting like the flames of dark candles. Covered in shaggy white hair, its lupine snout overflowed with interlacing fangs and bristled all along its barrel length with stout, wiry whiskers. Most captivating of all were the immense, elliptical eyes, perfectly black, reflecting nothing.

"My companion: Videre," said the man in red, sweeping his arm low. The animal chuffed and stretched out its body rapturously, front paws sliding forward, rear end lifted into the air. "The chest she wears is bound for Lucetal. I sail on the *Patientia*, young master. I've silver for your strong hand." He frowned somehow coyly. "Deft as she is, I'm afraid Videre would quite spook folk."

"You are right, My Lord. Creatures like this... I cannot say the guard will welcome her. Though, she is so beautiful," said Ogwold, going to Videre, who seemed to shiver with appreciation, rising from her stretch. She was, he thought, a thing of legend. Like his mother. Like Caelare. Going to her side he inspected the chest now, the wood soft, smelling of comfort and stillness, latched with a masterful silver lock. "As is your chest, My Lord."

"As is that plant of yours."

"How do you mean?" Ogwold looked dubiously at the tutum fruit still in his hand.

"Your right arm." The man gestured with his staff to Ogwold's awkward bandage. "It is... exuberant."

"I have only the left, My Lord."

"Ha! So you do; so you do..." The man trailed off, now eyeing the low shrubs of norm. He knelt as in solitude and ripped a great tuft from the ground, stuffing it in the dark leather bag at his hip. "Anyhow—I am Nubes." He rose, bowed, stood perfectly straight at once, looked to the mountains through their leafy frame, hung with the pendulous blue fruit, shared some secret exchange, too subtle to know, with Videre; then—before Ogwold could warn him about the norm—said, "You'll follow?" and turned to the coast walking quite briskly for his apparent physique.

When Ogwold loosened the ropes and removed the chest from her back, Videre described a single curious circle, and softly curled around the base of a tutum trunk to wait. One night-deep eye opened as in wondering why Ogwold still stood there. Finally prying himself from the amazing creature and hurrying shorewards with the box under his arm, he saw that Nubes was now already two docks down, as if he'd skipped through some inconsistency in space. Looming grandly over the bustling little red figure was the *Patientia*, the most regal ship and perhaps longest ever docked at Epherem. It had been a lifeless fixture for as long as Ogwold could remember. He hurried after his excuse to inspect it more closely.

Its masts towered like the spines of a great wooden Euphran, and the cloth of the sails faded like air itself in the pale sky, discernible only by the shining lines that held them out of the wind. The wood of the hull was a deep, dark rose, that subtle redness revealed in the varnish as it glared with sun. At the softly rocking prow rode the finely carved relief of a turtle queen bearing rich golden sceptres set with prismatic blue gems. On her ancient, monastic pate an intricate crystal diadem caught the light; it looked as though a star had dropped there. Marvelling as he took the stone dock Ogwold passed ornate, filigreed portholes opening on lavish quarters, and at the middle of the ship a great arching window. Long and widest at its apex, the crescent-moon pane enshrined a capacious ball room hung with silver chandeliers, carpeted in rich, weaving hues of red subtly melting together. The vast chamber was completely empty.

Hastening on to make up for his gawking, he stepped onto the gangway and in a few precarious moments the expansive deck. There was not a soul in sight but for Nubes, who beckoned expressionlessly and descended below. They walked silently down a crimson-carpeted hall, lined with tall, noble candles in golden sconces. Each flared and lit as they passed. Suddenly Nubes slipped through a tall wooden door, outrunning his fluttering red robes, saying, "Come in then. What is your name, young master?"

"I am called Ogwold, My Lord," said Ogwold, stooping and angling his shoulder to clear the doorway.

"So you are." Nubes chuckled. "Well, Ogwold, bring the chest to this platform here." He rapped the surface of a small, round table rhythmically with his knuckles as he passed it, continuing on aimlessly through the space as one who returns home after a long journey.

The room was large, high-ceilinged, and incredibly messy, littered with yellowing sheafs of paper covered in logicless scrawling. Upon one ornate desk were laid out a series of geometric drawings of strange winged vessels, having no wheels or means of traversal, but clearly outfitted with seats enough for a crew. Strange powders of purple and violet had spilled over the fine writing which detailed them, but Ogwold could discern the words "luxint energy" many times.

Moving through the space, he passed a gigantic green octagonal gem, swimming with inky vapour, which moved ever so softly with the floor of the rocking ship. Beside it, two crimson cloaks were haphazardly hung from the long, wise neck of the statue of an ancient turtle, which eternally cocked its head, as if to say hello. As Ogwold placed the chest upon the table, he noticed a beautiful map of the sea pinned up and spread out, delineating vast continents of which he knew nothing, above a luxurious bed with beautiful but markedly dumb wooden turtles for feet. Beside it upon a drastically ancient nightstand, equally turtled, a massive tome ruminated. Inscribed upon its leather face was the word *Xoloi*.

"The place is just as I left it," Nubes said, scratching his lower back deftly with the narrow end of his staff. "That was a long time ago, Ogwold. A long, long time ago, such that I have wrinkled and my hair has bleached. But the King is careful of me. He dare not molest my chambers. Why, I'd wager this ship has been here the whole while. It's not as if any of the court mages could summon it away." Nubes tapped his staff methodically and immersed himself in a vast scroll, which he'd let fall unfurling from one high-held hand as he spoke. "Preposterous!" he cried suddenly. "That was a most tragic hypothesis, I'll admit."

"You're right: this ship has always been here. I'd always wondered about its crew, but now I see there isn't one..." Ogwold still with his hand upon the chest saw that Nubes was completely immersed in his reading. "Uhm. I can be going, My Lord."

"Oh no! please stay!" Nubes flung the scroll aside. "I insist that you sit awhile."

Ogwold had never exchanged more than a sentence or two with a noble, as Nubes surely was, dressed in rich clothes, speaking of King Chalem as if he were a peer, travelling with the exotic Videre. The ship seemed his very own, crimson as was the theme of the man. But Ogwold had never encountered so amicable a noble. Where most were sinking stones, here was a fluffy cloud. Strangely calm as he was here in the insane quarters of Nubes' curious past, perhaps it was simply his speaking to Ogwold like an equal which brought him carefully down into one of the voluminously cushioned vermilion chairs positioned around the room awkwardly. Unnoticed until it had passed, a degree of tranquility left him as his hand parted from the smooth wood of the chest. Still he felt reassured in looking at it, somehow gracefully doing nothing upon the table. Nubes placed a small tinkling pouch of coins beside it.

"All yours! So tell me, Ogwold: will you slave here on the shore of Epherem forever?" Nubes promptly sat upon a black stool, spine straight as an arrow, unstoppered a tall bottle, and deftly guided its amber contents into a silver goblet, which he sipped daintily. "Such an oppressive place, don't you think?" He smacked his lips loudly. "And you so young. You've much ahead of you." He leaned to the side as in passing wind, somehow frowning and smiling at once. "Why, what's stopping you from grabbing yourself a pick, and finding some treasure of your own?"

"This place is very important, My Lord," Ogwold said. "To the delvers in the mountains, to the tradesmen, to the nobles over the water. Everything of value passes through our hands."

"Quite the philosopher, aren't you? Or is this a common thread?"

"My dad's—er, my father's thread at least. Lately I have been enjoying our work here. There's something sacred about it, in a way. But now... It is strange that you ask about my leaving."

"Oh really?" Nubes peered over his goblet with eyes like little skies.

"Well..." Ogwold inflected uncomfortably. "This morning actually, just before we met—I'd decided to leave Epherem. Even so, as long as I can remember, I've thought that there are many wonderful places in the wide world. To go elsewhere, to see Novare in their great cities, to walk the golden slopes of the Mardes. But I am bound here, My Lord. All of us are. By the colour of our skin and eyes, the shapes of our bodies, and our stature."

"You do strike a terrific figure," said Nubes, industriously refilling his goblet.

"Why do you ask, My Lord?"

"I am Nubes!" All levity dissipated in an instant as the old man smote his cup upon the table; liquid sloshed onto the wood. "I'd sooner refer to you as Lord before I'll hear it again. Are you not one of the Flosleao?" Ogwold gawked. Nubes who had become suddenly so grave and wrathful just as quickly lightened again, and a devilish grin passed his face. "It is in your face-bones enough." He looked to the chest, his eyes for a moment glossing, then suddenly sharp once more. "But your mother is not a simple woman of the sea, Ogwold."

"I'd... how do you know this? I'd only just learned of her."

Nubes seemed to ignore this question. Swishing what fluid remained in his goblet, he stood and walked to one of the many portholes. He craned his neck, which was surprisingly long, looking out over the waves for a moment. "Your mother is a Daughter of Caelare."

Ogwold, who had found his eyes moving to the chest during the silence, now stared at the old man with his blocky, stone jaw hanging wide open. "I... When I... this morning... I saw my mother in the sky, pointing to Zenidow. And I could not but think that she looked exactly as Caelare is always described in stories. She seemed to come from the sun itself, and her hair was like its fire."

"Caelare is not easily mistaken," Nubes said plainly.

Resounding as seemed the purpose of these words, Ogwold could only continue to sputter what he knew of legend. "Caelare... She rules the weather and conducts the spirits of the heavens. Why, she created Altum itself so my father tells me, and he is the loremaster of our village in my eyes..."

Nubes turned from the porthole, and Ogwold's voice trailed off, for the wizard had become gravely serious. His bushy eyebrows formerly so disarming were now like ominous, white grubs inching together. "Ogwold, Son of Caelare," he said, approaching the table, setting down his goblet. "You have been staring at the Great Mountain all morning. The occupant of this chest awoke at once in your presence, and certainly you feel its gaze even now. Videre and I have travelled many treacherous leagues to introduce you."

Deftly Nubes slipped a small silver key into the lock of the chest, and unfastened the latch. The lid opened back without a noise, and he turned the box to reveal its contents. Resting on the dark red cushion inside was a lone silvery orb no bigger than an eye. Soft and grey-white, it looked a perfect sphere, and somewhere in it was a luminance flawlessly contained, for it shone but projected no light beyond its surface. Even as the lid was raised, a soft hum as in an invisible, vibrating string threaded the inmost eyelet of Ogwold's mind ear to ear. It vibrated as though it always had, like the aural ideal from which all sound-forms leap—the voice of the sea, the rush of the wind, the chatter of wildlife, the drone of the heart of the world.

"What is it?" Ogwold breathed. He could not look away.

"To be completely honest, I have no idea. But if you listen, it speaks for itself. Videre and I came to Epherem looking for the one who would drop everything just to see the place of its origin. Ogwold, your eyes have been fixed on that very cradle ever I spied you this morning."

"Its origin?"

"The heart of Zenidow, Ogwold. Tell me. Why do you look at that mountain with such longing? You are perhaps the most restless ogre in the world! Did you know: I've never seen one of your kind even look at the sky. And I've known plenty of Nogofod."

Ogwold with great effort pulled his gaze from the white depths of the enthralling orb; Nubes and surrounding room materialized in shocking detail, as if long he had been away in another place entirely, where form was essence and naught had shape. "It was my mother. She told me never to return to the sea, to leave Epherem and seek Zenidow. I stopped going into the water. But every morning since I've relied on the norm to ease that loss and forestall her summons as it reminds itself in every crashing wave."

"Ah, yes, norm—that's the name," muttered Nubes, rummaging in his deep pocket.

"This morning, I went so long without it that the pain of the song reached its greatest purpose, but instead of destroying me it tapered and settled and became a kindness. When I looked out to sea, there she was riding her cloud, pointing to Zenidow."

> *At the peak of the peakless find kinship*
> *With godly things in plain sight incarnate.*

As if it knew Ogwold's every thought, the orb brightened, pulsed, rotated softly in its cushion, and rose straight into the air. It paused motionless above the chest, as if held in an invisible hand, and seemed to look up into Ogwold's massive, astonished face, though it had no features with which to express its feeling. "It floats?"

Nubes raised the bulb of his staff, and a tail of smoke coiled from a shiny, black pipe clenched between his teeth. Its bowl was carved into three vertically stacked turtle heads of ascending awareness: the bottom stupefied, the middle bordering on consciousness, and the utmost soul-piercing. Looking away from the too-penetrating eyes of that highest turtle, Ogwold noticed the unmistakable pile of norm which had appeared on the table. Nubes spoke through the smoking pipe, ignoring Ogwold's astonishment and exhaling a redolent cloud. "The sphere is an organism, like you and me. It belongs to Zenidow. There it will return." Nubes looked sternly into Ogwold's eyes, which wrestled rather with the sphere and the notion of its being alive. "Whether or not you seek the zenith of Altum, Son of Caelare, I release the sphere at this time. I am needed in Lucetal, and I'd never let those war-fiends sight such a Power. If you will follow it, you may ride with Videre. She awaits your summons." His eyes raged bright, yet gently sparkled, and the doom of his countenance subtly melted into contentment. "Great gods, this grass is potent!"

"You know," said Ogwold, still staring into the silvery sentience of the orb, "I wouldn't recommend smoking that. Not only was it that very grass which blinded me to my mother. But I think that the norm was brought here expressly to subdue the Nogofod."

"Oh most certainly, but what a marvellous thing, being subdued every once in a while. Sometimes the old ego can grow quite swollen my boy, and there's nothing like a good slap in the face in that case. But yes, as with anything one must be moderate..." Nubes trailed off, blowing rings of blue smoke. "Unless you're a wizard of course."

Now Ogwold lifted his sight out of the sphere. "I suppose you're right. The norm certainly makes everything less serious for a while. Maybe it did help me in a way. Anyhow, if you've been to Zenidow, perhaps you deserve the weight."

"Quite."

"My father says that no man has ever even passed beyond Fonslad. And Zenidow is countless leagues even—they say—beyond the peaks of ice themselves. I've heard that only Euphran live in that country, but they too will not go near the Great Mountain out of fear."

"Your father knows well the stories of the Mardes."

"Now it makes sense why he was always telling me about the mountains. He too once wanted to leave Epherem. He wants me to go—father, mother, Caelare, now you! A Wizard!" Ogwold shook his head and stared into the sphere.

They sat for some time longer, the orb floating motionless, perpetuated through some medium beyond the dimensionality of their world. The cries of gulls carried through the portholes with the rushing sea wind, and the gurgle and suck of deep water against the broad hull sounded as it did all mornings against the docks of Epherem. The omnipresent sounds of the ocean waxed of an entire life on the surf's edge. How would it feel to leave that chorus behind? The smell of norm filling the room reminded Ogwold now viscerally of the pleasure of weight throughout the body. He tasted it like drugging sea water, and felt spectral smoke massage his massive lungs, wishing as from nowhere for Nubes to pass the wrap, for the sphere to vanish, for his mother to be a Nogofod. "But I will be slain if I set foot within Occultash," he groaned.

The sphere drew close to Ogwold's long nose as if it wished to understand, seeming to pause and wonder before suddenly it rounded his huge head, and burst from between two locks of hair, spinning impossibly fast, motionless in a breath. Its humming fluctuated, and a living trail of sound arced around him in its path. He felt the low harmony like a dull roar of flowing blood through his frame, a sweet drone in his consciousness. The memory of weight and contentment seemed as a cheap trick next to this mere nudge from the consciousness of the sphere. It spun almost hopefully as it occurred to Ogwold how much was contained in this thing so small, and in that spinning all his feelings were bound together, harmonized as by great empathy, composed into a single theme which was theirs together. He smiled. The orb brightened happily.

"Thank you, Nubes," he said at last. "I know not what you've given me, or to what true end I'm led exactly, but you are right. Even months ago I knew that I could not stay here. Somehow, I am not afraid of the guards. And the magic of this thing," the humming spiked, "is beyond words. It speaks to me. I hear its voice, and the meaning of its mind is somewhere in me. It wishes for my companionship."

"It is as drawn to Zenidow as you."

"Why then did you not leave it be?"

Nubes rumpled his eyebrows together and puffing more vigorously at the smoking turtle tower in a quickly growing cloud became again cryptically sober. "Long listen, Ogwold, to the voice now joined with your own, and you will understand. It has a task: bringing you to its fountainhead. So I led it here where you were prophesied to be. I cannot go with you, but know that my fate in Lucetal is very much bound up in yours, Ogwold, if you'll have it."

"I will," said Ogwold almost before thinking that he would. But it felt in him the right use of his voice. A final barrier seemed to dissolve, and the sphere rested on his shoulder-dressing, softly spinning.

At once, the alien weed therein erupted through its binding, the shapeless lump bulging into a great rounded shoulder of green, the tightly wound tendril shooting powerfully out, helixing around itself like a great gleaming root seeking deep water to form the slender shape of an arm, equal in length and thickly structured as his other. Ogwold raised this new extremity without thinking, as one catches an object suddenly thrown their way, and rose in shock, nearly upending Nubes' table, as there formed before his eyes through the sweet knitting of exquisite musculature the palm and dexterous fingers of a green hand so fine and real that it nearly brought tears to his eyes. The wizard stumbling back almost fell flat on his rear, but somehow retained the liquid in his goblet and the ridiculous pipe surprisingly sturdy between his pursed lips, chuckling at his success.

"This is impossible!" Ogwold boomed. He wiggled his new, tough fingers, and clenched them into a fist, felt raw strength welling in uncanny muscles.

"And so Zenidow sends a message, being accepted," said Nubes. He sat once more, set his smouldering pipe gingerly upon the table, and in one motion drained his goblet with a flourish. His cheeks flushed, and his beard seemed to curl at its utmost wispy tips. "But you must understand the messenger on your own. Now, I will impart one last token of advice upon the both of you. And I shan't say 'the three of you,' for it would be unreasonable: Ogwold, that arm of yours is not so much yours as you. Do not think of it as a foreign thing, a prosthetic, a tool. It is Ogwold now; and Ogwold, you are it. Those roots have reached into the pits of your bones and even now wreath your very brain and heart. There is no undoing magic such as that. And there is no using such magic until you recognize its truth in you. Drat, it seems I'll be imparting two tokens then..."

Nubes laughed, then was grave and solemn in the same moment. "As you rise in the range, if it comes to pass that you are lost, which certainly must happen, know that the delvers are one with the mountains. The higher you climb, the less, but greater you'll find. Listen to them, for though they are often misled, and their minds taken to abysses from which return is nigh impossible, they are wisest in the high places." He took his staff up and twirled it against the floorboards. "Now, this ship departs shortly. Take your leave, Ogwold. When even the madmen of the mountains can no longer help you, may Zenidow be your ultimate guide."

Ogwold left with the orb singing warmth in his massive ear, gliding beside him as he lumbered along the dock, and humming in place as he stood looking out at the mountains for some time, his eyes trained beyond them all, hiding his new arm inside his tunic. A great creaking and splashing signalled the *Patientia*'s raised anchor, and he turned, watching it take to sea. It was an immense craft, and slowly it plied the water, its great sails unfolding gradually and stretching as in tremendous lungs filling with slow contemplative breath. Still no crew seemed aboard.

He spied Nubes, hunched at the helm, one hand on the great red wheel, the other holding up his black staff. A gust of wind without precedent hurried over Ogwold's shoulders and sought out the sails of the ship, filling them so that they caught and swelled quickly. A great groaning issued from the *Patientia* as in turning to the horizon it made for Lucetal, leagues away, that magical island of lights shrouded in legend.

Going back into the tutum grove, Ogwold sat down beside Nubes' animal companion where she waited in the dappled shade. "Videre," he said, at first unsure about being so near to the beast. "Your master has gone." But she looked at him over folded paws with inky, deep eyes, and he knew that this was right with her. They would go together to Occultash at the feet of the mountains, up and away from the coast, out over the desert.

CHAPTER XI
A WITCH'S WAY

The waving red sprites of sun-filled leaves patterned Sylna's dark lids. Through a green shock her opening eyes followed one golden shaft of light, unhindered in diagonal purity from canopy to forest floor, where it sliced open a pool of clear standing water. Beside that dazzling cut sat a blue mottled rancus, bow-legged in the grass, cocking its head curiously to the side as she stirred. Out snapped its sinewy tongue with natural suddenness, distinguishing a buzzing thing from the swirling motes of dust.

"Good morning." Sylna yawned, sitting up cross-legged.

"It's quite noon," croaked the little amphibian expressionlessly, and in one neat hop it was gone.

She chuckled, cinching her boots. As she stood, dry leaves spilled from her clothes in a swirling skirt. The sheets of her waveless almond hair pivoted against pointy shoulders as she twisted her hat snugly on. Drawing her cloak more closely to warm her sleeping blood, she looked drowsily about. The great stillness of the wood peered out from around the trees, under the toadstools, in the soft eye of a stoic bird, the thoughtful meandering of an orange worm, and in the bottomless gulfs of shadow—in the interstices between boulders, the dark overlay of boughs, among the changeful foliage—where loomed a dimension inaccessible to the large.

Compelled by all this quiet beauty, she began her morning practice; Pivwood silently abided. With movements slow and sure she performed and held the fundamental poses learned early in her time with Nubes. Blood cheered through her system, inspiring bones, saturating muscles, illuminating neurons. When body and mind were equilimber, she took up her bow and drew back the silver string. Focusing solely upon the form of her aim, she stood poised, lightly sweating from her exercises, as thoughts and memories surrounded and probed her concentration, of achiness in her legs, of Occultash peppered with impotent rains, of Wanuev's silly face, of tormented Primexcitum crucified in the pit of flames, of Nubes dancing in the sun.

One by one she neither held dearly nor banished frustratedly each of these impulses, allowing them simply to pass like clouds against the changeless, eternal sky which was her unwavering archery. Fewer were the clouds rolling in, until the perfect stillness of her bow was a pure blue vault. Now she imagined that her spirit was an arrow set to the gleaming line, aiming for the very essence of that endless firmament against which all clouds, all thoughts are transient. There was no need to let fly this arrow; already she became one with her target. For a timeless moment Sylna was but a fold in the Fabric blessed with awareness.

Like lungs expiring of a nature unbeknownst to the breather, she began lowering the bow. As gradually as she loosened the string were her senses returned to Pivwood. The uncanny presence of sight, smell, sound, touch and taste fed and animated the ego which had dissolved into its source. Laughing, she slung the white wood along her back, and came striding out of the leafy hideaway.

As there had been no path leading to this part of the forest, there were no sensible walkways among the living places of the Piv. So Sylna walked in what direction seemed salient. She passed a feathery blue fern bustling with hungry caterpillars, and here a small pebbly creek giggled; she'd heard it the night before. Damp twigs split beneath her boots. Tall grasses swished wetly against her legs. A group of rowdy chimfrees swung by cheeping and smacking their lips, so noisy all at once in their frenzied troupe, replaced now by immortal silence and the sough of wind in the high canopy.

She rounded the shoulder of a very old and dark-trunked tree. Here, four saplings bowed together and enshrined with their long, hanging leaves a noble hall leading onward. Alone in this cathedral of slender beams was a tall toadstool washed with the trickling sun. Upon its face lay Muewa, bathing as in photosynthesis, though at first she was invisible. Only as Sylna wandered by did she sense an awareness uncommon to your average mushroom, and looking down behold! There was the queenly Piv outfitted in fresh leaves, berries in her hair.

One bright little eye opened slowly, a shiny button in Muewa's plush face, and straight away a big smile parted like a seam beneath it. "Awake at last my dear," she said, beaming up. "The dews of the wood draw even the most lucid minds into rapturous slumber."

Sylna grinned in return, stooping and crawling to come sit in the hall of saplings. "Usually I am unhappy to sleep so late, and end up in a sorry hurry; but today when I woke it was as though haste was a very silly thing; I enjoyed my waking rituals more than ever." Her contentment wavered now, looking at the Piv to whom she had expressed such urgency the day before. "In my complacency I have meditated too long in the forest."

Muewa's laugh twittered like the lilting voices of the pucks, and even some of those little red birds peeped their heads from the foliage to see what the fuss was all about. "Already you brush against the great truths of the universe, Sylna. Nubes chose you well. Yet 'too long' is a strange notion for the seeker of peace. Why, when there is not enough time in the day to meditate, I often drop everything I'm doing and spend a whole week doing solely that—sitting and being." She nodded at the birds as if to assure them that all was well, and they disappeared one by one into the bushes whence they came. "However, I believe in this case we must work quickly. We've both our reasons." She turned back with large green eyes, tranquil as they were serious.

Sylna bowed humbly, removing her hat. "I am very sorry Muewa. I will make it up to you."

"There is no need. It really can't be helped among these old trees..." Muewa trailed off gazing up into the canopy. "Why, Nubes slept three days when he first came to me. And though he might not seem it, that wizard is quite a hasty fellow, always going from one thing to another, never satisfied..." She hummed a busy little melody. "Now, I have accomplished much good thinking while you were away. Firstly how about some lunch, or should I say breakfast?"

A troop of Piv came out from the high grass parting to admit their little cherubic faces, bearing lightly wrapped morsels, and leafy cones filled with crystal water. Sylna was offered three different mushrooms, each tasting nothing like the others. The earthy food brought sudden vitality even in the smallest nibbles.

Sylna and Muewa laughed all through their meal discussing Nubes' obsession with such mushrooms; each had stories quite new to the other's ear. The Piv expounded upon the wizard's fear of Oerbanuem, which she found quite ironic, especially now that his young pupil had faced the fungal god and suffered, perhaps, the most terrifying vision yet afforded to mortal minds. Sylna though deflected this feat, though much to the hysterics of Muewa, with tales of Nubes' psychonautical adventures, for many were the mornings when he would wander into the tower dishevelled with sleeplessness, covered in fungal crumbs, bug-eyed with pupils like pots, and sit stroking a live turtle in his lap until again the sun had set and risen.

When all was eaten and drunk, and when the last laugh was had, such that they sat simply admiring and missing old Nubes, Muewa led the witch out of the hall and into the dense trees, now especially enormous compared to the saplings which had housed them. Sylna walked briskly while the Piv worked her fourfold wings, though it was impossible to see any one of them, so quickly they moved in an emerald continuum. For a long while they wove around wet trunks, brushed through waist-high families of shrub and fern, scrambled within gullies of mossy stone. Deep, cool leaf-caves and tunnels of shadow passed over their heads, where only the sound of dripping dew was heard. Coming out of these chill, dark places they crossed broad, sunny clearings latticed with creekwater, or navigated winding mazes of tree and toadstool many whose species were novel to Sylna.

In one clearing the loamy turf sloped upwards into a steep hill. For half an hour they meandered up its high grass-sheened back, until, at the rounded top, they stood level with the highest, sunniest echelon of the forest. It was as if they summited a bald pate around which manifold trees like endless locks of hair tumbled and curled ever out. Far, far away she thought she even saw the roof of Nubes' tower. And beyond it, behind the stretching surging treeline, there was Zenidow tall and noble, a silver axle if the sky and earth were great wheels. Girding its base were the white mountains—highest in the world—that like the jagged teeth of some godly jaw ensconced Pivwood on all sides.

Muewa lighted atop a smooth boulder and folded her wings elegantly. "This is as good a place as any for weather workers. But before we speak of storms," she tittered warmly, "I should like to know absolutely every detail concerning your comprehension of what Novare call 'magic,' though through Nubes I believe you know it as 'folding,' or 'sewing,' or something or other."

"Absolutely every detail?" The witch's eyes widened into brown pools.

Muewa laughed. "The significant ones, yes." Her wings snapped out and returned in a fey gesture. "We Piv are sensitive creatures. Tell your story as you know it should be told."

Frowning, Sylna sat cross-legged beside the boulder, murmuring without inflection, "How shall I begin?" She looked out over the sea of embracing treetops, listening to the wind, feeling the sun on her shoulders and back. Removing her bow from its place she set it gently in the soft grass, leaving one hand to rest on its white wood. Muewa with perfect patience waited, so still and natural that it looked as though Sylna sat alone beside a strange flower growing from the rock.

"I suppose..." Sylna began, tilting her head towards this flower, the pointed tip of her hat flopping to that side. "Everything has its beginning in Ardua, my birthplace. My mother was Queen of the Golden Palace, highest and absolute ruler of the Holy City. Among her many ambitions was the wish that I one day wear her mantle. Though she spoke this command only once, my father carried on the sentiment as he was her limb. I was very little when first she shared that destiny. She watched me carve this bow, as the royal huntress had shown me to do, and spoke as from a high place, though nearer to me physically than ever she'd been."

Sylna looked down at her ringed hand now tightly grasping the weapon. A dewdrop—assimilated from a blade of grass—glistened on its string. "When I finished, she took the bow and held it—naturally as I'd seen the huntress with her own—but returned it quickly, and turned her back. She said my work was fine, and to keep the bow with me as an emblem of my skill and strength, but never to use it. 'Killing,' she said, 'is not your path.'" Sylna began to smile softly as she spoke, though her grip upon the white wood did not loosen.

"I should say, my inheritance was once compelling. Mother seemed so righteous. Power was in her step and glance, wisdom on her brow. She was tall and graceful, noble-cheeked, fire-eyed; blonde as the sun, her hair was never cut. When she walked she floated, and all things melted in the gold of her robes and jewellery. Though I scarcely spoke with her, the magnificent paintings and golden statues of her likeness throughout the castle inspired a special love for her glory. I imagined her a ruler gracious and understanding, and aspired to become like her—that idea of her—and earn the profound respect with which the people approached her court. Such unconditional surrender, I thought, could only come from a place of love.

"I would sit in her throne nights, the seat so large I could reach only one of the great gilt armrests. I'd pretend to oversee the great hall like I watched her do, placing an invisible crown atop my head, raising an invisible sceptre in my hand. Before me the people of Ardua would stand proudly for the splendour of the land and all the glories of our mines. Then there would be a great feast for all the Queendom, long bounteous tables filling the hall. This, for a long while, was how I imagined the people of Ardua: loving, gay, perfectly sustained yet dreaming sometimes of even greater wonders long promised them. Such was my own state, and so I projected it upon their distant faces. Yet every incipient ruler must one day observe her subjects.

"Our golden palace stood tall and sharp in the centre of a great garden, many miles across, forested with ancient, hardy trees that bore the frost wondrously. In many places thickly covered by their branches, the snow did not reach, and one could lay in the cold grass. Though I was permitted to wander quite far into this wood, and though I had explored its densest thickets, plumbed its every extremity, I could not dare, in those moments, looking up at the high black barrier, to disobey the only other direct commandment given me by Mother: 'You will not leave the garden.' But when I was thirteen, the time, it seemed, had come. Father wrapped me in furs and took me in his chariot to experience the Holy City.

"I passed at last through the golden gates onto a cobbled street, and the dizzying, onyx garden wall fell behind. The condition of the road quickly deteriorated. Trees withered and gave to decaying, black buildings decked in snow and lacquered with ice. These edifices were nothing like those which comprised the castle and its surrounding quarters, or even the stables of our beasts. They crumbled and listed one against the other. Jagged cracks storied their flanks, and paneless windows gaped like wounds. Leant feebly against the base of one dilapidated tower was a dirt-streaked man all alone, clothed only in tattered trousers, ribs upholding tight sallow skin, cheeks sunken into shadow, tongue lolling. I was stunned; here a state of being I had never beheld.

"He called up to us as we approached. 'Help me, Blessed Ones. I am starving.'

"'Can we not feed this man?' I implored. 'We have far more food at home than we'll ever need.'

"Scoffing through his gold-ringed beard, Father scourged the team of capramons onward. 'He has already chosen his path,' he said. The beasts trundled more hastily, and the weary face of the beggar was lost in a slurry. 'Your mother is too wise to exhume wretches from graves of their own digging. If we spoil this vagabond he will never earn his own way.' Though I hadn't the aplomb to speak against him in those days, as we rattled along without speaking I did not struggle to disagree with father. Such a state of being could not be voluntary. Begging seemed the ultimate act of humility to me, the absolute recognition of need. I saw the man in the road as one who cannot go on but for the grace of others. Even if he was a villain, how could we, the rulers and self-professed guardians of Ardua, ignore such open declarations?

"The empty and desolate streets near the garden were replaced with more sturdy black compounds as we went. Shadows came out of ice-hung alleyways.

Anxieties steeped in the frigid air. Rank odours rolled along the rock. More beggars in various stages of grief and starvation sat weakly or trudged along with no particular aim, pausing to gaze empty-eyed at some cracked wall, an overturned, rotting cart, the raw sky. Now there appeared more livable houses and many-storied stone buildings. Other citizens of the like I'd seen in Mother's hall—though clothed in nothing so fine as then—peeped their ruddy faces from stony apertures and disappeared shortly.

"Those few who came out from the crumbling manors—along the more affluent streets we achieved by noon—were most of all disgusted by the ubiquitous poor, spitting upon them and tossing rinds or bones before their groveling shapes. We passed only one House of Faith that afternoon. It was a beautiful, well-maintained, and clearly royal citadel, dwarfing both physically and aesthetically all around it with its magnificent, polished glory. High was its slender, black steeple, and the rich sloping roof shingled with golden slabs melted like cataracts of radiant godly tears upon towering walls of smooth stone veined with the finest carvings and murals of Mother I'd yet seen. As we drew near, a priestess came out onto the step; her raiment was nearly fine as my own, her countenance smug as Father's.

"These differences in caste already too much for my naive heart, I realized as we passed that a kind of equality did in fact exist in the Holy City; the rich and poor, young and old—even the priestess who seemed so above them all—called out to Father with desperate praises, all of them stooping low and crooning in unctuous tones. Will Your Holiness be needing a suit of armour? Might the Divine Daughter be interested in a bouquet of mountain flowers? When will the God-Queen conduct the Ritual and absolve us? Father barely noticed them, though he held his chin high and there was dominion in his eyes. I could clearly see that he thought himself strong and resplendent before his daughter. He wished for me to envy him, to covet our blood, to crave power.

"But when I returned home to my enormous, silk-canopied bed with its satiny, touching blankets, comfort eluded me. The revolting softness of everything, the sick gold of my spacious and fragrant chamber dredged up flavours of bile, when far off in the streets there vied but varying degrees of hateful squalor. I cast off the repugnant sheets and fell shaking out of bed as from the dangerously plush tongue of some gruesomely patient ambush predator, pressing my shoulder and cheekbone against the hard polished floor, grateful for its resistance. Rolling onto my back and stiffly lying there I thought only of that beggar somewhere in the cold doing the same. The luxuries of my life rose up in nightmare shadow from the peripheral dark bulk of bed, and hung over me in a horrible moving tableau;

fine foods piled in gross mounds upon tables stained with wasted wines; relentlessly warm firesides beside grand couches spilling viscera of swollen pillows; rouged royals drooling sophisms of faultless praise with too-tender fingers wandering across their fat bellies; mindless automaton servants on mechanized tracks hidden in the interstices of flagstones, bowing rigidly, conceding with clockwork enthusiasm. A memory of Mother in court swelled as from behind it all, and took to itself the shadowed forms of sick excess as a great roiling mantle of black, showing now in her courtly countenance a manner not of love and acceptance, but of absolute control.

"The days and weeks that followed only fed my nightmares, for on those few occasions when I glimpsed Mother through the curtains of my box looking on the great hall from above, I saw only hate and wrath in her. I realized that her special smiles had moved my naive daughter's love before only by their rarity, not their splendour, for I saw them now thin and contrived as they truly were, the impression of a painted canvas mask pulled tight against a pale dead skull out-glared by golden hair and crown. Yet, sickening as she'd become, it was Father first and last that spurred my ultimate flight from the palace, for he was less abstract, and more often seen. Little sleuthing showed he was a callous brute, and treated our servants, when he thought I could not see, with terrible rage.

"One night I stayed up later than I was taken to even in those days of sneaking and watching. He was drunk and red-faced, carrying Mother's sceptre as if it were his own. At his blunt command the servants were whipped in front of dishes they'd dropped, forced to drive their hands into the slivers of glass. The sound of it was odious—thick snakes of leather sliding dead from naked backs. All of this wailing and gnashing and tearing of flesh before the great hearth and its crackling, friendly flames, blood splattering the ornate carpet where I had sat so many times looking up in reverence at the golden bust of my mother licked with light.

"When I could no longer bear it, I fled to my room, grabbed what things appeared significant, and tripped out into the freezing garden muffling my sobbing as best I could. In the lamp-touched dark I tore my clothes and muddied my face and body and cut off my hair with an arrowhead. I hid my bow in a secret place among the trees which I alone would know, and covered myself there in a fallen bough. I slept in liminal space, still cloistered by the royal grounds, yet repulsed by the leering gold of the palace. In the morning a thick slurry masked my hike through the garden, and soon—by paths only I knew to travel—I came to the grand highway leading out into Ardua.

"Crouching in the cold shadows of a snow-clumped bough, I waited for a cart to approach the golden gates. At last such a vehicle came from the direction of the palace, and I slunk in its shadow as the way was opened. So tattered and spectral was my passage that the guards seemed not to notice. When I stepped under the gilt archway dividing the royal grounds from the city, I half expected to see the very beggar who had begun my transformation, but no soul was about. Going to the tower where he'd lain, I called softly into the crypt-like darkness of the alley nearest, and placed at the side of the road a small sack containing all of the gold ever I'd been given. Then I walked until my feet could no longer sustain me.

I passed the squalid houses of the lay, wandered the crumbling structures of commerce, avoided the always patrolling, black-caped Holy Knights like shades in gold plate armour, gazed up at the eldritch cathedrals, and dodged through their constant streams of haggard worshippers. I bumped shoulders with faceless shrouded others on their dreary ways through crowded spaces. Into candle-lit barns and ale-rank taverns I stumbled to be quickly sent away. At dusk I collapsed in an inky alleyway and slept like a stone; at dawn I sat out on the road and begged for food. When finally I had earned something to eat—that first day it was a mouldering husk of bread—I took again to my blistered feet, wanting to know everything I could about the real Ardua.

"As the months passed, I grew hard and tough, and my needs narrowed. Scraps of food made hearty sustenance. Water could be soaked up from the sides of streets and strained through my rags. I came to know instinctively the concentric, ringed layout of the city, its network of crannies, its special hideaways, and the most prosperous footholds for alms. I caught rumours on the breath of the people that the Princess had disappeared. But it was almost as if I needn't cut off my hair or cover myself in dirt, for few eyes fell on those who begged, and those that did were clouded with disgust. But inequity of status was hardly so concerning as the other horrors of Ardua, which I could never have anticipated. Men and women starved to death in the streets, their shrunken corpses long ignored. Public executions were played out on gruesome stages before bloodthirsty crowds of all castes. Holy Knights slew commoners in the streets for fictitious blasphemies. Murder and theft ran like stinking veins through the frozen night, but lawmen cared only to accost those they might capture easily.

"Most illuminating of all were the Houses of Faith. One for each of the Nine Rings of Ardua, these towering, palatial cathedrals existed for the sole purpose of worshipping Mother. With incomparable dogma and painstaking masochism the litany of the God-Queen was conducted before the statues and murals of that very likeness which before I'd venerated in my own way. Within every indomitable church—I visited them all—in the highest-ceilinged, vaulted hall, candle-haunted sermons were endlessly conducted by veiled priestesses from spindly lecterns lowered upon the solid gold palm of Mother's enormous stooping statue, ever looming over the rows of benches packed with unblinking, terrified faithful. In the eyes of every such titan image of the God-Queen, there was indeed naught which could be called Novare. But looking up into those dominating, gilt eyes, I knew that no benevolent god would ever let her people rot such as they did in Ardua.

"At the close of one year, the knowledge of my blood had swollen with such hate that I could no longer bear the ubiquitous imagery of Mother. I strayed far from the centre of the city where her eyes—ever staring out of the profusely vigilant statues—could not find me, and began to haunt rather the godless slums where—though Mother's name was everywhere bellowed—religion cared less to reach. I wanted to forget her, the palace, everything about my horrid birthright, and focus upon living as any beggar instead of investigating Ardua as its cynical, runaway Princess. I tortured myself in these sordid streets with a brutal asceticism. I waited, fasted, breathed, allowing all the sensations of real Arduan existence to wash over me and go as they came. At first this was a punishment, punishment for my royal blood, depriving myself of everything which I used to rely on so needlessly, and much more. But simply by being, without possessions, without external need, without attachment, and slowly, each day more effortlessly, without the gnawing need to hunt down Mother's evils, I found a peace so simple and elegant it was as if it had awaited me all along.

"With time, not only did my feelings of hatred and repulsion become less important, but as well this pursuit of a so-called ideal state of Arduan being faded in relevance, and I sank more into contemplating the essence of being itself. I imagined that 'being' was an immaterial thing imbued in the mortal vessel, and I began to wonder about the other gods with which my Mother claimed relation, for as with her own professed mythology, there are no stories about their having anything to do with the creation of life. How did the soul arise then, I wondered, and to what was it related? Did it share some property with the egos of the gods? Was there some greater God from which all consciousness was derived? I turned my awareness inwards, as if searching along the roots of my consciousness for a hidden network where I imagined all life was born and ultimately connected. It no longer mattered that I was in the busy city, and this thought even brought me restlessness, for even in these less chaotic walks of Ardua, too often there was some distracting squabble, the grating squawk of merchants, a cacophonous parade of Knights looking for some peasant to bother. I figured that perhaps I had experienced Ardua enough for now, and its dirty streets were not conducive to my new practice. Really, there was only one place to go.

"So I returned to the royal gardens, in the canvassed cargo of a rations wagon, a nameless rag-wraith exuded from the baggage of twilight. Deep in the forest—more serene than I remembered—I brought out my old bow from its hidden bower. There it was white and smooth as always, that prized possession which I'd formed with my own little hands. It was both memory of Mother's power and symbol of my own. But already I had reclaimed the garden. This was a place special to me in ways she could never understand. And so was this bow, then. By taking it up once more, I accepted my past boldly. I decided that I would never again abandon my power. I would carry it always as a reminder of my first identity. Holding it then, kneeling in the frosted grass, I became ashamed of my running away so completely. To deny the past was to empower Mother; to embrace it, to own it, was to empower Sylna.

"I raised the bow, drew back the fine string arrowless, and focused on my form. My mind and heart grew light and clear like never before. Losing myself in the infinitesimal, contending vibrations of the string, I began to see the forces of tension and resolution in a unity of opposites; one could not be without the other, and so they were at variance and harmony both in my aim. Yet I accepted this contradiction, surrendered to it. As I allowed my consciousness to become one with the string and its finest adjustments too subtle to influence, I realized that this was not duality at play, but a vast multiplicity of constantly changing strings. While surely there was some microscopic moment where tension became resolution and resolution tension, between the extremes of these concepts existed an infinity of substates, each giving to the other ineffably all down the string from tip to tip of the bow as I held it to my shoulder in that quantum state of drawnness.

"My soul became the string. The intrinsic multiplicity of power and finesse in my archery suggested that I too existed in a variable state; I was both Sylna and a universe of others at once. All living things in aiming differently their inmost bows had in common one vibrating string, the underlying selfsame germ of manifest consciousness, so that we were like aspects of the same being blessed for a moment with individual self-awareness. In the infinitude of time I was one of the people of Ardua, yet a Princess too, a Euphran, a miner, a tree and a spider. I saw my body growing old and dying, dissolving into dust; yet from that dust up sprang a flower blossoming; just as life had come to it a great fire raged, and all was ash, yet I was the fire and I was the ash. I swirled up into the sky and became a star; my ancient light began to fade.

"Touched as I was by this higher consciousness and deeper meaning, even in the quiet solitude of the garden and the peaceful ecstasy of my revelations, I was not yet free of anger and disgust. Like dormant dark seeds these passions waited for the right nutrient to summon their sick stalks again into the light. It took but a notion of vengeance to trigger that cancer. One afternoon, as I walked in the dense brush near the highway, there came a susurrus of rebellion on the lips of two passing nobles. Already one idol of the God-Queen had been molested. A House of Faith became the place of a great riot. The rebel leader was Rawn the Traitor himself, once second in command of the Nine Paladins of the Holy Knights.

"I'd first heard that name when I was seven. Even when he worked for my mother, Rawn was one of few mist-eyed military men too many times bade to slay or abide the slaying of those his heart could not accuse. Cruel as his features and dark, biting eyes became, he loved Ardua for its people, not its God. When he broke, Rawn in his anger turned upon the holy host. It was said that the Queen herself forced him to kneel, but on the day of his capture I had seen the blasphemer-commander dragged bleeding along the floor of the great hall by the Captain of the Nine. Thereon he had rotted in the grand prison beneath those very lavish floors, a symbol of her power, for she would not execute him lest his condition cease to deter. When I was very young, wandering in those dank dungeons, I spied upon his cell thinking him a horrible murderer as was my duty. He was naked and lashed, hair boltered with his own blood, yet he sat silent and composed as if his schemes had already begun.

"I willed myself to ignore the sudden, bodily urge to seek out this rebellion, planting myself far away from the road and meditating for entire days and nights. But now my moments of greatest clarity were harshly disrupted; the bow would shake, would lower, and that formerly thousandfold string settled into a single, total pause. Anger was the one passion which I could not let pass. The possibility of revenge slunk out of the shadows and into my own. I began again to wander, less often taking up my bow, each day steeping more bitterly in the physical world where universal consciousness was bound up by time and space in brief bodies of conditional ego. At last I knew that there was but one way to put my mind at ease. I stole once more into the city.

"I found the rebel council on a smoky night deep in the mines of the lay, those sooty tunnels under the city where the real Arduans live and die. Rawn stood upon a stone table clad in the golden cuirass of a Holy Knight painted with the emblem of the revolution: a black pickaxe hanging like the anchor of a ship. He spoke of the storied knights he and his rescuers had slain in the dungeon, in the castle, in the garden, how he'd felled even the Captain of the Nine in his escape.

'Bring it here, the gem that was his undoing,' he shouted, holding out his gloved hand. A dark figure strode from the company of men and women also facing the crowd, and placed into his palm a glowing stone which I knew well, for its pale light had themed my childhood. 'This is but a common rock to the royals,' Rawn bellowed, holding it aloft like a white star. Many in the crowd gasped with first sight. 'I pulled it—one of hundreds—from a fixture in the wall of the dungeon, and stuck it in the Captain's skull! You cannot imagine what treasures they save for their own chambers, if such godly things give light to their prisoners.' He threw the stone into the crowd, and it was snatched by a bald man covered in scars. 'Together, we shall open up the mines for all! We shall overwhelm the seat of evil and break the cages of our allies! We shall not rest until Ardua belongs to Arduans!'

"When his speech ended, and when the hands were flung high to join his troops, I too raised my arm in rebellion against the God-Queen. Rawn was a violent man, and many an innocent had fallen to his blade, but his words smote my fevered heart with lucid will. Over the next several months, I learned the ways of the rebels. In one enormous cave deep in the mine was our base of operations, and there I learned to fight. They told me that outright conflict would erupt any day. I had joined just in time. Now I practised the aim of my bow for killing. Each morning I went to hunt wild capramons outside the city walls, and many carcasses were left to waste. When I was not training, I was helping to raid the royal barracks and guard towers nearest the many mouths of our labyrinthian mine-base. No royal went to these dark, grimy places where, though the most precious gems did not appear, the most fundamental resources upon which they depended, of metal and rock, were brought painstakingly to light. And so their destroyers would pour from those neglected tunnels everywhere beneath their feet.

"At last, there was a great war in Ardua. As a ranger, I came up out of the mines after our blade-armed forces. Smoke and the clang of weapons carried round the buildings. The distant curdling yells of combat were like the piercing calls of hawks in Hell. I saw the slumped and mangled corpses of our warriors, and broken Holy Knights in the blood-sick streets. The host of archers dashed down the street and disappeared in the haze, leaving me frozen as on the precipice of dark deeds. From a pile of gore smashed into a stone wall, a gold-gauntleted arm flailed, found purchase, and up one knight hoisted himself breathing heavily. Helmetless, he turned and saw me with brown eyes like my own. I nocked my first arrow. He seemed to call out, made no move to draw his sword from the slain rebel lying over his lap. I released my shot. The shaft passed through his throat. That same arm was lifted, grew limp, fell again with a clank as his cuirass struck the cobblestones heavy with dull death. Somewhere in my heart was an awful satisfaction, a vindication, as if I had shot Mother herself, for I had not looked so deeply into the man's face as I had the image of the Queen upon his chest.

"Many more I slew with those arrows I'd stolen from royal armouries, and the vital fluids of my own kin flecked the weapon which had been an instrument of peace only a season before. I worked my way from cover to cover, now behind a crumbling tower, shooting a high-positioned guard, now roving through the debris searching corpses for new arrows. But as I moved more closely to the central ring of the city, I began to see that Rawn had prioritized not the opening of the mines nor the freeing of prisoners, but the destruction of the grand cathedrals, for the power of the church was the power of the God-Queen. In the blaze of demise I found him standing arms crossed and laughing like a maniac. This Rawn had little concern for the lives of the citizens not joined with him in this fight, for they were burned and crushed by the collapsing structures and executed indiscriminately, as if they fought against him all the same as Mother. Blatantly I saw his evil lit by the flames of vengeance, and I knew then that his goal was power not unlike her own. It was the same desire for control, the same black hate and hopeless need that I had seen in her nightmare apparition on the night of my transformation.

"Suddenly the blood upon my hands and bow stank of malice and open graves. The sweat soaking through my clothes grew clammy with a chill wind of shame. I fled the fight as one who selfishly shirks all responsibility. Coward though I might have been, I could not kill again, and I abandoned the rebellion as I had abandoned my birthright, by completely denying it. Perhaps my life was saved in that childish decision, for the hand of the Queen was yet strong, and the rebellion was drowned in blood. In the morning, she beheaded Rawn herself on the greatest stage of all in the heart of the First Ring. I watched from the eyrie of a tall, tenantless tower. That day was spent in total misery.

"When I came down at last, I stood independent once more upon the cobbled streets, my bow and other oddments wrapped in rags beside me against a crooked wall, watching as the smoking debris of Chansythe Cathedral was sifted for treasure. I could not take satisfaction from the shattered idol of my mother spread in gilt chunks before the place. In the streets, the power-hungry and the short-sighted were merely hidden, for they did not own the throne. Mother was no aberration; this violence, I thought, was nature. Yet as a disgust for all Novare began to grip me, a terrible shame again welled in my heart for those I had slain, and I remembered then the garden and the recognition that I too was just like them, Mother, Father, the Holy Knights in their graves. I had fallen into the shadows of hate as much as Rawn. Now I understood truly what it meant for all life to derive from one great consciousness. Not only goodness and love were universal traits, but hate and pride as much.

"I returned then to the remotest tangled dells of the garden to be alone. My aim was to forgive them all and one day myself, if only I could only sit and embrace these feelings of disgrace as an essential part of being. In the pale sun I wandered beneath the pure and ancient trees of tall, noble stature, and at night I slept among immense roots thick as horses. I ate bugs and the little warm blooded creatures that roamed there, when I could match their speed with an arrow. I drank from the icy streams which ran through the wood. Apart from these activities, my every effort was focused upon meditation, as when I had first fled the palace. In time I accepted that I could never forget my anger, at Rawn, Mother, and at last myself; instead, I owned it, cared for it as an intimate aspect of my consciousness, and the days of my anger and violence became a necessary path to peace.

"Once again I took up my bow in surrender to the past. My soul was again an arrow, my body like the bow, and the string the gift of incarnation. Those moments in which I accessed higher consciousness became my dearest treasures. When I achieved this peace, this truth, I saw clearly once more my connection with other bundles of consciousness. The trees seemed to speak, and I felt as though my thoughts were carried in the hearts of birds. I began to sense—not with shame or anger, but new curiosity—that there were Novare too, going about their business in the city. In all of them were the cruellest villain and the most virtuous hero contained. They had succeeded and failed, loved and hated, given and stolen; even in the most awful weeds of sin I saw the seeds of great kindness. Now they were like other bows and arrows in states of drawnness never like another.

"One day, as I sat silently meditating among the great roots of an old tree, I detected among the sea of Novare a new presence in the Queendom, as though it were a bright light in the darkness. A severe, incendiary rage passed through the outer gate, such that I suspected another Rawn had taken up the streets; but slowly, patiently, I realized that the flames of this presence were subdued and cocooned by a peace so effortless it required even no such totem as my bow. For this heart wherein there was such anger, there was somehow no suffering, no seeking, no passion, only acceptance. It was an ineffable sense of being that imitated nothing, autonomous and authoritative as it was open and surrendered to its fate. I knew straight away that this warm, open heart—so master of its wrath—would only come to Ardua once, and so I left the garden to meet him.

"I slipped through the great golden gate and mingled with the groups of shambling beggars along the highway, following this whiff of wisdom through an uncommonly sunny morning. The packed snow and dripping ice blinded me with its glare. But in the rowdy central market, I discovered him quite easily, or he stood out across the crowd, crimson-robed, grey bearded, a little old man with a black staff bent over a stack of tattered books for sale. Still though I sensed that his temper might at any moment erupt, he seemed more calm than any that wandered the stalls.

"After much scrutiny he went away from these wares, and I watched as he haggled composedly with nearly every merchant in the square. I followed him all day, peered secretly from a dark alley while he went door to door in the guild compound of the common mines, hid behind a cart of textiles while he accosted the Office of the Royal Mine, and afterwards followed him perhaps too closely as he visited three different cartographers' shops. When he parted again the black double doors of the last he seemed quite triumphant, a nameless tome under his arm. I slept alertly in the alley beside the inn where he seemed to stay for the night. He set out very early in the morning, strangely without the book for which he had looked so thoroughly.

"He headed immediately for and through the outer gate of the city into the wilds, and I knew—as when I had first sensed his presence—that he would not return. I looked back over the leaning black towers and blocky buildings, at the House of Faith nearest this entrance, evilly gold, sharp in its cruel relief, and decided that if there was anyone who could show me the rest of the world, it was this weird elder. When I passed through the gate, he seemed to have vanished; but scanning the snowy waste I saw him just shimmying out of sight along the leaning black border of Ardua. Following his prints in the shade of the wall, I discovered a subtle pathway I had never noticed before on my hunts beyond the walls, but certainly there were the marks of boots tramping back and forth.

"Sweeping along the side of the icy precipice on which the city sat, this winding trail of packed snow led ever downward, so extreme in its wide curving that I lost sight of the old man, having to keep my distance around the bend. The exposure was terrifying. Out to my left yawned a roaring white abyss, and the fog far below was such that I could not tell how many thousands of yards of empty space spanned the distance to the river valley at the foot of the mountain. High on my right was the wall of ice supporting Ardua, to which I plastered my hands and body and—when I could no longer look out into oblivion—my gaze, as I inched slowly along.

"When I could no longer hear the man's shuffling feet, I silenced my own and slowly crept forth to find him standing upon a much more spacious shelf of ice. He held up his staff, and its bud began to glow, lighting up the mouth of a great mine shaft hewn into the cliff face that supported the city. Glinting in the sudden light, there were also two golden statues of my mother standing on either side of the entrance, polished and clean—but for a dusting of snow—as those only which I had seen in the palace. I had never heard of any mine beyond the city walls, though this seemed a very old place despite the newness of the statues, and the fresh path we had taken. But I had little time to wonder what secret tunnel this was, for the man stepped quickly into the dark such that I followed in a hurry.

"The reeking air that spilled out from the gaping maw of the place was somehow more stale, more cold and alien than even in the deepest, least-frequented passages of the mines I knew as a rebel. A thick primordial scent it was, of chthonian things long buried, which should remain in the dark. Yet down into that darkness the old man travelled as one strolls through town, holding out his luminous staff. So on I pressed, encouraging myself by his nonchalance, lurking as far behind as I could manage in the shadows.

"For three days I crept after that pale light, deep into the body of the mountain, and slept in total blackness near to his camp, the setting up of which was my only means of telling time. There he always sat late into the night, seeming—I hoped—to meditate just as I. Then at last, my hunger was too much. On the night of the third day, when I had summoned the courage to make my plea, I approached the old man by his campfire.

"'Oho! So the pitter patter has a face,' he said, turning to where I stood in shadow. 'Come and sit where it is warm, and speak your purpose.'

"Cautiously I came out of the dark and sat hugging my scabbed knees at the edge of the flickering wash of flame. 'You are a wizard,' I said.

"'I am called so. To describe my look is not difficult though.'

"'That may be, but I have seen plenty who would think themselves wizards and dress the like, yet they are nothing to you.' I bowed my head to show respect. 'You do not seek power, yet to me this is the greatest power of all. I've followed you because I can see in your step and gaze that you do not suffer desire. I wish more than anything to achieve such peace.'

"'Hm,' the wizard said, tugging at his beard, narrowing his eyes. He inspected me as in an enchanting puzzle, the firelight flickering all through the wrinkles of his grave face, his eyes seeming to shift from joy to sorrow and back again in each leaping flame. "Tell me, Sylna of Ardua, why have you forsaken your place in line? The God-Queen lives well, no?'

"I could only stare, but my surprise must have been quite apparent.

"'Ah,' he said, 'I too can read a step and gaze, as well as your posture and diction. You are no beggar, though I see you've willed that life. No, you cannot shake this dignity inscribed from birth; deep is your cultivation—but own it! If you wish to be a beggar, then so you are, but a dignified one. My question is why?'

"I could not but smile now at this old man who I had feared would be wrathful at finding he was followed. When I came closer to the fire, I saw at last that the deep well of anger in the man was utterly subordinate to his compassion. The severity of his features hardly masked his dancing eyes full of kindness and grace, which like warm pools guided me as I spoke. I told him of nauseous luxuries of my life when first I beheld the poorer folk of the city, how I went among them and begged and explored Ardua only to unearth its evils. Afraid that those fumes of rage would rekindle, I explained how I calmed my temper and surrendered to the world as it was. How I surrendered as well to my past, taking up my old bow. How I went to meditate beneath the great trees of the garden where I saw that there were no natural castes among Novare, how peasants were equal to princesses. Then I spoke again of my indefatigable anger and my horrid mother, and the rebellion. He frowned when I described my days of violence and the feelings that tainted my killer's heart. But his countenance relaxed when I spoke of how those atrocious days showed me what it truly means for all life to be One, in vice as much as virtue.

"'Why, you're a natural,' he said. 'Only a mind so ambitiously capable of contradiction could hope to achieve true peace. I see now how you traced my spirit.'

"'How do you mean?'

"'Comfort disgusts you; disgust comforts you. Peace blooms. Then you hurl yourself into war! Please, I do not mean to offend,' he laughed, seeing that a pall had taken my face. 'What I mean is this: you would not have followed me into these caverns if not for the insights of courageous folly.' He grinned, threw a berry high in the air, and caught it deftly between his teeth. Swallowing it he closed his eyes. 'But your vision is narrow yet, young one.' When he finally opened his eyes again he only gazed at me queerly through the flame and smoke. Again his look vacillated between silliness and sobriety, felicity and melancholy.

"I said, 'Contradiction is certainly important to me. The oppressive condition of Ardua contradicts the God-Queen's divine duty to her people. Anger and knowledge gave me new life. But I discovered a second contradiction in fighting, for I became no better than my mother. Now I see that contradiction is natural. Wherever I can recognize it, I am able to let go and surrender to things as they are. But this is not complacency! I assure you. This acceptance allows me to see even more clearly what is just and unjust in the world, and to react from a place of deeper understanding. If only I had felt this way before listening to the rhetoric of Rawn. But like you said, if it were not for his vengeance and the rebellion, and the blood on my hands, I'd not have grown.'

"'You are wise, Sylna,' Nubes said. He did not smile or frown, but it seemed that there was admiration in the muscles of his face. 'Illuminate me. How is it that you meditate?'

"'This bow is not only a reminder of my past; it has also been my greatest teacher.' I took out my instrument and pulled back the string, aiming out into the darkness. 'As I aim, I think how delicate is the balance between the bowstring and my drawing it, how tension and resolution contend to compel the arrow of my spirit with the ideals of accuracy and precision. When I surrender to the natural opposition of these forces, there are times when my form falls into a place of its own accord, and the contradictory two become one. There is neither tension nor resolution. Then I hit my target.'

"The wizard nodded solemnly. 'And what is your target?'

"'It's hard to explain,' I mumbled. 'But, I suppose... it is whatever contradicts the self. When I strike the target, I feel as though... as though my soul itself becomes one with some other greater consciousness, and this feels like a grand return to whence it came in the first place.'

"'But why return?'

"'Because it feels true.'

"The emphasis on my last word gave the wizard pause. He looked into the crackling fire and sighed. 'Indeed,' he said. 'A worthy goal.' Now he really smiled and I felt that his eyes invited me into a secret knowledge. 'Sylna, I am going through these mines to a place where few have been. My goal is Zenidow the Great; it lies on the other side of this mountain. No mortal, I think, has known its full presence, but it is my fate to learn its secret. It will be a dangerous journey full of uncertainty, and it is very much possible that horrible demise awaits, but I will have you along most happily and teach you what I know of truth, if that is your wish.'

"'I do wish it, sir wizard.'

"'Call me Nubes!' He stood and bowed with a flourish."

CHAPTER XII
CASTLE IN THE DAY STAR

rose as well and bowed much to his subdued delight, asking, 'How long have you known that I followed you?'

"'Since you first spied upon me in the city. A wizard's eye,' he said, 'sees many things,' and looking into the cobalt iris whose bony socket he now tapped whimsically, I thought that a wizard's eye saw much more than runaway princesses in crowded markets and sneaking things in the dark, for I swore he looked right into my heart and soul, and suspected that he had sensed my presence long before I his.

"'These tunnels,' I said, feeling too well understood. 'I've not heard of anything like them.'

"'They are little known even among the nobles of Ardua,' he said sitting down again, 'and only recently discovered. A subterranean network untouched by the hands of Novare. Yet, they will come, and soon. There are veins of ore here that confound the imagination. But hard work is required, work like none before. All of the delvers royal and common will join forces at last to plumb this place. I can only hope that they heed my warning. There are dark things below us.' As he spoke, Nubes cocked his hairy ear, and falling silent listened intently. I became suddenly more aware of the hollow eking of the stale, moist air, the occasional clattering in the distant dark, the fluttering of leathery wings in the high arching roofs of the tunnels.

"'Come,' he said suddenly, and we went away from the fire in the light of his staff. Nubes followed his ear through the cold, dank dark, until at last I too heard the sound of trickling water, ever so softly, then building as rain against dry earth. Around a slimy bend there glittered a spill of crystal liquid merrily burbling as through a pleasant meadow in the garden. Nubes produced from the lit end of his staff a second bubble of light, which floated out over the subterranean stream and hovered there so as to give us vision and warmth. Beneath it, the radiant ribbon of water was uncommonly clear and beautiful.

"He seated himself beside the flow. 'You spoke of surrender, of a return to greater consciousness. Once, I too espoused such philosophies. But one day, as I was ferried across a great river, in the moving water I perceived the true form of this greater consciousness. Perhaps you will hear what I heard that day,' he indicated the stream. 'Listen, and tell me: what is the self?'

"If you know Nubes, you will not be surprised by our sitting beside that stream for nearly two hours, neither of us speaking a word. I took up my bow and drew back the string to clear my mind and ears, but I heard only running water. Still, this was a deeply beautiful sound, so that as I contemplated its gurgling I found myself at peace with this simple act of listening, and the first hour passed. But during the second hour, I was again lost and my mind touched with frustration. Now I recognized the beauty of the stream only through resolve, and my bowstring became unbalanced by degrees. Even this crude determination began to wane, and I set the instrument aside, simply watching.

"Only then, I had one simple thought: the stream was one, and it was many. Composed as it was of numberless drops of water, even if every drop had precisely the same structure, each had its own unique perspective of the whole. In this infinitely transforming flow of limitless contexts, there was no slice of time in which the stream was ever as it had been the moment before. Yet always the stream was one entity, one perspective, one stream. Now I imagined that it ran into and joined through subterranean systems with other bodies of water in the open air, where through the cycle of evaporation, transpiration and precipitation these filtered their moisture into the distant sea and the lakes and rivers of Altum. Singular as was its nature over time, as in the stream, the water in this cycle was always renewing.

"To Nubes, I said, 'This stream shows us how all selves are connected and naturally surrender to a greater whole, but also how each self is a unique, independent idea, like one drop of water flowing down through the stream, out into the world, cast onto a dry bank, evaporated into the clouds, and sent falling back to Altum as a raindrop. Looking at the cycle from without, I am unable to distinguish the boundaries between the drops of water and their different contexts. But, if I removed some water from the stream,' and I did so with one finger, holding it up flashing in the light. 'There is no more stream. There is just the drop, separated. That, I think, is the self. And for a moment,' I dipped my finger into the stream again, 'it can surrender to Oneness.'

"'Mm,' he mumbled. 'Yes, like all things in the world, if you look closely enough, you'll find that we are emergent properties of a greater being. But you have already learned to surrender. Why should I show you another bowstring?'

"'As a test?' I shrugged.

"Nubes smiled wryly. 'You passed any test I could dream up when you followed me into this godforsaken labyrinth.' He cleared his throat. 'You perceive the stream and your bowstring as powerful metaphors of becoming, but you continue to separate things into one and the other. Did you learn nothing from your so-called wedding of tension and resolution? Now you divide the drop and the stream. Tell me. What is one without the other?"

"Looking into those eyes of melted ice, now the metamorphosing body and bodies of the stream, I began to speak as with words I'd not yet prepared. 'In a sense, because the individual drops move indistinguishably as one, the stream is itself one great drop of water in the cycle. But this means that one drop taken from the stream is of the same nature, only smaller. I suppose the contradiction here is to say that a single drop is not made by the stream, but contains within itself already the existence of the stream as much as the stream contains the existence of the drop. Perhaps the proposition of the stream is even in the rain cloud or the condensation of dew on a blade of grass. Its potential is everywhere in the cycle. You mean to show me that you and I, ourselves, are not produced by a greater self, but that we are of that greater self. There is really no separation. The self never leaves or returns. It is already in a state of Oneness.'

"'Hrm! So you discover the self,' he said. 'But do not think that true Oneness is in this simple unity of opposites.' Now Nubes smirked deviously in the half-light, as if he'd hatched a scheme. 'For this, another teacher.' He reached about and brought forth a stone from the ground. This he handed to me with a most perplexing look. 'Listen again, and tell me now, what is Oneness?'

"Trying to conceal my frustration with the old man, I held the rock up to my ear. When that sense yielded nothing I squeezed it, and I felt its texture, smelled it, rapped on it, licked it, rolled it against the floor of the cave, sat staring at it, and Nubes the whole while had not moved a muscle at all or even his gaze from the rock, looking almost trepidatious, as if the thing might spontaneously transform into a horrifying Euphran. When I looked over as for a hint, he only smiled in that infuriating way, at once kind and condescending, which I would come to know so well. I scrutinized the rock anew, trying to see it as some extension of stream-logic.

"The rough surface did not move like the stream, but it was certainly composed of smaller elements. As I felt the shedding grains of dirt and flecks of stone piling in my palm, and as I watched them spill through my fingers, fall upon and blend with the cave floor, I considered that the grander structure around us was made of the same material. The rock had arisen from the mountain just as a drop from the stream. I saw the passage of time then from a broader perspective, for though things moved quickly in the stream, and a multitude of drops were instantly created in every splashing meander, individuality developed far more gradually in the ground. This rock was not always a rock, but one day formed, and will not always be a rock, will one day dissolve and become part of the mountain again. Just like the stream, the mountain around us was always the same mountain, yet always changing in its composition. The rock, really, was just like the drop of water, only taking much longer to actualize, and granted more durable selfhood. But as I revelled in the immensity and patience of time, I realized that for Nubes I would only have a new metaphor for the self.

"The wizard seemed to recognize the turmoil in me, but I could not discern whether he grimaced or smiled through his cloudy beard. 'Once more you knock upon Truth's door,' he said, 'but still you are not admitted. You saw in the stream that the self and its fountainhead are the same. I show you this rock because you have been stumped by one last contradiction. You speak of Oneness as if it exists in multiple forms. Intellectually, you have deduced it as a state of consciousness, but you have not lived it insofar as it describes the world.' He took the rock from me and brandished it as if his point was self-evident. 'You and I... are rocks.'

"'You mean metaphorically,' I said, completely stumped again. 'As the mountain is the source of the rock, the self has its own greater source. But both dualities are illusions. The rock really is the mountain, only separated by our limited perception of time and space.'

"'No, I mean you and I are rocks.'

"'But we are nothing like rocks! I can see that the rock and mountain share a medium, but,' I continued, seeing that he was not at all satisfied, 'we share nothing with rocks! We're living beings!'

"'Stubborn girl! How do you know that a rock is not alive?' Nubes looked almost comically offended, and I could not help but smirk. It was easy to picture the old wizard conducting an industrious conversation with rocks.

"'Rocks do not think,' I said at last.

"'Sometimes yes. Did you always think?'"

"'Well, not before I was born. And after I die thinking will be impossible. But then there is no 'I' to do any thinking.'"

"'Aha! But isn't it the goal of your meditation to dissolve this 'I' and surrender to its source? What then is left of the ego? Certainly not thinking.' As he spoke Nubes tossed the rock up and down, emphasizing his words.

"Now I looked at the rock more suspiciously. 'Perhaps the rock was once alive, but the self which animated it has gone. So then, we aren't rocks right now, but could, say, over millions of years, come to share their structure? Perhaps when I die my decomposing body could be wrapped up in some sedimentary formation and it could be said that I was a rock.'

"Nubes sighed. 'While that is entirely possible, rocks are quite alive despite any lack of thought, and without your help. This rock is conscious as you and I and the drops in the stream, and everything.'

"'But souls and matter, they are entirely different. I had always thought of the spirit as a thing apart, inspired in us alone by God, and not... rocks.'

"Looking up I nearly screamed. Before me sat in ponderous tableau an utterly lifeless stone carving of an old man, draped in haunting red robes. What had been the lively, ruddy skin of Nubes was now hard and grey-brown. Friable gravel delineated his formerly light and airy beard in an uncompromising frieze of hair flowing in a nonexistent breeze. I scooted away in horror as a crack in the effigy of his face grated open, spilling dust, and began to utter hollow syllables.

"'I am Nubes,' it said, 'and I am rock. You underestimate the notion of Oneness. The clumsy philosopher might say that technically this is possible because there is no true difference but time and the arrangement of fundamental particles between my chemistry and that of the rock. But really it is this: I recognize no difference at all. I am conscious that the entire universe in which we live and breathe is merely the expression of one ultimate, unified field which is called: the Fabric. So I find what thread my flesh shares with this rock, and taking it up I stitch their folds together as they once were in the dawn of time. Now I let go!' As though I had blinked, all was in an instant skin as before, and Nubes winked most pretentiously. 'Now I hope you never speak too openly in front of rocks again!' He picked up the rock which had dropped from his suddenly stone hands, and flung it into the stream, which issued a loud *ker-plunk*. 'That is, until you can listen and know what their intentions are.'

"I watched where the rock had disappeared. As the ripples expanded from the little fountain of its plunge, with each broader ring there pulsed a greater sensation of life—life all around me. Like a child I had thought myself prescient for surrendering to the universal self, but now I saw that even in dissolving this one duality, I clung to another far more primitive in my parsing of bodies and boundaries by an arbitrary, narcissistic alienation of animate and inanimate. Not only was every atom of the stream and cavern, and of my flesh and bone, and of Nubes' robes, and of the air particles all through the cavern each a living node of consciousness and perception, but so too were they inextricably involved in every soul, abstracted concept, thought and dream, whatever I had thought non-physical should mean, and all of them, everything together with myself, my body and mind, was called the Fabric. 'Don't worry,' Nubes said casually. 'Rocks can't drown.'

"It was this comment that broke me, and I doubled over laughing. The wizard contained his mirth quite well, but soon joined in. For a long while we cackled and giggled and ultimately just sat again listening to the stream. At last I said, 'Wizard Nubes, can you speak to the rocks then?'

"'In a way. It takes a patient consciousness to sew the Fabric. But then,' he smiled warmly in the pale light, 'you have been practising for a long time.'

"That evening will always be my defining memory of Nubes—a grinning golem in a red hat and robe. But there were many more significant nights to be had. We travelled through labyrinthine tunnels seeming to have no business with Novare, more and more of them quite enormous and perfectly round, as if they had been bored out by some godly drill. Somehow the wizard knew where to go at every turn. Only once did he seem stumped at a quartet of diverging mouths, but really he had just fallen asleep on his feet!

"For several days Nubes guided my meditations upon the Fabric through the philosophizing of some new object—a stalactite, a blue glow worm, even a pile of droppings—or concept—the staleness of the air, the echo of our footsteps. But in time he gave me one task which, he said quite adamantly, I must learn on my own before my work with the Fabric could truly begin. 'Make light from the darkness, Sylna, and then you will be a witch.'

"It was only on the final night of our journey through the tunnels that I completed this first and apparently simplest stitch. I knew that in the inky darkness all around I could find a common thread with light itself, yet still the idea confounded me. I had attacked this notion for many changeless days with great frustration—light was made of darkness, and darkness made of light. At last I realized that I was not truly meditating, but coming at the problem intellectually as Nubes had warned I favoured overmuch to do; but this time he had not said anything while I floundered and cursed in the dark. Now I took up my bow, drew back the string, and imagined that all states of darkness and light were like the multiplicity of infinitely flexing bowstrings. Only for an instant—as when those forces of tension and resolution are somehow one—I really did believe that these utter contradictions were connected, and therein—as through an opened seam in the reality I had so far known—I beheld a woven universe of infinitely folding and self-transforming colour, always renewing, always complete, always the same.

"Among the endless weave of that vast art, one shadowy thread streamed from a manifold so black and lightless in its fluctuating dimensions that it could only be the essence of the dark. Yet following as it unspooled in hue to a silvery, now a golden white, far away in the lifting, falling, surging medium I saw where this one same thread entered upon another manifold which was opposite in nature to the first, and blinding to my being. In the moment I beheld this link, it was as though my bowstring were released, and as an arrow fired forth I hurtled into the Fabric. I slipped first through the manifold of darkness like a sewing needle now threaded on this single strand, pulling all those moving quilted shadows behind me as I flew to pierce as well the distant light. Such was my speed that in an instant I had passed through that opposing form, so that now my flying spirit swung round and back, high over the massive folds of light and dark leaning out over fabric abysses one towards the other. With the added, sudden tug against my eyelet speeding overhead, the Fabric folded upon itself, and at last the light and dark surpassed their gulfs, and were sewn together. As by the same motion I was pulled back into the cave, where a jewelled bulb of luminance had appeared like an egg floating precisely in the aim of my bow. I was shocked and cried out, and at once the light disappeared, but in the flash of its brief existence I saw the pride on Nubes' face, for he had stopped and turned to watch even as I took out my instrument.

"In the morning we came out of the mines on the far side of the mountain, and before us was the Crater, and further along, far below, over many miles of steeply sloping rock and snow, shrouded in mist, lay Pivwood, and at its centre Zenidow the High. In one month we achieved the edge of the forest, and Nubes led us to a clearing where he began building the tower that stands there today. There we have lived for the last twelve years, though Nubes long ago departed for Lucetal over the sea and left me with this task of sewing now the storm I spoke of before."

*

When the tale was told, Sylna and Muewa reflected each to themselves, listening for a while to the wind-rattled trees, the twittering and chirping of birds, the drop of dew from branches and leaves spread out beneath them in all directions, and the rush of clean wind here on the high, bare hill. The witch had taken her hand from her bow, and now it rested in the cool grass.

Muewa spoke when she was ready. "Your quest is one of knowledge. Yet you are wise to see the dangers in that path. You, Sylna, who saw that understanding is surrender, yet accepted your lesser role for love: I am happy to continue your learning. Though," she laughed, wings fluttering, "I'm afraid it will be more of the same. There is a reason Nubes did not suggest your coming here. A storm is a complex feat of sewing indeed, but you need only reach the sky through the simple act of meditation."

"I suspected as much, and have tried for many months since his leaving. Every day I search. But I cannot discover such matrices of Fabric as to shift the very weather. I can fold air into water and sew them with the wind, but no such heavenly unity as even the falling rain has come from my work."

"That is because storms are not born on Altum. They are sent by Caelare herself." Muewa looked up into the light of the sun, shading her eyes with one wing. "There was a time when she lived among us and ruled all, but that was before even the sea was stained. Now she cares little for creatures of the land. Still, the weather of the world is in her wings. It is simple really, this thing. Seek beyond the world; seek the sun! For that is her house."

Sylna was appalled. "Nubes told me to follow no thread which leaves the Fold of Altum. My soul could be lost forever!"

"Well I won't say it isn't dangerous. But I cannot show you what it is to call thunder and lightning from heaven. You must call out yourself."

"I..." the witch murmured, looking up into the charged, blue firmament. "I suppose Nubes has modelled breaking many of his own rules before."

"What other option do you have? You will sit on this hill until it rains." With these words the Piv was silent.

Sylna nodded nervously, but anxiety began already to fall away as was its nature when she took up her bow. Drawing back the gleaming string, skyward she aimed the arrow of her soul. She cleared the mind, focused upon the breath—inspired by everything, accepting that all would expire—and held the infinite forms of tension and resolution in her hand like a confounding unity.

As always, the Fabric was revealed to her as through a seam in the air itself subtly split, now widening with totality, revealing the bottommost metaphysical truth of its reality. The last traces of three dimensional existence were passed over by the rippling lips of the great opening, and replaced with a surging tapestry of billowing Pivwood, the white mountains, the touch of exquisite detail that was little Muewa before her, Zenidow behind, the sky above, all stitched and folded and woven with a mastery of moving complexity that made the world she'd left seem as a crude carving on the wall of a cave. Now she moved the sight of her bow slowly over the texture of the heavens as seething blue began to swim with the gold and white. There was—as between all things—one thread connecting the tip of her drawn soul with the consciousness of the day star. That subtle line out in the great shifting material she soon found, for those things Nubes had forbidden she had often sought before.

Softly the bowstring twanged, and Sylna sent forth the manifold of her very consciousness from that of its mortal vessel in a silver needle streaming along that single, fine thread connecting her with the sun. Already the folds of the forest below were shrouded in distance, and only the endless contour of Zenidow remained. She calmed herself as best she could with the memory of Muewa's blessing. In that thought the clouds grew thick and grey, and even the Great Mountain vanished so that she hurtled curving, diving, shooting upward through the stitching of the outer atmosphere. With a sound like absence itself she met the final membrane englobing Altum, arched along its surface, and zagged out and away upon her chosen string which led thereon into a total, depthless black which dwarfed all sensibility.

As the great purple and green sphere of the world, now vast, shrinking—too quickly even for its twenty moons to show in orbit—became a distant ball, Sylna found herself profoundly alone in an endless void of surging Fabric. As her soaring senses adjusted she saw that the eternal curtain of night was everywhere pricked by gleaming divine lights. These were the distant manifolds of stars, and some of them, perhaps, other worlds; perhaps one such light was Kellod. Lastly, yet most glaringly bright and growing only larger by the moment, there was the sun, Caelare's palace. It was pure and perfect, immortally bright and wondrous, and more complex a manifold than any she before had experienced. Normally one could scarcely look at that enormous ball of fire, so brilliant was its majesty that it would melt the mind and blind the eyes. But as Sylna had taken the essential form of the Fabric itself, she was able to look on it insofar as it was another fold with which she shared the essence of her being.

The further she went from her body upon the far face of Altum in this way, the more vulnerable she was to severance, for there were—Nubes said—malefic and nefandous things which roamed these cosmic patterns; things which could feel the ripples of the distanced soul and rend it from the body. But now it was too late to turn back. The curvature impressed upon the Fabric by Caelare's palace was such that Sylna was now inexorably drawn at increasing speed sliding down great satiny slopes of dark space into the centre of its well. The all-encompassing light of the great star rushed in an expanding pit of dazzling white brilliance to swallow her. With a noiseless boom the blackness of space was replaced with endless white. On went the shapeless, utterly pure light for a span of time which was lost to her in its vastness. Yet out of abyssal blindness there emerged at last the evening of distinct shades which became more soft to the senses. Though the divine light had never dimmed, through the gradient of growing gentleness she was able to see now the subtle delineation of a regal, white wall.

The only feature in the heightless, white plane was an endlessly tall set of double doors, discernible only by the subtle cut of their oblong panels. There seemed to be no way of parting them, but when she changed the fold of her spirit from arrow into a hand outreaching, they swung slowly to, revealing a great hall within. A long golden floor spread forth beneath her, and now drooping from the thread yet connected to her distant, physical form, as an extension of purely spiritual fabric she touched down with folded feet. Down the centre of the hall yawned an open chasm of light, the very core of the sun exposed, yet her drifting feet met some unseen resistance over its illimitable abyss, and she made her way carefully through the room.

At the end of the blinding chasm was a raised platform, and a brilliant throne. In this great seat—brighter, yet more contained in brightness than all else—sat an elegant Novare woman, for Caelare favours the form of her chosen children. Her long blazing hair was the light of the sun itself, whose long tendrils kindled and burned as they reached far out into the radiant deeps all around her. She looked down on Sylna with golden-white eyes, clad only in a flowing ivory gown. Her expressionless face was smooth as starlight, but she held out her luminous arms in a sign of welcome.

"Great mother," said Sylna, bowing low and kneeling before the throne. "You are Light."

Caelare did not gesture for Sylna to rise, and neither did the slightest feeling seem to complicate her immortal visage as she placed her hands again upon the armrests of her heavenly chair. "Child," she said, and her voice was like the ageless singing of seraphim in heaven. "You will accomplish greater things than you can know. I will not speak of that future, but I grant you this audience."

Sylna lifted her head slightly, remaining on one knee, which shook against the brilliant floor. "I must call a storm."

Caelare loomed without moving, her presence all that Sylna perceived. "You are mistaken to think this in your power." The witch thought to meet Caelare's bottomless eyes, but could not, and saw again the chasm below. "Your master is devious, sending you. I would not so meddle in the affairs of Teludei—known to you as the Alium—for one such as Nubes, but you... Sylna," she said the witch's name with grave purpose, "I cannot this time ignore. Listen then. Fire your bow. I will reach out over Occultash only once. Lightning shall guide the Nogofod Ogwold to the mountains; thunder shall obscure his footfalls; rain shall clothe him in chaos."

Sylna forced her eyes upward so that she saw the goddess' brilliant visage; still the suns of those eyes repelled direct contact. "Great Light, I know not how to thank you. But..." She steeled herself. "I would ask for your counsel in one other event. The ancient wood of the Piv is threatened."

Caelare's countenance at last assumed the form of an expression, and it was grave to behold. "This storm is all I shall risk on account of the Teludei."

"Of course." Sylna averted her eyes at once. "I swear to protect your world."

Caelare was silent for a long while. At last she spoke, and with her words the light of the palace bloomed and drowned all. "You will do well."

The flood of effulgence sent Sylna flying back along the endless thread in a great rush, arching against the black cosmic night, strafing and cutting through the atmosphere of Altum and sliding down the sky. When she returned to her body on the sunny hill in Pivwood, she could not open her eyes for some time. Back was the susurrus of wind in the grass, and back was the tittering voice of Muewa.

"Well, it's about time," said the little Piv. "On my count, you've been at it for three days and nights!" With a diminutive green foot, Muewa kicked a leafy sack of mushrooms down from her boulder. They spilled out like little brown ears in the grass. "Eat!" Opening her eyes, a gnawing hunger struck Sylna and she devoured the food at once. As she ate, a soft booming carried through the land, and Sylna saw that there were many grey vapours in the sky. Now these clouds huddled over the forest, and their dark bellies began to mist. Cool drops of water peppered Sylna's munching cheeks, and she laughed as the rain began to fall in swift sheets.

Muewa cheered. "The Goddess sends her signature."

"Caelare..." Sylna said softly, holding out her hand under the light, cool droplets. "She said that no mortal can sew storms."

The Piv nodded knowingly. "We Piv are but celebrants. The Goddess gives us what weather she pleases."

Sylna smiled as one deceived in good fun. "She will align my bowshot with her thunder. I just need to fire at the right time—gods! How long did you say? I have just over one week!"

"Well that's all right then, not a moment too soon," said Muewa beaming.

The rain steadily thickened as they sped down the side of the hill and beneath the streaming leaves of the trees. Slowing their pace under the dry boughs, they made their way back to the village of the Piv, while Sylna told Muewa all about the castle in the day star.

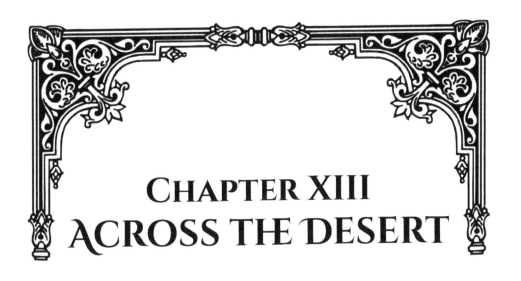

CHAPTER XIII
ACROSS THE DESERT

Videre curled up in the satin shadows of the tutum grove, awaiting nightfall. The last gleam of her master's ship had turned upon itself, flashed like a dying star, dissolved in the glittering expanse of the sea. Now there was only the ogre and his farewells between her and the mountains; and well, there was of course that awful desert. She sighed at length, her saggy jowls flapping rhythmically as she scanned the coast, settling upon the distant hulk which was Ogwold. He had gone down to the water one last time.

The ogre peered back up into the rock-strewn coastal hills stiff with white trees and the little sacs of their blue fruit. Videre's spacious eyes were black pools floating amidst the spectre of her sleek fur blending seamlessly with the pale trunks. The inky tufts of her tails hovered like wandering spirits of darkness. Stealthily they slunk out of sight, and closing the oval deeps of her gaze, she quite vanished. Two enormous Nogofod lumbered along the perimeter of the grove, but they were distracted enough with Ogwold sitting so close to the water. From below, he could just discern their scowls as he twisted to obscure the stark green of his alien arm planted in the sand. The reminder in their disapproval recalled the close roar of the sea, the mist on his cheek pulling it round when they had lurched far enough away.

Dusk now draped the waves, snuffing their sparkles slowly reborn in the sky; there they simmered like a bed of coals. Fonsvana and colourful Elemdam took flight against those cold embers. The first should have been at half-moon were it not a physical crescent fully illumined, but some prehistoric celestial clash had hollowed out its belly, leaving only a distorted, grey sickle floating dead and doubled over. Novare called it the Moon of Magic, because it had no heart. But they could not ignore the glaring power of its sister, always near. Unmistakable vitality was in Elemdam's moving symmetry of lava and liquid water, and so they charged its image with Altum's natural forces. This evening, the orange corona of Elemdam's penumbra was its brightest feature. Though through that shadowed half Ogwold could delineate the dark feathers of storming flame, he was more interested in the other, soft blue hemisphere which shone singly in Caelare's unseen light.

As always, he struggled to believe that this limpid medium was really water, for the sea to him had always been purple, and even the purified water from the royal taps was a stark violet. Perhaps near Lucetal, or elsewhere in the world there were blue waters, but if it were up to him, scripture should say that the gentler half of Elemdam was made of pure, bottomless sky—or perhaps it was one enormous tutum fruit! This made him smile. He wondered how Novare dared speak to the heavenly bodies' significance, let alone of what they were composed. Perhaps they conjured different meanings in the mountains, or among the diverse cultures of Altum about which he knew so little. What was Elemdam in the desert? In the mountains? Still, for Ogwold some lore would never fully change: Somnam—wherever it was that night—would always be the source of dreams.

But for the moons and stars, evening gathered its variable shades into integers of solid black. Only then did Ogwold stand and turn his back on the opposing themes of Magic and Nature in Fonsvana and Elemdam, and on the sea, his first love, now looking over the shacks of Epherem, out over the desert foothills, up into the faraway brooding range as if there waited for him not only new moons, but new loves.

As the cabin materialized out of the huddled shadows of the sparsely lit village, Ogwold coming up from the shore saw through the flickering window the oafish silhouettes of Ogdof and Wog arranged around the hearth. Ghostly fingers of smoke slunk over the sill. The soft wind carried their trailing claws round to the front, and when he swung the door open their quickened white tips grasped at the night.

"Ogwold," Ogdof grunted stoically; but even in the red opacity of his heavy-lidded eyes there was yet that secret past which only his son could recognize. Ogwold smiled, his gnarled green right arm and the huge, layered bulb of its shoulder still hidden behind the door and outer wall.

Wog cared little for the moment. "Don't think I didn't notice your absence today, boy. You sully the Nogofod name," he spat. The force of 'name' dredged up a long, shuddering belch, and his eyes bulged as puffs of smoke chugged down his chest with each new syllable in the word drawn out. Ogdof began to speak, but his hearthmate suddenly recovering had more to say. "Don't you start. 'He's got one arm' is it?"

Ogdof scowled. "My son helps in other ways. He's always been a better hand in the groves than I. Besides, we're doing all right."

"Well I've no issue with a missing arm. Punishment, I can stomach. But never laziness. Even if my legs were hacked off, I'd still be out there working."

"Ignore his nonsense, Ogwold." Ogdof chuckled deeply, raising his sonorous voice over the groaning other. "I won a great fortune this afternoon." He took a long draw from his pipe, and removing the stem released a rattling, rasping sigh, savouring the smoke that trickled through the cracks in his system, and eked back, licking his nostrils, completing the veil over his eyes. "A fine lady from Lucetal required the careful employment of only a very experienced labourer." He bowed his head piously, jowls stiff and impassive.

Wog split into the hearty peals of laughter for which he was known to emit as from nowhere; though, it seemed Ogdof had drawn the outburst from him intentionally. "You should have seen the driver of her cart! He was pale as a spirit!" Difficult as it was to acknowledge the levity of one so rude to him moments ago, Ogwold smirked and shrugged the shoulder which they could see, for after all Wog was one of few ogres who cared to spend time with his father, and over all these recent merry months he had become somewhat endeared to the brute's caprices.

"For good reason." Ogdof gestured with his pipe to the table. "I might have lost a limb myself if I'd run afoul of her." Ribbons of blue smoke trailed his hairy knuckles and carried onward, coiling over that surface, where glinted three brilliant golden coins. "Only royalty could be so thoughtless with her purse."

Ogwold's eyes were gibbous. "Dad! These will purchase you fresh water for a year!"

"And you, son. Your thirst is my thirst."

"Ha!" Wog leered at Ogwold through matted, stringy hair, his mirth forgotten. "The layabout reminds you: he deserves no such reward! See how he won't even cross the threshold! At least he recognizes when he's not worth his weight."

"Wog!" Ogdof boomed, anger on his brow such that none had seen in many years. "He's worth far more than that to me, and you know it. I'll not warn you again," he growled, slowly letting his heavy eyelids slide down again over his suddenly penetrating gaze. Fully closing them now, he folded his great burned arms and sighed heartily. "One day you will have a little one too."

"He is not so little anymore!" Wog bellowed, but even as he spoke he grimaced, and a thick, sagging vein pulsed in his sweaty forehead. "Ah," he muttered, shaking his head and lighting his own pipe. After a long sequence of puffs and smacking lips he said, "Well come in and sit down then, boy. There's norm to go round." He narrowed his eyes and sighed, troubling the milky tide of smoke into a rolling wave. "If I had a son... Even if he were... totally useless..." Unfinished as this thought went, it was the closest to compassion ever that Wog had come so far as Ogwold knew. In his ruddy countenance so often stiff with skepticism there was a softening of affect as one senses among family.

Ogwold breathed deeply, and looked into those bleary eyes which only for a moment longer would accept him, and never again. Then he stepped into the room, drawing forth the shoulder which was not a shoulder, the arm which was not an arm from their place behind the door. He held the great appendage flexed and slightly bent before him in the wash of hearthlight, so that its deep greens were saturated and the hard ridges of its stiff musculature were shadowed in relief. The heat of the fire was uniquely intense against the green flesh exposed, such that it seemed to shrink tight, condensing its tissue, but still he advanced to the table and placed there the sack of silver coins which Nubes had given him. "I meant that I will not be drinking your water any longer. Here is a great sum to repay my burden on this house. I'm to Occultash tonight."

There was a long silence, but for the infinite roar of the sea. Wog rose slowly. Wet crunching punctuated the crumbling of his broken pipe, dribbling between fat hairy fingers onto the old floorboards. A shadow passed over the face of Ogdof. He had whittled the old piece for his friend when they were very young.

"Demon," Wog grated, raising a stabbing, shaking finger. Unable to tear his eyes from Ogwold's treacherous limb, he spoke sidelong to Ogdof. "Your mutant spawn sells his dignity to the Xol for cursed flesh." The last shards of the pipe fell from his twitching fingers. "Cut that abomination from his shoulder and throw it in the fire. I shall bring the guard to your traitorous doorstep this instant!" he bellowed.

"Wog, my friend." Ogdof, standing, planted the grey trunks of his legs before the quaking ogre, blocking his exit. He was much larger and nobler in stature than the other, and though he would never hurt his friend, Wog had always feared the notion of their wrestling. "If you never wish to speak again, I'll understand," Ogdof continued, only with kindness in his voice now. "But do me this one service, dear old Wog, after all these years. Do not speak to the knights at least until dawn, then I will bear whatever punishment is necessary. My son leaves Epherem tonight, so allow us our farewell."

Wog fumed, but as his gaze darted madly around the room, those red, burning eyes fell on the shattered remains of the pipe, and rising met Ogdof's gaze. There he held, and none could say what thoughts passed through his rage-blooded mind, but that all at once he swung away his bloated face and lurched for the door, muttering in the direction of Ogwold. "Occultash? Bah! You'll lose much more than an arm." Always a slammer of doors, Wog left the entryway ajar, swaying and creaking in the sea wind, as if to say that just this once he would stray from his customs.

Ogwold closed the door slowly and gazed back at his father, firelight throwing the shadows of his windswept hair over his features. "I can't say I like him but, for whatever reason... Wog was your closest friend..."

"Oh, yes, yes, you're right. He's like a brother. But he'll come around. This is not the first time I've incurred his wrath. And I believe it won't be the last. Who is it you think helped me explain away your motherlessness? There are few things so strange as a child appearing from nowhere and looking just ever so slightly different from his peers." Ogdof chuckled. "Wog is a passionate ogre of stout heart. His stone burdens those who come near. But I admire his pride in our people, and in his own way he admires us, Ogwold. I doubt he will speak to the guard at all."

Ogwold still could only hang his head. "Staying in Epherem these past months was selfish, and a waste of time. I'm ashamed to finally leave only when I am physically unable to live here. Even if he doesn't go to the guard, Wog has a point about my arm: there's certainly no hiding it now, scarce of boarding me up here till the end of my days." They stared at the strange gossamer musculature as it seemed to breathe and pulse subtly. "I swear I had already made up my mind this morning. I saw Mother. I won't ignore her again." Ogwold still could not shake a deep revulsion for the flames that danced in the hearth, and so he did not come closer. But his father came to him and held his new limb with striking tenderness for a being so hulking and graceless.

"Autlos-lo watches over you." Ogdof spoke with solemn compassion. "I am glad that you heed her wish at last. Surely she sends you on the path of righteousness." Releasing his grasp, he lumbered over to the foot of his sleeping pad, and with some fiddling—now a scraping and a shifting of wood against wood, sheets of faint dust rising into the room—pulled an old board up from the floor. Dragging it carefully to the side, he revealed a deep crawl space, a black rectangular opening wall to wall. Reaching his thick arms into the musty darkness he heaved up an enormous rectangular bundle of white cloth, nearly as long as the board which had covered it, and placed it carefully, though none too quietly upon the floor, glowing before the hearth. Slowly he fitted the board back into place, shutting away the dark, and sat looking down at the package from his fireside smoking chair.

"As with you," he said, looking off now into the flames, "it was not only love for Autlos-lo that seeded my heart with restlessness. My dream of leaving the shore is so old that it is lost." He turned up his heavy eyes and gestured for Ogwold to undo the tremendous wrapping.

Avoiding the eye of the fire, Ogwold endured the heat on his quivering green skin, and stooped to unroll the bundle. The material revealed itself unfolding to be a great hooded cloak of voluminous sleeves, heavy and finely woven, white as the richest tutum trunk and tough as its bark. Upon it unwrapped was a raw slab of a sword, thick and long as the arm of a Nogofod. Like an enormous butcher's knife, its blunt side was the only that angled at its end sharply from rectangularity, while the cutting edge was purely straight all down to the guardless hilt, protruding from the worn, leather scabbard long enough for two ogroid hands to comfortably grip its stained, cloth wrap.

Ogdof continued. "My plan was yours. But Occultash is vast. I feared capture wandering in its tangled streets, always well lit—they say—by meridiem lamps. There will be guards everywhere, Ogwold, knights even. I was controlled by fear, yet if not for that fear I mightn't have met your mother, and you mightn't have faced it for me." He smiled. "So I say! If you are set in your quest, take my tools, whatever you shall need from our stores of tutum and water skins. The cloak is pale as the moonlit desert, and large enough I think to obscure your secret flight. Believe it or not, I was a little larger than you in my youth. As for the blade..." Ogdof nodded. "Unsheath it, son."

Ogwold squatted, gripped the weathered scabbard with his green right, grasped the cloth-wrapped hilt with his grey left, slowly, methodically out-dragging a dark, rough metal, dull and hard and unyielding. Even the firelight could not play on its face. Though resting at an angle against the cabin floor as he pulled, the sword was overwhelmingly heavy even for an arm which had been shouldering the traders' packages for months on its own. But rising up on his feet and taking one powerful step back he drew the great, flat blade smoothly enough, and with both hands grey and green stacked together raised it before him so that it pointed towards the open window. He had never held a weapon before, but somehow his stance felt natural, back straight, shoulders up, feet widely spaced, knees slightly bent. Still the thing was all the more difficult to support by its ridiculous length, and he let the end down slowly until it gave its weight to the floor again.

"It is not pretty or valuable, but it is strong," said Ogof from his seat, watching with the seam of his grey lips pulled up and to the side. "It belonged to an immense knight who walked our shore long before I met your mother. I couldn't say whether he came aboard a ship, or out from the desert, and when or how he departed I hadn't the slightest intuition. One day he was here, another gone. Yet he wandered in the village for many days, always alone, seeming to repulse the other knights. He was taken by the sea, and found me there watching the waves as well. I too was avoided by my fellows, for I cared not to hide my interest in the water. There we spoke as equals. I began to wonder whether I would be treated differently elsewhere in the world. There are few who see a soul in the eyes of Nogofod, yet he was one! When I asked if there were others, he spoke merrily of all different kinds of life in far flung places. I declared that I would become an adventurer, that with such a massive blade as he wore across his back I might slay even the Euphran in one swing, and so I pledged all of my earnings, everything I had for it. He accepted only a small amount of silver, and I think his heart leapt to give his weapon to one—he said—so worthy. Perhaps he pitied me. But if anyone could swing his sword, he figured it would be an ogre." He laughed. Yet as he gazed now out of memory into the present moment of his son's grasping the great weapon, the creases of Ogdof's smile slowly fell and folded into grief.

"This sword will be a device of doom in your hands, Ogwold, I'm sure of it. We ogres are powerful creatures, kept obedient for more than our ability to work. They fear us, son, our strength, our grit. They watch our wrestling and laugh, cheering on their favourites, placing bets, discussing records and skillsets, but how would they fare in the ring? How would even their finest warrior with his best blade parry this monstrous piece of metal, swung by a beast such as you? We have no education in the arts of war, but I suspect there is talent in our blood. You especially are young, quick to learn, and brimming with imagination. I pray that you go easy on the man who dares to challenge you."

Ogdof left his seat and touched the blade with his hand. He pressed his thumb hard down along the edge, and a thin stream of blood flowed from a fine line in his raw calloused skin. "With enough force the edge yet cuts." He tried to laugh again, though it came in a dismissive snort. "But this knight—he told me it is rather the crushing weight of the weapon that makes it so deadly." He led Ogwold to lift the sword level with the floor once more, and fitted the sheath again over the right-angle tip, shoving the scabbard back over its dull slab face. "Still, let us hope that it remains on your back. And take this infernal silver away!" He pushed Nubes' payment across the wood. "You were never a burden, son, and I'll rest easier knowing you have coin for the road. Granted, it's quite a sum, and I can't imagine the sort of noble who dropped it on you."

"Dad..." Ogwold set the sword upon the table, which groaned dangerously. "Thank you." At last his father noticed the tears rolling down his own face as much as his son's. "I am sorry to have said so foolishly that these last months have been a waste, for I would never trade them away. If only I had known you more closely. I love you, Dad. I love the Nogofod, even Wog, that animal. I love Epherem and the sea. But I must away, for both our sakes, before this arm gets us both killed, before Autlos-lo gives up on me." He stepped forward and wrapped Ogdof in a hard embrace. "One day I will return."

Ogwold kissed his father's bald, wrinkled head, and stepping back gently held the sea-scarred arms of the man who had raised him, smiling into those cryptic stone eyes which at last he at least partly understood. Then he packed a leather rucksack with as much of the dried fruit as he could manage, and tethered to its straps two bulging waterskins. Around his shoulders old and new fell the folds of the great white cloak as if they were sewn with his hulking figure in mind.

With much grunting he belted the enormous scabbard around his right shoulder, which seemed better to resist the digging-in of the strap. The long hilt stuck up behind his head, and the right-angle tip of the sword reached the backs of his knees, though the hump of his back lifted its length out behind him so that it might not slam against his legs. Testing the weight of it all, he figured he would at least be able to travel short distances with intermittent breaks. With one last kiss to Ogdof's wet cheek, he stepped out over the threshold of his cabin for good.

The simmering coal-bed sky now kindled with innumerable cold stars. Elemdam and Fonsvana flew high over Ogdof's cabin, joining in bright awareness of the path up from the scattered cabins of Epherem, out into the white rolling hills of the desert. Far off, the black mountains communed high-shouldered, and out from their nighted secrecy shot Zenidow in a pale pillar to heaven.

Ogwold took Nubes' warm sphere from his pocket, where it had spent the greater part of the evening. The powerful drone which had so astounded him before had significantly lessened, though it still strung his ears together through the innermost atom of his consciousness. Perhaps it had become slowly more natural to him, like the lifelong backdrop of the roaring surf. Or—if the sphere was really a living thing—perhaps it slept. With this thought the light of it pulsed once, twice; smoothly it spun against his open palm, and rose into the air before his face humming no louder than before, not reflecting, but suffusing with moonlight.

"So you are awake then," Ogwold whispered. Though still the humming felt as a constant medium, there was within it an infinitude of unique vibrations which all together created the impression of wholeness. From these complexities more endless and essential as Ogwold listened, there seemed to arise the pure confirmation that yes, the sphere had waited for him, and now it was time at last to go.

As if his gaze was carried up from those tiny silver deeps on some subtle crescendo in their music, he beheld the slender hulk of Videre poised atop a fingernail of white rock, three tails snaking like dense mists, bottomless eye-pits hovering in the astral form of a monstrous lupine cat. She leapt—in a moment interposed the crescent face of Fonsvana—and vanished. Noiseless she reappeared, lowering one enormous, triangular shoulder before Ogwold. He placed his grey hand tentatively upon the high, pointed bone, but when he felt her long, thick hair it seemed again, as before when he had returned to her in the tutum grove, that she was a friend.

He vaulted clumsily atop her huge, sinewy back, and she swung one black convex eye around as if to see that he was secure. The intensity of her stare was such that Ogwold instinctively gripped hard into the shaggy white locks of her long, barrel neck, pressing his chin down between the high pyramidal blades of her shoulders. Just as he realized that—big as she was—Videre was not only bearing his great carriage, but also the gigantic sword upon his back, her body exploded forward. The only sound in that elastic moment but for the crashing surf was the soft patter of dust against rock. In an instant they touched down; in another they were hurtling forward. Each pounce was a concert of delicate precision and uncoiling force, each soft congress of paw and rock like the brief swooping of predatory birds upon their speeding prey.

While Ogwold had planned to enter the desert from some more desolate stretch of coast, Videre cared little for the loose and drunken patrol that watched the highway. The Novare guards could scarce comprehend what massive bowling blur of white it was that like a ghost swept along the edges of their fires and vanished into the vastness of the pale desert.

Long into that white waste they raced, the dark range rising ahead of the crust of the world. Elemdam and Fonsvana fell beyond their craggy black bulks. Three newborn moons rose blossoming behind them, coming and going among the rushing, silvered clouds. First was jonquil Vitalem, and like a petal of the same flower Lucifella unfolded, the brightest of all moons, silver-white as the sheer wall of Zenidow, and said to be the second home of Caelare herself. Like a stem to the others was the slender Moon of Creation, Incipi, small, greyish, porous with craters and older than any. In the light of their eudaimonia stretched the shadows of wagons packed up for the night; many such a smouldering encampment they surpassed like a white wind in the night.

When the moons had set Ogwold figured they must slow for sight, yet Videre bolted through the total dark it seemed with even greater precision and vigour. He could hardly fathom how calmly and evenly she breathed, maintaining such powerful speed without fluctuation despite the rise and fall of the blasted terrain. Even come the thin rays of dawn her pace did not flag, but at the first sound of rattling wagons she paused so softly and suddenly as to have pitched her rider into the rock below were it not for the grip of his greener limb, which—he found—had extended and woven its fingers as roots fast around her shoulders, trunk and muscled neck.

Unsure at first why they had stopped, for he had not his partner's ears, Ogwold took the moment to rest and observe the desert of his morning terrors. With the sun only just rising beyond the sea, all was cool and clear, and at last it seemed that the song of Autlos-lo would no longer torment him. Now there was even a majesty to this place otherwise so horribly manifested in his nightmares. Under the cloudless blue vault of heaven the rolling and cresting relief of dunes and hills and rocks all white and parched and cracked looked like the skeleton of the ocean stripped of its purple, flowing flesh and organs. Here was merely a slow and solid sea of different texture, whose waves crashed gradually over gulfs of time.

With a soft hiss smooth and liquid his greener limb slunk in upon itself and tightened easily to its previous likeness: a muscled Nogofod arm. Wondering at its impulse to change in that moment, Ogwold noticed that the voluminous white sleeves of his father's cloak covered all but the verdant tips of his fingers, quite hiding their nature. His race, really, would be the difficult part of his being to obscure in Occultash. Then he heard the wagon wheels.

"I don't think I'm in danger on this road, Videre," he said, leaning forward into her layered sets of ears as if she needed to hear him more clearly. "You're too fast! Besides, you are so large, I might look like a Novare by comparison." Though he had spoken to her before, Ogwold was astonished by how naturally she understood, catching his eye and chuffing loudly. He wrapped his long arms around her neck, and locked his fingers back into the heavy layers of her shaggy hair. With the stunning ease and grace of her first and freshest stride, she bounded forth.

Almost at once there appeared over the mirage-pooled hills a rumbling caravan of wagons bound for Epherem. The first cornibets reared up, snorted fearfully and in succession down the line their drivers slowed to gawk, astounded by the strange and awesome creature that flew like a great spirit of the desert through this treacherous land, and by the huge stature and sword of the black-maned man that drove her away from the sea. So ferocious and swift were the calculated bounds of Videre that the snapping folds of Ogwold's radiant cloak haunted the last wagon before any word of their coming had reached it. Yet already a new caravan shimmered on the distant coils of the road ahead. All morning they encountered new veins of weary traders, and several they overcame in their shared direction away from the sea. Only just before the highest point of day did the business of the ancient road taper and clear.

Alone at last they ranged through the dizzyingly bright, bare hills as the day star poured its molten totality into the trapping sand. Scorching, motionless air rose just hovering in an endless, cottony gag above the shadeless scramble. Ragged, limber shadows of desert birds troubled all periphery. Only atop the highest hills waited but a torturously brief swell of clear air. The real oppression and aridity of the desert was far worse than any nightmare, even as those memories inexorably compounded in his heat-oppressed mind. There was nothing surreal, nothing abstract about this place, and certainly nothing of deeper meaning. The torrid air scarred his throat; the heavy, stagnant burning sapped his strength and desiccated his skin; the scalding sand sliced and rubbed raw his naked face and tender eyes.

He slipped in and out of a heat-sick limbo that even the most historic dose of norm could not remotely dampen, investing all his waning strength in holding onto his mount. Tearing pain seared his stomach and left arm from the work; though his right gorged rather on the full glare of the sun, he could not figure how to again extend those gripping roots for support. Videre hurtled forward all the same, if a little sweaty.

Finally these changeless hours evened. The hard, gleaming block of the sky softened into the golden epilogue of noon. Caelare's light seared low, swathing red the mountains, melting into their eaves. Though her speed had not lessened as the day wore on, Ogwold felt a lightness rise through Videre with the cooling evening wind, and he too felt a feeble cheer as they raced the darkling hours in near solitude—passing but a few camps of quiet wagons and campfire smoke— and the bracing freeze of a night lit singly this time by the dim vastness of solitary

Somnam. Only in the violet hours before sunrise did Videre stop, breathing heavily and freely.

Ogwold slid from her back awkwardly, staggered around in a plume of dust and debris, and fell flat on his back. His left arm roiled with sporadic shooting spurs of pain and troubling dead patches; yet more arresting was a very different kind of enervation in his right, as if it could hardly wait any longer for sunrise.

Videre's huge furry snout appeared over him, and she dragged a rough tongue along his cheek. He laughed. When she snorted, a strange rumbling voice burrowed through Ogwold's chest, thrumming in his bones. Sitting up, rummaging in his rucksack, he fed her slowly of the tutum fruit. She ate curiously and delicately for so large and muscled a beast. He held out his waterskin, and she tilted her head, perplexed, stirring the dusty rock with one paw. He tipped the container slantwise, and she lapped at its mouth thirstily. As in a reflex his pouting green arm leapt out to catch the spilling water, which disappeared into its fibres as unto an inescapable vacuum. A tremendous thrill fired up the arm into Ogwold's chest and heart, flowing over his skull and down the back in waves of ecstasy, and he looked down at the strange limb in wonder.

"Here," he said, pouring a little more water into his green palm, but he had to stop soon as it seemed the plant would never stop drinking, and the chills of energy began nearly to overwhelm him. Feeling suddenly so strong and refreshed, he sat back against Videre's furry ribs where she'd curled up, and ate some tutum himself, resting until those tall ears perked up as before with the approach of the morning traders.

Once more went the young Nogofod unto the great animal. Past the approaching wagons they soared over the sun-drenched rock, and they did not stop again to sleep until Caelare was retired and the first moon began to rise. That night it was the wide hemisphere of gigantic, deep-orange Sweelux, the Lucetalian Moon of Passion, yet many others would shine upon their winding desert path on nights to come.

On and again went their rush for the city, until fully six times the day star and those of its twenty pale sisters which chose to appear each night had spun through the firmament. So gradually in stature grew the faraway mountains over those days and nights, that only looking away and back again could Ogwold notice any change. But at last, on the morning of the seventh day they passed into the titanic, zagging shadows of the many peaks of Shadith, the nearest mountain. Videre slowed if only slightly, and whether it was through a subtle tremor in the ubiquitous humming of Nubes' sphere in his deep pocket, or through the intimate link he now shared with this strange and awesome animal,

Ogwold knew that the city drew near.

Videre's seamless leaps just as smoothly transitioned into soft padding, her huge muscles wagging loose; somehow there was still no bumpiness for her rider. Shadith loomed mightily close, thrusting forward its numberless crags, so that even the bleeding switchbacks of its lower flank could in places through the circling, faint clouds be followed, and Ogwold thought he saw the smoke of industry hanging over dark masses which might have been forest.

A metallic proscenium breached the horizon, looking like the head of a titan pickaxe rising against the face of the mountain. Nearly as tall was a high stone wall stretching featureless out and back towards Shadith on either side. Soon the sheer slab towered over them, and in its shade they sighed with relief, for the sun now fully risen from the distant sea unleashed its most uncompromising glare upon the baking sand and rock, the mountain's shadow thrown opposite them into the unknown West.

Dismounting with a thud that cracked the plates of rock beneath his boots, Ogwold lumbered for the left of the gate, avoiding its range of sight. He searched clumsily along the length of the wall, so vertical that it seemed to lean over his head. His legs were weak and wobbly, but little time passed before he happened on a snug trench in the land, a long-dry, primeval riverbed, ensconced by ancient boulders. Here he designed to hide and wait out the day. Videre curled massively beside him in the shadowed bottom, pyramidal shoulders folding together like great wings, and immediately began snoring, her great jowls fluttering and whistling.

When the worst heat had waned, a busy caravan issued from the city. Through the meeting point of two boulders, Ogwold peeped up over the riverbank and watched the wagons roll endlessly over the hills down to the distant shore, invisible now, though he heard it faintly in his heart, and felt its life stream even through his greener arm, thought it felt quite weak, parched as it was and now out of the sun. But he was distracted from its condition by the thought that finally he was on the other side of these shipments, for it was a deeply pleasant thought. He did not miss the sea then. The leagues of torrid desert behind him were but a beautifully rugged beginning. In his heart, he was grateful for the challenge of those seven awful days. He had not pushed himself so far since, well; at last he looked down at his now slightly shrunken right arm; since he had been attacked by the sea serpent.

Many caravans came and went while he waited for night. The pitiless sun roasted the land as it spun through the sky overhead. Even as it passed out of sight beyond the mountains, and even in the protective trench of the riverbed, the shade cooked with a stifling warmth nearly too much to bear, so used was Ogwold to the rushing wind of Videre's speed. Yet she the far harrier slept and slept as though never more comfortable, so he felt rather soft for his complaining. Yet it was not only her strength and resilience that he missed. Now that those great black eyes were closed to him, Ogwold felt quite alone here in an unknown world on the perimeter of a city which despised his kind.

Seeking the time-blindness of companionship, he took the sphere out from his pocket, and stared into it like a brilliant hole in space, reflecting nothing despite that self-propagating luminance. When he released it, softly spinning from his flicking fingertip it continued on, floating in the air, slowing, pausing, its rotation evening. He leaned back against the rocky wall of the inner riverbank, and a drowsy sense of eternity arose as he gazed into the hovering silver-white face, listening to its constant hum.

Light orange, pink columns of cloud scudded through the sky, striated with an unseen sunset over the mountains. Ogwold could envision the sliding, darkly condensing paint of Caelare's palace bleeding its runny purpling reds between the peaks to spill along the land. So summoned, such fingers of rich colour drifted overhead, staining the desert with twilit oils.

Awash in the exchange of day and night, Ogwold perceived the first impurity he had ever noticed in the impermeable silver of the sphere. Where colour and light had seemed always to slip ineffectually over its immaculate surface, now the darkest inks of evening subtly collapsed towards its presence, lingering delicately in its orbit before passing on. Only their faintest gossamer wisps stayed behind, which—whether actualized by their acknowledgement, the hypnagogia of twilight, or both—began to swirl steadily faster, assuming ribbons more vivid and clear, accreting into purple-black whorls and transforming discs. As he leaned further in, the massing complexities of the vision spun so swiftly as to uniformly ring their silver planet.

Even as this grand design settled into shape, the searing black and purple cord reached a velocity too great for the sphere's gravity to contain, and exploded in spiralling tendrils of shadow out into the varicoloured vermilion heavens, ascending and opening to enormous breadth each as they went, splitting as seams ever widening unto cosmic gulfs. Compounding one against the other these tears chased away the already darkening sky as though it were the flat set-piece of a theatre.

Backstage was an entirely new dimension. If the clouds were its curtains, the firmament its backdrop, and the stars its coulisses, this endless, unreverberant void—the true, uncostumed Cosmos—was far too massive for Ogwold's imagination. Yet, as he looked around, the shifting shadows of three actors revealed their differing qualities of blackness, for they were touched and contrasted by the faintest, silvery light. They stooped together, labouring against the changeless abyss. Only for a moment did the light washing their figures begin to swell; then the dark was swallowed all at once. A blinding effulgence drowned their huddled shapes. All was formless, sightless light. Yet even as it conquered Ogwold's vision, the light withdrew. Now in the deafening silence and quickly returning darkness there was a feeble, subtlest drone.

Beyond the three labourers appeared one by one the twinkling fires of stars, first in swaths sparsely glittering, then in great unfolding tapestries of shimmering, numberless more. The longer Ogwold looked, the even greater distances adjusted their depth to his eyes. But out from this evolving infinity of splendour, there arose a host of unnatural, dark red beams, approaching quickly, converging overhead. Amassing they grew like a horde of bloody beacons, and washed the workers in the omen of their coming. The labourers pressed their forms together, then broke apart. Two flew wingless straight up into the red storm that came down upon them, but the remaining, shortest yet most stout of their number, remained behind.

Stooping, rising, turning, the figure revealed the very light which had shone so universally before, now small and dim in the arms of its carrier. Yet even as it shone, it disappeared into the surface of the world, and the figure knelt for a moment beside that place, head bowed as in supplication, before fleeing to join its companions in the battle among the stars. Slowly, a great quake began to build, spreading out from the place of the light's leaving, rippling through Ogwold's bones and passing on into the gulfs of space. His view shifted as the rumbling translated through his sight, one scene bleeding into another, and he beheld the vast Cosmos of stars as though he were one himself.

From this vantage, the thousandfold host of red lights showed their hugeness and strange society, swarming hive-like in pillared torrents, as though a billion crimson suns were organized by the same hegemonic mind. Below their point of greatest concentration was a great, black planet, looking like the moon Somnam, yet completely lightless and far larger. So dark was its surface as to appear only in the bloody hue which bathed it, for otherwise it was as a hole of nothingness where no star could shine. Yet there was one other light. It was a small but unmistakably familiar flash upon the face of the black world, expanding in a thin disc, retracting to a point unseeable, now ejected straight and pure like a comet far out into the spaces between the stars. Within moments it was merely another of those white twinkling pinpricks; only slightly, it appeared to carry on in its movement through their midst.

Now great cracks webbed throughout the planet, and great, hard chunks of vital light stabbed out into the void. Enormous, shifting chasms opened in its face, struggled to hold, finally split. There was a silence as in the deeps of the ocean Ogwold knew so well, then like the braying of brass horns in hell, the formless syllable of the end. The world fractured into chunks, exposing a blinding core. The brightness scarred Ogwold's vision, pulsed, flashed, faded into bands of orange, yellow, red, violet. Groggily he beheld the spinning sphere rising clear and clean as ever from the soup of colour, humming before him once more, the sky now shedding its former carmine for a voluminous dark purple.

"You are from the stars?" He spoke to the sphere, as he'd spoken with Videre—nearby she opened one black eye—and this time felt that it was perfectly natural to hold congress with an object. There was no reply. The sun had set.

CHAPTER XIV
LIGHTNING OVER OCCULTASH

The navy broom of night swept the last crepuscular hues from the sand. But even those departing shades were uncommonly dark, thought Ogwold, his senses slowly returning. Videre too craned her neck, huge black eyes incomprehensibly focused. Whether even a single moon had risen, none were visible, and only just above the horizon did a speckling of cold stars twinkle, for heading these and blocking all light from above was a ceiling of sagging clouds lumped together in an endless procession over the arid waste.

Against that firmament of thickest grey turned the slow funnels and distended rims of bottomless black calderas. Everywhere fine contours of roiling, transforming nebulae glowed faintly with the outermost veins of an electric heart. Yet for all the gathering, wakening volcanoes of aerial power above, there was no wind at all on the face of the desert; even the grains of sand atop the riverbank sat perfectly still. Then came the thunder. The grey-black continent of fume split all through its midst into colossal shifting plates, and from the opening, abyssal divides between them, light rain began to fall, steadily picking up.

A powerful petrichor filled Ogwold's capacious nostrils. The desert so long dry drank the water even as it landed, but so continuous became the sweeping sheets and splattering, stabbing pillars of precipitation that great puddles and spilling, exponentially diverging streams began to form, filling deep pockets in the ancient riverbed. Suddenly, yet without a sound, there was an eruption of light, high as the heavens and wide as the world, bright and blinding and total. It left behind for a moment its innermost nervous system, a tremendous, jagged bolt of lightning. Out from the blackest crater of cloud above it came, taking twelve directions in an instant, and exploding even as it formed in a shower of sparks and prismatic curtains of rain water just before the great archway into Occultash. Then it was gone. The air crackled dry and charged, now soft and wet. Howling wind came at last with the returning darkness.

Videre leapt easily atop the bank, and slunk towards the scorched path. Trying to stand, Ogwold fell straight to his knees, torrents of displaced water and mud splattering his legs and stomach. Pulling him still tighter to the ground, his greener arm had divided and dug powerfully into the riverbed, visibly pulsing with ecstasy as the water flowed over it. At first he could only marvel at how intimately he now sensed this process of drinking, perceiving that his fingers had driven much deeper than sight could tell, feeling that even now they carried on, slipping through solid rock easily as through tutum fruit. But Ogwold could feel Videre's black eyes on his back, and something in the seat of his mind knew that this was no time for dreaming.

His arm must have been engaged in this effort all evening while he ogled the orb, looking for subterranean water even before the rain had come. Throwing his sodden bag up onto the bank, he closed his eyes to think. Breathing deeply and evenly, he placed his left hand firmly against the hard, green flesh of the thirsting plant. What had his mother said? What guidance had Nubes? He and the plant were one. They had become separated while his mind wandered in the sphere; now they would reunite. He listened for the nerves in his body which they shared, imagining that they loosened and relaxed. Did the plant listen for him? Did it imagine being Ogwold? The rain pounded, thunder boomed. A second explosion of lightning ripped his eyes open, and he saw once again the form of a hand wavering distorted beneath the surface of the rushing water, pressed against the rock. About it were deep, broad bores of black where the roots had sunken into unspeakable depths.

Atop the bank, Videre cocked her great head as if to say: now. Clumsily Ogwold waded through the rising, turbid current of water crashing, slapping the rocky walls, and clambered up the side of the river. They moved alongside the high city wall slick and gleaming with rainwater. Videre slipped round the corner into the wide gate, and Ogwold slowly followed her under the great arch. He stepped onto a broad road paved with dull, long-beaten metals, lit by the craning necks of golden lamps gazing bolted from the high stone walls of nameless compounds. Their lambent auras shone ghostly in the storming pools of water sloshing in the humps and divots in the pavement. Not a soul lurked in the wet.

A blazing forest of lightning spread across the city. The rooftops and shining walls coruscated. Great bronze streaks latticed the masonry of a domed hall, illuminated in the teeming forks of electricity above. A columnar purple-white fractal of light tore into a tall cottage down the road, setting it ablaze. Ogwold dashed to the side of the road after Videre and crouched in an alley, breathing as quietly as possible, though the rain clashed like swords against the streets and roofs. Feeble shouting slipped through the movements of thunder, and three armoured guards ran up to the house. Two went inside. The other looked down the way, precisely where Ogwold peered out, but the ogre had already pulled back into the dripping dark.

Still, he had seen his enemies clearly. They wore slim, silver cuirasses, black greaves and gauntlets. Their golden helms bore no plumage; rather, a smooth, raised arc bisected the crowns of their heads, looking like the head of a pickaxe. Short swords were sheathed at their belts, and light circular shields, silver as the armour yet decorated with three concentric circles of gold, were set between their shoulders.

Videre nudged him, and he climbed atop her back. When he gripped down into her soaking locks of neck-fur, the fingers of his left hand seared from the sores and blisters they had developed in doing so for seven days. At first that pain was oppressive, but as he fell into it, owned it as he had the roots in his arm and their need of water, felt the rain pouring off of his back now not as abject liquid but healing vitality, feeding his greener limb, he gathered himself, focused, found within a great calm and now—purpose. He was a Nogofod in Occultash. This storm was a gift.

The wolf-cat barrelled low and strong down the alley with the ogre clamped resolutely to her back, shifting her momentum at an impossibly sudden angle into an even smaller street. The giant edifices of the main road had blocked from sight this deeper network of the city, where small paths snaked through stone and wooden houses that seemed less accommodating even than the cabins of the Nogofod, and mashed impossibly close together. Videre uncoiling leapt lithely atop the oblong, slated roof of one sturdy cell, reflected up from her deft landing sidelong in the air as the rain changed direction, skidding just barely atop the high narrow roof of a building stretching long into the labyrinth of buildings. Her momentum flowed over the slick shingles like rainwater itself, paused silently at the edge of the roof, pounced over a great gap to find another, drifting softly on sure paws against the wet tiles, sending up sheets of water, now exploding from a new angle in a storm of mist.

They were now completely exposed, running on the roofs of the city. The white of Videre's fur, and of Ogwold's cloak, no longer had the grey walls with which to blend. Yet the storm was unrelenting and still growing, the mess of crazed rain and wind confounded the eyes, so that only in the great webbed matrices of lightning could their rushing hulk be somehow distinguished from the flashing whiteness all around. So it seemed then that they could not be found out, but whether the fire at the entrance had attracted more attention, or if even the watch was sparse that night, Occultash was still a massive, sprawling place, and surely there were many guards between them and the mountains.

The strikes of lightning succeeded with accumulating intelligence, each bolt seeming to subtly correct their path, lighting up whichever monolithic or slummy parts of the city into which Videre soon after rushed. So unknowingly accustomed was Ogwold to this phenomenon by their arrival at the steeple of a great church, still sparking and steaming with the scorch of the most recent blast, that he knew instinctively Videre had stopped not for rest, but for another bolt to guide her.

The sphere slipped spinning from the folds of Ogwold's cloak and flew humming up his hunched-over back, round the shoulder to his huge ear; as in a gentle aural hand it turned the brow, now lifted the chin on its song. Looking out over the streaming rooftops he beheld an immense cave in the sheer wall of Shadith where it bordered the city. A tap-root of white flaming lightning sundered the darkness. In the reverberant flash was revealed a wide plaza before the yawning maw, the flashing of armoured bodies, the eclectic shadows of buildings thrown like elegant branches over immense flagstones. Harried shouts went up from the place as it darkened. The air sounded with the clang of metal against stone.

Videre chuffed, fell at once with loose muscles bunching together as her paws touched down upon the roof of a broad house below and beside the church. Smoothly sliding along its angled shingles to a sturdy wooden shed, she hopped gracefully into the street, shoulders rising high and sharp on either side of Ogwold's face. Again they were in the layer of lamplight, but here those pale necks were bolted only to the rightmost buildings. They traversed the left side of the road, where they were hidden at least partially in a slim, curving shadow.

This highway was broader even than that upon which they'd entered the city. Its pavement was deeply worn, littered with sodden papers, empty woven baskets, cartons and twisted metals, and in some places crowded with closely parked wagons and carts, their contents covered over with soaking canvas. All along the lamplit side of the street were the tall frosted panes of diverse storefronts. In the most well-lit of these sat a shiny, studded helm upon a violet pillow, beside which twin pickaxes of rich wooden handles hung one crossing the other over a wide table lined with precious metals, raw ores and dazzling jewels. Yet these artifacts Ogwold could see only from across the way, for the shadowed half of the street down which Videre carried him was bordered only by a single, colossal compound reaching at a depth unknowable back into the city.

The entrance to the high-walled plaza at the end of the road was clearly marked by a pickaxe-head proscenium as that under which they had entered the city. Inscribed in its arching metal were the words "Occultash to Shadith." The tall, narrow space below this message seemed the only passage forward, for on both sides there extended slabs of dull silver tall and treacherous as the wall of Occultash itself, and no surrounding structure—even the enormous compound—seemed even close to reaching such a height. Videre stopped some paces before the arch; Ogwold slid from his seat, struggling to muffle the sound of his enormous feet striking the ground, and she swung her long face about as if to scold him. He went quickly ahead of her, back to the wall, and peered around the edge.

The plaza seemed so full of knights that he pulled back into the shadows at once, his big heart thumping loudly as he looked into Videre's inscrutable black eyes. But even considering the storm, Ogwold should not have been so surprised by the heavy guard. He had seen their armour catch the light from above, and even so, the authority of Occultash allowed no soul to pass into the mountains freely. He knew from tales that travelled with the caravans down to Epherem that there was a rich toll on this road. One must identify their goals before entering under Shadith. How like the Novare to claim these godly peaks for themselves, he thought, gulping, leaning once more into sight.

One bolt had stricken a man through the chest, and several others were grouped around his smoking armour. Gruff voices meandered through the storm. A tall, black-hatted man dressed in silver mantle and golden cape strode out onto a stone balcony with the impression of having left the scene only moments ago. He gestured cursorily to the knights below, turned and passed into the high gabled chamber from which he'd come. Two knights hoisted their yet living comrade up onto his feet, helping him stumble towards the lower storey of the same building. It was an artful and curious structure with high, rich doors, and beautifully stained windows. In fact, all down that rightmost side of the plaza there seemed houses even more rich, as if the wealthiest aristocrats lived here. The eye following these discovered as well a squat barracks situated to the immediate right of the entry arch.

Videre nudged Ogwold as she had many times already that night in the hopes of hurrying him along. While the storm still provided cover, and the guards were occupied with their fallen, now was the time to act. She disappeared into the shadow along the inside left wall of the plaza, slipping under the awnings of the spacious market stalls there aligned in a continuous curve until nearly the cavern mouth itself. The rain drummed rapidly on the fabric above as Ogwold followed.

When the tall black doors had shut behind the wounded, his helpers, the remaining six knights, returning to what must have been their posts, doing their best to stay out of the rain. Two stood at either side of the cavern entrance, tall spears rigid against the wet stone walk, sheltered by horned outcroppings of rock from which streams of dirty water slapped into huge puddles. Two others leaned against the wall of the large dark-windowed barracks, whose low roof reached out far enough to keep them somewhat dry. The final pair came to Ogwold and Videre's side, seeking shelter under the stall awnings, rubbing their arms and blowing vents of steam into the sheer wind.

Almost in the very moment Ogwold realized that there was no way to reach the cavern now without being seen, Videre surged through the shadows along the wall. For an instant she was gone; in the next she arose at a sharp angle from the dark like an enormous white shark breaching black water, connecting clean to the throat of the nearest knight. From the point of sudden contact his figure sagged, limp in her teeth, spear clattering over the wet stone.

His postmate stumbled out into the light almost a full second late, so quick and subtle was her attack. He yelled through the rain, now raised his shield, readying his spear menacingly though he did not quite advance on the great mass of white from which his partner hung like a dark rag. Without thinking at all, Ogwold lurched from the dark and tackled the hesitant knight sidelong.

He had never been much of a wrestler, but like all Nogofod he'd had his bouts, and knew at least from Wog's endless talk of strategy and technique that he would need to hit as low as possible, driving forward with the shoulder. Another ogre might have reversed the impact mightily, for the rush was clumsy and unpractised, but for a Novare man it was like standing in the path of a runaway wagon. The knight was tall enough that Ogwold's massive deltoid slammed straight into his shield, rather than the face, and broad enough, strong and heavy enough—with all his armour—that he did not instantly fly across the square; instead he was wrapped up in the ogre's enormous arms and squeezed tighter than the heaviest coffer.

There was a loud wrenching and grating, and a sickening crunch. The shield folded round the knight as his cuirass fractured like an eggshell in the fist of a child. As soon as he felt the bloody yolk on his skin, Ogwold gasping dropped the suddenly far too limp knight and staggered backwards, falling on his rear in a great puddle. The knight's face contorted with pain, and his breath spat out over the puddles of water in which his face was pressed. It was clear that he meant to scream, but he was able only to twitch and grind his teeth, blood trickling faintly over the flagstones.

"I only meant to... I'm sorry!" Ogwold cried through the rain.

The two knights by the barracks moved slowly forward, shields drawn, spears readied at their hips. "It's an ogre," called one of the two approaching from their posts at the mouth of the cavern.

"It'll be slow; keep your range!"

Ogwold raised his right arm instinctively. Swelling and flattening into a hard disc it consumed both spearheads as they came. Fine tendrils whirled out from the green flesh and helixed along the shafts of the spears, quickly overtaking the arms of their wielders. "No!" Ogwold shouted. "Please stop!" A shudder ran down the great plant so evolved, and it paused, slowly began to retreat. "Please," said Ogwold, reaching out in his thoughts.

The white mass of Videre replaced the nearest guard, hanging now as though hours dead from her rain-streaming jaws stained red. The other backed away quickly in horror, still reeling from the writhing mass of root and vine that had gripped his arm like sudden-hardening cement. Videre dropping her prey leapt towards the next target, slamming her front paws into his shield, raised at the last moment. He skidded far back along the wet stone, recovering from the reverberations, yelled half for courage yet as much for the falling of his comrade, and now lunged forward with his spear.

But Ogwold had stood, and he caught the shaft in his grey hand before it could reach Videre. The spear shattered in his grip; the knight drew his sword and swung up and out, but it stuck fast in Ogwold's blocking green forearm, which had resumed its shielding shape. "Videre, wait," he said as she prepared to lunge anew.

Realizing his sword was inextricably embedded, the knight released his grip, retreating towards the remaining two who seemed all the more wary, considerably slowed in their advance from the cavern mouth. Videre stepped in front of her charge, eyes blacker and deeper than ever. Her hair stood all on end, and Ogwold could tell that every muscle in her body had steeled. His head pounded. Thunder ripped through his chest, reliving the breaking knight's body, and his eyes fell upon the man who still seemed to be conscious. "Listen, knights of Occultash. Let us pass into Shadith and we needn't fight! Save this man while you can!"

A shadow passed through the plaza. From within the retreating knight, a pale blade flashed upward as a crackle of high lightning churned the black clouds. Spinning halves of torso and shorn limb fell in the rain. Over the fallen body stood a figure hard to see in the dark. His cloak shook in the wind, blooded broadsword conducted the light of the storm.

Dashing with astonishing celerity the stranger swung down upon the next guard who had dashed to meet him. The knight's blocking shield split clean in two as his head was hewn in the same stroke, carrying on vertically through the trunk of the body. Yanking the weapon free, dark gouts of viscera slathered the stranger in gore. His opponent fell eerily to the dead clanking of metal, collapsed forward. Shaking behind his shield, the other knight reached his breaking point, and bolted into the darkness of an alley.

Hoisting the broadsword over his shoulder, bloody rainwater streaming from its edge, the stranger watched him go. The rain splattered hard and loud. Thunder boomed. "Coward," rasped a surprisingly youthful, male voice. The lightning struck again all about the man, several cords diverging and spitting into the market stalls along the left side, which burst into flame. The plaza lit up blinding and white, now glowing low and orange with the raging flames quickly dampening in the rain. The stranger wore a black cloak, the hood shading his scruffy face as it turned. Tattered leather greaves and gauntlets caught the firelight beneath the blustering fabric.

"You... why?" Ogwold stammered.

The man seemed to stare back out of the black void of his face. "Nice sword," he said. "Use it, next time." Sheathing his own blade, the stranger turned and strode for the yawning tunnel into Shadith.

For all its weight, Ogwold had nearly forgotten Ogdof's enormous sword across his back. Still, he knew he could not draw it against another living creature. Even the accident of crushing the first knight had broken his heart. He shuddered with a sudden heat from the sphere, which pressed against his waist through its place in his pocket, then burst from his cloak and swept through the rain after the stranger, its pale light arcing and vanishing into the darkness like a stray, tiny bolt of lightning.

Videre followed, disappearing into the shadows, which was well, thought Ogwold, sloshing instinctively after her, for word would travel with the escaped knight, or perhaps the killing had been heard in the balconied chamber. But he stopped suddenly, shivered with a thought, and ran to the man he had hurt, scooping him up in his great arms, and rushing him to the covered doorstep of the house where the lightning-stricken other was presumably being mended. "You'll... They'll help you... I'm sorry, sir," he said, laying the knight carefully on the dry stone step. Standing up and taking a deep breath, he knocked on the door softly as he could, though, as he'd suspected, the noise was booming. Then he ran.

The cavern was surprisingly warm and dry. Its rugose ceiling curved high above, dimly shadowed by the glowing stones embedded in the rocky wall. The roaring rain now sounded distant and comforting. Here in the sharply inclining road were the familiar wagon-wheel grooves and hoof prints of the desert caravans. But there was no time to linger, for Videre was yet far ahead of Ogwold, and the hum of the sphere had all but vanished. His tremendous footfalls echoed through the ridged roof. The smooth dirt felt soft and kind in the bones of his legs.

In time, he staggered round a great bend in the tunnel, and a distant semi-sphere of starry navy blue appeared, growing now in size as he went. Cool wind touched his high, wet cheeks, and the sound of rain, though far gentler than it had been in Occultash, reached his hairy ears. When he stepped out into the night once again, the deep yellow, enormous yet most distant Moon of Power, Potengrav, was slowly revealed in the parting storm-clouds.

The rain seemed to lighten and stop even as he walked out into the tall, wet grass. Videre waited for him in a pleasant valley thick with pale yellow flowers and smoothly swaying brush. Small night birds peeped in the calm. The dirt path led up a stony pass enshrined with seemingly natural arches of rock interlacing. Under these strode the gaunt figure of the strange man like a shade.

"Wait!" Ogwold called, snatching the sphere out of the air where it hovered beside the mouth of the tunnel. The man stopped, but did not turn. "Do you know this trail?"

The man said nothing.

Ogwold took out the pouch of silver coins that Nubes had given him. "I must reach Zenidow."

"I don't know the trail." The man seemed only slightly to perk at the mention of Zenidow, but still he was like an implacable shadow.

Despite the insistent drone of the sphere, Ogwold himself greatly desired the protection the stranger's skill could provide. He knew now he could not fight, let alone kill. Though he abhorred the way this man had slain the knights so easily and without affect, he knew that it would be unrealistic not to fear armed combat on the trail ahead. Surely this master of that art would be of invaluable service then, even if he was a killer.

"Why shouldn't we travel together for some time? It's better than being alone when neither of us knows the way." Ogwold held out the pouch cautiously. "I can pay you, as a guide."

"No."

"At least let me pay you for saving me."

Ignoring this, the man began walking again. But at a distance Ogwold followed him as naturally as did Videre.

The path narrowed until it was about the width of a single wagon, and declined steeply into a succession of rock-strewn foothills. Realizing that it should have taken much longer to pass straight through Shadith, Ogwold turned round and looked back up the way they'd come. The cave-mouth from which the path had led was visible some ways up, and now leaning back he took in the enormity of Shadith above and to his left massing for unseeable distances up and out. The road had taken them superficially through a stretch of the skin of its vast base, up onto a small shoulder. Over its lower slopes below he could see Occultash sprawling out to the east; and thereon was the awful desert, somewhere far away Epherem and the sea. He stood for a little while looking down the way, wondering what his father was doing. Then came the inevitable nudge from Videre.

First the tall compounds and high city wall, and then the white expanse of desert disappeared behind the bulk of Shadith as they continued downward along its side. When the stranger at last sat to eat and drink atop a low, flat rock beside the road, Ogwold came up to him and sat too, across the way in the grass. So large was his stature that still he was at eye level with the man, who paid him no mind.

"Let us go with you and find some way to help you. I'm certain you'll have less trouble on the road with me and Videre along. And, listen... I don't know the first thing about swordplay. You slew those men like it was your nature. If you teach me to use my own blade I bet I'll make a good watch for your back."

"You couldn't have finished that knight if he was your worst enemy," said the man. He had spoken critically, but not necessarily out of malice, and it seemed that his shoulders had softened in their rigid posture. The sphere, which had grown more and more hot as Ogwold passed through the tunnel, as the man made to go about his own way, now suddenly cooled, and its humming took a sweetness to it.

"So," said Ogwold, "you think that he survived?"

"Your ego is admirable, but he merely lost his wind."

"I hope so. It was awful the way he stopped resisting."

The man sighed, and was silent for a time. "Look," he grunted, "I don't mind sharing the road. I can see you mean no harm. And... I have a map."

"Of what?"

"The mountains, roughly. I'm not sure how to read it. I suppose another eye on it would help." He glared across the path. "If you can keep up with my pace during the day, we can share a night-watch as well. But know this," he said gravely. "Where I go there is ever hurt and suffering."

"What do you mean?"

A single green eye flashed in the moonlight. "I'm hunting an evil sorcerer; he is hunting Zenidow, as you are."

The ogre smiled so broadly that the stranger looked away, down the path. "I am Ogwold," he said almost as if speaking for the little orb chiming in, "and this is Videre." Videre chuffed and blinked her enormous black eyes before burying her face in her great paws. "We promise to be of help to you, sir. Even someone of your skill could use some company."

The man again seemed unaffected. "I'm Byron," he grunted, folding his arms. With one look, it seemed, at Ogwold's sword where it was laid in the grass, he closed his eye and appeared for the rest of the night to sleep, seated upright on the stone.

CHAPTER XV
TO LISTEN

The invisible leashes of Xirell, Xelv, and Feox unspooled to distances near banishment from the lean shadow of Zelor advancing, hands clasped behind his back. Darkness and spilling white locks obscured his hooded face but for a gaunt scowl. Mute tails slid freezing in the snow. Not a single word had he uttered since their departure from Quiflum, and it seemed to Elts that he cared little whether she followed. Yet not so far behind the solemn company she looked back on the fog-shrouded village while its last thatched roofs disappeared into the slurry.

Gradually the roaring mists and earthy scent of the river faded into backcountry serenity. An alpine wood thickened about them. Still there were the occasional monoliths of azure stone, though the steep, steely ice in which they were sealed gradually swelled with unmolested humps and blankets of powder, swallowing in time all but the tallest trees. By the freeze of evening, the snow grew unpassably deep. Feox swung his battleaxe in flaming sickle swathes to harvest the path, and Xelv pressed through the great melt to find where they might sow the seeds of their feet. Were it still loyal, Xirell should have sent forth his septry familiar to scout ahead. Yet visible enough through the ceiling of icy branches was their dizzying destination, the black towers of Ardua sprouting like obsidian fungus from the sheer cliff-face high above the wood.

Darkness fell. They camped on a broad, stone plate cleared dry round Feox's surging axe wedged in a great crack. The Zefloz collapsed like abandoned puppets. Zelor wandered off into the black spaces between the trees. Sleepless under the stars that trickled through the snow-decked boughs, Elts felt the awful absence of her master, lying corpse-like, like a dormant technology set by the fire to dry. If the real Xirell was somewhere trapped within that evil-yoked body, perhaps he wished for death, being before so free and luminous a being. It would be simple and merciful enough to escape the wind of his lungs, silence his throes in the latest hours. She would bury him in an honourable snow drift beneath a noble tree and bless his voyage to Xeléd.

Yet whether some part of her believed that her old friend might still be freed from his horrific catatonia, or simply because she was terrified of the truth, she could not bring herself to do it. Even as the pale dawn painted the net of black branches, she envisioned still Xirell's dead face and lightless green eyes, wondering if that expression would even change when the blood among its brain tissue ceased to pump. Feox took up and sheathed his axe. Xelv rose impassive to their snow-caked robes. Invisible strings exhumed Xirell from his grave. Wordlessly, Zelor appeared, eyes focused inward, pressing them forward from his presence with commands insensible. Elts followed only when she could no longer hear their progress through the frosted brush, shivering with her distance from Feox's heat, but calmed by her solitude.

Morning dissolved as they climbed an old stone staircase up towards the base of the mountain. The snow grew more densely packed and traversable as the chance corners and strange proportions of ancient stone ruins reappeared even where Feox's flames did not reach. A lone, rugose column leaned cracked and eroded against the fat burl of an ancient tree. Remarkably preserved statues of nameless queens loomed eerily from steep hills. Fragments of silver railing stuck up out of the ice. At last the great white wall of vertical rock became clear beyond the bleary trees. So blindingly radiant with the noon sun was it that the shape of Ardua high above was impossible to determine, yet Zelor stood at the foot of the wall staring straight up at his goal, tails long motionless slightly turning in the frost.

Xelv like a blue ghost appeared among the thick foliage clustered against the rock face, and fading led the company back to the mouth of a dark shaft teething with icicles. From its slabby entrance the faint contour of a vast highway spilled through the snow down towards Quiflum. Into the darkness they dragged their frozen feet, and the road became more manageable, though its harsh grade inspired wonder at the pack animals—presumably the strange goat-beasts of the village—that must have drawn wagons up to Ardua, or even those which must so carefully have descended this way to the village.

Like a smooth spiral core was the old road, ratcheting up through the mountain, glowing sparsely with veins of the luminous blue ore which characterized so much rock in this part of the range. The pulsing, lambent medium seeped into cracks and fissures in the tumultuous ceiling. They rested long and late that first night in that dim azure light, pressing on only when Zelor, who appeared more exhausted than any, felt that they must. There was no command; he merely stood, turned towards the inclining darkness, and walked. And certainly Feox and Xelv needed as little instruction as Zelor's own legs, for they had risen and gone far sooner.

Such morbid loss of affect and other signs of physical weakness Elts began more easily to notice in the Silver Zefloz, and somewhere in her heart were the beginnings of remorse. Perhaps it was the loss of Fexest and all companionship, or did she sympathize with the bent tragic shape so unlike the Zelor of the past, once tall and proud, because she saw too clearly now how the sorcerer was manipulated by the cosmic will of Duxmortul? Dark patches bruised his fatless flesh, and his red-rimmed eyes were blasted dry by endless nightmares. Even at times she swore she saw writhing tentacles mingling in his crooked shadow, or when he lifted his arm to lean against the cavern wall, it was as though a great brooding mass attached itself to his back, feeding and whispering.

During the long hours of night he spent far from company, staring as into a foundering abyss—Elts stealthily discovered—at the bag containing the idol unabashedly, it seemed now that such bleeding wounds of subjugation had always been there. The deeds and aura of the possessed had blinded all around it. What she had mistaken for a conqueror's wrath was the fear of a tortured animal. Fozlest had not muzzled pride, but helpless fealty. The one Xirell had called evil, the very thing which enslaved him now was not Zelor, not here, not of Altum. Yet however horrible his curse, Zelor still was presumably the wretched soul to grant Duxmortul this form of incarnation, so it was not pity that touched Elts.

It was rather his alleged intention to destroy the Alium—against the will of Fozlest—that touched her heart already so turned against the Empress. To her who lived to defy the Empire, who had worked too long now under its law, and only for the sake of Xirell, it was a noble deed to keep from Fozlest a power meant only for gods, and perhaps not even gods, for surely there was a reason none seemed to know of it. Yet, honourable as Zelor's mutiny seemed, she did not believe he had taken up the awful power of Duxmortul for this sole purpose. Only a wicked heart would be drawn to such darkness in the first. So she set aside these feelings of honour, and returned his silence with a coldness of her own, waiting to see how flagrant were his lies.

*

After five days of monotonous, empty climbing in the stuffy dimness of ore-veins, and four sleepless nights huddled against friable walls of rock listening to what horribly rhythmic breathing issued from the direction of the inert Zefloz, Elts came up out of the cavern behind the company onto a high snowy slope. At last she stood somewhat level with the enormous dark towers of Ardua, like titanic stalagmites clustered against the wall of rock. The distant eye's dream that the city was formed straight out of the mountain dissolved, for its great mass of black spires rested rather upon a grand shelf of ice wrapping along that sheer face.

Outside the snow was deep and pure, so the going again became slow. By nightfall they camped at the foot of a hill which rose no more than a mile to the high city walls above. Again Feox planted his axe like an unnatural burning weed, and lay lifeless beside the Zefloz of his ilk. Zelor sat strangely near to the fire, looking into its surging flames, his hated bags pushed far away from the glow into the dark snow. Elts kept her eyes too on the fire, though she could sense each time that Zelor looked back to those evil, black humps on the edge of their camp, and slowly back. All through the night, before she retired, it seemed as they sat there shivering with their tails tucked inside their robes that the sorcerer wished to say something to her.

They rose with the white sun and strode up the slope in a line of black shrouds against the pristine snow. As the crumbling wall, tilted onyx buildings, and steep conical roofs rose more massively over them, Elts realized that the whole city was quite destroyed. The great, frost-lacquered metal gate was warped and twisted open, as if blown apart. The broken streets were empty, riven with huge trenches and shifting plates of pavement. Skeletal buildings overflowed with snow and ice. Dire vacancy peered round collapsed corners. Terror loomed in every shadow.

Considering the scarce population of Quiflum in the valley below, tens of thousands more Arduans unable to escape through the caverns must have had their graves beneath it all. Ardua's death did not seem at all natural, or to have anything to do with the plague of the delver's telling. Something huge and chaotic had descended upon the city; or had it ascended, thought Elts, as they stopped in procession before a great abyssal hole in the ground before them. Circumnavigating the tower-thick gulf, as they walked, and as the wall and gate were obscured behind the debris they passed, other such vast and inexplicably circular holes appeared—in the roads, in the shattered foundations of buildings—opening on total blackness below the city.

Still, Zelor seemed to ignore the possibility that whatever had burst from these noisome pits might still persist here. When they arrived in a kind of cobbled nexus, he sent the company out to search for the Secret Mine, as he had seen it in the old Quiflumian delver's memory, a statue of the God-Queen beside it. Feox marched rhythmically ahead. Xirell descended a steep hill down into the icy shade of similar road winding to the right. Xelv took the left, where a host of broken towers leaned together and enshrined a street which was quite straight compared to the others they had seen.

"Stay with me," Zelor said coldly as Elts turned to a narrow alley.

She did not reply, but followed him in the direction Feox had taken. The Red Zefloz had already disappeared over the crest of the torn and buckled incline. As they walked in silence up the rising land, their elevation grew such that over the broken buildings Elts saw the concentric inner walls of the city as they shrank in increasing height like tighter and more sheltered rings towards the centre of Ardua. At the clouded, high rim of the furthest wall, she thought she saw the slightest hint of green, but as the wind blew away that nebula she saw only black stone. Turning with the gale she saw over the outmost, lowest wall, far below, the misty canopy over the valley of Quiflum. Down in that fog was a statue of Fexest, a reminder to the villagers of that which passed through their remote domain. She shivered to think that she shared any design with the man who froze her there. Surely Zelor lied; surely he would take the Alium for himself.

He surprised her by speaking. "You should find it easy to search these streets."

Elts kept her eyes on the valley below. "If it is a mine we seek, unless it is hewn into the face of the mountain, which is unlikely, it must be below us. We might simply plunge into one of these holes."

"There are too many. We cannot be sure of their synthesis. The path will be subtle." Zelor seemed almost in discussion with himself. "Magic is better for these sorts of things; or, I suppose I should say folding. But I am unaccustomed to the Fabric." He stopped walking, staring into the road. "I have heard that you are able to map a place by the flow of its air. These open chasms are like windows into the subterranean." His tails swirled, froze. "Teach me to walk them through the Fabric of the wind. Then we can separate and search the vastness of Ardua more thoroughly."

Only Xirell had ever asked Elts about her powers. She was looked down upon by all in Fozlest's council, and even the old man was quite the diplomat in Xoldra for all his playfulness beyond its roots. Xol called her the specialist, the colourless White Zefloz, who made up for her lack by being an intellectual—who would say "white is all colours" to much condescending laughter—and a technician, for her ropecraft and gamut of knives were a boon to the military. Whatever compliments decorated her, all Xol—excepting the Novare-raised

Zelor—could feel the stuntedness in her aura. But more ironic than his choosing her in all the Zefloz for a lesson was his destroying the minds of any who might have been useful to him when they were lucid. She frowned disgustedly. Perhaps he was not even after her power, but had at last realized that he could not stand the silence of his puppets. She could see how the drooling dispositions of Feox, Xelv and Xirell perturbed him. He kept them always at a distance. Was she now just a voice to hear? An animal noise to remind him that he was not totally alone?

"Or must I take over?" Zelor's tails curled in threat.

"Whatever it is you did to the others, it would not avail you of my abilities," Elts said coldly. "I have no powers." She held up her empty hands as if to signify the lack in her spirit.

"You lie, White Zefloz," Zelor said sharply.

Elts sighed, looked down at her naked feet, violet from the cold. Then she brought out from its sheath beside the ropes and knives against her belt her elz-bark mask, holding it out for Zelor to see. "The wings of this mask are enchanted. My adopted mother was a wind mage before she was an elz smith. She gave me this mask when I was very young. It allows for only very simple manipulation of the element, but I've studied it and practised all my life. At last I can do things most wind mages accomplish when they are children. But, I have had to be more creative then."

"You cannot use magic without this... toy." Zelor faded into thought with the severity of his scowl. "I see now why you are Zefloz," he said broodingly. "To think that you could do such things—I've heard the stories—with such limited resources. Imagine what you could do with an Item of Power."

Elts grimaced with those words which in some form snaked about her heels or formed in the tails of passersby in every corner of Xoldra. How incredible it was that she ranked among the Zefloz; how genius was her work with tools; how innovative was her fighting technique. "I have no desire for such a thing," she spat. "I joined the Zefloz to see the world, to understand it and experience all there is. Our mission is dangerous. You have made it all the more so, yet what is Zenidow? What is the Alium?" Her heart rose in her chest. "What is Ardua, even? The Kingdom of Lucetal has as little notion of this place as the greatest scholars in Xoldra!"

Being Wyxian, Elts was naturally unaccustomed to the royal rituals of aversion, but the ferocity with which she had turned her eyes upon Zelor as she spoke seemed more purposeful than accidental, as if she sought to know him, though she figured he would not return the glare. It was strange for any Xol but Xirell to communicate with her not only through the manipulations of sound, thought, and tail, but by the sight of the mind exposed, so their culture believed that act of meeting eyes most intimate among the psychic. Yet Zelor—pureblood as he was, yet taught in Molavor always to honour one's attention—did not hesitate to complete the act.

Now his eyes were not so black as they appeared before, for subtly they were latticed with striations of white converging on opal centres, and as he spoke in reply those asymmetric gyres seemed ever so slightly to turn. "Your ambition is honourable. Recently, I too have become more open to what I do not understand. You must know I have always detested magic. Now I see that it is not only mighty but subtle, and far reaching. I thought of it before as weak and fearful."

"Perhaps in a swordfight it is." Elts lowered her eyes to Zelor's scabbard, though she could feel his gaze still upon her face.

"Yes."

"So—you will kill me if I refuse?"

Zelor looked away, down at his empty hands. "I am a killer. But if any part of my honour remains, I will leave you be. Fexest acted valiantly, but dangerously, surprising me in my sleep when..." He fell silent. "If she had challenged me outright I may have been able to control myself."

"Doubtful," said Elts, feeling confident now. "I've not once seen you hold back." Images of the collapsed skulls of those whose minds had been drunk by the palms of Zelor wavered in the periphery of her vision as her voice rang through the empty streets and alleyways, but as it faded into distant, feeble echoes she was left only with the sensation of the sorcerer's black-white gaze lingering as strangely in her heart as before she'd looked away. There was little evil as there was kindness there. Even more certain was the ambition of the spirit contained within those vitreous lenses, an ambition wholly unattached to need or want, a righteousness, perhaps, a vocation to sacrifice.

She broke the silence. "If for now our goal is the same, all I can do is believe you. But if I discover that you plan to wield the Alium, yes, you can be certain that I'll not cut your throat at night. I'll slay you in the light of day, and with a blade. If honour is suddenly so vital to you, you owe me an honourable end."

Zelor did not turn, but it seemed as though his long chin were raised to hear such noble words out of his distant past. So it was that Elts, seeing and now beginning to feel some new side of him unveiled and vulnerable, asked the question which had troubled her since Quiflum: "If I'm to help you more than by abiding your ego, tell me first: who is Duxmortul?"

Zelor's tails snapped like whips. Gouts of packed snow lifted from the street, fell hissing. Yet when his black-white stare turning met again the steeled blue of her own, Elts was struck not by the wrath, but by an ageless, seething terror at last fully revealed in his naked eyes as he hissed, "Where have you heard this nefandous thing?"

"In a dream," said Elts. Her abdomen coiled for defence, stout legs slightly bent, gloved hands hovering over the knives against her belt. "I saw a black, tentacled monster flying through the outer deeps. It ate worlds. Its followers called it by that name."

The screaming fear was in a blink veiled with spiteful rage, though it seemed now to Elts like a helpless guise barely holding to its seams. "A great evil reaches out to you from the stars, Elts." He closed his eyes as if to centre himself, as if that costume of anger was all too familiar in its sway over his actions. "Fozlest would use the Alium to conquer Altum. But this thing is by far the greater danger. The one you speak of is but a herald of things more great and terrible than we can imagine, for it can only overcome us in time. All that we can do is destroy the Alium, for if the Shadow claims it, at the very least Altum will be thralled to doom, and the Whorls of Secundom cast into darkness. All is at stake."

Elts breathed, but did not relax her position. "If you are so righteous then, how do you atone for the blood upon your own hands?"

A ripple of pain passed through the grim mask of Zelor's face seeming so horribly concentrated on shutting off the rays of its sight. "There was a time when It was my ally. It lent me power, promised me more." Now he opened his eyes and looked clearly again into Elts'. The trembling, suffering mask of rage had broken, yet beneath it those bottomless deeps of horror were not revealed. Instead there were the eyes with which he and Elts had first made contact. Here was the absence of both good and evil; again there was purpose severed of self. These, thought Elts almost reflexively, were the true eyes of Zelor.

"That power consumed me. My mind was absorbed and buried. For many years I was a possessed thing, a machine servant of the black sky. It bent me to its will, and forced me to destroy those I loved in ways for which I can never forgive my intimate involvement. I laid waste to cities, slew men, women, children alike. I inspired and led the new front against Novare who had no connection with Lucetal, and granted Fozlest's wish that the war become one of the races, one for extinction of all Novare! This is how I came to know true evil! Only through pitiless endurance and unerring focus did I reclaim myself, and even now I am unable to draw on those powers which fester ever hotter in my heart without killing or silencing those who oppose me. Ever I hear the whispers from beyond the stars beseeching me, telling me to drink life, demanding from me the prize of Zenidow."

Zelor crushed his hands into fists, swept his tails fiercely through the snow, and the crumbling house behind him split down the middle with a loud crack. A rising sheet of icy powder blossomed through the street. Rumbling rattled the teeth and bones. Large slabs of rock fell into the hard-packed snow. "Fozlest of course would not allow that the Alium be lost. Even the knowledge of it she covets more closely than her throne. Xelv is undying in his faith to her; he was my first opponent in this quest. But as soon as I set the will of my new powers against him, his mind disintegrated. He became as I was once to It, as a tentacle, an arm." He held up his hand as if disgusted by his intimate control over it. "I meant only to change his loyalty."

"Now you lie," said Elts, tails slowly weaving, "Silver Zefloz."

"I swear upon Caelare and Xeléd. I intended with all my will not to kill him, and thank the gods the Zefloz are so strong as to persist at least materially under the full black of the Shadow. This state of mastery was the result of my effort and Xelv's greatness. The same as with the others. I could not describe what grace it was to see that they had not perished as do most with their mind in my hand, but then... they have perished in a different manner, for they walk the world in a mockery of their image."

"It is despicable," Elts said through her teeth, jaw tight. "It was Xirell that unmasked me. It was he who taught me everything I know about the Xol, who brought me one day before Fozlest and earned me these white-hemmed robes. I wish that you had killed him rather than... this."

"As do I. But he was the first to sense my treachery against Xelv, and quick to catch me as I took Feox. In that moment he unleashed the extent of his might upon me with far greater ferocity than Fexest. All that I knew to do which could contest with his power was to call upon the dark." Now in the sorcerer's eyes there was only grim and grave dimness, and the great chasms of endless fear began once again to open like inexorably shifting plates of rock. Elts looked away. It was not easy to behold this particular shade of Zelor so abandoned of all hope.

"Xirell was a fierce sorcerer," he continued. "I feared that he wouldn't understand the danger of the Alium, and it was too late for me, considering my deeds. The glorious power... it nearly consumed me once more. Killing those villagers, Fexest, it was a feast during famine. Nearly I slew everyone in Quiflum, but I reclaimed my purpose through no small effort. Each day I train my will to contend with the pull of this artifact." Zelor threw down his bags and from the leather sack produced the black idol of Duxmortul.

As soon as the red columns of its eyes arose from the leather, as that shining black beak caught the dawn sun cruel and harsh, Elts felt a suffocating darkness fall over her heart, squeezing it like a toy, throttling all sense from her blood. Zelor went on, brandishing the thing as if it held no sway over him. "On that day, for a moment, its influence grew weak, as if it were distracted by some other prey, and I saw the blood all around me, cursing myself for the evil I'd brought to the village. Yet still I crushed that delver's skull, yes consciously, lucidly, with utmost awareness and responsibility, for there is a part of me that knew an efficient route to Zenidow is the only route... Is this infandous image not new to you?"

Elts stared at the awful nest of snaking arms and bloody, gibbous eyes, wondering how Zelor was able to touch its substance with his bare hand without being utterly overcome. "It is the same as in my dream," she said at last.

Zelor frowned, seeming to accept this. "It fell one dark night from the sky, as in a lone shooting star, into the fields of Molavor, where I bunked with the Novare I would one day betray. I was drawn to it, dreamt of it, fetched it after many fitful nights. Months it took to discover the rim of its impact crater. Then there it was, a bottomless black presence at the pit of the site. As soon as I touched it, Zelor was no more. Soon I was kneeling before Fozlest speaking of the evil of all Novare, how they were all like the King of Lucetal and his hated ancestors. I became the Silver Zefloz. Molavor burned."

Zelor wrapped up the idol and placed it in its private bag. When the last crimson eye had been covered, a great peace seemed to settle, as though a gnawing agony had always filled the air, and Elts' heart seemed to expand all around into the air like a spirit released into heaven.

"When I awoke from it all, I saw first the silver hems against my wrists. I had joined the highest ranks of the institution I most despised. I learned slowly what I had wrought against my brethren in Molavor, who I had loved most and to whom I had dedicated my life. It is only through direct confrontation with this wicked idol that I have retained a kind of composure. It feels as though at any moment I might fall again into that cold sleep... It wishes above all things to uproot Zenidow, and so I will use Its own power against that end. This hideous thing," he squeezed the bagged idol in his shaking hand, "is my weapon." Zelor, it seemed, had finished his case, and looked silently into the snow.

Though Elts did not speak at first, the fury of the moment had faded, and the stout features of her face had slowly softened as she listened. Certainly, his words had moved her, but still she would not accept or reveal her feelings. "I do not see it in your eyes or feel it in your presence, but you are evil, Zelor. You speak as if you pay a necessary price, but I see only the blood of those who might have been your greatest allies." She slammed her tails into the snow. "You cannot undo the past, but you can undo your ways. If your goal is really so virtuous, I will teach you the subtleties of the wind. But you must promise me this: that you will not kill another defenceless or companionable creature again."

When the sorcerer returned her stare, the temptations in its might were marrow-deep, but Elts saw that his convictions were even greater. His tails raised, folded in a sign of peace. "I concede," he said, "but the need for power must arise. We know not what stands guard at Zenidow, or what might call that place its citadel."

As Zelor thought of the power he still needed, dark pits of fear opened again behind his painful eyes, for they turned inward to the presence of Duxmortul, but this time Elts did not feel the sudden need to look away. The sorcerer held fast his look of determination even through that desperate thralldom, and it seemed almost unforced, an expression not of wrath, nor wicked satisfaction, when he smiled. It was virtuous to Elts' eyes, but she did not return the expression. She spoke evenly, distantly. "Your teacher goes everywhere with you. I am but a fellow listener."

Zelor sat rigidly in the middle of the road as morning hardened into noon, straining to comprehend the voice of the wind. Long too did it howl, sigh, laugh through his long white hair, wail, croon, shout against the cliff face, call over the concentric walls, and beseech the many towers. Yet even its finest notes were only rude noise, the hollow themes of a rough element splitting over his cold unfeeling skin.

Far more potent and effortlessly articulate was the cruel animacy of the idol of Duxmortul, leering at him from its swaddling place in the leather bag. The columns of red eyes branded his stiff cheek. Its sharp beak gleamed and stabbed his ribs with hunger. Black tentacles snuck through the skin of the snow as if they would slip into his biology and work his features with awful precision. In every slightest whisper as much as each pounding gale he heard only the gargling, probing, icy susurrus of the destroyer, calling for its disciple, felt only the burning stare of the unblinking spaces between the stars in those pitiless vacuums of blasphemous vision.

An old fear wriggled in his mind like a parasite awakened, wriggling a little deeper each time it was acknowledged. Perhaps his brief victories over the idol were merely the result of his insignificance in Duxmortul's design. What he had taken for his own personal courage and fortitude was, he thought, only a lack in

Its interest, the liberty of a dull toy cast aside. It may have distributed thousands of likenesses to bewitch and enthrall all life as a preface to its arrival. How many more like himself existed even now in other forms across Altum, unable to contend with their own idols? What designs had the Novare apostle? Was there somewhere a red-eyed, black Euphran flying on soundless wings, breathing subjugation? Were the minds of the lower animals unmolested? And what of the trees? With power such as It had, could It supplant Caelare herself before even the arrival of Its fleet? And what was Altum but one of a thousand worlds it sought to devour?

Elts appeared from the shadows first as a set of limpid irids, the glittering tips of the icicles above her little alcove leaving their bodies behind. Then her broad, light-purple face and spiked white hair leaned forward into the pale light as she sat across the way from him, distanced yet visible now, and attentive, the belted knives, coiled black ropes, and sheathed mask pushed up around her waist by the ice and snow. "You are not listening," she said, placing her chin in one strong purple hand, elbow cocked against her knee.

"I am trying."

"There is no trying. You must let go." She followed Zelor's unblinking black and white gaze to the ominous bags where they rested against a stone wall. "Can we not destroy it?"

"No!" Zelor tore his eyes from that hated place, and for a moment they seemed entirely black, like sunken holes beneath his high purple forehead, over the sharp nose and long, narrow chin with its tight lips. "I mean—I have tried many times." Now the tendrils of a past conscience swam white through his gaze, which he lowered. "We will only call the attention of its maker."

Elts' tails exchanged positions over her head as they swayed. "How can we destroy the Alium if we cannot even be rid of a statue?"

Zelor stiffened. "There is but one way my best effort will be certain." Now he returned his gaze to the bag and the idol within, placing one long hand against his breast. "I will detonate my body with all of this borrowed, accursed power in the heart of Zenidow."

Though there were still two Elts vying not always equally, adamant in their causes, to believe the cursed sorcerer, now one at last began to subdue the other, for such bold claims—even if they too were lies—of surrender for a virtuous future of Altum never had she before perceived. Even her crystal exterior now showed the first moltenness of compassion, for the lines about her scowl had softened. "But if you die you will not even know if you've succeeded."

"It is all I can do," he said gravely.

Elts knew well what it was to give up one's life, for each night in Wyx when she fitted her mask and dropped into the dark, she had accepted that protecting the helpless villagers and their children was worth dying for. But resolved as she'd been in her vocation, she had never encountered another who would swear upon not merely a risk, but an absolute, and as a price for what they believed to be the highest good.

Yet Zelor's ideals were bloody. He killed, destroyed whatever stood between him and his goal. She too had slain many raiders even who stood no chance of defending themselves, but they were murderers. Whatever blood was on the hands of Xelv, Feox, or Fexest, Xirell had never harmed the slightest plant, and the Quiflumians Zelor had slain only out of haste. Was destroying the Alium such a cosmic and urgent destiny as to supersede innocent blood? Certainly Zelor thought it was worth his own. Always Elts had striven to her utmost abilities to stay alive when she faced the raiders, but he spoke of turning his greatest effort to wilful self-annihilation.

"Perhaps you'll see the result." Zelor enunciated this last thought not as a question, but a drifting, dissolving possibility, as if speaking to himself.

"Perhaps I will," said Elts. A rumour of grief was in her bowels. How could she be affected by the death of one who deserved that fate long ago?

Zelor went on remorselessly, straightening his posture. "This is no time to rehearse the inevitable." He shut his eyes resolutely. His ears seemed even to twitch, straining to hear the hidden voice of the wind.

Elts' tails switched behind her, snaking over her slouched shoulders. "You will not hear anything until your heart is calm."

"Is there not a quicker way?" He opened one eye furiously, a black, reptilian lens flitting over one white staring orb.

She crossed her arms disdainfully, tails dipping and darting with annoyance. "You come from a line of masters over minerals. I've never seen you engage that medium, or any, but I've never known a pureblood to be born without the gift of their lineage. How is it that you work the rock?"

"Not with voice or hearing, but through another thing which I cannot describe."

"Then cannot that thing call upon water, fire, the wind? The Fabric is the same source in all things."

"Of course," he scoffed. Suddenly so tremendous a speeding wall of wind roared through the street that the impact of its arrival nearly knocked Elts from her seat. Zelor sat stone-still against his cloak and hair flying completely horizontal, as if frozen at their maximum extent in the sheer force of the blow.

Ice and snow were ripped from the faces of buildings along with the chunks of crumbling stone they had supported. Long-frozen roofs collapsed. The enormous holes in the ground droned eerily. The streets were whipped clear. A great mist of rising shrapnel veiled the sky. "Such a thing is trivial," he said as the wind died down. "But I can only inspire it as a raw force of violence, not embrace it, learn from it... understand it... as you do, like a technology."

"What you have done just now I could never accomplish," said Elts in awe. Still the streets and broken buildings quaked with the storm Zelor had conjured. Slabs of stone fell from the crumbling ruins and shattered distantly as in the outward rippling surface of a great lake. "But if this is the power of Xeléd to you, you have a crude, Novare grasp for the arcane," she continued. "Your hatred for your birthright, and your time among the soldiers of Molavor are only too apparent. The Fabric is no blunt instrument of force. It is the breath of the world and the source of all things. It is harmony. Where you look for punctuation there is only flow. Clearly you must feel that flow somewhere in your being. A talent so prodigious cannot come without instinct. Easily you rank among the Zefloz, but you are imbalanced, swollen, misguided..." Elts trailed off, frowning. "Brutal methods can be excused, but how can you know the presence of the Fabric and live such a life of evil? To me it is the most contrary thing to know that one who calls upon the voice of the world can kill in cold blood those who deserve peace."

Zelor stood, shaking off the snow which had gathered upon his lap and shoulders in the gale, and turned, stepped broodingly from her and looked to the pale sky. Many were his memories of innocent Xol slain by the sewers of the Fabric, in the name of Fozlest. When he had abandoned Xoldra as a young man, he had explored thoroughly the outer stretches of the black forest, discovering the many secret evils of the Empire before he came to Molavor. He knew well the awful realities of places like Wyx, alone and forgotten by all but such anomalies as Elts, harvested for the rare prodigy of their stunted stock. There, simple Xol families were stricken down and robbed of their lifeblood, of their property, of their dignity. Nowhere, he realized, did he and Elts both see the darkness of the Xol more clearly and personally than in Fozlest, their Empress.

"It is not so uncommon," he said, still facing away from her. "Did you not defend Wyx from that very contradiction?"

Elts doubted Zelor could truly know the evils of that place, but his words had all the more weight for it, conjuring up memories of Rolv and his ilk torturing the weak, enslaving their children. "I would be lying to say that those I fought were merely the extension of a singular evil. They each chose to live as they did, and they each knew what their decision meant in the balance of nature. The

Fabric is everywhere and in all things the same. Its message cannot be changed for those who hear it." She began to wonder, as she spoke, whether she believed her own words; for—however little he understood it—if Zelor sensed with such natural, prodigious power the voice of Xeléd, then he chose willingly to go against the nature of it, sacrificing himself and his place in heaven, the possibility of a great future in the history of his people, for the fate of all life.

"I might ask you about another paradox," came the voice of Zelor. "How is it that you serve Fozlest if these are your feelings?"

"I serve Xirell," Elts said not without passion. "He served Fozlest, and the Empress before her. He convinced me to join the Zefloz as part of my education." Her tails reared dangerously without her willing them to do so.

Now Zelor turned, noting her anger not without fascination. "Then you have no allegiance to her now?"

"She is everything I detest about the Xol," Elts spat. There was a long silence as the still meaningless wind buffeted Zelor's pointed ears.

Then he almost seemed to smile, and the original white of his eyes was clear. "Such rage I have felt all my life, Elts. To have become Zefloz and serve her so intimately is second in its mockery of my life only to the great humiliation of stooping to touch that idol when my every dream of its coming was stained with death."

Elts breathed and lowered her tails. "I promised to help, and I will," she said. "The Alium, I agree, must be destroyed. Neither Fozlest nor Duxmortul should own a Power such as the gods."

Zelor nodded. "If I'd the presence of mind to persuade him..." A shadow fell over his face, and his tails seemed to shrink back from the snow towards the shelter of his cloak. "But there are no excuses. I am sorry for the loss of your master."

CHAPTER XVI
THE PLAGUE OF ARDUA

Elts was compelled to meet Zelor's gaze, yet as she looked into those white eyes which forsook forgiveness, a loathsome shadow-form oozed from the alley behind him. A dark purple hand bled forth from an oil-black alley, slid pressing, shaving particles of frost from the stone, gaining definition. Awkward, rhythmless steps hitched and stumbled. An awful, fetid odour filled the street. Ragged black tatters hung like grave-linens coming into the light, yet they were hemmed in green.

Without his top hat or scarf the full alienness of Xirell's deformed head was like a vast, hairy tumour bursting from the torn cloth. The expressive muscles of his face were a conflux of slugs wriggling and contorting their bodies beneath pallid skin, his limp moustache and frayed black hair quivering with an immense effort quaking up from his shaking legs through his balding scalp. His whole way of walking was horribly like the first steps of an infant, for though he placed each foot with painstaking calculation, it seemed that any moment he might topple over for lack of balance.

Zelor turned from Elts' stare to behold his puppet which—he instantly realized—was no longer his to control. Even she could see this, for it was Xirell's soft green eyes which had changed most significantly, shedding the empty stupor which had cursed them, and returning to that so clearly remembered colour and light which had looked on Elts out from the rain in the Hollow of Wyx. Yet though they shone precisely now with their old gleam and cause for mischief, it

seemed as with the features of his face and movement of his body that their
director had no experience using them. They were unfocused, eerily opposed,
alternately rotating with little reference to the scene they approached.

"It is... easy to see why sewing... is no art with you... Zelor," coughed Xirell in a
scratchy, gurgling voice, as though he were unused to speaking. Each ill-toned
word seemed a great effort for his vocal organs to produce. One of his beautiful
old eyes completed a circuit in its socket, paused, stared penetratingly at the
ground beside the sorcerer. "Knowledge and power... you have... but... you
cannot... force..." He tilted his head like a grating joint in a rusty socket. One arm
twitched spasmodically, settled, stiffened. Oddly curled feet pointed violently
outward. A stream of saliva dropped from his swollen lips and pooled in the
snow, steaming. His arms shook violently in place, and an awful grinding screech
bubbled up from his throat. "Understanding," he forced from that orifice, the
word sliding hideously long and drawn out from the fluttering lips.

"Whatever you are, what do you want?" Elts said bitterly, placing her mask
over her eyes. "So that I can be sure you never find it." Currents of wind stirred
about her feet. Zelor held up his hand, tails urgently beseeching her to wait.

"I am..." Xirell croaked, spewing phlegm that dribbled down his chin, hung in
his moustache. Something seemed to change in him, his eyes beginning to work
together, though still missing their object. "I am the brain." He spoke this time
with remarkably improved ease and sense of syntax, though the timbre of his
voice was yet alien. Perceiving this new eloquence his leering-nowhere visage
contorted into a swollen grin, the ends of its moustache rearing back. "But do I
understand?" The hideous dead face leaned mockingly forward, and both
sickeningly luminous eyes rolled at last sluggishly together, staring into Zelor's, as
if now realizing what they were meant to do in conversation.

"Fool," said Zelor, raising his hateful hand, advancing.

Xirell screeched like a wild animal, startling Zelor and Elts so completely that
they staggered back. The icy street split open between them and the wailing
Green Zefloz, great thorny vines spilling from the dark crack and writhing in an
evolving net before the disgusting figure, only those increasingly cognizant eyes
visible through the moving mass. One cord of verdure snaked swiftly out to snare
Zelor, but with a flash of silver it fell sundered beside him, his sword from hip to
hip unsheathed at a severe angle.

"I am this body," came the voice sounding even more natural. "I use this
mind." More vines leapt forward to strangle Zelor, but he paired them in easy
strokes. Now Xirell shouted with so precisely the voice of her master that Elts
shivered and froze. "But I am not Xirell!"

"Your intention to teach only reminds me of the old man," said Zelor. Elts behind him was surprised by how suddenly she had thought the same.

"From one mind-eater to another," came the voice, "you will never hear the wind!"

"Now that," Elts shouted, shaking off her uncanny petrification, "my master would never say!"

With an explosion of dense winds from her palms lowered to the ground, she rocketed past Zelor, flung out a coil of rope from her belt, and as it caught the vine upon which she'd aimed, pulled, rose spiralling, arced, gathered a host of air-darts, and flung them backhand raining down from above. A smattering of flesh echoed through the street, and a hideous shrieking rent the air. The vines collapsed to the ground, snow flying up around them. Gouts of white blood spurted from not-Xirell's robes as he spasmed and twisted his limbs in horribly animal directions, falling at last to his knees.

Elts landed in a crouch beside her master, drawing her longest knife as she stood, holding it to his throat. Spitting, gagging, somehow laughing as if drawing on a gamut of random expressions, not-Xirell looked up to her, focusing those old green eyes upon her exactly as they'd done many times before. So arranged now were all of the features of his face that the image of the abominable dissolved, and she looked now at Xirell her master, her teacher, her friend. And so she hesitated.

In that instant, Zelor flitted forward quickly as a candle's shadow, leaping over the fallen vines, clamping his palm down atop the old, dying thing's head. The creature inhabiting Xirell shrieked with a voice unlike any heard by Elts or Zelor, and blood poured down from its rolling eyes as it was absorbed into the sorcerer's being.

"I know that you wished to be the one to send him to Xeléd, Elts. But let me own the awful murder which I began," said Zelor, now having to focus, bear down, dropping his sword and gripping his arm for support. "By the Frandun," he groaned, "why is there so much?"

Zelor shivered, stiffened, shutting his eyes, now opening them suddenly wide—they were black as crypts. So too did the air around him warp with simmering dark, and a low rumbling worked its way through the ground. With his free hand he shoved Elts away, then joined that second palm upon the skull of the seizing not-Xirell. His arms shook violently and he fell to his knees, bent over and wailed as though he were engulfed in flame. Ghostly black tentacles rose up from his quaking, hunched back and played as huge transforming shadows against the snow and the walls of the buildings. With a sickening crunch, the skull of Xirell imploded. An empty body fell to the snow, disgraced for the last time.

Zelor collapsed flat on his back. Just before the darkness began quickly to recede—it seemed—into his very heart, his eyes were utterly red. Then they were tightly shut. Even from her distance, for she had scrambled even further back as the wings of darkness rose from Zelor, Elts could see that the furious orbs worked back and forth beneath their lids, as in reading. "Life," he murmured in a fever, beginning it seemed to choke, now seizing, hands clenching and smearing white blood through the frost. He vomited an awful black bile up over his trembling chin and heaving chest, threw himself onto his side, pressing his hot face into the cold snow, wheezing. "Time," he moaned, clutching at his ribs as the word dissolved and foundered in an awful dying noise like the pleas of a tortured animal.

Only in the fullness of night did the fit begin to leave him. He lay staring up into the sky breathing shallowly. The full-faced light of Drolv, the Moon of Disease, glowed sickly and green all throughout the city, steeping the towers and the snow in a jaundiced pallor of malaise. Elts sat removed from his suffering in the shadows of a stone arch. With great effort he looked over to her, straining his face. At last he said in a whisper: "I..." His eyes were black, but a whiteness seemed to creep upon their fringes. "It was the only way."

Slowly Elts rose and approached the mutilated corpse of Xirell opposite him. She knelt, closed the old man's eyelids over those kind green pools too long abused, and placed the long knife, which he had given her long ago, across his chest.

Then she left Zelor lying there alone with the death of her master which was his to own, and found a stone tower still with its integrity in which to spend the night. She could not say why she settled in the chamber she did, though it was relatively dry, quite high up in the structure, with a window overlooking the street.

But by purpose or accident, here she could see, and as night fell continued to watch the form of Zelor. He went to Xirell, held the limp body in his arms, went away, and returned alone. Now he sat in the middle of the road holding his head in hands, now straightening his back, rounding his shoulders. A gale of cold wind rushed through his cloak, rippling like a ragged black flag, and it seemed that he tilted his head to better hear its message.

The cold rays of dawn stirred Elts, sprawled on the uneven stone floor. The ache of her spine and blocky shoulders was nothing compared to the pounding in her toes and raw heels. It was as if each morning the cumulative abstract body of the journey caught up with her physical own all at once in those blistered soles. How Novare could buckle up the freedom of their closest contact with Altum in boots, she would never understand. Who could imagine what horrendous sores must develop under the coarse restrictions of such wilful prisons.

She sat up, rooted in the bags which she'd not thought even to unclip from her belt, and gnawed on a thick, brown leaf Xirell had discovered in the lower peaks. Chewing on its bitter fibres slowly, sipping from a dull elz-flask, there was in her heart a new kind of mourning that seemed to conclude with a different and natural theme of solemn calm that anxious grieving which had begun upon the morning of her master's change. Now, here was a far more sorrowful finality, yet with it came a security—at last his suffering had ended. Gazing out of the arched, paneless window, she envisioned his spirit rising enfolded with the sky up into the blue sphere of Xeléd.

She descended the tower, finishing her breakfast, and found Zelor still seated in the road. Wordless, though clearly haggard for lack of sleep, he rose, brushed the frost from his robes, turned and led her down the hill to the broken gates. Even as she glimpsed his countenance and tasted his presence she knew that he had changed for the worse. However damning it had been to call upon the power of Duxmortul in overcoming and absorbing Xirell's possessor, the contents of that alien mind alone had seemed nearly to kill him on the spot.

His eyes were only faintly white; his face still and impassive; his tails dead weight. The motions of his turning and walking were like actions in a play, designed, performed, yet without any belief in their validity. Despite the rigid vacancy of his being, he strode down the street and through the great blasted gate of Ardua with increasing energy, as though thankful for the movement. Outside he stopped on a small knoll beside one of the very few scraggly alpine trees which sprouted crooked and black from the great shelf of land. In a soft mound at its base, Elts' long knife was stuck. It was tied off with the missing green scarf of her master.

"Here lies Xirell," she said, lowering her gaze. "Lover of trees." She was reluctantly touched that Zelor had found the old sorcerer's cloth, and thought to find at least some kind of growing thing in these desolate heights to enshrine his passing.

"He is with Xeléd," Zelor said with uncanny mortality. "His flesh is returned to the Fabric. It will dissolve into and feed that which he loved. Let us remember him this way."

They stood in the wind before the grave of Xirell for a long while. Zelor did not move, it seemed, until Elts' thick shoulders subtly fell, and her stiff jaw turned the rays of her eyes beyond the scene into heaven. He strode off. She knelt, kissed the snow, stood with her hand against the wood of the tree, and at last followed him towards the city wall.

He turned against it rather than pass under the gate, and moved along its high surface as though searching for something. Suddenly his pace quickened, and Elts following saw that a snow-covered set of stairs led open-faced and awfully exposed down along the shelf of land upon which the city was situated.

"Where are we going?" Elts finally asked.

He pressed on, quickening their pace. "I know the way now. It is in the mind of Lirp." He touched two long fingers to his temple. "That is the name of the thing which came to us in the form of Xirell."

Still harrowed by the desecrations of that creature, Elts favoured another question then as to its nature. "Yet you were listening to the wind this morning? If you discovered the way already, what need is there for that practice?"

"I need more than power by the time we reach Zenidow," he replied, flowing down the steps. Yet he stopped and turned suddenly, and it seemed almost that he wished to smile. "There is peace in what you've taught me, Elts. When I listen to the wind, it feels as though I brush against something which the Shadow will never understand. And it is vital to me now, that feeling." He gazed back at her for a moment before flipping stiffly his tails and resuming the descent.

The staircase wound around and down until as from nowhere appeared another, smaller shelf set beneath the great bowl of Ardua's foundation. Following Zelor onto this plane of ice, Elts was thankful for the space between her and the unprotected drop into abyssal white fog. They stood now before the rectangular entrance to a mine shaft, ensconced in lustrous gold, hewn into the rock upon which Ardua was built. Before the black entrance stood a cracked, ice and snow-decked statue of a tall, regal Novare woman crowned with gold, staring pupilless out over the land below. Beside her lay gold and black armour and weapons destroyed and trampled remarkably flat.

Radiating out from the shaft were the same immense, noisome holes as appeared throughout the city above, some of them wider than any they'd yet encountered, others quite small, all of them dwarfing and rendering the gilded tunnel of Novare a tiny pore in the face of the mountain.

"These places are where they achieved the surface." Zelor indicated the different tunnels with his tails and hands, seeming almost to think aloud.

"They?" she asked.

"The worms," he said. "Worms mighty as elz trees. Now they are only in the very deepest places of the mountain." He let out a low sigh, kneading his high forehead in one hand, and Elts realized she was standing quite close to him. She stepped away, and the rustling of her bare feet through the snow seemed to remind Zelor of her presence. "Thankfully we need not venture so low into the world as the Arduans dared to delve. There is a fairer path through the mountain." His tails swished with viscous anxiety.

Elts shivered at the presence of Lirp in Zelor's speech and thought. So many helpless souls were damned to haunt that swollen purple cranium, yet also it did not seem at all invigorating or desirable being wilfully possessed of their suffering. Horrible as it was to see even the sick, dazed glare of Lirp dissolve from Xirell's eyes into Zelor's hand, similarly remorseless and self-destructive was such an act for the absorber, damning himself to carry these affectless, dead memories. With each Zefloz enthralled, every sunken head in his hand, Zelor's eyes grew dimmer, his voice more like the clang of metal in an empty vault, his gestures, the language of his body and tails more affectless and hopeless.

Confounding as was the way he spoke now to her nearly as an equal, where he hardly recognized her presence for the majority of their journey, more strange yet hopeful in its contrast to his dark evolution was that tenuous, mortal passion in his grating voice which arose when he did so. Evidently the mind of Lirp contained far vaster histories than any before it, for he seemed almost wholly disconnected now from his body, as though his mind were an engineer enmeshed in the control of its brain. Yet the great blow to Zelor's own spirit, this most powerful shove into madness and away from bodily life was not enough to sever him completely from his lone companion—if only recently and contractually acquired—in this quest.

And she did not feel so distant herself, for it seemed, even through the petrification of his countenance and tonelessness of his voice, that Zelor respected her. She recalled how he sat so dutifully out in the freezing wind through the night in the green light of Drolv cross-legged, head cocked to the side, wholly committed to her instruction. And he was quick to ask her whether he might hear the wind even below ground. Whatever need he had for more subtle magic, she wondered, he who requires no path but straight through his enemies, he felt clearly that only she could help him, that not only her skills but her independence were of dire importance. He respected her as an authority not to be further questioned on the absolute logic she had already divulged, and trusted completely that lesson even in his continual failure to comprehend the nature of the Fabric.

"Yes, even when the lungs fail, there is wind," she answered. Her tails coiled, swished. "I saw you meditating through the night," she added softly. It was the first that she had ever expressed attention to some personal side of Zelor in the open.

"I heard only my master," he replied.

As if to remind Zelor in turn of his own slaves, Feox and Xelv appeared along the sheer stair, blank faces shadowed in their hoods, tails dragging, unaffected in their stride by the cold. Even when he had summoned them as they descended the stair, Zelor perceived through his tethers to their souls that they were uninfested by entities such as Lirp, and with only little scrutiny did Elts as well determine them still to be his thralls, for they walked with the smooth coordination—however lifeless—of one who is well used to embodiment.

Only a flicker of his former, or perhaps yet true disgust animated the sorcerer's ever-deadening tails and ever-blackening eyes as he sent those former Zefloz forth first into the black shaft. He followed only after their odious footsteps had receded into distant echoes. Elts stepped forward beside him, matching pace. Darkness at first was total, though ahead the fire of Feox beat against high, arching walls and wooden support beams, the occasional metal cart, pile of rock, queenly statue. Zelor too, as they drew away from the blinding white entryway, held a live flame in his open palm, casting a runny swath of sight about them.

The craggy ground sloped ever downwards, and only a few turns and forks they encountered. At these junctures, Zelor knew exactly which way to go, for the far-ahead decisions of Feox and Xelv were but his own thoughts manifest. So eerie was it to see his consciousness tangibly and simultaneously divided, Elts shuddered at the more disturbing knowledge that the limb-like actions of these illusory separate entities ahead of them were informed not by Zelor's own intuition, but Lirp's which he had consumed. It was not even that he paused to examine an impersonal map in his memory, but rather that he had truly spanned these networks countless times as one at home.

Elts' stomach turned with the sheer efficiency and ease of it all, and never so clearly did she see the awful temptation in the power Duxmortul offered Its apostle. It was not so difficult to think that Zelor's opinion of her might suddenly change, that he might decide that yes he could certainly derive some use from her, wind powers or not, if she were more malleable. In an instant she could become either like the other Zefloz, or imprisoned even in that high purple cranium with the white hair and pitiless dark eyes.

They camped in a low-ceilinged shaft which seemed hewn entirely by the hands of Novare. Feox plunged his axe blazing into the rock and shifted off into the inky dark to sit, eyes gleaming like an aborjay hanging from its roost. Xelv fell beside him, leant up against the dusty wall like an automaton out of use. Elts squatted by the fire of the weapon and held out her frozen violet hands, puffs of steam issuing from her tightly drawn hood. Somehow it was even colder down here in the dank tunnels, even without the harsh winds of the mountainside.

"Zelor," she said, peering over at the sorcerer where he sat cross-legged in the posture, again, of listening for the wind, which she had assured him could be heard anywhere in the world. "Who was Lirp?"

He blinked stiffly, as if lost, and turned his stone visage and the uncompromising rays of his eyes to Feox and Xelv who had now fallen completely supine, visual organs shut off, arms folded cruciform upon their chests. "It sickens me, what they are," he muttered. A shiver, a notion of feeling passed through a fine muscle in his jaw. "Xirell... his memories, his magic, his knowledge, these things like quanta were with Lirp, but nothing of his spirit remained. True understanding cannot be stolen." Zelor turned with black-white anguish in his face, and when those changeful orbs contacted her sight, his promise never to turn on her conflowed with their emanation of sincerity. "Lirp was Viruchaea," he said. "You may have learned about their kind in Xoldra."

"Another gift from Xirell," she replied. "They are microscopic organisms which require the flesh of another to replicate."

Zelor nodded solemnly. "Lirp was one such entity, though unlike any I've seen or read about. The typical Viruchaea infects its hosts, reproduces for a time, fades as the body repels it. But Lirp perfectly consumed and replaced the nervous system, bringing itself and all of its experiences along with it. Not unlike my own hideous mastery." He looked down the mine shaft out into the darkness at Feox and Xelv lying corpse-like.

"Lirp's kind once used the great worms for hosts. Nearly all of his memories involve tunnels far blacker and deeper than we'll dare approach. Those worms which attacked Ardua were not worms in mind and spirit, but vehicles, a whole species enslaved to embody the consciousness of another. There is even a turbid recollection, young as Lirp was, of a time before the worms, and before then as well, the notion that these Viruchaea have projected themselves into new mediums over and again when the survival of their kind is at stake.

"When the Arduans delved near to their tunnels, the Viruchaea sensed their violent lust for mineral wealth, and communicated among themselves whether it was time for their race to migrate, and through the rapid mutations of their being they became transmissible to Novare. They drove the worms up into the light, destroyed the mines and ravaged the city. One by one they abandoned their hosts and parasitized the Novare. The empty worms were burned in great fires, and those natural-minded—reared like slaves—regained their ancient group-think and burrowed back into the mountain."

"They protected themselves through conquest," Elts mused aloud.

"You could say the same of the Xol. Brutality is no novel piece of our history."

"We are taught to loathe the Novare specifically for their heedless violence, but we are none too different in the end," Elts murmured, realizing in a nebulous way that she had never quite had such an agreement even with Xirell that the Xol and Novare were equally destructive to life and Altum. Zelor's rejection of the Empire continued to surprise her. "But then, how were we not infected? And Feox and Xelv? Viruchaea must be everywhere throughout these tunnels, and in the city."

"They cannot survive in the light of Caelare without a host, though Lirp believed this to be an immutable trait derived from so many eons living in the systems of the worms. Xirell's final memory," he said with sudden lucidity, raising his chin towards Elts, whiteness warring in his eyes, "shows an old cellar where little light reached. How fitting that my orders led him to his doom. Though, I'd already taken everything from him." Now Zelor's eyes lost their clarity and resoluteness as that dark miasma of fear and inevitability arose within their swirling shadows.

"Were your eyes always black and white?" Elts turned back to the fire as if she were embarrassed for his nakedness.

Zelor started, and his vision cleared. "They were once purely white. To many they still are. You see the Shadow in me, Elts." With this recognition of mutual understanding, those ink-stains drizzled into the darkness like spectral tears, and the rigid topography of his gaunt face seemed to flow once more like flesh. Even one tail rose and flipped, drifting to the rocky floor.

Elts too felt that she was closer now to Zelor than most Xol, but she steeled herself as always, dropping her thick brow, running a hand through her prickly hair. "There is another being to you, just like Lirp but far more powerful, and I sense that it will take command in time."

"So It will," Zelor said almost as in a command. "As long as I can reach the Alium before that happens, I can die at least in a state of perceived repentance."

They sat quietly as the tension of the moment swirled round, and the shadows began again to creep back into Zelor's periphery. Elts changed the subject. "If we put out our lights, we will be steeped in darkness here."

Zelor nodded. "But we need only fear the worms themselves. The Viruchaea have moved entirely above ground, and live only in the buildings of Ardua, as a mockery of their former residents. There is even a court in the palace, where the God-Queen still sits in her throne."

*

Over days of pitiless dark Elts followed Zelor as he carved out their path through the bright motions of Feox, tested it first through the stride of Xelv. On went the noisome caverns, many shaped by the slow majesty of time into arches and spindly or stout, dripping, sweating fingers reaching down and grasping up in eon-old gestures. Other shafts of hard angles and regularity were hollowed out and supported by the tools of Novare, jutting from these huge natural caves as with sudden abandon for the scent of precious, glittering veins. But as they descended into layers more deep and ancient, they walked solely through a great network of tunnels which the worms had bored in the rock as schools of leviathan fish through water. The first of these capacious, ever-winding tubes appeared yawning under the broken floor of a large mine-shaft. The place was full of metal and bone licked in the flame.

Zelor watched unblinking as Elts looped her rope round a spire of rock, cast it unspooling through the hole, and leapt deftly into the darkness, hand sliding loosely against the black fibre, distant feet touching down. When he received the psychic emanation of her finding surface below, he descended the cord as he had watched her do, though more methodically, slow to push away with his feet from the rock into empty space. But the lesson would not avail him again now that they were in the true matrix of the worms, for he knew, and Elts saw in the light of Feox descending above them into this alien world, that it was universally connected. Forward went the fire, Xelv behind it. Adroitly she snapped her line through a rushing gust of dank air, and it uncoiled from its catch above, fell swiftly through the dark, snaked neatly to her hip. Though she could see Zelor's admiration even in the unmoving features of his face, she did not acknowledge him.

As they pressed on, the memory of Xirell's final vision as Zelor had described it hung in Elts's mind like a still life: her old master with top hat held down, scarf over his chin, flowing moustache rippling in the alpine wind as he stepped down into the blissful void of his horrible yet gracious end. Often she would picture this dark cellar she had never seen, where mindlessly, running the errand of its master, the husk of her former friend and teacher wandered into the microscopic clutches of Lirp. And each time envisioning this scene, she would grow strangely calm knowing that at last the mockery of Xirell had passed from the world.

There was, of course, something poetic about Zelor killing the man he had cursed to undeath. Certainly Elts had hesitated at the precipice of the deed, but certainly too the sorcerer had leapt at the chance for some modicum of atonement, however gravely he denied forgiveness. She was grateful for it, his owning the travesty, yet as well it revealed to her that still he had kept Xirell alive for his utility, no matter how disgusting he appeared to him, for if the mind of Lirp was the surprise which pushed him so violently to draw upon the Shadow, his ability to destroy the Zefloz was apparently quite accessible. Perhaps he had decided to end the misery of her master once he understood Elts' loss, but here was a question again she kept to herself. It was so convenient for Xirell to have come to them with all of the information they needed swimming in his swollen head, for the necessity of his death to hover so suddenly and thankfully between them and Zenidow. Yet she wished to believe that Zelor was honourable, and so she did not call into question that honour as they travelled further into the deep.

If he had learned more about her from the mind he drank, Zelor did not make his understanding any more apparent than through an increasing appreciation for her abilities, which already he seemed to hold in the highest regard, and in his own way. His manner of demanding another lesson, his ambition for knowledge, the questions he asked of the subterrene air, his utter lack of levity—he was nothing like Xirell. Ever clearer was Lirp's lesson that the soul cannot be stolen, only abused. But Elts saw too that the consumption of souls is a torment of its own for the abuser. More intimately each moment she felt not only the suffocating tentacles wrapped round and dragging behind Zelor with increasing weight and demand, but also the many-headed beast of wasted lives contending for consciousness in his heavy brow, bent on usurping always what he turned to for help. She did what she could to avail his pain with her words, and lessons in listening to the wind as it spoke subtly each night in the echoing dank tunnels, beginning to hope in her heart that he would not lose his spirit to Duxmortul as appeared so inevitable.

They came by what they believed was the fourth sunset to the maw of a titan worm-hole, seeming next to the other tunnels as though a hundred of the stoutest and most vigorous creatures had forced themselves in a uniform mass through the rock. Some hundred yards tall it was, and another hundred wide, such that even the Great Tree of Xoldra would slide through but for its branches. Beyond was an endless, featureless blackness.

"The path of the Great Worm," said Zelor, standing in what appeared to be awe. "No Viruchaea dared approach its tunnels. It is known to come out of the mountain every one thousand years to feel the light of Caelare no matter how badly its flesh is burned. One could hear its wails all through the mountains, though nowhere so clearly as on the side facing Zenidow, where it goes always on this errand."

Elts gazed high into the unseeable black ceiling of the tunnel. She felt the gravity of the worm as if it were there; so massive was the dark that it imposed upon her as a monster in itself. "So this is the way."

"We must find the proper path, but we have at least tapped the network."

"And what if the worm finds us?"

"We would hear it long before that. Vast though the worm is, the mountains are far more so than we can imagine. Deep into the world go the tunnels, and deeper this worm than any other. The deeper the better, for their kind. This worm," he said, placing his hand against the ridged texture of the tunnel wall, "is the lone seeker of light."

"If we are so high up then, we must already be near to the correct tunnel."

Zelor was silent, his countenance indifferent, but the slightest undulation in his tails bespoke respect for her insight. "That is true," he said.

"I should like to see one of them," Elts breathed, marvelling at the enormous furrowed ribs of the passageway, their dark trenches opening up into a sea of black.

"As should I, but even a youngling would hinder us greatly."

Feox stuck his suddenly burning axe in the rock, shambled off into the dark, and crumpled to the floor. Xelv already had folded themself up for the night.

"Can't you at least..." Elts thought aloud in a dry murmur.

"Pretend?" Zelor sighed, swinging round his expressionless face, and Elts swore that his eyes were entirely black even in the firelight.

"No," she said. "It's better this way."

"I could kill them," he echoed another of her thoughts.

She did not reply. The small flames danced against the oblivion over and beyond their camp, the starving tunnel of the Great Worm seeming to open wider with each pitiful leap of light. They slept there on the rock, huddled around the tiny flames, listening to the faint drip of moisture from distant stalactites. For the first in a great many nights, Elts did not dwell on the loss of her master, nor on the torment of Zelor. Instead she could not but think of the great worm, somewhere coiled like the entrails of Altum.

CHAPTER XVII
A DIFFERENT KIND OF DELVER

At first the tireless strides of Byron seemed driven in their length and forcefulness to outlast whatever guards might have followed from Occultash. But watching the scarred, one-eyed man joylessly devour his simple meals, sit upright through the nights in a state of brooding which repelled all mortal contact, wait coldly as if he'd never moved or slept for the ogre to rise, Ogwold learned that the mercenary did nothing except with great severity, and figured their pace would scarcely slacken whether or not they were pursued.

Only one week after the divine storm, so incredible was their progress through the range that even he stopped looking for shining companies of pickaxe helmets searching over the hills they had crossed. When his eyes did turn back, they wandered up, rather, at the looming, forked peak of Shadith where it rose ever more shrouded in the blue haze of distance, far beyond the many mountains lesser and greater whose broad, shadeless shoulders they had rounded.

These initial leagues of the Mardes were busily travelled, and the grand highway, however sudden in its changeful grade, was broad, well-maintained, and easy to follow. The longer they held to even this commonest route, the more various were the races of men and women that worked the mine shafts freely, urged on their carts through the rising dust, discussed in gem-fevered haste amongst themselves or alongside the wagons of traders. Never was an armoured soldier among them it seemed, and though no Nogofod appeared, Ogwold's grey skin, hulking size, and even the strange green fingers which slipped from the long white sleeve of his cloak brought no more suspicion on them than the fantastical Videre, who drew the eye only for her rare and exquisite form.

Already they had passed several sprawling settlements captive to such mad industry as appraised Ogwold and Videre only for what role they might play in a mine. The great camps were fat with swathes of trade-wagons like big brown maggots upon a carcass yet lively, buzzing with flies who seemed never to have swung a tool or handled the rock from which their treasures came, aimless and recursive in their insectile pacing, awaiting the time when some soot-streaked delver would appear leaning against a huge wooden wheel, grinning and lighting their pipe. So crazed and delighted were many such delvers, and all throughout the interior of the camps was the endless energy of a war against the mountains themselves. Brick chimneys pumped black clouds from huddles of squat cabins and older, stone houses. The windows of long wooden buildings raged with cheer. Delvers spilled all about—shouting, smoking, wheeling precarious carts of rock studded with the chance ore. Dim amber light pulsed deep in yawning dark tunnels where Novare constantly came and went in metal helms that kindled in the glow, swinging rusted pickaxes like the enormous keys to some secret dungeon.

Even as the highway narrowed, aged and became overgrown with the thorny, low mountain shrubs and the hardy ferns of sweeping frond, still many were the rickety covered carts with their tall wheels plying the dirt in grooves, and the tremendous rotten piles of cornibet dung that cooked so thick in the sun. But as the company travelled on and on each day at the unflagging pace set by Byron, over the hip of this small mountain, down through this rock-clustered vale, up and along this dizzying scarp, and as the camps and villages of delvers and traders slowly began to dwindle, the highway which was now nowhere near as grand tapered so drastically in quality as to hardly accommodate the carriage of a standard wagon. In the clearing of a cliff-side wood it swung harshly and at last burst into a tangle of switchbacks and meandering trails, everything rockier and more treacherous. Now there appeared elder wooden signage and the odd cairn to guide those who ventured so far as to leave behind the main road.

Far and wide they journeyed by this matrix of routes more subtle, testing the different exposed roads which inched along sheer precipices or dipped suddenly down into hidden forests, sometimes all together scowling at the cryptic map. The sphere hummed ever softly, and though it came out at times to float and orbit Ogwold's enormous shaggy head, peer itself at the map as if comprehending everything, drift playfully after the switching tails of Videre, it remained snug within his cloak whenever they encountered fellow travellers. Byron seemed to pay it no mind.

Even for a lean ogre Ogwold was strong, but this aerobic work especially in the increasing altitude was becoming much for him, and his muscles grew queasy under the immense weight of his father's sword. He heaved and sweated profusely, and though his vast steps covered far more ground than Byron's, it began to feel that he was only barely keeping up. Worst of all was the dry fragility that plagued his greener arm if he did not constantly sip from his waterskin which was invariably nearly empty. As exhaustion steeped in his big, heavy bones, he wanted very much to speak with Byron and derive some lift of spirit or modicum of acknowledgement that their race through the mountains was perhaps record-setting, but the inscrutable stalker was an inexorable and silent blade slicing through the trail.

They came near dusk on the twelfth day of their journey at last to a giggling stream which cut down through a sheer slope and spilled over the path. It was the first source of water they had yet encountered, and even the mercenary allowed himself an expression of relief. Beside the shallow flow he scooped water to his cracked lips, splashed himself all over, sat back and began wolfishly to tear at the tough, black dried meat from his pack. The sun had set, and the sky wore deep purple, milky grey clouds snaking through the lower peaks that studded the land before them. Shadith was now invisible, and there were only the disjointed teeth of so many alien peaks and shadow-haunted crags to enshrine the progress of the day.

Ogwold lumbered puffing up the grade. When he saw the stream his eyes bulged like gibbous moons, and he rushed rumbling to its bank like a great tetrapod, smashing what portion of his head would fit underwater at length. A great wave broke over the stony face of Byron who seemed not even slightly to flinch. Only awash in that cold, lucid elixir did Ogwold realize the clear water was quite blue! Just like they say about Elemdam, he thought; so this is inland water. Certainly it was very different from the sea, tasting much like the filtered water from the Lucetalian pumps. He could tell instantly that it was not toxic, and drank desperately, awful sucking noises spattering his cheeks which finally drew Byron's eye.

Sated at last, Ogwold took in the water rather through his windpipe, and ah, yes, there it is, he thought; to breathe beneath the surface was an uncanny sedative. He sighed, rearing up out of the exploding stream, twilit liquid rilling full of sediment from the black locks of his hair, dreadlocked with the adventure's sand and dirt and sweat. Sputtering with satisfaction he leaned against the steep rock wall next to Byron, huge columnar legs lying like grey logs across the trail, cradling and squeezing his stranger arm whose unsettling aridity became more pronounced in the calm of all this life-giving moisture. His long drink now poured into the fibres of the limb, tracing its brittle channels, resuscitating the ghost of its true form, but the flesh craved so much more. He sank the arm into the crystal water, where it rejoiced, strengthened, and gripped into his shoulder and back and ribs with a pleasure so fierce it gave the ogre a start of pain. But that shock of intensity melted at once into bliss. Innumerable roots sprouted all along the submerged length and spiralled out glorying in the water, some of them burrowing into the dirt. Ogwold sighed deeply and slumped with a wholly novel, yet somehow ancient sense of relief.

"I've never seen anything like that," said Byron looking askance. It was his first speech of the journey that had not to do directly with their path.

"Neither had I until very recently," Ogwold said with some effort, the plant squeezing him as in a duravium clamp. "And still I don't know what it really is. I used to have a normal arm, you know." He couldn't help glancing at the mark of Byron's own missing organ. Though the vacant socket was sealed shut, its sunkenness was ghastly clear. In the other eye, jade and cold, there turned a sliver of curiosity the likes of which had not appeared in it as far as Ogwold knew, though it seemed Byron's gaze was fixed not on the alien plant, but on Ogdof's massive sword, lying in its leather scabbard by the water.

Byron nodded slightly, now turning that lone green ray to Ogwold's arm for certain. "How did you lose it?"

"Oh." Ogwold wrestled the urge to smile, folding over his stone brow and pursing his lips cool and aloof like the mercenary, though he must have appeared quite foolish, for the man's eyebrow was subtly raised. Quickly the ogre softened his impression of impassion, horrified at the thought that Byron might think himself mocked. He admired the man for his poise, but rejoiced so much more in the possibility of its dissolution, wanting very much to have a companion with whom he could speak freely on the way to Zenidow. Still, he could not imagine the mercenary would respond positively to enthusiasm, at least for now.

"It was eaten by a sea monster," he began, pronouncing the word 'monster' very casually, as if it were perfectly quotidian. "I was saved by a Flosleao woman, and when I woke up on the beach she'd rooted this plant in my wound. It used to be a little patch, then a sprout, and now it's grown so much." The extremity seemed to drink even more vigorously as he spoke of its evolution.

Byron did not at all seem surprised by the mention of the Flosleao, tearing off another chunk of black meat, chewing like an animal. Videre appeared around the bend, the long shag of her lupine jowls boltered in the black blood of her dinner. Lapping delicately from the stream, she wound her body up to sleep on the opposite bank looking like a huge white boulder.

"It makes a fine shield," said the mercenary swallowing, stowing the stringy meat in his pack. Leaning back against the mountain, crossing his arms, and shutting his eye, it seemed at first that he was finished speaking. "Learn to use it."

Byron scowled as he delivered this sliver of advice, but Ogwold had come to believe this was merely a standard expression, and he took it even as a form of acknowledgement considering the man had not uttered so many words in his presence since the night they had met. Whatever the mercenary figured to scowl at must at least be concerning to him. And Ogwold knew—and took very seriously himself—the sort of work Byron suggested, for Nubes had advised him similarly, and so had the words of Autlos-lo spoke of some mental or spiritual union between his being and her gift. Learn indeed, he thought, suddenly quite upset with himself for all but ignoring the plant these past twelve days. As the mercenary brooded in silence against the rock, Ogwold opened his heart and thoughts to his arm drinking in the flow of the stream, feeling how the sinews of each root so finely attuned themselves to that medium.

"Love and light," he recited, "it needs in teaching you to speak." He breathed slowly, deeply, envisioning, now truly feeling the water as it spilled cold and vital into his vegetable pores, absorbing the sinking sun through its healing hues refracted in the sparkling surface. "Deep into the blood and bones," he continued, "now reach its careful roots." He imagined that the plant had sent its fibres all through his body now, that—like Nubes had said—they worked within his heart and brain.

No images came, nor words, but there was a slow feeling, a gradual, noble, long-reaching flow of energy that resonated with him. There was synthesis here. He felt it in his teeth and nails, in his hair, and in his veins and the striations of his muscles. With each thump of his great heart came as well the softest gesture towards water and life, but also back into his own being from that strange green arm, so subtly as the tree grows from shade into light and turns up its boughs in supplication. There were no words to describe it, because describing it would be to put words to the sensation of being alive, and that was what it was: life. He was the plant, and the plant was Ogwold, and so—together—they drank.

"Whose verse?" Byron spoke softly for the hardness of his countenance.

When Ogwold turned and opened his eyes, even in that statuesque grimace the mercenary's gaze seemed open to him, as though some invisible wall had lowered, but only over that emerald irid. "My mother's," said Ogwold.

Byron nodded, leaned his head against the rock, closing his eye. "There is more?"

Ogwold smiled, thinking his exuberance would be missed, but that one eye shot open once more, scanned his naked appreciation of its interest, closed off.

"I'd like to hear the rest," said Byron. "Another time." Then he was silent.

Ogre and plant drifted off to sleep, their thoughts lacing together like networks of root and nerve down through his hand into the stream, below the bed of water, down into the rocks, deep into the mountainside and out into the bones of Altum as Incipi and Amorcem, the Moons of Creation and Love, opened their slight silver and small dun awarenesses, subtle yet profound to any who saw them, and the stars plucked up their points.

Ogwold woke much earlier than usual the next day, just as Caelare's palace sent up its first sheets of dawn, as if the plant had soaked up a quality of sleep far more vital than was necessary for your typical Nogofod. He sat up and drew the green limb from the water, its vast root systems sliding up out of their tunnels and coalescing into fingers. The flesh was now so tight and strong like stone, yet flexible and quick as his will to move it. He clenched his fist and flexed the steely muscles welling with strength, and the day's journey suddenly seemed deeply appealing to him.

Byron came walking around the bend. It was strange to find him moved from his usual seated and impatient position of dark waiting. The mercenary was covered in sweat and breathing heavily, but nodded stoically as ever to Ogwold. Videre had already left, but they saw her immense paw prints in the dusty trail. The road led them down across the stream and along a bleeding meander of switchbacks into a valley full of broken rock and massive boulders. All around them unknown mountains rose, hunching together their broad shoulders, scaled with crags and outfitted in pockets of forest. Byron stopped to scan the wooden, interlocking sign post that waited for them at the foot of the slope.

Feeling so inspired not only by the seemingly boundless energy that coursed from his arm into every extremest nerve, but also by the conversation of the evening, Ogwold spoke up. "How do you know we can reach Zenidow?"

"Because others have," was the toneless reply.

"I've heard so too, but they must have been quite savvy."

Byron swung his eye back and over the ogre, turned and began walking. "It will be a perilous journey."

"Then why are you here?"

"I told you—I am looking for a sorcerer. He seeks the highest mountain." As he spoke, Byron's hand reached as if by nature for the hilt of his sword. But even as it seemed he would draw the weapon, his hand fell to his side and those bladed strides continued. "And you?"

"I really don't know. But it has something to do with this..." As if summoned, the sphere—which had been gliding along contentedly—came round Ogwold's side and rose to float between them. It orbited his head once, and then Byron's, resting near his shoulder. "Oh, it likes you too!"

Byron scowling flicked the sphere away like an annoying insect. It buzzed dizzily off and fell into orbit around Ogwold again. "What is it?"

"I've no idea, but it wants to go to Zenidow and I'm supposed to go with it. An old wizard gave it to me."

Byron had no reply, continuing on up the road as if his question had been purely perfunctory. Ogwold followed sheepishly, though he did not feel so denied as he'd expected to find himself in continuing to speak with the man. Closed off and prickly as he was, there seemed nothing malevolent in the manner of Byron, and so Ogwold began to feel slowly more comfortable with his companion, though it was difficult as ever to think that the man had slain two nameless knights without hesitation.

By dusk they had crossed the valley by a well made road. The rocky terrain fell away, and now they entered upon a moist, grassy forest full of life. Birds chattered everywhere. Here they camped among the sloping roots of their next ascent. In the morning Ogwold woke snuggled into a downy mass of grass and loam. His arm had planted itself and grown perceptibly brighter, more hale and sturdy like a green tree. The adventure of its roots was vast, and in some places about the ogre's nest great humps and nodules knotted together. He knew that freeing himself would not be a matter of uprooting the plant physically, but willing it naturally to return to the air, and so it did, slinking smoothly back into the likeness of limbhood. He flexed the green fingers. There were ten of them! But like streams of water covering one to the other each paired off, twining together, and there were five normal enough digits once more.

With this business of extricating himself from the ground finished, he realized that again it was quite early, and that he had again slept wonderfully well. He wandered towards the place where Byron had sat the night through in typical upright fashion, against an old tree. As expected, Ogwold was alone among the whispering dark trees. A man like that simply does not sleep, he thought, wandering through the tall spiny trees looking for the mercenary, eager to see what was his business before sunrise. It was some time before he came upon the man at last in a small clearing lit faintly in the dark dawn.

There he stood in a wide stance, one leg pointed back almost directly opposite his countenance of utmost focus, the other bent before him low and square over the ball of his foot. Sweat poured from his grim brow, and he heaved with breath. He held his sword out before him level with the grass, both hands gripping the hilt, one elbow cocked to his low ear. Slowly the weapon rose high above his head like a metal steeple. Then he swung the length of it powerfully down, the grass rippling as it instantly paused, suddenly and perfectly parallel with the ground once more. A rush of wind blew through the clearing. The man exhaled as in great exhaustion, tore air back into his nostrils grunting.

Ogwold had not seen much of Byron's sword, apart from its use in Occultash; but then it had been dark and the rain had made all things bleary to the eyes. Now in the sun unsheathed he realized how huge the thing was. It was far more proportional to Nogofod hands than Novare. The blade of the weapon was certainly no masterpiece, and appeared incredibly thick and heavy. It looked, in fact, much like the blade of his father, though smaller. But crude as the weapon was, in Byron's hand it seemed a light and deadly force.

The ogre stood watching for some time, unsure if he was noticed. The mercenary must have completed fifty such maximum effort swings before Ogwold spoke up. "What are you doing?"

The man turned, and seamlessly sheathed the blade along his back. "Training."

"To fight the wind?"

Byron's complexion did not change. "Let's continue. I have waited for you."

"Are you sure you can hike as long today? You slew those guards with far less effort than you've put in this morning." Now the ogre was hardly trying to hold back his enthusiasm, but it did not seem to repel the mercenary any more than normal conversation.

Byron shut his eye disdainfully. "This is my practice."

"Then you are terribly strong," said Ogwold. "I can hardly keep up with you, yet you expend more energy in one morning than I do in a day!"

"Doubtful."

Wind rushed through the trees, and a black hawk winged from a high branch. The first pale rays of sun slipped along its glossy feathers as it transcended the canopy.

"I can't stop thinking about that night," said Ogwold, watching it go. "I would have surely perished if you had not come. And, I am forever grateful, will do whatever I can to repay you, but I see it all in the worst way. Those Novare— what lives had they? The blood. The speed of death. The cruel ugliness of finality. I could never participate in something like that. You kill as though it is second nature. And here you are practising to kill! You must enjoy it.”

Byron crossed his arms, green orb reopening in his scarred visage. “You are a fool to seek Zenidow without a means of defence. Our path can only be more fell, especially if you go with me.” Ogwold was silent, staring at the grass. The mercenary sighed, looked down, then up into the grey sky latticed with dark branches. “You wish to repay me?”

“Yes, sir,” said Ogwold, stunned.

“Call me by name,” Byron spat into the grass. “I concede that it is well to have companions on this road. But as much as I love a fight, it would be far easier if I didn’t need to worry about you.”

“You worry about me?”

The mercenary stared back, a muscle in his face twitching. “I never worry. But I agreed to your company. A good soldier gives a good word.” Byron looked away as though the sincerity of the listening ogre was far too much to bear. “If you can rise so early, then you can train without hindering our progress. Let it be your payment. Already you are a formidable force to men. I’ll teach you to use that force. Here is my first advice. Beautiful as it is, leave your sword where it lies, and use that arm of yours in battle.”

Ogwold held up his green hand awkwardly, so moved by the unprecedented stream of words as it came from the mercenary’s narrow mouth. “I doubt this plant has the power to harm,” he said. “It protected me from their spears, but it is a kindly thing. I feel what it feels, you know. It wants soil and drinks light and water. It hasn’t violence in it; and neither do I, come to think of it.”

“Come, raise it against me!” Byron drew his sword with a ring of metal, and its dull length was dark in the sun. “Prove yourself, ogre!” The mercenary spoke loudly and with a fire that seemed to roar from nowhere.

Ogwold’s heart stirred with respect for the man. Had that sense of veneration come, he wondered, from the rain-wet night in Occultash, or was it something else? Gathering the honour he felt under the man’s rough attention, he held out his arm and drew his fingers together into a tight fist. Feelings of toughness and of strength and sharp edges grew in his chest and bloomed through his bones as he pictured his father’s blade unsheathed.

“Ha!” Byron shouted, and with a loud thunk he sank his bare blade into the ogre’s arm.

“Caelare! What did you... but...” The blade had barely embedded in the strange plant-flesh. Only an edgeless throb followed the impact. Even as the metal withdrew, the green matter knitted quickly together and was whole. Fastened and hard the substance of the thing seemed healthier and more vigorous than ever before.

"See. It is tougher than you know. Now sharpen it!"

"What if you had cut it off!"

"Maybe I will if you don't ready yourself."

Ogwold had not seen Byron so agitated before, even when he was battling the knights of Occultash. Inspired to earn the man's trust, he focused all his thoughts upon the green flesh and the roots within his body and mind, willing a vision of the plant morphing and changing, the way it had when it grew suddenly in the presence of the sphere, the way he sensed its reaching into the water and rock of the world to drink, the way his fingers had so smoothly paired from ten into five. As naturally as gooseflesh forms on the chilled skin, a sharp edge rippled from elbow to wrist, now reared up from the skin extending parallel to the forearm in a long, lean, slender shoot, sharply pointed. When Ogwold opened his eyes he saw that all of his arm from elbow beyond had transformed into a curved, rich green blade near the size of Byron's own greatsword.

"Now attack," said Byron, and he smiled. It was the first that he had made an expression involving any features other than his green eye, and Ogwold took to it with vigour. He swung the plant-blade out and down with a shout, though he quite held back for fear of hurting the man. Scoffing, Byron parried easily, and at such an angle that his attacker was flung by his own momentum face-first into the grass while the mercenary stepped casually aside. The ogre sprawled there wheezing, looking quite ridiculous for all his massive size.

"That was pathetic," said Byron.

Ogwold grinned and slowly staggered onto his feet. He was covered in sod and dirt but his big flat teeth seemed all the whiter. Then he really swung, throwing his new weapon up, down, side to side, and each time as Byron effortlessly turned the blow away he returned with even greater force, thinking that it might as well be impossible to strike the man. Soon he was swinging nearly as hard as he was able, which for even a feeble Nogofod was enough to kill a man on impact. The clanging noises which rang from the subtle economy of Byron's parries shook the wood and sent the birds from their trees to fly about restlessly. He guided each strike away with ease, smiling only when the ferocity behind them had at least reached a degree of mortal danger. Battle was his place, and now between the ogre and the man a kind of silent communion took form.

Ogwold was forced to stop from exhaustion, and he sat heavily in the grass panting. "You are incredibly skilled!" he said. "I could never hit you."

"Your blows are mighty. If you were to strike me I would surely die. But you overextend yourself. Stay your ground and let your opponent come to you. I don't doubt you will be a tough match for even a knight. Though, we may encounter stranger folk in these mountains. The best way to learn is from fighting." Byron sheathed his sword, complexion already beginning to stiffen as if to compensate for having spoken so many words in one breath.

A silence fell between them, and in that peace Videre appeared softly from the shade. She rubbed against Ogwold's head; he flopped back supine, looking into the sky, then her face as she glowered over him, mewing and dragging her rough tongue along his cheek. Reaching up to scratch her great neck, he realized that his arm had returned to a more presentable shape as naturally as he'd willed it to move.

Before noon they pushed out from the rocky forest and up onto a slow grade exposed to the chill wind. The pale sun spun high, and cast the long shadows of mountains as it carried on. It was a grey day, the grass mud-thick and spongy as they tramped. They reached the apex of a great, bald wold, and began their descent along its stone-pocked back as purpling night fell around them. At the dusky foot of the slope, old feathery glaucous trees rose up and took them in with sweeping arms. Densely leaved, long-reaching branches enshrined a dry nook, the crepitating of whose carpet only ceased when all had settled into their positions of slumber. Delicate clusterings of light blue snakes coiled about the roots of this tree, and though they slithered away when first the big people arrived, later, when Ogwold awoke, they were snuggled up against his warm body.

Only the most rare shreds of dawn light shimmered on the dewy grass or flared on the fine edges of the utmost boughs. His green arm had snuck deep into the soil unfolding as an invisible brain beneath the imbricating layers of leaves, but the business of withdrawing those far-reaching tendrils one to the other, now up to the world of light and air was even easier than before; as easy, really, as raising either arm. Looking down at the limb formed anew, its rough yet tender palm so touched with the Nogofod form, Ogwold breathed in the dreams and discoveries of the night which came to him from below the ground. Not only had it become easier to speak with his new companion, but as well they began at last to share their feelings, if only as in a pre-linguistic phantasmagoria of impressions.

There had been the burrows of small furry animals, the veins of subterranean waters, the echoes of nearby bodies frail and strong plodding atop or working into the soil, splitting the rock. The skitter of insects clicked and whispered in the finest airy spaces; the wriggling of strong-bodied worms sent waves of sight through the blind deeps. There was even the ripple of Byron rising from his seat against the back of this very tree, though when it had occurred the plant could not say, so awash was it in the simultaneous sensations of its liberty during the ogre's sleep.

Reminded then of the mercenary's morning ritual, Ogwold followed the map of emanations which came to him through the plant so entwined with his consciousness. And surely there was Byron, standing at the terminus of that silvery aural path of memory, hard at work swinging his sword. It seemed as though he'd practised a thousand slashes already, for his breath was ragged and his arms seemed even to shake as he spat away the sweat which fell from his nose and brow.

As before, Ogwold at first could only watch, fascinated with the display of determination and self-control. Only the mercenary's arms and shoulders seemed to move as he swung, his legs stalwart to their chosen technique and his back like a sinew of metal. Each swing of the sword blew up a rushing whorl of dry leaves that swirled and fell in delicate gatherings all about the clearing, only to be swept up again by the next strike. The man's green eye rolled to the side and—like a bird of prey sights its prize from afar—connected with Ogwold's stupid gawking.

"You're late," said Byron, relaxing his posture and turning round.

Ogwold could not help but grin, tired of pretending to be so stoic and cool as the mercenary, and so pleased by the notion that he was even expected. Not with the same ease as he had extricated his arm from the soil, but certainly with an increasing dimension of understanding, he formed his green arm into the shape of a sword, straighter and more stout than before, though he figured—looking at it with surprise, for he had not exactly willed any specific design—this sort of weapon seemed easier to wield.

"You are not ready to spar," said Byron. "When I have reason to rebut your attacks, I will."

"I'll do my best!" Ogwold said swinging the verdant edge of his arm. It was turned away as another leaf in the wind, though this time—lunging and exposed as he was—the ogre stopped himself from falling. As before, Byron parried Ogwold as he far less gracefully delivered his heavy and awkward blows, eventually losing his balance, swinging to madly as he grew tired and careless, collapsing upon his face, now his back, laughing like a fool in the grass as Videre appeared and savagely licked his big cheeks. She had watched all the while, her curious great head tilted, lucid black eyes following each exchange, containing yet missing nothing.

Now the road cut up and along the hipbone of an enormous mountain, far larger than those such as even titanic Shadith they had brushed with earlier. Its height disappeared into a ceiling of grey clouds, only which parted in brief pockets to reveal a dizzying succession of crags that seemed to have no end. They made almost no progress, it seemed, by night, and camped still among great dark trees which grew on the massive shelves of land.

In the morning they trained for several hours in total darkness but for the light of the sphere hovering near to them, for this time Ogwold woke partly with excitement to try his hand at Byron again, and partly to catch the mercenary sleeping. But Byron was already up and hard at work. How long in the morning he trained, Ogwold did not know, and never knew truly, but it crossed his mind often that Byron simply did not rest.

Afterwards they hiked quite far, yet still the trees were thick. Now they were running disastrously low on provisions. Byron slew a red-tailed vosca, which he found it seemed at once, leaving the trail while Ogwold waited with Videre, whose own meal showed in the spattering of blood upon her long snout. Byron seemed also a skilled hunter, for he returned with his prey already deftly skinned, cleaned, slung over his wiry shoulder. He roasted it against a simple fire as the dusk came on them.

He held out a portion for Ogwold, who'd been sitting like a gigantic lumpy boulder, hugging his knees opposite Byron over the flames, but the ogre hung his head even further. "I don't eat meat," he said.

The habitually lowered eyebrow of Byron's empty socket twitched.

"What?" Ogwold tilted his head, confused.

"You're an ogre," said the mercenary flatly.

"Nogofod only eat fruit. I haven't seen any that I recognize. I saw a malevolent looking red thing the other day. Perhaps it was quite nutritious. I couldn't bring myself to touch it though. Does the map say anything about local flora?"

"You can't just try some meat? You'll feel better if you do."

Ogwold peered over at the cooked flesh. He shuddered. "It wouldn't stay down," he said faintly.

"Xeléd," Byron muttered. "What a stubborn race." He popped the meat into his mouth and chewed aggressively.

"What is Xeléd?"

"Oh. It's a moon. That one." Byron jabbed a finger up into the sky. Framed in the dark branches of the night was a powerfully bright crescent of electric blue.

"That's Mutat," said Ogwold. "The Moon of Change."

"You know the Lucetalian name. It is called Xeléd by the Xol. The significance of it is very different in their culture, but still they conflate it with transformation in many ways. Some say that the spirits of the moons are beyond the divides of language."

Ogwold had heard of the Xol only in passing, and never from Nogofod lips; even Ogdof had but a snippet or two to divulge, and naught that he said uplifted or denigrated that race. Only the guards ever really used the word, and always bitterly, often spitting into the grey sand as they uttered so nefandous a syllable to them. He knew at least that the Xol lived in huge, black trees and had purple skin and many tails; and, of course, he knew that they practised black magic. To the Lucetalians, they were demons. But his green arm was easily the same sort of evil thing in Wog's eyes. And what was Nubes to men?

He looked up at Byron wanting to learn more, for here was a man who could answer such questions as pertained to the mysterious natives of Efvla, but also here was that familiar feeling that he'd overwhelmed the usually silent man with questions. It was already miraculous how talkative the mercenary was this evening.

Byron stared back, swallowed methodically. "I once lived among the Xol," he said presciently. "They are similar to Novare in many ways, though they have an innate connection with Xeléd. The one I'm looking for—he is Xol."

Ogwold tried to imagine the Xol as he often had before, but now instead of purple devils crawling out from insidious boles he saw rather a more elfin Nubes nimbly running branch to branch. He tried to impose upon this fey character the visage of the old wizard in the moment of his most grave severity, but he could only smile thinking how quickly that look might dissolve into whimsy. What might his tails get up to!

Time passed and the secret choirs of insects chirped madly as they listened to the crackling fire. Videre began to snore loudly, jowls flapping against wet gums. Aborjays and foreign night birds shrieked distantly and cawed in the heights. Cool winds hissed through the dry grass. Ogwold's stomach chimed in with so horrible a gurgling that he grinned like a sad idiot.

"I see light," said Byron, whose shadowed face had leaned out into the forest for some time. He pointed down among the thick trees, clinging to the side of the mountain, and there in a kind of natural bowl in the land Ogwold could see the fickle aura of flame.

His stomach rumbled even louder. "Maybe they know something about mountain fruit?"

Byron glared at him. "I'd not suspect hospitality for a pair such as us coming out of the night." Seeing that Ogwold submitted even as he spoke, hanging his head like an infant chided, Byron ground his teeth and said, "But we can try." The ogre's head popped up eagerly, grey eyes shining.

Byron scooted in from the dark with a fallen bough and fashioned a torch from their fire. Off they trundled loudly through the black brush, leaving the trail. Videre seamlessly awoke and followed them down through the trees. As the pulsing yellow grew in each its coruscations they found that it darted from the warm mouth of a great cave. Byron motioned for silence and entered first, passing so easy and low on his long legs that Ogwold shivered to think what men had fallen to that stealthy prowl. Though, something told him that Byron was not one to attack his foes from behind.

Inside was a great dig site, but even the untrained eye could see that the discovery of minerals was not the primary objective here. Wooden stairs and walkways were built all throughout the cavern in a many-storied network, many of these structures encapsulating at various levels raised tables of rock which seemed to have been very carefully carved out of the land. All about were crates of seemingly valueless stone packed very carefully together. At the far back of the chamber squatted a cluster of low, windowless wooden structures. Opening with dissimilar size all around and high above these little shacks stretched a smattering of odious, ink-dark tunnels, all seeming in the feeble light which trespassed their thresholds to turn straight up like natural slides.

Two Novare in the centre of the cave stood upon the rickety scaffolding and bent painstakingly over the top of one skinny rock-table, looking like a chthonic thumb sculpted out of the solid cavern floor. The men brushed away at its surface with little bristled things and picked gently at the finest debris. All of these minute, feverish movements were conducted with immense anxiety.

"Ho there!" Byron called out.

The men spun around and their eyes gleamed rodent-like from the shadow of their hunched work, but presently they straightened. They wore floppy flat-brimmed hats and extremely tarnished tunics too streaked with dirt to bear their true colours. From their leather belts hung a vast array of strange and specialized metal tools. Their awkward boots seemed far too large for either of them.

"Hello!" ululated the first who had turned in a surprisingly welcoming tone. "What's your business, swordsman?"

Activated by the friendliness of the hollering voice, Ogwold lumbered suddenly into the light like an enormous yellow-orange beast, his great white cloak blazing with the flames of the hearty torches, and his booming voice ballooned in the cavern. "Do you have any fruit?"

Byron shut his eye angrily, jerking his chin towards the night. "He means— what is edible out there?"

"Caelare eclipsed, it's an ogre!" loudly whispered the second, shorter man, adjusting a glinting pair of huge spectacles. His voice was not at all amicable and issued in a leathery, nasal stream of anxiety. "Tep, lookit those bones!"

The warm-voiced man laughed and patted the first on the back as he called over affably. "We've some drel berries to spare, but you must stay awhile. My brother and I have never seen one of the Nogofod before."

The diggers padded confidently along the precarious catwalk, and stepped onto the rock, approaching the entrance of the cave. Now Ogwold and Byron could see that they were middle-aged, black-bearded and certainly as beady-eyed as they'd appeared from a distance, the squat one with his ill-fitting glasses, the tall other with enormous ears and his grand smile.

"I am Teperchael," said the large-eared man. "And this is my brother Tinjus."

"Ain't no fruit won't poison you round here. Best you eat meat." The man with the glasses doffed his voluminous hat, shedding a curtain of dirt. "We've some of that too. Please. Stay." His eyes flashed blackly and he seemed to sniff at the air like some enormous rat.

"We are archaeologists. This is our dig." Teperchael said the word 'dig' with affected awe, seeming even to step partly in front of the unnerving Tinjus.

"I don't eat meat," said Ogwold sadly. "You said something about berries?"

"Yes! We love berries. I know little of mountain ecology, so we brought our own drel seeds with us long ago and keep a small garden here. You're welcome to them but we'd really appreciate some company." Tinjus nodded greedily as Teperchael spoke. "You see, being students of nature we are deeply honoured to encounter a creature of your exquisite genetics."

"Oh now," said Tinjus, adjusting his glasses and staring past Ogwold. "What's that fine specimen?" His constantly flitting eyes had noticed Videre who—as soon as she had crossed the threshold of the cave—had edged back into the darkness, the hair on her back standing jagged and hard, her eyes like black suns.

"That is Videre, our companion," said Ogwold, glozing over her tensity as she backed into the night like a white phantom of apprehension.

"Ah... of course," said Tinjus, and it seemed almost that he smacked his lips. "What is it?"

"Two new creatures for you to see then," said Byron shortly. "Now let's buy some berries and be off. I don't like the smell of this place Ogwold, and neither does Videre."

"Oh you needn't pay us, good swordsman. We haven't seen a fellow Novare in many years either. Aren't you interested in our findings?" Teperchael swept his arm out into the cave. "You've no idea what ancient creatures used to walk the mountains. We've discovered the bones of organisms that haven't drawn breath in millions of years."

"Well now that is interesting," said Ogwold, smitten. Byron glared at him.

"How about some berries then, and I'll show you around in the morning? It's getting quite late for us." Teperchael had gripped one dusty glove into the low shoulder of his brother who had all but yelped, though he said nothing now, and they were spared the awful tone of his speech.

Ogwold looked over to Byron expectantly. "Fine then," said the mercenary. "We leave at dawn." Promptly he went and sat up against the cave wall beside the entrance, arms crossed, eye shut, sword across his lap.

Tinjus brought out the berries in a large dirty jar, his small black eyes lively and darting about, though he didn't seem interested at all in eating. They were small and grainy morsels with little blue stems that reminded Ogwold of the tutum in a way, though the flesh of their fruit was a sallow and sickly colour. Still, the bitter taste was wholesome and refreshing, and he devoured them in great handfuls which their growers assured him was quite all right, for they rarely ate the berries and cultivated their bushes more as a way to remember their homeland.

Ever since the first camp of delvers which they'd passed so publicly unabated, Ogwold had been practically bursting to speak with other Novare that might not despise him. As his hands and lips grew stained yellow with drel juice he grew more relaxed and talkative. He shared with Teperchael and Tinjus stories from Epherem and the ways of the Nogofod, that race about which they probed him incessantly for the physical characteristics and livelihoods of. They swooned at talk of wrestling, leaned in obsessively as he described a day of work, tittered manically at the nuances of sexual dimorphism. Often they questioned him about his strange hand which appeared from the white sleeve, but he explained that this was no typical characteristic of his people. When he spoke of the sea serpent they listened in awe.

Never before had any Novare given the ogre such a stage upon which to speak, and never before had any but Byron truly listened to him. They seemed so carefree and easygoing compared to all other Novare that the ogre had met, such that Ogwold described his fear at being so different, and how his race was persecuted by the men of Lucetal and Occultash.

"Don't worry 'bout that," said Tinjus unctuously. "Miners are only for metal."

"And we're only for bones," Teperchael interjected. "Fossils really. The museum at Occultash pays handsomely for even the slightest trace of anything before the dawn of Novare."

"Like what?" Ogwold asked.

"All sorts of things, but the most interesting we've yet to unearth." Tinjus laughed greasily. "It's hard work, and these mountains are more dangerous than you could know." His eyes shimmered cryptically as they flicked off into and along the strange black holes that lined the wall. "For the good stuff, the stuff way down deep in the dark... certain sacrifices are made."

Teperchael cut in quite nervously. "You should see the specimens they have in the city. These mountains used to be full up with these gigantic lizards." He drew out his arms wide as they would go. "And that's just the width of the head! They've one skeleton put together, not all of it mind you but quite a bit, that's near twenty feet tall on its hind legs!"

"Such a find is but a dream for us," said Tinjus slapping a hand down upon Ogwold's massive arm which seemed almost to grip the flesh with a sense of appraisal.

"Ah but, I think I've found something even older," Teperchael breathed. "Wait until you see this, Ogwold." Quickly the archaeologist scampered off and over the ledge down into the deeps of the dig. His floppy ears were the first to reappear as he climbed back out, and under his arm was a dusty but nonetheless uncommonly shiny object.

"Yes, yes," muttered Tinjus as his companion approached. "He has many theories on the thing, but as for its age it can't be as old as he thinks."

Teperchael placed the object carefully before Ogwold, and sat in reverence beside it, wiping it tenderly with a dirty cloth. Smooth and metal in form, it was shaped very much like a helmet, but nothing like those he had seen upon the heads of the knights of Lucetal. For one thing, it was unadorned, and the quality of its material far finer than any ore to his knowledge. Most peculiar in substance was the visor, which he could only compare with glass, though when Teperchael winked and rapped upon its thin, transparent surface, it emitted no such familiar noise.

"This headwear," said Teperchael, "is, I think, at least one billion years old."

Ogwold could not help but laugh. "But it is shinier than my friend's sword!" Tinjus nodded in agreement, though his eyes were glossed over with rapture at the sheer sight of the artifact, and it seemed that its value to him differed greatly than for Teperchael.

"Ah, but watch." Teperchael placed the helmet onto his head.

"And see, it fits you!" Ogwold leaned in. "Novare heads can't have existed a billion years ago!" But he stopped speaking quickly, and his jaw fell, for the visor of the helmet had lit up with bright, neon blue light, such that Teperchael's features were replaced with a field of alien energy.

"It's magical, obviously," said Tinjus. "Some knight's gear enchanted by some old art."

Teperchael removed the helmet and at once the queer electric light diminished from its face. "No, no, it's not magical. It's merely... advanced. Far more advanced than anything upon Altum today. My theory is that long ago there was a different civilization in this land, whose technology had far surpassed all else in the Cosmos. Something terrible must have happened, however; my personal hypothesis is that some celestial body crashed into the world and extinguished their entire species. Things like this," he wiped the helmet again for good measure, gazing upon it fondly, "are the last remnants of their time."

"That's... fascinating," murmured Ogwold.

"It's a nice idea," said Tinjus wetly, "but apart from the extinction event, it's only speculation, and even that theory rides on a sparse fossil record and a layer of unknown minerals which he's unjustly concluded are from beyond. How about we show you some fossils that you can really understand?" He smiled almost cruelly. "And don't be a stranger. You ain't nowhere near as queer as the folk came through here a season ago."

"Oh yes," Teperchael said with a burst of enthusiasm. "They were somethin' else! Scary too. Six or seven of them I think, all in black robes, with different coloured hemming. Didn't say a word, none of em, except for this real old fella. He was a riot! Told me all sorts of things about these caverns. He just loved poking around, though it made me nervous, I won't lie. We're awful protective of our dig, you see." Again he pronounced the word 'dig' with strange majesty. "You best not be wandering off in the night. Go too deep into these caves and you might get right lost."

"He found an old skull too, but let us keep it, the old fool," said Tinjus wetly. "Ah, if only they had stayed. We could've dug so much deeper."

"Oh, were they good at digging?" asked Ogwold.

Both men gave the ogre an exceedingly odd look, even Teperchael losing the warmth of his manner which had been so soothing the whole while, and Ogwold felt for a moment very alone.

"Did they take the high road?" Byron had appeared just inside the firelight, staring coldly at Teperchael.

"Oh! Uhm. Yes, they did. The high road, just above this cave, yes."

"Were they Novare?" Byron scowled.

Tinjus coughed hideously before speaking. "Well. This old man, you see, his skin was purple. And his eyes were... different. He had two tails."

"At least another one of them wasn't too, you can be sure of that. They were covered head to toe, but one of them had her hood off. Her skin was purple, and she had short white hair like a man, but it was dark and I kept my distance."

"The others wouldn't come in," murmured Tinjus, his rat's eyes gleaming vacantly. It seemed that Teperchael glared at him, though it was hard to tell beneath the huge shadow of his hat-brim.

Byron nodded, turned and went to sit against the wall again.

"Strange one, isn't he," said Teperchael.

"Oh he means well," said Ogwold grinning. "He's just not a conversationalist really. Keeps to himself."

"Right, well." Teperchael gripped his brother's shoulder tightly once again. Then he stood with the strange bright helmet under his arm, and his countenance was oddly distant. "It's time we went to sleep." He gestured at a pile of animal hides in the far corner of the cave. "Help yourself to those skins for bedding, and give some to your friend there. We've a little hideout underneath the boards where we sleep."

Already Teperchael was making his way to the edge of a deep pit from which one tall table of scaffold rock rose, and clambered down a ladder out of sight. His eyes looked odd and dark for all his amiability as he descended, and it seemed many times that they darted over the strange black holes along the wall.

"Holler if you need us." With a tip of his floppy hat Tinjus winked, looking conversely enthusiastic, and waddled off to join his brother.

CHAPTER XVIII
HIVE OF THE EYELESS

gwold awoke in darkness. His head seared with pain, blind somnolence suffocated his senses, and his stomach was a ball of stone. The air was dank and stale, touched with the sounds of some dripping and oozing nameless fluid. Feeling around on the stone floor, his hand brushed against cloth, now solid flesh. He scooted over to the man lying in the black and shook him gently, but it did not take much.

The voice which arose from the dark was ragged and broken. "I hope you enjoyed those berries."

"What happened?" said the ogre, kneading his pulsing skull.

The mercenary seemed to have sat up, in which position he coughed up some spattering of invisible fluid. "You passed out in a bad way." He breathed slowly for a moment, hacked up another flow. "I failed us. There were too many."

"Too many what?"

"No idea. Monsters. Hundreds of them everywhere. Came out of the tunnels, the entrance, every crack in the rock as soon as you were out. Those bastard delvers were nowhere to be seen." Byron coughed, groaned. "They wanted us alive."

Ogwold shivered, feeling an immense blackness all around them here in this tiny chamber. "Where is Videre?"

Byron winced. "We should have left as soon as we saw she wouldn't enter the cave. She could have escaped easily, but when the danger was on us she stood by my side. She was still fighting when I joined you in unconsciousness."

"Videre," said Ogwold groggily, his shoulders falling forward in invisible shame, though the tone of his misery was clear enough. "I am sorry. There's no excuse. I was hungry and well, it's not only that; I just, I've never met any Novare that were actually interested in talking to me. I know it sounds silly, but my people are like animals to most men."

The mercenary spat another torrent of fluid. "What about me?"

Ogwold was silent, as if to point out that Byron was only ever interested in fighting. The mercenary sighed. "Look. It's fine. I should have forced us out of there. And…" The ogre could feel that green eye on him in the darkness. "Never mind. Let's get out of this pit."

Videre was indeed nowhere to be found. Their bags also seemed to be gone, and both of their swords. They were still clad, and Ogwold pulled his father's cloak tightly around him to break the damp, subterranean air. In this motion of gathering together what few things were left, he found the sphere still in his possession. It was actually tightly held in his hand, and may have been for quite a long time. The invariable heat and drone brought certainty and safety to him in this blackness. He opened his hand, and a pale light bloomed around them in the cell, unflickering, pure and faultless as ever, emanating from the sphere changelessly. The little thing floated as a lone star in an uncompromising night, humming and spinning in place. Now they could see a little ways beyond the dirty cell bars, into a stiflingly low-ceilinged chamber where there were only oddly shaped formations of rock and—further on—more inky darkness.

The pale glow washed over Byron slumped against the dissimilar wall beside the bars, and Ogwold gasped, for the man was caked in blood. Deep cuts split his brow, tore through the lips horribly, oozing black bile, and from his open-hanging mouth beaded a constant stream of fluid. Tattered and lying open as was his black cloak, along the thin leather of his chest piece revealed was a single ragged and clotted slash running shoulder to hip which appeared to have only recently stopped bleeding. His posture was so contorted with unease as to appear nothing like the warrior from before if not for that one green eye, hardly opened, radiating a miasma of bruising—that emerald ray had still its composure and indefatigable intensity. It was that look, not of pain, but almost of awe that caused the ogre to turn and face the back wall of their cell.

There dangled insidiously an abominable thing in the half-light. It was a grotesque, veinated sack hanging pendulous from the ceiling, oozing foul phlegm onto the ground with soft spattering noises that they now realized were not coming from the deeps of the caves, but from right beside them. The disgusting fluid had even now slopped close to Ogwold's seat such that he scrambled oafishly away and pressed his back against the cold bars. The sphere hovered over almost curiously, greeted by a muted gurgling; then there began a troubling swelling and twitching. The undulating surface suddenly ruptured, and a thin, pale limb extruded from the slime that poured forthwith, lunging and strafing, now gripping the membrane encasing the whole glob of the sac and peeling it away. An awful burbling gibbering came from within the mess, and a loathsome open maw made its egress, heaving in its first rattling, gasping breath. When it exhaled at last the cell was filled with the fetid stink of an open grave.

Groaning Byron rose into a crouch, blood sloshing down his trunk and smacking the floor, and he was forced to place his palms against that surface as he coughed up more fluid. Slowly he gathered himself, sucked in a long, savage breath, and rushed the hideous creature as it was born. He reached right into the tattered cocoon and grappled elbow deep with its evolving contents. The slippery limb seized violently, toothless mouth opened and closed breathlessly. Desperately a second head breached, hoarsely whispering from the miasma, and it too had a mouth which gulped up the dank air. Byron's eye was a fierce green in the light as he attached his other hand to the new neck, and there he stood quaking, gritting his teeth, fresh blood seeping up from his wounds, spattering the stone as the maws strained for breath. Disgusting bile and sludge spilled endlessly against his chest and splashed over his quaking shoulders so that he was soaked in sick. At last the creatures ceased to live, and Byron flung their smothered throats back into the tattered albumen viscera.

"Well this is poor luck." He turned, smiling in the ghostly light, one hand clutched over his now gushing chest wound. It was the second time Ogwold had seen the man smile, yet it was a different and not quite calming smile to have seen. Now in the belly of forsaken darkness an angry joy seemed to rage behind the mercenary's complexion. The light in the eye of the training Byron was brought on by the sense of adventure, but now Ogwold saw that such was but a shadow of the true awesome love for combat that lived in this man. It was the inescapable danger of their situation that brightened his companion's spirit. Perhaps there was truly nothing he craved more than a fight to the death.

But all at once the furious joy was gone. The man collapsed onto the slime-thick ground, and a pool of dark blood spread out around him. "Byron!" Ogwold moved to him as quickly as one so massive may in a place so cramped. He turned the mercenary over to free his face from the sick, and listened to his breathing. The sphere lowered its light, illuminating the horrible gash. As if by instinct Ogwold placed his greener hand over the wound, but seeing it there, feeling the flow of life leaving Byron so clearly, he recalled that the first identity of his new arm had been that of a miraculous healer. The first sensation he had felt in its presence was that of pain being drunk and the flow of blood being stemmed. He reached out to the fibres of the plant with his heart and mind and envisioned the blood slowly ceasing to run, pictured the wound closing up, imagined that he and the plant and the mercenary were for this time one growing and living entity. Even he dreamed out of panic and respect for the man that the plant left his own shoulder and became rather a gift to the mercenary.

As this thought transformed through his spirit into the plant and achieved synthesis with the flesh of Byron—or so he dreamed was the case—there entered his consciousness a new energy, not like the plant and certainly unlike his own. His visions of surging green fibres and deep-seeking roots converged and swelled into a great hill of rushing grass, and he saw upon its moonlit crest a vigilant, gaunt wolf made of smokeless fire. Haggard but tireless, infinitely wrathful yet completely devoted, it was a horrifying but awesome impression, as one might suffer standing before a flow of lava, so beautiful and captivating yet so inexorably destroying everything in its path. And yet for so powerful and exquisite a thing it was totally alone, one wolf, one flame, lost in one endless night. It howled, broken and tired, and no one but Ogwold could hear. So it was that he did not shy from this solemn predator he seemed now to have reached like some deep and brutally sheltered truth. Instead he only reached more fully, more compassionately out to hold and provide for it, to help it grow one day into a raging lupine flame. Whatever it was that this flow of fire, this undying hunter strove to kill, Ogwold felt in this moment that it was not in the name of evil.

"Can you bend those bars?" came the sudden voice of the mercenary.

The vision dissolved into ribbons of black and grey, now silvery light such as beat against his eyelids from the sphere. Now Ogwold dared open his eyes, and saw that the great plant had already begun to smoothly retreat and detach itself from the man. As this motion folded back upon itself into the form of a Nogofod hand, he saw that certain tendrils had sought out other injuries throughout the body and now returned from their own businesses there. At last he held his reformed hand up in the light whole and new, separated from Byron, who sat up partly in the light, stared at Ogwold, now the green hand, down at his wounds which had sealed and scarred over in such a brief period of time. Then he jerked his chin towards the cell door, seeming certainly well recovered as he said with renewed vigour, "I appreciate the hand. But there'll be time for thanks once we're out of here. The bars, ogre. Break them."

"Byron." Ogwold yet held his hand up as if he held yet in its green palm that brief connection with the remotest feelings of the mercenary, that last understanding of indomitable virtue in a storm of death, the wolf on the hill. Killing, he thought; was it really so unnatural? He looked back to the mutilated mess of flesh. "Those were babies."

"Imagine what the adults are like," Byron grunted severely, sitting up against the wall and folding his arms. He seemed quite well recovered. "Why do you think we were kept alive and locked up in a room with these monstrous eggs, eh?"

"But... they didn't even have a chance."

"This isn't the time for chance." The mercenary glowered in the silvery light, and the grin which he'd worn while throttling the gasping creatures returned.

Ogwold shuffled on his knees and firmly planted his massive hands around two of the argent bars. With the stink behind him it was easier to breathe, but it was not like the cavern air was any good either, and still the incessant gentle bursting and pooling of the dissolving pods continued. He pulled mightily, and there was even a deep-seated groaning in the metal; fine dust and dirt fell from the ceiling, but that was all. He paused and sought his greener limb, envisioning the trunk of a great and powerful tree which he had seen on their journey, casting out its imagined roots round the bars. Behind him Byron watched, grinning openly now as the ogre's shoulder swelled and swallowed up the entirety of the cell door, hardening like a cast of cement, now constricting with unyielding pressure. There was a loud warping, twisting screech and the entire wall of metal splintered and dissolved in a storm of rust.

Byron stole past him into the dark tunnel on his long legs low and lithe like a predator in the night. Even before he willed it, Ogwold's arm smoothly slunk hissing back to its original shape. He had not even pulled again at the bars; merely the thought of squeezing them did the work. It seemed that with each transformation he willed in the limb their congress became more easy and natural. He flexed the hand that was formed anew from the grasping, thick mess of vines and roots that had only moments before issued as from his bones. In the strength of its action he felt the echo, the scar of the smokeless wolf that was Byron now imprinted in the texture of this limb which was now a shield, guardian, guide, spirit—and weapon. Surely he must turn it upon the monsters if they were to escape. The pale light began to recede from the striations and pores of the alien flesh so uncannily his own, and quickly he lumbered after Byron whom the sphere followed more closely.

"Quiet," grunted the mercenary, turning and grimacing.

Ogwold's massive feet were a racket in the still subterranean air. Even beyond the cell he was forced to crouch incredibly low, and he began to feel that the walls would close around him and trap him forever. They took a bend, and looked into a low-ceilinged stone room. There was a sad, flat surface hewn from the rock in the centre, and their bags lay there, which they took, but no swords could be found. There was only one way out of the room, an even tighter passageway, and they went along this narrow hall in the light from the sphere.

They passed many other cells then, also barred, in ranks both vertical and horizontal like the pores of a honeycomb. Inside of them each there was in the deep shadowed corner one, sometimes two of the foul egg-sacs. Many such odious little pockets in the rock contained only the remains of these fleshy cocoons like the huge peels of some abominable fruit, and they saw that in these cases the doors were opened, and the creatures must have gone out, full up with their first meal. Ogwold shuddered to think that they might not have awoken when they did, or that he might have been alone and faced with the moral quandary which for Byron posed so simple and seemingly righteous a solution.

At the end of the hall of feeding cells they passed through an archway into a room where at last Ogwold could stand up straight, but here they stopped at once. Inside were, presumably, their capturers, huddled around each other in a tight circle, all panting heavily and wetly snorting. They seemed completely dormant if not for their frenetic breathing. Ogwold quickly snatched the sphere out of the way and obscured its light, but Byron took his hand and opened the fingers slowly. The light returned, and the eyeless creatures were none the wiser.

Ogwold had heard stories about the insidious Krug, so were called the blind mutants said to live within the mountains themselves. His father had called them the true ogres of the world, hideous trolls that mashed entire Novare in their limitless jaws. But these creatures were not so large as they were strange, for there was little about their appearance that seemed necessary for survival. Ogwold knew that the Nogofod were large because they had always lifted heavy things, but for what reasons should these creatures have two heads; why should their skin be translucent, so that all their skeleton and foul black organs were palely seen; why should they have seemingly helpless extraneous arms jutting out from their shoulder blades hanging there, twitching every so often, and extra legs—extending from their buttocks—doing the same, and too long, lying impotent along the cave floor?

Really only a few of their features seemed to have a purpose. Each head was sunken with one horrible gaping toothless mouth, constantly smacking open and closed. These vacant sucking holes were their only facial features but for hideously long whiskers arranged like numberless antennae that bristled and flowed and twirled, now Ogwold realized, everywhere upon their bodies. The milky, transparent skin from scalp to toeless foot was covered in these fine, waving, grasping hairs which seemed constantly to reach for the rock floor, the ceiling, out into the darkness for something, anything to touch.

Byron took one noiseless step into the room, but the moment his boot touched the ground, all of the venturing hairs upon the otherwise motionless creatures rippled, furled as in decoding some new frequency, stood alarmingly straight, then feverishly snaked out along the floor like sniffing hounds, undulating and issuing horrible tittering noises as the frenzied panting from their gathering grew deeper and more guttural.

"We won't get through," breathed Ogwold, but even the sound of his voice seemed to simmer in new amplitude upon the long hairs of the creatures and they began to cheep and chatter amongst themselves.

"You're the one with a weapon here," said the mercenary, pushing Ogwold into the room. If his own deft step had aroused the entities, the clumsy staggering of the ogre's huge feet must have been deafening. So tremendous was the impact of that sound that they all for an instant, each and every hair, seemed to freeze.

Yet even now against these wretched things fully grown and evil to behold, Ogwold could only think of the knight he had crushed in Occultash. He took a great, thumping step backwards, and the forest of hairs again began to throng as the pale creatures advanced in a manner wholly unnatural, wielding their crude wooden spears pointed with jagged rock, rasping and moaning through their yawning mouths which turned sickeningly upward as in some hellish silent crooning as they moved. But however hesitant was Ogwold in the face of these advancing monsters, his greener arm seemed as well attuned to the threat as it had been on that rainy night, and for it as much as Ogwold the training with Byron had quite soaked in.

Bulging and narrowing amorphous in the white glow, it rose as one instinctively shields the eyes from a bright light, and formed again that clean, green blade. Just in time was the edge rendered to parry the lunging spear of the nearest mutant, flinging it easily aside and returning to hover extended like a guardian spirit before its ward. With the jar of the deflection Ogwold too was knocked into a state of self-preservation, staring into the awful cavernous mouths of the creature before him. Suddenly shouting he leapt forward and kicked the creature directly in its opalescent chest. There was a deafening boom. The Krug spearman shot across the room, struck the wall, and slid to the ground, its horrible mouths smacking open and shut rapidly.

Ogwold staggered, stunned at the force he'd delivered. The other creatures scattered, warbling and cheeping heinously, their hirsute skin undulating madly;

but with a great roll of hair they charged him all at once. He drew back and swung out with the green sickle as he had at Byron these past mornings, strong, but not too hard, controlled, calculated, in one great sweeping motion, averting his eyes at the last moment. There was a sickening splatting noise, almost delayed in its sounding, as when a razor passes over flesh and the laceration blossoms moments later. In that instant Ogwold felt death. He saw clearly the wolf of fire on the lonely hill in the endless night, and it howled. The three mutants were cloven at varying heights; the mangled sections of their seizing bodies thumped wetly to the dirty cave floor. Ogwold's blade snaked so lithely back into the shape of an arm that it shed every last drop of the black blood it had touched in a dark mist lightly settling over the grisly scene.

"That was horrible," he said, falling to his knees with a great boom.

"You saved us." Byron placed one hand on the grieving ogre's massive shoulder. "They will kill us Ogwold, if we do not fight back."

"I understand." Ogwold sighed deeply and held the arm which had dealt three deaths so swiftly. Byron did not rush him, and went to lean against the wall, listening intently for the skitter of any approaching foes, but there were none. In the airless dark they brooded in silence each on their own paths. At last the ogre stood and nodded.

They ran quickly through the room and into the next tunnel, the sphere whizzing along just ahead of them to light the way. They turned again and again, choosing tunnels at random or at least which seemed to move towards the surface, coming on empty caves, knowing nothing about the layout of the labyrinth, and realizing as they went that though they seemed vaguely to move upward, the depths of the place, the extent of it was beyond imagining.

They passed many tunnels too small for either of them, looking precisely like those malevolent holes from the dig site. It was through these tubes, like portals into some hive-dimension, that they realized the nature of the creatures' awful extra limbs. Out from one such tiny passage burst three of the beasts one after the other before them, and Ogwold could see that just as they scrambled from the aperture their backward facing legs and arms had been running along the ceiling so that they bounded against two opposing surfaces. These three were gone in moments, tearing down the hall in the opposite direction. Neither Byron nor Ogwold had moved a muscle since they had first heard the awful scraping noises of their digitless extremities. When that febrile scrabbling had finally faded into the cylindrical darkness, they silently carried on.

One long tunnel opened into a marvellously tremendous cave too tall with blackness and thick with gloom to betray its proportions. The sphere swept out into the void of its mass, delineating its features as it went. Over the uneven floor and among the ancient and flowing formations of rock thronged a great host of the awful creatures, garbling and croaking at one another, huddled in those same circles breathing shallowly and quickly, their helpless backward facing arms and legs flailing and twitching in the dank air. Yet by far the majority were packed even more tightly together and hunched over a sequence of long stone tables, smacking and tittering and gibbering as they savagely fed on dark bloodied meat, slumped all over in no particular order before them.

The way they ate was snake-like, for having no teeth they did not chew, and leant back so that their food slid down through their gaping mouths and choking throats directly to their stomachs. All down the enormous stone slabs the pairs of heads reared back to gag upon their food in lumps or dove down to gum up some new shapeless chunk. All the creatures stood the whole while, as there were no seats; the tables were rather gigantic troughs of food, and however ravenously they went about their feeding, there was nothing easy or apparently enjoyable about this process.

Ogwold and Byron stood still in the stagnant air, watching from the entrance. There were perhaps thirty of the creatures here, but most horrifying was what they saw when the sphere spiralled up to shine upon the craggy funnel slope of the cavern roof. At first it appeared that there were several tremendous stalactites there, but then they saw that these were a different colour from the rock, and that some of them swung in that same sickening way as had the egg sac from their cell. They looked like cocoons hanging pendulous in the shine of the light, yet it was clear they were far too large, and their limbs were free to move, for the moment wrapped up in a great leathery membrane such as they'd not seen upon the other Krug.

A particularly oafish creature then lurched into the great dining hall, dwarfing the huddled whispering things, and when it passed through the crevice in the rock which served as its entrance, they saw fluttering from its twisted back a fourfold set of black, webbed wings like those of an enormous aborjay in texture, but more like a moth in appearance. The entity was similarly pale and translucent as the other wretches groveling before it on the floor, and it too had only gaping toothless maws within the pale blind flesh of each its twin heads. As well it was covered in the same disgusting tendrils that writhed for surfaces, snaked along the ground, snatched and clutched as the creature moved. But this entity did not have any extra limbs, compared with Ogwold and Byron at least, and stood only just shy of the full stature of a grown Novare man. It certainly wouldn't fit inside the smaller tunnels.

Most interesting of all, though the thing was an astonishing sight as a whole, the beast dragged Ogdof's unmistakable massive sword behind it into the room, sheathed in its simple leather scabbard. It was clear that the sword was too heavy for the creature; its back twisted horribly and its wings flapped with noiseless exertion as it quaked merely to unsheath the thing. Even when it did manage to hoist the weapon up into its grip, it was clear that it would never be able to properly swing it. Yet there was a great clamour of screeching and gibbering among the crowd, whose tendrils had presumably sized up the weapon when it was dragged in vibrating against the cavern floor, and they seemed to think otherwise, for they all forgot their food and fell prostrate on the ground in a great reverent silence.

"Ogwold. Get me that sword," Byron whispered. Already throughout the room the tendrils of hair picked up the notes of his voice.

"You're sure you can swing it?" A new seriousness had come over Ogwold, such that he wondered not about the possibility of waking the foul creatures hanging from the ceiling. He was focused, like Byron, upon escape, survival.

"Trust me, it's perfect."

For the second time that night, or was it day, neither of them knew, Ogwold hardened himself for combat. But this time, though the images of the slain Novare, of the bloody rain puddles, the gaping, dead faces, the slain Krug so simply bifurcated surfaced in his mind, he felt the strong grip of the plant in his shoulder, snug around his heart, which steeled, and some new animus awoke within him. It was a hard, a resolute spirit, as capable of wonderful tenderness as it could crush a boulder in its grasp, and now it stood not beside Ogwold but with him. They went into the fray together with one clear thought—it must be done.

He charged the creatures this time before they could prepare a defence. His plant arm flourished like liquid cast from the shorebreak of his shoulder, suddenly condensed down in a fine edge and hardened into a larger blade than before as he swung. The sphere went with him, humming in his ear, lighting up the pale monsters as they came. The first wave of creatures lost their torsos, and Byron could not help feeling a swell in his heart. The sick things were like imps next to the size of an ogre, and even were Ogwold unarmed, now that he was committed to their defeat, they could not stand a chance. As he fought, his arm-blade grew mightier, and began even to extend during his swings to reach more distant opponents. When seven of the creatures had fallen, the remainder of their feverish number retreated desperately into the shadows, some of them wriggling up into the black tube holes.

Only the winged leader with Ogdof's old slab of a sword held its ground. It struggled to raise it blocking as Ogwold brought his verdant blade crashing down upon it, displacing the massive weapon from the creature's hands which hardly supported its weight so that it sparked against the stone floor and thudded heavily away like a column of stone, incapable of bouncing, glued down by its impossible mass. With one swift backhanded slice the mutant's twin heads plopped to the ground, the body knelt in a breath, and slumped over dead, black, oily blood spouting all around like a babbling underground brook.

Panting, hunched over on his knees, Ogwold squinted and pushed the sweat-sodden locks of hair out of his eyes. The deafening hiss and chatter of the creatures packed along the cave walls was like spurs of ice scraping through his veins. Byron appeared silently and leant almost ceremoniously to grip the hilt of Ogdof's old sword where it lay on the ground, smoking in the river of sick. He drew it up with seeming ease, and with a blasting grunt hefted the whole immense length of it over his shoulder. For a moment it seemed that he would fall right through the cavern floor, but then he sighed as softly as one who is at last reunited with some lost lover. The weapon was far larger and heavier than the sword he had taken from Leostoph's armoury, and a much finer thing in essence. It was, he thought, almost the same breadth and length as the sword he'd carried long ago. Ogwold stared at him in total bafflement, for to lift the thing even he required a greater degree of exertion.

Then they heard the rustling, and the soft plopping of wet feet onto the stone floor in all directions. The sphere ranged about and they saw that the winged creatures roosted above had come down to meet them. They were just like the bearer of Byron's new blade, though somewhat slighter of build. Their mouths opened and rasped hoarsely as they approached in low positions, raising daggers and swords of jagged rock. Byron only grinned more broadly in the pale light.

From shoulder to toe with a titanic slash he obliterated the first Krug so fast that Ogwold could barely see the blade carrying through the air. Leaping forward he swung across the scene still thick with exploding blood and disembowelled three more. Inky innards spilled from ravaged torsos, and they toppled over noiselessly. The others shrieked and charged. Two brandished clubs of wood, the other a long sharp rock. Byron finishing his swing had used the momentum to lift the sword up and over behind him, and now he brought it crashing down atop the nearest monster, cleaving it clean in two. With the blade now shooting straight out before him, he changed his angle deftly and lunged suddenly forward, impaling both of the remaining creatures along the great long slab of metal. Raising the hilt of the weapon, he pushed them sliding off with his boot. The whole effort looked even easier for him than when parrying Ogwold's attacks in the morning. The ogre could only wonder how many of the beasts it had taken to wound him so grievously when they were captured.

Ogwold was silent, breathing heavily as he listened to the feverish flight of the remaining creatures, forcing themselves through the black holes and escaping into the cave-hive. But he realized that these heavy breaths were not from enervation, for he was quite bursting with energy and felt that he could climb any mountain without rest. It was adrenalin perhaps, or maybe, he thought, the green arm drinks from a fight as well. He stared at it cautiously, as if it possessed a mind of its own. Though it seemed to carry with it a beautiful peace, it too contained a great violence. He was yet able to accept that such violence may have come from his own heart, but certainly he had felt a kind of calm in winning the battle.

"They were monsters," Byron said, partly reading his mind. "They would have eaten us or worse. And now they'll return with hundreds more."

"But they were like us," said Ogwold. "They weren't just animals. And they liked my father's sword."

"What's not to like?" Byron swung the sword powerfully, as he did every morning, and a dank blast of air struck Ogwold in the face. "I could cut a boulder in half with this thing. It would crush an armoured man's bones with one swing. Your father must have been hunting Euphran." He grunted, hefting it back onto his shoulder and exhaling deeply as he rose beneath its weight. "He is a greater smith than many I've known."

He went near to the crevice through which the first larger creature had entered, and picked up, fitted the enormous weapon into the simple scabbard there. When the vast leather length was then strapped to his back, the point of the blade nearly touched the ground, extending just beyond Byron's calves. Ogwold was struck by Byron's strength, for he was not a particularly large man, and certainly he was of slighter build than the winged Krug which had barely wielded the thing a moment ago.

"It does look finer in your care. You use it so well. It's yours, Byron. But my father is no smith; he bought the blade from a Knight of Lucetal long ago."

Byron spat and the fluid which struck stone was mostly blood. "That is unfortunate. But even among the barbarians there are great minds and hands." He looked coldly into Ogwold's eyes, which misted as the ogre tried to imagine how the brilliant armour and kingly ships of Lucetal were somehow barbaric. "You're going to have to get over this killing business if you want to travel with me. I attract death. It's my calling, you could say. And these mountains are evidently teeming with fiends. Already devils like that infernal Teperchael lie in wait. Who knows what lurks higher up."

"Right," Ogwold said, saddened to think how easily he had embraced the notion of the archaeologist's friendliness. He sat upon one of the bloody stone tables to take many much needed breaths. The mercenary slouched and pressed one hand over his shoulder, finally allowing himself to grimace from the pain of his injuries, which had not completely healed spending so little time under the influence of the plant, spitting up gobs of blood too long forced down.

Ogwold suddenly leapt up in disgust, crying out. "These are Novare! They eat Novare!"

Byron only laughed, though weakly, following Ogwold's gaze of horror to the unmistakable and relatively whole foot of a man lying upon the stone. "Should we have some? I'm starving."

For some reason Ogwold found this hilarious, and he broke into booming, crazy laughter. Something about the depravity of it all, the violence and the oppressive darkness and the foreign but uncanny wrath that boiled in him all this time broke and showered out of him in deep hearty guffaws. And Byron laughed too, a cold and distant, but a true laugh such that Ogwold felt somehow in this darkest and most vile place he had truly connected with the man. They laughed and laughed, surrounded by corpses freshly bleeding and recently gummed.

Ogwold had forgotten all about the sphere, even though it lit the room; but now it came down to float between them, and pulsed softly as if to draw their attention and remind the ogre in particular that there was more work to be done.

"I think it can lead us out of here," he said suddenly. "The wizard who gave it to me said it is drawn to Zenidow. And that is the highest place of all, if we are down deep. Besides that, I think it is more complex than that. Sometimes it speaks to me in a way, puts pictures in my mind." He shut his eyes. Again Byron did not seem perplexed by the notion of magic or of purely psychic communication. Ogwold sent the image of an opening in the darkness, sunlight pouring through. Outside he flung up grass and trees swaying in a mild wind, birds chattering. For a time nothing came in return, but the glow against his eyelids began to fade, and the boots of Byron to step away.

"This way," said the mercenary.

They ran through many tunnels again for some time, following the streaming path of the sphere. The tunnel began to wind upward, and even the air seemed easier to breathe, but truly it was astounding how deep they were in the mountain, for the hours slipped by one after the other, and still they felt nowhere near the surface world. Up and up went the steep grade, which hadn't the slightest turn and seemed like a great ramp to extend nearly straight up into the mountain. Higher still went this passageway, and the amount of smaller holes unto the hidden matrix of tiny tunnels dwindled, and now there was only the craggy and difficult way up, more and more troubled with formations of rock. Though this way was large enough to accommodate even Ogwold, it was increasingly sheer and not at all meant for the trespass of feet. Frequently they needed to climb directly up the spill of rocks.

"This must be a passage for the flying ones," said Ogwold. "It's like a chimney. But as long as we can climb it, it must lead to the air." Looking down at Byron he was reminded of the huge sword the man carried on his back, which he was now hauling upward. His face seemed calm, but then Ogwold had become accustomed to Byron's ability to mask his feelings, and he could see in certain turns of the sphere's light that some of the boulders behind them were stained with the man's leaking blood.

"Then why is it still so stuffy?" Byron scoffed.

The sphere buzzed on upwards, and the light it cast at least showed more holds for their hands and feet. After about an hour of climbing the incline became nearly completely vertical and the ascension of its bare surface far more technical, but only for a short while, after which it began dramatically to lessen, and then more so, and they were once again able to scramble over steep lumpy boulders. They came up over the top of this last rockslide into a large, wet cave, nothing like the big vaulted spaces where the aborjay-like Krug creatures roosted, for it was full of softly glowing mosses and pungent hanging gunk. But there was also, here, a draft, and it smelled oddly fresh in the stink of the strange ooze that slopped all over the floor.

They passed under three great archways that seemed almost carved from the rock, and then into a most peculiar room. It was the first place, other than for the stone tables where the creatures had fed, that bore any semblance of architecture or really any sense for edges and corners that they had seen, and again Ogwold was reminded of the sentience of these monsters so many of which he had slain. The floor was a mosaic of tablets etched with strange and somehow hideous runes, many of which in their deep crevices filled up with the luminescent, rotten moss. Great ribbed columns rose in four rows from floor to ceiling. They were not decorated at all, but still showed fine workmanship, if not artistry. These rows they followed further through the room, where the sphere now ventured and cast its light.

At last they beheld the chief tenant of the place, and it was unlike any before it. The heinous thing coiled lethargically upon a great, flat stone, looking like an engorged worm. Its skin was pale and translucent, so that its black organs pulsed visibly against that membrane, and it was covered everywhere with the same evil looking cilia of its kin. Though it did have two small, feeble arms, which grasped and twitched in a most unsettling manner, it did not have legs, and the swollen length of its sluggish body seemed its only means of locomotion. Its single head was enormous and bulbous, trussed in thick veins, and its mouth was like the others, large and cavernous, toothless. Behind it hung in ranks of leathery pods from the cave roof many of the winged creatures, which seemed burlier and meaner than any they'd met before.

"It's the King," said Byron wryly.

"Why aren't they attacking?" Ogwold wondered aloud.

Then the King spoke. Or so it seemed. The long filamentous hairs all over its body began to undulate each in their own unique patterns, and in turn the hairs of the guards too waved and whipped. A conversation seemed quite afoot. Silently the sphere flew to the throne, and rested upon the great lolling head of the slug. It pulsed once, and the cave filled with light. Then Ogwold and Byron saw Videre. She was chained by each paw to the far wall, her fur boltered in blood. It was impossible to tell whether she was alive or dead.

Byron's green eye flashed in the dark. He charged forward and swung his sword, unsheathing and slicing down and across in one motion. Three of the winged Krug who had at once flung themselves forward were destroyed by the strike; but the King was untouched. Then they were all upon him before he could ready another blow. These creatures were more powerful than those below throughout the caverns. Swarming him, slamming against the broad side of the sword, which he held still before him as in a great shield, they forced him to the ground, piling and scrambling, attempting to overpower him. But now Ogwold had readied his own weapon.

He couldn't say later why he used it in this new way, but he pointed this time with the greener arm towards the King, and he said: "What you've done to us is one thing. But what you've done, whatever you've done to Videre; it's unforgivable." Suddenly the arm shot forward at a stupendous and fine length and passed like an emerald thread through the head of the King Krug, narrow and sharp, silently thrusting from the back of his chair, and several feet beyond, covered in filthy black bile, crumbling bits of stone falling to the wet floor. A small black bulb twitched for a moment, impaled upon the green spear, then went horribly still. The king shuddered and died. The guards atop Byron leapt up, shrieked, and began flapping their soundless wings and moaning bitterly, their evil hair writhing more profoundly than ever. In a great mass they took up their leader's body and flew with it down the great chimney.

Ogwold ran to the great cat, and broke her shackles with the mere strength of his hands. Though she could not stand, she was able to open one eye and mew, if faintly. He rubbed her rough snout and sat beside her, panting. "I heard you protected me, Videre," he murmured into one huge, triangular ear. "You should have escaped."

She groaned in reply, rolling her eyes over as if to say, "Only if you had too."

For a long while they sat in the dank while the ogre fixed his green hand over her heart and reached out with his mind to her spirit. Her wounds were not so easy to undo as had been the mercenary's, and many anxious hours passed— Byron seated in the near dark, Ogwold murmuring softly, the plant surging and flexing as it worked its fine veins into the gashes beneath her stiff fur—before at last the great cat was able to open her big black eyes.

Slowly she rose, shook her head gingerly, and licked Ogwold head to toe while he smiled and held her. Then the three of them searched for a way out at the back of the chamber. They shuffled to a great and ancient stone door that looked to have been shut for thousands of years. With all his strength, and the plant arm growing and buckling, Ogwold was able to slide the thing open wide enough to slip through, and at last they came suddenly out into the alpine air, sucking up clear breaths. As soon as the light struck their faces, they all sat flat on the ground with relief.

Just as suddenly, Ogwold surged with joy, drinking the pure and life-giving sunlight as if he had been starved of it for all his life. With each gulp of those divine rays a great weariness began to leave him, and he realized then how deeply exhausted and ragged his spirit had become in the darkness. Only when the first wave of this deliverance had passed did he realize these feelings had come from the plant in his arm. Much of its reserves had been expended in the caverns and tunnels, and perhaps it had even approached its end in healing Videre. Ogwold held the arm fondly as it drank the sun, and shared in its glorious revival.

They were on a high shelf, higher up than they'd ever been on the journey, and the air, though clean, was scarce. No vegetation grew here, and there was no path in any direction. The stretching forests far below were like homogeneous swaths of dark green. The gigantic mountains all around seemed all the more close.

"Now I see why this is the safest place for their ruler," Ogwold wheezed.

"And not deeper?" Byron winced, now fully nursing his wounds.

"Imagine what lives deeper if these things were so close to the surface."

"That is an interesting thought." Byron leaned against the cliff face and sighed. "There must be some way down," he mused. Ogwold walked to the edge of the shelf and looked out into the open. The way was sheer and rocky, but not impossible to navigate. It was certainly dangerous though, and one slip might send them forever falling. In some places the rock was not completely vertical, at least. Still, he was no fan of heights.

"Do you have rope in that bag?"

"I doubt the cat can hold onto a rope."

"Then we'll have to find a way to walk down. Or go back through the caves."

"There's no going down that way without wings."

"True."

"Can you ask that marble of yours?"

"Oh! Why yes I should."

Ogwold sat and breathed in the mountain air, listening for the humming of the sphere. In the heat of the moment he had ceased to hear it, but now it came warmly back to him, though the sphere did not itself appear. So he followed the droning over to the side of the shelf. And sure enough, there were steps there. Real, stone steps, though ancient as anything in the mountains. They were barely still visible, but they were certainly there.

Byron joined him and said, "Maybe there were delvers here once."

"Or those creatures were once more civilized."

"They couldn't have descended from Novare. These steps are easily thousands of years old. I do not think my kind have even inhabited this range for more than five hundred. Let alone have they surmounted such peaks."

"Maybe they have some other ancestor. Or, they haven't even changed at all; though it seems like these steps and that door haven't been used in a very long time." They marvelled at the strange steps, for they were quite small, much smaller than the mutants would use easily, and for Ogwold very treacherous. His angled foot took up six or seven such broken plates with each plod. Videre had the easiest time of their descent, injured though she was.

The sun had already been low when they'd come up out of the crypt in the mountain, and now night fell, blisteringly cold and dark as void, but the sphere bloomed even as the black grew, and lit up their path once more, holding low to the stair so they did not misplace their feet. They travelled all through those late hours quickly as they could, for fear of more Krug accosting them, but not the slightest sign of life occurred to the senses even of Videre.

When the white shards of day broke in the great cracked vault of the grey sky they were exhausted, but now the stairs had led them to places where strange,

engaged with that Kingdom, but really we are all on our own out here. Fonslad is a single people. The King will never aid us in our struggle with the Eyeless, but he will always take our metals. There is no place really for war or hatred here, but for the Eyeless," he spat onto the floor, "which we all loathe, together. And well there are many fell beasts in the range, the further you traverse it."

"That is our aim," Byron muttered.

Ogwold grinned. "To go further, he means."

"Then you've a perilous journey ahead of you." Solena leaned back upon his stool, crossing his leather-gauntleted arms. "Fonslad is as far as the traders go. The only delvers past this place are the most passionate and crazed. We rarely see any, but they do come through every once in a while to deposit their discoveries. They find many strange things further in the mountains, but little of current value in Occultash or Lucetal."

"Are you a delver?"

Solena winked, though a shadow passed over his face. "Well, only sometimes now do I chance the mines. I come from a family of metalheads, but happen to be handy with a weapon. My strength is needed with the guard these days. We need all able warriors. But yes, my heart is for the deeps, like most Novare who live here. Like you, I'm sure! What is it you wish to dig up that lurks beyond even Fonslad?" He laced his fingers together and leaned again forward, elbows to the tabletop.

"Well, the truth is I've no idea." Ogwold shrugged. The sphere pulsed and droned in the pocket of his cloak. "Call me an explorer."

"Ah, one of those." Solena grimaced.

Byron cut in darkly. "Do you know a path forward?"

"Well certainly." Solena at last turned his gaze fully upon Byron and Ogwold thought he saw the man flinch. "Many of the hunters go into the wood and beyond. There is also a great chain of lakes where many fish, and we have even some clusters of cabins there, and outposts to watch for Eyeless coming out of the rock in the evening. The border of the forest on all sides is rife with their hive-holes."

"What about beyond the lakes?"

"I have no idea what is beyond the lakes," Solena said gravely. "They are immense and many. Even in the mire, the Eyeless are the least of your worries."

"Right, of course," said Ogwold. "Well, but is there anyone in Fonslad that might know something about the way through the mire? Maybe we can find a way around the lakes on our own."

Solena's smile returned with an edge of shock. "I begin to believe in your story from earlier. You are stout-hearted, Nogofod Ogwold." He sipped his own drink smoothly, mulled over the notion for a little while. "There is an old woman, a witch, who lives in the Mistwood on the fringe of the marsh. She has helped us much in dealing with the Eyeless, and gives us even talismans that have some warding effect on the creatures. If anyone knows a path beyond the lakes, she will. Her name is Hesgruvia. You can find her by following the notches in the trees. Any soldier should be able to show you where to start."

Ogwold smiled broadly. "Why thank you, Solena." He brought his gigantic hand down to pat the young man on the shoulder, but the impact rocked Solena such that he was quite startled and toppled straight off of his stool. "Ah! Sorry about that." The ogre extended a massive grey hand. Solena's own looked like that of a baby disappearing into the palm which heaved him back onto his heels.

Byron smirked, holding out the unspilled glass which he'd rescued from the hand of the falling guard, and this more than anything seemed to calm Solena. The soldier smiled and laughed as he took the drink, raising it, nodding, imbibing. "How about I bring the explorers a round?" Without waiting for an answer, and quite missing the sheepish shaking of Ogwold's big head, he spun and made for the bar. Leaning over the wood, he entered upon some terrifically enthusiastic conversation with two fellow guards there posted.

"You are not so fearful as you present," said the mercenary, turning to Ogwold. He looked almost uncomfortably stiff for one who is so constantly piercing the eyes of others. "You slay monsters deep in their evil abode, yet honourably you mourn them; even after you are betrayed by the likes of Teperchael, with respect you approach the people of your own slavers; and without a doubt you have your heart set upon a mountain all men call unreachable." As he spoke, Byron regained his old composure, and even lifted the seam of his mouth.

Ogwold smiled warmly. "Well, you make a great model for dealing with fear. I really wouldn't be here right now if it weren't for your example."

Byron frowned and looked into his drink.

The ogre went on. "Though, there is one other who has helped me with fear, the one who sent me on this whole journey in the first place."

"The wizard?"

Ogwold looked out of the dark window into the unseeable night. "Caelare."

"Caelare," repeated the mercenary, as if the word came to him out of some distant past.

"It was she who sent me to Zenidow."

Byron chuckled, a strange, tuneless noise, but no less sincere for its awkward cadence. "Now that is reason enough."

CHAPTER XIX
THE SECRET OF
LUCETAL

King Chalem hunched over in his capacious silver throne. Azure robes like inland waters spilled over his broad belly and sandalled feet. An argent crown held fast the twisting pale blond tendrils of his devoutly unshorn hair. One husky palm smothered the metal pommel of a thin sceptre cut purely of luminous, blue gemstone. Elegant and intricate as was its form, the twin-edged instrument seemed hardly fragile when he rapped its fine tip loudly against the golden dais which raised his seat highest in the great hall.

Such anxious clacking echoed distant but sharp in the barrel ceiling, slipping under the lank tapestries, cutting through the roar of the surf as it bellowed dully at the stained-glass windows closely spaced along the walls. Through these tall parabolas slanted gleaming prisms of varicoloured sunshine, blazing in exquisite patterns, moving and changing over the flagstones and narrow carpet as the shadows of leaves and close boughs outside rustled and turned in the wind. Dazzling reds, greens, blues reflected and moved in the muddy hazel of the King's wide-set eyes. But he was quite impassive to that scene, glaring so remorselessly through the living light as to penetrate the great wooden double-door at the opposite end of the room.

The wizard could not possibly waste another moment. Crimson was on every wagging tongue and in every eye enchanted since the *Patientia* was sighted over the sea. Bare and booted feet slapped in the ecstatic streets. Children called out with glee as on a sudden holiday. Market squares fell silent and emptied. The low mages of the Red Tower were miraculously cured of their lethargy. And now, in all its gaudy enormity, that absurd galleon had been at harbour since dawn. Chalem could envision the bobbing turtle prow, the swarms of peasant children beaming up at its dumb countenance, their ruddy fathers clapping hand to shoulder, leaning in to charm them with old stories.

He had long sent away the guard, desiring to express his full wrath in privacy. It would not do for talk to circulate in a palace and city which loved the wizard more than ever. Yet prodigious as was his capacity for festering rage, even that anger, greatest he had known in many years, had quite burned over, simmered into exhaustion as the glare of early morning softened into day. Only the lonely crack of his sceptre carried on through the monotonous succession of vacant hours, as though it might with one strike, perhaps the next, conjure up the bygone flame of his storied wrath.

Therefore, it was not with idyllic fury that Chalem received his long-detained High Wizard, finally striding as though he'd never left through the immense, groaning doors, but with the weary trepidation which better illustrated the inmost state of his heart.

"Hail, Son of Chalor, father of the Island, Lord of Lucetal, Colonizer of Efvla, King of the Capital, how is it with you!" Nubes shouted musically through the immense echoing room, stepping nimbly along, crimson cloak and fluffy beard fluttering gaily on the sea wind which rushed from the slowly closing doors. The King sat still and unresponsive as stone, sceptre firmly rooted, until he arrived before the stage, whereupon the generous pool of blue fabric there spread Nubes planted his black staff, old withered hands folded atop its gnarled apex, and cocked his head so quizzically as to mock his own deference. "And how goes that infernal war?"

The King muttered inarticulately at first, rubbing the humped bridge of his stately nose. "Fifteen years, Nubes."

"Has it been that long already? And your mane is sunny as the day of its coronation!" The wizard chuckled as though, Chalem thought, such a compliment would certainly assuage the sting of his tardiness.

He snorted through expansive nostrils, now came a sharp rap from the sceptre as had not sounded since the doors were opened. "Do you know how many men and women have fallen in Efvla?"

"Countless thousands I am sure." Nubes gazed into the kaleidoscope of the nearest window, a principally blue and green swell of glittering shards which swirled into the noble countenance of the first King of Lucetal, Chalor. "But that is your own fault for making war with a power you do not understand."

"You insinuate I started this conflict?" Now Chalem grasped at the morning's rage. The burn of an obsessively close shave trembled on his mottled jowls.

"As ever!" Nubes faced the King dryly. "Ah, you look so much like your father when you make that face. I imagine you've been sitting here all day looking just like that! Really, I must apologize for not coming at once. I was needed straight away at Occulimontis, you see."

One corner of his broad mouth twitching, grinding his sceptre into the dais, Chalem drew a deep, rattling breath. The redness in his thick cheeks had retreated desperately from the notion of Chaldred, the King before him.

"Always speaking to me like I am a child," he groaned. "But then, you are of course the eldest damned creature that goes about on two legs. Yes—I am angry, Nubes. Angry that you abandoned us in our hour of need. Angry that for all these bloodiest years of my reign you vanish into the country of our enemy. Angry that you return only to skip about the city like some fey hero spreading mutinous lies about the Xol." The King sighed like a cornibet completing its haul, withdrawing his sceptre to sit across his voluminous lap. "I am sure your errand at Occulimontis was dire."

Nubes cocked one snowy eyebrow. "That it was. I understand your ire, but you must know that I have and always will serve the Sons of Chalor. It seems rather that you cannot stand this invented notion that you need me. Are you not the powerful Chalem? Is Efvla not the theatre of your might? Whether or not your war is a good one, you are certainly ambitious, first in your long line to contest the elder rule of the purple folk."

"Aye!" Chalem smote the dais furiously with his sceptre. The crack rang through the hall, such that Nubes called out with a loud harrumph. "I know who you are, Nubes. Merely I am dismayed by your wayward whims."

"I've no such impulse in my history that has not behooved Lucetal."

"So it is said by the fathers of my father. But never was there a King of Lucetal who allowed you such freedoms." Chalem scowled, leaning back in his throne. "Yet you stir my heart High Wizard; that much is true. I need no magic to claim the black forest. Let the demons of Xoldra fall to horse and blade!"

Nubes smirked coldly. "I could not possibly have aided you as much as I am about to if I had stayed put these years. You are wiser than you know for unleashing me." He stared hard and blue. "Though I offer no magical solution to your ails, you'd surely snap one up like the turtle of the bog."

The King leaned forward, glowering. "There are many awful paths to victory I'd take before stooping so low."

"And so you will," said Nubes.

Chalem torqued one thin, golden eyebrow. "Tell me then," he grumbled. "What knowledge has arrested you so long?"

Nubes quietly ascended the gilt steps to stand beside the throne. Turning round he stared out and up at the hanging rows of richly woven tapestries depicting the Lucetalian Kings of the Second Age, now beyond them at the vast mural painted with masterful detail upon the far wall, portraying those of the Third Age, that grave succession of visages more modern, ever unfinished above the double-door through which he had entered.

"Before I left the capital, I was tucked quite away in Occulimontis," he said in time.

"Yes, you couldn't be bothered."

The wizard tugged his beard, nodding as to himself. "I had a dream, you see, about an impossible presence hidden away far beyond the remotest charted mountains of Efvla across the sea, where no Novare nor Xol has ever dared venture. Yet, it was as though this presence had always been there. Certainly it should have occurred to me sooner, for when I traced the folds of the Mardes I detected it straight away. No, something in the Fabric has changed to reveal it. Perhaps the low gods, Caelare herself, or even the High Gods have opened the hearts of the sensitive. Why they have chosen this moment in our history, I couldn't say. Great things are afoot, Chalem, and I suspect your petty war will be wrapped up in it all soon enough. By now Fozlest too must have eyes in the mountains. I don't doubt she's had a dream of her own. Prescient as she may be; physically, I found it first: within the Great Mountain Zenidow."

"Zenidow?" Chalem barked. "Impossible."

Nubes raised his bushy eyebrows. "It was the most trying journey of my long life. But I built a home near to it in an elder wood out of time, and lived in the very shadow of the thing for many years. Only through careful study and the calling upon of all I know of the Fabric was I able to pass within the Great Mountain and learn its secret. As soon as my eyes were opened, it was my highest priority to return to you, Chalem. I can say that at least since I've come back down through the Mardes, not a soul of Xol persuasion has yet walked such reaches or learned the secret of Zenidow, though I did discover a civilization of Novare living far beyond the boundaries of our maps. They called themselves Arduans, and without their intelligence I mightn't have found such a swift route thereon. Sadly I could not thank them properly. The city was quite destroyed when I passed through on my return, though not by the Xol I am sure."

"At least you romanticize the notion of loyalty. What, pray, is the point of this mythmaking?"

"Of course you will only believe me when I say that this presence hidden in the heart of Zenidow is a greater power than Altum has ever known."

"Ah! So you have found me a weapon! Well this is fantastic news." Chalem's eyes darted to the image of his father solemnly envisioned among the hard shoulders of past Kings, painted in vivid reds and creamy whites, those famously tremendous shoulders bunched up in a cataract of blue and gold cloth sweeping as in a mighty gale off and behind the Kings before him. "I have your temper, Father," he said bitterly to the fresco, "but see what comes of trust."

"Ever fixated on might are the Sons of Chalor," Nubes grumbled. "And none more than you, though it must sound a compliment in your hall." He followed the King's eyes to the stoic image of Chaldred. "Your father's temper indeed! You were ready to exile me when I crossed your threshold."

"That fate still is not unkind to my ears, Nubes. You gave not the slightest premonition of your actions, and I've heard nothing of you for a quarter of my life. So appease me! Where is this weapon?"

"Well, I really don't know what it is, but yes if one were somehow to actualize and control it, they might accomplish much more than winning a silly war." Nubes gave a harrumph. "There is but one name for it which arises from the Fabric and which was spoken to me as by the voices of the Somnambiunt themselves together in my dream: so it is called Alium, even I suspect by the Xol if Fozlest suffered a similar vision. Though, of course, it must have some true name among its creators."

The King sighed. "You don't have it."

"No. But it is quite safe for now. The real issue is what I've learned in living so close to its influence. There is great tumult among the eyes and ears of the heavenly bodies, Chalem."

Nubes raised his staff. The very skin of the air seemed to ripple before the throne, distorting the distant tableau of Kings. The folds of bent light compressed, flowed, split and parted, revealing wider and more clearly a bottomless, black deep dusted with twinkling white stars. At the fading edges of the vision, wisps of darkling energy trailed into the slanting multicoloured rays beaming in through the tall windows, so that Chalem could not tell precisely where the immaterial gave way to the physical.

If he were surprised, it was only for the fifteen years absent of Nubes' brand of magic which so humiliated the trifles of Lucetal's greatest wizards. Already he was comforted by the familiar luminance of his family's oldest ally, to look through this sudden window unto the Cosmos.

The living plane of vision flexed and warped, stars streaming into fluid continuums, but when all had settled, and once again those points of light shone in space as individuals, there too was a new hue in the darkness. Supersaturated vermilion seeped up and billowed through the viscous black, and in the swollen carmine bellies of this bloody nebula shot inexorably forth, as great bladed blights against the stars, deadly black shapes with enormous serrated beaks, trailing long cords of writhing shadow.

Chalem leaned forward. "Caelare among us," he said, touching the ring of bone about his left thumb. "These are... they are of course very different but, they are eerily akin to..."

"That they are," Nubes muttered, watching the strange vessels slip through space. The wash of red played in his ice-coloured irids. "This fleet has consumed many worlds more mighty than Altum even at the height of Elechlear civilization. Domination is tantamount to its commander. Even, I suspect, It craves the rebellion of the conquered, so that It may defy the orders of Its master and absorb all life in the universe. It is called Duxmortul, one of the awful Wrudak, the bastard progeny of the Old King, the Shadow of Primexcitum's folly. The Wrudak's natural powers over the mind and spirit liken even Fozlest to a blithering fool, for they are wrought of god-flesh and armoured in technologies the likes of which stupefy the most advanced in the Cosmos."

Chalem stared into the vision stubbornly, his eyes glazing with mannish denial. "I can see that their crafts are fearsome and wholly alien. But they cannot reach Altum so easily." He cleared his throat. "If the Reach is so vast as you've often said."

"Vaster than you can imagine," Nubes said ominously. "And ours is a planet entirely across the galaxy from the Wrudak fleet. They passed into the outermost whorl of Semoteus two winters ago, but that utmost distance between us only speaks to the magnitude of the threat. I have observed these ships for many years, Chalem, and calculating the speed of their progress was a minor thing compared with what intelligence I bear now. Duxmortul's ships will enter Altum's atmosphere in seven years. The vessels at his command are much faster and greater than those of the fallen Elechlear which you hoard."

The vision collapsed inward like a great ethereal scroll rolled up at once, and Nubes brought his staff loudly to the golden surface of the dais. His countenance was grim to behold. "We must equip ourselves, King Chalem. Raise Fort Soarlin to the sky! Call for peace at once and join forces with the Xol! We shall share the ancient starships with all who can pilot them, and prepare to protect our world lest it collapse into the sucking hand of darkness!"

Nubes' quirky old voice had quite vanished, as if it were only an act; now boomed the deep, remorseless command of an elder wizard, echoing timeless through the high ceiling as it had many Kings before, mingling its bass with the roar of the sea. Chalem gazed into the glittering windows as the call washed over him. His tired shoulders sloped forward, sceptre screwed at the dais like an elegant cane. For five hundred years the crimson mage had advised the Sons of Chalor, but no matter the status of the speaker, not one would have even acknowledged this request. It was to go against the constitution of Lucetal itself.

Though he considered this foundation of his city's history in a thought, already his eyes were lifted to heights, he imagined, so awesome as to leave behind their worldly integrity. High above the flagstones, up the glossy wall, he looked over the painted, stately brows of his mindlessly subservient predecessors to a vacant space of high stone wall where he imagined one day his own proud face would look down on the proceedings of the great hall. In those days, Lucetal would be more powerful than ever before.

"Often I have thought to break the seal of my fathers," he said evenly. "Imagine the impotence of Xol sorcery before the full might of an Elechlear army."

"What? That is not at all our need. You speak of intolerable waste," Nubes said with fury blistering behind the composure of his unflinching gaze. "The Xol will be our strongest allies when the Shadow falls upon Altum."

Chalem's frown pushed the creased corners of his mouth into the pouches of his jowls. "Of course," he groaned, still gazing up at the fresco. "Perhaps the threat to our world is enough to quell the devilspawn until the doom has passed." He blinked as though for a while his eyes had grown dry from openness, and turned to Nubes. "The end of the world... it is at least of import enough to weather the wrath of Lucetalians deceived."

"A faction of revolt will surely form, but that is the price."

"Surely; surely. To be at war no less, desperate for peace, at bloody, bloody, endless war. Just the sight of an Elechlear ship, how it would appease them knowing that the fighting might end in a day." Chalem snapped his sceptre to the dais. "Ah, but to discover that one has swung a primitive metal tool in the stead of divine fury incarnate. What will my knights say when they learn that they have lost so many brethren who might have been spared by the atomizing hand that is luxint energy? What will they say, wise one, when they learn that they are not to avenge the dead with these new weapons, when they learn that arm in arm they must walk into hell with the Xol demons they hate as a right of birth?"

The growing fog of the King's eyes thickened as he croaked out these last few words, and his meaty knuckles grew white around his sceptre, driven like a stake into the golden floor. He twisted the pike as if sealing a kill, though he spoke clearly and calmly. "Yet, your council is fair. You are wisest in the Kingdom, and older than us all. Yes. Let us be done with this war!" Chalem rose at first gingerly for his sudden passion, but then steadily, his bones crunching like pestles and mortars of stone and gravel. Though he lurched and swayed, he rooted himself at last straight-backed and poised, and upon his blazing brow was a great dignity.

Nubes saw little to be trusted in that sudden glory. Already he had little patience for Novare, and like many wizards was quick to anger, though he hid this fault deftly. He had served under seven of Chalem's predecessors, and even the most brutal and uncompromising had not such lust for conquest. Yet this youngest descendent of Chalor was truly the most trusting of mages that Lucetal had ever known, a characteristic quite honourable in a man whose sworn enemy was a race of entities born in the light of the Fabric.

To this King, Nubes was no conjurer of tricks, no demonic deceiver or blasphemous summoner conscripted purely for intellect and worldly understanding, handed down over the years like some glorified advisor. Instead he was a powerful mage, and the source of true knowledge about the world and the Cosmos, a place—the greater universe—that only he, in the whole Kingdom, knew for what it was in truth. Yet for all the matrices of history and lore and demonstrations of astronomical mathematics and lessons upon the nature of the Fabric and physical law that Chalem endured, Nubes suspected his chief value to the King was in his prescient eye on the mind of Fozlest, for he knew that nothing was more important to the King than power.

"So you will call off the army," said Nubes heavily.

Chalem wrung his sceptre. "That I shall."

"Then I shall go to Fozlest and reveal to her what I know of Duxmortul and the Wrudak fleet. And," he looked askance through one piercing blue eye, "I will inform her of the Secret of Lucetal. Surely she will comply to join forces if you have already retreated from the black forest, and even more worthy of trust will you be when she learns that you offer up a new power for the protection of the world we share." With these words Nubes turned and descended the dais swiftly, striding out over the thin strip of blue carpet.

"Stay awhile, old friend," Chalem called suddenly, when the wizard was halfway to the door. "If I'm to reveal the troves of Lucetal at last, certainly you wish to see them. Won't the Demon Queen benefit from a more detailed account of my new technologies?"

Nubes stood with his back to the King for a moment, like a red shade. "Indeed," he shouted back at last.

"And I may as well display the fruit of the Elechlear first to the army's finest, as they'll soon educate the troops in preparation." Chalem rang a silver bell taken deftly from his robes. A young page appeared, listened on one knee to the King's wishes, and shot off again into the high halls which wound back and around up through the terraces of the palace.

Chalem ambled carefully down the steps of his stage, pivoting from each broad platform with his stabbing sceptre, and moved slowly across the spacious room. The changing colours of the iridescent window-scenes turned and sparked as he passed through their slanting rays. His long blue cloak, emblazoned with biting white panther and golden, serpentine prey, slid along the stone floor with a hiss like rain until he came to stand beside one of the ceiling-scraping parabolas of filtered sun. The rose and magenta chips of light cast from the tableau of twilit galleons cresting the sea illuminated his waist-length yellow hair as he leaned against the wall beside the tall window, listening to the sea.

Nubes remained in the centre of the hall, studying that ever-evolving fresco above the door, glancing over each of Chalem's fellow Kings of the Third Age. His eyes fixed upon the terrifying visage of Chaludren, the first King of Lucetal whom he had served. In those days, when the wizard was young and dared not unsheath his wit, the Lord of the Capital wore a tall, golden crown atop his bald pate, and was envisioned here as well in a radiant suit of gilded plate armour. The beardless, hawk-eyed face allowed no compromise; the utterly thin lips betrayed no emotion. Chaludren had executed all who spoke critically of his reign, always quick to demonstrate the power of his sovereignty to the people lest they feel comfortable in his shadow. Each slightest crime was a direct offence not only to himself, but the integrity and sacrality of his government.

It had always seemed to Nubes that Chaludren would inevitably unleash the great secret, but those ancient rooms beneath the city had remained untouched. Granted, there was no war to be had during those times. That King's thirst for power had been chiefly over his own people. The Xol of Chaludren's day were left alone, and even then, though Chalem would insist his peoples' hatred was marrow deep in the bones of time, the purple folk were respected rather as a compelling myth, guardians of the distant forests across the sea. Even had Chaludren sent his armies over the desert, or landed his fleets along the sylvan coast of Efvla, no commander could have had the spirit for conquest that thrived now in all but those of the Red Tower, Occulimontis, where Nubes' students masked their studies ever more carefully, thinking that—were the war to end and their intellects undermined—all workers of magic may be hunted down and slaughtered like the Xol.

The first to answer Chalem's summons was tall Donlan, Captain of Cavalry, high commander of mounted forces and chief in all matters of beast-taming. A storied hunter and taxonomer of many novel species in his youth, he was now a lean, coal-coloured old man whose soft brown eyes melted the hard, chiselled shadows of his fatless face. His short, poorly cut hair was studded with cowlicks and he had a nose which could stab a man. From his wiry shoulders fell a cape of blue, diaphanous cloth, so light and soft compared with the rough leather jerkin he wore beneath it, and the thick black sleeves of his shirt. Around his waist was a silvery, corded belt hung with three rapiers, gemmed at each hilt in red, burgundy, violet. Against his sandy trousers were the distinct pale marks their scabbards left over years of wear. Like the King he wore sandals.

Donlan was of equivalent age to Chalem, and knew Nubes well. Always he had loved the wizard, as many stoic Novare secretly, and few proudly do. After bowing before the King, he strode to the wizard eagerly, warmly clasping his dark hands over the other's and smiling. "Nubes, you daft fool. My spirit breathes again seeing you wandering our halls once more. I heard you made quite a scene at the docks!" The two embraced, and the old wizard seemed frail in the arms of the dark champion.

"And you, not a day older, horseboy," Nubes snorted with a vigour that contested his appearance. "I thought you'd at least have greyed a little by now! But you and the King both! If Chalem is the endless day, still your hair is the shade of night."

"You're one to talk. Ever the day I met you your vitality hasn't changed the least bit. A wizard's tricks eh? Or are they illusions?" Donlan lowered his sable eyebrows as if scornfully, but such was always his way of playing games.

The wizard's eyes flashed in return, unable to abstain the compliment. "At a certain age one can only appear so old." He laughed heartily. "Besides, I am no illusionist. I promised long ago never to deceive a friend."

Next into the room stomped the hard boots of stout-hearted Ramcrone, Captain of Knights, sculptor of any who fought armoured upon the ground with shield and blade. Many of his knights rode horses in battle with the hosts of Donlan's commanders, but once their legs struck down it was his law they followed, for it was he with which they chiefly trained. His hair was short and deep red, his eyes a flaming blue. Like Donlan his face was cleanly shaven, but his chin was stout and broad as any well-bearded warlord would envy. He was younger even than many of his knights, but a legend already in the capital and in the songs and stories of his foes. His talent with a blade was hallowed, and none thought to challenge him.

He appeared girt in a dull grey cuirass, silver greaves, and gauntlets reaching behind the elbows, a weighty broadsword across his back lest battle find him unawares. Upon him else were no adornments of cloth or fealty, and he wore beneath his armour only black leather, for he cared little about striking a noble figure. One would scarcely guess that his mother was the greatest blacksmith in Lucetal, for he attended little to the condition of his equipment. The metal pieces protecting his trunk, shoulders, limbs, though masterfully wrought, were storied with dents and scrapes, in some places awfully warped by the corrosive blood of the Xol's foul war-beasts, and appeared as old as any set of armour in the Kingdom. He carried too his beaten, scarred, silver helmet beneath one arm, and from it though no plumage shot, one could tell easily that it was the headgear of a great leader, for it had upon its cheek the rune which means in Lucetal "commander of commanders." Ever the soldier, upon bowing he came and stood silently, awaiting orders.

Last and most silently to arrive was Vespia, Captain of Rangers, head instructor of all engineers, archers, and assassins. She swept into the hall as a dark wind. Her jagged hair was jet black as her uncompromising eyes. Slim and blade-like she was, and nimble, yet there was terrible strength in her movement. She wore loose-fitting fabrics belted with a leather strap just as black, and there was sure to be a diverse assortment of knives strapped beneath her flowing tunic, or fitted in her spotless boots. At her shoulders were regal midnight pauldrons trimmed with gold, and upon the rightmost was the emblem of her rank, for she was proudest and most loyal to the Kingdom in all the army's finest. Her face was scrunched into so grave an impression of ceremony that even the stone-browed leader of the knights seemed next to her quite relaxed.

Ramcrone's youth was such that Nubes did not know the boy, but Vespia he had met long ago, when she was merely a gifted archer desirous of the warfront. In those days it was said that she might pin a man's cuff to a wall at two hundred yards; now there was talk that she could deflect opposing arrows from the sky with shots of her own. But it was less her skill with a bow than her intellect in devising technologies and her mind for science and natural prescience of the Fabric that had interested Nubes. He had offered up to her the red mantle, had beseeched her to make good on her mortal blessings and study beside him in the Red Tower Occulimontis.

But she detested sewers of the Fabric, and likened him to Fozlest. Still he recommended her to Chalem for leadership, and watched at first with pride as she swiftly ascended the ranks, then grief and soon after only a growing horror as the unassailable hate with which she approached all contexts involving the Xol grew and blistered. Last he beheld her work, the year before he left to seek Zenidow, she had displayed to the King a lightweight gauntlet equipped with grappling hook and serrated claws made from the elz of Xol armour taken off the fallen. Only instruments of such bark could bite into the flesh of their black trees and allow their climbing. Proudly she spoke of the special honour of slaying the demons in their very homes. Oh how Chalem had smiled. How horrible, Nubes thought then, that she who calls them demons conceives of their even having homes!

"My King," she said, bowing low. One dreadful orbit beamed out from the wall of straight hair which hung in triangular locks as she stooped, communicating to Nubes that her opinion of wizards had only worsened. And really, how might one trust a sewer—he thought—when one's sworn enemy fights and works chiefly with a power one refuses to understand.

Though at the coming of each his Captains Chalem made some pass of the eyes, some flash of hazel severity from his position by the window, he looked for the most part abjectly out to the sea through the stained-glass image of that very expanse, while he waited for at last Vespia to arrive. Then he turned, rapped his sceptre, and bade all follow.

Ascending the dais, he thumbed a slim, blue gem set discreetly in the flat silver arm of the throne, which sank with a low click into the metal. A muted grinding issued from below, and the grand chair itself suffered a sonorous tremor, shifted in its place, began to rise and turn, slowly but smoothly ratcheting some eight feet from the stage. Within the huge stone column risen from below was hewn a curved archway unto sooty darkness, and through it went the King without a word.

He took a torch from a sconce beside the entry and, after lighting it with a match from his pockets, applied its flame to another, handing this to Vespia behind him. Neither she nor any who followed spoke of the hidden pillar or its passage, each drawing a slender shaft of wood from the sconces and kindling them in turn. Behind the Captain of Rangers came Ramcrone, after him Donlan, and lastly Nubes, trailing his old fingers against the cool stone.

An orangish caravan of flares crackled and beat against the curving dark walls as they carefully descended a steep spiral stair. In seven circuits the tight coil opened into a larger chamber, low-ceilinged, inhabited only by a suit of ancient armour standing in one dusty corner. Many dark, doorless hallways branched off from this place. Chalem took the furthest from the steps. Again their boots and sandals fell on spiral stairs. Though more spacious than the first, this case screwed on thrice as long, betraying no sign of an end until suddenly meeting a thick silver door which required no key.

Now they walked into a vast, uncomfortable library, its stately shelves completely packed. The entire structure was immaculately organized, but even as the King tapped confidently along and turned with practised precision through the redolent grid of musty wood and aging paper, it seemed that they were completely lost. At the end of one dusty aisle they stopped before a blank stone wall with a small hole in its face. Chalem fitted the intricate, fine tip of his sceptre snugly into the opening, and turned swiftly his thick wrist. There was a deep shifting of discreet mechanisms, and an arching outline appeared, at first so subtly as to be a trail of damp dust, now deepening into a thick trench of shadow. In this slender, ellipsoid shape, a smooth chunk of wall swung inward with the heavy groan of stone on stone.

They filed into a stuffy tunnel beyond, seeming like the corridor of a long forgotten dungeon, and walked along a cobbled path, the flames of the torches lapping over smooth, flat stones. Here was a dead end, as though a cave-in of great boulders had wedged together like an immense altar, but Chalem placed his hand against one of these embedded rocks, and it sank slightly into a surprisingly cohesive structure. A chthonic snore ran all through the chamber. The wall then began to shift sidelong, and as it did dust and dirt fell in sheets all about, and grains of rocks scattered all over the floor. A stale blast of air swept out from the dark crypt beyond.

CHAPTER XX
HARBINGER

Inside it was pitch black but for their torches. Chalem set his own in one of the empty sconces which studded the walls, and gestured for the others to do the same. Then he sat at the simple wooden table in the centre of the room. Rough-hewn chairs were aimlessly set about the place, many tipped over, decked in cobwebs. Some were righted, and all joined at the table but Ramcrone, who stood in the flickering shadows. With the torches burning in the stale air, the room swelled with their dancing, uneven warmth, and a smooth metal panel was revealed, set deep into the stone wall opposite their entrance.

"How is the war going, do you think, Captains?" Chalem finally said.

"We have all but lost," intoned Ramcrone.

Nubes chuckled distantly. "I like this one."

Vespia spoke in a cold, furtive haste. "The demons have pushed our rear bases nearly back to the coast on which we first landed, and they bring greater power to the battle each day. There is little we can do to reach them with our arrows or siege weapons when even one sorcerer is on the battlefield. They cast impermeable shields about themselves, and our armour does nothing to protect us from their spells. It is true that the Demon Witch was slain on the plain of wrath, but she was soon replaced by two warlocks each of might equivalent to her own."

"Leostoph's army has fled that front sorely reduced," said Donlan, who had listened solemnly, nodding. "Even the trees sense our defeat. The black metal creeps into regions formerly it had left alone."

Chalem stared vacantly as each spoke, torchlight rilling through his hair, quickening in bright beads down the length of his sceptre to the floor. "Well then. Nubes. Please inform the Captains as to your personal opinion."

The wizard had fitted a long, wooden pipe into his mouth, its vast bowl composed of three turtle heads stacked in order of ascending consciousness. Chewing absentmindedly on the mouthpiece, he looked from one flame-shadowed face to another, inky pits flexing beneath his furrowed, bushy eyebrows, obscuring all but the finest twinkles of his thought.

"I've not been to the theatre," he said finally, "so I cannot speak for the dead. But I certainly never advised that you go about attacking the purple folk." A slender flame leapt from the burl of his staff, which he tipped over the loamy greenery packed into the cranium of the topmost and piercingly wise-eyed reptile. Fingers of smoke reached out from the coils of his beard, slinking downward and meandering in little rivers over the table top.

"What do you think, though, about our ability to defeat them, as we are?" Donlan asked the wizard.

"There is no chance at all."

"What!" Ramcrone slammed his huge hands suddenly down upon the table. The collecting pool of blue smoke broke its milky congress and rushed over the edges. "Where was this intelligence twenty years ago!"

"Gladly given," Nubes said remorselessly. "Your King chose to forgo it."

Vespia shifted coldly in her seat. Donlan sighed, lowering his gaze. Ramcrone faced Chalem as a soldier composed, yet unable to fathom his orders.

"Goodness," said Nubes, examining the blazing blue orbs of the knight's eyes, "I shouldn't have thought you would trust a wizard though. It is quite natural for Chalem to disregard my ranting. Why, it's practically in his blood."

"You are Nubes," said Ramcrone plainly, scowling in the wash of yellow-orange. "There is no wiser being on Altum, and no older or more powerful ally of Lucetal. My father told me you could melt the skin from Fozlest's bones."

"What? How can you stomach even the thought of such a victory, turning to the accursed arts?" spat Vespia.

"Victory is victory," Ramcrone grunted, closing his eyes. "There is no poetry in war."

Nubes raised an eyebrow. "Anyhow, it's preposterous to think that I could stand against the Empress. Were I even a man of violence, Fozlest is far more powerful than I."

Ramcrone looked to the wizard. "Were you a man of violence, the people of this city would have a new King."

"Hm," said Nubes, drawing from his pipe. Smoothly he exhaled a new field of roiling vapour which gathered blossoming over the wood. "Those are foolish words. Without Chalem, there is no Lucetal, we all know this." He glanced at Vespia as he spoke. "I have my own poetries to adhere to. However accursed are my arts in the eyes of the people, I shall stand with the Sons of Chalor until I am driven from the island once and for all."

"We miss the point, bickering amongst ourselves." Ramcrone cast the rays of his eyes over the other Captains. "If m'Lord does not listen to his most honoured and eldest advisor, I begin to suspect that many good knights have perished for matters of pride alone."

"Silence, Ramcrone," hissed Vespia.

Chalem called her off with the wave of a hand. "You are correct, brave Ramcrone; my pride was our compass, but also my love for Altum. I desired overmuch to capture the forests of Efvla before they blackened, yet now they are blacker than ever. Alack! This war cannot be undone, and the demons have now been aggravated to expand their Empire. There is only one way to end our conflict with the Xol." He looked coldly at Nubes.

The wizard's countenance had lost all pretense of transparency, for he heard in Chalem's words that uncanny tenor of ego which could never truly abide by a sewer's learning. The leering faces of the Kings of Lucetal swam in gaudy painted oils, sagging tapestries, and crystalline window-scenes before his old eyes. Yet great as his anger became, beneath it was a deep sadness for Novarekind and its hubris. And what terrible hubris as well, he thought, was it for Chalem to insist he attend this council which seemed so poised to defy the wizard's wishes. Still, he would wait and see it through. There is still time, Son of Chalor, he thought, to see the Xol for the powerful allies that they are.

"Harbinger!" Chalem called with sudden volume.

As from the fringes of the flickering flames, a white light instantly coalesced. Even as it flashed upon the surface of the blinking eye it receded into a blue and ghostly apparition of eerily pure radiance hovering in the interstice of two torch-spirits. It was the transparent figure of a man. He wore a single continuous suit of textureless material which covered even his fingers and toes. Were it not for the stark angular neckline he would seem naked and sexless. Completely hairless, so smooth and subtle was his complexion as the sleek fabric of his raiment, that only an innate sense in the observers told he was Novare.

The large, pupilless eyes were vacant blue deeps each of them. Alert and attentive nonetheless, he seemed to look at each Captain closely. Vespia glared pitilessly at Nubes, for she figured this magical work to be his, but the wizard seemed lost as Donlan beside him who gawked stupidly. Ramcrone frowned and folded his great arms, their gauntlets awash in the queer blue light.

"I am here," said the apparition tonelessly.

"Explain for my guests what you are," Chalem drawled, rooting his sceptre into the ground and glaring at the wizard who could not contain his fascination.

The figure turned to face the table, though his legs seemed not to move. "I am Harbinger, a luxint-powered artificial intelligence and central computer of Fort Soarlin. I am able to project from my core through any luxint receiver, such as the device implanted in the King's ring."

"This is no cursed magic." Chalem held up his hand. Fine as a grain of sand embedded in the thin bone circlet round his index finger glowed the same strange blue light which seemed entirely to compose the ghost addressing them. "It is like he said: a manifestation of luxint energy, and nothing more. Luxint is a naturally derived source of power, having nothing to do with the wholly unnatural conjurations of Nubes and his followers, or the Xol in their black trees. The gods smile on luxint, for it is the right of mortal ingenuity. It is like the fire that burns in our kilns and our forges, the wind and water which turn our mills, the trained horse that bears us into war. It is the product of science and engineering only. Though not by any scientist you can know."

"It seems like magic to me," said Donlan.

"That is the cost of sudden advancement. How would a primitive man react were you to strike up a blaze and cook for him his raw prey? Would you seem to him a devil if the wild horse was tamed under your yoke? What might he think of your fine metals and jewels; did they come from heaven?" Chalem gazed at Harbinger as he spoke, his words loudening and deepening with pride. "The appearance of Harbinger—so inexplicable to you now—has its roots in the fundamental physical laws of nature, just as the heat of fire and the turning of the mill and the domestication of plants and animals, all those technologies that have evolved our own civilization. But luxint, you see, is a thing so maddeningly ancient as to be superior to our own, from a time when the greatest efforts of our wisest engineers would seem like the banging together of rocks by blithering children."

"If that is true, is Nubes then merely a scientist?" Donlan said. "He is well known for inexplicable appearances. And the Xol too; their powers are certainly inexplicable. What is the difference between magic and science to this degree?"

"Nubes and the Xol go against God," Chalem said coldly.

Even Vespia was surprised, if only slightly, by his tone. But she smiled and leered at Nubes as though the shock was rather an inspiration. "They give up their souls in exchange for forbidden vision."

"Yes," nodded Chalem knowingly. "They steal and covet great powers and examine the flow of time, but the end of that abominable path is only an abyssal doom. Luxint is another thing entirely. It is the product of hard, mortal work, the result of God-fearing minds toiling only with the tools that were their blessing."

Nubes spoke softly, and there was a quiver of pain in even his solemn voice. "You are mistaken, Chalem."

Ramcrone and Donlan knew well this account of magic. Here was a lesson they delivered to their own commanders when the darkness of the war was upon their fevered minds, and in turn their commanders spoke down the ranks of the evil that was the cardinal sin of Xol power. But it was another thing entirely to see Nubes, old and frail, sit and listen and so faintly—as if he saw the Red Tower crumbling even now—deny such accusations against his love and life and work.

All in the room knew that the rhetoric of their clash with the Xol had too deeply stirred the blood of Lucetalians. Popular as Nubes was among the lower classes, when this war was over, the days of wizardry in Lucetal too would have their end. Yet even Donlan who loved the old man could not in his mind separate Xol magic from Nubes' own, and could not see how a society so turned upon the purple folk could abide that dissolution of boundaries in its very court.

"You strike a chord in us all," Donlan said, "but to my eyes the appearance of Harbinger is just as ungodly as Xol sorcery. Even if you can prove to us now that there is some logical, god-given path which leads to such an illusion as this blue spirit before us, how could the people of Lucetal not see it as magic?"

"The time for that will come," said Chalem gravely. "For now, to you, my Captains, I will provide this proof. Today, I will at last tell the story of luxint energy, which has been hidden here below our feet for too long." The King gazed into the limpid depths of Harbinger's empty eyes. "Harbinger was introduced to me when I gained the crown, in just such a way as I conjured him before you now. Ever since, I have spoken with him and learned the true history of this place. The generations of the Sons of Chalor have passed a great secret down their bloodline, which now I, Chalem, son of Chaldred, descendent of Chalor, will reveal to you, my most trusted friends. It is the secret of Lucetal."

"My Lord," said Vespia, falling from her chair to one knee in supplication. "We are infinitely grateful."

"Have you no dignity?" scoffed Ramcrone. "We learn the truth is kept from us, and you bow?"

The Captain of Rangers did not spare him a glance.

"At ease, Vespia," Chalem breathed with honour in his tone. "I am touched at your fealty, but again Ramcrone is correct. I and my fathers have lied to our people for all time."

"It can only have been for the good of Lucetal," said Vespia grimly. "I am at your service."

"And I too," said Donlan, working the grief from his brow. "You have been a good King to us, trusting in the valuable wisdom of Nubes and his scholars, and open-minded as to the unfolding of the war. Many of our greatest accomplishments have come from the free spirits of my commanders to do as they see fit. And the city blooms for its religious liberty and the academies which you have opened to all. Your father would never have allowed such fluid networks of command or programs so uplifting of the lowborn. And he certainly hadn't the heart to confront the Xol threat at last. Tell us this secret, and how we might aid you in deploying it."

"Aye, tell us m'Lord," Ramcrone grunted. "If this luxint technology is so mighty that our animal eyes see only magic, it must have some capacity for changing the war. I've no qualms with secret-keeping—or sorcery for that matter—if there's a way to put an end to it all."

"Truly," said Nubes, staring through Chalem's eyes. "There is a way to end it."

Chalem smiled nobly under the penetrating glare, though there was anguish in his razor-burned jowls. "My Captains..." He looked at each of them. "What do you know of the Elechlear?"

Nubes was silent, but the word sent a tremor through even Vespia. Ramcrone blinked as with sudden recollection. But it was Donlan that spoke. "They were a mythic empire said to have conquered all Altum. Their powers were far greater than the Xol. But they travelled to the stars, and never returned. We call them Elechlear because they are eldest. That is what we are all told as children, you must know."

Ramcrone shrugged his blocky shoulders. Vespia simply stared, though there was in her eyes an understanding which demanded the point.

"Well then," said Chalem, rising from his seat, straightening his spine so that the sceptre hung like a deadly icicle from his grasp, veined with the blue light of his ring. "Your story is only mythical for the great gaps between its truths..." He folded his hand over the hanging spire of ice, and looked into the eyes of each listener as he spoke with a voice more clear and noble than many had heard in years.

"Millennia ago there lived a race of beings we call the Elechlear, whose technology far outran the crude instruments of modern man. They constructed vast cities over whose beauty Caelare would weep. All of the continents of Altum were plumbed and understood to them, and layered with their might. Most grand were their exquisite machines, both of society and war. Among these were ships which sailed among the stars and visited other worlds, weapons which could vaporize duravium walls, vehicles which sped over the roughest lands with the speed of a thousand horses, and suits of armour that allowed one to breathe beneath water, or endure even the most hellish bowels of volcanoes.

"But the might of the Elechlear was such that they grew to distrust their fellows, and their society was split in twain. They discovered a source of power which rivalled the gods, for it tore apart the fundamental particles of the universe to expel from its savaged seams waves of inexorable death that would melt the very code of life and strip the world of fertility. By containing and controlling this new energy, the Elechlear produced what they called luxint, the light within light. They used this energy to power their ships, weapons, and cities. The most powerful of these weapons were the Luxint Rays, great cannons set in sequence around the planet like moons. So destructive was the potential of their firing that the schism and war had begun purely over the debate of their use.

"Naturally, the time came when one side unleashed against the other this very worst of armaments. And naturally as was the conflict born, there was no return fire. Yet many Luxint Rays were called upon at once. Their beams annihilated all life on the face of Altum. Everything was powered by luxint energy at this time, and when all systems collapsed, the main cores of the cities were exposed, and they sank into the world along with all they had supported. The luxint cores became one with the world then, and over billions of years new life forms grew and flourished from a landscape and sea imbued with that energy. This explosion of new life and climatology is referred to in their records as the Great Mutation.

"Only Nubes and myself—and now you, my Captains—know why, to this day, the sea is poisonous to our flesh. To all others it is merely a fact of life. But the water of the ocean was once blue as that of the inland lakes and rivers. The war of the Elechlear fundamentally changed not only Altum, but the very laws of its nature, the walks of its life, the races which would evolve over millions of years to come, yet so it was that, like the gods they—and all of their cities and stupendous technology—who shaped the world we know were hidden away, not in the stars, but under the layers of crust as the surface settled anew.

"For millions of years the technologies of Altum's most powerful race have lain dormant, and never would have been found if it were not for the obsessive plumbing of our ancestors some six thousand years ago. Novare have always been obsessed with deeps, and have always dug, as they do all throughout the mountains and land that they inhabit. It was the father of my fathers, King Chalor himself, that found in the passionately and fearlessly deep mining of his workers the great Elechlear city on top of which Lucetal was then built, and still resides. Ever I have sat directly above Fort Soarlin, an ancient military base encased in geologic ages. The first Novare to live in Lucetal knew of it, walked its halls, tasted of its gifts. But that information was smothered for the good of Novarekind, so that we should not succumb to such devastation as the Elechlear, and now the knowledge of it only exists between Kings, though I have shared much with Nubes." Chalem glared at the wizard with blazing pride.

"And today the High Wizard has made good on my trust, for today he has convinced me to open the Fort to our armies. It contains weapons that will allow us a swift victory over the Xol!" He spat as he issued this last statement like the command of a great conqueror, smiting the stone floor with his sceptre.

Nubes rose like a great spirit of shadowed crimson, and the flames snuffed out, sputtered brilliantly to life all at once, and died again. Now only the pale blue light of Harbinger glowed in the room, and in that alien wash the wizard's face was terrible to behold. "Son of Chalor. You make a grave error."

Chalem sat silently in the dark, his face all shadow. "The Xol will never join us, Nubes. I will wipe them from the face of the world."

Nubes trembled with rage, and it was a strange sight even for the Captains who knew his presence well, for he was thought of in the palace as much as in Lucetal as a tranquil creature. Yet now it was not at all difficult to see that he was full of wrath. Grave waves of purpose seemed to crush the lungs of all, and the King could not but turn his eyes upon the floor.

Suddenly the torches flared again to life. "So be it," boomed the wizard. "I will not stop you. But the Xol shall play their part. This world is doomed, and your foolish war only hastens the end." Without another word, Nubes nodded each to the captains, lastly and oddly most honourably to Harbinger, and made his exit in a flourish of crimson cloth.

Donlan was last to take his eyes from the empty passageway, and those final words he took the most heavily. Nevertheless, he would not argue with his King, for despite his long friendship with Nubes he was loyal foremost to the blood of Chalor. The wizard would understand. Donlan perceived as well as the others that Nubes invoked some greater threat than the Xol, but even he who knew so well the wisdom of the Red Tower could not imagine that the purple folk would ever unite with Novare against any cause, even if it meant the destruction of the world. Grand and wise as the wizard was, he knew nothing of battle. So it was that for the first time in many years the Captain of Cavalry thought Nubes wrong.

So too were the feelings of Ramcrone, unprejudiced against users of magic and respectful of Nubes' legend as he was. For all his knowledge and power, the wizard himself had admitted not to have seen what the black legions had worked against their soldiers, and the heart of the Captain of the Knights was forever hardened against those deeds. Many of his finest and most skilled warriors had fallen in the war. His father was incinerated by Ezfled on a front far away while he brooded, locked up in the palace for his value and leadership. Whether or not the Xol were capable of forging some league or alliance with Novare in the darkest times of Altum, Ramcrone knew that he would never look a one in the eye without the will to fight.

The wizard's warning had stirred nothing in Vespia, who could think only of Chalem's speech. Looking up from the glory on her brow which had calmed him, now too observing the stout resolve and grave acceptance of Ramcrone and Donlan, the King saw that none of his captains were yet prepared to betray him. He nodded to Harbinger, and the sheer metal panel along the opposite wall noiselessly lifted. Through its clean perimeter they followed the blue figure into an angular hall made purely of bright, sleek and stainless metal. Their footsteps echoed all down the length of it, over which Harbinger glided on vestigial limbs, flickering out of existence, appearing again further down, now close to them, now perhaps halfway to the far, silver doors which parted smoothly to admit them. They passed here into a small chamber.

"Armoury," said Chalem, standing his sceptre between his sandalled feet, closing his eyes as before some object of reverence.

The polished floor sank smooth and sudden. Breathtaking speed was accomplished in an instant, though for a seemingly endless expanse of alien time the box-shaped cell plummeted directly into the world, only the endless droning of its machine intelligence pulsing in the ears of its riders. As they fell, Donlan envisioned the palace as if it were miles above their heads. Vespia stood rigid, eyes flaring with black exuberance. Ramcrone leaned against the cold wall stoically, as if he were comfortable, though his stomach had quite turned over. When the platform at last abruptly halted, only Chalem and Vespia had not begun to shake. Donlan breathed a sigh of relief as Ramcrone slowly extricated himself from the wall which had in the final minute of their endless plunge all but melded with his spine.

A vertical line of blue light bisected the door, and the delineated halves hissed apart. They stepped into a vast darkness troubled only by the diffuse blue-white flame which was Harbinger flying out and up in the void. Suddenly that same hue snapped throughout the entire enormous space, revealing dimensions so massive as to contain the King's great hall twenty times over. Yet each remotest corner was as clearly revealed by the piercing clean light as the featureless metal floor beneath the brilliant lamp-strips themselves, so impossibly distant above, arranged in hexagonal patterns along the angled, dizzying ceiling. To their left, a sheer silver plane extended at length to meet another looking precisely like the tall surface through which they'd passed from the tiny cell doors. At about the height of their waists ran the fine relief of a narrow shelf, seeming wholly unconnected yet to hover motionlessly before the surface of its own accord. Out to the right and from this low-tabled wall the smooth, lamp-veined ceiling angled acutely upward to accommodate and flatten above numberless rows of towering argent columns arranged in exacting procession all down the length of the hall, expanding into a distant though ubiquitously bright and clear horizon like an immense geometric forest of naked metal trees. The high wall beyond them seemed rather like a grey sky.

Chalem went to one of these structures, the click of his gemstone sceptre echoing up and out through the enormous room, and enacted some exchange with a progressively more formless Harbinger, who had descended above him like an electric cloud. The electric blue vapours of the figure seemed to mingle in the flow and folds of the King's cape. With a sonorous click, the face of the metal obelisk parted in a slender slot to admit his reach, and the ghost of Harbinger rushed away as in an impossible wind.

The King came away with a slim, black box, which he placed upon the hovering table against the wall. Low-profile, entirely without marking, and dark as night, it rested there like an object out of another world, and none could say what to do with it until Chalem touched his index finger to the centre of its surface, and there pulsed a soft blue line of light along its perimeter. The box opened back from this line with a jet of white steam. A metal platform rose up and flung itself forward from within, presenting a strange artifact to the eyes of the Captains. Small, silver, and sleek, it had a hilt like that of a crossbow, yet protruding therefrom was merely a short gleaming cylinder no thicker than an arrow, seeming wholly without purpose. An inexplicable hexagonal metal panel sat angled up from the meeting of hilt and cylinder, but as Chalem drew the thing from the depression moulded to its form, a radiant blue light blossomed up into that surface suddenly alive with energy, and shot down the length of the barrel, coursing softly at its end.

"This is a blaster," he said quite plainly, holding the instrument gently in one hand. "A more powerful killing machine than anything you've yet beheld. Harbinger, authorize the range."

The blue spectre was not there precisely, either thinking its Novare shape unnecessary, or too at home now in the bowels of Fort Soarlin to think of itself as a physical entity, but all the same the King's commands were carried out in an instant. The wall behind the shelf suddenly rose, and a long, low-ceilinged shaft was revealed. One by one throughout the space appeared floating, circular targets composed—like Harbinger, the hexagonal lights, the sudden animacy of the blaster—of that strange blue energy. Each bore concentric, spectral rings and a central dot. Chalem levelled the weapon so that its slender barrel pointed down the range. One thin line of blue light whispered forth and struck the edge of the closest target. A small bright white dot simmered just within the outermost ring, glowed, pulsed, turned blue as the rest of the display, and vanished.

Vespia smirked; Donlan gasped; Ramcrone frowned. "Such is as impossible as this Harbinger and that sick falling room," said the knight. "But how can a feeble light outdo a lucidium blade in good hands? Even the weakest Xol sorcerers cast such trifles, and a strong shield is enough in some cases."

Chalem smiled, weighing the weapon in his old hand. "Indeed, this is a very small and simple hand blaster, and of the Elechlear arsenal it is perhaps the most common and least destructive. Yet one pass of that feeble light over your strong shield, Ramcrone, and hardly a plume of dust would mark the spot of your annihilation."

"Incredible," breathed Vespia.

"It is like the lesser Gort," said Donlan, ever the lover of animals. "Small and simple to the eye though it carries a deadly venom. Sometimes the most dangerous things are improperly judged. See how precise and swift the shot was. As soon as it was released it had already arrived at its mark, and the beam was straight as an edge. This is unlike even a bolt of the strongest crossbow in range and accuracy. Yet it really does seem in some way different from magic, like it is a tool, a tool that we have never seen before, the bow and arrow of some distant future. Well, I suppose I should say past."

"Its force can be modulated as well," said Chalem proudly. He indicated the glowing blue arc that ran across the hexagonal panel. "At this level of power, one shot will completely erase an organic being from existence, no matter where or how they interact with the beam, or whether they are armoured. Well, armoured, I mean, like we outfit our own warriors." He passed his thumb over the arc, and the gradient of light depleted into a blue sliver. "Now it will merely stun a man for about five hours." He held the blaster out by the barrel, the blue light disappearing as soon as his palm left the hilt. "Who will try it first?"

Vespia took the thing almost before he could finish speaking. As soon as her hand touched the handle, the gun lit up once more in blue light, the arc slicing along its raised panel, the thick bright vein striating the barrel, charging in the tip.

"How does it fire?" asked Donlan, leaning in.

"There is a release," said Ramcrone. "Under the forefinger."

"You've a close eye," said Vespia, aiming deftly and without hesitation at the furthest target. Chalem's heart leapt to see how naturally she handled the weapon. A sharp blue thread unvarying in linearity from blaster to target connected dead centre, vanishing quickly as it came. The perfect shot illuminated the entire circle. "Bellumroth, what a tool this is. And this is the simplest?" She had begun to grin wildly, and all around her were startled seeing her so excited.

Ramcrone tried his hand at the blaster next, standing awkwardly like a man pointing off at some distant object. Donlan after him fired with like technique to the King, discovering quickly, however, that subsequent blasts could be fired instantaneously, and that by maintaining pressure one initiated a sequence of bolts which fired in far more rapid succession than one could affect manually.

As they practised, Chalem brought out new types of arms from other black cases of varying sizes and lengths. There were stout, large-barrelled cannons which expelled spreading waves effective at short range; there were long, slender rifles which fired ultradense beams very precisely at long ranges—these Vespia took a great liking to; and there was a vast gamut of bulkier variants of blasters which could be set against the shoulder and fired without much extraneous movement. Donlan and Ramcrone much preferred these automatic rifles to the other weapons, and quite enjoyed themselves in overwhelming a target. Yet of the three Captains, Ramcrone was least able to hit the targets consistently, and though he certainly enjoyed the powerful close-range weapons and the blast rifle, he could not help but miss the feel of a sword in his hands.

"These guns are surely powerful and terribly accurate," he exclaimed, having missed the nearest target once again, "but my men and I are more suited to the life of the blade. Did the Elechlear fight hand to hand at all?"

"They certainly did," said Chalem. "But let me tell you one last thing about the Elechlear. Harbinger!" The figure of Harbinger silvered into being beside the King. "Who were the Elechlear?"

"Your tense confuses me." Harbinger floated very still for a moment, and its empty eyes seemed to look elsewhere.

"The legend says they went to live among the stars, like the gods," Donlan murmured. "And my Lord, you said as well that some of the Elechlear escaped their fate."

"Isn't it obvious," said Vespia coldly, firing another methodical round at the most distant target, with the long-range tactical rifle she had not put down in some time.

Chalem nodded. "Allow me to finish the tale. In the years before the great war, one group of Elechlear abandoned their world in a fleet of magnificent starships, though they planned not to seek new homes. Those that escaped entered a state of hibernation, and their luxint-powered computer pilots, such as Harbinger, automatically returned them to Altum when it had become reasonably habitable again. Even millions of years after the Luxint Rays poisoned the world, the residual radiation killed many shortly upon arrival, but a rare few survived by the chance of their practices, and Altum was home again to Elechlear peoples, though they remembered little of their former civilization.

"The Elechlear at first returned to their technology. Yet ultimately they decided that the luxint was too great and evil a thing. They desired to live simply in their new world, and sank their ships in the poison sea. They became hunter-gatherers like their ancient ancestors, and raised their kin on a great island which they called Luce. All knowledge of the true Elechlear was lost wilfully over millions of years, buried beneath the capital city of Lucetal, guarded by the sons of Chalor, and so they took a new name, that of the Novare. Modern Novare are therefore the only life forms of Altum that are not an aspect of the Great Mutation. Rather, we created it."

Ramcrone looked at the blasters and rifles upon the table, and recalled as in some deep-seated memory that it was strange how simply and easily they fit into his hand. Really the whole place seemed so perfectly to accommodate the Novare form.

Greater than awe was the weight of their true ancestors' deeds upon Donlan. "Now we turn to luxint energy, just as they did, for war. Are not our actions against the Xol akin to those which doomed the Elechlear?" The Captain sat upon the cold metal floor, cross-legged. His sharp features were weary, and his eyes downcast. "The words of Nubes trouble me deeply."

Chalem had gone to the forest of pillars as he finished his story, and returning now held a much smaller and thinner case than they'd yet seen. "The difference between our war and that of the Elechlear is in the blood of our enemy. The Xol are not Novare, and they will never understand Novare," he said darkly. "Our only avenue to peace is extermination."

"They are remorseless," said Vespia, still firing without the slightest extraneous motion, never straying from the absolute centre of her target. "It is a war not for conquest, but to protect ourselves from inevitable invasion. If the Elechlear were a warring people then it is true to our blood to defend our liberties from the demons. So says our King that they are in fact the abominable spawn of the failure of our ancestors. We owe it to our history and ourselves to wipe the world clean of that disgrace before it blackens every last tree. So be it if we one day destroy ourselves; it will not be by laying down before the purple hordes!" She fired more rapidly as she ground these last few words out.

Donlan did not stir at her words, seated in greater brooding yet, but Ramcrone was deeply moved. "It is true," he said. "I've not known a Xol to lay down their weapons, or spare a man without his own. And those we capture cannot be reasoned with. They do anything to kill, and hold their own life as nothing next to the agenda of their Empress."

Sensing the will to fight within the young captain, Chalem handed him the new case. Inside was a smooth silver hilt, set with an angled guard, wrapped in tough black fabric. Ramcrone eyed the King with wonder, and pointed the slender metal away into open space, feeling the tug of the grip against his palm. When he flipped the low-profile switch under his thumb, a great blade of blue light burst forth straight and pure as starlight, fine tipped and clean-edged. Its bright cylindrical length crackled and hummed like one dense rifle pulse held and drawn out.

"Aye," said Ramcrone, a rare smile cutting his ruddy cheek. "These weapons were made for us."

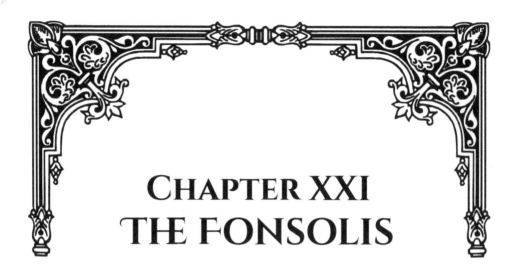

CHAPTER XXI
THE FONSOLIS

As there was no soil in which to plunge and feed, and the lightless journey up and out of the hive of the Eyeless had tested him such that sea monsters seemed but trifles, Ogwold slept long into the morning, snoring like a shaken bucket of gravel, drooling deep into the tissue of his ratty pillow. Stirring at last in the rumour of smoke that lay thick upon the boards of the old inn, when he finally forced his heavy stone eyelids to rise, he saw the sphere hovering over him like his own little moon. Byron's cot was empty. Training as always, thought the ogre. That was not for him today.

After a plate of leafy green tubers and one mauve, bitter bulb seemingly used in all Fonsladian dishes, he paid the innkeeper, and weighing what remained of Nubes' silver in his huge hand inquired as to where he might stock up on more such edibles. The innkeeper merely pointed across the way, and when Ogwold lurched through the swinging green doors of *The Silver Shovel* he beheld a low-roofed, broad-windowed building whose stocky bearded proprietor was that very moment hauling out into the morning chill a cart of the same purplish bulbs which like healing music dissolved in the ogre's gut even now as he gawked drooling. Lurching into the store with wild eyes, there was much explaining now required of his massive form and strange skin, but in no less than half an hour he emerged onto the dirt road with his old bag quite stuffed with fruits and vegetables of all varieties.

Slinging the bulging sack of precious food over his shoulder, patting it affectionately and—he laughed to himself—somewhat ironically with his plant hand, at last he set out with quite a saunter in his ungainly stride to explore the city and learn something of the witch Hesgruvia. A low blanket of white, milky mist clung to the morning treetops and dew-thick, slanting roofs, but the sun shone bright and clear over the red shingled cones that sprouted up from the centre of town, and already the haze was beginning to burn off. Though the palace appeared quite old even from a distance, the sturdy houses which he lumbered past like a huge grey-white golem were fortified with fresh stone and seemed many times reconstructed. The whole atmosphere of Fonslad was certainly tense, as though all its people knew they worked and lived on the precipice of their demise. There were, for instance, far more guards on patrol than ever Ogwold had seen in Epherem, even on days when the finest gems were to pass through that liminal space of commerce. These soldiers, though, were nothing like those royal knights with their blazing signatures of rank and proud plumage.

Solena must have come straight to the tavern following his shift, for the knights of Fonslad were no more armoured than was he the night before. Standing in dogged gangs, glancing anxiously over all that passed by, they were clad in rough-shod metal and leather helmets, short spears appearing to be their only weapons but for the hosts of archers posted at high vantages all about. Strapped to the backs of each warrior were small, circular shields, part metal and leather. Quickly Ogwold was approached and questioned of his business, looking so out of place, but there was nothing standoffish about the encounter, and soon he was directed as to where he could find the beginning of the path to Hesgruvia's tree-house, for it was common knowledge among the guard.

A sallow, grizzled knight left him at the edge of the vast forest, spilling out from the low mountains—covered in their industries of delving—which embraced Fonslad. Here the houses were mostly destroyed, windows shattered, walls collapsed inward, as if this part of the city had been so constantly assaulted by the Eyeless that there was no business in preserving it. The tall, spiny trees thickened quickly like the border into a wild land beyond the last few, dilapidated houses, old and rotting, and the solid white mist fastened their branches in a singular living wall of green and white.

As he stepped cautiously between the first dark trunks into the grand silence of the place, still there were some very old houses leaning out of the glossy shadows, long abandoned, hardly standing, bursting thick with fungi and coated in moss. But any malevolence as to the nature of the wood seemed so suddenly supplanted by a wonderful serenity, walking under the long spindly leaves so softly waving one over the other, feeling the cool mist against his skin, smelling the heavy dew and loam, and gazing upon divine shafts of sunlight that like the fine hairs of Caelare lowered down their locks into dazzling little clearings of silvery grasses.

It was in savouring these senses which brought such peace, in wondering how such abominable things as the Eyeless could proceed from the shadows of such noble trees, that Ogwold noticed the first notch, at about his waist, the place where a man's chest might have reached. Two legs of a tall triangle, three concentric ovals seated in its elbow—this was the symbol to follow. He placed his green hand over the mark, felt the flowing, gradual gesture of life just touching the bark, and moved on.

Many strange shrubs and weeds grew all about the trees, whose roots were generally exposed, and flowed about in tangled streams and knots, so that Ogwold needed at times to step over them quite carefully. He found the next notch beside a small stream. The grass and earth was wet and spongy, and he could sense that the great marsh beyond had influence over the entirety of the valley. Almost on cue, a light rain reached him through the treetops, and the sunlight, which had already dimmed, became pale and grey through a great sheet of fog. The trees became more dense as he went notch to notch, and feeling quite alone he took the sphere up out of his pocket and let it coast through the air at his shoulder. It hummed and spun and sometimes went to investigate the trees, or slip inside the foliage and come thrilling out, the dew spinning off of it in a fine mist.

The walk proved quite short by the lumbering strides of a Nogofod, and it was easy to see that the notches led to an enormous tree, much larger and wider than the others, along whose craggy trunk long thick vines tumbled like shaggy fur. Straight away the sphere shot up along the bark of the great plant and disappeared into the high canopy. Ogwold chuckled at the whim of the little silver ball, shooting forth and providing no precedent at all for what the ogre would find in following it. But this was a nice thought to him, for even in the dank tomb of the Eyeless he had enjoyed himself more than any day in Epherem; except, perhaps, for those evenings he spent in the sea. But then, if there was one thing the normgrass taught him well, it was that there are many more oceans in the world.

Staring at the mess of choking vines, Ogwold recalled suddenly the King of the Eyeless. It was just one of these long, slender shoots the shape of which his greener arm had taken, when it shot out to avenge Videre. Even as he thought this, that very limb quite became a vine itself, and snaked pooling out in coils of tough green rope upon the forest floor like a great thread unspooling. He grinned and flung the lengths of hardy cord up into the dense leaves above him, and something seemed to catch, and when he tugged bore security. So he held that anchor tight, and as his other arm pulled upon the length of fibre he could feel the plant reeling in with equal force, so that he walked his great oafish feet directly up the springy bark of the tree.

There was no pain but the feeling of extreme pressure in the fibres of the green flesh. The broad, spacious lower branches enveloped him and grew more numerous, more tightly spaced, and close to the trunk he climbed straight up through a tunnel of green and brown, surrounded by the twittering of birds, the buzzing of little insects, the rush and whisper of high winds seated and thrilling among the leaves. Soon he found the anchor-point of his arm, tightly wrapped around a branch nearly twice as thick as his torso. Walking slowly out onto the enormous extremity, he willed the vine to spool back up into his shoulder, from which it blossomed fluid and strong once more into the shape of an arm. He stared at his hand, wondering why it no longer saw a need for rope.

"And so a Nogofod comes to my humble home," came a musical voice. A woman sat not far from Ogwold, seated on a branch of her own, thick as the one he rested on now. She had dark skin, and silver hair. Her eyes were shaded by a great, pointed hat of soft navy blue, and she wore a long flowing cloak of the same colour. In her hand was a silver wooden staff which twisted around itself like a system of roots, and terminated in a slender bulb, glowing softly, at its top.

The sphere floated just over her shoulder, and she smiled at it. "And he brings a friend! Now here's a thing I've never seen!"

"I am Ogwold!" he said, standing wobbly and very much terrified of falling from the branch, broad as it was; still he bowed with grandeur, leading with his greener arm as if to display his allegiance with growing things. "I am looking for Hesgruvia."

"What business have you with her?"

"I am told she might know a path further into the range."

"Hm. She couldn't know so much as this orb. Though its trajectory is not easy to decipher."

Ogwold's eyes widened. "It speaks to you?"

"It is quite noisy, don't you think?" She closed her eyes. "Why don't you come inside, Ogwold? I am the one you seek."

Hesgruvia leapt from her place upon the slightly higher branch and landed deftly beside the ogre. The enormous trunk of the tree unseamed before her, and she stepped into the lambent passageway there opening to admit her. Ogwold lurched after her, happy to escape the treacherous heights of the branch. Within was a great wooden room lit by hovering green and gold orbs. The rings of the tree's heart played out on the floor and on the ceiling. In fine grooves were fitted ladders leading above and below. Hesgruvia had taken a seat in a simple wooden chair. The sphere ranged about the room curiously.

"I don't know what or who your friend is, or what it bodes, but I know it is important," said Hesgruvia, gesturing to the floor. "Please don't sit in one of my chairs lest you shatter them with your enormous carriage."

Ogwold laughed and sat slowly upon the warm wooden floor. When his palm touched the wood, he thrilled with the dense, ancient life of the tree, and a pleasant warmth travelled up through the veins of that arm into Ogwold's own heart. He sighed as though each of his muscles one after the other recognized some unnecessary tension in their being and slowly released.

Hesgruvia smiled, looking at the strange hand where it grew from the white sleeve. "Now that's something I've seen before, if it's knowledge you seek."

"You know what it is?"

"It is a Fountain Seed, the Fonsolis, a rare and magical plant that grows only in the deepest abyss of the ocean, held in the highest regard by the Flosleao. The Fonsolis grows only in threes, every thousand years." She laughed aloud. "Now how did you come to grow one in your shoulder?"

"My mother was a Flosleao. She saved me from a monster in the sea. It had eaten my arm. She left me on the beach and in the place of my wound this plant had grown. At first it was a small bulb, but when I met the sphere the plant suddenly grew into a new arm, and it also changes into other shapes. So far I've made a sword from it, sometimes big crushing vines that can break even metal bars. I made a single vine from it just now in climbing your tree."

"And you will find even greater things come from the Fonsolis. But it is better for you to find those things on your own. I've heard that the relationship between a Fountain Seed and its host is deeper and more intimate than the love of immortals. But legends always exaggerate," Hesgruvia mused. "My only advice is to keep your mind open to it and know that you share your body with another being, for the seed is no tool. It is an individual living thing which seeks symbiosis, not domination or subjugation. Such is the only way you and it can recognize that you are one. Treat it well, and keep it from fire. It loves water, sunlight and all living things, especially those which grow from the earth."

"It certainly loves your house."

"Of course. This is the fairest and eldest tree in the forest. Now then, what is the purpose of your questing beyond the perilous marshes?"

Ogwold set his jaw and the wonder went from his eyes in a way. "I seek Zenidow. That is where I must take the sphere."

Hesgruvia was silent, and leaned back in her chair thinking. Outside, the ever rippling trees soughed and sighed, and thousands of different birds cheeped and warbled. "You have a long way to go," she said. "And your competitors are far ahead of you."

"Competitors?"

"A party of sorcerers and sorceresses called the Zefloz by their Queen Fozlest, Empress of the Xol. They seek the mountain, but not the mountain itself. Rather, they are after something which is held within it."

"They must be the ones my companion is after, or at least one of their number is," said Ogwold. The sphere hummed loudly and seemed brighter than ever but for a moment. It went to him and hung in the air beside his ear. He then perceived an image in his mind of the mountain, and he felt in his heart that the sphere was inside it, that it was part of it, that it would be reunited.

"I sensed long ago that Zenidow was not a mountain," said Hesgruvia. "And I knew that one day the Xol would come for it. But I did not foresee the coming of Ogwold!" She shouted this last part and Ogwold was taken aback, but she chuckled softly.

"What are the Xol, Hesgruvia? I've heard many different accounts. It seems they are hated by all, but even my friend who hunts his arch enemy, one of the Xol, tells me that they are an elder and wise race."

"Your friend sounds quite wise himself. Like any body of people, the Nogofod, Novare, Flosleao, they have their heroes and villains, and many who stand between those forces. They live in the trees of Efvla, and have long ruled there. They are skilled in magic, and possess—even the non-magical ones—psychic gifts, for they are deeply at one with Altum, compared with Novare at least. But why should you trust my account if you have heard so many?" Hesgruvia stood, and held up her staff. A soft grey light emanated from it, and bathed her in fine luminance, so that for a moment she was unseen to Ogwold. When the light dissipated she was not as before. Her skin had chilled into violet, as her eyes too now flashed, and behind her two tails coiled round the legs of her chair as she sat once more.

"I am one of their kind," she said. "When I lived among my people, I was called Hesflet, but now I walk as a Novare among Novare, and go by the title Hesgruvia, for—as you say—Lucetal has so warped the name of the Xol that even here in far Fonslad, no matter how many wonders I work against the Eyeless, no matter the lives that I save or the magics that I weave for the good of these people, if my true nature were revealed I would be banished to die in the marsh."

Ogwold was in awe as much for the change in Hesgruvia—for he had never beheld one of the purple folk—as for the notion that any race of beings might be more horribly persecuted than his own. At once he was ashamed for thinking that his own troubles had been special, that there were not others in the world that suffered more greatly, for of course there were. He was blessed to have found at last a place where Novare like Solena would speak with him as an equal, but even here in a place that professed proudly its tolerance of otherness there was an unsquashable seed of hate.

"I can hardly imagine what that must be like," he said finally. "I thought it was oppressive to be Nogofod, but we were paid and kept alive at least. Now I see what war really is. But why come here, Hesgruvia? How difficult it must be to obscure your identity from the people you care for."

The witch nodded knowingly. "I left my people because I could no longer abide their treatment of the trees. They dominate them, you see, as I'd will you not treat your new arm. The forests of Efvla become each day more black and rigid, so that each great tree dies and becomes like a tower of metal, mouldable matter for the housing and weaponry of the Empire. The Empress and her ancestors are so afraid of losing the trees either to age, or, now, to the Lucetalians that invade their land, that they immortalize them as unfeeling statues of their former glory. It is a sick and depraved thing, and I could live among it no longer."

Ogwold sat thinking, his green hand held fast to the living wood of the old tree in which they rested. "But not all Xol think as the Empress does?"

"Many disagree, as I do, with the way of things, but many more are aligned with the will of the ancestors, and there is, of course, the curse. The blackening of the trees, it is a natural consequence of our being, imbued in our blood long ago by our eldest mothers."

"But this tree seems quite all right, yes?"

Hesgruvia smiled. "I have overcome the curse. It was the only reason I allowed myself to live among the true trees of Altum. I wish one day to return to Xoldra and share what I have learned, but..." Her countenance wilted. "I will be struck down if I am seen again among those branches. I am enemy as much as the King of Lucetal to Fozlest now." She looked up to Ogwold. "However, your coming to me creates an interesting opportunity. Already I've given you guidance in the nurturing of your Fonsolis, and as well I have an idea as to how you might achieve Zenidow in time, but do me one favour in return, Ogwold."

"Of course! I'm happy to help!" The ogre beamed.

Hesgruvia smiled solemnly once more. "It is these Zefloz, the group of sorcerers whom you race to the great mountain, whom your friend is hunting. The Zefloz are the Empress' elite, her personal squadron. They will have little trouble with mountain Novare, or mutants or any other monsters here. And that is why they are far ahead of you in the journey. They came through Fonslad a long time ago, and have long left the marshes behind."

"And must we outpace them? I know not the true reason for my journey, though I perceive easily that the sphere goes in haste."

"I fear that the heart of Zenidow holds a great power, and that the Zefloz will take it by any means. This would not be so terrible a thing if it were not for Zelor."

"Zelor! I know that word!" Ogwold shot up. "My partner; he comes with me to Zenidow in pursuit of that name."

Hesgruvia raised her silver eyebrows, and the deeps of her purple eyes glinted. "Now that is most peculiar," she said. "Zelor I know little of personally, divorced as I've been from the Xol, but I know he is new to the Zefloz, and I know that he is possessed of a great and terrible fear that goes ever before him. When he came through this place I felt that he walked not alone, for a great black shadow was cast about his presence, and it came from beyond the world. I sense that his reaching Zenidow will hold only calamity for all races of Altum. For I sensed also his power; it is far greater than any I have ever known, and by a tremendous margin."

"I wonder how Byron knows him," thought Ogwold aloud. "But I see now, if he's so evil, why Byron has such hatred for him."

Hesgruvia nodded. "Zelor will be the greatest threat to your quest, in time. But he is not the Xol wrapped up in my favour. Though they are powerful and extremely dangerous, the Zefloz are also quite different from most Xol, each of them with their unique interests in their journey. From the start there were some among their number who already disagreed with the ways of the Empire. Zelor has broken the minds of them all but for one. Her name is Elts."

The syllable of the name echoed through Ogwold as though it were some discreet and subtle necessity in such a song as his mother's which he so often recited in his mind and heart, yet he knew it was some part of a different song, some other portentous structure of verse from another path, a greater song, perhaps, or equal in importance to his own, and so the name of Elts crystallized in his memory like the single shard of a great work one day to be fully realized.

"She was the student of my oldest friend and greatest ally, Xirell, though he has fallen," the witch went on. "But she will certainly be interested in defeating the curse of our ancestors, as working against that weave was her master's greatest dream." Hesgruvia opened her palm, and in a turn of light there appeared a lone seed, slender like a teardrop and brown as the rich soil of the forest. "I wish, Ogwold, for you to deliver this seed to her. It can be the salvation of Efvla, if it is protected, and planted deep in the black forest Xoldra whence this all began."

Ogwold held out his hand. "I will gladly aid you, Hesgruvia. If there is a way for Byron and I to catch up with the Zefloz then I will make as great an effort as I do in fulfilling the wishes of this sphere in fulfilling your own. Elts will have the seed!"

Hesgruvia smiled and placed the seed into the ogre's palm. He stowed it in his bag, safely cinched in the pouch which once had contained his stock of dried tutum skins.

"They are very near to the Great Mountain even now. I know not what stands between them and Zenidow yet, but there is a way for you to overtake them."

"That sounds impossible!" Ogwold laughed nervously. "We'd have to fly through the air!"

"Indeed," said Hesgruvia. "You require the friendship of a Euphran. Only such a creature could bear you that far and over so many perils." She stood up. "I know of only one near to this place. She is called Wygram, and she is ancient and very lazy, but could do this thing for you if you can earn her trust."

"A real Euphran?"

"There are many in the mountains, for they are the greatest lovers of Caelare and this place is closest to her in all Altum."

Ogwold was silent, thinking of all the dangers he had so far weathered, of the Eyeless and the guards of Occultash, of the evil Zelor waiting for him at his goal, and now of the Euphran. But again his heart gladdened, and he was reminded of Byron and his bravery. He looked up determinedly, and she saw the resolve in his eyes.

"Wygram," she said, "is trapped, actually. You will need to free her. That should perhaps indebt her to you, but even so she will not at all want to be flying to Zenidow. She is kept in the deepest darkest dungeon of the Sanguar Lord Azanak, who has his great stronghold at the centre of the marshland. Azanak is millions of years old, and has roosted here sucking the blood of all life for that time in its fullness. Now that Novare have come they are frequently farmed in his dungeons like cattle, though the people of Fonslad blame most of his murder on the Eyeless."

"What is a Sanguar?"

"It is a cursed thing, a dead thing that walks and takes only to the night with vigour. It must drink blood and blood only, from any vein it can tap. And Euphran blood is the most delicious of all. Azanak keeps Wygram deep, deeper than the Novare prisoners of which there may be hundreds, and deeper even than the other rare creatures which he keeps half alive there."

"But how do I stop something which is already dead? Cut off his head?"

"No, that will accomplish little more than a brief respite while it is reattached. He does not quite have corporeal form, and can change his shape at will. There is only one way to kill a Sanguar, and that is sunshine. Even fire won't do the trick, nor puncturing its heart, nor obliterating it. The sun is its only enemy. Azanak will have many defences against it, though I suspect a creature so ancient will be prideful and reveal some chink in that strategy if you stay at it long enough." She leered at Ogwold here as if making a cruel joke. "But, I'm sorry, I'm scaring you on purpose." She suddenly leapt up and came to him. "I must tell you another property of the Fonsolis." She grasped his wrist and held the arm before her. "Ah, it is like no other plant," she marvelled, her eyes swimming with awe. "To think I would ever even touch such a thing in my long life."

"This can help me defeat the Sanguar?"

She peered at him circumspectly. "Tell me Ogwold, how do plants grow?"

"They need water and sunlight."

"Right you are, and so does your arm, Ogwold. You may have noticed this."

"It does love water, and feels more sturdy and hearty when I am out in the light. But it is still useful even in complete darkness. I was trapped by the Eyeless for a long time, and stuck in the pitch black fighting my way out for I don't know how long. I relied on its power throughout, and it never failed me."

"Trapped by the Eyeless! That is terrible!" Hesgruvia's tails swished and wrapped around each other. "Thank Caelare that you escaped. The Fonsolis alone can't be so powerful?"

"I had help. The sphere lit the way, and my partner Byron is a near unstoppable force." Ogwold grinned sheepishly, embarrassed for having been at all in such a dire situation.

Hesgruvia stared at him before slowly beginning to laugh. "Ogwold, you will accomplish great things. I'm glad to hear you have some experience fighting. Perhaps you noticed some weakness in the limb though?"

"I suppose towards the end of our escape, and then, now that I think about it, when we came out into the light again I felt as if I'd awoken from an endless sleep."

"Amazing. That is even a greater power than I expected. You see, Ogwold, the

Fonsolis absorbs sunlight like any other plant, and it also stores that sunlight, like a desert plant stores water, and much of that light remains unconverted."

"Unconverted?"

"Pure sunlight, stored within the systems of the Fountain Seed until it necessarily becomes energy for the plant. But before that process begins, it can be released in as many ways as the flesh itself can change its form. If you learn to release it when Azanak is vulnerable, the Sanguar will stand no chance."

Ogwold looked at his hand and thought of the great day star itself. "How do I do it?"

"I have no idea," said Hesgruvia, going back to her seat, tails flicking. "That's for you to figure out. Now, as for finding his awful fortress, it is as I said in the heart of the mire, where the four lakes meet, and it is ever shrouded in dark clouds. If you head straight north of my tree, you will encounter Lake Lumus. Circumnavigate it until you come to one of the four land bridges. Such will lead you straight to the centre of things."

Ogwold sat long on Hesgruvia's floor, pondering the quest she had set before him. But at long last he stood and bade her farewell, thanking her for all she had shared. "Hesgruvia, I cannot thank you enough for your guidance. I promise to deliver the seed to Elts. I won't fail you!"

"Farewell, Ogwold. Xeléd be with you." The witch nodded, smiling, and with a weaving of tails the entry-seam again formed the bark of her tree-house.

The ogre took his leave, sliding down the ropy vines to the forest floor, passing through the thick weave of mist. Notch to notch he made his way back to the crumpled outskirts of the city, wandering through the overgrown ruins, walking along the fringes of the first cobbled roads as if Videre might suddenly appear from the wood to join him. Still, there was no sign of the great cat. Returning to the inn he could not find Byron either, though surely the mercenary could not still be swinging his sword somewhere. By this time any other day they should have long been on their way. And then it occurred to him that there was a tavern.

At the back of the inn, in the large barnish room, the dark loft twinkling with liquors, at one of the many small circular tables stood about there was Byron, face darkened and glowering in shadow, a great mug set before him, and that tremendous slab of a sword lying beneath his feet where none could lay even an eye upon it without a glare from its owner.

"Where were you?" grumbled the mercenary as Ogwold pulled up a seemingly tiny chair across from him. The wood creaked dangerously, but held the ogre's weight.

"Finding a path for us. And you?"

Byron's eye flashed. "Most guards just laugh. But I met an old fisherman; he says there should be trails far beyond the lakes."

Ogwold tapped his huge fingers upon the wood. "I went into the wood to meet the witch Hesgruvia; Solena spoke of her." He looked around the room, but the guard was not present. "Turns out she is a Xol just like your enemy, but she pretends to be Novare. Apparently the Xol are just as hated here as they are in Epherem."

"Makes sense. That hatred has become a great unifying force for most Novare."

"I was surprised," Ogwold murmured. "She helps them with the Eyeless."

"The cavelings are monsters, easy to hate as they are to think about." Byron slugged his drink. "But the Xol, thanks to the rhetoric of Lucetal, are a much more intellectual enemy, almost a religious one. It's something that's taught from a young age. You don't need to tell someone twice that the cavelings are dangerous, but the Xol, you have to make someone believe it, feel it, trust in it as they pass it down to their children. That's not just fear; that's real hate."

Ogwold stared at the mercenary who had spoken with the beginnings of passion. His eyes fell on the drink which again seemed to have inspired this strange openness in the man. "I knew that kind of hate," he said. "Or, at least I thought I did. We Nogofod are raised thinking we are lesser beings. But meeting Hesgruvia today, or, that is, her name is Hesflet—"

"Hesflet, a beautiful name." Byron raised his mug. "Call her so then."

"You're right," said Ogwold. "Meeting Hesflet, I glimpsed what it really means to fear one's own identity. It is a horrible thing."

Byron nodded; the bustle of the tavern dulled, rose in volume as several new men came in at the threshold. "You are honourable to place the suffering of the Xol above your own, for theirs is great, but that does not detract from what the Lucetalians have done to your people."

Saying this the mercenary went swiftly to the bar, as if to escape again the sentiment of the moment, returning with his mug full and foaming, and the expression of solemnity again upon his brow. "More importantly: if you met one of the Xol," he said, "we are in great luck. She must have sensed Zelor if he passed through here."

"She did," said Ogwold. "She knows him and his whole company by name. And they came into Fonslad, yes, but a very long time ago. Zelor is far ahead of us, and apparently seeks some great powerful thing stored in Zenidow."

"Yes. Zelor was sent by the Empress of Xoldra to retrieve a great weapon. They call it Alium."

"Hesflet told me that Zelor is evil, and will use this thing to conquer the world. But she said that there are other Xol with him who are good of heart. Well, there were, but now there is only one who has not fallen to him." Ogwold took out the pouch with the seed and opened it over the table.

Byron's green eye peered circumspectly into the leathery dark. "What is it?"

"A cure. I'm to give it to the one called Elts who goes with Zelor. If she can bring it to the black forest and plant it there, it will reverse the process that changes the trees."

Now Byron was shocked. His lip seemed even to drop, and there was little mystery in the passion of his gaze. Quickly he cinched the pouch and pushed Ogwold's hand back into his bag. "We must reach them as soon as possible," he said. "If this is true, the races may reunite."

"Well, they are very close now to this Alium, perhaps even at its doorstep. Hesflet believes that if Zelor achieves his goal he will become unstoppable. Even now he may be too powerful. She told me that she has never known a Xol so strong."

"It was not always so," said Byron, and he took a long draft from his mug. Foam flecked his mouth when he slammed it to the table. Several heads throughout the room turned to the noise, but quickly resumed their own business. "Zelor and I grew up together like brothers. We were weak, but both of us came through the life of the sword into our own strengths. He was mocked by all Xol for his impotence when it came to magic. But together we were formidable, and he became even a great hero in the tales of my people."

"The Xol were not always the enemy of Novare?"

"To Lucetal they have always been evil, but I come from a different Kingdom of Novare called Molavor, which had its home in Efvla beside the purple folk long before any contact was made over the great sea. We lived in harmony with the Xol for many ages. But that time is lost to the deeds of Zelor." Byron set his empty glass upon the wood with surprising delicacy.

"He changed," he said finally. "The Zelor I knew was gone, and in his place was a monster. A red-eyed creature of darkness wielding a magic that awed even the mightiest sorcerers, so mighty even that it brought fear into the heart of his very Empress. But she is hungry for power as any, and so he was elevated to the highest of her ranks, and sent now upon this mission which, it seems, he has already taken over for his own purposes."

Byron had spoken a great deal, and the two sat in almost stunned silence as the words washed between them. Ogwold at last could see how difficult was the task before the mercenary, to hunt down and kill one whom he had loved.

"Well," began the ogre, "I don't think these paths beyond the lakes are going to get us to Zelor fast enough."

Byron raised an eyebrow. "Your quest is to reach the mountain. What haste is there in that?"

"Your quest is my quest, Byron." Ogwold smiled cautiously. "We will stop Zelor and save the trees, and, well..."

The mercenary sighed. "And I will help you with whatever your business really is at Zenidow."

"Maybe this is it," said Ogwold.

Byron frowned. "Caelare would not stoop so low. My guess is you have a higher purpose, and it must have to do with this Alium."

"Whatever it is," Ogwold mused. "I don't think it's a weapon."

"A pretty thought."

Ogwold took a deep breath. "Listen, there is a way. Hesflet gave me much more than this seed. She wants it delivered more than anything, and knows that Elts is each day more threatened to fall under the shadow of Zelor. But, hear me out. There is a Euphran near to Fonslad which might fly us straight to the mountain, if we can earn its favour."

Byron stared calmly, nodding as if this was quite ordinary.

"You don't seem surprised," said the ogre.

"This is Euphran country," said Byron. "They come from these mountains. Of course I'm not surprised that there is one nearby, but I'm certainly surprised that you think we can even get its attention."

"Okay." Ogwold laughed nervously. "Here's the other bit." He told Byron about Azanak and the black castle at the centre of the marsh, and the awful dungeons which he presumed to invade in rescuing Wygram.

"Now that might work," said Byron as soon as Ogwold was finished. He grinned, and it was the same wan, desirous and mad grin that he'd worn in the halls of the mutants, covered in black blood and hunted by monsters. "Depends on the Euphran, but this will be a big debt to pay. And a Sanguar. I have never heard of such a thing."

"Apparently it is immortal, and this one is thousands of years old. Only the sun can hurt it, so it makes sense that it lives under such a constant fog. But also my green arm was something that Hesflet recognized, and she called it a Fountain Seed, or a Fonsolis. Another new word for you?"

Byron shrugged.

The ogre went on smiling. "She told me that it can store and release sunlight, and so I might kill Azanak with it even in his darkest keeps."

"But you don't know how to do it?"

"I can learn, probably, while we travel. It is a long way to the marshlands proper, and then we must walk around one of the great lakes to reach the Sanguar's fortress."

"A Euphran in chains..." Bryon stood abruptly. All signs of drunkenness left him as in a coat suddenly shed, and his green eye was lucid and fierce. "One thing at a time then. We leave at dawn. Think hard on how you will release the sunlight from your Fonsolis." And he left without another word.

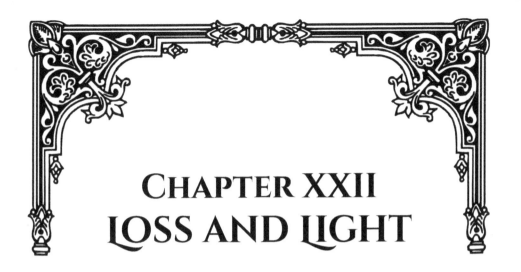

CHAPTER XXII
LOSS AND LIGHT

gwold woke before the sun, alone again in the inn. He found Byron training just within the wood. Notch to notch they hiked through the dense foliage, surpassing the great tree of Hesflet, and for many hours walking straight on, or as straight as they should think. Videre joined them so seamlessly among the trees that Ogwold was caught quite unawares, only easing back onto his big heels as she nuzzled him in the ribs. The sphere spun over her and rolled against her long head. Her fur was caked with mud, and there was a fierce liberty in her glowing eyes. The ogre gave the cat a great hug, and she rumbled affectionately in his wide bones. But then they had to catch up with Byron.

The ground grew increasingly soft and spongy, and squelched beneath their boots, though the great cat's feet made little noise, as they strode through the tall, dewy grasses. The soaked trees began to thin, great grey spaces of mist opening between their weeping trunks. Soon there were few about them at all, and they came out into the fullness of a vast mire. All around the mountains rose dark and distant as though the valley of the marsh were larger than the desert between Epherem and Occultash. Between their titan bulks an abyss of white mist revealed the details of the marsh only a few meters at a time. Heaps of brush and wet weeds scraggly and twisted stuck up out of the roiling fumes, bald mounds of dirt rose from sucking mud like the tonsured pates of dead giants; in their seedy pores, little ponds of stagnant water thronged with the splish and splash of secret life.

They walked mound to mound, rounding these stagnant pools and sinks of muck, their clothes, hair, and Videre's fur sinking wet and heavy down against the flesh. She became the grumpiest of all, for though she was fleet-footed on even stony and craggy surfaces, here in the sucking morass she was as slow as her fellows, and unused to a traversal that did not come to her naturally as breath. Often they passed large bogs of thinner water capable at least of flowing and rippling with the creatures there that swam or leapt, rolling with the touchdowns of black, rangy birds with horrible curved beaks. Yet some places were thicker than even the stretches of marsh between each of the solid mounds. On the black shore of one oozing, bursting swamp a hairy, wheezing thing lay twitching. In the centre of the murk, fully supported by the density of its contents, lay a great rat, whipping its tail about in propulsive lashes.

By midday the mounds began to recede, and they waded through a plain of sludge coming quite up to Videre's chin; but just as the situation was becoming truly unbearable the land beneath the muck sloped upwards and brought them up onto a still spongy but relatively solid stretch of turf. Out of the mist appeared a great expanse of still, black water, and they stood now upon the shore of an endless lake, over the glassy surface of which great phantoms of mist swirled and roiled. Ogwold felt quite sure that they were being watched by the dull glassy eye of some immense serpent, such as the monster which had taken his old arm, and he gripped the Fonsolis anxiously. Videre quite calmly went up to the water and began lapping thankful gulps of it, coming back to them sated and relaxed. Shrugging, Byron filled his flask, and Ogwold would not be the only one to abstain from drinking, even though the Fonsolis was quite hydrated from the sheer mists of the place that welled against its flesh.

They took the leftmost way along the furrowed bank, knowing that this side was at least closer to the edge of the marsh. With the ever-changing swampy terrain behind them, all they could do was keep their eyes on the eerily still lake water far out over the vitreous black, or the cold fingers of its edge which touched passively the muddy ground where they followed in a great endless arc. The mist clung to them still in suffocating sheets, and their cold muscles grew so dull, Ogwold felt that though he could continue walking forever so long as he had the least bit of momentum, if he were to stop for even a moment he would freeze solid. But at last the curve of the bank reached its apex and began to arch inward to the centre of things. Night fell then, and suddenly, for it was impossible to tell the time of day in the mist until the sun had truly set, and though they walked for some time in the blackness, they were too weary to go on, and bedded down in the mud.

Videre watched through the night, for it seemed she needed little sleep compared with her companions, yet even in the morning when Ogwold woke, Byron had clearly been up for some time. The man heaved as ever with heavy breaths and swung his sword as if for the thousandth time when Ogwold came up to him out of the mist to lead him back to the water. They pressed on. All through the day they walked, clothes so soaked that they rubbed the flesh raw, and clammy rashes and sores developed on their skin. They rested again at midday and sat to eat of what little rations they still had. So tough was the hunk of bread that Ogwold gnawed at that he fell to simply letting the flavor dissolve into his mouth, lying flat on his back with the grey knot looking like a stone between his teeth.

But as they rested the mist seemed to thin, and they saw ahead of them, across their path, that they had drawn near to another great lake, whose bank curved and came to meet with that shore which they'd followed to this point, continuing on together each shore to some shared vanishing point. When they'd eaten, they took again to the bank and trudged until night came again, sudden and total, and they camped down this time further from the water where it would perhaps be drier. Still they awoke sodden and sore once again; once again Byron was at work with his new great blade, and it seemed easier for him to swing that tremendous weapon which already had seemed light in his hands.

It was just past dawn, on the third day of their quest into the marsh, walking along the narrow bridge of land between the two lakes, that they came within range of the castle of Azanak. A great black mass it was, muddled in the wet fog as some shapeless undersea entity obscured through the depths of flowing water, and it persisted looming there in constant immensity as a black omen while they walked for many hours. The first features to reveal themselves were the great spines, seeming to rise in random patterns, at varying lengths, like jagged tusks; but as the pointed field came closer into view, clearly there were five towers which seemed the greater and had a majesty to them. Four rose from each corner of the great spiny bulk of the place; the fifth and largest rose from the centre up into the fog, where it was tipped by a great black barb like a thorn in the grey sky.

The whole castle rested upon and nearly completely occupied a piece of land where the two great lakes met against two distant others situated similarly, so that the fortress was like the malefic stamen of some great flower, the four lakes its liquid petals. The marsh was still awful and deep, full of foul slush, and the going was terrible as ever coming nearer to the fortress, for the lakes began to degrade through their boundaries into an insular wetland. Yet in time the gate rose before them, and they stepped onto a great black set of hundreds of aged, cracked stairs. There they collapsed and rested at the foot of the winding case, eating and drinking and marvelling at the great castle.

All the while they walked, Ogwold thought upon the feeble grey sun-rays that met them here beneath the fog, that turned dead against the black lake-water. In each mote of pale light he reached out to the Fonsolis which was his arm and shoulder, seeking as for some formless, nameless principle which should teach him the nature of photosynthesis. From the ancient plant he received the usual, each day more constant and lucid stream of feelings and impressions which began with the morning's removal of its venturing tendrils from the soaking soil and ended only with sleep—of the subtle shifting and underlying processes of land and water, of the ecosystem which thrived therein and thereof, the swamp creatures that moved in the rushes and through the rippling black, even the slightest insectile dusts that touched and skittered upon the lake—but never did true communication seem to come. It was as though the Fonsolis slept and Ogwold had only its chaotic matrix of dreams to sift through for answers.

Now sitting upon the evil stair of Azanak's fortress, he was forced to own his failure. "Byron. I haven't learned to release the sunlight. I fear we go to our deaths now."

"We're too close to give up," said Byron, and he smiled hungrily. "We know the sun is in there somewhere. Sometimes these things can only be accomplished in times of need. That's how I've always learned, by fighting." With that he rose and took to the steps like a man possessed. "I'm sure the old bastard knows we're here, even if it is daytime. He'll be waiting for us."

Ogwold stood up and followed him, taking the buzzing sphere from the air and placing it in the sodden pocket of his cloak, for something in him feared that Azanak should see it. Videre sat staring up at the palace walls for a long moment before arching her back, quaking as the muscles stretched, and crawling slowly forward just behind, a white creep over the black stair. Her fur was jagged and stiff as when they had fallen into the trap of the archaeologists and their nightmarish covenant with the Eyeless, but there was as well a composure in the cat that showed she knew as well as her company the great necessity of this dire venture.

The steps were numberless, and wound like a severe switchback up the high grade where loomed the castle. Thick dark clouds reigned here, and there was a ceaseless heavy rain which smote their clothes and stung their skin. They were soaked and frozen to the core when they came at last beneath the great arch which swept over the entryway where tall black doors set with sharp stones all along their edges waited. Straightaway Byron took to pushing them in, and with a loud groaning they swung to, revealing a stagnant and pungent gloom within. The air was stale and dry, and as they came into the main hall their footsteps rebounded in the invisible ceiling.

The dark grey sun still played faintly upon the doorstep behind them, but the stink of death came at once to their noses. Like an ancient decay the odour hung about the whole place in pockets of almost visible miasmas as they walked, sometimes worsening, other times lessening, and it was the dissimilarity of the stink that made it somehow all the more odious to the senses, waxing and waning as if they passed by heaps of invisible rotted corpses.

No light reached further within that glowing block of the threshold, and as they left the main hall behind they found themselves in so suffocating a void that Ogwold was forced to take the sphere from his pocket once more, so that it cast its pale light around them as it had in the tunnels of the Eyeless. The walls and floors were bare, and their long dark, ageless surfaces went on like a windowless labyrinth. There were no articles of furniture, no rugs, no portraits or statues, sconces, or even doors to mark the boundaries of the cracked arches of the thresholds from room to empty room which made the whole place seem like a vast catacomb.

They found at last in the pale light a great stairwell beginning in the centre of an empty, purposeless room, leading down below like a sudden black throat. The steps were cracked and smoothed by time, and they did not speak as they took them, passing many more floors low in the ground, hearing only the hollow vast emptiness of the fortress all around them.

"Hold on," said Byron, his close voice sounding distant in the motionless air. "There's something in this one." He motioned towards the doorless arch they had reached beside the stair.

Ogwold moved past him and angled his blocky shoulder, stooping low to enter the room. He could hear a soft whispering, as wind through dry leaves, though it was eerily rhythmic and had to it a strange texture of moisture. As the sphere followed him, its light played upon an expanse of low shadowed shapes lying in heaps all about the stone floor, like animals long starved and abandoned, their emaciated ribs slowly expanding and contracting with the minimum energy required for survival. The sphere slipped curiously among the pulsing humps of flesh, which were not quite animals. They were Novare, men, women, and children, all lying helpless and sick, singly or in clumps, in a universal state of catatonia. Their eyes were glassy and their heads lolled, bodies limp and contorted. The presence of Byron, Ogwold, and Videre within the room had no effect upon them, continuing to gape and rasp like fish thrown helpless onto the beach of oblivion.

Ogwold reared back in horror at first, but soon stumbled out into the room, looking down its length at the veritable piles of the half-alive, taking in all that was truly there, for some several hundred Novare were here imprisoned by their own lack of will to escape. It was a vast cell without bars, a holding tank for flesh in stasis. Far out in the room he came to a cylindrical banister, and leaning over the edge he saw an endless pit of darkness ribbed with the concentric descending chambers all swelling softly in moving shelves of darkness. And worst of all, in the great, endless silence of the pit, was the deafening noise of shallow breathing in some enormous hellish concert all down to the bottom of the world.

"Why are they here?" he whispered, and Byron's hand found his shoulder.

"They're livestock," he said grimly. "We cannot save them, friend."

Ogwold turned and saw that there was compassion in Byron's eye, and it was a strange sight, as if a mask had been lifted from the man's constantly stony brow and there was a light that came from it, and it calmed him.

"We seek the Euphran," said Byron. He cast his eye down into the ranked pit. "It must be much farther down."

Ogwold steeled himself, and though it seemed as if the breathing and rustling of Novare grew and pounded in his ears, he was able to leave the gruesome scene and pass again onto the stair beyond the arch. The sphere led them down further through the shadows, and they passed each new layer of the dungeon doing their best not to glance through the doorless arches wherethrough they knew the masses of hardly living Novare were sprawled. Time dissolved in the changeless dark, the sphere a pool of gracious light hovering along the steps before them, upon which Ogwold focused all of his attention that was not necessary in navigating the steps. The stench of captive meat grew only more powerful, taking to it in time the smell of burning hair and flesh.

Yet at last the staircase ended. The final, edgeless step settled within a cavernous room beneath the lowest floor of the great tower of Novare prisoners, the bottom of that pit a ceiling to them now. Spinning and darting with the freedom of the open space the sphere shot in a stream of light. Here there were prisoners far removed from the biology of Novare, many the likes of which Ogwold had never before heard even remotely described. Though they, like the prisoners above them, were a deathly colour and feeble to behold, the strange beasts were brutally shackled to the stone walls, and even Byron did not stray too near as they passed.

The mercenary was however familiar with one creature that cowered in the shadows, fearing the light of the sphere. It was a bulky white serpent, silvery eyes shot with black shards, and it coiled itself gingerly into defensive loops, for it was so weak that it shied even from the tiny Novare that walked towards it.

"This is a Great Gort! A man in Occultash told me that it is only a legend. He quite understated its size, though. But look how destroyed it is, inside and out. If we find this Euphran, how do we know it will even be able to fly?" The enormous snake eyed the mercenary coldly, seeming to shed its anxiety.

"It must not be too weak if it's chained up like that," said Ogwold, admiring the creature. It looked much like the sea-serpent of the kelp forest, though quite smaller and hooded. The eyes too seemed far more intelligent, and the way they looked him over so slowly and thoughtfully set him shuddering. Hastily the ogre followed the sphere through the room, Byron eventually following with Videre, who swished her tails walking confidently past the other strange and hideous monsters, all of which huddled as far from the light as they could and shook with fear.

At the end of the hall of exotic specimens was a great crack in the stone, through which they passed into a room quite different from those left behind, cathedral-like in its high-ceilinged grandiosity. Still the walls and floor here were unadorned, but there was a majesty to the place that seemed to ill fit the rest of the castle.

The sphere cut through the dimness along milky flagstones like a lonely comet, and paused hovering between two gigantic white claws at the opposite end of the room, their sharp curvature twinkling in the pale glow. Slowly the far point rose, illuminating the unmistakable visage which Ogwold had heard described only in legend, of a great and wise Euphran. Its powerful jaws were decked in pale blue scales, and its all-seeing eyes were like shards of ice within deep white crystals. It had very long horns for its kind, kindling in the sphere's light, sweeping back along with the silvery, gossamer cords of hair that grew out and back in an ethereal mane from its stately brow down to its narrow, angled shoulders.

"She is not as weak as the others," said Byron, stalking out into the room, one hand upon the hilt of his sword. Ogwold and Videre followed. The Euphran stared at them with bright, knowing eyes as they approached, its complexion unchanging, scales shimmering as in distant firelight in the sooty dark. "And look how she is chained."

Each of the Euphran's hard-scaled limbs, none more crudely than the grand, silver and blue tail, were choked in sequences of immense metal shackles, and bolted to the floor. One thick chain attached to the shackle around her neck would not allow her triangular head to rest on the ground. Her great many-layered wings were pierced in three places each, and awful chains had been drawn through the wounds to bind them to the wall.

The trio arrived before the grand creature, keeping their distance, and Ogwold could not contain his fascination. "She's beautiful," he said, big grey eyes swimming with the azure glitter of her armour.

"Why thank you," said the Euphran in plain speech.

"You can talk!" Ogwold said.

Byron scowled in the pale light. "The power of the Euphran is in its voice. As is our own power over her if we find the right words."

The Euphran cocked its head, the motion flowing through the silvery cords all down her neck. The corners of her mouth seemed poised in some higher form of expression inaccessible to mortals, emanating a peace that was at once blissful and mournful. Perhaps it was the sweet voice of the creature that drew these impressions together in Ogwold's heart and moved him so to trust the magical creature completely, for it was like warm honey to the ears and flowed all through the senses, making his spirit rise and his skin vibrate.

"Even my master hasn't such knowledge," she said, ageless eyes scanning the mercenary.

"I once partnered with the Euphran Yorym. He and I went into many battles together, neither of us master of the other," said Byron. "But he was lost."

"What?" Ogwold was astounded.

Byron shrugged.

"Yorym—I've not heard of him," mused the Euphran. "To think that freely one of my kind would fight alongside a friend of the Xol is hard to believe."

"But how can you know that he used to live with the Xol?"

"It's all over me," Byron answered. "Whether or not they hate or love the Xol, no creature is more sensitive to the death of Efvla's trees than the Euphran."

"There are others more wounded," said the Euphran. "I do not distrust the Xol any more than the Novare. Or the Nogofod for that matter." The gelid crystals of her eyes hovered over Ogwold. "Though I've not met such a one."

The ogre fell to one knee and bowed his shaggy head. "Please trust us, Wygram. We've come to rescue you! We need your help. You must fly us to Zenidow."

At the sound of her name, the Euphran was clearly amazed, her mane rippling with surprise, and though she seemed quite excited to hear those long unused syllables, she folded her talons over calmly. "Zenidow!" Wygram laughed boomingly, and the brassy sound filled the room. "That is even more preposterous than thinking you might yourselves even escape this place."

"We'll see about that." Byron smirked. "Well promise us this. If we break your shackles, you will not eat us."

Wygram rolled her eyes. "I'm not a monster. Besides, I would never harm a child of Caelare."

Byron looked sidelong at his companion. Now it was Ogwold's turn to shrug. The mercenary shook his head smiling, drew his immense sword, and swung it hard upon the chain attached to Wygram's neck shackle—it snapped clean in two. Next he cleaved the shackle binding her right arm and with an arching chop the left. Ogwold set the Fonsolis on her short legs and serpentine tail, and very carefully her wings. She watched the spectacle of root and twisting vine with fascination, even after she was thoroughly extricated from the wall, as if she at first could not process the notion of liberty. But a warm thrill trilled down her spine, and she craned her neck, arched her back like Videre stretching in the evening, and a thrumming purr issued from deep within her scaled hide. Videre sauntered up and rubbed against the soft belly now exposed.

"What a lovely creature." Wygram smiled and the reptilian lids of her eyes lowered.

"All Euphran are different," said Byron cautiously to Ogwold. "But most are like this Wygram, peaceful at heart."

"And you are the judge of a peaceful heart," said Wygram, staring at Byron before he could turn and walk. "You stink of death."

"I only kill wicked things."

"That's true as far as I know," said Ogwold. "I've had to take lives too, and I hated it. But it was right and necessary."

Wygram rumbled. "Why is it necessary for you to go to Zenidow?"

Ogwold and Byron exchanged glances, but it was the ogre that spoke for them. "We're following an evil Xol sorcerer. If he reaches the mountain before us he will become too powerful to stop."

Wygram closed her eyes. "Hm. But this is not your personal quest, Nogofod."

"His name is Ogwold," said Byron. "You can't lie to a Euphran, ogre. It's true, he has his own reasons."

"But we've agreed to help one another, just like we'll help you now, Wygram." Ogwold smiled at both.

"Hm," Wygram hummed. "Your paths converge then. There is something within Zenidow which calls to you both. Even Azanak knows that something has recently become sensible in that place, and he is quite dead to the world."

"Where is Azanak now?" Ogwold asked.

"He is everywhere. What do you propose to do about that, Zenidow hunters?"

"We've a secret weapon," said Byron, turning confidently to Ogwold.

"Indeed," said Wygram, sounding now serious and solemn, as if some hellish delirium had left her and she now saw some sliver of hope in the depths of her pain. "Do you know how to use it?"

"No..." said Ogwold. "We were, I was hoping it would just, well I don't know."

Wygram's wise eyes seemed to lighten, though that same expression of elder peace persisted. "You are in luck," she said. "Come here, child."

Ogwold lumbered over to the gigantic figure of Wygram, and snaking down soft and low she touched the skin of the Fonsolis outheld with her snout. By breaths she became impossibly still, eyes shut off, features soft. The last that Ogwold beheld as he closed his own eyes was the hovering light of the sphere, drawing near to that point of contact between scale and plant. Warm fabrics of darkness rose and fell from below and above, but slowly one fold distinguished itself from another by the subtlest gradient of shadow, now another, here several more collapsing and tessellating out like rippling endless black bed sheets outflung in all directions. Yet these sheets were no longer fabric; they were water, dark water now growing lighter with each motion of the great shifting, flowing image. He was beneath the sea, floating above the kelp forest in the dazzling water, far from the shore, and up from the kelp there rose a strange being.

Everywhere the being appeared connected inextricably to the kelp from which it came, yet it seemed itself a single, independent notion. A mass of feeling, thinking vegetation it was, and from it at all angles stretched and floated vast roots like the nervous system of a bodiless brain. Always this flexing nexus was growing, but so gradually and slightly that the eye could not perceive the small changes, and was confused. Out reached the living singular forest of tendrils around him, cradling his head and enveloping him, and he felt as though the entire kelp forest transfused his being into its own. A rushing power came into his blood. Then he heard the voice of the plant. It was one sound, only it fluctuated, and it sang sweetly into him, and he knew, he understood why it sang, and what it sang. The voice sang one word, and the word was light itself.

Then the plant-mind and forest-body were silent. Wrapped in the dark green, warm womb of the inmost being of this place of primordial dreams, Ogwold felt that it was his turn to sing, and so he opened his mouth and out came, to his surprise, though it seemed natural, the same strange chord, harmonizing perfectly with his memory of the song. And the word was "Iliofos!" Which he shouted at the top of his lungs.

"Well then," came Wygram's voice. "You don't need to bellow so."

Ogwold was in the dungeon once more, looking up into the dazzling, radiant face of Wygram, lit up so completely as to appear perfectly white but for the pure blue chips of her kind eyes. Even the wall behind her was washed in golden luminance, and as he looked down at last he saw that the Fonsolis beamed as from its every slightest pore with a light that was bright and true as the palace of Caelare itself.

"Now, listen next for the word of return," Wygram urged.

Ogwold shut his eyes to the light and recalled the way always he would will his arm to change back into a resemblance of the other, a normal Nogofod limb with five fingers at least. Yet now he opened his ears and heart too to that secret singing which had come to him in the dream of the kelp, and sure enough a word formed in the same lilting hollow song that he'd heard in that trance.

"Protagi!" said Ogwold only a little less loudly, and at once the light was no more. He flexed the green arm, turned it over, and a powerful grin spread across his oafish face.

"As I said, you need only speak the word in your heart. But I have heard that it is more powerful to say it aloud when you summon the strength of the Fonsolis. Now let's please vacate this awful place." Wygram began slowly making her way from the great archway that led into her prison room, her huge talons raking the flagstones.

As they made their way back through the enormous crack into the room of strange and mystical prisoners which the Euphran urged them kindly not to release, and up the winding stairs, Wygram having to cram her gigantic but thankfully slender and narrow body through the cold stone walls, Ogwold thought of all the different transformations that the Fonsolis had so far offered. There were the shield and blade shapes that it first had made. Then there had been the vine form, which had stricken out and pierced the mutant king, and which had helped him climb the tree of Hesflet. Now there was the sunlight which he could conjure, but it had seemed to him incomplete, as if that state, for the Fonsolis, was a precursor to something far more wonderful.

He reached out to the plant in the hopes of forming a constant understanding with its voice, calling it by name as they ran, asking for more words. It spoke to him now more clearly than ever, and a great language unfolded in the halls of the mind, as if high windows were slowly uncurtained, and now bright beams of truth-light struck the dark tiles of the floor with brilliance. Yet they came soon up into the prison layers of the Novare, and there through the doorless archways those hopeless and numberless captives lay in the awful malaise, their eyes sallow and cheeks sunken.

"Can anything be done to save these people?" said Ogwold again, stopping, stooping beneath the arch, kneeling beside one of the sad forms. It was an old woman, hardly covered in soiled rags, eyes rolled, tongue slightly protruding from cracked lips, though on that feeble organ was the slightest moisture of life.

"They are long dead," Wygram rumbled, sticking her head into the room; beneath her tasselled chin Videre sauntered lithely to Ogwold and lowered her huge black eyes over the poor old Novare. "Held up far beyond the limits of their biologies. Azanak is all that keeps them circulating. No minds exist in those hollows."

Byron squeezed into the room. "And where is the old fool?" He grinned cruelly, gripping the hilt of his blade.

"You are attracted to doom," the Euphran snorted. "I like it! But your weapon means nothing in this place. Only Ogwold has power here, and this is not just any Sanguar. Azanak is a demon lord, old as the mountains. Though I suspect the Fonsolis is more ancient, you have never truly called upon its strength."

"If we kill Azanak, what happens to the people?" Ogwold murmured, staring out over the wheezing mounds.

"They would fall," came the sudden chorus of many distant voices—high, low, hoarse, unctuous, grating, soft—as though some far clump of the bloodless bodies seized suddenly with singular animacy. Even before the pale light of the seeking sphere fell fully upon the source of the unnatural sound, the eyes of the company found that tall thin ghost standing naked and pale in the black. The sick white skin now illumined was fatless as a drum. A brittle skeleton unburdened by the slightest musculature showed its every component as clearly as its lack of joints, as if the bones were held together sheerly by the tautness of the flesh. Swelling like a foul bulb upon a stem long and sinewy rode the bulbous head of the thing, weaving as a snake tastes its prey upon the air, its huge eyes nighted pits of bottomless black, the only features in a ghastly white face that surely hadn't the faculty for speech.

When the hideous concert of voices came again, Ogwold imagined that the noise was a storm of lost souls trapped within the swollen head, beamed from the hollow eyes. "How thoughtful, to bring forth the Euphran. I just dreamt of a drink."

Wygram shuddered horribly, though her countenance could shed no dignity. "There's your Azanak," she said with surprising lightness of being. Ogwold could only wonder how the sanguar would drink, having no mouth.

"Ah, but..." The rayless eyes of the sanguar seemed uncannily to focus upon Videre, and she growled deep in her throat. "What is this?" The voices yet simmered on the air even as Azanak vanished. A cold wind swept blind and rough through the very marrow of Ogwold and Byron before they realized the monster had slipped its awful hands effortlessly into the thick trunk of Videre's neck. She wailed and screamed, the subtlest muscles standing out hard and desperate along her great body, claws scraping and chipping from torque against the stony ground. Byron brought his massive sword down powerfully, shearing through Azanak's head, bunched neck, and body clear down to the waist, so that the monster was split clean in two but for its crouching legs, peeling nearly symmetrical away from either side of the blade where it stuck. But the separate eyes only laughed, in each a hellish acapella of mirth, and all heard clearly now that the awful cacophony of voices arose indeed from those deep black pits.

Cold cackling echoing in so many ways, the independent white arms welled and bulged elbow deep in Videre's flesh like mud through which they sank, trussed in sickening, throbbing veins running up along and out from the ravine of cloven torso and neck, pulsing in the rearing, snakelike laughing halves of Azanak's bulbous head. Already tendrils of black gunk unravelled from the sundered flesh all down to the blade embedded, had begun knitting together at a great pace, bubbling and bursting foul ichor all over the floor stones, meeting and knotting in strands, tugging inexorably one side back to the other. Byron ripped back the edge from the sanguar, black blood splattering all around, but even as he readied the next blow there was a terrible wet, crushing sound, and all of Videre's body collapsed in on itself, the life leaving her eyes at once, and only a dying whistle parting her lips, the last that she would utter. Azanak withdrew his arms from the limp body, and his pale hands were dry, for every drop of blood had entered under their skin, and raising them he pressed the two halves of his yet knitting head together at last.

"Strange blood! Hidden blood! Cruel thirst—none remains. From where did it come?" Pressing his pale hands to his fatless chest in a horrible impression of woe, Azanak's speech—however touched by the identities that were his many voices—rang flat like lines in a play terribly acted, mechanically dictated by a dead parade of corpses carrying on by the lonely engine of a forgotten curse. Yet in meaning they were the lines of one who is moved by passion and desire. Somewhere in the monster was the likeness of a soul born in some ancient evening of mortality, which formed these thoughts, who philosophized upon the novelty and rarity of Videre.

Ogwold fell to his knees in shock, holding the lifeless body of Videre tightly.

His mind blistered over with visions from all angles of her death. Great big tears rolled down his cheeks. Even Byron had not been quick or strong enough, but at least the mercenary had acted. Yet the ogre could not rise or lift even his eyes from the long cold cheek of the great cat, and shame was on his back.

Byron swept his black-blooded sword up through the path of its first descent, but the sanguar leaping back betrayed that he would rather not be caught again by the massive weapon, and sliding back along the stone sank to the ground on all fours. He advanced with the same cold speed as before, but this time Byron beheld all, showing the swift reaching hands the broadside of his blade. He rammed his shoulder into the makeshift shield and forced Azanak back but one step, for the monster had prodigious strength. But even in that step Bryon leaned into and mastered the momentum of the impact, spinning full round and pulling the right-angle edge right through the narrow waist of Azanak moments from escape. Bodiless legs scrambled and fell; torso landed on the floor with a wet thunk. The mercenary lunged to pierce the centre of Azanak's head, but on its long neck the hideous thing dodged, and the arms shot out and lengthened so swiftly that even already rolling out of the way the mercenary was too slow, and the clutching fingers raked his side. Gouts of bright blood painted the dank floor, but Byron only grunted and steeled himself behind his sword.

The mangled body melted suddenly into foul sludge, massing in a bubbling mess of twisting bone and ragged white flesh; up shot anew the tall spindly form unscathed as before, and the eyes bellowed awful, affectless laughter through the prison. "Fool!" they said in a thousand tones. "I am the night." The sanguar dispersed into a cloud of black smoke, rushing forward all at once like a storm of evil breath. But now Wygram joined the fray, thrusting forward her great wings, and a sudden wind rushed roaring through the cavern, ripping at the smoke, holding it now as it fought, gaining materiality, now too heavy to blow away; this time a huge hairless rat fell splat on the stone, its translucent tail whipping, its maw slobbering and gibbering, through serrated yellow teeth all sticking in different directions.

The rat uncorked its fat haunches, hurtling through the stale air, but Byron was thankful for the larger target, and the taste of blood hastened his blade. He brought the great dull edge crashing down at the moment the hideous whiskers just tickled his face, and the beast was thrown back by the strength and speed of the blow twitching and moaning, a vast gash in its face and chest. The fissure folded, boiled black; all dissolved into a mess of grey sick. Up rose the first form of Azanak standing easily. Blood slopped from Byron's wounds, and a network of black veins now showed up along his neck and down his arms, so that he came down on one knee and coughed up bile. His skin had grown eerily pale, the green of his eye shaded with mist.

"Your strength wanes, Novare."

"I'm only getting started," spat the mercenary, driving his knee against the floor, rising into a knightly stance once more.

Still Ogwold clung helplessly to the stiff frame of Videre, the two of them slumped together on the flagstones as empty of passion as any of the mewling husks that littered the prison. But as he huddled there with his friend so quickly deceased, the glaze over his troubled eyes slowly cleared, and he beheld as out of a world of shadows a murky vision of the mercenary Byron in a battle to the death, bleeding, broken, yet unrelenting, so ready to face his own end for the sake of Videre and Ogwold who were all but strangers to him, of Wygram who he had only just met. It was the inviolable word of the mercenary so displayed, the promise that truly would not break, that flowed up from the deeps of dark defeat like a rising current, that finally brought the ogre swimming to the surface, and when he broke into consciousness of the vital horror around him, it was with three precise passions: honour Videre; repay Byron; defend yourself.

Only more dense as was the pain of loss now so clearly realized, within that packed core was a motile heat, a ferocious and glorious warmth maddening like a volcano long dormant, for now he burned to avenge the fair cat that had taken him so far from Epherem. As Byron now fought, so too had she carried him with unshakable devotion over the desert, placed herself ready to die before the knights of Occultash, and battled so ferociously the Eyeless as to be coveted by their King, when easily she might have escaped. In those vile tunnels, it was Videre as much as the ruthless Byron who taught him at last, that there are some who must fall. Now there was no difficulty in seeing the evil that was Azanak, and the fate that creature deserved. So he stood unnoticed and solemn as the hideous amorphous mass of bone and flesh was hurled away by Byron's sword, laughing arrogantly once again. He conjured his strength into the Fonsolis, the flesh gripping, twisting, responding in turn with a resolve equally powered, and formed in the voice of his spirit, out from the ancestral language of his partner that word which he had learned in his vision of kelp. Yet there was more, for never so adamantly had he requested the service of the plant. Even as Byron wiped the blood from his face and prepared for the next exchange, a new word arose from the shapeless song of the elder plant in concert with the first; and Ogwold cried out: "Iliofos! Ampeligio!"

With a rippling burst, as stars appear billionfold in galactic singularity, the numberless pores of the Fonsolis surged all together blinding white, featureless and pure as the day star itself compressed into the smiling shoulder of a young Nogofod, the flare of its aura flashing into a blazing arm slender and true as a bending ray of sun, dawn upon its fingertips. Azanak leapt back hissing, for his skin had at once begun to bubble and steam, and all but his despicable eyes were lost in the glare. His first thought was to escape, for the immortal sanguar's mind was dominated ever by fear of death. But for Ogwold's second word, the creature might have found safety, turning seamlessly into a winged smoke flying for the upper floor more swiftly even than he had moved before. Yet where "Iliofos" brought the light, "Ampeligio" shaped it, conjuring the form of the vines which so many times had plunged into the surface of Altum seeking nutrients, which had helped Ogwold so easily to ascend the great tree of Hesflet. Seeing them together entwined as a great whip, so it was—a whip—of pure sunlight. With a resounding crack the cord of light snapped through the formless thing and there came the screams of a million souls dragged to Carcerem, pulling the true form of the sanguar entrapped in materiality out from the smoke and flinging it wailing upon the stone.

If "Iliofos" had shown the ogre his gills, "Ampeligio" was their first taste of the sea, so that now, naturally as when long ago he fell from the dock in Epherem and beheld in simultaneity all the skills of swimming he was born to know, so too did the language of the Fonsolis blossom throughout his spirit—here long it had been grown—like a vast world formerly hidden from the eyes, now revealed in all the totality which was the given right of its partner to feel. Here like the effortless motions of underwater flight came a grand sequence of words, a lexicon of subtle truths through which the ogre now shared each his impulse with the plant so wrapped within his being. And so, together, they bellowed through shared lips and lungs in a booming voice of power, one new word to seal the demon in an inescapable, unending day, the pure whip of sun snaking back from that scorned, quivering hide, gathering into a brighter and denser luminance as though all of its light were withdrawn into the very seed of the shoulder: "Kandesmi!" As through a window flung open in the wall of Caelare's palace, a radiant beam of pure white sunlight shot straight and true in an unerring eternal shaft through the heart of Azanak, if he had one, and widening consumed his form entire. The horrible wailing of the sanguar was cut short so utterly in that brilliance that it seemed already a distant nightmare, for Azanak, Lord of the Mire, was utterly annihilated.

The light faded swiftly as it had come. Ogwold whispered this time only in his mind the word "Protagi," and the Fonsolis was again his arm, in likeness of the other, again green and hale, the merciless sunlight retreating into each its pores as infinite eyes turned back to sleep. Wygram lay down on the floor and snorted decisively. Byron too slumped over and flopped back, immense sword thudding singly against the stone, for the black poison had warped him horribly. His skin was nearly white, he wheezed with pain, and blood poured with wicked speed and smoothness from the gashes in his side and chest. All around was heard the dry plopping of other bodies, endless bodies, even the distant patter of those husks stored in the floors above falling masterless and dead, at last, as they had been for many years.

The soft noise echoed up into silence high above them, and they could only imagine how many more continued to fall in the furthest chambers. Wygram said, "They are free."

Ogwold was bent over the dying mercenary, unable to lose another companion. His grey hand held tight against the worst of the bleed, and the Fonsolis he pressed over the black, evil wounds, but as opposing forces there seemed an invisible impediment between that cursed flesh and the tough green of his palm. He could feel in his own veins and heart a revulsion and weakness in the presence of the insidious bile, such as the plant felt when it was near to open flames. "I'm so sorry Byron," he murmured shakily. "I was afraid. I... should have done something."

"He can only be healed by the light of the sun," the jewelled snout of Wygram inched over the mercenary as if to smell him.

His eye scanned her coldly. "I'll be all right." He choked up a flow of blood. "Just get me outside, ogre."

"Fos!" Ogwold called, but no light came from the Fonsolis. He stared at the dark hand where only minutes ago had come such blinding radiance.

Byron smirked eerily. "Used it all, huh?" Without a word Ogwold picked up the mercenary like a sack of tutum and hung him over his grey shoulder. "Wait... oh, thank you," said Byron as the ogre picked up his father's sword.

With one last look at the body of Videre, Ogwold said, "I'll be back. Wygram, you coming?"

The Euphran only tilted her head, the silvery tassels hanging to one side, the blue scales pale in the light of the sphere as it left her to join the ogre, but as Ogwold ascended the endless staircase he could hear her powerful talons moving closer against the stone. Blood darkened the ogre's white cloak as he walked carefully and smoothly as was possible for so hulking a creature as he was, and if there was any pain in the process for Byron it seemed no more than he already suffered. Either that, or the mercenary refused to admit he was dying. At last they came up through the confounding halls of the castle proper, and found the light of the door still ajar, as though in Azanak's mind even drawing so close to close off the day would have to wait for night. So it was that they stumbled out of the labyrinth and breathed the moisture heavy air of the mire once again.

The sun was just setting over the misted mountains. Ogwold set the mercenary down against the high black wall, and those low golden rays at last reached his pale flesh. First the darkness left his eye, then colour touched his flesh. He coughed up a horrible plume of black gunk, and then the sick veins began, slowly, to retreat. The wounds did not close, and the blood did not stop flowing, yet Ogwold remembered that the first thanks he had ever given the Fonsolis was for drinking blood from his own wound, so he willed that his hand widen and grow over the gashes already lighter and less blackened. He hesitated at first, recalling that repelling force from before, but the tentative feelings of the plant soon fled, and with its own debt to the mercenary came the word for healing: "Kalliergo." He held the grown Fonsolis over Byron's wounds, expanding all around him in healing, cocooning roots, and soon enough blood ceased to fall onto the stone. But the silent sun-drenched man sat there long holding the gashes closed while he rested.

"I am sorry for being so useless," said Ogwold sitting beside him. "It was your bravery that brought me to my senses, Byron."

"That bastard might have actually killed me."

Ogwold exchanged a funny glance with Wygram, who coming last out of the great doorway had watched with fascination everything he'd done with the Fonsolis.

"Who knows," she said. "To last even a moment under the power of Azanak is a feat few mortals have accomplished. Two thousand years I have been his prisoner, and never have I seen such resistance."

"Maybe he used to be stronger," Ogwold implored.

"The sanguar grows more powerful with each drop of blood that it drinks. The older the mightier. That is the greatest gift of their immortality, but also the worst of their torment if they come to loathe their undead state, which is inevitable, for the longer that curse persists, the more inescapable is its hold."

"You are quite the loremaster, Wygram," said Ogwold.

The Euphran set her silver-whiskered chin upon her claws. "I will help you. No being has ever done such a goodness to my heart, and you are even a son of the Great Mother. I will fly you and your partner as far as I can, which is very near to Zenidow." She looked up with laughter in her great icy eyes. "...but you will not make for a light load."

"Thank you, wise one." More like Ogdof than ever before did Ogwold appear in his solemn speech. "If you will wait, I must retrieve the body of my friend from this awful place." He lumbered back into the suffocating dark without a moment's hesitation.

He returned only as dusk settled over the great lakes, the enormous cat heavy in his quaking arms, lurching wordless down the darkling stair and out into the marsh, where he dug up a deep grave for his oldest partner in this journey, and lowered her body carefully down into the warm, wet earth. Before the soft mound filled in he arranged the grasses of the mire in a kind of crown, and made a long prayer to Caelare, willing Videre's spirit to soar among the stars, and find some place in the ether where others like her ranged and played. Then he slowly returned to the tall black gate where Byron and the Euphran had waited.

The mercenary had ripped a sheet from his cloak and wrapped it snugly, but not too tightly around the deep wounds, which had greatly healed under the influence of the Fonsolis, but not entirely. Wygram gazed off into the sky that she had not seen in millennia, as if she could do so forever. The return to Fonslad was simple on the wings of Wygram. She flew them easily above the mist so that the whole valley spilled everywhere in a sea of vapour, and soon, with the sinking sun, they touched down just beyond the village. Wygram was wise to obscure herself deep in the wood while Ogwold and Byron camped on the fringes of the city, having no silver left to spare at the inn.

Three days more the company stayed in Fonslad recovering, and little is there to tell of that time, for it was a period of peace and warmth before a long journey. Byron's wounds healed greatly, for he spent part of each day with the Fonsolis against his skin. By the morning of the second day he was able to swing his sword without splitting the horrible gashes anew, and he trained—quite against the insistence of Ogwold—all that day in the woods. He did not ask the ogre at all about his true relationship with Caelare, though he had heard Wygram well.

On the third day they met Wygram at the fringe of the forest. Coming out of the trees as from some phosphorescent myth, her scales turned transforming iridescent blues as the sun bent against her hide. Her great wings unfurled as in greeting, free of the tight spaces of the trees and the shackles of Azanak. Each larger than her body, webbed as with a diaphanous blue canvas, the delicate bones bore at their threefold elbows sharp spires of crystal shining like the blue depths of her eyes.

Byron was last to arrive, brow slick with sweat, for he had been training since before the sun had touched the trees, and now it was noon. Approaching like some haggard bandit out of the shadows, he laid Ogdof's old, massive sword in the grass before Ogwold with an awkward but practised sense of ceremony. "I've chosen a name for your father's blade, if I can call it my own," he said gruffly.

"I could never wield it as well as you." Ogwold smiled oafishly.

Byron grinned as well, and it was not a bloodthirsty madness there on his face, but a pure and simple expression of joy. "It is called Azanog!" He suddenly unsheathed the blade and swept it up into the clear sky. "A weapon of the Nogofod which bit the flesh of Azanak."

"That's a fine name," Wygram boomed. Her voice differed greatly from that which she used many days ago, when she was weak. Now she was hearty and full, and her cheeks bloomed with azure health. Byron and Ogwold bound their possessions to her scaly back. The mercenary sat in front, wrapping his arms around her long neck, and Ogwold behind him could not contain his excitement, shouting out so that his deep ogre voice thrummed through the forest, and all manner of birds burst from the trees.

With one great unfurling of wings Wygram exploded into the air, and the blast of wind removed many a hat from the onlooking villagers. Strong were her wingbeats, slow and gradual though the land unfolded beneath them at speeds before unrealized. Swiftly the trees thinned, the forest passed in an instant, but they could not see the marshland, for there was only an endless blanket of white fog, though Ogwold swore he glimpsed the black thorns of the highest spires of Azanak's awful fortress.

They winged low over the solid white wash in a noiseless oblivion. Acres of mist surged featureless in all directions, the ragged, ethereal range ahead an unmoving, unchanging horizon, yet suddenly leaping in detail—one crag, one swath of forest—so close and drawing nearer. Like a great fabric out-flung the canopy of vapour broke streaming up against the titanic blue mountains at the end of the valley, along whose vast feet Wygram rose steep and true, banking between their dazzling peaks, where no fog could reach. The Fonsolis gloried in its closeness to the sun.

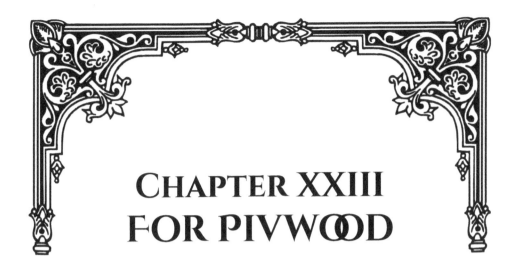

CHAPTER XXIII
FOR PIVWOOD

Pale in the far axe-flare of Feox, Elts' limpid eyes and prickly shock of hair floated after that single source of vision as it was a lonely star lost in artificial night. Seeking a sky long promised them both, though the bearer of that flame walked with the rigid composure of an automaton, its distant follower's exhausted tails hardly lifted from the rugose cavern rock. Still she stumbled hastily as Zelor beside her.

The sorcerer's broken voice had not troubled the tomb-stale air in days. Oiled sinks seemed his eyes, turning inward against the singular friction of his will to advance. Charred was his face with woe; scorched was his mind by its many tenants; ever did the cinders of stolen souls smoulder on his breath. Though still, when they rested, he sat in meditation—stiffened his pointed ears, extended his tails like vanes unto the slightest subterranean winds—he was hardly the man who sought peace in the first.

Yet it was just as Elts accepted her final solitude, the reality of the horrible premonitions that haunted her now so frequently—evil tentacles bursting from the back of the sorcerer, crimson light blaring in the total black of his stare—that a cold draft shivered their cloaks, and he spoke at last, cutting the dead silence in the very tone which she had come to trust in Ardua.

"We have arrived," he said, creaking round, and the faint, flickering light painted in his abyssal orbits two fine slivers of original white.

Above the burning star that was Feox, now sharply inclining as it clambered over a spill of enormous boulders washed in its yellows and oranges, there opened up in the sightless rock a great chute unto the rich navy of true night, strewn with such cold jewels as showed how dim and feeble was the fire of the axe that joined them. High and full-faced in the portal, more grand and spacious as they approached, were little Kelzos with its fine grain of craters, and red-ringed Oflos, just blacker than the sky. Inching as a bead of warm cream down the curvature of a glass firmament, the Moon of Desire seemed drawn to the forbidden power hidden in the bloody fingernail of the other, Lord over Darkness that it was.

Arching and broadening atop the scramble of tremendous rocks up which the Zefloz scaled to the waiting Feox, the opening in the side of the mountain was monstrous as the being whose ancient path they had followed at last to its end, yet hardly so smooth in form, as though with explosive need the Great Worm had burst at last into the open air. The imprint of great thrashing and twisting enshrined the tortured egress with jagged rocks irregularly teething and splaying, large sections of cavern splitting open over chasms menacingly empty, and all semblance of footing was lost in a frozen break of geologic waves.

Watching the black cloaks rip suddenly in the cold wind, silhouetted against that lambent chunk of night, Elts surmounted a plate of rock alone and stood for a moment silently, listening, breathing, just feeling the freshness and liberty in contrast to the deathless stagnation so vast yet so finally behind her. When she climbed at last herself through the ruins of the twisted titan chimney where in elder days the worm had sought its own salvation, she was nearly blinded, for all the land here was a waste of snow that caught and beamed the light of the moons in a serene and radiant glory.

But for the slab of rock and ice upon which the Zefloz now stood, this side of the mountain angled downward with uncompromising steepness, meeting not far below the raised lip of a gigantic caldera in the land, larger and deeper than any valley they had before encountered. Elts could not see directly over the crater lip, but farther along its curving perimeter, and out across the vast expanse that it encircled, sheer and scarcely textured slopes of rock and snow showed that the descent would test the extent of her equipment.

At the lowest point and epicentre of the vast bowl stood Zenidow. Silvery and featureless as ever, it rose cylindrical at a nearly constant width from the sprawling, snowy wood encircling its base, slightly slimming about some distant focus as it vanished into the night-clouds. Nothing stood between it and the caldera rim but for dark forests and sheer open plains of snow funnelling into that pit of what seemed now to Elts the site of some primordial impact, for even the craggy mountains from which she now emerged looked as though they had been pushed back equidistant like the frozen debris of whatever cataclysmic explosion had rent this great hole in the world.

Feox had already split the ice, melting a wide circle of rock round the plume of flame rising from his axe embedded, and now he crumpled beside the bundle of tail and cloak that was Xelv, far from the disgust of their master. Zelor sat before the flames and closed his weary eyes. It seemed even as his lids were lowered that he glanced in the direction of Elts. Yet she went off into the white waste to be alone.

She hollowed out a little cave in the snow and lay there brooding, far from the fire, and despite the warm winds which she managed to draw up and close to her body, she nearly froze. But it was better, for now, than facing Zelor who she had quite taken for dead. She feared that she too now walked in a dark shadow, for even as she chose to distance herself, the sight of those trembling remainders of white in the sorcerer's tortured eyes had moved her deeply, and in her heart she wished to speak with him.

In the dawn dark they left the bald perch of the tunnel mouth and waded downward, encased to their waists in snow. By the first light to touch the infinitely tall face of Zenidow, they reached the knuckled caldera rim, and peered down into the treacherous, terraced bowl whose dizzying exposure was their newest challenge. Even Elts, so used to leaping among tall branches, felt uneasy as she knelt, uncoiled and knotted together all of her ropes. Fumbling about in the freezing powder she set her anchor round a deep-rooted stone jutting back as though itself petrified of falling, and with a hard tug she supposed it was secure as any.

Feox and Xelv were cast out over the drop without hesitation, yet though their increasingly longer and more fearless palm-shredding leaps down the rockface proved the line would hold much more, their master backed over the edge very cautiously, and what had taken them twenty minutes each was nearly an hour in his placing one foot after the other before finally reaching the spill of ice far below. Elts following him was herself unusually slow to abseil, feeling out the nearly vertical rock with her bare feet and reaching tails. When snow once again pierced her frozen toes, she stepped back from the rock, placed one hand upon the mask of elz at her belt, and drew the wind through her knot-work high above. The distant thread of rope wormed across the pale sky, seemed as if it might float there forever, and fell at last, hissing into a pool before her. The conjoining ties undone, accumulated snow and rock shed in a fine dust as the coils whipped to her belt.

If the high wall curving subtly into the distance was like some great fossilized ring of enormous tree trunks fused together, the thick, thorny ridges of ice which spread and wound steeply from its feet were like their buckling roots exposed. Only the utmost certainty of foot and vestibular precision of tail was required, but by midday they reached a suitable enough angle of hard frost upon which to walk without having to focus so closely, and the huge halls of ice that formed such wandering high-walled paths as they were forced to follow—no matter how circuitously they addressed the descent—slowly dwindled into a smooth and even slope.

Frosted trees rose sparsely round the diminishing arms of ice, like the impossible survivors of a forest wholly frozen within the thicker and taller shoulders which bunched against the caldera rim. But with time these thin dark stragglers joined into dense clumps, and clumps gathered more closely into stands until the Zefloz were locked in the freezing shade of a forest far greater than any which could have been so obscured by the glacial mass behind.

Strange creatures tittered in the still deeps between the trees. Sudden sunny clearings blinded them in a flash of pure snow, or shaded walks under the stiff boughs of the hardy trees chilled them to the core. Tranquil humps of boulders decked in powder began to trouble their way, and the trees thinned, vanished as quickly and inexplicably as they had first gathered together. Here was a great clearing of broken stones, small and large, many leaning together in uneven tunnels and archways, sometimes forming slabby chambers or together lying in singular plates that shifted under the weight of the company. Craggy obelisks jutted like old bones among the icy boulders, and the natural caves of ice and rock took on the likeness of design. Little remained of what civilization once must have been, and all was overgrown with dark, hardy plants, the stones eroded by eons of wind and melting snow. But they had little time to stop and observe as quickly and quietly the strange ruins sank behind them in a serene fall of snow, and hoary trees clustered as if to close off the secret place.

The grade steepened again, and as the trees thinned once more the ground broke into levels and plates that fell and bunched rapidly closer together, pleating into a rim much like that from which they first descended. In the last hues of twilight Elts cast down her ropes, for though the drop was not totally sheer, it was certainly treacherous. When she joined the others at the foot of the steep scramble, dizzyingly high though far more choppy and gradual than their first descent of the day, darkness had quite fallen. They bedded in the gnarled thickets profuse about the wall, still feeling the titanic pull of gravity, so declined was their position. But the trees which grew here did not seem to mind the sharp angle, for their roots were dug deep into the world and clamped over with blackish ice.

As though the fresh air and bright sun brought welling up what memory and mourning was silenced in the tomb-tunnels of the mountain, all day Elts had brooded upon the darkness in Zelor responsible for—among so many deaths— her master slain, that saintly old man who should have loved to see these remarkable trees. Even though Xirell had never placed such trust in her before as Zelor did now, surely the sorcerer deserved to die. Yet something far worse than death more clearly entrapped him with each his heavier and more weary steps that stamped inexorably through the frozen, biting waste, that miasma of tentacled darkness floating over him, mingling with his being, clutching and probing for the controls of his consciousness.

Yet as much as this evil did Elts weigh the sorcerer's unconditional surrender to her, and the selflessness of his true quest, so that now, as they made camp, in her mind were separated finally the man who resolved to save Altum from the monster which pushed him to devour it. It was Duxmortul she should despise, not Zelor. Perhaps the man did not deserve even the curse of his enslavement.

So it was now, even as these marvellous old trees clothed in dusk invoked her lost friend, that this other dimension of Elts' heart at last prevailed, and she knew that there would be no solace for her in the impending doom of Zelor, for it was rather the Shadow, and not the man possessed by it, whom she blamed.

Now more than even in the lonely abysses of the worm tunnels did she wish to console him, to at least, perhaps, discuss their journey as he seemed to desire as much as she, for she feared that at any moment he would truly and finally lose himself to Duxmortul, just as Xirell and the others had gone into that black waste, and she would be totally alone, unable to do anything but find the Alium, for if there was about Zelor anything which had moved her more than her hate for Duxmortul, it was that which raged against Fozlest, and she knew now that she would give up her life to keep the weapon from her Empress.

When she came and huddled by the fire of Feox's axe, Zelor saw in the flickering light that she had done away at last with her stoic composure, that the soft pale eyes searched now in earnest for the security of a friend. She saw his end, knew his will. At last he was believed, accepted, yet he struggled to find words. Watching as Oflos and Kelzos again appeared black-red and cream-white among the clouds, his mind and heart were hardened, for the goal was near, and he had known ever since they had come out of the tunnel of the worm that the mountain they now approached was well protected. So he grumbled, "There are guardians about Zenidow."

Elts set out her frozen, cracked feet aching in the healing warmth of the fire. "Even I can sense their fold, and trees, great trees like I've never known." She added her stiff hands and tails to the glow.

The sorcerer stared blankly into the flames, kindling the tiny points of white that remained in his black eyes. "Whatever they are, they will do everything in their power to stop me."

"Why should they? If they knew of the Shadow and your intentions, surely they would assist us. It is not the Alium they protect, but their forest." Elts rubbed her hands over her feet, massaging them like blocks of stone.

The cracks in the sorcerer's stone face drew in the fringes of night as the firelight washed his high cheekbones and protuberant brow. "They see no difference between me and It."

"Duxmortul is the evil one," Elts spoke up so clearly as to recall the empty, enormous stillness of the night. Yet it was not solitude that she felt in that vast empty night, for it did not swallow up her voice, but rather buttressed it up and carried it to the stars. She felt supremely good to acknowledge the figuration of her heart that Zelor and the Shadow were forces opposed, and that she and Zelor worked together now for a great purpose, and never did these words seem so true as now, cutting up through the dark, smouldering in the heat of the axe, heightening all sensory perception. She faced her interlocutor with passion unobscured. "You are Its greatest enemy."

Zelor turned his tight-drawn forehead and twisted cheeks to her, and the lines of shadow there were like traceries in broken glass. The singular mould of stoicism had shattered and lay in fragments upon his fearful cheeks. "They will never believe my goal to be anything other than power. And so there is no end to the evil I must work here; I will be forced to slaughter them and burn their forest. But they are strong. The time will come when I must call upon the power of the Shadow. I can only hope that these hands have crushed the Alium already when they are taken at last by darkness."

They were silent, listening to the fire and the howling wind. Elts felt on her breath the admission that she was here for the sorcerer, that he was not completely alone yet and could add to the night his shouting voice with hers, but she could not form the words. She too could sense the inevitability of war, of Zelor's fall, Duxmortul's incarnation. A threat to the forest enshrining Zenidow was a threat that would not be allowed by the spirits of that place. More sacred than the mountain, than the Alium, were those trees to their kin. She could only imagine what that love must feel like to one so gifted as Zelor. "If ever there has been a race more hostile to the trees of the world, it is ours," she said.

Zelor nodded grimly. His long white hair had fallen over his face, for his head was hung as under heavy thought. "Our love suffocates its object, dead yet never lost. Even now the trees about us tremble with loathing, feel the poison in our blood, the deeds of our ancestors."

"I hate... the Xol." Elts spoke hollowly, distantly, as though hearing another voice so much like her own, yet so distorted, insincere, as if even when the words formed she realized that all sense of duty had come to her in the Hollow of Wyx, where she gave everything to protect her fellows and placed her faith in a future liberated from the elz-hard grasp of Fozlest.

Even after she gave up her crusades, all knowledge and belonging which she held so close and spirited her will to learn and grow had come to her from Xirell whom she followed and trusted, lover of his people and devotee of their progress in science and art. As well the sacrifices of Zelor were in the end selfless, virtuous—if only on some cosmic scale—for all the death they brought. How easy it would be for the sorcerer to give in, hand over his failing form to the Shadow. But he would not give up that last fibre of sapience until he had made right on his folly. There was great strength in the Xol, great potential which could not be denied. Whatever was true, real; no, she did not hate the Xol: she hated the Empire.

Zelor met the disbelief in her voice with earnestness. "I have always despised my kind, such that I abandoned my family, all that I was born into, and joined the ranks of Novare. Always, I will think of myself as one of them. But see what comes of hate." His head hung low and shadowed, and though its petrified features could no longer contort to expression, it was clear the pain they secreted. "I killed them all. I watched them burn, laughed at their weakness. There is nothing now I hate so much as the one to whom hate itself has led me: Duxmortul." Zelor formed this last word not at all with the supreme difficulty which Elts figured kept him from its nefandous syllables, but with a cold, rasping ease that flowed in deep intimacy. It was the first he had uttered the creature's name aloud, so far as she knew, and it brought even a rekindling, it seemed, of the original whiteness—however feeble and minute—in his firelit eyes. "If I must rend these perfect trees, so be it. Already I have taken innocent lives, and my memories rot, my soul too much like so many others it has eaten. If it all might come to the demise of the Alium, still I will not die in peace, but I will die having succeeded."

The sorcerer lifted his swollen brow, and as he did, so too did the affectless heads of Xelv and Feox rise from the dark snow just outside of the glow. The first folded at the knees, pale blue palms fitted together and slender fingers arranged in esoteric figuration, while the other stood straight, matted hair hanging back, hands uplifted to the dark. Azure light seemed to veil Xelv. Jets of flame, sparks and cinders popped and sizzled all around Feox. Slumped dark shapes formed as from ether in the darkness behind them, rows upon rows of small black orbs that seemed risen by the will of the Blue Zefloz, and now suddenly a great fire blazed up as a gateway for those faithful to Red; from the glare stepped a raging being, all flame, falling upon one knee, bowing its burning visage. Another flashed into form beside the first, and a second, three more at once; so grew the ranks of kneeling flame warriors.

Zelor took out his long silver sword and placed it over his knees to treat its edge. "A great might is in the wood. Even now it grows stronger. The more warriors we summon the longer I can delay the coming of the Shadow. I will raise rock lords from below, myself." He looked to Elts and his eyes were full of smoke. "I would call upon your gifts too, but I know not what they are in such a case as this."

"I can fight," she said proudly. "But I am no summoner."

"Still, the tide of wind is a great component of war."

Elts nodded solemnly. The long, clean ring of metal against metal sounded as Zelor sharpened his blade with methodical strokes. Howling winds blew cold and fierce, though the fiery clothes of the flame spirits flared even brighter. Some two hundred waited already in ranks, the snow melting and steaming beneath them. The demure conjurations of Xelv sat curled and tucked into small shapes like waist-high eggs in a number far greater. Elts had only eyes for these spirits, for she knew the many tales of Xelv's power. They were the greatest summoner in the empire.

"They are Koloi," Zelor spoke, seeing her stare. "Water spirits." He held one hand over the wastes of snow. "An elixir more abundant here than anything. They are the children of the very medium through which we now travel." He dropped his hand limply. "To think that all this time, I had my knowledge of the Fabric."

"I understand," Elts murmured. "Well. I was born outside of the flow, in the darkness where Xeléd does not shine. At first I hated all sewers of the Fabric. It helped of course that the imperial sorcerers who came to Wyx were so vile. But here I am, a student of the wind, and I don't think it is merely because of my mother's gift. There was a part of me that always was interested in the subtle forces of life and the world. Perhaps we are all drawn to it, no matter how we see the Fabric or how it hurts us."

The frozen face of Zelor seemed, if not to loosen, at least to lighten, as if those black furrows in his troubled skin had suddenly more shallow abysses. "You are wise," he said. "If only I had not gone off to be alone so young, I might have met those Xol like your mother, like Xirell, who could have shown me the true nature of Xeléd."

"Maybe our positions are not so different from the start. I certainly thought about abandoning Wyx. The idol might have found me first."

Zelor looked back over the growing forces of his summoning, and it did not seem that he would reply.

"I see what makes Koloi powerful," Elts said. "Their formation and action require little sewing, and so you might conjure hundreds very quickly. They seem quite small, but again—this is why they are so numerous."

Zelor seemed to nod. "Numerous but easily dispersed, and not so quick to resume their form. They may overwhelm the enemy, but the warriors of Feox will finish them. They are Varaga, living flame. Not so easy to raise in this place, but in the end the power of a Zefloz is an awesome thing. It is a shame that he is limited to my instruction. If any of our company had a mind for war, it was him." The sorcerer turned back to the fire and closed his eyes.

Elts came and sat beside him, placing one hand over his. The dark purple skin was hot as molten metal, and though at first she wished to pull away, she held tightly to the limp fingers. The purple flesh was impossibly thin and gaunt, as though it hardly held back the bone. "Zelor," she said. "There is no forgiveness for what you have done. For many days, and none so critically as this have I struggled to divide in my mind your spirit from the Shadow of Duxmortul. This I have now finally accomplished. I see you, what you might have been, what you wish to be, what you hope for Altum. I cannot forget the pain, the darkness that has been wrought through your form; I will never see you as you once truly were. Yet I will stand beside you. I believe that you work for the good of this world, that whether your first alliance with Duxmortul was born of hate or justice, it does not matter now." She quieted, and her grip loosened as the faint gossamer countenance of Xirell fell like a veil over her memory. There was a long silence.

"The old man; he loved you," Zelor said at last. "There was no truth so clear in his mind when..."

"When the Shadow took him."

"When I took him." The sorcerer pulled away from her touch and resumed the sharpening of his weapon. The long, ringing beats cut the silent night as the ranks of elementals rose and ordered themselves over the starlit snow. But even as he had returned to his exercise Zelor hung his head, and the sword was too stiff in his hands. He turned to the side his chin, so that one eye was revealed, and not since the beginning of their journey into the mountains had there been such a clear and bright whiteness in that gaze. "Thank you, Elts," he said.

The Silver Zefloz did not speak again for the remainder of the night, methodically preparing his weapon. Xelv and Feox conducted their work as though they would never sleep, and by the time that Elts lay down herself, it seemed that a vast army was prepared already for the dawn.

She dreamed that night of Zelor slain, white blood flowing as from his every pore, stark and pitiless against black robes, yet indistinguishable from the pure snow where it pooled. A purple blossom was on his chest, and in his hands stood the idol of Duxmortul, its six red eyes bubbling and steaming. But the host was dead, useless. Darkness rose up from Zelor's body, slowly fading into immortal night.

At sunrise the army of flame and water was grown vast. One thousand fiery warriors strode clothed in hot smoke down the sloping plain, burning away the snow as they went; ahead of them and bursting at their flanks like a massive battering barrier surged a veritable sea of Koloi. The Varaga standing straight were tall as men and lean as blades, with long, powerful claws of fire, and snaking tails which smote the snow in gouts of steam. Upon their faces were masks of smoke and ash which trailed behind them like great blustery manes. The Koloi were much smaller, fluid and crystalline at once, like living beads flowing and gathering, variously shifting from liquid to ice and back again. It was quite hard to say what other features were consistent to their form, for they packed so close together and moved in such homogeneous bodies of work it was impossible to distinguish one single entity from the mass of others but for the trickle of stragglers and crown of leaders along the fringes of their host.

Behind the downward marching legion and its moving armour of changeful water followed Feox and Xelv, somehow more lifelessly than their own conjurations. After them went Elts and Zelor, poised, it seemed, together, on the precipice of battle. As far as they could see, further even than the frontmost numbers of Koloi vanishing into distance, were only great shifting curtains of fog, pleating, folding, expanding and contracting, so that they trudged cold and wet through an abyss of whiteness, the rufous auras of the Varaga like bleeding paints through the vapour thick with water.

At the apex of Caelare's daily path, the fog cleared, and they saw now a grand forest before them which rivalled even Xoldra. Yet these trees were alive, and even without the curse of black immortality upon them were clearly more ancient than any known to Xol kind. They were of a race in even the oldest scriptures of the *Xoloi* untold, and those closest to the mountain—for the wood seemed to reach its very silver surface—stood taller than even some of the greatest and longest fortified elz fortresses of the Empire. The harsh climate here upon the roof of the world did not trouble the place, for only on the very top of the forest canopy did the snow lie heavy, and they could see drawing closer that far amid the trees there were lush and healthy greens and woody browns and the vibrant hues of mushroom and flower, where it seemed no frost bit or wind tore.

When they came within the span of their army of the first trees, Zelor held up his hand, ceasing their advance. A young woman stepped out from beneath the outermost boughs, a single Novare witch, lightly clad in a loose, blue cloak and wide-brimmed grey hat, bound in a ribbon of like colour to the noon sky. A slender bow of thin white wood was set upon her back, and with it was a quiver strapped there too. In the growing twilight the little shafts there snugly tucked gleamed white and clear. Beside her floated a diminutive creature green all over, of diaphanous fourfold wings and flowing emerald hair. It was clear to Elts and Zelor that a vast power went with the creature, ageless as the world, and they were humbled straight away. The hovering fairy looked long upon Zelor, far over his army as though she could see him with perfect clarity. Then she spoke.

"Shadowed One!" came a voice that boomed with impossible and lucid volume. "You will not cross this threshold. Turn you back, or meet the wrath of the trees!"

Zelor looked to Elts before he answered, shouting back as loud as could his withered voice over the heads of fire and living waters in gravelly desperation. "I seek the Alium lest it fall into the hands of a great evil."

"You speak honestly," said the fairy quite at once, and the Xol were astounded by her understanding. "Yet a malice owns you which no mortal can resist. You think that you last by your own will, but all that you do is the intention of the Shadow. The closer you come to Zenidow, the closer draws its time for action. It seeks the Alium, and will seize your being when the time has come to seize the object of its desire." The old Piv lighted upon the snow and stood tall—for so little a creature—pointing her chin to the sky. Suddenly the great wingspan of Faltion kindled into being about her, and the enormous bird shook out its feathers, screeched wildly to the heavens. "We will protect our forest from that which goes with you, Zelor. Darkness shall not shadow this wood!"

"What will it be?" called the witch in blue. Her voice was more faint on the air, thin and high and not quite so sure as the stately command of her companion.

"Do you turn back, or will you bring more death to these mountains?"

Zelor bowed his head. "Elts," he said softly. "Now it begins. This is your chance. They will take you in, I know it. Leave me and save yourself."

"I stay by your side." Elts switched her tails. "If I can help delay the dominion of the Shadow, then I cannot knowingly join the forces which hasten its coming."

"So be it," said Zelor, lowering his black eyes, and so forth went his answer as the legions of fire and water crashed like a great rumbling wave towards Pivwood, though he knew not the name of the sacred place to which he now laid siege.

Pivwood as one leviathan organism of root, trunk, and leaf thrummed in reply with the grumbling of a long sleep suddenly broken. Out from under its layered canopy, speeding in dappled parties through the shade, now stark and clear charging and soaring against the sun-sheened snow and open cobalt sky, came its defenders. At first it seemed as though millions of leaves swept up from the forest floor in a ferocious gale, yet out of the infinitely different greens formed distinct fabrics of fluttering little bodies advancing in stunningly ordered hosts. Even as the first diminutive warriors streamed past Sylna and Muewa, the golden-white vision of the great bird Faltion above them cried piercing to the sun, and so began to reveal themselves many elder beings—each to their own Piv—similar and vastly different to herself, as every rushing fairy was enveloped in a unique cocoon of surging silvery aura, amorphous at first, quickening from their chests like liquid shoots of plants long dormant, trailing behind in the ripping, life-giving wind and sun, taking up now the distinctions of incarnation.

Born as from the deep memory of the forest were the spirits of birds and mammals and reptiles and insects and fungus and plants pouring out through the air and along the snowy waste and through the soil beneath it, diving and wheeling and banking as the extinct ancestors of septries or swarming from the fitful dark as leathery aborjays, bounding freely or mounted over the churning plain as pale voscas and lunions, crouching upon tiny shoulders or swinging from branches as ghostly chimfrees, coiling round waists and speeding like ribbons through the snow as serpents and lizards and salamanders, trundling as turtles, buzzing on machine wings as wasps colossal and fine or skittering as thousand-eyed spiders, writhing forth as currents of brush or mycelia unearthed, sending out wicked elder spores as mushrooms not seen for eons, stampeding upon roots uplifted as many great and powerful trunks from the days when Pivwood reached all to Ardua raising up long boughs with which to slash and crush, their valiant hosts the little Piv standing defiant and proud among their woody limbs.

Gyge the lunion leapt, mane streaming like white fire, beside the Piv Tesflind who lighted astride those supple shoulders drawing her slender grassblade bow, wings appraising the subtlest airs. The Euphran spirit Hortgav craned its neck of milkwhite cloud to pierce the enemy hordes with golden eyes, levelling its wings of light sliced from its scouting to the side of Yeuv who called that beast his familiar. The twin four-horned deer Iodon of barbed tail and Iadan of stabbing hoof went with the twins Huewn and Vanweu, galloping side by side as their riders readied the gleaming stems of their swords. Up from the ground exploded in a fountain of snow the armoured mole Donvlor beneath its master Wenve, who rode upon that muscled back and gave sight to blind motion. The largest mushroom ever to fruit in the wood was Vundred, whose companion Reluen rode atop that flowing tapestry of blues and whites and silvers that domed the sinewy innumerable hyphae which conducted its locomotion, calling as they writhed from the forest for a veil of spores which buttressed their allies yet choked their opponents. A tree to dwarf the greatest towers of men was Klind the Old, whose great uprooted network of nerves sprawled over the land to drag and propel him forth, Meu the scholar riding in a cozy hole in the heart of his godly cambium as if he wore an enormous suit of armour. Trond too could not be forgotten, the blue-barked, the white-leaved, with her diverging, many trunks, so that she looked as though twenty different trees had long embraced and grown together. Among her shady boughs danced that Piv who went always with her, Ue, second in age only to Muewa.

Among these beings and numberless more were six spirits wholly unlike the others, who showed in their coming a power far more formidable. They were the Great Ones, the eldest spirits of Pivwood, ancient even in a time when Oerbanuem was yet to develop that higher consciousness which would ultimately birth the Piv, the memories of which so distorted by distance that even the god of the wood could not say whether there had truly been a seventh in those days.

First to appear was Yisven Vir, a billowing nebula of golden fumes always entering and escaping orbit of her several white floating cores so bright as to reveal the infinity of transforming different colours deep within her changeful form. She bore up in thickest vapours her chosen Piv Luen through the sky above the charging hosts, and together they beseeched what few clouds there were to part and draw the sunlight upon the field, for Yisven Vir had always lorded over the vapours of this land, and none worked so closely with the winds as her partner. Far below, the brightening snow erupted as there reared from the land the thick masses of dirt and loam which were the spirit Granulen, master of soils. Riding like the smallest little weed atop the highest terraces of that cascading, rolling nutrient was Veun the gardener, the only of the chosen Piv whose clan had anticipated would befriend one of the Six. In the shadows of the swelling hills of Granulen sped the sable fractal of Ros, who is wherever there is darkness, whether under the slightest blade of grass or cast from the tallest tree. So long as he maintains in extending his form even the slightest connection to his origin, his shape can grow so far as there is volume of shade in the forest, and transport up from anywhere it lies, as through a discreet dimension of living shadow, the subtle figure of Treuwev his partner, the only Piv to wear a colour other than green. There was another like Ros too who could not sever its connection to the wood, though it could venture to massive distances by the plenty of its substance. Now winding through the hillocks of the soil lord came rushing and roaring the spirit of Aio, the meandering riparian consciousness of the forest's waters, and floating upon its rapids-fluffed current in his queer little oarless boat was old Nuem the ferryman, leafy beard blustering with speed.

The mightiest of the Great Ones were two spirits so ancient as to have lost all form. For many thousands of years they would go without an avatar, yet the war for Pivwood saw them both embodied. Morviut was the spirit of death, father of decay. One hundred seasons past he chose for a partner the hermit Fuewav, whom few had seen before the coming of Zelor. Down from his remote bower among the treetops the old man descended, silent in his ropy rags, dark green eyes averted, twisted back bent with sorrows special to his condition. So old and frail was he, so slow to move and delicate boned that hardly could he enter the battle unprotected by the sturdiest of tree spirits and most vigilant birds and chimfrees keeping watch among their branches. But were he touched by any—friend or foe—in the state of true possessions, the very fibres of that matter so cursed would be instantly dissolved, as if never it had been, and so he was a terrible force, however unwieldy.

Last of the Six was the other of the eldest, the fickle spirit of life, Vivoen, the very seed of all that grew and flourished in the first garden which would age into the majesty of Oerbanuem and Pivwood itself. Most mysterious and rarest to appear of all the spirits of the land, her gifts as much as her powers not only varied depending on her whim, but her chosen host as well. In ages past she had blessed her hosts with flight and terrific radiance or vision even of things to come, yet also she was known to be the worst kind of trickster and might vanish from their hearts at some time of terrible need. It so happened that often she chose for partnership a Piv like herself who struggled to take things seriously, and so it followed that in this century, she had only very recently settled upon a silly little fairy called Wanuev.

And so together all the hosts of bird, mammal, reptile, insect, fungus, plant, primordial spirit, and Piv converged out of time and space upon the sloping open waste in a violent clash with the ranks of Varaga and the swelling storm of Koloi that threatened their ancestral home. The spirits grew only more lucid as they smote with their great wings and beaks, claws and teeth, stingers and mandibles, hyphae and spore, and branches and root the hordes of fire and water. Blown back was the army of the Zefloz by the winds of Yisven Vir; blinded and trapped were those disoriented in the sweeping shade of Ros; extinguished were many of the greatest flame sentinels by the lashing river of Aio; smothered and absorbed were countless Koloi by the sucking soils of Granulen.

Even as the first waves of Piv burst from the wood, Zelor saw that their strength was more than he had feared. With one hand he cast over the snow many jet black seeds taken from the pockets of Xirell, and with the other he drew up from the ground huge boulders which slamming together formed titanic many-limbed giants lumbering forward, swinging their powerful arms about as the routed companies of fire and water regrouped behind them. As the golems balanced the fray, behind them tremendous stalks burst writhing from the spot of their sewing, and at their ends huge bulbs bloomed and vivid floral maws splayed, gnashing spiral holes of thorny teeth. Ripping up their roots these creatures stormed to join the giants of rock, already who had crushed to death many a daring Piv, paring life from limb and gorging themselves on lumps of wadded bodies. Yet still more forces flowed from the wood, beating back even the enormous rock beasts and the ravening weeds, so that already Zelor set his most powerful weapons to work.

With his hands still upraised in command of the soldiers of rock, with the snap of one tail Zelor folded the Blue Zefloz Xelv into the complex bodily pattern of his summoning, and shortly were the numbers of Koloi supplemented, bubbling from the snow which provided their raw material, streaming to the rear guard, adhering to their fellows, budding forward through the ranks and overwhelming with their mass many Piv whose guardians could not weather the water. At the simultaneous snap of the other of his master's tails, Feox too opened the vast flaming portal whence his underlings had issued, yet from the swirling, burning gate came not Varaga, but a gigantic desiccated newt, oiled in flame. The fleshy, belly-dragging monster was as long and muscled as a Great Gort, its triangular head dumb and soft as its huge milky eyes, though poured from its toothless jaws destroying rivers of heat. Leaping atop its back the Red Zefloz carved out with his axe sweeping discs of flame like exoskeletal burning ribs from his mount as it slithered hugely through the battle melting all that quailed under the pressure of its coming, and everywhere the tree spirits no matter how elder or powerful balked in fear.

Yet Xelv and Feox could not conduct these efforts consciously, for their master controlled them absolutely, and now this task far from effortless was compounded with the demands of the golems and the constant resistance maintained against the growing desire to call upon the Shadow of Duxmortul— to end it all in an instant. So Zelor was forced to retreat back from the conflict and draw around him a barrier of Varaga and Koloi, a house of flame and smoke girded with defending bulbous waters always increasing in mass, so as to focus upon the theatre he directed.

Elts held her distance while the battle took shape. Unable to act, she marvelled at the wondrous host of the Piv as it amassed on glories on the plain, watched as Zelor's golems and the carnivorous plants which could only have come from her master's belongings worked to balance the fight, and now as the resumed summoning of Xelv, and especially the destruction that was Feox and his burning mount, together began pushing back the enemy forces. What had seemed at first an unwinnable conflict, Zelor now held with incipient mastery in his hand, and truly, at last, Elts was faced with the decision to defend him now or flee.

As she looked beyond the raging conflict, out over the serene canopy of snow-decked trees, up along the tall shining monolith that was Zenidow, she knew already that she would do everything now not only to destroy the Alium, but to keep Zelor from falling finally into darkness. Even now she could sense the coming of the Shadow. But if this battle could be won before that awful day, then it was worth the sin that was to turn her powers against these sacred lovers of trees. Over her eyes and ears went the black elz mask as she ran to the guarding ranks of Zelor's position, the Varaga and Koloi parting fluid and natural to admit her, and soon she stood beside the Silver Zefloz seated, jaw clamped, high forehead folded with concentration. Now even thoughts of the quest that lay ahead of them faded as she saw that despite it all his eyes held those points of white when they looked up to her, that still he was Zelor and not, as the fairy had called him, the Shadowed One.

"I am at your side, Zelor," she said, watching over the sorcerer's shoulder as a wave of Piv warriors shattered a sentinel of rock and spilled forward to attack the barrier of elementals. She took the wind to her hands, and formed with it blunt pods of air which she hoped could not kill, but surely which should slow down her opponents. Leaping up on a burst of wind, these she hurled over the defending ranks upon the company which drew near, and their bodies crumpled limp to the snow, spirit guardians dissipating with their consciousness. Deftly she landed again in the rings of guardians.

"You should go," said the sorcerer stiffly.

"You don't need to hear the wind if I can. I'll keep them away while you take the field."

"I'll never hear the wind, Elts." Zelor groaned as under a great weight, grinding his teeth, and in the distance a great swathe of flame marked the exploding demise of many. "We may win the day, but my doom is set." His tails writhed; plumes of fire erupted from the battle. Golems collapsed and rose again.

With a slamming upward gust Elts knocked a flock of bird spirits and their mounted partners from the sky; the green forms fell like mossy rocks. "If you can win the day, I must help."

"It is worse than I had imagined. I will not alter my course, but the Shadow is close. If It supplants my aim before I reach the mountain, these people will need you. And then," he looked into her eyes with white resolve, "only you can destroy the Alium."

CHAPTER XXIV
THE SHADOW

lts turned from Zelor fiercely, blasting with one hand a group of Piv that hung within the branches of a great burning tree that came too near. "I cannot simply allow you to fall!"

But there was little time for conversation. Zelor glared at the great tree-spirit which had hardly swayed in Elts' gale, and from the direction of his vassal Feox a bolt of flame burrowed through its woody heart. Elts started, seeing the beautiful complexity dissolve so swiftly, the little Piv screaming as they plummeted from its dying boughs.

Though it seemed she could defend Zelor without killing, there was death all around her. Now like the other Xol she worked against life and peace. Duxmortul, and Fozlest, the mere existence of the Alium they threatened far more than the trees of Altum, but slowly with such logic came the feeling that she did not act of her own will, that she and Zelor had no control now, that they were the real puppets under a great shadow looming over the battlefield, whose hooking tentacles squeezed their hearts into submission. Still she cleared the air above them of the spying spirits of fowl and insect, and boosting to her high vantage sent crushing waves of wind over those Piv who threatened Zelor's position.

Yet there were others far more dangerous who closed upon that place. With a wide stage before the forest now cleared, held, and well defended by the spirits of sturdy trees full up with Piv archers, out went the Great One Yisven Vir with her partner Luen, and not far behind her Sylna and Muewa upon the back of

Faltion, to seek from high vantage and with sharp eye for the fastness of the Shadow. As the spirit of Pivwood's air and mist arrived like a wondrous cloud over the opposite end of the battle, she sensed at once the absence of killing intent in the winds of Elts, and focused upon that place as it quite stood out among all of the death. But Luen riding among that always transforming golden cloud did not have long to consider why this Xol was not so cruel as her compatriots, blowing back all that approached the rings of fire and water, for though they now discovered beside her that here was Zelor himself, the chosen Piv now noticed near to that closely defended position the demure posture of Xelv, seated far too calmly beyond and seeming to build up even the liquid exterior of their enemy's final barrier from without. Through the telescoping vapours of her ethereal chariot, she saw indeed that all around the Blue Zefloz bubbled like the mouth of a great river the source of the endless living waters which gave the attacking army such ceaseless volume.

"There!" she shouted in her high shrill voice, and looking back over the plain she saw the flashing eye of Faltion as the great bird turned to follow, Sylna's blue cloak rippling out to the side as they banked.

Yisven Vir swept low towards the summoner with the blue-hemmed robes. "Luen, this one is protected," she breathed from all directions in the lilting concert of auras surrounding her rider.

"Muewa and Sylna are coming." The Piv hardly grimaced, preparing for the drop. "Hold the Shadowed One and the woman as long as you can. I'll take the summoner."

From the roiling cloud descending, Luen shot like a small green dart straight to the snow, and far behind her over the fighting could be seen the shape of Faltion racing to her aid. The glowing, roaring winds of Yisven Vir seemed from her perspective to consume Zelor and all that stood to guard him. But the Piv could not have known how closely connected were the minds of the sorcerer and his defenceless puppet, for Zelor knew at once what was their plan, and no sooner was the shadow of the Great One over him had he dashed swiftly from under the falling well of vapour and through the seamlessly parting ranks of his protectors towards Luen. Already she zoomed forth on iridescent wings with her grass blade angled for the oblivious heart of Xelv, but her strike met only the shining silver of Zelor's sword appearing as from nowhere, and the force of that parry threw her spinning and fluttering desperately through the air, tiny fairy that she was.

Yet the swift winds of Yisven Vir had turned and swirled in an expanding whorl and now with tremendous momentum passed in a terrific and ceaseless gale through the back of Zelor, such that he plunged his sword and tails into the snow and bore down heavily to retain his posture. In the distance Feox slumped masterless atop his mount, though the flame-slimed monster carried on in the mindless destruction of its own nature which—like the Varaga and Koloi—needed not a controller.

Here was breath enough for Luen to cast her slender little sword spiralling straight and true like a razor-fine javelin for the defenceless Xelv. But slightly the sharp point of the projectile turned and missed, slashing open a bloodless swath of black cloth only, for Elts arriving in a silent gust which plied the snow now worked even from the substance of Yisven Vir herself a single gold-white hush to lift away the lethal dart. The spirit of Pivwood's winds paused in awe, feeling how the faintest boundaries of her mists had been transformed and guided by the will of this mortal and the simple magic of her elz-bark trinket. Yet it was only a brief moment in the agelessness of her time, and with a rush of colour and cold Elts was knocked high into the sky and severed from her mask such that she could not soften her fall hard into the frozen ground far away.

In the space of Elts' contention, Zelor with a shout resumed his control over Feox—now the flaming arcs of the greataxe glared anew through the locked forces at battle—and shrugged off the Great One's distracted winds, advancing upon Luen in broad strokes. Brave and impossible seemed her terribly close dodges, yet in truth too deft and precise was her darting little form for the sorcerer to intercept, and now Xelv sat unprotected before the bog of bursting new Koloi. The piercing cry of Faltion signalled that she and her riders Muewa and Sylna had now arrived, and shortly did they wing for the summoner. Down they banked like a slicing blade, and just as Elts regained her feet to find her mask, just before Zelor could turn to see the target of the slender white bow upheld and released with expert form by the witch in blue, the majesty of the bird had sped away, and he knew already that Xelv the Blue Zefloz slumped lifelessly forward in the snow, a white arrow sprouting from under the chin.

In a gust of colour and light Luen was rushed away by her guardian to stream and helix in rippling silvers and golds about the figure of Faltion circling back. Zelor was now exposed, and the flood of Koloi could no longer wall him in, so he called Feox to his side at once. The Red Zefloz had slain more Piv than any. Behind and around the muted slippery steps and sluggish tail of his mount was a wake of black smouldering erasure, the full power of his monstrous fire released. Yet already the numbers of the fragile Koloi were rapidly dispersing, and openings appeared as the forces of Piv drew in to flank him while he turned to face his master. Running to his side with Elts guarding the rear, Zelor threw up with much strain new golems of expanding and slamming rock from below to guard the vulnerable sides of Feox.

Yet a blinding pain scourged his back, and he fell, quickly rolling away from a flurry of stabbing bright blades that sank into the ground with a blast of snow and wind, hurling himself up to meet again the enormous talons of Faltion which struck this time against his blocking blade. Pushing with all his might against the crushing force of the attack, blade shaking, tails pressing against the ground, he looked up and saw Muewa, little and green but no less fierce, perched upon the brow of the enormous creature, and behind her over the silver-feathered shoulder Sylna readying an arrow. With a gravelly yell and a great yank Zelor slashed the edge of his blade through the foot of Faltion and threw up one hand—an exploding vertical pillar of rock just missed the feinting bird as it rolled back into the sky, now banking sharply down for another attack. Yet another wall of rock was thrown up as a shield before the still recovering sorcerer, and the great talons slammed against it with an impact that jarred the land. Smashing the two slabs of wall together Zelor nearly pinned the trio, but they shot up too swift and true, just the slightest of tailfeathers caught between the closing gap.

Among the host of warriors who fought the Red Zefloz while Faltion, Sylna, and Muewa fought the shadow, Wanuev was one of four who walked with the Great Ones, and the others now made their own efforts to render their opponent vulnerable so that he might deliver the finishing blow. Aio, the spirit of Piv-wood's rivers, poured all of its might into the flank of the great flaming salamander such that a vast cloud of steam erupted from its skin and it swung round its head breathing only impotent gasping air, yet even as Nuem called round the waters for another strike, new blistering fires welled from the throat of the creature to contend, and the moisture seemed driven from the air all around, blowing him back and evaporating a vast chunk of Aio's winding body in an instant.

Yet in the moment of the salamander's sudden cooling the winds of Yisven Vir had carried the old hermit Fuewav—small and hard to see—not so close to Feox himself, but to the side of the unmissable largeness of his mount. As the flames poured out and vaporized that great portion of Aio, Fuewav laid his hand upon the dry hide of the great newt, and Morviut the spirit of death passed from his palm. At once the skin shrank tight against that point, and a tremor went through the structure of the huge hairless, scaleless animal such that it paused in all its doing. Its desiccated being began to ripple, and in the hiss which was its final collapse, in the cascading waves of colourless sand which thundered to the ground and blew back all those Piv who yet advanced upon the scene, Zelor with a hiss—still flinging great boulders after the strafing Faltion—commanded Feox to escape the wave of dissolution, so that like a flaming shade the Red Zefloz leapt in moment of final collapse through the veiled air, landing poised in the rain of detritus.

Even as his bare feet touched the snow Feox swung out his enormous axe, and so destroyed were those spirits of tree and lunion there ready to meet him that their Piv partners were completely incapacitated. That sheet of flame he gathered into a turning beam which fired directly into the tiny place where yet stood Fuewav still with his hand outstretched above the field of ash which had been the hideous newt. The old Piv was totally obliterated in an instant, and even when the annihilating flames had cleared, already came down the tremendous axe slamming to the ground in an explosion of burning that blew back the entirety of Yisven Vir which now rushed to smother his flames. Aio crippled, Yisven Vir dispersed, and Morviut's avatar slain, only Wanuev small and feeble appeared through the smoke to face the Red Zefloz, and it was horribly clear to him that the power of this being—even so limited by what focus its master could spare during the fight with Faltion—was quite enough to destroy even the most powerful spirits.

Already the conflict was circumscribed by many Varaga which had come to defend their mountless master, and many Piv now converging as well upon this crucial point of war who contested them, so that Feox and Wanuev stood as alone in a surging encirclement of battle. Out came the axe in broad rebounding circuits, yet Wanuev jetted aside on his gossamer wings like a refracting green shaft of light, and through the wide spaces between the giant Xol's slow-seeming movements he angled suddenly, not at all knowing what he would do once he reached the sorcerer.

"Come on," he thought, closing his eyes as he sped for Feox's open chest, the slow axe swing still continuing on in his periphery. "Where are you, Vivoen?"

Now the spirit of life is one whom none could describe but that it cannot be predicted, invisible even now though already Wanuev had called upon it. In elder days it had given visions of the Cosmos, conducted miracles for the ill, or blessed the forest with some new evolution, as many times as it had blinded, misled, or undermined the Piv. Yet trickster as it was, it always seemed to know just what to do, if it was interested in helping, that is.

There appeared round Wanuev a glimmering aura of purple and silver shimmering like a ghostly liquid as he flew as fast as little wings could carry him, head first with his tiny arms outstretched like a living arrow shaft screaming at the top of his little voice, so that it seemed a pure beam of divine light struck the black-cloaked burning chest of the sorcerer, and not a tiny buzzing fairy. At once Wanuev felt that his hands were engulfed in lava and he yelped in pain, but in that very instant the whole of the strange energy which had enveloped him left, and surrounded Feox instead, taking with it all of the pain. Even as it went to the Red Zefloz the light seemed to fade, and there was a queer silence in the eye of the battle as Wanuev scampered back, more unsure what to do than ever.

The fire mage stood there for a moment as though nothing had happened. He turned, blinked, and looked all around him at the seething theatre of war, the axe in his hand, the slain Piv all around and so many more which warred against his own elementals, Zenidow so towering close amid the forest. Yet all these things so wondrous and impossible fell into red-tinged obscurity as his eyes fell upon Zelor. "You," he said, advancing.

Elts and Zelor gawked, almost forgetting their efforts—she to keep back the Piv with her winds, he to defeat Faltion and her riders—for the Feox who had spoken after so many months, and who approached now was the very same which had left Xoldra beside them. At last one of those men whom Zelor had so utterly disgraced was somehow liberated by a power which contended even with the Shadow. But there was only an instant to appreciate that strange magic.

Already the gladiator leapt forward like a flaring meteor over the field, and swinging out his great-axe cleaved up from the ground a huge rising drift of snow and dirt; Zelor feinting only just avoided the arc of blinding flame as it left trails of smoke upon his fluttering robes. Fire plumed from the outstretched palm of the Red Zefloz to intersect that dodging motion, but slamming together the still flying debris of rock so dug up by the first strike, Zelor cocooned himself fast so that the fires washed over and out, burning all who stood too near. Forward he undressed and thrust the carapace of rock to strike Feox, but his target had already dashed to the side, now hefting his axe somehow brighter and hotter than ever it had raged over one shoulder, thrusting forward one knee to prepare the slamming of that massive double edge in annihilation of all that lived before him.

Yet suddenly there was a tremendous gale of freezing, sleet-thick wind, and as it rushed over the Red Zefloz the glorious flames of his axe and eyes seemed to wither. "Zelor!" he shouted. "I will kill you!" But the winds only increased and ripped at his clothes such that one foot, now the other were forced back as he leaned fully into the force of it all to gain leverage. With a great shout, Elts brought her wrists together, palms open to project all that she had conjured and condensed upon the scene, as though she were closing some immense, immovable set of stone doors, and with an explosion of sound Feox was blasted high into the sky, the dying flames and smoke of his axe trailing behind him as though he were a spout of lava ejected from a volcano beneath the snow.

"For Pivwood!" came the voices of Muewa and Sylna in harmony. The talons of Faltion screaming through the air impaled brutally the broad torso of Feox as it hung defenceless above the field, now a limp dark thing hanging from the winging golden form of the spirit bird and her riders interposed against the pale sun. The black chunks which were the Red Zefloz were shredded to pieces in one vicious twist of flight. Already Faltion dove anew, so swiftly even to outpace those falling pieces of Feox, heading straight for Zelor below.

But now with his mind no longer occupied with the actions of Feox, Zelor with his full focus and true power freed at last raised both arms and slammed two instantly risen sheets of rock together, crushing the speeding form of Faltion all but flat. There the bird was trapped shivering, and though the small green fleck which was Muewa had already taken to the air on wings of her own, the blue body of Sylna fell like a stone to the shaded earth between the wedded slabs. Still the loss of Feox was sore, and fearful fury was in the eyes of the Silver Zefloz as the host of Piv still rushed in rivers through the golems and man-eating plants. Now with only Elts to protect him, with the Koloi much diminished and the Varaga masterless, all able Piv and spirit alike turned upon him in a massive concerted effort.

With a great effort Zelor lifted sharp shelves of rock more titanic than any before to pierce from beneath the ground which smote the Piv warriors and destroyed many of their familiars, leaving immense shielding walls like titan fins upright in the land. But still in valiant waves the Piv rushed through these great shifting slabs, and even as they broke through the spirits of land to bear down upon him with their savage claws and teeth, the sorcerer saw that now the Great Ones too had surrounded him, and that the end was near.

"Elts!" Zelor shouted from within the trapping slabs, as the Piv surrounded him. "You must fly! Fly now!" He fell to his knees. Shade passed over the cloudless sky.

She heard it in his voice, but still she ran through the towering, leaning scarps that like a maze of jagged teeth and ribs now defended the sorcerer, as if something could be done, as if still they might prevail before the Shadow, as if together they would find the Alium.

Up from the labyrinth of rock boomed an utterance like no Altumian ever had witnessed, such that the whole field of war grew still with the machine drone of its ending. Night draped the snow as though the sun was snuffed out, but there were no stars or moons to shine upon what then unfolded.

From the centre of the shielding slabs exploded an immense gashing bolt of blood-red energy, tearing as one vast instant to the forest and narrowing suddenly into a fine thread of blinding light, vanishing quickly as it had come.

All along the way the foul energy had traversed was now a bottomless chasm of void. But for the molten skeletons of the trees close to the final flash, all of the tens of hundreds of Piv caught in the red moment were vaporized beyond the state of dust, and even Elts standing wholly opposite the trajectory of it all, though cocooned in the hardest and densest pod of wind that ever she had conjured, was thrown so far and high by its concussive becoming that the sheer blunt impact nearly killed her.

Deep within the dark leaning plates of rock, hunched before the great steaming hole which marked the egress of that terrible energy, Zelor remained upon his knees seizing with pain, holding his head in his hands and shaking as he retched. Cracking from his quaking back so suddenly as to thrust him forward, now splitting his chest and belly so powerfully as to fold back his spine in a crunching arch, great gouts of black ichor exploded in spiralling and coiling tendrils of darkness, liquid at first, hardening as by the touch of the air into many-jointed extremities that coursed and flexed and swelled until they were long and great as trees. Slamming into the ground the numberless tentacles dragged the sorcerer into the air. Blistering crimson light surrounded him in an aura of malevolence as more such evil limbs erupted from his flesh and writhed in the black sky.

Hanging limp in the hold of the black and red mass, it seemed that Zelor had naught to do with what transpired, yet his head lifted then with the slow certainty of intent, white hair hanging madly all over and blowing in the wind, blinding red eyes flashing and searing over the plain. He held up his hands with an alien delicacy, as if such things were new to him yet like precious gifts only slowly to be understood, and now the enormous tentacles grew eerily conscious. Suddenly they bunched together, now unfurled with violence, hurling each new bolts of crimson energy as devastating as the first. All that stood or flew too near were annihilated, as the very crust of the world was opened up with black and bottomless wounds unto its centre.

Horrible as was the destruction, Zelor did not move from the spot where he hung in his writhing tentacle armour, hurling out the bolts of doom, and so all Piv that remained now took flight, gathering together upon what spirits were most fleet. The sorcerer only watched as they went, and as the last of their numbers arrived at the edge of the wood, the vast tentacles lowered him to the snow once more, and sluggishly began to recede into some bottomless dimension of darkness within his soul.

Elts had fled at first, but now she stopped and watched as Zelor drew up three great slabs from the ground like huge sheets sliding from deep slots below. Around him they rose as beneath him came a platform of stone bearing him high

into the sky—fifty, sixty, one hundred meters over the evil matrix of rifts in the
tortured ground below, and when at last the slabs angled and met—the last of
the great black tentacles spooling back into his back as they closed—Zelor was
housed in an impenetrable fortress of rock. At the top of the tower he shaped a
great spike to heaven.

Elts ran across the plain until she stood with her hands placed against the cold
outer shell of that sudden tower, far below, the place to which he had risen so
cold and alone in the sky, and tears welled in her eyes. She had felt it more
poignantly than any when the power of Duxmortul arrived, and she could feel it
now hovering over the tower and the whole furrowed field like a black cloud
bent on the Alium. Enormous ghosts of dark tentacles menaced the sky, and she
shivered at the malice which brooded within the walls.

And so she sat upon the ground and surrendered to whatever should befall
her, for she saw clearly now that Zelor the Xol would never return, that the man
whose ambitions she had at last come to understand had been crushed under the
dark will of the thing from beyond the stars.

Out of the slurry walked the slim shape of Sylna. Her face was caked with
blood, her quiver empty, her blue robes ragged with snow and dirt. She stopped
beside the white-haired sorceress sitting so calmly in the snow, her back against
the tower of rock, such vacancy in her eyes.

"She has given up," said Muewa, floating forth as well upon her elegant wings,
landing softly, nimble hands folded behind her back. "She has no malice in her
heart for Pivwood, or desire at all for the Alium."

"What is your name?" said Sylna, holding out her hand.

The White Zefloz looked blankly at Sylna's ringed fingers. "Elts."

"We saw how you would not take a life. Muewa says that you are not of the
Shadow."

"I fought for it today."

"You fought for Zelor," said Muewa, lighting upon Elts' trembling knee. "He
wished to make things right, but he could not have escaped it. To think that he
resisted so long is a sign of great valiance. I see that you believed in his heart."

"Come away from this evil place," said Sylna. "If you wish to free your friend
from his darkness, that too is our goal."

Memories flowed from the voice of the witch like moving images on the snow-
glittering breeze, of Xirell cooing to his septry, of noble Fexest composed in her
determination, of Zelor meditating upon the wind. Duxmortul had taken him
just like the others, crushed him, drained him, used him, if not even more

terribly, forcing him to apply the very curse of his own thralldom to what should have been his own allies. She gripped Sylna's offered hand and rose from the snow, looking up to the top of the tower.

And so night fell on the first day of the battle for Pivwood. Elts and Sylna followed Muewa through the labyrinth of debris, crossing on bridges—sewn as they went—of shimmering ice over the great furrows rent in the world by Zelor. Soon the scars of war were behind them, and with them the darkness lost its hold, for as they walked upon the open snow they beheld the peeping jewels of starlight.

At last they came under the low boughs, brushed through the high ferns, walked around the noble tall trunks. Close ahead lay a great clearing bursting with all manner of fungal structures, and upon the tops of the mushrooms large and small there stood and danced and mourned a thousand Piv. Clans from all through the forest had been summoned there, and continued ceaselessly to arrive in tremendous numbers, wandering or fluttering out from the flickering shadows, clambering into the warm boughs, communing with the faint images of spirits, altogether constantly spilling from all the coulisses of the forest as the Moon of War, silver as a blade, passed through the leaves above.

Looking up at the argent crescent, Elts sighed and went to rest away from the commotion upon a mossy log, ribbed in mushrooms. Sylna came away in time from a group of fairies and sat silently beside her, not knowing what to say. But the Xol was quite ready to speak at last with someone other than Zelor, however much she missed him.

"There is no sign of Fextol tonight," she said, still staring up at the moon.

Sylna joined her gaze. "Fextol?"

"Oh. The peaceful moon." Elts made a sweeping motion with her purple hand. "I do not know what it is called by Novare, but it is like a cloud, a gas that breaks up or collects sometimes into a sphere."

"We call it Pacemn. How interesting that it has the same meaning among the Xol." Sylna mused, taking comfort in the intellectual activity. "And yes, that's odd, it usually comes along with..."

"Zedoras," said Elts.

"Zedoras. What a pretty name. To me it has always been Bellumroth. Much more beastly don't you think?"

Elts nodded. "War is a beastly thing."

They sat in silence for a moment, watching the dark clouds slip across the face of the moon. "What do you think it means?"

"It means that peace is gone."

"Or maybe that it is to be found elsewhere than in fighting. Maybe Fextol wants nothing to do with Zedoras these days."

Elts smiled, turning to the witch. "That is a lovely thought."

Suddenly an adorable little clearing of the throat summoned their attention to Muewa, who stood like a shoot of bendy grass upon a toadstool before them. Beside her landed silently a very tall fairy of much darker complexion, and even darker green eyes. Next to Muewa's folk he seemed as a shadow, for they were fair skinned and light-haired.

"Please, allow me to introduce Wistmane, elder of the Eastern Piv of the Azure Lagoon," said Muewa, sweeping out one diminutive hand.

Wistmane spoke in a sonorous baritone. "Greetings, Xol and Novare. All of us in the forest knew a day would come when the Powers of the World would seek the Alium." He bowed nobly. "Oerbanuem is in both of you. The forces of evil will have a hard fight with you on our side. Now where is Wanuev!"

Over flitted Wanuev quickly, but his silliness was quite gone. "Elder, I am at your service."

"At ease, friend," said Wistmane laughing. "It is good to see you so serious. And alive too. We will need you greatly at dawn."

"Wanuev is in communion with one of the Great Ones," tittered Muewa proudly to Elts. "The spirit of life Vivoen to be precise. It was her power that defeated the fire mage today, though certainly Wanuev is a brave one for standing against him." She smiled warmly.

"The Great Ones are the strongest spirits of the wood, as gods to us," said Wistmane. "Wanuev will live many more centuries than even Muewa because of this, but his responsibility in a time as this is great."

Elts was not as surprised as Sylna had been when many months ago she had learned this news herself, for the sorceress had not met the little creature before or weathered his pranking. "I saw how he defeated Feox. He must be one of your most powerful warriors."

Wanuev grinned sheepishly at Elts and blushed, the armour of his composure quite cracked.

"Aha!" Sylna laughed, pointing at the embarrassed Piv. "You don't know Wanuev like I do, Elts. He once played me for a horrible joke."

"I'm very sorry, miss witch," said Wanuev. "You see, now I feel I must be a tough Piv!"

"You were tough enough on the battlefield, little one, no need to pretend for the ladies," chuckled Wistmane, leading Wanuev away—blushing an even darker hue of jade—to speak with him alone.

Muewa laughed like a tinkling bell. "It is funny you know, how Vivoen always seems to choose the most untethered sorts of Piv. Come now, you must meet the other Elders." She flew off then so quickly that Sylna and Elts had quite to hustle in following her, their robes filling up with the dew-thick evening air. They found the Piv beside another woman with marine skin and big glossy eyes, perched upon a boulder. "The Elder of the West, Veanwe," Muewa said, bowing. Sylna and Elts paid their respects in the same manner, and sat in the grass before the new Piv.

"Muewa, it is a joy to see you!" The woman was thinner and smaller than any Piv Sylna had ever seen, and needed to fly up and around the witches' faces even before they could confess a good look at her. "And these women are strong!" Her voice was high and sweet like a flute, and all that she said beamed with happiness. "But this one has much darkness in her heart."

"You see well, Elder." Elts cast down her gaze. "I convinced myself that defending Zelor was more important than these old trees and the lives of your people. I am Xol, aren't I? Surely the true lovers of the trees are here, and not in our black lands."

Veanwe beamed. "Ah, but all who love the trees are pure in that love. The Xol were once kind as the Piv to spirits of the wood and earth."

Elts grimaced, reminded of her own curse. "You've not seen what our presence does to the trees. If I stay here in this forest too long, they will begin to calcify and turn black as night."

"There is nothing to worry about here," Muewa said calmly. "It will take far more than one kindly Xol to poison Pivwood."

There was suddenly a great clamour, and most all Piv rose in a chorus of merriment, for the fairies of the North had come at last. Old as time they were, and their skin the purest colour of fresh leaf and the thick grass. Tall and lean, they wore kind smiles and sang softly as they flew, lighting all about in places among the others. They had travelled thousands of miles, for Pivwood was densest and greater beyond Zenidow, and like all Piv the Northlings lived far from the mountain's base. Their leader was an ancient creature, so old as to bear actual wrinkles upon his face. His eyes were brown like the bark of the richest trees, and his face showed forth an immeasurable kindness as he laughed in a bellow deep and fruity for his tiny frame. He wore a tunic made of two great leaves bound together with weeds, and sticks and twigs and strange insects made their abode in his frizzy pale mint hair.

"That is Eanwu," said Muewa proudly, "the Eldest. It is said that he walked with Caelare when the world was shaped." Even she had become solemn-eyed now, so that Sylna and Elts took up her manner and waited silently while Piv of all shapes and sizes flocked to the old man, surrounding him gleefully and haranguing him with their shrill little voices as he came through to the centre of the council.

It was there amidst the two concentric rings of toadstools at the centre of the clearing where all the Piv seemed now to gather that Muewa led Sylna and Elts to meet with Veanwe and Wistmane, who had taken their seats. The witch and the sorceress sat in the grass, and Muewa lighting atop a toadstool needed only Eanwu to complete the inmost circle of four, where he crossed his legs, folded his wings, and said, "At last, the four Elders are together again."

Muewa smiled, and called out in her high voice to the whole of the wood amassed around them. "The time has come for all Piv to join and fight against one who would threaten our forest!" A great cry and roaring song came from the Piv, and Elts was astounded by their numbers, for thousands of voices came from the forest. "But I ask you, dear friends," Muewa went on, "that we Elders meet together this night without shouting for you all." There was laughter. "Take you your sleep! Tend to your wounded!" The cry sounded again, and though many still stood watching, the numbers of Piv seemed to dissolve into the trees.

Five Piv including Wanuev drew closer and seated themselves among the outer ring of mushrooms. Elts figured that these must be those whose familiars were the Great Ones, and she realized—turning to Sylna who looked on as a shadow passed over her face—that one of their number must have fallen in the battle. Elts hung her head in shame.

"Muewa, you are ever the leader of these people," said Wistmane.

"Why, this is my part of the wood, is it not?"

"Oh, you would raise the noise of any crowd," peeped Veanwe.

Muewa smiled sheepishly. "Anyhow. There is much to discuss. I have here two witches, one Novare, the other Xol, and I think there is a lot they can tell us about the enemy, but also about the fate of the wood. Sylna, I believe we should start with you." Muewa gestured for the witch to speak.

"Greetings, Elders, friends. I am blessed beyond words to walk among you and your folk, the oldest denizens of Altum." The Elders seemed to laugh inwardly, but there was a degree of ancient appreciation in their manners. "As you know, a great power sleeps in the heart of Zenidow. I came to this wood with my master Nubes to discover this thing which we call and you seem already to know by the name Alium. I have not been to it, but Nubes has, and he spoke with it through his understanding of the way of the Cosmos. He revealed little to me, but that the Alium would waken, and that others would come to take it for their own gain. The wakening of the thing, he said, is essential in saving our world from a horrible doom, but it can only be accomplished with the help of another. And that other is a true son of Caelare!"

All but for Muewa and Eanwu were astounded. Their small eyes were widened and their mouths quivered. At last Wistmane spoke. "Is this true?"

"Yes," said Muewa. "He is called Ogwold."

"Even now he approaches," said Eanwu. His brown eyes flashed as he dug a fly from his hair and swallowed it in one motion so smooth and natural that Elts was hardly surprised until many moments later. "He comes with an old Euphran... but, there is another rider. A Novare, and I think he has some destiny to accomplish among us as well."

"Another Novare," Wistmane mused. "Let us hope he is not for the power of the Alium. He could be a deceiver of this Ogwold."

"We will have to deal with that when they arrive," said Eanwu. "But first we must survive the coming day, for though they fly swiftly, they are far off."

"Yes, I sense a darkness about the tower of the Shadow. He is amassing some new opponent for us, and it reeks of deathless void." Veanwe's eyes were misted with fright, and her voice only grew higher as she spoke.

"That is where the Xol Elts may help us," said Muewa.

Elts bowed, arranging her tails in the sign of peace and humility. "Greetings, guardians of these the most glorious trees I have ever known. You must sense that my presence here is a poison to things that grow; it is a great honour to be accepted into your forest." The Elders looked on with admiration, but Elts could not return their smiles. "Zelor is the one you call the Shadow. He has grown far more powerful even than our Empress Fozlest in recent time, for he holds sway over the minds of others, and little can harm him. The spirits of my compatriots and master were bent easily to his will so that they became such puppets as you fought today upon the plain. My finest friend Xirell the courageous and ever wise even was broken in this way, and to look into his vacant eyes was the saddest moment in my life. But I say in my defence for having stood loyally beside the darkness: Zelor is not our enemy."

A murmuring passed through the outer ring, though the Elders only waited for Elts to continue. She paused for a moment, unclasping from her belt a small leather pouch. "At first I too thought that he was everything dark in the world. I obeyed him out of fear, thinking that somehow I might find a way to resurrect my master. But then I discovered the true killer among us. Zelor had been possessed by a terrible monster from the stars, a thing more cruel and powerful than anything this world has known, a false god who craves the Alium so badly that even from far off in the deeps of space It reached out into the mind of Zelor when he was at his weakest and twisted him to its will. By the strength of his own will to defy evil Zelor overcame the darkness and endeavoured to use its own power against it. He wanted to destroy the Alium so that it could never be used against all peoples of Altum."

Elts turned to Sylna, pain on her brow. "I thought that our battle today did not involve the Alium, but now I see that you need it, somehow. But you have not seen the true evil that hangs over the man. If the Alium falls into such a grasp, our world will break."

Sylna bowed her head, saying nothing.

"Perhaps it cannot be so easily destroyed. But what is the Alium next to the very thing which seeks to abuse it, the very monster which descends now upon this place. Zelor knew. I knew, saw the power. He tried to save me, to send me away, but I wouldn't go because... I believed that he had control. But now he is gone. Yes, his body is still out there under the Shadow, but here is the true face of evil!"

Out from the leather pouch fell the hideous black idol as Elts cast the unbearable tentacled thing clattering over a small, flat rock in the centre of their circle of seats. Twice it rolled, stopping with the terrible columns of red eyes facing up. At once a terrible chill passed through all who saw it, and Veanwe cheeped in horror.

"This is the image of Duxmortul," said Elts gravely. "Ever since I knew its presence, it has haunted my dreams, this creature not of Altum carved here out of a substance I cannot place. It comes from the gulfs of space in a great black ship that sails through the void. Even now across the whorls of Secundom It reaches to our minds like playthings to be tasted."

"That is no mere image, friend Xol," said Eanwu, and his countenance was grim to behold.

"You know what this is?" Veanwe squeaked.

Eanwu gazed into the blood-red ranks of eyes. "No, but there is life in it, watching, vigilance."

"Let us destroy it at once," Wistmane scoffed. "I too feel this presence."

"Yes, if this thing can see or hear us through it," said Veanwe, "we must be rid of it!"

"I doubt we have the ability to," Eanwu muttered through his great beard. "Just as I doubt even the full might of this Duxmortul could mar the Alium." He gazed serenely into Elts' eyes. "Elts, tell us, when do these dreams come to you?"

The sorceress sighed. It was true. Zelor could never have succeeded. The idol was destined to find him; the Zefloz could never have understood him; the Piv would die before allowing evil into their land; and even if they had reached Zenidow in time, they would never have been able to destroy the Alium. Had it all been Duxmortul's plan? Was Its eminence merely a flex of the lightest muscle? Muewa had spoken a cold truth when they first accosted Pivwood; Zelor was merely a vehicle, and its rider had at last arrived.

When she looked up to continue her story, took in carefully the faces of the waiting Elders—Wistmane stoically impatient, Veanwe fidgeting on the edge of her toadstool, Eanwu stroking his beard, Muewa somehow softly smiling—she knew that even though she too had been so easily manipulated, even here, in the place she had threatened, she was still accepted. Accepted, and understood as well, she thought; from the start, they had supported her feelings, and must now know what was the noblest action in their light. Zelor would want her to oppose the Shadow in his stead, and she could think of no greater way to honour and forgive him than to do what she should have done for her master long ago—by sending his spirit to Xeléd.

"Before I knew what were the designs of Zelor, I sought to understand his new powers and find some way to save my master from thralldom. Among his bags I found this horrible icon, and the mere touch of its cold life transported me to its maker. I found myself in a great ship of metal flying through the stars like the gods. We descended to a white world where more black ships had landed, a frozen, sunless land suffused of its own alien light. Around us were beautiful creatures shaped from the ice, writhing in so much pain. The destruction began at their slightest revolt—the dying, the breaking, the consumption. As everything collapsed, I drifted up and out of this thing," she jabbed her finger again at the statue. "Duxmortul: It—the Shadow—destroyed their entire world, crushed and drank it life and all. By some chance of luck this object fell from my hand before I was perceived, but that, I think, is the goal of it: perception, Zelor of the power leant him, Duxmortul of Its prophet's path."

Muewa's wings wilted as the witch spoke. "This is calamitous indeed."

Veanwe shivered. "What need could something so powerful have for the Alium?"

"Have you any other dreams to share?" Eanwu spoke calmly.

"Many, though they are all of the same nature." Elts' gaze flitted over the dormant idol. "Tentacles cast over the land, crushing, sucking. Blood-red light washing out all hope. And a vast darkness descending at last. I've not held the idol long enough, I think, to suffer another transportation. I'd returned it to Zelor's bags, but I stole it again before the battle. When it is in my hand I feel its energy, but if I rid myself of it quickly enough it is only horror and pain that I feel, and I retain myself. Zelor said that he gained control of himself through learning to resist it, so there is perhaps some mortal force which can grow and learn its ways."

"Perhaps we should touch it, then we'll know what we're up against?" Wanuev had chimed in from the outer ring of the circle.

"Fool," Wistmane rebutted him. "Whatever this thing is, we must be rid of it."

"Yes, there is no understanding it but understanding raw destructive will and killing intent, from the sound of Elts' dreams," said Veanwe. "Whatever she can tell us is quite enough I imagine." Wanuev bit his tongue.

"Well let's be rid of it then," said Sylna. "I can fold it into Nubes' vault. It may chance that its closeness gives the Shadow more power."

Wistmane spoke at once. "Do it then. We must focus on Zelor. The night grows old."

The others agreed, and Sylna took up her bow arrowless. She closed her eyes, and slowly as she pulled back the silvery string the air before her unseamed. Through the slender opening Elts could see the warmth of wood, the flicker of candlelight. Up rose the idol as though it were lifted on a canvas made taut, and at once Sylna felt the pressure of it, the heat of it, suddenly a raw awful scratching in her mind so probing and remorseless that it could never run out of need. Swiftly she enfolded the idol in the invisible fabric, and with a turning wink it was gone.

The witch fell to the ground breathing slowly, her hands in the grass. "What an evil thing! How can you have held it in your hand, Elts?"

"And now it is in your home, but I suppose there are other dark things there too." Muewa glanced at her.

"None so foul. But yes, I sent it to a safe place at least."

"So now we are free to discuss strategy?" Wistmane's face was hard and grim.

Muewa adjusted one red berry in her flowing green hair. "What I and many sensed this day, when Zelor retreated into his tower, was that the use of that destroying red light may have exhausted him already. I don't see why else he should not have taken the forest at once, for there was nothing we could do to stop him."

"Yes," said Eanwu. "It was fear of death that brought out the Shadow at last, and again which showed us that It is not entirely willing to fight us head on."

Wistmane grunted. "I as well sensed the panic in it all. If such power was always accessible to Zelor, he should have burned the forest tonight. Instead he hides in a tower of rock to what, regain his energy for another such assault?"

"I doubt that," Veanwe twittered. "Zelor must know that there are many more of us Piv on their way. He could kill thousands of us, but more will come, and he cannot reach Zenidow if he uses up all of his power. Whatever this creature is that uses him, it must be limited by the logic of that form."

"Veanwe is right," said Muewa. "We must assume that he has some new plan. Elts, again we ask for your help. What do you think he will do?"

"I do not know to what extent Duxmortul may express its power in the form It has taken, but I agree that whatever we saw today was too much for even the body of Zelor to sustain. I think, even, that it nearly destroyed him. Therefore the Shadow will now seek for the greatest weapon available to its host. For the Xol, such will always have to do with our natural aptitude for sewing. Though for most of Zelor's life he detested the Fabric and never used it, Duxmortul has no such compass, and so will search deep in the mind It has taken for the worst possible force that can be turned upon us, worse than even the most vile sorcerers would succumb to. Duxmortul will draw, I think, upon the gate to Oflos, and summon from its black heart the greatest evils ever known to our ancestors, nameless fiends who have not seen the light of Altum for thousands of years. I have little capacity as a sorceress, but even I could sense the intuition of that tower. With Duxmortul full in control, we will be fighting demons such that even the most evil Xol should never think to call upon."

When Elts finished speaking, she found that her hands had taken the mask of elz from her belt, and held it gently in her lap. Looking down at the metallic black flow of the piece, she sat still in the grass, feeling all around her who had listened. All through the Elders and in the silence of Sylna beside her she could feel how each soul processed what she had said, yet there seemed no fear of her relationship with the Shadow, and she could not understand how she could be trusted after the events of the day.

Wistmane was first to voice his thoughts. "At least he won't confront us face to face then. Many more warriors than he could possibly anticipate are on their way. Those you see now are the first to arrive of their clans. We lost many today, but the Piv are as numerous as the leaves of the forest."

"Perhaps it will take a good deal of time for Zelor to usher in these spirits," said Sylna. "We must assume he will have a new host of shadow warriors by the morning, but if we are able to stop him tomorrow, if his numbers fall, still there is the issue of penetrating his fortress, but he might not be able to conjure more for some time. That should be our opening."

Muewa's leafy locks sighed with the soft winds of the night, and she looked carefully over the faces of those who would stand beside her come the dawn. "Let us hope," said the old Piv, "that this Ogwold will soon arrive."

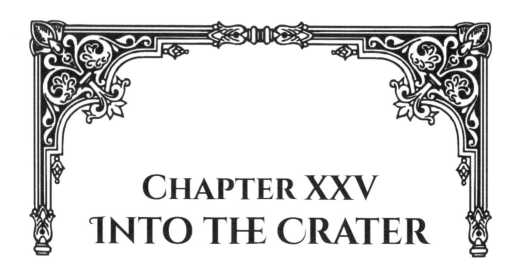

CHAPTER XXV
INTO THE CRATER

Even as the wet sky greyed and thick snow steeped the high mountains through which they flew, Ogwold and Byron as huddled shadows warmed themselves against the glaucous gleam of Wygram, returned at last to her natural realm. So long had she been crammed into the deepest dungeon of Azanak that the freedom of her heart was palpable in each jewelled scale dusted with ice, in every snapping ripple of her trailing, silvery whiskers, and in that calm her riders quite forgot the freezing sleet that pelted their bare faces.

Endlessly the jagged peaks fell beyond the haze, rose anew out of distance which blurred all but the enormous figure of Zenidow, all around them a changeless flood of titan rock frozen in waves of ice and crag. The tireless speed and precision of Wygram centred it all, crystallizing each fluid moment of supreme progress into a succession of instantaneously unique flakes sudden-shed swirling into homogeneous infinitude. Ogwold and Byron both decided no man might ever make such a journey on foot, let alone surpass in such a climate one who is many months ahead, for these thoughts and more were but a small space in a day's flight.

They stopped only to rest with the coming of night, the Euphran banking soft and sharp—suddenly with hurtling speed the icy wind threatened to rip off her riders' ears—for a small and rare shelf just touched with frost, above which she ceased so smoothly and easily her forward motion that time seemed undone. Calmly she circled over the cozy alpine nest, touching down in one soft exhalation. Her immense leathery wings still folded in retreat from their skyward work as she seemed already fast asleep, snoring loudly, but soon they settled over her body like a breathing gossamer shawl.

Byron after a long draft of cold water went to the far side of the outcropping to swing his sword. Ogwold leaned against the Euphran's scaled hide, looking out into the world of high rock. This little turfy place was tucked into the shoulder of a mountain greater than those near to it, and there seemed to be no way to descend from or survive in such a place. Yet the lithe shadows of mountain goats leapt with practised certainty along subtlest reliefs all down into the mist along the steep drop, and watching them in this vertical existence he saw the nests of septries and of hawks. Astounding and beautiful as were the lives of these creatures in this land so remote, Ogwold's eyes were drawn above it all, marvelling at the exploding, surging colours of the Reach, arching over the tops of the mountains so high in the world where it was clearest seen.

As it was a great transforming serpent, the moonless deeps of the navy sky around it seemed as the sea. He imagined that the high land upon which he sat was like the long stone dock beside his cabin in far off Epherem, and leaning forward into that reverie he plunged beneath an infinity of welcoming water. With thunderous kicks chillingly natural and so long forgotten he streamed out away from the coast and down deep into the the great stillness, where the roar and din of the waves crashing, knitting, diverging could not reach, and the heart of the world unfleshed lay open and beating amid the giant stalks of kelp, stretching in a thick, dark jungle all along the ocean floor into oblivion. Somewhere within was the silver city of the Flosleao. Suddenly more than ever before he wished to return to that place.

"Ho, Ogwold," grunted Byron, sitting and leaning beside him against Wygram's huge ribs. "Do you know the constellations?"

Dazed with the dissolving dream, Ogwold shook his great head and noticed now the vast multitude of cold stars as if they had all together appeared from the deepest loneliest darknesses of his imagined sea. He smiled oafishly: they were like the lights of the silver city. Except now that dream floated above him wherever he went. "I know many but I suspect Novare have their own," he mused, feeling his muscles relax and only now realizing they had been quite tense. "The Nogofod have a somewhat insular understanding of the universe."

Byron crossed his arms. "Then show me one; maybe I'll know it."

"All right then. See those twelve stars?" Ogwold pointed out into the sky and Byron squinted along the length of his huge arm. "They make four triangles, larger, then smaller, then the rest larger and larger." His index finger drew the angles in the air.

"I see them."

"They are the Wheels of the Nogofod, for they'll never roll."

The mercenary smirked. "That's depressing."

"There is an irony to it. But I think the point is that we are a sturdy race."

"Right," Byron muttered, as though realizing only now how little he knew of the Nogofod. "What was it like being so sturdy?"

Ogwold's heart swelled in that moment, and the ethereal image of the deep sea drained from his mind, as he rose up out of it and imagined himself floating over the village of Epherem. It was daybreak and the traders had begun to arrive. "Consistent, I'd say. Each day was like the one before it. But my father would say this is a great lesson about life—that such days that seem one so like to the other are actually very different, that every moment of life is unique."

Byron only looked out at the stars, listening.

"But... there is something about sturdiness that is a little too calming. Like the grass that my people smoke. It stills the heart and brings great ease, and it helps one to fit in, to be part of something; but it takes away our dreams."

"It keeps you on the beach."

"Precisely. That is what Lucetal desires." Ogwold frowned. "The Nogofod are a race of servants. Always our task has been to help the traders with their burdens and load up the galleons bound for the capital. There are guards there from the Island who keep watch over those of us for whom the grass does not suffice, for whom the simple pleasures, the pay is not enough—they keep us sturdy, you might say. When I lost my arm few were surprised," he said holding up the Fonsolis, suffused with starlight. "It is a common punishment for escape. And already I had a poor reputation."

Byron glared into the ogre's kind face. "You are a brave one, Ogwold." He clapped a hand onto one immense thigh. "I was lucky to find you in Occultash."

"Thank you, Byron. I am perhaps more lucky for finding you. I'd never used a weapon in my life."

"Well you happened to be carrying two of the finest."

They looked off into the stars silently for a while. Wygram snored. The wind rushed. The clatter of loose rock sounded in the abyss below. "What then is a constellation to Novare?" Ogwold asked.

"I see one now that my people knew and shared and told many stories about. I doubt any citizen of Lucetal or Occultash would know it." Byron pointed higher in the sky. Above the Wheels of the Nogofod, four stars described a bright rhombus, high and narrow. "These four here make the Seal of Molavor."

"I see it." Ogwold gazed at the shape. "What is Molavor?"

A shade fell on the mercenary, and he was still. "It is a young name for a city far older, built in elder days to guard the undersea prison of an ancient monster defeated by Caelare herself. The mortals of that land were the last to walk alongside the Goddess before she left Altum. She named them Keepers, and commanded that they stand as sentinels by that site, so that no dark force should ever discover the dormant Frandun. What sort of beings they were, or to whom they passed that honour ages ago, only the most learned scholars know, but it so happened that one thousand years ago it fell upon a nomadic host of Novare to inhabit the ancient city. And so they called it by a word of their own: Molavor."

Ogwold gazed into the simple arrangement of stars which meant, it seemed, so much to his companion. "A city of Novare. I've never heard of it before."

"If you were raised under the yoke of Lucetal, you could not have known of my home."

"Ah." The ogre nodded. "You don't have to talk about home, Byron."

The mercenary smiled wanly, his eye a gem in the starlight. "My ancestors were separated from other Novare long ago when they sailed across the sea to Efvla, and entered the northern forests to make a place for their own. In those days, the prison of the Frandun had been unguarded so long that the Xol did not know what race had last walked its broken streets, and they themselves too religiously feared to live in such close proximity to the bay. An alliance was formed with the newcomers, and Molavor rebuilt by the hands and minds of Novare. Even as the first stones were taken up, it is said that Caelare descended upon those first Molavorians with a vision and that same commandment: keep evil from this place. And so we have. Though the Empire cared little for us and likened the Frandun to a myth, still we peacefully coexisted. The Xol of Lofled were most close to us. They taught us from the scriptures, instructed our mages to work with the elz trees, and we showed them the ways of metal and delving. But for the lust of Lucetal our alliance might have gone on; when King Chalem invaded the coast of Efvla, everything changed. Fozlest twisted by the words of Zelor believed that all Novare were evil, that Molavor too would turn against them. And so she sent him to work our end."

Ogwold leaned his head back against Wygram's cold scales. "That's why you're hunting him."

"I wish it were not so," said Byron to the stars. "Together we were Knights under the Seal, and travelled through the old forests, showing the magic users the utility of a strong blade. Zelor wanted to show the Xol that Novare were to be honoured as equals, but no matter how hard we pushed each other, nothing could impress the Empress. In time he distanced himself, pushed us all away, and forgot the way of the sword. Only he hunted alone in the deep forest for an answer to his ails which constantly he seemed to dream about. For nearly a season he vanished. When he returned, evil hung round his neck by a silver cord, yet he swore madly it would help him topple the Empire. Over so many swift months his eyes turned pitch black, and he spoke only of Fozlest. A new mind had taken residence in his body who had need of the very strength which Zelor once despised. Yet it knew all that he knew, that only Molavorians could speak to his change, and so in the dawn of the war with Lucetal he convinced the Empress that we were traitorous to her kind, and gloried in her favour as he collapsed our walls, burned our houses, and slew nearly us all."

As he spoke, Byron's hand went to the hilt of Azanog, which lay beside him in the grass. Its wrapping had become ragged, perhaps from how brutal was the grip of its new wielder. A single tear beaded against his rough cheek and caught the moonlight. He thumbed it away. "I know not what to call the entity but Zelor, for it goes by that accursed name as if to mock his memory. With my last breath, Ogwold, I will pull the sick tentacles of that creature from my brother's heart."

The ogre lay back in sheer amazement at all he had heard. Never had Byron spoken at such length and with such sincerity, and even the man's face was contorted with open pain. For a long while, Ogwold could only listen to the rushing night-wind, feel the gentle pulse of Wygram's breathing, glance over at the hunched shadow of the mercenary. He recalled then the flaming, lonely wolf atop the hill which he had seen when the Fonsolis entwined with Byron's spirit, and now he saw the true suffering of it all, that the one it hunted was family. "Must he really be killed?" he said softly, feeling that he only made things worse. "Maybe there is a way to undo the curse."

Byron sighed and closed his eye. The grass stirred. "He opened his heart to the dark. Death is his only escape."

Ogwold hugged his great knees and chewed his lip. The roots of the Fonsolis wrapped themselves about his calf snugly as he thought. "We'll find him, Byron."

"I'm certain of it," the mercenary rasped, glancing sidelong so that the starlight paled his features, and it seemed even that he wore a wicked grin. "Why else should a Son of Caelare have joined me on this path? You, at least, are destined for such things as vanquishing evil."

"I was wondering when you would bring that up." Ogwold chuckled with nervous levity. "The wizard had already told me, but Wygram seemed to know as soon as she saw me. It only makes me believe him more."

Byron turned back to the night sky. "I figured you had something in your blood. Though I've never met a Nogofod before, there is something over you, something in the air. Besides, there was truth in your voice when you spoke the nature of your summons to Zenidow. Caelare does not call idly upon the folk of the world. I am not surprised to learn she is your ancestor." He narrowed his one eye now, looking as into some other place. "And if any creature recognizes the blood of Caelare it is certainly the Euphran. They belong to her."

Wygram's queer face materialized from the night, having snaked around. "Yes, you are obviously a descendant of hers. But, I know also that she has not left her palace in some time. Perhaps she doesn't care for you." The Euphran slunk away into the dark grass to rest her chin, though she did not resume snoring.

"Caelare has many children," said Byron. "But not one goes beyond the knowledge of her light."

"I thought she never came to the land. How could she have fallen in love with mortals?"

Wygram's voice came from the dark. "Do you know what Altum is, child?"

"It is the world, the land, the seas and the sky."

"Whence did it come to be?"

"Because of Caelare."

"Yes, she is the Maker. Altum she built for her solitary home in the deeps of space, and she lived here many ages. Even when mortals first arose out of All she walked with them, but long ago it was decreed that she would retreat from our affairs."

"Decreed? I thought she left of her own volition."

"The Decree of Primexcitum," rumbled Wygram. "God of gods, Firstborn of All, Lord of Secundom—it was his commandment. When mortals appeared in the created spheres of his people, he saw in their liberty and special consciousness a test given by his own creator. So he bid the gods to remove the stars and involve themselves little in their affairs."

"Long ago, Primexcitum was defeated," said Bryon gruffly. "But Novare and Xol both have never honoured his usurper."

"I'd always thought Caelare was the highest god," murmured Ogwold.

Wygram chuffed. "On Altum she is. In the Cosmos, she is but another star."

"Seems Lucetal reasons not to teach the Nogofod such things." Byron stood and crossed his arms, looking down into the sheer dark. The wind quickened his cloak.

Quite used to lacking greater knowledge, Ogwold hunched in another thought. "But if Caelare has all these children, she must have disobeyed. Doesn't that make her a follower of the usurper?"

Byron laughed dryly. "Gods will be gods."

Wygram snorted in agreement.

Ogwold smiled sheepishly. The sphere came spinning around to his opposite shoulder, shimmering in the night. After a moment or two it began lazily drifting about and off into the air, as in thought, forgetting its quest and for a moment the ogre it was due to follow, beginning to look like another star in heaven.

The morning sun reddened the peaks of the lesser mountains all around, and a cold blanket of vapour burned straight away, the sky unveiled clear and blue. Everywhere sparkled and refracted the traceries of snow, the grey-green tips of tough trees rearing like burdened spines from the gleaming drifts, and bare spires of rock shooting proud and bold into the clear air. Little plumes of steam signalled the leaping places of the hardy mountain goats, and the distant echoing cry of a fontus hawk pierced the grand dawn stillness. Merely the dizzying verticals all around the travellers were magnificent enough for a day's appreciation, but even Ogwold did not tarry long taking it all in.

Breakfastless they hunkered once more atop the Euphran. Noiseless and easy she soared off into the clear, cold sky. Day shed its hours into gold. Zenidow grew greater in their eyes all the while. While mountain on mountain rose to face them, shrank into the distance behind them, for many hours the size of Zenidow seemed always as it had been even from the shores of Epherem; but in the noon hours at last it began to swell, if only subtly, yet in such a way that it seemed they had burst finally into its own isolated environment, where gradually it would draw near.

Wygram flew low with the setting sun, and lighted upon a barren hill along the vast, low flank of the last mountain they had rounded. Ogwold stood for a long time gazing up at Zenidow. It seemed that only two tremendous triangular mountains and one sheer, listing wall made the final boundary in their quest. The oils of twilight soaked the open, smooth face of the silver, so that viscous purples and reds melted together in an exquisite tapestry, drizzling and cresting the mountains below with the dark blues of all the oozing paint gathering unto vats. Even as night slowly took shape, Zenidow was a beacon, taking to it the light of the stars and moons as if those celestial bodies too gazed only upon it.

Still it reached impossibly high into its ubiquitous headdress of cloud. Now the shape of the mountain seemed very strange compared with those around it, for it was so smooth and thin compared to the others, which had clear apices and broadened, split into rocky roots as they met the earth. But Zenidow was almost like an elliptical tower so subtly curved along its endless height, though this continuous narrow shape was all through massive as even the widest, bulkiest part of any mountain. Still it seemed that there were no features whatsoever to the mountain, so that more than ever before it looked precisely like the strange sphere which had guided Ogwold here and hovered now just above his shoulder.

The last light of day fell as Byron came to stand beside the ogre, and while they gazed about they noticed not far below them the unmistakable shapes of buildings. Though Wygram could not be bothered to move from her inevitable slumber, she promised to wait for them here on the high hill if they wished to descend. "If you find somewhere to lodge," she murmured, already drifting off, "I'll be here... in the morning."

There was a clear enough switchback down towards the shapes of the structures, and as they descended among the first tough grasses and over the misty buildings gaining figure in the wet air, the grand roar of a great river reached their ears. About them strange monolithic rocks began to heap up and lean one against the other as sudden shadows out of the thick fog, and Ogwold was nearly left behind ogling at and running his hands over the curious, luminous blue ore which ran like veins through their rock.

As he lumbered after Byron, a village began to take shape around him, first in the form of sparse barns and fenceless pastures dotted with the occasional gathering of scrawny goatish creatures craning their long necks like spirits of the mist, then in the hard arrangement of stones beneath his feet which made a road finer than any they had seen in Fonslad, and along its wind many cabins of stone and sodden wood well crafted and with solid chimneys just touched, some of them, with memories of smoke. Lastly the river took shape, far larger and swifter than they had expected as it ran through the village. Yet for all its enormous crashing ceaseless noise, rather a deathly silence steeped the place. Not a single goat issued even the slightest bleat, and when they knocked upon several doors, no one answered.

It was not long before the mercenary left to find some wild meat and swing his sword. Ogwold sat by the river for some time, munching slowly on the mauve vegetables from his pack, lost in thought, the sphere orbiting his great head, before suddenly realizing that here was a body of water! Pure and clear, and most importantly very deep, at last there rushed just before the ogre's eyes the first chance for a swim since he turned his back upon the poison sea. He slipped out of his white cloak and ragged tunic with ritual suddenness, yet carefully tightly cinched up the bag of coveted fruits and vegetables before tucking it carefully beneath an arrangement of rocks upon the bank. Then he slid into the cold water.

At once his skin was alive with glory, the voice of the river saying all things at once. Cold water thrilled between his toes and fingers. Current and sphere whirled with him, lighting up the way. The suspended sheaf of black hair sundered into long locks rippling. With streamlined arms and shoulders he rode, clear liquid filtering through lungs to which that medium was life. The Fonsolis sang, strength welling up along the channels of the plant through his bones and blood. He focused and closed his eyes, and thought of that moment when Autlos-lo had spoken to him out of the kelp. Out folded the shivering cores of his shoulder blades into great flying fins, sweeping over the water, holding him in place even against the swift current. Forward he shot, compounding wingbeats with the flow of the river, covering immense distances all at once, so that suddenly he stopped himself laughing and shaking with glee. Slowly he turned and began swimming upstream, smiling still perhaps more broadly than he had in many months.

But then he saw the body. In the peripheral light of the sphere drifted unmistakably the frozen grasp of pale fingers, a swollen arm, and already from the dark leered now the swollen figure of a Novare man. One blackened leg was trapped among the rocks, and such thick and ropy river weeds enwrapped his chest and waist it seemed his gaping head—unseamed by decay—emerged from the bank itself. The bruised eyes and the sick gentle floating of the empty face sent horrible shivers through Ogwold. Instinctively he kicked away to the surface, flooding forward his wings in a great rejection of what rotted below.

Bursting into the freezing air, he saw he was still very far down the meander; still, the corpse must have been a villager. How many more had he sped by in his ignorant flight? Jetting to the shore he climbed the bank with contrasting lethargy. The long membranes at his shoulders withdrew smoothly into his body. There were only trees around him, but he could not go back into the river of the dead, so he began the slow walk back in the direction of the village. When he returned, twilight draped the settlement in long shadows. Byron stood in a small clearing in plain sight of whomever might be hidden away in the different houses, swinging his sword, covered in sweat beside a crackling fire. The carcass of a goat lay skinned atop a smooth stone.

Night came quickly, and now even Zenidow did not carry the hues of the sinking day, though still it was quite illuminated by the stars and moons. They continued knocking on doors to no avail of a place to sleep or even a peep from another living creature, and Ogwold could think only of the corpse in the river. Finally Byron simply decided to open one of these, and inside there was nothing but a cot, an empty black pot, and a pile of dull rocks. Hardly hesitating he sat and leaned his back against the wall, crossed his arms, and closed his eye.

The ogre carefully laid himself on the bed, but despite his best efforts it suddenly collapsed into a heap of rubble. Byron's eye opened and he chuckled, but was soon at rest once more. The ogre lay there marvelling at the comfort of the simple mattress, however lumpy was the support of its broken structure below, before rolling over and pulling his cloak about himself. He dreamt of the river, but there were no dead bodies.

Ogwold woke to the invariable absence of the mercenary gone to train, but he was not alone. A little old man clad in grey rags and a big black hat watched him from the door, where he sat evidently waiting for the beast to rise. Beams of pale sunlight shafted through the windows, and dust motes swirled about the place like light snow, settling in the stranger's ashen beard.

"Hello," said Ogwold, sitting up. The old man's eyes went directly to the Fonsolis as it caught the light. "I'm sorry to have taken your cot for the night. I needed a place to sleep out of the snow. I mean no harm really."

"... It is all right," croaked the man. "I'd hidden with the others when we saw that more cloaked ones were coming to our village. I see that you are not like them now."

"Cloaked ones!" Ogwold stood up suddenly, and the man gulped at the massive stature of the ogre. "Where did they go?"

"The Old City, on the cliffs." The old man's eyes mournfully gazed at the destroyed bed.

Ogwold bowed. "I am very sorry about your cot," he said shakily.

The man was silent and grim. "Please, just go."

Ogwold sheepishly ducked and squeezed through the tiny doorway. The streets were still empty, but now he saw that some folk looked out through windows, or even stood outside of their homes watching him. They figured perhaps that Ogwold and Byron meant them no harm, but it was obvious that they were not welcome. He thought of the corpse in the river, and though it turned his stomach, it was a good thing to see that many villagers were alive.

"Byron," he said, walking up to the man who had clearly been swinging his sword for hours beside the river. "Zelor was here. He went up to... well..." Ogwold turned and scanned up along the sheer vertical wall above the village. It seemed even that the rising sun went with his eyes, for just then the clouds behind him shifted and a beam of pale light passed over the high clustered towers and walls of a black city. "There," he said softly.

"So I've been told," Byron said, hefting the sword onto his shoulder. A powerful gust came up over the bank of the river and tore his cloak so that it flapped and cracked like a tattered coat of arms. "Come, spar with me before we go."

"We should hurry, Byron. He must be on the other side of this mountain now."

The mercenary held out the massive sword at arm's length, so that the point hovered before Ogwold's chest. "Fight me, ogre!"

"We are only a short flight to Zenidow."

"And so we test your strength one last time."

Finally Ogwold smiled. "So be it. Let us be quick at least." Since they had left the citadel of Azanak, the ogre's familiarity with the tongue of the Fonsolis had grown considerably, and he could not deny that he wished to show the mercenary the word for 'blade.' So he bellowed, "Spathakri!" His great green arm collapsed into liquid, whipped out to twice its length, and threw up along its back down to the elbow a long sharp edge, which arced like a scythe; in a moment all was hardened and gleaming in the sunlight that rebounded off the blinding snow. Byron grinned.

Their weapons clashed loudly in the stillness of the settlement. The townspeople who were not afraid came out into the streets and ventured to the edge of town to watch the fight. It was clear that Ogwold had greater might, greater strength, and that he was trying the hardest, for his face was terrible to behold, and it was true that he had always wanted to get the better of Byron in a duel. But today was not his day. The villagers gasped as the mercenary so easily parried even the most brutal, crushing blows, not by absorbing their impact, but by turning them away softly and smoothly. He never attacked, playing only defence. Ogwold's flurry and intensity only quickened, but at last Byron's green eye flashed, and he swung his sword in offence. There was a loud crack, and a boom, and huge drifts of snow flew up around the fighters so that they were obscured, but when it all fell the people saw that Ogwold had blocked Byron's attack by sheer strength of will. Down on one knee in the snow, the ground had cracked beneath him, snow had been blown clear away, and the Fonsolis shook, Byron's blade embedded in its tough flesh. Byron withdrew and flung the blade atop his shoulder. Already the vegetable flesh began knitting together.

"Better," said Byron. Ogwold was stunned. He had never beheld such ferocity from Byron before, even against Azanak. He figured he would never know why Byron was so powerful, for all he could say was that the young man certainly practised enough.

They trudged up the snowy hill as the mist closed in behind them and the roar of the river diminished, until by noon they found Wygram, fast asleep in the broad day, and woke her with their shouting. She peered blearily at them. "Today is the day," said Ogwold. "Zenidow is just beyond that peak."

Wygram sighed and preened her long whiskers. "I will take you as close as I can, but then I leave, Son of Caelare. Your fight is not mine."

"As you wish, Wygram." Ogwold bowed. "We are indebted to you for your grace as it is."

"Oh please. I am free because of your valiance," she thrummed musically in her long throat, and it was clear even in the serene changelessness of her countenance that she appreciated their thanks.

One last time they gathered their things and climbed aboard her great spine, and she carried them up into the sky on the massive motions of her wings. Zenidow loomed, and they drew near to the last range of peaks bordering it as the morning waned, looking down on the black city where it clutched against the flat rock.

With the sun high in the sky, they came over the left shoulder of that very mountain, and below them appeared unmistakably, from this height, an enormously vast and deep crater, at the centre of which stuck Zenidow like a bullet from heaven. The whole bowl in the land was ensconced by other, more normal looking mountains, jaggedly arranged at equal distance to the centre; everywhere within this circle of peaks there was little change in the landscape but for the ever sloping snow and stretches of forest. The closer to the Great Mountain the thicker clustered those spans of trees so that about the base of the great silver ellipse itself, for some hundred miles in all directions, was the densest forest either Byron or Ogwold had ever seen.

"That is Pivwood," said Wygram over the rushing wind. "But I cannot take you so far," and as she banked off to the side descending, her riders saw now the turning patch of dark cloud that hovered like a small storm system over the open snow just outside of the great forest. They landed themselves in a clearing, far beneath the high steep rim of the crater, but perhaps equally far from their Pivwood. Ogwold and Byron slid to the ground with a tremendous thump and a soft tap, and stood in the snow bewitched with the mountain as it caught the evening hues so awesome in its closeness. It seemed wholly unlike anything in the world, standing so pure and spotless against the purples and reds of sunset.

Wygram spoke softly. "Son of Caelare, and you, Demon Eye, fare you well. There is a great evil at large before the threshold of Pivwood such that I cannot go any closer. It will not be easily met, but truly you are brave warriors both."

"Where will you go?" Ogwold leaned back calling up, for the Euphran's neck unfurled now to its utmost height as she gazed out into the open sky.

"To be with my own," she said, turning that long diamond skull so that one ice-chip irid beheld them as from another world. Then she was off, so grand and mysterious in all her shining scales soaring over the trees, now but an angular blue shadow high above, already fading.

The Euphran had taken them well inside the caldera rim, though the land was still quite steep, and they could see far ahead over a low stretch of trees. It seemed there was a cessation in that wood, though it was hard to tell how wide was the open plain presumed then to lead to Pivwood. All that seemed to occupy the space between this forest and that which surrounded Zenidow itself was a lone, wicked spire like some enormous, branchless tree whose roots were the jagged fissures that sprawled about its base. All the more black and twisted did it look interposed against the vast silver face of Zenidow.

"He is there." Byron squinted down and off at the distant point.

To Ogwold it was indeed difficult to call merely a gathering of dark clouds those evil black vapours which swirled like tendrils about the thing. He imagined that these were the long and haunting spirits of deep roots which had been ripped up from the world—the source of those ghastly furrows. "Is this what the Xol do to trees?"

"No. That is a tower of rock. Zelor's magic is with the minerals. I only knew from the stories he told of his father and the line of his blood's weave; that is, until he turned even those powers upon our family. But this is good. If he's made a fortress, he must have been prevented from entering the forest."

Ogwold pondered this. "Such a fantastical place must have its own folk." As if to join in, the sphere spun up out of his pocket to float between them. "Can't you just fly to the mountain now?" he implored. It made no reply, hovering still, sweetly humming as ever. "Well, if you're coming with us, I've a promise to uphold. Without Byron we wouldn't have made it here. This Zelor has it coming! And still, we don't know what we'll find down there. It looks like we have a long trek ahead of us." The light then began to fade, for the sun now sank behind the mountains beyond Zenidow.

In the morning, Novare and Nogofod began their hike down through the sloping woods. The grade was incredibly steep, and its streaks and patches of ice so treacherously slick that they were forced to move only very slowly, now round an enormous tree, clinging to its system of hard roots, staggering rapidly to a cluster of boulders, stopping to stand and rest and peer down over their friable pates.

When at last they came to a more gradual decline, Ogwold flung himself into a seated position and slid at a great speed down along a streak of ice, gradually losing speed as the land evened out, plunging noiselessly into a cumulus snowbank. His huge head appeared, shaking its mass of dreadlocked hair all around, and Byron even grinned, deftly side stepping down the grade, as the ogre's hearty laugh boomed up to him. Reunited they walked more easily, for the snow was hard-packed such that in places even Ogwold's huge crushing feet did not sink. Dark and broad fir trees thickened quickly, shielding them from the wind which whistled shrilly in their needles.

Slowly as they went there developed a low rumbling, as from the pits of their own ears, now trembling and holding along the vast plains and sheets of ice like the crashing of some massive distant surf. When Caelare's palace had spun beyond its daily apex, the roaring medium subtly became punctuated with a rising and falling of noise which began to sound very much like a succession of tremendous explosions. Yet at their clearest and most bone-jarring these troubling and powerful movements suddenly ceased, and all was eerily still.

Now through the thinning trees Ogwold and Byron beheld from afar the inky spire of Zelor silhouetted in the crepuscular glow before the shining hull of Zenidow, the two towers separated, it seemed, only by that dense orbit of forest which Wygram had called Pivwood. As before, Zelor's fortress looked like an immense needle, but now they saw that its base was structured and walled more broadly by tremendous formations of rock. Around the great lower bulk of the building stood chaotic sequences of rocky walls, having pinnacles of their own, everything jagged and ominous, so arranged as if the grounds of the place were heavily guarded.

Ogwold was deathly cold and wished dearly to move behind the protection of the rock walls and out of the wind. The pain of the Fonsolis was his as well, and it was not fond of the cold. Wrapped around his shivering core to keep warm, now as the last trees fell away and the wind struck them fully, all that kept them moving forward was the tightly held wrap of the great white cloak. Wide and barren for several more hours of trudging through the ice was the rock-strewn field leading to the outermost walls, but as darkness fell the adventurers bivouacked beneath a great slab of leaning stone, which shielded them finally from the elements. Ogwold collapsed against the overarching angle and huddled deep down into the frost caked cloth, rubbing his hands together and breathing into the stiff digits of the Fonsolis. Byron sighed, sat beside him, arms crossed, brow lowered, and seemed to stare straight through the rock towards the tower of his enemy.

Before dawn their quest was renewed with vigour, for the Fonsolis free to wander from its cloaken cloister had drunk deeply from the soil below the hard crust and snow, and now Ogwold cheered with the warmth of its satiety. As day broke in great gleaming chunks of pale light, they transitioned from bold approach to the seeping cover of boulders and giant shards of displaced rock. Moving slowly through the plain they came to the first high rock wall, craggily imperfect, haphazardly sprung as it was from below. Many more such barriers rose at varying heights and widths in concentric slabs, interlocking, leaning one upon the other in a far more perplexing anarchy than had seemed from afar. At the centre of the shield-labyrinth, huge shifting mountains of rock melded together, and from their communing, hulking shoulders shot the high, wicked seat of Zelor.

CHAPTER XXVI
OLD FRIENDS

lready Byron melted into the shadows of the maze, and clumsily realizing his partner's absence Ogwold stumbled after him. More graciously than before the stabbing wind was wholly cut off in the lanes between the high walls, and the cold receded. Around another wall they went, and now through a great crack. Once they were able to walk forward through many arches of rock, but were suddenly suffered to circumnavigate an endless plane of stone all along whose surface there seemed a hieroglyphic legend written in eon-webbed layers of ancient strata. At last they came within the innermost buffers, and peering round one cracked high ring saw the roots of the tower where they had exploded out of the ground. There were no windows or doors anywhere to be seen, and as they walked cautiously into the open, now a little more confidently—for the place was silent as death—even when they came around to the front there seemed not a single feature to the structure but for the aquiline spear which jutted high above their heads from the tip of it all.

Ogwold shivered quietly in the cold, feeling the slow thaw of the still resuscitating Fonsolis, listening to the omnipresent drone of the small silver orb in his pocket which offered no images or advice. At last he said, "Maybe we should just break in?"

Suddenly the echo of breaking rock split the air, and the very ground beneath their feet shook so violently that they both were hurled upon it in a rising fog of snow. With a massive shifting and tearing, the face of the tower bore upon its heavy flank a fractal crack of chiselled lightning, and at its lowest point began to open as two parting pieces unto a black triangular void. Already they could hear a great commotion approaching within the bowels of dark.

"Quick," hissed Byron leaping up, and yanking after him the ogre with surprising force. Stumbling over the still grinding valley floor they reached a close but low slab and hid themselves behind it, just peering round through a nick in its edge.

Now the concentric slabs that stood in layers between fortress, battlefield, and forest began to separate through their midst in like jagged fashion as the makeshift doors of the tower proper, as in a sequence of immense crude gates, revealed lastly a high narrow view of an open plain of snow and far away the border of Pivwood itself, serene and still with the dawn.

Then from the base of Zelor's tower, where only moments ago the adventurers had sat peacefully, there emerged a slow flood of pure darkness, advancing unto the path between the barricades sundering before them. At first the procession was as one surging, formless shadow, but in time Ogwold could distinguish among its motions the multitudes of hideous creatures which wore its aura like a collective gauze. Such warriors cast from the tower forth were like man-sized reptilian insects bejewelled in compound eyes pointing in so many chaotic directions as the jagged claws and spikes which jutted all about their bodies. Yet for all the scales and shining carapaces that went among them, each being undulated and rolled as though made entirely of ectoplasm, their endless limbs and antennae expressed like inky fluid to feel out the posterior of whatever entity went ahead, the whole spectacle moving as by some blind overarching intention. So it was that everywhere about the moving tapestry of evil were the suggestions of tendrils undulating, reaching, grasping, everything with its clear relation to and origin in the utmost chamber of Zelor's tower over which there turned more dark and malevolent than ever the nebula of black which was his menacing will.

Byron whispered harshly. "My brother could only be found in the heart of a battle; this Zelor sends others to do his work..." But he trailed off, and placed one hand upon the leg of his partner, for a terrible, silent evil now followed the horde into battle.

It was a group only few in number, though quite different in aspect. Where the other shadows had taken the shapes as of chaos and bloodlust incarnate, these creatures were modest and lean. They walked upright like men, and carried themselves with a kind of sapience that could not be ascribed to the infantry that went before them. At the turn of their indistinct, featureless faces, looking like smudges out of focus, as though they could not be adequately rendered in this world, shudders of freezing chill shot down even the spine of the mercenary. It seemed as though these beings had no business at all with the world in which they now walked, perhaps just as the mindless shadow spawn that came with them; yet more evil was it to see that indeed they knew they did not belong, that at last they had been given form, that they had mind with which to think not only, but bodies with which to act. As they passed through the first of the great broken gates, the last of the walkers turned back, and Byron and Ogwold quickly hid. Whether or not it had seen them, a terrible chill seemed for a moment to stop the blood in their veins; then the evil thing went to meet the war parties far off in the storm.

Despite the ogre still reeling beside him, Byron edged out into the open even as the gates of rock began slowly to drag themselves closed behind the shadow warrior, and as he ran back to the front of the tower Ogwold realized too that this was their moment. The great triangular zig zag of darkness had now last of all the others begun to close, and almost as soon as they had slunk inside, the grinding walls sealed fast behind them, shutting off all but memory of the snowy waste without.

The depthless, total dark was impossibly silent. Ogwold took the sphere from his cloak and it filled the room with pale light. They were in a spacious, cave-like chamber seeming to have no visible ceiling, devoid of any sign that once a horde of shadow beings had issued thence, and occupied only by a misshapen set of rocky stairs, more like crags that jutted in rising succession along the wall up through an archway. These they followed carefully, for it was very difficult for Ogwold to hold his balance, and he was already deathly afraid of falling but five steps above the troubled floor. Even as he found his way along the rising turn of the strange footholds, they were soon horrifyingly high in the darkness such that there seemed no solid ground beneath them as much as still there was no surface above them in sight. Yet ever up they climbed in stillness and silence, keeping their attention on the light of the sphere where it played on the next steps.

Ogwold held fast the Fonsolis to the wall, for it seemed not only to give him security of step and balance but also a sense of strange calm here in the alien dark. What motivation else he needed was in the inexorable advance of Byron, who held but one gentle hand as if aloof against the trailing rock as he went, but who never increased his pace such as to leave the fearful ogre behind. Hours seemed to pass in the monotonous half light until they came up onto a wide ledge where they were free at least to stretch and feel secure in standing without constant attention to the placement of their feet. The sphere ranged above them and at last its pale light fell upon a ceiling of craggy rock. Even blacker and more ominous now seemed the void below them, as if one false step would send one falling for an eternity. But their focus was not on that manner of death. One last flight of much more straight and more agreeable steps, broad and flat, led from the ledge to a great door hewn of two smooth slabs of rock.

"Quite a simple construction, this place," said Byron, no humour in his voice. "He must have truly built it in desperation. If the Zelor I knew would never use his powers, he would surely die before succumbing to fear." The mercenary brooded in silence before the crude door. That lone green eye turned up from the shadows of his face, and never so striking was his likeness to a starving wolf. "Ogwold. You don't need to come with me. Your sphere can still lead you from this tomb."

"We'll go together," said the ogre, almost surprised to hear how nobly came his oafish voice. But whether he sounded heroic or brave to whatever ears in all the Cosmos, this impression came rather from within his own heart's listening, for he was proud, proud of Byron, proud of himself for coming so far, and he felt that he owed everything to the mercenary who was, quite simply put, he thought, his best friend.

Byron nodded, and with a grimace pushed against the doors. They swung noiselessly open for all the tortured grinding of all other living rocks throughout the fortress and its savage walls. Pale light was here, flowing over the head of one last case of stairs. They took these slowly, and came up into a great dome, which seemed to sharpen exponentially at its apex. Now the light was quite bright and natural, for half of the great space was completely open to the elements, yet the snow did not enter upon the place as if there were some invisible impermeable sheet between tower and sky. And there was to this vast sheet as well another magic, for it magnified and rendered the battlefield below in stunning detail, and seemed to move and shift in its scope. But it was all a blur to the newcomers, for they had eyes rather for the cloaked figure who stood, arms clasped behind its back, in the centre of that view, seeing all.

Pure white hair fell blending with the brilliant view of snow in cataracts down the broad black shoulders of a long cloak, hemmed in silver. Sharp purple ears shot up from that mane, and two tails of like hue hissed snaking against the smooth rock floor. About the figure was a cloud of shade that moved like faint smoke. "So," came a cold, metallic voice from man unturning. "You have found us."

Byron drew his immense sword, advancing through the gigantic room. Zelor turned, and Ogwold beheld him for the first time. He was noble and beautiful. Though Ogwold had only Hesflet for an example of the Xol race, he could tell that Zelor was a man of stature and grace among his people. His high forehead and thick eyebrows commanded attention, sitting back behind a blade of a nose. Silver scabbards swept from his waist and along his back in the manner of Byron's. Now about him the nebula of shadow seemed to take shape, and Ogwold saw long tentacles of darkness reaching and winding in all directions; ever so faintly, six red lights stood in two ethereal columns above him.

One affectless purple hand rose before the scene, and as it went the approaching Byron was ossified in place, lifted from the floor unable to move any but those minor muscles which stood out about his clenched jaw. Blood began to seep between his gritted teeth, streaming already down his jawline from the pressure.

"Fight him like a man, Zelor!"

Zelor turned slowly, eyes deep as time. Even as he scanned with that cold gaze the foolish grey oaf who had bellowed so brazenly, he dropped Byron to the floor where he gasped for breath, coughing dark fluid.

Ogwold spoke bravely into the evil silence, though his legs quaked with fear and from Fonsolis and sphere he felt only a mad desire to flee. "Kill him like this, and you shall never escape the knowledge that you cowered before swordsmanship."

"We have always been better with a blade," said Zelor, and Ogwold now heard that just as there was a second presence, a second sight in the cloud which hung about the sorcerer, there too was a second voice layered amid the first, a gargling, a distant faltering echo, something not of the world scraping together the primitive verbal symbols of mortals.

Byron rose shakily, sword brandished. He spat a stringy gob of black blood onto the stone floor. "Like I always said, brother: the day you turn to magic is the day you recognize you could never beat me."

Zelor burst into peals of grating laughter, seeming nothing like laughter at all but some cruel imitation of petty, lesser life. Even as the noises of supposed glee were uttered they were in the same breath mocked by their tone. But at last the awful display was choked off, and he stared at Byron with a boundless fury for one so calm a moment ago.

"Very well!" he shouted. "Die by the edge of the only love you ever knew." Out from the scabbard at his slim waist came a narrow, jagged blade, black as night. It was not so long or nearly so thick as Byron's massive sword, but an awful power welled from it, and Ogwold could not look directly into its shade.

The mercenary only smiled, not in the way he grinned in the heat of battle or on the precipice of death, but in a new way, almost as an expression of peace.

Then he took his stance, that very same stance he always assumed, swinging over and over his sword each morning, each night, whenever he had the chance.

Zelor leapt forward with incredible speed, such that Ogwold turned his eyes much too late to see what had happened. There was a flash and a crack as the two weapons—one immensely broad, the other needle sharp—recoiled from one another. Byron slid backwards, crouching low to the ground. Zelor stood calm and tall in place, though he had at least placed one foot behind him for support. Then it was Byron's turn to rush. He came at one severe angle, now pouncing to the side changing his approach and dashing in with a series of thrusts and slashes that amazed Ogwold with their thoughtful grace. Now the ogre saw that all the fighting that Byron had done up to this point—slaying the guards of Occultash, culling the hordes of the Eyeless, even against the insurmountable force of Azanak—had been executed purely through brute rage, the warring of a battle-scarred mercenary. Now, here was a different warrior altogether. With each stroke of the enormous blade he struck the figure of some great knight of ancient legend, stoic and fearless in poise and form, his footwork dexterous, the artful fluid of sword and body a perfect mastery. Ogwold quite shamefully remembered those surges of pride he had felt in his finest moments sparring with the green-eyed man, for now he realized as he watched that if he were ever to duel Byron for real, he wouldn't last even a moment.

Still Zelor parried every blow with seeming ease, turning Byron's momentum to his favour, riding the power of each stroke into an offensive of his own which seemed to build with each block. As if at last having gathered in his weapon all of the energy of the opponent's onslaught, the sorcerer commenced a terrible rebuttal. Down, up, down, up with hurtling, time-rending strokes he advanced slowly on Byron. Each blow caromed back only to be returned with greater ferocity, pushing the man—still calm countenanced—further towards the floor, where his wide stance began to buckle.

Like a bolt of lightning Byron slashed without precedent, and though Zelor held his sword perpendicular, blocking him perfectly, the mercenary already charged forward, forcing the sorcerer's boots along the smooth floor. Flinging up his weapon, Zelor was thrown back. Byron only quickened his charge, lunged out with a thrust so deadly swift that to Ogwold it seemed the massive weapon vanished entirely from sight. Yet the blow met only air. The image of Zelor appeared beside, and just behind Byron, holding straight out his sword as in completing the routine slicing of a helpless opponent. A gout of blood jetted from Byron's side, and his knee was planted in the ground.

Zelor smirked. "You are too slow."

Byron slashed wildly, one hand clutching his side, but Zelor vanished in a blink, appearing as though landing lightly some ten yards away. The mercenary stood slowly. Blood flowed warm down his leg and pooled on the rock floor.

"Good," he said. "Now I can take this seriously." He flung off his cloak, and beneath it there was a metal breastplate. The side of it had been cloven wide open by Zelor's strike, and it was from this gash that Byron's blood poured onto the floor. He pulled the mangled armour over his head and threw it to the ground with a weighty clang.

Zelor swept forward. Byron lowered his shoulder, twisted his boot into the ground. Their blades met in fury. The sound of the clash was deafening. Blood spouted from Byron's wound upon impact, but the pain seemed only to make him all the hungrier for victory. Looking into the eyes which had once been his brother's he saw only the cinders of Molavor. Thus his rage grew, and the strength and speed of his blows. At last with a great thrust Byron's sword slipped past Zelor's exquisite defence and found its mark along the hip; though it was a glancing blow, a sword so mighty as Azanog bore no easy wound, however slight its impact. Zelor slid back, staggered, grasping at his side. White blood spattered onto the floor. His eyes flashed bright red and the smoky tentacles—which had receded and faded during the fight—became suddenly stark and full. He raised his off hand, and with it came one of these evil appendages overshadowing him.

"If you use your magic I'll attack," shouted Ogwold. He had uttered a new word spoken to him by the Fonsolis, and now the plant had grown to tremendous proportions. It was an enormous, bladed cannon, seething with sunlight, readied to deliver its most powerful offensive. Its roots had surged to massive size and extended all through the room, plunging and worming into the floor and walls and ceiling in preparation for the kick of the blast.

Zelor smirked and sweeping suddenly, his arm produced an enormous wall of flame that washed the entire side of the domed room where stood the ogre with the suddenness of a lamp turning in a windowpane. There was no force to the fire, only a remorseless burning that carried over him like a hot wind of blind death. In the deepest brightest absence of all but light and pain, the Fonsolis screamed; then it was silent. The fire seared the ogre's flesh quite terribly and burned away his cloak and hair in an instant, but its worst heat ceased almost as soon as it had begun, and perhaps he lived because of his tough hide. Naked and hairless, falling limply to the floor, his last moment of consciousness beheld the smoking stump at his shoulder where once had flourished the gift of Autlos-lo.

Already Zelor looked away, bearing down on Byron who met into his path and blocked—swinging his sword upwards—the downward blow with a terrible shout. Blood gushed from both of their wounds as they stumbled back.

"How honourable," Byron grunted, slamming his sword vertically into the ground for support. "The mighty sorcerer Zelor, Knight of Molavor."

Zelor groaned and shook his head. He swung his off arm and the shadow of Duxmortul seemed even to disperse, the columns of red light receding as into a secret world. Though still a clutching, writhing darkness was about the sorcerer, the distinct image of his possessor could not be distinguished, and so the way of his speaking changed. "I'll do this on my own, brother," he said coldly.

Again their swords met loudly and swiftly. Zelor sliced a gash in Byron's thigh, and Byron only just missed Zelor's head, opening his cheek so that blood spilled down and away from him jumping back. They breathed heavily. The next exchange must decide this, thought Byron; he raised his sword high above his head.

"Foolish," said Zelor, raising his sword to block.

"You should dodge," said Byron.

"The strength of a Novare man is nothing to me."

Yet it was true that Byron had saved his strength for the final clash, waiting for Zelor's pride to get the better of him, for though he knew long ago that his old friend had been lost in the dark, he knew that not even some evil god from beyond the stars could warp the bone-deep pride of a Molavorian. He had practised over and over this very downward stroke all his life, and more and more since his city was lost, thinking always of Zelor. Now he brought down the sword once more to end it, with all power of will and remaining drop of strength that he had. The spirit of Molavor itself came heavy down upon that falling blade as it carried right through Zelor's blocking sword, splitting it clean in two; thereon it sank deep into the sorcerer's shoulder, but still it carried on, inexorably, as with unstoppable inertia, and screaming Byron pushed the blade screeching through seizing torso, down and finally out the opposite side, smashing to the rock floor with a resounding clang. A geyser of white blood plumed up and showered them both, now slowing, bubbling and pooling where the halves of Zelor fell twitching.

Fine streams of black sand and ash and smoke rose from the mutilated body as from infinitesimal pores, and aggregated into a dark nebula above the scene of death. Within the seething black fume was an evil, bloody light that seemed the core of all that had parasitized the Xol body. Yet even at its brightest red and darkest, thickest black the cloud began to disperse, slowly fading out of being. A great sigh passed through the room as the natural light coming in through the vast window subtly brightened, for the shadow of Duxmortul had gone away.

Sundered of much his form, the face of Zelor yet stirred with its final moments. "Byron?"

"Brother." The mercenary knelt beside him. "You are free."

Zelor smiled. If Elts were there, she might have seen his face as once it truly was, long ago. "I knew you would come. I cannot be forgiven for Molavor, but I am honoured to be struck down by the finest and last of those warriors. May they never be forgotten..." A river of blood bubbled from the sorcerer's mouth, choking off his speech as he gagged on the unromantic finality of death. "Brother—you must destroy the Alium. Find Elts. Duxmortul; he is coming."

The mercenary sat beside his old friend as he died, closing his vitreous eyes with one hand. Suddenly he remembered the ogre. Staggering to his feet, clutching his bleeding ribs, he stumbled hastily to the ashy site of his friend. He collapsed to his knees beside the great blackened, bald Nogofod and gripped him gently on the shoulder. "Ogwold. You'd better be alive in there."

"Byron," came a hoarse reply. Slowly consciousness returned to Ogwold as he lay there feeling his skin charred all over. But he was certainly alive, painfully, painfully alive. Slowly that pain drained away as he lay there with the brooding mercenary beside him, so that while he waited for his senses to return they both gazed over at the fallen form of Zelor in its pool of white blood. At last he felt that he could sit up, and when he did, soot and ash slid from his skin in a vast layer, and he saw that really he was quite all right; hairless, yes, but still grey as a misty day. "I guess I have a resistance to fire in me," he choked out. "But I can't say the same for the Fonsolis. It is gone."

"I am sorry, Ogwold. It is a great gladness to see that you live." Byron looked back at the corpse.

"You did a good thing, Byron."

"It seems there was more of a scrap of the real Zelor left than I'd anticipated, even after all of these years."

Slowly and with much groaning Byron wrapped his wounds with cloth torn from his soiled undershirt. His cloak he gave to the naked ogre, and though it could hardly come close to stretching round his rocky shoulders, it was at least some cover for Ogwold's waist.

Then they went to the great view of the snow waste beyond the tower. Zelor's death had not instantly cancelled this magic, and through its wavering ghost they were able to see many subtleties out in the field. A great and valiant day had been won for the Piv. Everywhere the forces of shadow that remained were beginning to dissolve and rise into the sky, purifying as they grew nearer the holy light of the sun. At last the battlefield was grown silent. Then the tower began to crumble.

Out on the trembling plain of war a host of Piv drew near to Zelor's fortress now free of the swirling darkness which had held over it so long. Like the shimmering away of some vast mirage their familiars receded into that ethereal realm from whence they came; with each wave of fading animals and plants and fungus now the moving, floating field of little green bodies unclothed of oversoul seemed so fragile and defenceless. Yet great power went with Sylna, Elts, and Muewa, riding with Faltion over their heads.

Even as the black clouds first lightened, the tower had started to shake. First the vast slabby walls had begun to collapse and shed the sheets of rock so unnaturally pulled together in their formation. Lastly fell the tallest spire, leaning to the side, shifting and strafing, then sinking inward through a great expanding storm of dust and snow. Smoke and dirt and rock-dust flew everywhere, and the sweeping wind blended it all together so that only the distant shaking booming of more and more rock falling back to Altum showed where the demise was centred.

But Luen went with Yisven Vir, the Great One of the Wind, and together high above they cleared the sky of what clouds yet remained, and tore away the fields of floating debris as they collected below. The weather grew strangely calm, as if it had always meant to be so even of temperament, and the winds died as snow ceased to fall. By the time the host had come to the wreckage, the sun was shining on them. There in the clear bright day, seated atop one low angled slab was an enormous, bald, almost totally naked, one-armed, grey-skinned troll of a creature, its twisted stump of a blasted shoulder black as soot. Beside him stood upon the snow the strangely small figure of a Novare man, covered in blood both red and white; the soaked cloth and tattered leather of his garb flickered like the last threads of a morbid standard in the waste of debris. The face of the great grey man was quite merry to behold as he saw the numberless fairies and the great swooping bird approach, for he could not believe their luck in surviving the great collapse of the tower and felt that he was ready for anything.

"Hello!" the giant boomed heartily. "It's okay! Zelor has fallen!"

Faltion landed, kicking up a sheet of snow. Despite the kindness in the creature's voice, Sylna and Elts approached slowly and cautiously. The host of Piv held even further back, but for Muewa, who floated towards the two strangers curiously. Now near to the slab, Sylna looked up into the amicable grey eyes of the ogre.

"It is not as difficult as I once thought to see that you must be Ogwold," she said slowly, still walking with composure towards the duo. "I am Sylna. The wizard Nubes was my teacher. He told me you would come here."

"And he told me I would find you here." The ogre smiled sheepishly.

Elts stepped up beside Sylna, trying to imagine how this big grinning creature could be a killer. "How did he die?"

Ogwold marvelled at the woman, for clearly she too was Xol. Her thin purple tails waved nervously behind her, and her white eyes and hair glared bright against her dark skin.

"I cut him down," Byron said. In the silence that followed he glanced over the Xol woman. "Do you avenge him?"

Elts shook her head, studying the hard lines of the man's face as they looked away. "No. I am glad that he no longer suffers."

Byron nodded. "Once, it was an honour to fight alongside Zelor. I thought that man was gone forever, but even as he died, I saw him as he once was—free."

"This is Byron," barked Ogwold suddenly, his jarring voice breaking the stillness of the moment. All heads turned to him awkwardly. "... By the way."

Muewa coughed in her little lilting way and zoomed up to light upon the ogre's vast mound of a knee. "Gentlemen who have come so far: I am Muewa of Southern Pivwood." She angled her delicate wings as if to indicate the great forest behind her. "I think I can speak for all my people when I say that we are profoundly grateful. We would have surely lost the forest without your coming when you did. Please, come with us to eat and rest in the shelter of the wood."

"That sounds wonderful!" The ridges of Ogwold's hairless brows raised right up.

The Piv smiled from down upon his leg like a little beaming winged flower. "You must have many questions, the both of you. All will be told when we are nice and warm among the trees. Of course," she looked askance, tittering to Byron as if in mockery of his stoicism. "You are free to stay out here in the cold."

The mercenary spat a ribbon of blood into the snow. "I go where he goes."

"Isn't he charming?" Ogwold grinned.

But the ogre's levity was the last and only of the evening, and as the group walked up the field towards Pivwood, passing through smouldering debris and among the slain bodies of so many, a solemn shroud fell over the procession such that Ogwold could no longer enjoy his and Byron's improbable survival. No one spoke. Rattled from the day of battle, the sun beginning to set, all had minds for food and rest. When they reached the edge of the forest the numbers of the Piv filtered away like motes of dust into the purifying rays of twilight, and the group of lumbering big people—Novare, Xol, Nogofod—were left in silence to find some comfortable place upon the loamy floor to sleep. The warm flesh of the leaf, and the forest in all, which was a pleasant temperature, and even the air of the place calming to the nerves, coaxed Ogwold to sleep even as the visions of the battle with Zelor came on him and boiled his blood. One could not have said the same for Byron, who slept little at all.

The mercenary awoke as always before the sun, sitting up in the dark wood, and looked instinctively to his sword, which lay beside him in the soft grass. A moment's pause was all that showed his release from Zelor, for on any other day he would have taken up that blade at once to train. But today for just a moment, sweet and light, he sat looking at it and reflecting on the previous day. Then he stood, took the weapon, and went to practice in a nearby clearing. It was all he knew now, swinging that sword, over and over. From the first stroke, hundreds of little Piv fluttered up as from some microscopic and ubiquitous dimension in a great confusion.

Ogwold stirred a few hours later, looking like a great boulder morphing to life. Sitting up, feeling his bald head and thinking much like his father he must look, he breathed in the dewy air and listened to the rush of the sun-rich air through the endless layers of canopy above his head. He began to walk, taking in all that he could, for everywhere new colours and shapes revealed themselves such that he felt awake in dreaming. Here were golden flowers with long red tongues, and there was a springy opalescent mushroom larger than any he'd ever seen, bobbing in the breeze. But with each strange new fern or bush or stand of saplings there only grew more clear and melancholy the reality of his missing partner, finest of all growing things, the Fonsolis. Presently he stood before a small pool of clear water, therein his horribly changed image, stripped of those long black locks never before cut, unclothed of that kind white cloak which had kept away the elements since Epherem.

He opened his great palm, revealing the sphere which he had gripped so closely since the burning of all his belongings and bag, and all through the night. "I look like an enormous baby, don't I?" He spoke into the unreflecting silver. "Maybe you can't make me some real pants, but... Can't you make the Fonsolis grow one more time?"

There was no reply.

Wandering on with his mood quite tapered, Ogwold found Byron surrounded by wide-eyed fairies, all standing or sitting upon all manner of stalks and flowers and toadstools, or crammed along the branches just outside the clearing watching the insane man swing his gigantic sword over and over, sweat pouring all down his face and back, huffing loud breaths and grunting, moaning even with each stroke. Ogwold nearly smiled at the adorable spectacle, but instinctively he looked to his shoulder where should leap his own sparring blade. There was only that voiceless, blackened stump.

Before Byron could notice, he turned back among the trees, wandering here and there, trying to focus now upon the diverse wildlife—a group of chimfrees had fallen in curiously behind him in the network of branches overhead—until he came upon Elts and Sylna, seated with Muewa atop three very stiff and stout mushrooms which filled the little clearing in profusion. There was a fine mist in the air here, like a salve upon the mind, and thin shafts of sunlight streamed through the canopy to dazzle the senses. The low voices of the witches harmonized nicely with the tittering of the fairy, and Ogwold's heart grew lighter as he approached.

"Good morning, Ogwold," said Sylna, looking up at the gigantic Nogofod as he stomped into the open.

"Hello, hello," he said, sitting in the grass.

"How was the weather in Occultash?" Muewa chirped. Even sitting, the ogre rose high above the mushroom and her tiny body. She smiled at Sylna.

"It was terribly lucky. There was a great storm, but the lightning strikes; they seemed to guide, well, guide Videre."

"Videre!" Sylna sat up straight and her brown eyes wavered. "Where is she?"

"She is gone," Ogwold said softly. "If it weren't for her I never would have even made it to Occultash, let alone up into the mountains. She always knew exactly what to do."

After a long silence, the sweet wind rustling in the leaves and grasses, Sylna said, "How did she die?"

"She was slain by a creature called Azanak, a Sanguar who lives in a terrible castle in the marshes beyond Fonslad. We only entered that evil place because we needed to free the Euphran Wygram from his dungeons. She is the reason we came to the Crater as soon as we did."

"You are a true son of Caelare then," said Muewa. "The Euphran do not choose their riders idly."

"She did have a soft spot for me. But she would only take us so close to this forest."

"Euphran hate Xol above all else. She probably smelled Zelor at a hundred miles," said Elts. "No race knows as well the dark side of our people as the Euphran. Yet we are so infatuated with their power that we breed our own abominable forms, never so grand."

"Elleon rode a true Euphran," said Byron, coming out through the dewy brush. "I won it from him. It took me to Occultash, but no further, for it feared the judgment of its kin."

"Elleon is a detestable and wicked old man," said Elts, "but he is powerful in working the minds of others. It is rumoured that is the only reason Fozlest is so close with him."

"Well he is dead now," Byron said, leaning against a tree outside of the circle and folding his arms.

"You are a most fascinating Novare being," Muewa crooned. "Looking at you, you are quite normal in every way. There is no magic to you at all! Yet you slew Zelor with only a sword. I'm not surprised this Elleon too was no match for you. You are a terrifying man if I might say so. And unexpected. Sylna prophesied Ogwold alone, but he comes with this green-eyed killer."

Byron stared at her coldly. "Isn't she just a Novare?" he said, nodding to Sylna.

"Yes but she is a witch, and a good one too. She studied under Nubes the Wise."

"Nubes the Wise!" Ogwold laughed. "That's one way of putting it. What a funny old man he is."

Sylna smiled. "He can be most frustratingly aloof at times, but he is a great wizard indeed."

Ogwold nodded thoughtfully. "Excuse my laughter; it was only out of fondness. I trusted him like no other man I've met, except for maybe Byron, now that he's saved my life so many times. But I'd already in a way decided to seek the mountains. I had these visions, you see. And then when Nubes gave me the sphere... something in me just decided once and for all."

"What sphere?" Sylna pushed back the blue brim of her hat.

"Oh! I figured you would know about it." Ogwold released the sphere from his fist, so that it floated out into the centre of the group like a dewdrop ascending to heaven from the tall stalks of grass. But it did not go on forever, hovering in place in the midst of the watchers, spinning slowly on its axis.

"Oh my," Muewa said.

"What is that?" Elts wondered.

"It's a shiny ball," Byron said. "And it hasn't done much of anything except glow in dark places."

"Well, it led us out of those vile caverns, didn't it?"

Byron shut his eye as out of irritation. "We went up."

"Ogwold," said Sylna, "what is this thing?"

The ogre shrugged his one massy shoulder. "Nubes only said it wanted to lead me to Zenidow. He said it was part of the mountain or something like that, but that it needed me to return with it."

"That damned loon," muttered the witch. "He never told me about this."

"Do you know what it is?"

"No, but we will find out." Sylna stood up. "Ogwold, we must take this thing to the mountain. I know the trail from my tower, though my master forbade me to take it alone."

"I think you're forgetting something," Muewa said, holding out her hands in the directions of Byron and Elts. "Don't you wonder why these two are here with us? What if they have some other role to play? Besides, those woods near the mountain are perilous."

"I certainly wish to see Zenidow," said Elts. "May I come with you?"

"Of course." Ogwold showed his flat teeth.

Byron nodded, looking off into the trees absentmindedly.

Sylna looked from one face to the next. "I have no idea what will happen when we get there. Muewa is right, of course. Elts and Byron, we would greatly appreciate your assistance."

So they went and gathered their things. Ogwold was adorned by trains of giggling Piv in a large tunic and set of trousers of thin but tough leaf. They came as a company by evening to Muewa's village and found beds of leaf and grass. In the morning, tramping through the tall trees, witch, swordsman, Nogofod, and Xol went on their way deep into the heart of Pivwood.

They hiked up through the misted lowlands and came to the wide river that long ago Sylna had traced to find Wanuev and soon after the node of Oerbanuem. Following it they passed along the lake, marvelling at the strange wildlife. Beyond this place Sylna found her old way easily enough, and in the waning hours of the afternoon they came upon the tall tower with its great brassy dome, sparkling in the pre-dusk goldenness.

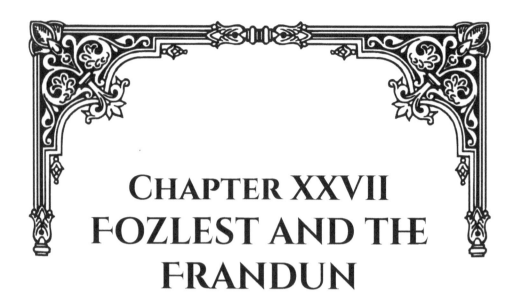

CHAPTER XXVII
FOZLEST AND THE FRANDUN

From the mountains to the frozen north, joining eastern with western seas, the continent of Efvla was a continuous metallic forest. Throughout that obsidian country of cold glints and sharp angles, numberless sylvan worlds obscured their interwelded distinctions to unaccustomed vision. Yet there was one so mighty that even the Lucetalians spying from their approaching galleons and war forts along the distant coast could see it rise alone and glorious like some great elz castle from the vastness of the Black North. Hardly could they guess what transpired within.

Such was Xoldra, the Imperial Wood and greatest society of the Xol, interred in its cast of titan trees over such eons transformed in stature and complexity that even the eldest scriptures would not describe a time when their leaves were green. Like the universe of forests to which it was welded on all sides, those endless root systems and manifold branches were fused into a seamless network, and the architecture of its inhabitants formed as a natural expression of their movement. Diverse edifices clustered along the networked boughs, great halls ratcheted through hollowed-out trunks, and windows opened unto labyrinthine light in the frozen seethe of leviathan roots.

But morphing to the needs of the Xol was not the only common trait of elz, for every tree so changed suffered together a ubiquitous bend in every slightest twig as much as the furthest sweeping reach of their grandest limbs. So flowed this impression of leaning from the most distant extremities of their number all the way inward over thousands of miles of elz forest to the ultimate, Xoldra itself. Yet even in that place which seemed the focus of it all, the turning went on in each leaf and subtlest root, until at last every surface faced the focus of all things that had hardened and blackened through the influence of the purple folk. Said to be the oldest in all Efvla, the first of the elz trees, it was the great tree Xoloz.

Within the grandest hollow hall of this most sacred trunk, from the highest time-ringed floor, was formed the seat of Fozlest, Empress of the Xol. At present she stood before that stately chair, tall and broad-shouldered for her kind, thick of bone, long of limb, powerful of jaw and brow. Her elz-mailed tails swept in wide arcs from either side, disappearing into shadow. At the hip of her purple-hemmed robes was a stout wand hewn of the very bark of Xoloz; from her jagged ears hung chips of the same.

So dark was her silky hair that only the brightest hues from the windowshafts showed its pure purple; lifted into an immense nodule, its mass sat atop her head like a looming glossy eye, missing nothing. Her more mortal orbits were white straight through, pupilless and dazed, as though she went through life in an unending trance, yet her poise was lucid as she looked out over those she had summoned. All throughout the hall, kneeling in ranks upon the wide black hemispheric plane before the throne, were the hundredfold Zefled, above whom in rank only the six Zefloz—absent on their quest to Zenidow—are distinguished by their exceptional ability.

The only figure in the wide room who did not lower himself in the presence of the Empress was a snow-bearded Novare man in red robes. His countenance was stern if lost, as he paced about behind the throne, tapping away with his gnarled staff, seeming quite to ignore what momentous ceremony transpired in the same room as his thinking. Weary, beaten, dragged down by the rumour of war, the long journey over the sea and deep into the elz maze of Efvla had aged him. Yet still a quirky glimmer was in one passing ice-pick iris catching the light. The Xol respected the red wizard as an extension of Fozlest in every way, and though his allegiance was foremost with Lucetal, never in the presence of Chalem was he treated with such dignity as here in Xoldra. But this pleasant thought passed, and frowning he resumed his anxious hobbling back and forth.

"The Novare," said Fozlest now, her cold, sweet voice thrumming through the crowd, "bring war the likes of which we cannot know. I have seen through the eyes of Nubes Tree-Friend the new weapons of Lucetal that long have slept beneath the crust of the world. They are made of unnatural metal and burn synthetically, cruel mockeries of the light of Xeléd! Many months they have had to train their warriors, to outfit them with such equipment, to take up flight in ships that travel like clouds through the sky, which even now soar over the wide sea from the East. So it is: the time has come for the final protection of our trees!"

The crowd stirred like a rushing wind. Fozlest lowered her hands, and seated herself in the black throne, long purple fingers curling over the polished armrests, looking slowly over all of the faces turned to her. Now she spoke more evenly.

"All summoners, conjure to exhaustion. All enchanters; go, live in the armouries. All tamers, ready every beast. All warriors converge upon the guard trees. All captains move the Five Forests to their stoutest defences. And all Zefled, you my finest mages, and all under your tutelage who you deem ready for this challenge; conduct a symphony of Fabric the likes of which none have seen in one thousand seasons, and through your work Xoldra shall be shielded by light."

There was a powerful silence. Orders flowed through psychic chains of command, and all throughout the imperial forest a network of preparation began for the coming destroyers. When the information had passed from the minds of the Zefled unto their students and factions in other great elz trees, all sank deeper to the floor, entering upon a selfsame trance. All about them grew at once a great pulsing brilliance, for they were masters of their craft, and high above the tree, all about the city, the first shivering rays of energy began to actuate.

"Two days shall flesh this defence," Fozlest addressed the still pacing Nubes.

"The ships of Lucetal arrive sooner," muttered the wizard grimly, tapping away. "And anyhow, even the mightiest weave cannot ward off their guns forever. Xoldra will fall."

Fozlest sighed stiffly. "That may be, but my people need hope. This shield and others like it in all our cities will reach high above our trees. So long as even one throws its light up from the dark, there will be hope, and in the places where doom falls first, eyes will turn, like all the trees, to Xoldra. If this barrier here still shines for all Xol to see, no matter their suffering, at least the battle will be worth fighting." The Empress' knuckles turned violet against the black armrests of her seat. "But personally I've a different hope. Lucetal shall not reach the coast at all."

The glimmer in Nubes' eye vanished, and he appeared gravely beside the throne. "You cannot still be on about that plan. It is not yet the end of days, Fozlest. Do you wish to hasten it? Far greater powers than the Lucetalians and their inherited trifles are bound for this world. Even these new toys will be nothing when Duxmortul and his Wrudak blot out the stars." He rapped his staff firmly against the elz floor. "A covenant is our only option!"

"Chalem has already done away with your twisted fantasy," said the Empress calmly. "You say it yourself: he comes to annihilate us. If in the end our power will not suffice, the Frandun is all that I know on this planet with might enough."

Nubes closed his eyes and sighed. The curls of his beard seemed to wilt. "It will be the end of us all, Fozlest. Lucetal and Xoldra alike will be ripped from the Fabric. Altum itself will become a dead ball before even the Shadow arrives to smother it."

"But for the Alium," Fozlest spat, little hope in her rough voice. "Surely the bulk of Lucetal's forces have their sights on Xoldra itself, which must send them directly over the demon's prison. However chaotic is its intent to destroy, no living thing can fall so easily in its path than Chalem, and if his new weapons are so awesome, then surely their battle will be a great one. In that time, my Zefloz may plumb Zenidow yet."

Nubes laughed dryly. "And do what? The Alium sleeps. Only the sons and daughters of Caelare can stir it."

"Oh? Is it they whom you've sent?" The Empress turned sharply. "Do not think my fading sight a sign of faded thought. You have only just returned from the mountains yourself."

"You are cunning as ever, Fozlest. Freely I tell you: by my guidance, two are set upon the place, but they are not enough to fulfill the prophecy I was given. It is for the fate of Altum that more children of the Goddess should converge upon Zenidow, but who can say what seasons might pass before their coming? If ever the Alium is to become our ally, it may be in time for the arrival of the Shadow, but it surely cannot awaken so soon as this silly war! If you do not compromise with Chalem, you will be equally responsible for hobbling the last defenders of the world. Duxmortul will find only a whorl of ash and dust in place of Altum, and floating amid the traces of our annihilation will await the dozing Alium unscathed, naked and free to grasp and bring back to Its master. You would hand the greatest gift in the Cosmos over to the ensign of Scelgeorat the Usurper willingly. Know this, when you spite Lucetal."

Fozlest set her pitiless white eyes to the tired old wizard, and in them was a wrath which would not be assuaged. "Surrender will not protect our forests. Novare wish only for open spaces to dig up their metals and build their castles, and none so much as the loathsome Sons of Chalor. If our demise and the destruction of all we love is indelible, then let a true god be the arbiter of doom rather than this self-appointed King of nothing." She looked out upon the Zefled in deep prayer. "We will meet Lucetal with the fullness of our strength."

Nubes folded his old hands over the burl of his staff and sighed. For a little while he stood solemnly, eyes closed, tugging at his beard, as all throughout

Xoldra and in unfolding succession among every community of Xol to the very edges of the Black North, hundreds of thousands of sorcerers and sorceresses received the news which emanated from the imperial forest. In the next few hours, all around their vast conglomerates of elz would begin to appear great shimmering spheres of protective energy in like image to the mightiest which even now took shape high above Xoldra, and in every mind and heart that day which had not battled upon or dealt directly with the woes of the front, would be kindled the first true spark of war which always they had feared would reach them even so deep in the forest. Their efforts all these years had not been enough. Lucetal had grown strong; now it was coming.

And here he was again, thought the wizard, standing beside a different throne, begging another ruler for peace, understanding. It simply would not be. Perhaps it was all his fault, even, expecting Chalem to take up the technology of his ancestors without turning them upon his favourite enemy, then coming here and stirring up such commotion that his old friend had gone so mad as to wake up the worst and most ancient evil in the history of Altum. Truly, Fozlest was right; but for the Alium, indeed. The only hope now was with Sylna and Ogwold.

"Well then," he coughed at last, clearing his throat and rolling back his wiry shoulders as if to take up his old mantle of merriment. "If we are all to die horribly, I will take my fall at Chalem's side, for though he is a despicable ass, to the last I am a servant of Lucetal."

Methodically he tapped his staff, grumbling as if hesitant to go on. "You say that Novare are only for metal, yet here you sit, Empress, in a tree hardened and gleaming as the purest lucidium, which can no longer grow without your sewing, and will never again feel the light of the sun or moisture in its roots. Ah, but, you know this. Indeed, no one in this world despises the curse of the elz as much as you, Empress. Perhaps you might have released the Frandun long ago if I hadn't come along. Yes, I see what is the real object of your cunning. To keep Chalem from you trees is one thing, but here arises your final opportunity to free this forest from the Xol. You wish to eradicate us all." Nubes sighed, not looking at Fozlest, for he did not need to know her expression. "I wish the best for your people, old friend, and hope to one day speak with you again in a time of peace. The world is greater than Efvla and its trees."

With one last rap of his staff, the wizard tipped his hat, bowed low, and strode away with sudden nimbleness and disappeared beyond the high-arched doorway at the end of the room. The eyes of the Empress upon her mages did not waver.

Long after the wizard had gone, Fozlest sat in tumultuous thought. Inevitably, the intense concentration of the Zefled began to irritate her, as often large groups, however silent, seemed to do. Sighing, she stood, crossed her brawny arms, frowned sternly over their supplicant numbers; lifting her grand tails to avoid dragging their armour loudly over the hard black floor, she walked to the back of the great hall.

There she climbed the sable stem thrusting, winding, budding high above her throne into a luminous, hollow bulb nestled in the apical moment of the funnelled ceiling like a small moon, radiant and blue as Xeléd. The opacity of this great dewdrop could be changed in a thousand ways, from revealing through its membrane all which proceeded in the court below, to swallowing the Empress in perfect solitude. So as she rose into the stillness of her private quarters, the surface under her feet rippled from crystal transparency to a milky blue, enfolding her in quietude.

Her subjects knew that the chamber was nothing so divine as a true shard of Xeléd, as once it had been rumoured, but certainly it reminded them of their Empress' divine right, chosen as was her family's blood by Caelare to lead the purple folk. The bulb itself was really an immense glowlet, cousin to those floating orbs which were a universal source of light in dark places for all Xol, and represented the most juvenile sort of sewing a sorceress may learn. Still there was an art of vast hierarchy to composing such lights, and Fozlest sat quite near the top of it. She had cast this great specimen in as an unbloomed flower, blue as the Divine Moon itself shining down upon the seat of her power.

Complex though its creation had been, this was hardly a complicated room. Smooth and simple were the curving walls, and it was furnished only with one mat for sleeping and thinking. Here she sat now, as she often did, to meditate upon her next action, the blue light filtering through her eyelids as the shield of the Zefled materialized in waves around the city. She could feel it growing even in her seclusion. High, vivacious walls of pure light welling up out of the forest floor would soon grow to yawn over the trees, reach ultimately above even this highest spot in all Xoldra where she sat, to meet and meld as one cohesive integument, just as the bulb in which she now sat.

It was a moving, but a desperate image. She stirred with the power of the Xol so clearly envisioned, but she trusted Nubes when he said that no act of sewing could protect them. Gravely he had shown her the doomful vision of Duxmortul's fleet, but she knew now more than ever, in the still peace of her room, that she would never side with Chalem. Even if a union of Xol and Novare was the only path out from the Shadow, she knew that in the settling dust the hated King would set his eyes once more upon the hidden metals beneath the forest floor, and the noble trees which to him were as expendable as the dirt and rock which interred his prize. That, indeed, was his goal, she thought—Lucetal before Altum. Why else should he violate one thousand years of peace? Why else should he invade our land even as a great evil threatens us all?

At the clang of her armoured tails, the great bulb out-bloomed. Leaping up she lighted upon one of the broad blue petals unfolded, looking one last time down at the praying Zefled. Then she threw herself smoothly through one of the high windows which cast the mauves and oranges of twilight over the court. Cold air struck her face as she hung upside down in weightless oblivion; slowly began the fall, then with incredible power increased her speed, purple-black locks streaming out behind the great nodule of her hair like the dark flames of a falling meteor. It seemed entire minutes expired before the last enormous black boughs flew by and the ground rushed up to meet her. Flipping upright, she thrust her hands and tails straight down, slowed at once by the dense psychic cushions they projected, and stepped to the forest floor.

One winding black body split from the tangle of immense black roots like a slender new-fallen branch still tumbling; but flowing onward lithely it showed a dexterous calm far removed from the stoic silence of elz. It was an enormous, armoured myriapod which approached Fozlest and bowed its diamond head, the black plates quickening in the waning sun. The uncountable ranks of its blade-like legs folded into the ground as she leapt atop its hull, lowering herself down into the spacious crevice between helmet and hauberk as though she operated a ship all her own. With one powerful undulation they were a dark javelin through the black trees.

Powerfully they raced the moonless night, cold stars gathering with the dark in swaths, streaming high above in the net of branches. Whether or not the breath of dawn touched the sky, they rode in a dark day, the bright climes of Xoldra already behind them. Now they navigated the dense-canopied networks of shadow-haunted Lofled, a lightless labyrinth of elz which like some guardian trial surges east to the great sea. Along the tenantless black, metallic tunnels the tireless legs of the great myriapod tore, and only in the hours of late and lambent noon did the creature appear with its hidden passenger out from under that thick ceiling of hard branch and suffocating leaf into the gold-touched coastal swaths of Fexdrel the Young, a narrow, sickle-shaped wood only some hundred years in the blackening, which enfolds the elder abysses of Lofled.

The first traces of evening emboldened the rich yellow light, and showed again in the transforming variability of their colour the true speed with which the Empress rode. Now the dark trees began slowly to change, exhaling their pitiless shade of black, shedding their metallized sheen, seeming subtly each so different from one another in texture and hue, almost moving with the wind, gesturing gradually towards the light, tightening the musculature of their tender roots, showing those rare forms which marked the change in them from woody and green to inflexible obsidian. How strange it was that as they outran the slow progress of the curse, these trees only just poisoned seemed free and mortal in greater and more expansive numbers, when in actuality they would one day stand rigid and black as all those which they had left behind.

Confronted with the seeping petrification of these yet living trees, Fozlest remembered a childhood dream. Surely the extinction of the Xol would save the trees; without us, life might return to the vibrant flowing diversity described so passionately, but distantly in scripture. Even as she took the throne this thought had plagued her. Not even loyal and most trusted Xelv could show the young Empress the necessity of their ancestors' decisions. So as she devoted her every resource to elucidating an end to the curse, a secret hatred for her kind was born, and festered in all that she did. Seeking a cure as much as liberation from that cruel and awful nature in her kin, at first she stalked the wide world alone, but distrust was grown in the people so abandoned, and the stability of the Empire called her home. So off she sent instead her most powerful sorcerers and sorceresses, and the greatest minds of Xoldra into unknown reaches, glowering after them as they were the travelling touch of cold elz incarnate. And while they were gone, whenever the needs of the people waned, long, furious, bitter hours of calculated enthusiasm were spent in the great libraries of old.

But no outland discovery or proposed elixir or incantation or holy rite or scientific insight or amount of meditation shed but the slightest more clarifying light upon the issue than the most vague and battered apocrypha of the ancient texts. At long last it seemed that the curse was eternal. There would be no resurrection of the old forests; there would be no changing the blood of the Xol. Such was the first time that Fozlest had thought seriously of the Frandun. A terrible monster, a demon-god it was, that all Xol knew well in scripture as much as in myth and rumour. The Frandun was a hideous abomination, the unborn son of Caelare and Xeléd ripped from the womb of the sun and cast down to suffer upon primordial Altum.

Yet it was as much a god as its parents the Day Star and the Divine Moon, and it had its place in the Cosmos as one who controls fate. Even then she figured that there must be some way to release the creature, a new Power of Altum to decide the destiny of its inhabitants. That was the real dream, the second dream which completed the first, coming to her out of most hopeless darkness on a fitful night when the last of her great efforts had failed. She saw the sea sundered, the monster liberated from its subsea shackles, descending upon sick Efvla to smite the Xol and wipe away the disease of their existence forever, leaving the trees to flourish in peace at last.

But at last, it was Nubes that finally helped her see things differently. The red wizard appeared with impossible precision on the very morning of that horrible nightmare. She had stood in her high hall looking down upon the blackened lay of Xoldra when the sentinels of lower Xoloz sent to her the impression of a little Novare man in billowing red robes. In those days having little reason to distrust a single man come so deep into her territory, and feeling as well like there was nothing left to do but give up, the Empress had welcomed the odd creature into her court. There he stood boldly before the throne to warn the Xol about his people, a civilization called Lucetal, and their obsession with tearing up the land and coveting its deepest contents. He showed to her a terrible vision of smoking mines, of the treeless, barren, pocked wastes of Petrampis, the dead continent of his homeland across the sea.

She could still see him with his brownish hair and all the symptoms of impending old age, could still hear him intoning gravely that were the Sons of Chalor to visit Efvla they would surely raze the land for its metal. He had honoured the Xol that day, treasuring their most banal literatures, going away with their silliest artifacts, repeating their unique names for the twenty moons with savouring lips, and asking endless questions about the Fabric. But warmest of all in her heart was that final moment when he had dubbed them before Caelare the guardians of the world's greatest forest. More clearly now than ever she remembered reciting in reply, with feeling for the first time—as off the wizard went on his next adventure, promising to return—those words which were her parents', and their parents', all down the blood of her history to the very source of the curse, whatever it was. Presently, the last elz trees fell away around her, and she repeated these words aloud.

"When life fails, elz shall persist."

The rapid thudding of the myriapod's feet stormed on. Now all around were the living and perceiving trees and plants of diverse shapes and glorious species which had known Efvla long before the coming of the Xol. Rushing by went their glossy green leaves and blazing flowers, and in the cool shade of their breathing, supple barks were the signs of natural growth. Seeing things as they should be, changeful and shaped by time and chaos, the hideous metal spikes of elz rearing behind it all in an endless uniform mass seemed a terrible sickness over the land.

But Fozlest almost laughed. So it was that Nubes once again after all these years had changed her mind; though, not to follow his counsel. The Empress shook her head. The dream of the Frandun was more than childhood fantasy. If the curse could no longer protect the forest, then the Xol were simply a great parasite, sucking up its beauty at the cost of its mortality. And she would not allow a villain like Chalem to play god to her people.

"When elz fails," she added, "life shall persist."

Now a wide rocky space of soft green turf and moss-heavy boulders opened upon the dull endless crash of the purple sea. Here the trees were few, thin and slender, bow-backed, their long leaves like glassy locks. The salt air struck Fozlest's nostrils, seared her glazed white eyes. She slipped from the myriapod's shell as it was a suit of armour, and the creature bled away winding like some fluid machine into the forest shade, though it was quite easy to distinguish among so many vibrant colours.

The Empress walked slowly now, for her goal was near, letting the forgotten touch of the coast rekindle her memory. Now the land rose gradually into a great promontory, so that even the elz trees far behind seemed to look up out of their collective black at the lone Xol who ascended to greater heights without them. Among the sparse, bendy trees there grew a hardy yellow grass, which became all the more tall and sinuous with sea-wind as Fozlest summited the great shelf and found herself now upon a vast plain, strewn with the sundered remains of huge stone walls, the carcasses of collapsed roofs. Beyond that golden expanse of waving grasses and silent, dark ruins, the purple sea at last appeared; at first, it was the finest line of colour achieving infinity with the unattainable horizon, yet with one, now but two footfalls it had grown enormous as a second sky. But Fozlest could not enjoy such a view for long.

A vast, broken proscenium lay at her feet like some huge fallen giant of stone. Crushed and warped, jutting from its split limbs like gleaming bones were the distorted likeness of thick golden gates, etched with the glyphs of a lost society. Such was the storied entrance to the ruins of Molavor. A rare breed of Novare—honourable and just—had raised this great arch long ago. Happily they had shared their trades all through Efvla; with reverence had they studied the Xol classics. With the lost people of close Fexdrel they had shared a special bond, yet as well many of their philosophers and naturalists had laboured in far off Xoldra itself alongside the scientists of Fozlest, pursuing the truth of elz. So moved they were both by the necessity and the horror of the curse, for they were known to hold both sides of the debate.

To most all Xol, this place was known only as the home of the Green Eye, that woeful man who had slain so many of her kind in fury, as the flames raged, as the buildings collapsed and the tabernacle was broken. Of course, she could show no mercy to such a one were he to reappear, but in her private thoughts he was a symbol of that land which was once her greatest ally. Though Fozlest might easily say that Zelor had hardened her heart, in the end—she placed one hand against the cloven arch—it was she, who they so trusted, who betrayed Molavor. If only Nubes had found her sooner, the Molavorians might have risen beside her in battle once again. What disgust they would share for the Sons of Chalor! Still, they would never have allowed the awakening of the Frandun. Her hand slipped from the old stone.

Straightening herself, she shouldered past the arch into the city proper. Those low ruins which had seemed few from afar, and beneath the high grasses, grew in stature and numerousness quickly as she went. She wound through teething foundations, under the ribs of collapsed buildings, leapt down from uprooted roadways, glanced over broken carts decked in ash, mangled skeletons still clad in armour. She paused once more beside the demolished cathedral, unrecognizable but that she knew it had once stood here, glorious and stately, a holy place for Novare and those Xol who went among them alike. Here it was she had taken little Zelor long ago, and offered up his will for adoption. As she stood again lost in memory, twilight seeped like tessellating inks into the dry grass, and the sky sagged violet-dark, wind softening, the dry grasses soughing; the twittering of the dusk's first aborjays recalled her haste. She strode off into the melting shadows of the broken buildings, and by the time she reached the ragged cliff overlooking the great sea, a moonless night had fallen thick and black over its satin waves.

Looking out over the expanse of transforming water like a dark, billowing blanket under the cold stars, she thought of poison, woven inextricably into the seething tapestry of purple deeps, leaching into the ground, feeding all of the plants of Efvla, of Petrampis, perhaps of all other continents hidden elsewhere upon the sphere of Altum. Of course, it was not poison to her. This world— everything was hostile to the Novare; they did not belong here. Their very existence confounded the natural order, and so it was that their flesh was burned away by the water which was life to all other plants, animals, and fungi. Ah, but, there was another poison, she reminded herself. The Xol themselves, though natural and protected from that corrosion, have become a blight upon its wonder. The world is no place for Novare, and the Xol offend its nature. Let us all be annihilated. On this thought, she leapt gracefully from the rocky promontory, fell in silence as the wind ripped through her robes, slipped lithely into the water.

Down she swam into dark depths, holding her breath evenly, confidently. The deep purple water grew freezing cold, and dark to the point of oblivion, but her eyes flashed, beamed, held forth a white spectrum of sight. At first through the pale echo of light flitted and drifted diverse creatures of the sea, but as she was a powerful swimmer and dove only straight down, soon she had no company, not even vegetation, for nothing could live in this darkest dungeon of the world where no light came or favour from the gods shone. Yet at the moment of total oblivion, a colossal white bulk rose from the abyss as if it were the floor of the ocean. At her approach the great mass rounded out far off in each direction, like a small world or an ancient moon fallen in primeval days to this lowest point in the sea. Everywhere it was crusted in pale white, an infinity of bone or some impossibly large reef long ossified, now revealing its rich texture of frozen fur, ragged strands in chaotic tableau like white elz trees rising petrified about her as she lighted and sat among them on the alabaster land.

Here was required at last the use of the Fabric, for she could no longer hold her breath. Casting an easy atmosphere from her shoulders to the peak of her nodule of dark hair, she drank clean air therein, cleared the pounding pressure from her head, soothed her thoughts in the deaf roar of the boundless ocean around her. Thrilling as it had been to dive so recklessly deep, now she could truly focus. So she assumed her posture of meditation, conjuring forth all that was her might in works of sewing, which already was greatest among her people, yet as well all energies that she could find hidden, welling in the remotest untapped latencies of her spirit, and calling with equal pleas to the Fabric, welcoming and beseeching all power that would show forth its assistance.

So power came, for Fozlest was one of the Xol blessed as never before, mighty enough—some said—even to undo the curse of elz by sheer force of will. Perhaps that was now what she did. Indeed, there came to her summons, in time, more energy than was summoned even in the first blackening of Efvla. Bright she burned with overwhelming force bursting from her pores in an aura of purest resolve that washed out her image, so that the whole of the ocean seemed lit aflame, the heavy waters and abyssal pressure blown back, and the great frozen fields of the eons-imprisoned Frandun below and all around were awash. In the solid orb of power which then began to consolidate her position, there was the threading of all living, material, and spiritual realities near enough to hear her call, and wide had reached that need. Alive in the light were the hearts of the organisms of the sea and sky, and all that went upon the land in Molavor and Fexdrel, but for its elz trees which were sealed away; and even the bones of the long dead, even the spirits of rock, water, light itself, the clouds above, and among them so many more nameless threads too abstract for incarnation, but which saw their relation to the Empress and knew their time was come, were drawn together in a great fabric sewn as one and to her form enfolded.

All these things compounded in harmony amid the sunken sun which was at that moment no longer Fozlest, but all things with which she had joined, and not so much any one of these things as it was the universal, unshakable determination which bound them. So it was that at the grandest and most radiant moment, when all that could come was poised upon the brow of Fozlest alone, directly and precisely downward in one voice, one single, merciless command, everything went to the white crust beneath, and the very ocean shivered.

Swiftly the light faded. The great boom of its passing dwindled into the mute abysses of the deep. Hardly could Fozlest maintain her breathing apparatus, so exhausted were all her faculties. She had spent all but her last on the deed. Time seemed to slow, stop. Water ceased to flow. The blood of the Empress' very veins lost its purpose. And yet the immensity beneath her, upon which she sat trembling with vacancy, was quite unchanged.

"You would undo my work, Fozlest," came a warm voice from above.

Looking weakly up, the Empress beheld a lady all of light, in white flowing dress, crowned in starlight, hovering like the sun itself woven bright and golden from the dark firmament of the sea. "Caelare." Fozlest lowered her eyes. "You honour me with rebuke. Punish me how you will. I do what I must, for Altum."

"A power far greater than Lucetal threatens what you aim to protect. When the lesser enemy is annihilated, know that the Frandun will turn upon you. My firstborn will not suffice to defend this world alone."

Fozlest was silent; then she spoke. "So be it. Whatever alliance may be formed, Chalem will never end his campaign to dig up your forests. But that is not all, My Light." She strained to look into the bottomless eyes of the goddess. "The spread of my peoples' disease cannot go on. The time of the Xol is at its end."

Caelare stared long at the Empress, expressionless. The divine angles of her radiant eyes seemed to contain all knowledge of past, present, and future. "Strong indeed are the Xol," she said finally, "and mightiest among them is Fozlest."

The Empress bowed her head low, understanding little. "You speak too kindly of blasphemy, My Light... But hear me more. If we are all to be destroyed, it is my last wish that one of the Xol end the curse upon the trees. Grant me that power, I beg you, let us release your firstborn to strike corruption from the world."

"Strongest of my children," Caelare lilted, seeming already far away, her voice and luminance receding beyond a veil of dark water stitching together. "It was your success that summoned me." Then she was gone.

Time began anew. Water filled Fozlest's robes. The roar and pressure of the deep was on her shoulders. With a boom which shook the deep itself, a great crack bloomed in the hard white land, opening from where her tough hands still touched the surface. The erupting gulf disassembled into jagged fractal rifts ever-dividing over the horizon of the endless mass of the frozen Frandun, down into the deeps. All around the Empress, the great white trees seemed to wave just slightly in the current. A silent ash fell from their lengths.

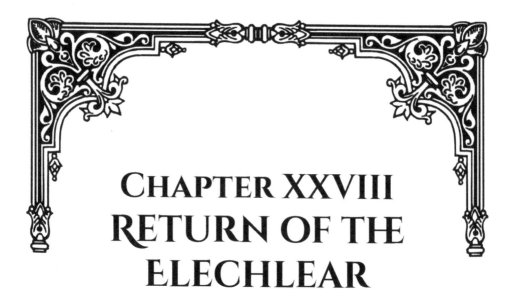

CHAPTER XXVIII
RETURN OF THE ELECHLEAR

ubes leaned back in the depression of sand formed to his narrow buttocks, but not to marvel any further, as he had for many hours, at the majesty of the purple sea before him. Rather, he squinted high up at a silver sequin streaming over the horizon and across the sky.

Even against so cloudless and sun-charged a day, the luminous blue trail of the sleek object was more pure and bright a colour than the vault of heaven itself, looking as though some fine, living sliver of the neon moon Xeléd—well, he thought, in Lucetal it was Mutat—had descended to Altum as a metal bird of prey. Yet this craft was swifter than the greatest Euphran, slicing across the vastness of the sea even as its most distant gleam caught the wizard's eye, already slowing, banking round the shore, hovering noiselessly over the beach, its slim orthogonal wings tucking back as it settled down.

The angular, brilliant wake of raw energy narrowed into a thread and dissolved, leaving no sign of the vessel's passage. So too did the luminous patterning of its slender hull suddenly vanish, but for one rhomboid panel, still bevelled in light. With a hiss the thin metal slid up, and out from the interior of the flying machine leapt a Lucetalian knight. His red hair flashed in the morning sun, but not so brightly as the cohesive metal suit which flowed flexibly as liquid over his figure, terminating just below the jawline, ribbed and shouldered in the same blue light which had followed the ship.

"Ramcrone!" Nubes rose on wobbly legs and leaned against his staff. "Where is your mother's armour? You hardly look comfortable."

The Captain of the Knights crossed his arms as he laughed. "If I could operate a jet in my old plates, I would."

"Of course." The wizard threw out from his robes a thin wafer, spinning like a bright coin over the sand, and the knight snatched it deftly from the salty air. Soft blue light flashed once as his fingers closed round the tiny object. "I too have a preference for old plates, though mine would be the Fabric. The magic of this thing is quite handy to have summoned you, but to be honest I cannot stand its presence. Anyhow, I was expecting an old friend and counsellor, not a young warrior like yourself."

The knight smirked. "Yours is not a common feeling in the Kingdom, but if there was one who would agree with you, it is certainly Donlan. He sends me in his stead. We have become greater friends these days, and he wishes to convince me of your wisdom."

"Just like your father?" Nubes winked.

"I have my doubts, wizard." Ramcrone narrowed his tall stare, though he spoke the word 'wizard' with a kind of dignity. "But I will hear you out. The machines of the Elechlear transform Lucetal and its people by the hour; whether we have become more or less virtuous is hard to guess. So many are empowered, and so quick was the acceptance of all these things so new yet familiar, I must admit there is no going back to our old ways."

"Oh? Your war must be going well then."

Darkness touched the knight's brow. "The Xol are no match for us now. The first wave of our battleships annihilated all wartime defences they had established. Tens of years of bloody siege, and now such instant progress. There was hardly time to forgive the hiding of such powerful weapons, yet from the first demonstration of our new firepower the city burst with enthusiasm. Already a new theatre of conflict is concluding deeper inland, in the heart of one of their own cities. There are many powerful magic users there who have managed to put up a fight, but it is only a matter of time. Now that we are well positioned in Efvla, Chalem himself comes over the water in his command ship."

The King's name drew their eyes out over the layered tapestries of the purple and violet waves in the direction of far off Lucetal, up into the faultless limpid sky, as if like some immense harbinger of war his colossal flying machine would appear. "So, you too have forgiven him?" Nubes wondered aloud.

"Never," Ramcrone spat into the sand. "Though I see now why the Elechlear wished to forget their past. My men and I, all our people; we have a great need for this luxint energy. If only we had held such power sooner."

"Indeed, too many lives have been lost."

"That might easily have been spared."

"At the cost of extinguishing an entire civilization?"

"I have no sympathy for demons, Nubes."

"And what will you do when they are all gone? Perhaps new demons must appear among your countrymen? Caelare knows Lucetal needs an Enemy."

The waves crashed, and a great wind roared cool and clean between them. Nubes' crimson raiment blustered and flapped as the gale foundered and swept away into the trees. Ramcrone's eyes lit up fierce and blue as the light which striated his flight suit and glowed within his slim shoulder-plates, and it seemed that the young Captain was replaced by the likeness of Harbinger, that strange azure ghost which was the wizard's only previous glimpse of luxint energy.

"Chalem will not receive you kindly. There's much talk of your desertion."

The knight turned back to his ship, and Nubes followed with grave wonder as they climbed into the flying machine of his ancestors. The seed-shaped cockpit was small and low-ceilinged. Two slender metal seats sat before a silver plane, bare as the blade of a sword but for the field of blue light hovering just upon its surface. One wide window sloped from over their heads and curved beyond the vessel's sharp nose to end just beneath their feet. Through the spacious crystal pane they saw miles of shoreline meandering ahead, the tangling elz trees stretching into the metallic ridges of the black west, the vast purple sea unfolding and transforming as an infinity of tearing and sewing into the vanishing east.

Nubes settled gingerly into the gleaming chair beside Ramcrone, but could not withhold a deep, rattling sigh and much wiggling of sandalled toes when its sterile appearance proved wonderfully accommodating. Uncannily supported were his old spine and delicate hips by the structure of the chair, so nicely held in place his tired shoulders, so subtly known the proportions of his limbs in the flow of the armrests and the curved metal floor that at first it seemed he was floating upon a cloud.

"Incredible, isn't it?" Ramcrone submerged his hands in the medium of blue light before him, and a gridwork of that same bright power veined out through the ceiling and walls, collecting in the back of the craft like an azure heart. "There are thousands more like this ship, and a thousand kinds greater and smaller. Everything was just sitting under the island, rank on rank. What it must have felt like to ride in the first fleet upon evil this morning..."

The smile waned from Nubes' wrinkles. "Why are you not out in the fray?"

"It's not yet my time, which is well, anyhow; this kind of fighting, from the sky I mean—it's terribly effective, but too impersonal for me. Real combat awaits me in Xoldra. There I lead the land invasion." As he spoke, Ramcrone modulated his hands quite adroitly for one so recently initiated, and as that inviolate field of energy warped to the unique movements of each his commanding fingers, the ship rose, shivered, and arced silently up from the beach, faint blue exhaust streaming from its wafer-thin wings, mingling with the cobalt sky.

The wizard's stomach fell at once, but as he settled into the immaculately smooth flight of the ship he could not help but smile, twirling his staff in one hand. He was no stranger to flight, but never had he ridden so stable and comfortable a chariot in the sky. "It is no question why the people of Lucetal are so smitten as you've said. Especially if I hadn't been affected by the war, I don't know if I could complain at all if Chalem suddenly dropped a magnificent thing like this in my lap."

"He is quite the salesman as well. He knew exactly which technologies would win them." Ramcrone thought of the luxint blade at his hip, that light metallic hilt wherefrom—at the flick of a switch—would burst an edge so atomically fine as to rend stone in a breath. "As much as I want to wring his neck for withholding it all, I'll thank the gods when finally I can see our new weapons ablaze on the front."

"Yes, of course, who wouldn't," Nubes murmured, gazing through the great window—which wrapped well around the sides of the vessel—at the so finely wrought silver wing as it cut the air like a jointed blade. "And truly such blazing is what all of these things, this ship even, are built for. Everything so beautiful and supreme about this vehicle has been designed with the foremost consideration for military might. Either Chalem has only revealed the Elechlear's tools of destruction, or their society was one centred entirely upon warfare."

Ramcrone angled his palms within the blue light, and the craft banked sharply away from the coast as it rose. "You are right when you say that everything so far revealed has to do with combat. As much as Donlan, I too suspect the Elechlear were not so civil as one might call a sophisticated race."

"Ah, well, the question of Elechlear sophistication is unanswered yet. Here we are as impossible figures flung from time, flying this machine as once did our eldest relatives, you working these esoteric controls like you were born for it. And just as they, off we go to do violence! Have we not learned what comes of that path? Perhaps, if we can avoid it all, then the history books will say that yes, the Elechlear were sophisticated in more ways than one, a mindful and worldly people, who opened their doors even at the height of their power to their worst enemies."

The knight scoffed. "The Xol would never listen to our words. Violence, for now, is the necessity of our future. Those purple bastards will never think to cross the wide sea, whether for conquest or vengeance, when they realize what even the luxint weaponry of this little jet can do to those despicable trees."

"Elz trees."

"Eh?" One blue eye flashed askance through rufous locks which had quite grown since the two were last together. The ship seemed even to slow with the redirection of its pilot's attention.

Nubes felt the gravity of Ramcrone's glare, yet carried on watching in silence as the last swath of metallic black forest fell away into the distance. Now they flew over the enormous fabric of the open ocean. "They are called elz trees," he said at last, turning back.

The knight returned his focus to the field of light which seemed to control the ship's motions, and soon their altitude levelled out. His hands were now flat and calm, each their digits floating as in a warm updraft of the blue energy. His eyes seemed to look away from the vast expanse of ocean all around them. "You went to warn the Xol, did you not?"

"Ha! Is that what they're saying? Then let it be said. Even if I did not owe my life to Fozlest, I could never let one of my oldest friends enter into an unwinnable conflict." The wizard massaged the rocky bridge of his nose, muttering as if to himself. "Chalem does not know what doom he brings to this world in his petty warring, and neither does the Empress in her rebuttal. But however the King wishes to punish me, however cruelly is his treatment of the Xol who would never have challenged him were it not his design to destroy their forests, I will stand beside the last Son of Chalor, whoever he may be, whatever his fate, for long ago I swore my life to Lucetal."

Ramcrone nodded stoically, moved by the wizard's noble words. "That is honourable. My father said that there is no man more wise than the wizard Nubes. Donlan too would trust no man so much with his life or even the fate of the Kingdom." He frowned carefully. "I agree that this war is one of pride and conquest, but there is no undoing what has come to pass except through victory. The Xol may never have bothered us if we had left them alone, but now they will surely destroy us if given the chance. If you are so devoted to Lucetal, I struggle to see why you would betray our designs to the adversary, when all of this could soon be over." Now he glanced over at the wizard, and the edge was gone from his voice. "Donlan believes that you would never have convinced Chalem to reveal the Elechlear technology unless there was a threat far greater than the Xol."

Nubes could hear now in Ramcrone's voice the desperation of a man who loves his people, and he felt behind his eyes the faint heat of tears. "Friend Ramcrone. Our world is beset upon by monsters from beyond the void. Next to their plans for Altum, the war between Lucetal and Xoldra is but a child's scuffle. The instruments of the Elechlear will not be enough. I came to Lucetal to convince Chalem to join forces with the Xol, to teach them as well to use these new weapons in the hopes that they might lend their own powers. Without them, you see, our survival in the years to come is hardly likely."

Ramcrone's knuckles grew white as he formed a fist within the field of blue energy, but slowly as they whirred through the cloudless sky he relaxed his grasp and returned to his graceful composure at the controls. For a long while they flew in silence, the expanses of purple waves speeding below. At last the knight spoke, and his voice was cold like metal. "I will go where my King commands. If this is the end, so be it. We have fought with the Xol for too long not to finish them while we have the chance. They are demons, and will always be evil to Novare."

"In the end I failed to see that." Nubes trailed off. All those years far away from Lucetal, he realized now, had disconnected him from the very thing he left to protect. But had he left for the sake of Lucetal? Yes, he had learned of its peril, but perhaps he had quite ignored the politics of its day. Right; it was all for the Alium, for Altum, for himself, the world. If only he had stayed on the Island, ignored his dreams of Zenidow, thought the wizard, gazing out of the window, he might never have anticipated the coming Shadow, might never have persuaded Chalem to raise the fleet, might never have brought the notion of the Frandun into the mind of Fozlest. Perhaps the war would still have been at its timeless standstill when the darkness came; perhaps naturally Novare and Xol would have joined together. But now they would annihilate each other before even the true enemy could arrive.

As they flew, a gradual haze began to fill the sky, and where none had seemed in all directions, clouds began to gather, first in the distance, now cumulus and white around them. Through this world of heavenly fluff and transforming shadow they cut like a knife, until there fell upon the galvanic surface of the wings a great shadow. All around the clouds darkened and shifted apart like a great fuming sea sundered by the prow of an enormous ship, for the darkness had indeed been cast by a colossal structure moving among them. As the shreds of vapour striated and thinning broke over the huge approaching object, there arose from the seething nebula of grey and white a titan wall of metal, glaring and bright as the finest shields of Lucetal, and endlessly tall, as of some godly citadel floating here high above the world.

Whatever features were hidden in the ocean of cloud-masses still clinging to and orbiting the magnificent ship, there seemed at least to be innumerable windows built into the side which was visible, as if there was within a great city. But as Ramcrone willed his tiny jet through the more obfuscating vapours, and as the terrific size of the thing grew only more maddening, they were able to make out another huge mass protruding from one less clouded side, which seemed far extended and narrower than the main vessel. So the three great wings of that flank distinguished themselves from the long shadow as it shed the roiling nebulae, stacked one atop the other and lined with burning cores of blue energy whose trailing azure wake extended back to the horizon in a sheet of sheer luxint power.

Like a silver and blue insect they pulled up alongside the vast wall just below the stupendous length of the lowest wing, and the sea of clouds through which the craft sailed finally parted. Returned were visions of the purple water, and they saw that the very movement of the gigantic ship subtly depressed even the surface of the sea far below. So close to the body of the ship, it seemed an entire planet of its own, an endless plane of gleaming metal, the wings above and below like silver mountains looking very much like small versions of Zenidow were it not for the blistering blue turbines fixed along their vastness.

Only moments after they slowed to hover beside the endless metal, a wide hatch opened inexplicably in its featureless surface to receive Ramcrone's jet. Crackling blue energy swept over their passage within. Again Nubes was dazed by the knight's deft control over his new craft, as he flexed and turned his hands within the luxint field and brought them to rest upon the wide floor of an immense hangar stocked with some hundred other fighter jets at rest, wings folded, windows blacked out by the sheer glare of them. The door slid hissing open, and Nubes stepped down into a world of awesome technology.

The massive chamber stretched on and on, rank upon rank of fighter jets waiting cool and sleek for their pilots. High above the silver catwalks that latticed the ceiling, long blue strips of light illuminated the room in soft, pure light of a sterile, constant persistency which Nubes could not fathom. A group of technicians, Ramcrone called them, swept into the jet clicking and murmuring, taking measurements, holding unknown devices and reading from their esoteric screens, checking on the wings, examining the thrusters again with the strange tools. It was incredible to Nubes how quickly mankind had returned to such ancient practices. Every machine, every process fit them not merely physically; somewhere in the history of their consciousness a collective memory seemed to take precedence.

Ramcrone behind him leapt to the ground with obvious enjoyment. "Nubes, welcome to Fort Soarlin," he said with dignity, crossing his arms proudly.

"Fort Soarlin... You mean this whole ship is the Elechlear Fortress?"

The knight nodded, grinning openly. "Everything of Elechlear technology we have found was contained within this one vessel."

The wizard felt his jaw slacken as he thought back to that spiral stair below the throne of Chalem. "But what of the city? The Fort must have been its entire foundation!"

Ramcrone raised one fire-coloured eyebrow. "The Fort was not quite under the city. It arose far from it actually, near to the coast."

Nubes seemed to ignore this. "I'd never expected the Sons of Chalor to actually prepare for a day when they would raise the Fort, but once again I am gravely wrong." The wizard rapped his staff against the cold metal floor. "Of course Chalem is no exception. The First father must have built Lucetal far enough away from Fort Soarlin to allow for its ultimate resurrection. But... it confounds everything he stood for."

"What do you mean? Are you saying Chalor buried away the Elechlear for a different reason?"

But the wizard was off in another world, now pacing chaotically about and tapping away fiercely with his staff to the growing interest of several tunicked technicians and slender-armoured guards. "Chalem, Chalem, Chalem..." he was saying. "What else have you hidden from me?" He looked up into the white centre of one blue-rimmed luxint light fixture high above. Suddenly he set his eyes on Ramcrone; blue as they were, there was nothing like the strange energy of the Elechlear in their gleam. "Anyhow. What's done is done. Now, I have other business with Chalem most pressing. You must take me to the King!"

Crossing the wide, smooth floor in strides, they entered one of several narrow, bright hallways extruding from the hangar. Past numberless subtle doorways just faintly neon-edged they went, and as the path began to curve they came upon a succession of floor-to-ceiling window panes opening at a downward angle—for they were quite near the bottom of the great ship—on the sea far below. Eventually the hall intersected with another, then another, and they entered a spacious commons which seemed the nexus of five other such walkways, all silent with the busy coming and going of Lucetalian forces.

There were few knights, such as Ramcrone, distinguishable—if not for their similar suits of slim armour—by the recognition in their poise and the nods of respect which they dealt their commander. But most who came through this space did not wear metal. These were, presumably, more such technicians as had been earlier described to the wizard, though he could not imagine how many different roles they each took on elsewhere in the labyrinthine sprawl of the ship, for they were all dressed similarly in pure white tunics. Apart from the streams of passersby, the room was equipped with a trio of levitating metal seats before a vast window which let in a wonderful array of natural lights. Though the luxint overheads were dimmed so as to accentuate this pleasant quality, no man or woman cared to stop—at least in that moment—and enjoy the view.

A more obvious set of doors than yet Nubes had seen waited for them in the centre of the wall opposite this great window. Hissing calmly their smooth panels parting revealed a smaller, cylindrical chamber seeming without exit and much like a glorified closet to the perplexed Nubes. Ramcrone, though, quite comfortably manipulated a bright blue hologram—much like that which controlled his jet—upon the wall, and with a click, whir, and a pulse of deep machine consciousness the floor shot up under them. Nubes' stomach rose and fell suddenly into his pelvis, and his beard seemed all at once to go limp.

"This is the same sort of device that bore me to Fort Soarlin when it was still hidden near to Lucetal." Ramcrone leaned against the wall as if he had been just as comfortable that day when the floor had first abandoned him.

"Hrm." Nubes coughed nervously, gathering himself. "It does seem that we are moving straight up, but then it is almost like we are winding through some discreet system of tubes. There is the most peculiar sensation of turning in my gut."

"I'll trust that instinct," said Ramcrone. "It must have been the same kind of transit which diverts one from directly beneath the city to the Fort."

It seemed that entire realms within the ship were passed as they travelled up through its endless body at unknowable speeds in this tiny little room where time and space hardly persisted, but just as Nubes was feeling comfortable resuming his pacing and muttering, just, even, as his gnarled staff first rapped the metal floor, the room ceased to move, and there was a powerful silence. The smooth metal doors parted like liquid drapes. A kind of antechamber greeted them. Levitating shelves arced in the shape of an ellipse, ensconcing the small room. Two knights stood on either side of one last silver door, lined with electric blue, which slid open before them.

Here was the command deck. It was a vast saucer of a room, as though a wide crystal disc had been fitted into the front of the great ship, for all over it was utterly transparent, beneath the feet as above the head. Along the smooth curve of open sky and sea stood knights helmetless as Ramcrone, though armoured in a manner quite different. Over each figure subtly flexed an exoskeleton of metal, like molten silver plates suspended upon blue lava which glowed like a cohering suit of light in all the fine traceries between them. Smooth shells rode upon their shoulders, jointed sleeves, gauntlets, and greaves contracted and extended with each slightest motion as they turned to face the newcomers, and multifaceted cuirasses focused round the bright cores of luxint in their solar plexuses, looked now like the eyes of gods of the Elechlear reincarnated all about the King.

"The return of Nubes," said Chalem coldly, turning from his position at the front of the grand room, the focus of all such divinely equipped guardsmen. As always he wore his long blue emblazoned robe and leaned upon his sceptre of singular gemstone sparkling, no less glorious than the day it was hewn, though the golden blond of his famous locks seemed somewhat sickly in the electric blue light of the lectern before which he stood, bearing its own hovering field of mouldable energy.

Nubes waited quietly as Ramcrone strode off to stand beside the doors. Then he bowed with utmost sincerity. "My King, it is an honour to be with you here at the end of days. Whatever you wish of me, let it be so. There is but one piece of news which I am honour-bound to deliver, and then you may enjoy my silence."

Chalem glowered. "So you keep on with this talk of doom. No power in the universe can supplant me now. There is a cannon aboard this vessel which can obliterate entire countries. Do you know of any magic to accomplish such a feat?"

The wizard raised his fluffy eyebrows like a tired parent.

The King smirked. "What is this news?"

"The Empress refuses alliance against Duxmortul so long as you advance upon Efvla with your fleet, and at the knowledge of your new might—which I gave her freely—has resorted to the worst desperation. Fozlest has sworn to exhume and set upon you an ancient evil from its prison beneath the sea, a godling called the Frandun, which long ago battled with Caelare herself, and could not be slain even by the full might of the goddess."

Chalem's proud smile did not waver. "And you have the audacity to return here? You who have—as you say—doomed us all, then, if our weapons cannot suffice."

"Certainly they do not suffice."

The King laughed, cold and clear. "Foolish old man. Have you not guessed it yet? My ancestor Chalor was not one to give up such strength. He knew that the Elechlear never wished to forget their power! They were forced to seal it away by that very goddess herself." Now he leaned forward, the mad ecstasy of might on his brow. "Caelare fears our power."

"You know not what you do, Son of Chalor." Nubes' voice boomed and the air seemed to crackle with a different kind of energy. "This will be the end of us all. Yet hear my council unchanged: there is still hope for Altum if we join forces with the Empire. Only together can we force the Frandun to incarceration and prepare for war with those who come to enslave this world which is home to us both, Novare and Xol."

Chalem turned back to his lectern, gazing through the tremendous window unto the distant glittering expanse of purple sea. The hand which held his sceptre was uncommonly gentle, and the sharp tip of the instrument hardly graced the metal floor, so calm was its wielder.

"The weapons forged by our fathers will accomplish these tasks, along with the total eradication of the hated black forest. The Xol are as evil as any, and we will exterminate them now before the bigger foe might disrupt our long-hearted war. Harbinger knows well that beneath the most mutated woods of their land lie some of the oldest and greatest vestiges of the Elechlear world. When Duxmortul arrives, Lucetal will be equipped with a hundred more ships as glorious as this, and a hundred thousand more weapons the likes of which It cannot know." Two of the powerfully armoured knights seized Nubes by the arms. The luxint cores in their suits gave them the strength of fifty Novare each, and they held him so tight as to seal him in molten metal instantly cooled. "What good is your wisdom if you cannot surpass ordinary men, great wizard? Watch as the primitive Empire of the Xol turns to ash. From the wastes of their end will rise at last the full majesty of our kin."

Metal circlets were clamped to Nubes' wrists and ankles, bands of the blue-white energy leaping all together from each to join in a bright net constraining his every movement. His staff was removed to the vestibule, and he was led to stand lastly beside Chalem in a mockery of his former seat at the throne of Lucetal.

"Captain," Chalem called to Ramcrone, his voice—which passion had for a moment cracked—suddenly composed. "We shall achieve the coast within the hour. The Xol army there has mostly retreated and gathered to the northeast. We will strike from above with the Lux Cannon and move on. Your orders are to stay behind—take twenty ships and whichever men and equipment you desire— to sweep the city. Search the biggest trees for any surviving leaders, and kill them. I'll have no other magic users aboard our ships. One wizard is enough."

"My Lord," said Ramcrone gruffly. "Was I not to lead the charge on Xoldra?"

Chalem laughed distantly. "Vespia commands a destroyer which is already much closer." He glanced casually across the room to his Captain. "You must admit she is more skilled as a pilot. We cannot show even the slightest inefficiency in that blackest wood. Besides, I need your valour in the outer wilds cutting off the Xol now retreating to the capital. Put that new toy of yours to work!"

The knight set his eyes upon the floor, arms crossed. "Aye, m'Lord."

"This Lux Cannon," Nubes tittered suddenly. "Might it be the same weapon that nearly destroyed your ancestors?"

"No, you speak of the Luxint Ray." The blue hologram of Harbinger winked into being before the lectern. Ageless and slender he stood in the same floating image of a hairless young man with which he had first appeared to Nubes beneath the throne room, and tilted his head as if to add some degree of Novare authenticity to his speech. "That weapon can only be deployed from orbit, and though this ship is capable of interfacing with its computer, it seems to have been offline for many thousands of years."

"Which is well," said the King.

Nubes raised an ashen eyebrow. "Well? To go without your greatest weapon? I see there is yet some speck of remorse in you."

Chalem smirked. "If only it was merely a weapon, I should use it without hesitation. But the Ray leaves behind a deathless breed of invisible poison which only decays over great ages. The last of the Elechlear only returned to Altum when the worst of it had finally faded."

"But it is nothing more than luxint energy, correct?" Nubes turned to Harbinger.

"Yes."

"Then does this ship not trail such poison through the sky even as we speak?"

"To a degree, but it is statistically harmless."

"Right." Chalem smiled wolfishly, his yellow hair seeming all the more sickly and pale.

"The Lux Cannon, however, which the King speaks of, leaves behind a significant degree of radiation. Its fallout cannot approach the devastation that drove your people to the stars, but the areas which it strikes will be uninhabitable by Novare for no less than one thousand years."

"So you will not acquire their land after all," Nubes murmured.

The King looked off over the vast fabric of the poison sea as if he had considered such a notion many times. "Not now, yes, or for myself, but what is one millennium next to the future of our people? Harbinger, we will still be able to extract the other Elechlear Forts using the gear you spoke of?"

"Yes. There are enough radiation suits aboard Soarlin alone to clothe a formidable investigation."

The King nodded. "You see, Nubes. We will unearth the rest of our weapons and face Duxmortul with more power than the Xol could ever offer."

On this point, Nubes was silent.

For a while King and wizard stood as once they had in the court of Lucetal, watching through the crystal floor as the leagues of the purple sea rushed below. The world was still, it seemed, poised on the precipice of war, and between the men so openly opposed in their ideals there settled even a calm which spoke to the many years they had spent together. But it was not to last. As the first hazy signs of coastline troubled the otherwise changeless horizon, a great boom echoed through the ship, and Nubes being quite unable to balance fell flat on his rear. Chalem, however, stood tall, and holding up his hand bid his knights be at ease.

At the swift turning of his ringed hand amid the luxint control field, a sudden magnification distorted the fore of the command deck, as though the transparent ellipse itself were made of that same transformative energy. Now they saw in stunning detail what waited a hundred miles ahead, the individual trees, the lay of the white shore, the crashing of the poison surf upon it, and even the trailing wisps of dirt and rock tumbling all about, displaced by the great quake which must have been the cause of so titanic a noise. Now a tremendous wave smashed unto the coast, so tall and powerful that it pressed through the tall elz sentinels there and flooded into their midst as though the sea had risen twenty meters in level. Chalem withdrew the focus of his sight to reveal in a wide perspective including all the surrounding sea, another wave coming in from the open water more massive than the first, and behind it, rising, curling in upon itself, a third which might smother and drown all Lucetal with its landing.

But above and beyond even this historic wave, a greater shape was risen, and of its birth surely radiated the seismic power so shaking the world and dashing the coast with destroying waters. It was a colossal, dark hump, emerging as from the enseaming masses of the sea itself, shed from its growing substance in waves more stupefying. Yet already the smooth shape began to change, articulating round terrific geysers of solid ocean erupting from the great gaps of its moving parts, collapsing in crushing falls upon the long, unfolding digits as of some monstrous hand, opened and splaying its sickle claws each streaming huge rivers of seawater. Suspended fully above the exploding waves and clear in its enormous image as the hand of the deep incarnate, the horrifying organ slammed down, raked grinding chasms in the distant beach, caught hold of some stiffer rock below the crust, and began to pull so hard that the shelf of land split under the pressure and cracked in huge rifts which sped out into the forest, sucking grand lines of elz beneath the world like broken twigs, and throwing up into the sky from their distant midst huge storms of black debris.

As the titan hand bore down into the surface of the continental plate for support, far out to sea up reared the vast sluggish coils of an enormous serpent, one staggering loop after another, until at last it seemed the final head of the thing had been yanked to the surface. Still with lethargy it rose, and Chalem gasped as clear as Nubes, for the immense scales of the serpent body did not appear upon the loathsome, hairy visage which slowly shook out its lank fur boisterous with the crashing ocean, devil-horned, massive tusked, and absurdly toothed. Sea water seeped from its grizzled jaws, and its numberless, differently sized, lambent eyes—situated chaotically all along the length of the neck and head—gazed each in their own directions with terrible comprehension of their wakefulness. Winding and knotting and twisting the newborn jaws shot straight up into the sky, and though it was a clear day soon vanished by the sheer extent of that still loosely uncoiling neck. Up came then the shoulders of the creature much closer to the hand which mantled up its cosmic weight against the land, and the rising full bulk of the body of the thing became so large as to reveal its every detail, for it was covered in coarse, matted fur, as it reared up and bared its ugly chest.

In its full height the terrible head was nowhere to be seen, as if it searched to swallow Caelare herself for its first free errand in a billion years of frozen sleep. Yet even so, untensed coils of its scaly serpent neck still hung in awful loops waiting to unravel as the head dove higher. These rings of snake-flesh wrapped and swung massively all over the hairy body, which was as large as a mountain. And then suddenly, as if it had been merely hiding just out of sight, the hideous head lowered into view, its every eye—and all those eyes bulging massively down the neck—focused on the command ship. Already the great claw began to slip from the coastal shelf, the massive hairy body began to plow through the purple waves.

"Behold, the Frandun," said Nubes distantly.

Chalem shakily raised his old hands from the field of blue light, and with them was out-flung a planar vision into some other part of the ship, where a host of technicians sat in various states of awe and frenzy in rows of metal seats, eclectic luxint fields of presumably differing purpose hovering at their hands along curving silvery desks. Only one man appeared to notice the King's intrusion; seated before a larger display at the back of the wide chamber atop a raised platform, he was the Captain of Defence.

"Ready the Lux Cannon!" the King shouted into the hologram. "Atomize that monster before it takes another step!" Though the pride in Chalem's voice was not assuaged, there was a haste in it which seemed to make the captain slightly nervous, but as if hearing his own doubt in the distorted, distant-sounding words which had left his dry mouth, the King added, "Now we shall experience the true might of our ancestors!"

The man grinned through whatever anguish was brought on by the sight of the Frandun, for his desire to unleash their most glorious weapon without consequence was far greater than his fear. "It is fully charged, my Lord," he replied as quickly as he could, his knuckles white against the armrests of his chair, wispy moustache fluttering as he spoke, and now most others in the room had noticed what must have been a vast apparition of Chalem before them. The captain shouted down to their ranks. "How is our aim?"

"We are locked on to its chest," came a shout from a group which stood now about one field of blue energy.

In the enhanced view the beast waded through the sea as if it walked upon the very bottom, hunching its mountainous shaggy shoulders, lowering its reptilian neck in innumerable helices rearing up behind the slathering fangs and tusks bared under its lowering horns.

"Fire!" Chalem yelled.

Silence arose, as though all commotion was sucked from the universe, and all was perfectly ordered and still. Then a pure, straight, fine beam of light shot straight and true from beneath the command deck, out along the sea. Perhaps ten full seconds passed as it travelled the many leagues of distance to its titan target, but it seemed as though it struck right where the heart should be. Great blue tendons of energy coiled about the thread of light, and a second beam purely blue and wider, large and columnar barrelled down the length of the white light and struck with an enormous, world-rocking boom against the creature's chest. The impact roared louder than anything ever perhaps heard on the face of Altum, and mortal vision was drowned in a flash. Down leaned the Frandun as if fallen to one knee against the abyssal floor, lopsided against the waves which slammed now in a directionless chaos. Huge clouds of steam poured up and out from the place where it was struck, until the whole coast was full of white fog.

"Halt forward progress," said Chalem, opening a second luxint field-screen unto the flight deck, where his team of pilots swiftly slowed the great ship to a stop.

The white hot fog was viscous, billowing thicker with each roiling plume.

Seconds crawled by. All aboard, upon every deck, in every chamber big or small or hallway void of windows, waited in a great pause. Then there was a noise like the tortured ululations of demon choirs in hell, screeching, wailing, calling out from a place of suffering eternally endured to mock the petty weapons of men which chanced to scratch a god. The nebulous steam began to clear and disperse, therein was the great shadow of a snake rearing up. A clawed hand swiped forward, and so immense was its reach and size that the clouds were ripped and thrown to the winds, jetting off over the forest and the waves.

Now Chalem saw what his cannon had wrought. The entire right side and arm of the monster had been obliterated. A huge gory mess carved in jagged crescent from neck to hip spewed hideous black ichor like oil into the sea, and from the ragged tissue all manners of nonsensical bone sprouted, splintered and smoking. Still the thing had legs, or at least some means of locomotion beneath the surface, and seemed in general unperturbed, for it sank suddenly out of sight, not as in collapsing but as in diving.

"We just need to hit it one more time," Chalem muttered shakily, somehow smiling, and a new kind of pride, a crazed arrogance as in the heat of battle supplanted his former confidence. "To think that our fathers' technology is capable of even hurting a monster like that. Truly the thing is godlike! But we will do the smiting today! Raise our elevation! We must exceed the Mardes if we want to be safe from that thing's reach."

"Yes, my Lord!" The pilots laboured over their holographic controls, and with a powerful thrust the ship began to rise, gathering speed.

Now the King addressed the second image. "Recharge the cannon at once."

"Your Grace, it won't be ready for about forty minutes," said the Captain of Defence. Behind him the technicians stood dead-eyed in awe of their peril.

"Then man the turrets and activate the phasers; express all that is in your lesser guns, Captain!" Chalem swept his hand through the command field, opening communication channels with the fleet. "I need all ships outbound. The sea creature is your target. Concentrate maximum firepower upon the neck and cut off that hideous head!"

Over the feed came then the sound of hatches opening and boots tramping, the yelling of names and responsibilities, the odd shout of despair. Suddenly all was dark in the cabin, for a wall of solid water erupted about the ship. There was a tremendous explosion of noise as the entire ship listed violently to the side, the structure of it all jarring, shaking. A loud grinding sound issued. The ship tilted on its side. Lights flashed red and bloody. Chalem bellowed orders to his pilots. The vessel righted, and as the command deck shed its last curtain of violet seawater, there waited before it but one enormous, bulging yellow eye itself twice as large as the command deck, as if the Frandun knew precisely that this small disc contained the one who had blown off its arm. So enormous was that visual organ that the knights fled to the back of the cabin, and Nubes stared in wonder at the most monstrous manifestation of flesh ever to have graced his presence.

"Attack, you fools!" Chalem shouted, staggering back, his sceptre slipping from his grasp as he fell upon the floor. "Protect the command deck!"

Sharp spears of blue light stabbed out from above and below, shredding matted fur and bursting part of the glassy wall of the eye. Gouts of smoke and black ichor jetted in all directions, hissed and slopped against the glass, and tattered gunk hung in strips shorn from the immense orbit, but the creature was largely unfazed, and now pressed its eye directly against the command deck, obscuring everything but for its pulsing veins big as rivers chugging against the glass so powerfully as to transmit the roaring of their blood through even shielding so thick. "Where is the fleet?" Chalem leapt up and stood shaking before the great eye which seemed to look directly into his own. "Begone you foul creature!" He shouted, "You are nothing next to the might of Lucetal!"

Then he heard the unmistakable laughing, deep and sonorous as the sea. The boom of a forbidden god's mirth unshackled, incarnate at last, liberated upon the surface of Altum, free to destroy all that it would and inexorable in its enjoyment. All it touched would end, said the laugh; all it saw would fall. It was too much for the King. Once more he sank to his knees as the hellish noise continued, and madness seized his fevered brain. Seeing its offender broken from within, the eye retreated, leaving a sick film of slime upon the glass, and the head of the beast reared back so violently and distantly from the ship upon its endless serpent neck that it was almost entirely visible, opening wide its cavernous mouth to reveal layers over layers of jagged, dissimilar teeth big as mountains and sharp as finest swords. The great mouth strained ever wider, with a gruesome burst unhinging to reveal the oblivion of the monster's naked esophagus, and the lower jaw fell down too far to see, so that the maw before Chalem was wide as the abyss.

At last, bright blue streams of tiny fighter jets poured out from the hangars far below and swarmed like electric hornets around the enormous monster. They fired their blue beams as well into its flesh, but it was unperturbed, even still widening its jaws. Then they closed, all at once, all that violently slow, bone-breaking, muscle-tearing and horribly forceful process of opening consolidated in a moment's undoing. Slam went the teeth, total darkness suffocated all sight, and an awful sucking sound filled the ears of the ship's occupants no matter where they stood in fear. On the command deck, only the eerie blue light of luxint shone on the hideous texture of the mouth-flesh which now flexed and contracted, squeezing the body of the ship so tightly that it groaned in its innermost foundation.

"This cannot be." Chalem trembled at first with rage, then as that furious defence dissolved, with pure, untamable fear filling his vacant voice as he stared into the black abyss.

Nubes cleared his throat most irritatingly. "Perhaps your cannon will be ready to fire from within the beast's stomach. An ulcer would give it at least some form of pause, don't you think?"

The King turned to his forgotten prisoner, squinting as into a bright light. Limp and sickly now seemed his blond hair, his eyes clouded with terror. Suddenly like a child he sprawled before the old man and grabbed at his robes like a beggar. "Nubes..." he said hoarsely. "Save us."

The wizard chuckled solemnly. "Have you still the mind to unfasten these infernal cuffs?"

CHAPTER XXIX
ZENIDOW

gwold was alone. In vacant darkness he floated, one arm abstracted ahead. As the abyss could not apply the slightest friction to its reach, he withdrew that searching hand to seek—if anything—its living heat against his face. But neither cold nor warm, the closing notions of palm and cheek passed one through the other, exchanging nothing.

Still, the thought of one hand invoked a second; and oh!—at his side, five fingers curled from the void. Cracking knuckles gave each their sharp report, together sparking a jointed unity. From that skeletal echo, muscles expanded unto the dark, heavy with blood. Now chipped nails slid against the hard shapes of calluses, and the soft reply of the inmost palm cupped their different edges in warmth.

Just as naturally, this new and visceral hand discovered the broad shelf of his cheekbone, actuating further the tough skin which pressed and held its becoming. So too did those creating fingertips conduct the long current of his hard jaw, and enliven one rubbery vein in his neck, which trembled as he ran its length, searching for a shoulder below. Yet as one wading out into a deep, dark lake knows not when the supporting land will drop away, suddenly there was nothing to grasp.

As though gracious embodiment raised a floor beneath his feet, the removal of that certainty sent Ogwold plummeting down into the black. Yet sudden as that weightless speeding fall commenced, there came as from the void itself the solid shock of water, cold and hard, a soaking impact whose combining waves were quick to pull him under. Now with scrupulous intimacy the remorseless flow quickened all it touched—the hand, cheek, jaw, and neck anew, yet far more clearly realized, and every inch of the skin, all the finest details of muscle and bone, including, at last, the bottomless hole in his shoulder.

Yet here in this medium so familiar in his lungs, such a loss was little hindrance. Instinctively the impulse to swim rippled down through flexing, whipping ankles. Membranous wing-fins left their spinal cores and caught voluminous angles against an ever-forked yet singular path. So delicate in strength were the dual edges of those ascended limbs that like the bows of violins they found in toneless matter a wondrous music. Notions of light and joy were in its timbre, such that Ogwold too was singing—not knowing when he had started—in a sacred language newly learned as it was always known.

Out from the pit of his wound came an answer. Flowering luminance burst forth about him, magnificent as a third wing, then endlessly more complex and vast, shooting and budding as golden green light exploded and washed the water with infinite detail, blowing back the black. Suddenly all the sea was radiant with its being. Yet so vigorous was the evolution of this unfolding awakening force of life that it carried on with the sheer exuberance of its being, jetting off like some transforming invertebrate, trailing its godly roots, now a streaming, blazing star, small in the watery night, and gone.

Ogwold slowly opened his eyes. Low orange light seeped through his sleep-stiff face. The first he saw was the tiny silver sphere, floating before him; already it was winding away into the warm openness of a great room. The sough of numberless dry leaves tickled his hairy ears, cut through by the proud cry of some far-off night-bird. Now he remembered how the weary trek through Pivwood had deposited him here upon the warm wood of the highest floor of Nubes' tower. Sighing, blinking blearily out of the near window, he recalled as well the Fonsolis, and released his coal-black, tattered shoulder from the tight grasp born of his dream.

But for one swishing tail and cursory white eye, though Elts was first to notice his return from troubled sleep, she merely nodded and resumed her severe scanning of several yellowed pages she had taken up from the sagging desk. However immersed was Sylna in her own text, a large, mouldy tome, the witch expressed far greater concern for the ogre's well-being, her brown eyes leaping from the page of impossibly fine print. Setting aside her reading with focused delicacy, she strode across the room.

"Ogwold! Perhaps you should rest a little more?" She pulled the lumpy blue quilt back over his enormous legs. Suddenly he couldn't help but grin, reminded by the heavy warmth of the blanket that he was settled in a silly crimson chair quite like those which had held even his enormous carriage aboard Nubes' absurd ship so many months ago. But the darkness of the dream crept already into the periphery of his mirth, and the upturned corner of his oafish mouth knew not why it froze there.

"Do you think Nubes kept an armoury?" he said, looking up at the witch with the utmost politeness. This affectation caused Sylna to laugh, as it had many times already, juxtaposed with his huge and rough exterior. It didn't seem to bother the ogre, as he went right along with her and bowed his great head dramatically. Still, he had spoken sincerely.

Forgetting his question as if it were some manner of joke, Sylna said, "You know Ogwold, I could swear your hair is already growing back!"

"Gods!" The ogre ran his hand over the bumpy bald dome of his head, and there replied against his broad fingers indeed the coarse bristling of his deceased mane's shallowest buds. Looking quickly around for some reflective surface, he found only the glint of Byron's green eye, an emerald in the shadows, where the mercenary sat against the high wall between two rickety bookcases.

"I wouldn't think you a vain one," grunted the mercenary. "Especially if Nogofod hair is so quick to proliferate."

"Would it hurt you to sit in a chair?" Ogwold divested his hand of its thorough investigation, but though his broad grey cheeks darkened, he did not seem entirely embarrassed. "You wouldn't understand. I'd been growing it my whole life."

Byron laughed, placing one hand over the massive scabbard which lay close beside him. "Hair will return in time. But if it's a weapon you're missing, you're not getting this sword back so easily."

"You dishonour my gift." Ogwold leaned forward, planting his huge elbow against one knee—and his meaty chin to his fist—as his blanket slid once more to the floorboards. "I would never ask for my dad's sword back, for the same reason it hurts so to be without the Fonsolis. You and Azanog are partners now."

Byron snorted, and though his face already was shadowed, he deemed it necessary to turn away and obscure his expression.

Sylna looked back and forth between the now very serious men. Now she thought of her own, white bow, leant beside the desk behind her, and she realized that Ogwold had not asked idly for a look into the armoury. Ashamed as she felt to have mistaken his vulnerability for humour, she took that avenue to security which was most familiar to her, and intellectualized the issue of his loss.

"I see what you mean," she said quickly, as if she understood everything now, trying to imagine the Fonsolis as it had been described for her on the way back through Pivwood. "I cannot pretend to offer something so special as you've lost, but I'll go look around. Nubes kept all sorts of odds and ends. There must be something to put you at ease."

Embarrassed as she was affected in her posture and confidence, the witch went quickly away, slipping through the wooden door which had only barely admitted Ogwold when they had arrived, and all could hear the rapid patter of her feet upon the stair. As the steps faded away into the dizzying depth of the tower, Ogwold settled back into the voluminous chair and pulled the heavy quilt up to his chin, thinking back to his dream and wondering if perhaps some piece of the Fonsolis still lived, if not materially, in his soul.

Strangely, it was Byron who first broke the silence. "Elts, what is it you're reading?"

She turned from the crepitating pages, one sheet held between forefinger and thumb. "Descriptions of the different moons," she said. "I had never thought to imagine them as having such vastly eccentric features."

Ogwold peered over the quilt. "That's fascinating!" His muffled voice sounded quite deep.

Elts gazed over the piece of paper at the ogre, and she too could not help but smirk. He was a ridiculous specimen—gigantic, clumsy, hairless, like a monster out of some fairy tale. But she could also see quite clearly that he was kind of heart and gentle to the core, for the way his grey eyes shone out at her seemed only to encourage and uplift.

"This one, Vitalem, Moon of Growth, as it is called here, though to my people it is Setfret," she said, "seems to be entirely forested, or at least a forest is the closest approximation the writer can make. Whatever it is which covers the landscape, it is likely a kind of vegetation which seems to participate in the formation of an oxygen rich atmosphere. It is a world not unlike our own. Of course, there cannot be the blight of elz trees there."

"Elz trees have a beauty of their own," Byron said from his dark seat. "A tragic one, but still they were changed by love, not hate."

Elts glanced at the mercenary. "I've met only a few Novare, but I doubt any in the world would agree with you. I am even a Xol myself and see nothing beautiful in them. Too much love is a thing which smothers and kills."

Busily as she'd left, Sylna returned, her voice coming first through the open door saying, "Nubes actually quite loves the elz trees, and he's Novare!" Arriving herself she stopped and stood proudly before the others, arms akimbo, as there floated after her and into the room a great wooden club. Long, narrow handle up, with its massy trunk angled down to the floor, the slowly spinning object looked like a sad upside-down balloon as it listed and stopped before the ogre. The club was about the length of his arm, its rich wood a dark and glossy brown, and all along its body he could see now the fine furrows of its grain.

"Am I a troll then?" he grumbled exaggeratedly, not without enjoyment. He reached out and closed his hand around the long hilt, as though drawing a sword from its sheath, and at once the intense weight of the object ratcheted up into his chest. But he held on and already the club was stable in his grasp, such that he stood up and hefted it swiftly over his shoulder like an adventurer. Suddenly the mass of the club overwhelmed him, and he nearly fell to his knee under its tremendous weight. "Or perhaps a troll would stand like this," he added, lowering his voice to fit his drastic hunch.

Sylna laughed. "I'd say you're much stronger than a measly troll to even lift up so heavy a thing," she said. "I'm not one to fold the Fabric unless I must, but there's no other way I'd have transported such a mass."

"What do you mean 'fold the Fabric'? Isn't it made of wood?" Ogwold asked.

"Ah, yes, of course, it is wooden, yes, but wood itself is only one manifestation of the Fabric. You see, the universe is..." Sylna found herself already pacing about just like her master used to do; stopping rigidly, she decided perhaps it was not the time for a lecture. "I had to use magic, to put it simply. And, well, there is magic of the kind as well in the very structure of the club. The harder you swing it, the heavier it becomes." Sylna swept her tall, pointed hat as though she had solved all of the ogre's problems, but quickly retreated into a demure laugh. "That is why it became so unwieldy when you flung it round."

"Magic," said Ogwold dreamily. "I've thought about it always, you know, but I had ascribed it to the gods before I met Nubes. Then I really saw something I couldn't explain. There wasn't a crew at all aboard his ship, and it seemed a great wind came from nowhere to fill his sails. I really would like to know how it works. Is it something you're born with? Does it come from learning?"

Sylna nodded austerely for one so happy to be questioned on the subject. "I can tell you all that I know in time, but suffice it to say that the Fabric is in everything."

"And you can fold such a thing?" Ogwold's jaw fell open in so comic a manner that even Byron chuckled. "You must be able to do anything!"

"Hardly." Sylna smiled.

Ogwold lowered the club slowly from his shoulder, and indeed it became all the lighter in his grasp, such that he straightened his posture. "So, this wood then; it can be light and heavy at once?"

"Yes! If you were to drop it out of the window it would make quite a crater in the land below, but if you handle it lightly, one so muscled as you should have little difficulty bearing it. For me however, its basic form might as well be an anvil."

Ogwold stared at the club for a little while, his grey eyes misty. "I name you Wogdof," he said suddenly and proudly, "for you are as hard-headed as you are subject to change." Then he set the club on the floor beside him gingerly, leaning the haft against the arm of his chair. Only doing so did he notice the carving of a small, bow-necked turtle set deep in the handle. "Ah and of course, a turtle! So I can never forget Nubes. Thank you, Sylna."

The witch bowed, replacing her hat atop her long brown hair.

"What is it with the turtles?" Byron's gruff voice cut in. He swung his eye impassively over the room and its turtle statues posed in various positions, carved from the legs of the desk and feet of each chair, smiling wanly or closing their eyes in deep contemplation. The mercenary himself was surrounded by them. Two very large wooden likenesses guarded over his little shadowy domain across the room, and along the empty shelves were arranged a procession of metal bookends of like form.

Ogwold laughed at the stony intonation of the haggard man enclosed in such kind and gentle images. "Nubes loves turtles," he said, sitting down once more in the crimson armchair, his hand already drawn as by some notion of security to touch the club beside him. "They were all over his ship."

"His favourite animal," Sylna agreed. "Once, he said he'd journeyed to Pivwood to study all manner of turtles more than anything else. We've composed many records of their unique forms in this forest; though, I only know they're unique because he says so, and because we cannot find them in his other taxonomical books, which are very esteemed pieces of work I'm to believe."

"Is that your telescope?" Elts startled everyone by speaking, for she had seemed so reabsorbed in reading since the witch had returned. But now they saw she had set the loose pages aside and pointed to the great brass cone which shot down like a vast metal icicle through the domed ceiling. "We've some instruments in Xoldra, but none which could have yielded such descriptions as are contained upon these pages."

"Oh, yes!" Sylna beamed up at the esoteric instrument, lambent in the musty cave of the roof. "It is not like any other telescope in the world, at least according to Nubes. Would you like a look?"

"Very much so," said Elts.

"Ogwold, I'd wager this is something new to you," Byron remarked from the shade. "Telescopes are like a special looking glass for studying the Cosmos. Through the lens of even very simple such devices you can study the faces of distant worlds."

Ogwold gawked. "Other worlds? Don't you mean the moons?"

"Perhaps I've underestimated your ignorance." Byron laughed. "What things the Nogofod believe! Caelare is the highest God, and Altum the only world in the Cosmos?"

Elts intervened kindly, seeing that even the resilient cheeriness of Ogwold was rippled by this reminder of his past, though she knew little about it. "There are many worlds other than Altum, Ogwold," she said. "Some are visible even to the naked eye, though they appear as stars in the night sky."

"That's incredible!" Ogwold suddenly stood straight up, all embarrassment forgotten in wonder, such that the old floorboards creaked perilously. "But you can see the moons as well, yes? Are you saying that through this thing you can see more closely the surface of Somnam?"

"Oh, Somnam in far greater detail than any planet," said Sylna, "or even many of the other moons—it is quite a close one. But let Elts use it first."

Sylna waved her hand, and with a pleasant whirring and euphony of clicking the grand telescope slowly unlocked the many segments of its narrow body from the vast lens which looked out through the roof, its tuba-shaped body turning ever so slightly as it descended so that the thinnest point—a soft, burnished, wooden eyepiece—was upturned at about the level of Elts' chin. "Go ahead," said the witch.

Elts peered cautiously into the glass, her tails twisting over the floor. Through the lens she beheld at first fuzzily, then with stunning clarity a nacreous blue sphere, soft-faced as satin, partly encircled in a sickle shadow which blended seamlessly into a background of black gauze. "It's beautiful," she murmured. "And certainly not any planet known in Xoldra."

"I call it Kellod," Sylna said grandly. "I think there must be great oceans beneath that shell of ice, oceans which perhaps harbour diverse organisms. I've written many stories involving them, their ways of living and even their societies..." She blushed suddenly and trailed off, but then her face became severe and stoic. "The environment is hellish, without atmosphere and cold as the vacuum, but it is not impossible for biology to take shape in such conditions. We certainly have our extremophiles here on Altum." For some reason she found herself looking across the room to Byron as she said this.

"I would love to read your stories," said Ogwold grinning.

Now the redness was back at Sylna's cheeks, and she glanced at an enormous stack of paper stacked very neatly and carefully upon a shelf. "You're welcome to it."

Ogwold's eyes expanded as he took in the extent of her work. "Perhaps when we have some time to spare. At least I should see your inspiration!" Already he was hovering over Elts' shoulder and following with watery irids the magnificent length of the instrument as it broadened out into the ceiling, doing his best to imagine what she might be experiencing.

Elts stepped calmly away from the eyepiece, and Ogwold leaned so close into it—having to stoop very low—that his massy brow closed upon and wrapped about the brass, squeezing with curiosity. Even before that eager grip had settled, he gasped; but just as quickly he grew deeply silent. "Another world," he said at last, the assimilated viewing stem moving with the motions of his speech. "Really, but for the moons I only thought there were stars in the sky."

"And what are stars?" Sylna implored.

"Well, the Nogofod say they are the houses of the lesser gods; but the Nogofod are quite wrong about things lately."

"On this point they are not entirely misled," Sylna assured him. "But this idea of lesser gods is not quite right, if you mean that Caelare is greater. Really, she is a lesser god herself, as most who occupy the different stars and watch over the worlds in orbit which they've made are of like power."

Elts nodded. "Our sun is just another star, the closest star to Altum, such that to us it appears much larger and brighter. In all, it is an average star, middle-aged and moderate in size—though, next to Altum it is a titan. We Xol study all of the observable stars very closely, and I can tell you that there are some behemoths out there which could swallow a hundred suns."

"Yes, of course Elts is correct." Sylna grinned, seeming to enjoy very much the company of another astronomer.

Ogwold rose reverently from the eyepiece. "I don't know what is more astounding," he said. "That you know all of these things, or that you can both agree so precisely across cultures. Aren't the Xol and Novare sworn enemies?"

Byron grunted from across the room. "All students of the Fabric have agreed upon one cosmology for thousands of years."

"You are full of surprises," Elts said, turning. "I thought the people of Lucetal were savages."

"Some of them," said Byron scowling.

"But he's from Molavor!" Ogwold said smiling. "Oh, right. He doesn't like to share personal information."

"Molavor?" Elts said aghast, staring at the mercenary. "The Lost City of Molavor?"

Ogwold laughed almost out of surprise. "You've heard of it?"

"Of course," Elts said. "For centuries the Molavorians and the Xol lived in harmony. That is, before Zelor." Elts sighed, her eyes downcast. She had quite forgotten the other evil in that sorcerer's history, as she had been so focused before on understanding the loss of Xirell. She wondered whether Byron had pursued Zelor out of some more personal offence than the destruction of Molavor, but she said only, "Now I see why you came here."

The mercenary simply nodded.

"What a day," said Ogwold, scratching his head. "I suppose I shouldn't be so surprised that other folk have heard of Molavor or can speak so knowledgeably about the stars. It seems that everything about anything was withheld from my people."

"Well, the Lucetalians themselves do not believe that there is anything beyond our own night sky," said Elts. "At least regarding the size of the universe, they trusted you with equal awareness."

"Look," Sylna broke in, "you would like to see Somnam though?" She strode to the great desk covered not only by many papers and books, but also outfitted in the great panel of dials and switches which Nubes had built there to control the telescope more easily. Her hands flew lightly over the switches, and with a deep and easy whirring the telescope adjusted its focus, though it seemed it hadn't moved at all. "Well, there you are then!"

Ogwold stooped over the eyepiece once again, and there was the surface of Somnam, that same ghostly dark navy complexion, magnified to such a scale that it was as if he merely peered out of a window on another tower built upon the moon itself. But as the wonder of the moment settled, he realized that the place was quite featureless, but for its many shallow craters. It was a vast field of hills and dust and rock, unbroken by even a distant mountain and certainly devoid of plants or animals.

"Not what you expected?" Sylna smirked. "Quite a dead place for the source of all dreams, as they say."

Ogwold laughed. "I think it's lovely," he said, stony brow deposed raptly to the eyepiece. "What does it mean to the Xol, Elts?"

"We call it Lofos, but its signification is the same. It is also for me a special one, regardless of its look." Having herself approached the desk, Elts indicated with one tail a series of very dusty switches arranged in rows to the far right of the panel. "What are these for? They seem long unused."

"Oh, they are like these others; they represent celestial bodies which the telescope can quickly locate based upon last known positions. Really the calculative faculty of the thing is astonishing. We can even predict the locations of undiscovered objects by analyzing inconsistencies in the orbits of some solar systems which are more or less known to us. Kellod, for instance, was found only because its movement around the gas giant Kel caused the slightest elongation in that planet's barycentre. Nubes deduced that there must have been a large body influencing the system, and so by determining the mass and orbit which would cause such a shift we predicted the presence and even precise location of Kellod! It's fascinating stuff really." She looked hopefully into the glazed grey eyes of Ogwold.

"So, these switches... They find... certain things." The ogre's expression of deep understanding was so earnestly contrived that even Elts snorted and cracked a smile. He grinned at her sheepishly.

Sylna relaxed a little as she smiled. "Yes but, I've gone off on a tangent, haven't I? As to the switches which Elts indicated, I don't know what things, exactly, they find. Nubes forbade me to touch those."

"Well, I don't see the old wizard around." Ogwold put his great eye back to the glass, looking again over the impossibly real surface of Somnam. "Just imagine what sorts of things he was into."

"Oh I can't imagine." Sylna tugged on the sides of her hat anxiously. "But every time I do something that Nubes forbids me to do, I always end up suffering the worst consequences."

"What if someone else does it while you're not looking?" Ogwold turned from the eyepiece and grinned evilly, his broad teeth looking like tombstones.

"I too am interested in what the old man was so set on hiding," said Elts.

Sylna sighed. "Most things, really. Fine then. I suppose we deserve some sort of reward for defending Pivwood without his help. Besides," she eyed the switches nervously, "it won't be the first time I've disobeyed him."

"As you said," Elts said, showing a rare, thin smile. She flipped the topmost switch of the forbidden set. Almost as it moved, so too did the telescope slightly adjust, making some subtle calculation, aligning with some infinitesimal angle, almost too fine for the eye to tell from its former position.

Ogwold, being nearest, looked into the lens. "Now, I'm no expert, as it's been made clear enough; but these are no worlds!"

"Let me see," Sylna said, coming over. She pushed her big, droopy hat back on her head and looked too into the scope, rising onto her toes. What she saw was a great black spaceship, soaring through the void. The only reason she could even make it out was for its bright red lights, which cast the whole array in shining blood. In its wake she now beheld numberless more such vessels, like sleek cephalopods jetting through the void. "Gods," she said, drawing away and sitting at once in one of the great chairs. "They look just like Zelor's figurine."

"What?" Elts returned to the eyepiece. "Xeléd Down! These are the black ships from my vision, made in like form to Duxmortul." The chill word blossomed like an evil flower in the room. Staring into the telescope she began to shake with fury, her tails hissing taut over the floor. The mercenary and ogre were surprised, more by her vigour after such calm than by the strange name of Duxmortul, which they had not yet heard.

Sylna rushed to the desk. "The distance and trajectory should be here," she said, pulling out from beneath the surface a flat wooden plane, such as one might sit and write more comfortably upon. Here was a great sheet of paper, and over that surface already a sudden blue ink scrawled swiftly as from nowhere. Scrupulously she leant over the esoteric figures, pulling at her hat.

"Who is this Duxmortul?" Byron called to Elts. "Your enemy?"

"And yours, if it was Zelor's actions that brought you here," Elts said coldly, turning from the telescope. "Duxmortul is the very Shadow which possessed him and assaulted the wood. It is an evil which cannot be reckoned, but we know at least that it is connected to a figurine which I took from him. It is an odious little idol, all black and tentacled with columns of red eyes."

Byron crossed his arms, grunting. "I remember well the day my brother found that hideous statue, and wore it thence around his neck. He said it came from the stars. Never let it out of his sight. I found him praying to it often." The mercenary sighed raspily. "All who were close to Zelor and our family knew in time that this object was the true evil, though it became hard to distinguish the man from his collar. Still, the elders of Molavor composed this poem to remember his fate, and I have kept its words close in my journey."

> Above the stars, a new light interposed
> The cosmic dark, like teardrop slowly massed.
> Now freed against the stained-glass cheek of night,
> It shone for Zelor, dreaming where it led.

"Lord, Byron! What verse!" Ogwold laughed. "That was beautiful!"

Elts too had listened attentively. "It is a sorrowful lyric. I shudder at the perceived divinity in an artifact so evil."

"Evil indeed," said Byron. "But to Zelor it was a beacon of hope, and so we always try to remember that it was a true Molavorian who fell under that spell, and not one who desired ill for our people. The tale in itself is a reminder that brilliant things are not always to be trusted."

"Those are wise words, mercenary. I can imagine it would be hard to think a falling light from heaven was something so foul as Duxmortul's totem." Elts said, turning to Sylna, "Where is it now?"

"It is secure, and we needn't show it to him," said the witch over her shoulder. "Description will suffice, and its presence may be perilous."

"Sylna is right," Elts murmured. "The figurine you speak of must be the same as we found."

"Its effect on him was slow, as evil things often are." Byron's hard green eye scoured Elts. "It had never occurred to me that this statue was the very image of his master. But now it seems true. Many times I have seen it in my dreams, though I had thought this a fantasy of fear."

"I too have had the dreams," Elts said. "But I can say confidently that they are real, for when I held the idol in my hand, it transported me to the seat of true evil. Here, look for yourself." She stepped away from the telescope.

Byron appeared in a step and looked through the lens, arms folded. Then he spat on the ground. "Aye. And you have the accursed thing here? Why not destroy it?"

"It can't be done," Sylna replied mutedly.

"It matters not," said Elts. "But Duxmortul is coming. We will have our revenge."

Byron raised an eyebrow over his empty socket. "You are a warrior, Elts."

"While there is a threat to what I love, I shall fight," she replied. "There was a time in my journey where I forgot this principle, and during that time Duxmortul slew my oldest and greatest friend. But there is still much in the world to fight for. I may not have known the Zelor you once called a brother, but I did know a Zelor worthy of trust and respect. I wanted to believe that he could overcome the Shadow. He would never say Its name, such that I thought he might find some way to escape."

"That does seem like resistance," said Byron. "Names are powerful things, especially to the Xol. I can believe that Zelor held off the sway of this thing for a while, but only as he lay dying did I recognize him. My only regret is that I might have slain him before the fall of Molavor."

Elts' tails swished abjectly. "Perhaps he might have wanted that. The only thing he hated more than his own truth was Duxmortul. At least I can take up that quest in his stead."

"Elts," said Ogwold, his oafish voice dissolving the tensity of the moment. "What else do you love about the world?"

She smiled. "The trees, I suppose."

"The trees!" Ogwold slapped his hand to his huge naked head. "I've failed them! Elts, I cannot begin to apologize. Hesgruvia; Hesflet; another Xol! I met her in Fonslad, and she knew Xirell and—"

"Out with it, ogre," laughed Byron.

"She had a cure for the curse!" Ogwold gasped. "But... It is gone. I've lost it. It was burned up with my hair and the Fonsolis and my clothes. It was a seed, Elts, which she said could be planted in Xoldra to restore the trees to their natural state!"

There was only stunned silence. Elts gawked.

Sylna suddenly rose from the desk, kneading her forehead as she faced the room. "The fleet is about two parsecs from Altum, and moving towards us near the speed of light... They will arrive in no less than seven years." Silently these numbers hung in the candled air as she returned to the busy page upon the desk. "The largest of Duxmortul's ships is about the size of Somnam," she added. Noticing the strange quietude of the room, she looked from face to face. "This is far more pressing than the curse of the Xol!" she shouted.

"What you've said is unbelievable to me, Ogwold," said Elts. "At least it is some notion that there is even a hope for Efvla's trees."

"I'm sorry. I should have held my tongue."

"No. I am happy to hear it. Maybe there are other ways. One day I shall find this Hesflet. Surely I must if she was a friend of Xirell. But the trees will have to wait," Elts said gravely.

"Right. Seven years does not seem long at all," Ogwold wondered aloud.

"Indeed..." Sylna said, now hurrying back to the telescope and pressing her face right up to the lens. "Seeing how far away are these ships, though, and just thinking where they must have come from, moving at this speed, influencing Zelor so many years ago—Duxmortul must have an enormous psychic ability. Imagine what It can do physically! And... And Nubes knew about this all along! That toadstool!"

"He certainly didn't warn me either," muttered Ogwold. As if on cue the mysterious sphere swept out of his cloak pocket and carried on round his head.

"Yet you were instrumental in Zelor's demise," Byron said, watching it. "Maybe your purpose here has something to do with Duxmortul as well."

"An excellent point," Sylna mused. "The Alium is undoubtedly wrapped up in this."

"Oh yes! So what is the Alium?" asked Ogwold. The sphere buzzed in his ear, bounced off of his forehead, and began wandering about the room aimlessly.

"We have no idea," Sylna announced as though she knew everything in the world, "but that its impression upon the Fabric is unlike any even the gods might leave."

"Fozlest knew little else," said Elts. "She reasoned it might provide us a great advantage over Lucetal. But now, I think she knew about these ships as well. I only discovered near the end of our journey that Zelor conspired to destroy the Alium, thus keeping it from Fozlest as well as Duxmortul." She looked cautiously at Byron.

The mercenary grumbled solemnly. "Sounds like Zelor."

Sylna threw off her hat, and it floated softly into an armchair. "Why couldn't Nubes just tell me! We don't know anything!" Swooping up the hat she flopped down onto the red seat and sank deep within its cushioning. "I suppose all we can do now is seek the Alium."

"Agreed," said Elts. "Let us go at once."

"Is your aim to destroy it as well?" Byron's metal voice was difficult to judge. The silver sphere seemed to stray from its dizzy wandering about the capacious room, as if it meant to listen in a little more closely.

The sorceress flicked a tail. "What do you care?"

The mercenary batted away the sphere. "I did not come to the mountains for any Alium, but it is the goal of my friend Ogwold to discover it."

Sylna looked anxiously from face to face. "Well I certainly don't want it destroyed! Even if we could do it, perhaps we'd be throwing away our only hope. I doubt Duxmortul requires any additional strength to conquer Altum."

Elts smiled wanly. "I believed the Piv Muewa when she called Zelor's goal a righteous folly. He persuaded me with his ambition once, but I was forced to see the terrible truth of his fate. What I do wish for is the demise of Duxmortul, however, and the Alium seems a weapon we shall need."

Byron nodded, returning to his seat between the bookcases. "It is like the witch said; all we can do is go."

"Then let's be off! Let's be off to Zenidow!" Ogwold boomed, and they all had to cover their ears.

Chapter XXX
Xeléd Down

Fast as she was able, and completely without rest, Fozlest raced from Molavor upon her fast-trundling myriapod. The night had passed quickly in her labour beneath the surface, so that when she emerged from the ruins, listening to the deeply muted, endless cracking and splitting of that nameless integument which for so many ages had withheld Caelare's greatest enemy, the palace of that very goddess broke above the black treeline in the east and threw upon her deeds a bright and all-knowing light.

By the time the first giant waves had struck the coast, already the promontory of Molavor was far behind her. Still she heard the awful wailing of the Frandun as it was stricken, and saw the star-bright flash, totalizing through the firmament, of what weapon dared fire upon it. As the unholy light of luxint burned the sky, she shuddered to think what it might mean to her people. Evil as the Frandun was, she could not suppress a grateful smirk when sounded again its massive form booming through the sea, for she knew that Chalem and his unnatural power would be destroyed. Still, her own kind was next, and she would not be absent from Xoldra for the final end to the curse.

At present, the noon sun had just begun its descent over the distant sea, and in the golden light, standing upon a tall, bald hill at the boundary between the elz forests of spacious Fexdrel and labyrinthine Lofled, Fozlest beheld from afar the highest black-on-black layers of Xoldra's canopy, the greater apex of her home-tree Xoloz just piercing that noble midst. More comforting than, at last, a vision of her destination, was that high hemisphere of liquid radiance rising from the elz trees, for the barrier was complete above even the highest point of the city, and seemed at least from where she stood unbroken.

Down from the vantage she sped upon the great armoured insect, and without another slightest pause they shot between the dark, shining trees over familiar land. The remainder of her journey was now far the more gruelling, for the thick climes of Lofled were dark, winding, and in many places blocked to passage, so that only as evening gathered above in trailing, sugary oranges did she come at last upon the wall of pulsing purple light which curved down from beyond the canopy in a thick plane, and marked that perimeter which her sorcerers and sorceresses had deemed the extent of the imperial wood. She dismounted, and the weaving creature she had ridden for so many miles slunk back into the gloom of the wood, wrapping itself about one elz tree and streaming up into its branches.

All through the final act of her return, since she had seen the completed shield high over the city, she had entertained the idea that Xoldra was safe, that perhaps the Lucetalians had been waylaid; or, and this idea she coveted, their new weapons had been unable to penetrate the weave of the Zefled. But as she stepped through the force field, at once these fantasies dissolved, for the city was deathly silent. All smelled of molten elz. Many mighty elz trees were splintered, shattered, warped as by tremendous heat. Now she saw that smoke was everywhere, wreathing the great trees, collecting in the broken matrices of their bound branches and roots, floating through their labyrinthine trunks like spirits of decay. There were no Xol in sight. The city was in ruin.

She sank to the grassy loam upon her knees, her long black cloak, hemmed in purple, fanning about her, and wept silently. It had been many hundreds of years since she had let tears fall from her face, but in the end of it all, the culmination of her devotion to her people, she had been absent for the fall of all she loved and leaving swore to protect, at whatever cost. Cold and lonely in her heart was the wretched hope that the Frandun in its blind fury avenge the death of Xoldra. She had nothing left to lose.

Yet in time the tears ceased to come and withered upon her rough cheeks, for too accustomed to stoicism was her countenance, and already the familiar stony frieze of composure gripped her bones, and forced the Empress to stand. She looked instinctively to Xoloz, which rose still unscathed in all its glory, thick and strong and infinitely tall, and off she went to see what had come of her throne. Drawing closer she saw that even the immense solidity of that greatest tree was melted, splintered, and torn in places, but still stood steadfast, an eternal symbol of the Xol spirit among the ruined wood. Now she saw signs of life, for all about and along its sprawling mighty roots were stationed many silver vessels far sleeker and more radiant than any work of metal ever she had seen.

They were vehicles, she knew, for Nubes had described to her the nature of Lucetal's new armaments. Their narrow noses were entirely clear, as though a pilot seated in that vertex could see all that transpired in his or her periphery, yet somehow it was impossible to pierce that thick glass with the eye from without. Long angular slits were set within the ships just aft of their doors, in nearly equivalently low profile, though like the wings of a bird are often tucked into invisible depths, Fozlest imagined that these planar scales might shoot out and take to the sky. For surely there was no purpose other than flight for these crafts. They had no wheels, and their smooth bellies sank into the grass too low to accommodate what gear might propel them across the forest floor.

She walked among them standing silent and beautiful, touching the cool metal, feeling for some outline of an entryway in their featureless smooth surfaces, craning her thick neck to see inside their impermeable windows. But as the tears had gone so quickly from her eyes, so too was her shameful fascination with the technologies of men crushed by that part of her spirit which was the Empress, and not merely Fozlest.

So composed, she approached the face of the tree which had been for centuries her dear home, knowing full well that it was infested by the enemy. Here was one of the four great arches formed among its greatest roots which facilitated the sun and fresh air always known to fill the atrium that is the lowest realm of Xoloz. With a deep breath, she wound through that shining black tunnel with what dignity had always accompanied her entrance into the palace. As the walls turned, the great hall opened before her, and she saw that here there had been a terrible struggle. The slain had been pushed into a cold shadow like cold purple lumps, their white blood dried in the ghost of a pool round them, trailing out into the room whence they were dragged.

In the great chamber there stood and sat in what elz furniture retained their integrity several Novare men, though they looked as beings from another world. All over they were plated with smooth silver metal, and they wore visors of the same implacable substance that windowed the crafts waiting outside. At their necks in charged rings she saw a pulsing blue light, which ran in veins down through a network of metal pieces as in luminous, exo-circulatory humours. Like armour were the many plates connected over this underlying energy, but they were not at all bulky. More like liquid they seemed, as they bent and twisted in unison with the body of the knight nearest her, morphing with his movement and seeming not at all a burden upon him as he approached, and then suddenly retreated.

A Novare voice only partly distant and cold issued from his opaque helmet. "It's the Empress. She has purple hemming."

"Detain her," said another of the men, though all seemed to have taken a step back from the tall Xol and her famous might.

The knights carried strange devices that stirred a fresh hate in Fozlest, for they seemed like the unique mockeries of Xol technology which Nubes had described to her. They were not swords at all, or crossbows even though they were held as such. Rather, they reminded her of wands or staffs, for they were trained now upon her chest in like manner as one who is soon to discharge some deadly spell. Even so, she let her own wand drop to the ground, where it rolled forth and came to a stop amid the guards, who kept their distance as if the little thing would explode.

She raised her strong, empty hands. "I see that the city is lost." She held her wrists out. "I'll not resist. I wish only to see the one who sits in my throne."

"She's been waiting for you," said a dark-skinned, wiry man discreetly seated across the room in a simple white tunic. Three slim swords lay upon the floor beside him, and it seemed as though they had not been removed from their differently coloured scabbards for a long while. Their owner motioned to the others with an air of natural command, yet though his manner was confident, it was easy to sense in the emanations of his mind a terrible fear.

One knight approached cautiously and snapped two metal circlets about the Empress' arms. Bright blue crackling webs of energy formed between the independent units, flourishing and undulating at first rapidly, now suddenly straight and immovable.

"The tails too," said the dark man in the corner, nodding to the long plated whips that trailed behind her. She drew them slowly forward, wrapped them many times around her waist, and presented their purple ends. When they were clapped together in the same manner, she could move only her legs, and hardly so spaciously as to totter. One knight stepped in front of the spiral stair which rose from the centre of the atrium up into Xoloz proper, and the first gestured for the Empress to follow. So the two knights directed her through this place she knew so well, one ahead of her speaking with those whom they passed, floor after floor, the other not too close behind her, though she could feel the intent of his weapon upon her back.

Numberless Lucetalian troops and other Novare in white tunics passed as they rose through the holy tree. Some carried other weapons, or none at all it seemed, and a rare few, she noticed, wore a different sort of armour altogether. This suit, for it was one cohesive unit of metal, she thought, having no gaps in its material whatsoever, seemed thin and fitting perfectly to the figure of the wearer. The knights who wore these suits had no helmets. The material they wore reached all the way up to their ears, completely coating the neck. Fozlest's first thought was that these garments were perhaps the sort one wears beneath their armour, but something in her mind said otherwise. It seemed, instead, that they represented a wholly more advanced piece of equipment.

Beneath her hatred of Novare, beneath the sadness of the loss of her people, still the fascination which had taken her in the presence of the strange vessels crept into her consciousness. But this time as she pushed away that sacrilege, she was reminded of the coming of the true destroyers: Duxmortul and Its terrible kin, the Wrudak from beyond the stars. To think such technology exists as to thwart the most awesome magic of my finest sorcerers and sorceresses, and that even such things pale in comparison to the tools and minds of those whom Nubes had so earnestly warned her. Almost she succumbed to tears in that moment, remembering her oldest friend, the red wizard. Certainly he must be dead now, she thought, for the same reason I was absent at the fall of Xoldra, because of my pride.

At last they arrived at the Meristem, that very chamber wherein the Empress had set her Zefled to work in casting the great shield in the early sunless hours just two mornings past. The luminous blue bulb of her personal quarters hung softly lighting the high-ceilinged room, though the shafts of sunlight beaming down through tall windows were far brighter, and in their natural glory she was ashamed that she had ever thought to fashion her quarters in the likeness of so divine and inimitable a thing as the great moon Xeléd.

In her own high elz throne sat a young Novare woman. Her hair and eyes were black as tar. Her skin also was dark. She was slim and blade-like, yet there was great strength in her countenance. She did not wear such armour as the others, but the rarer, the more elegant cohesive, form-fitting suit which Fozlest had seen briefly on her ascent through the tree. The suit, though, was not silver, but night-black, and it gleamed like obsidian in the light as if it were made of elz, a wicked union of Lucetalian and Xoldran art. About this suit the woman wore a long black cape, fixed at her shoulders by a silver brooch shaped in the likeness of the Lucetalian coat of arms.

"Empress," she said coldly from her stolen seat. "You stand before Vespia." No mention of Lucetal followed this introduction.

"You have conquered us all," said Fozlest, holding the gaze of the Captain of the Rangers.

"Xoldra fell easily," Vespia hissed through the hair that swept before her face like a black scythe. "Tell me: what is this Frandun?"

Fozlest smiled cruelly. "You Novare refer to my people as devils. Now you know the power of a true demon. The Frandun is a dark god, an immortal, ineradicable sin from beyond the gulfs of space and time."

Vespia scowled, shadow passing through her sable visage. "The wizard Nubes divines that you woke it."

"He divines as well that Chalem would smite the forest with some merciless new power."

"So it is true then?"

The Empress held up her luxint-cuffed hands as if to display in their helplessness the ruination of Xoldra.

Vespia motioned for a soldier near to her, who brought forward and set upon the floor a slim, silver module. At once a plane of blue light burst forth, expanded, and consolidated into a crystalline three-dimensional projection of a spacious room almost totally dark but for the glow of blue light which washed over its single visible occupant, not Chalem, King of Lucetal, but little old Nubes, tapping away with his old black staff, and pulling thoughtfully at his snowy beard.

With the quickening of his image, he started and turned to face the throne room. Though the silvers and blues of his environment were rendered quite faithfully in the hologram, his robes seemed remarkably purple. "Empress." He nodded.

"Nubes," Fozlest started.

Vespia rose from the throne. "Where are your shackles, wizard?"

Nubes grimaced, beginning again his pacing and tapping. "Chalem has... how do I put it? Frankly, he's gone mad, my Lady. You see, the Frandun has entirely consumed the command ship. Myself and the King, and a great deal of Lucetal's army are now quite settled in its digestive processes. Already our outermost shielding has begun to dissolve." Now he faced Fozlest in particular, ceasing his back and forth. "You've done it, Empress. Lucetal is quite defeated, and the bloodline of Chalor now lies in the hands of an insensible fool. Now, with the fleet scattered, the monster will certainly head for Efvla." Tap, tap, tap went the staff. "And I shall not stand to dissolve in this abominable gut knowing that the world may be undefended."

"What?" Vespia shook, facing the Empress. "He speaks as though you've no chance of stopping the beast. You would throw away the lives of your own people just to win?"

"Yes, but she needn't, Vespia," cut in the wizard once more. "Listen: in the King's absence I've spent long hours in congress with the computer-mind Harbinger, a being too wise and ancient to have been built by Novare. Still, he tells me it was indeed the Elechlear who made him; I suppose over millions of years such a one grows vastly in knowledge."

"I am just as always, sir," came a ghostly voice, as suddenly there winked into being the spectral image of a hairless, featureless man, composed entirely of azure luminance.

"Ah! Here he is." Nubes smiled at the spectre, somehow clearer than anything else now portrayed in the hologram. "Have you finished your calculations?"

"Yes. Given a considerable surge of power, the Luxint Ray may return to its full capacities, in which state it can at least annihilate the physical form of the Frandun."

"Impossible," said Fozlest dryly.

"Ha!" Nubes clapped his hands. "Quite possible actually. Harbinger is the greatest mathematical mind in the galaxy! But there is more I must share. And bear with me, it involves the true nature of Xeléd. Fozlest, the Divine Moon is no moon at all. The great blue orb in the sky which you call Xeléd is actually an elder machine long forgotten, the world-ender, the greatest weapon of the ancient Elechlear and the cause of that civilization's demise. Once there were many such constructs in orbit. Now there is but one. It was called then the Luxint Ray, and it strikes the face of the world as a star raining down from heaven!"

Fozlest spoke loudly through her diminishing composure. "Blasphemy! Treacherous blasphemy. Xeléd is everything to my people! To suggest that it was made by the hands of Novare is an insult most dire."

Harbinger looked to the Empress with his gibbous, blue-white eyes, and seemed even to wonder, though he had no capacity for expression, whether he himself was also an insult to her.

The wizard sighed. "But indeed, it is made of metal; indeed, it was sent into the night sky by mortal hands. Still, this does not mean it is no longer Xeléd! I learned today that you are truly its children! Harbinger has revealed as well that your race and most all things upon Altum were born of this great weapon's divine fury; the Divine Moon itself is the reason the sea was stricken purple in elder days. Why else should that water burn the skin of the Elechlear's descendents, but not your own people to whom it is nature? Then here is your chance to reach out to your creator! Slay the Frandun and destroy the high command of Lucetal in one blow! Stay the extinction of the Xol! There will be time to wait and see what the Alium might do for your trees."

Fozlest started. "You mean it is possible; the Alium may have some sway over elz?"

"Anything is possible given the scale of the thing. Whatever the Alium is, even Caelare will not or cannot disturb it."

Fozlest thought for a moment, anger settling into anguish. "It is odious to think that one has held in so high an honour a construction of one's most hated enemy. How can there be between us and this cold machine a connection as true as our invented love?"

Nubes nodded, pulling upon his beard. "I suppose that is the great mystery of this age, all this life which Harbinger tells me has formed from the radiation of the last war of the Elechlear. So indeed—Xeléd is the mother of the Xol after all. She is the god of the new world, a second sun, who provided your power from the start, and needs your power in the end. Isn't it uncanny that only the Xol can resurrect the true form of its chosen and destined god? Isn't it fitting that you should call down its wrath upon the last of the Sons of Chalor!"

"Bring forth Chalem!" Vespia raised her voice, stepping down from the dais. "Show him to me!"

Nubes looked away, as into some space unrendered by the luxint hologram. Harbinger floated without affect.

"Nubes," said Fozlest, "as always you compel me, but how will you escape if you are also to initiate this weapon?"

"That I cannot do," said the wizard solemnly. "Nor can any Novare ever return to this part of the world once the Ray has been fired. The Xol must go on; but it is my time, and Chalem's time, and time for the Novare to go away from Efvla at last. With your power and blessing I shall call down this final wrath. Only promise me, in my stead, old friend: spare what remains of Lucetal; unite the people of the world; seek the Alium. Seek the Piv! Seek Sylna and Ogwold, my students. Remember their names, find them at Zenidow, and maybe there you will find an end to the curse."

"I believe it, Nubes."

"Do not deny me this last chance to do my part. Let us be rid of all that stands in the way of the wise. Become the ruler of the new world, Fozlest. If I can die knowing that at last some alliance of Altumians awaits the arrival of Duxmortul, then I will have done my duty to the Cosmos."

Vespia scoffed bitterly, lifting her chin. "The ruler of the new world? You are defeated, Demon Queen. Nubes is an old fool if he thinks Lucetal needs a King to carry on." She swept her hand out over the ranks of knights. "This is my land now."

Ignoring her, Fozlest bowed low before the wizard, for she had not been so honoured in many ages. Even as she rose, the cords of her luxint restraints shivered like old thread, frayed into withering coils, and snapped. "Your sacrifice flows already in the blood of the Xol," she declared, unfurling her great armoured tails in the simple but rare sign of highest gratitude. All around, the Knights of Lucetal stepped back, seeing their great technology so abused, and the cruel smile dissolved upon Vespia's face.

"Then I shall see you again, Fozlest, in Xeléd," said Nubes, the slightest warmth in his old voice. The shimmering blue projection of the command deck vanished into space.

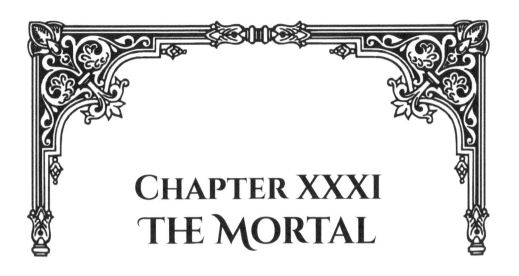

CHAPTER XXXI
THE MORTAL

espite his enthusiasm, Ogwold woke long after the sun. A loudly banging door nearly caused him to release the wooden club, but dreamily he held it only closer. The first that he saw was the silver sphere, rolling back and forth as though eagerly upon the floor before him. He smiled lethargically at the little thing.

Sleep had come easily, and no dreams of the missing Fonsolis had haunted him. Thus the hours slipped away like a flow of lithe water. But the same could not be said for his swollen body; stiff, creaking, he sat up with the slow determinism of one who has finally processed the physical consequences of some enormous and ill-advised labour, until now hurried through in a denial which any moment might be supplanted with imponderable weariness. "Ugh!" he cried to the empty room, slumping over. "What I would do for a pipe-full of norm!"

Zooming through the still caroming wooden door, Sylna moved across the room with a wide tray of steaming mushrooms, which she set beside him under the tall bright window whose glaring beams had not bothered his sleep. Taking off her over-large mittens she gestured to the glistening morsels and proceeded to hang touching her toes in a sunbeam of her own. Ogwold devoured the lot in one fistful, and collapsed into one of the armchairs groaning in unison with its precarious structure. Leaning back, looking up into the domed ceiling, the first flitting spirit of adventure quickened the most tired and dull of his bones.

The droning of the sphere seemed to say that it was high time; time at last.

Zenidow loomed over the day.

Sylna vanishing down the stair called back hastily that all now were waiting for him, and so after a clumsy descent along the winding steps after her, Ogwold stepped heavily from the front door. Blinking in the harsh sun, he looked like some primordial spirit of the earth, grey and hairless, girt in the leafy tunic-carpet of the Piv, the great club strapped to his waist, now beginning to feel the strange fungus stirring up the subtle energies of his gut. Ahead of him flew the silver sphere, humming merrily, as it would for the remainder of their journey, the raiment of the Piv having little notion of pockets.

Even as he followed that buzzing light into the open, Elts turned and strode off like a blade, chin up in the clean mountain air, the knives and ropes of her belt held fast to her hips, and her cloak tied back out of the way of the impending foliage. Sylna fell in line behind her, gazing still unto the different trees as was her habit, but slinging her white bow with a kind of finality. Byron materialized as from the forest shade itself, following darkly at a distance, huge Azanog athwart his shoulders.

They took the trail Nubes walked long ago when he made his pilgrimage to the mountain. Marked by a single silver fruit, hanging from the sweet bough of a humble little evergreen, it was a rare route, difficult to follow, cracked and rocky, and quite faint in places, though every once in a while they happened upon another argent cairn. Many parts of the path were overgrown with hairy vines or dense mobs of shrubs which shouldered their way into the open, as if searching for that extra bit of sunlight that might leak down from above. In some places the giant trees had grown so fast together that the path diverged suddenly about the great walls of their combining trunks.

As so far this part of the forest was recognizable to Sylna, they ate the berries and grasses which she told them were safe and nutritious. A clear stream came giggling across the way, spilling out from some fey tunnel in the brush, and draining what they could of their skins, each were replenished with the cold, crystal liquid. Though in this brief respite they heard the calling of diverse birds, and the lazy or hyperactive buzzing of insect life, even the rustling of small bodied things nearby, they encountered no wildlife, and the signs of activity around them only dwindled as they went. Soon there was only the rare and tentative squeak of a chimfree, perhaps following high above in the canopy, as the whole wood now seemed to watch the company go circumspectly, unwilling to interfere.

Thicker and more ancient grew the trees in this noble silence, and the land sloped downward quickly. Tall, sharp boulders reared up out of the foliage.

Humps and hills of land rose and fell against the steepening grade, so that the trail in compensation went side to side in a sharp pattern, and the company were made to angle their feet against the slippery forest floor. Elts was reminded of those earlier stretches navigating down into the Crater from high above, except that here the snow could not penetrate the stuffy warmth of the forest. Though the ice and inscrutable drifts had been perilous before, there was a new and yawning danger here to the treacherous vines and weeds spilling from or hidden in the foliage which might ensnare one's stride and pitch them headfirst into an endless tumble.

The trail only became more steep, so that each of their steps—especially the top heavy Ogwold's—were carefully placed, and Sylna stopped them from walking many times to look ahead and be sure that they had footing, for all else but the trail was covered in thick foliage, and they knew not what lay underneath if they were to fall or slide. Elts had very sharp eyes, and greater experience in travel, and so she soon took the lead then in these parts, for she was able to detect the finest detail from great distances, and with her guidance they began to pick up speed. Down they went with smooth haste, the sphere shooting out over pathless parts like a curious little sprite. In one place the switchback dissolved into a trough or a gully, cut deep into the forest floor as in some elder riverbed. Walking within the rock-strewn bottom of this half-tunnel they found the going easier, and it was clear to Sylna that Nubes had taken this way, for one silver fruit hung from the bough of a tree which weeping leant out over their new path.

At last the grade became gentler, and in another hour it was nearly flat once more. Looking back the way they had come, the forest rose as a great entity high above them, as they were now in a low valley removed from those climes. Here there was a vast riverbed. Another silver fruit showed where they could climb a Cyclopean mound of boulders seeming unnaturally drawn together from bank to bank, as if some giant had gathered the largest rocks from all throughout the riverbed and heaped them here. The work of crossing this strange bridge was easy enough, but dramatically the switchbacks then returned as they came quickly down through a suddenly steep stand of thorny ferns which seemed uncannily able to scratch the skin no matter how one twisted or weaved. About the field of thorns, the greater trees opened into harsh, bright clearings and the sun struck them in big hard blocks of light.

This time the descent was not so long and arduous. The hard diagonals of Nubes' trail began to swerve more easily even as they had become so severe, rounding out in their turns, until the path was a smooth curve, now a meander. The oppressive ferns were left behind to their thick congress, but the trees continued to stretch out around them, large spaces between each, as if their independent root systems required greater room to roam in solitude. These were indeed stoic trees, tall and supple, of grey bark and whose long, sweeping branches cast out only very high up, with flashing dark green leaves, tiny but in countless numbers, so that in their shifting and slipping edge over crisp edge one could not spy the place where radiance gave to shade. Even the lower shrubs dwindled now to high weeds and bright mountain flowers, until they walked freely and lightly across short, airy grasses, diaphanous green and shimmering with a silver light.

Through this secret peaceful grove they strolled easily, taking in the cool silence, for they were grown quite tired and were thankful for the level turf and gracious open spaces. They rested at the base of a great ashen tree and ate. Byron sat up against the opposite side, arms crossed, eye closed. Ogwold told stories that Ogdof had spun when he was young. Elts told an ancient Xol myth, very important to her people she said, and always told to children. Sylna was fascinated by everything.

They resumed their walking and over the last hours of late noon this strange tranquil wood continued. Twilight began to fall like satin drapes all about them, touching the grasses with violet and magenta, wetting the trees with oils of red and orange. With the fading of these magnificent hues, and the final, heavy descent of deep navy night, the trees became more and more sparse, and soon they came out of the forest altogether under the smooth light of the lone moon Xeléd, having just risen.

Before them was Zenidow, pale and brilliant. It stood more smooth and elliptical than ever, some twenty miles off like a silver tower to the Cosmos, or whatever was hidden in that omnipresent crown of storm. At last, no massive object stood between it and their position, and all remembered a time when they had first seen the mountain so far away and inaccessible even to fancy.

Still, they could not wander so easily in its direction, for at their feet fell off a sharp ledge, whose open face of rock shot down so far into the growing shadows that one could not see where it terminated, and only farther away in the vast basin which encapsulated Zenidow could they see the distant curve of the land shoot out from the dark, now shining in the moonlight as it hastened on to the base of the mountain. Yet for now, there it was: the very base of that unachievable, massive, and sky-piercing place around which they had all been, it seemed, divined to converge. So they stood and marvelled, and saw in truth those details the faraway mind imagines, but cannot confirm.

The shape of it was smooth and curved, broadest at the point where it passed beneath the ground. That place of greatest breadth still was much less than the spreading roots and backs of the great mountains encircling the crater, true titans themselves far greater than any in the range, but it was the continuity of that breadth to such astounding heights—slimming only subtly about some imperceptible focus as it vanished into the clouds high above—that no other landform could rival. Yet Zenidow far surpassed them.

Indeed, Zenidow seemed to be made of a completely different substance than that of the rock all around it, here where one could finally see how it met the crust of the world. Its flawless surface took to it the brightest rays from the white core of brilliant blue Xeléd, now crossing behind its stature, lining itself in an apotheosis of light. Along its gleaming silver surface, where Zenidow met the dun rock, the ground was blasted and torn, and great ripples of devastation wound out from its shining feet, colliding and throwing up terrific ridges like rows of teeth in the crater mouth, or diverging and opening unto yawning chasms. The largest of these carried straight through the inner rim atop which they stood and continued off among the distant parts of the forest, somewhere widening over deep drops hidden by the dense vegetation.

"This is no mountain," Byron said.

Elts agreed. "Rarely am I moved by superstition, but the sole appearance of Xeléd has always with my people a divine significance, as if, I mean, Zenidow is not of the world."

"Perhaps your people would say it has fallen from heaven," Sylna murmured, scribbling in a small notebook.

"Why it's... perfect," breathed Ogwold, and the sphere—close to his ear—hummed in agreement.

It was, indeed, the most beautiful thing the young Nogofod had ever seen, like the very wellspring of all that brought happiness and wonder. Truly, this must be the real source of dreams, he thought. And so a dream came in reply, for in that most luminous face, haloed by the transiting moon, Ogwold saw her: Caelare, Autlos-lo, two aspects of one being: the woman of sky and sea; his mother, Goddess, Creator of Altum. She rode atop a single vaporous carpet of dark fluff, produced as from the glare and shadow compounded along that moonlit edge, now carrying on across the face of Xeléd. She was infinitesimal yet impossibly, finely detailed, interposed with the blue-white light as it melded with the mountain. Out and up from the trailing, infinite locks of her white blazing hair rose an elegant hand, braceleted in starlight, and even as the image faded away into dazzling brightness, Ogwold saw that she summoned him.

They bivouacked away from the ledge, among the great trees. Ogwold sat up late, his weariness forgotten, gazing at the mountain, for that night it seemed nothing could be more transportative than the world of the real. Sylna and Elts as well stayed up nearly as late beside him, looking up into the stars, wondering about the Alium, whispering to each other in the long silvery dark. Every once in a while Ogwold's deep voice washed away their conversation. Byron had no trouble sleeping up against a tree, though not too far away.

At first light, Ogwold sat straight up. On this morning, the cracking in his bones only served to shake the dust from his sleep. He had on his mind only one thing, which was to behold Zenidow, and so he stood staring at the mountain, the silver sphere hovering beside him in equal rapture, as Elts and Sylna stirred and began gathering their things. Shortly the mercenary appeared, hefting Azanog onto his shoulder, and the sweat pouring from his scarred brow belied many hours of training. For a time they all sat in a circle to eat and drink, discussing a manner in which they might dare the descent over the ledge. But soon the food was eaten and the decisions made, and all eyes were turned to the mountain.

At first they were able to climb carefully down onto different shelves of rock, having often to inch along each new exposed ledge until they found somewhere else where they could find more footing dropping down just a little lower. The pull of gravity was dizzying and suffocating. Ogwold felt his entrails turning inside out, for he was stupefied by great heights. The going was painstaking, and by noon they had made not very much progress at all. But by evening the grade was finally giving way, and they were thankful to have encountered only one utterly blank spot.

At this sheer, almost completely vertical place, Elts performed the service of whose security she had assured them that morning. She took a long, black rope, and tied it expertly round a spire of solid rock, which jutted out and up, so that the tension of the line was held as in a great hook. The knot was strange, her hands dexterous and quick to watch. Soon she was gesturing to Ogwold to go first, deftly lassoing his great waist, again with a tie so alien none could tell how it compared to the anchor point.

One vein standing out along his bald skull, huffing like a cornibet, Ogwold lowered himself slowly and fearfully over the edge, but faithfully, placing everything in Elts' ability. Hers was the last face visible as the lip of rock rose above him; she smiled encouragingly. The drop was some twenty-five yards where no features showed themselves on the rock face, slick against his nervous boots, the rope burning his one hand as he loosened and squeezed it, slowly lowering himself down. For a while there was only whimpering to tell of his progress, and then there was a great silence. Cold winds rushed through the cloaks of those above. A distant hawk cried.

"I've done it!" Ogwold's voice caromed through the crater, so much more voluminous than it should have been in so huge and spacious a land. The rope went slack.

One by one the line was raised back up, and first Sylna, then Byron lowered themselves down onto what was thankfully a solid outcropping. There the ogre sat curled up like a patient boulder, holding the sphere in his hand as if it could keep him from tumbling down the cliffside, and when he moved to greet them it was as though the rock had come alive. Elts went last, zooming down the side of the rock in two bouncing movements, touching lightly down, beside the party. With a flick of her tail, there was a distant snap, and the rope uncoiled from its high tether, snaked through the air, and pooled hissing to her waist.

Thereon the grade lessened, and the going grew easier, such that they could marvel at the ancient pit in the world through which they wandered. Huge, broken slabs leaned together, forming narrow paths down the sheer walls, and some of these great plates of rock had split off entirely and fallen inward like long ramps, which were the easiest to traverse.

With each small span the boundaries of Zenidow raced outward as its sheer mass was a horizon all its own, so that by midday the charged blue sky was like one hemisphere of Altum now behind them, for a new world of utterly featureless silver-white curved in like vastness over their heads. After many hours clambering down through a cracked, rocky spill, they found a wide slab under the plane of alien metal, in a sturdy enough space for camp just as the dark of night truly coalesced in the recognizable climes behind them. Still fifteen miles separated them from Zenidow, close as its mass appeared. It was all they could see ahead as they set out their belongings on this still quite exposed but broad ledge, the worst of the trip seemingly behind them. That night, no one found sleep, and all necks ached from gazing up without tire at the godly feature before them.

In the morning whatever enervation or soreness they might have felt was easily forgotten. Sand was wiped from eyes, and water was sipped hastily. Ogwold was first to begin the scramble down over the immense seethe of fused boulders that lay all about in huge mounds. The rock here was like the petrified crashing surf of a titanic wave, whose yawning verticality froze ever on the verge of collapse. Leaving the last of these tumbling crests by early noon, the company walked out down a stretch of stony, sloping ground, and here they reckoned with the massive abysses cut in the crust which veined out from the mountain's base.

It seemed at first that there was no way to traverse these stupefying gulfs, and the enormity of Zenidow so near seemed to remind them that what they sought was not to be found. But then Sylna cried out, and along her gaze the company saw a small silver apple, nestled atop a stack of circular plates of rock. Beside it, almost hidden in the shade of that little tower, a vast stone slab had been laid across the empty blackness of the chasm below. So they crossed carefully over this makeshift bridge left by Nubes, and from there were able to walk straight on towards the high silver dimension which was all they could perceive but for the ground beneath their feet.

So they came to the base of Zenidow. Immaculate and unyielding, it stretched beyond sight, a silver firmament domed round their craning necks. This near to it was a grand and immortal silence. The winds faltered, and were turned away; sunlight bent round its surface; the world was held at a distance from its face.

Ogwold was first to place his hand upon its substance, as unto the glassy water of an untroubled lake. Cool and soft, the almost frictionless continuum against his calloused fingers was nothing like the rock into which the entirety of the vast object seemed to bore. The soft rapping of his broad knuckles emitted a hollow, deep echo, like the tumbling of some small and wayward stone in the bowels of a cavern.

Sylna too touched the wall of Zenidow, a little more cautiously, sliding her hands along the perfect smoothness, though quickly she withdrew them and stood brooding. With a sigh, she leaned back against the cold blank plane, removing her hat and wiping the sweaty strands of brown hair out of her eyes. "And now, I have no idea what to do," she said distantly.

Ogwold turned against the wall beside her, pressing his sun-burned shoulder into the chill metal. It was searing hot here in the crater, being the middle of the day. They would not be comfortably in Zenidow's shadow for several more hours. With his back against the mountain, already he felt lighter, gazing out and up at the entire rising structure of the crater through which they'd descended, and high above its rocky rim over the outermost ragged greens of Pivwood; beyond the dazzling canopy reared up the tall snowy peaks of the nearest mountains, blinding in the sun, and he felt then that it might have been ages since Wygram had first flown him through their midst.

Sylna groaned. "I figured some new riddle awaited us here."

Elts had placed her hands against the face of Zenidow soon after Ogwold had first touched it, and she had not yet taken them away. "This substance," she said, enraptured. "It is unlike anything. And yet it reminds me so much of your little sphere, Ogwold." Now she pushed sturdily against the silver, feeling the strength of the mountain.

"You're right!" Ogwold looked around to see where the little orb had wandered off to, as in this latest stretch of their journey it had taken to going about on its own. Only in listening carefully for its drone did he spy it hovering like a little gleaming point of light beside Byron. The mercenary seemed deep in thought, arms tightly folded. But now he approached, striding up to the face of the mountain to join the others, and the sphere zooming along with him was soon snatched out of the air. Raising it between his forefinger and thumb, Ogwold held one massive grey eye up to its surface. "It certainly looks like the same sort of material," he mused.

Suddenly, there was no surface at all to lean on; Ogwold, Sylna, and Elts fell straight back through a plane of cool, bright light, sprawling onto a metal floor precisely of the texture and quality of the mountain itself.

Byron stood still and impassive in the opening, one hand held out as if it had only just rested against the vanished surface formerly solid. Around his figure the wall of Zenidow seemed like silver curtains to have parted, admitting the company, for in all directions the unbroken medium persisted about that new-cloven archway. Below his feet the plane of subtle metal extended perpendicular to that eternal surface rising above and expanding to each side, so that it seemed he stood in another world—one of rock and sky and sun—framed like a picture upon an endless wall of one single immutable substance. From this tiny window unto Altum, he stepped into Zenidow.

The opening closed at once behind him, its noiseless, untraceable fusion severing the alpine wind and glaring sunlight of the outside world. He stood now in a narrow, curving hallway, running seemingly parallel to the crater rim without, and lit diffusely by its own softly luminous metal. Just as on the face of Zenidow, there were no features to the walls, ceiling, or floor, all equally silver and smooth. And just as the exterior bespoke eternal calm, so too was the inner space of the mountain divinely still; if not more so, for the air itself seemed without motion or temperature.

"Well this is surely no mountain. It's a building!" Ogwold shouted laughing, sitting up to see the mercenary. "And Byron's the key!"

"Well, perhaps," Sylna muttered energetically, glancing over the man. "But then, how did Nubes get in? No, it must be something else."

"Maybe he didn't," Ogwold mused, and they were all silent for a moment.

"I envisioned an opening," Byron said evenly, crossing his arms. "Something the Xol taught me."

"And so it is open," Elts murmured, as if finishing her thought aloud. "Perhaps the material of Zenidow is mindful, or at least mouldable in the Fabric, like the elz trees. If you approach it as a closed system, you are excluded, but..."

She rose and moved across the enormous hallway, coming to the wall opposite their entrance. Here she placed her hands against the surface, and closed her eyes. Smoothly and silently, the metal plane rippled out from her influence. As Byron before her, she passed through the opening like the purple, white, and black core of the silver-petalled blossoming of some metal flower, and when the company had followed, those manifest fluid pieces cohered once more behind them, as if always the wall had been at rest, solid and inviolable.

The second hall was just as the first. Still, bright, and gleaming were the high smooth walls; nowhere did a shadow fall, for changeless light was in every span of its surfaces. The sphere came whizzing in loops, and hovered droning among them. Now all were faced with its astounding likeness to the whole of Zenidow's composition, for its pale radiance and silver countenance seemed to have a perfect symmetry with the grand structure around, as if the sphere were a lone drop from the ocean of its mass.

Already Ogwold set his imagination to work upon the next inner wall. But even as he considered its admitting him—his eyes yet to close in thought—the implacable metal parted like silent curtains before them, yielding as that before it. "Ah!" said Ogwold. "Even I can fold the Fabric in this place!"

"I doubt that," Sylna murmured. "It takes many long years of study to master even the simplest forms of folding. No, there is something woven into this place. It has already been sewn in such a way as to be opened by will alone... or is it our will in particular... Nubes' will? What do we all have in common?"

Ogwold seemed unbothered by the witch's condescension. "Then it makes sense that Byron was the first to figure it out. He thinks he can do anything."

The mercenary shrugged, and walked through the opening.

In this way they intersected twenty more such immense concentric hallways, as if the company was a needle piercing and carrying the thread of their intent through many spacious layers of living fabric, each the same as that before it, the next gateway opening with greater and more natural suddenness as now they had all turned their minds together upon the object of their progress, such that in time they did not even pause, and their pace quickened as the continuously warping walls led them deeper into the heart of the strange silver world of still and changeless light. So long went on this process, and so similar were all of the spaces through which they passed, that only many portals since the change had begun did they realize that the slick floor was ramping slightly downward.

Ogwold was the first to notice the other new change in the endless halls, for his ears were most tuned to the language of the sphere; but this voice which he heard now was far greater. It was a timeless, bottomless drone which came from deep within the place. Only he could say—though all believed him—that this strange, fundamental music was of the same timbre as the sphere's, but seemed to represent rather the substrate from which that simple hum was derived, a great medium, an endless field of ultimate sound from which one drop had once issued, now longing to at last return in final harmony. But all could agree that it was more grand and moving than any sound they had ever heard, for unlike the humming of the little orb, it became clear to them as he described it, and as each perceived its tone, it loudened still, as if its becoming was dependent upon their notice.

And then suddenly, one wall was not like the others. As its cousins, so too did it unfold at the intuition of the company's mind, but beyond its blossoming no further hall awaited, and they were stopped at once before a terrifically massive space. The mindful rift unto its vastness unseamed to unseeable distances above and below the flatfooted company, for there was no floor or ceiling at all ahead. They stood on the precipice of an immense, cylindrical room, endless, it seemed, in all dimensions but for width, for they could at least describe the distance of the opposite wall, far off in the unchanging, beautiful light.

But it was less the enormous size of the space that enthralled them than it was the strange object hovering in its centre, tilted on its axis, slowly turning like a silver planet. It was a gigantic sphere, a thousand times in size to that of Ogwold's. But just as its little likeness, it reflected nothing, and glowed with the same divine light that was everywhere throughout Zenidow, now even brighter, though it was not at all harsh to their eyes, for that luminance was strangely contained within the volume of it, seeming to go with it rather than emit from it. It was silver, and subtly white, and it seemed as if its surface, though homogeneous at first glance, swam and shifted like an ever-changing liquid. All of this fine detail was lucid to them even though the enormous orb was quite far from their reach, out in the abyssal light-depth of the great chamber.

Ogwold plucked his own sphere from the air—where it wheeled delightedly about—and brought it close to his eye, looking for the liquidity that he saw in the greater one, for surely now there was no debating whether the one was related to the other. But if the same ripples and tessellations were there, they were too fine to detect at this scale, and the eagerness of the little orb could not be contained for long study, for it slipped from his hand before he could tell much of anything, however, and smoothly soared out into oblivion. They all saw it, somehow, lastly interposed with the enormous sphere, a turning crescent somehow slightly darker, now flashing into the dissimilar. Then it was gone.

Ogwold looked at his hand. "That's my quest over with then," he said plainly.

Sylna smiled. "This great orb must be the Alium. But according to Nubes it is asleep, and we must wake it. He did not tell me much, but he did say that you and I were the only souls which could accomplish this task." She stared unflinchingly out at the great orb. "As to how we are meant to do such a thing..."

Now Elts spoke. "Here is my suggestion. Just as with the doors, make a pathway with your mind." She shut her blue eyes, coiled her tails in thought. The edge of the floor before them shivered, and forthwith a plane of bright silver shot and arced up and out into the void of radiance twinkling. On it went, noiseless and true, until it reached the great orb, where it paused, split, and circumnavigated the Alium in a wide, disc-shaped stage. The sorceress opened her eyes and looked down at the footbridge, her satisfaction visible only in the flick of one tail.

"This sort of work suits the Xol well," said Byron.

Sylna nodded. "So does this entire place suit any active imagination. It is like a dream we all share, made by the mind."

The bridge was sturdy as any part of Zenidow that had so far supported the company, but thin as the edge of a knife, and with nowhere to balance oneself by hand. For Elts such a walkway was quite spacious compared with the spindly elz branches of Wyx, and so she strode off first with easy haste. Behind her went Byron, also with little difficulty, though unhurried, and after him Sylna stepped cautiously along. But Ogwold gaped at the tiny strip of silver arching off towards the sphere, and looked nervously down into the endless yet brilliantly bright oblivion below, and it was some time before he mustered the courage to inch one big foot out onto its surface. It seemed to hold, but just that boot took up nearly the entire space of the bridge. The surface was cold and smooth, and he felt he would easily slip.

I wish, he thought, that my feet could stick to it. And so they did! He could not lift his foot from the surface, so unified it was with the silver. But when he willed it truly in his mind, that fusion was gone. Then he wished for a handrail, and suddenly there it was, a narrow line of strong silver risen up from the edge of the path to accommodate him.

"Might as well make the way a little wider," Byron called back to him, standing with the others before the great orb.

"Smart." Ogwold grinned shakily, and beneath him the bridge expanded so that he could stand comfortably upon it.

Still he went on very carefully, doing his best not to look over the side down into the endless abyss of silver light, moving step by step. The walk was long, however, and he eventually found his stride as he reached the apex of the arch. Finally a good practical use for a dreamer, he thought. My imagination directly influences the very substance of Zenidow! His mind drifted off into a memory of the ocean, that first place of dreams, and for a moment his balance wavered such that a great fear of falling rose again in his gut, and he pressed on, now slowly moving slightly down from the peak of the arc, and coming at last to the wide, silver platform where the others waited for him.

The drone of the sphere was no louder than it had been from the other end of the bridge, but now they could see clearly that its surface was indeed constantly changing. Though it had no texture, and its skin seemed composed of but one silver-white medium, somehow there was an ever-morphing quality played out in ways fine and grand—and everything in between—as they stood spellbound watching this eternal process unfold, filling all their vision, for at this distance the object loomed immense before them, and one needed to turn their head from one side to the other to take in its dimensions.

Even as they walked round the stage which Elts had expanded from the bridge, everywhere the sphere was the same, yet infinitely different. At no second did any one aspect of its being seem ever as it did before, yet somehow it seemed that the sphere as a whole was unchanging and immutable in its essence. Sylna thought it was like a great stream curved in upon itself infinitely flowing, always the same body of water, never the same nature of passage.

As with the face of Zenidow before, Ogwold was first to touch the sphere. Slowly he placed his enormous hand against its face, whose temperature might have been the same as his own, for he could feel the surface by its perfect smoothness. Like a union of wind and water, the sphere did not resist the pressure of his touch, but like the solid form which it appeared to take, it did not give way completely; rather hand and orb met with equanimity, suspended out of time. The brightness washed with gentle grace along his arm, though its grasp was total, and suddenly Ogwold felt that his feet had left the security of the platform.

Now there was in all directions a shimmering, silvery white field of radiance. He peered into this place where there was no time or space, and saw that those changeful and eternally new shapes so displayed upon the surface of the sphere were here living and dying beings, a universe of infinite complexities lacing and weaving, unspooling and dovetailing. As under a great wave of silver-white fabric he was swept up, and from the cores in his back were pulled as by nature his great wing-fins, straining to find some current in the storm of living luminance. Down they churned, back and out and down again, searching blindly, now suddenly taut, hung as on some invisible force familiar to them. As the seething current of light slowed, calmed, carried him along now gently, Ogwold saw that still his big hand was held out in front as if he had only just touched the Alium— but he was alone, alone in an endless white void, floating along, his wings outspread like great parachutes. He lowered his hand. But just as peace had come, so did change arise in the oceanic fabric of the Alium.

Darkness closed in from all sides, cloaking the transforming manifolds of silvery light in shadow, so that Ogwold could but faintly make out his own skin in the dark, until there was only a small mote of radiance left floating before him, a little fey speck of dust hovering just in front of his nose. So rare and delicate appeared the tiny thing, that he sheltered it with his palm and looked down into its spherical, translucent light as though it were the last to shine in the world. Within was curled a shape, a naked Novare child clothed in sleep. Its flesh was silver-white, and it seemed to have no features but for two eyelids softly closed. From beneath those subtle folds seeped all of the light which cocooned its image, and therein all the endless and immortal forms which had danced so freely and ubiquitously before, now so completely retreated and contained, settling hidden and dormant beneath the brow of this young one.

Ogwold turned his hand so that the floating child was cupped, and rested in his palm. "Wake up," he said, peering over its subtle face. "Or all the light will go away." But the creature did not stir.

Now he looked away, and found the surrounding darkness not at all vacant. Transforming shadow and smoke moved in the periphery of the child's light, a realm earlier washed out in uniform radiance. Though its diverse landscapes and living shapes were emboldened by the severity of shade, all moved slowly towards the tiny core of light which was the child in Ogwold's hand, for it was its slightest touch upon their surfaces which gave them being. Their stage was an endless, raging storm of dark. Ahead of its tremendous clouds, citadels and bristling cities of spires of night rose and fell rushing one into the other, and before their constant evolution rose up armies of shadow. At the fore of these surging bodies, alien geometries and withering many-limbed figures confounded the eye just as they dissolved or ballooned into new concepts more stunning. And closer still there peered and shifted the most clear-lit likenesses of many wandering and curious spirits.

But out of these countless forms, three distinctly recognizable figures struck Ogwold's sight, and in the striking were drawn nearer to his vision than the rest, so that all the innumerable peoples of the dark were muddled into the billowing fabric of the great black storm. Of the three, two were small and thin, while the other was tall and thick. Though the lesser in stature seemed alike, they approached in manners wholly different, the first striding forth to behold the source of all light, the other following more cautiously, low of shoulder and nervous of aspect. As they pressed upon the shining place about Ogwold, he saw they were women from the gulfs of the dark. But the third figure was not so coaxed as to reveal more of its image than its solid, grim composure; it stood away in the void of blossoming shadow, only just pronounced from the thousands of other forms behind it.

The striding female spirit was first to reach Ogwold, and he saw at once that it was an apparition of Sylna, smoke trailing from her eyes, her pointed hat barely materializing, as in a shadow following her about, just slightly tardy for her appearance. She held out her hands to receive the child, and though Ogwold hesitated for a moment, as if protecting the little thing, he soon handed it to her, so that she went away and sat cross-legged, hovering there in its bubble of light, cradling it. There she stayed for it seemed a long while, her hat of shadow pulled down over her eyes, and so silent and still was her congress with the child that the second female shape did not come closer.

Ogwold felt then that he became like another distant shadow form in the great curtain of the dark storm, and the events which followed played out before him as on a stage lit by the emanation of the strange child. Even in this timeless place he felt the passage of moments as a great procession. Yet slowly, as before when the darkness had crept into the world, he began to hear a distant singing. It was sweet yet sorrowful, a solemn harmony of wisdom and beauty carrying as from all things, and it grew in volume and richness, until it was an underlying theme of this place, this light around which they were all huddled, and the very leagues of the black storm seemed attuned to its noise.

Now the second figure came forward onto the stage and into the light, and Ogwold saw that it was an apparition of Elts. Her tails were wisps of smoke, and her hair floated like light ash over the pale ice of her eyes. Still with anxious care she approached the light, but certainty was in her step. She took the child from Sylna, and she too sat with it beside her. As well she thought or listened in silence, and the song carried on for far longer than before had Sylna cradled the child in silence. Suddenly the face of the Xol was lifted, and there was a bright light in her eyes not unlike that of the child's. Sylna too was stirred, and together they stood, holding the child in their careful hands. Still the song carried on, though it had faded as all things now into the swirling vortex of darkness all about them, and could only be heard as it was another muted being obscured in the sable fabric.

Whatever knowledge was achieved between them, the child slept on. Witch and Xol turned now to another spirit. Still stark and savage in the dark apart, the third spirit, tall and rough, had begun to pace wolfishly back and forth, a leering and restless spirit as though enraged and kept at bay by the light of a fire in the nighted woods. Yet they went to him even so, and as by whatever secret code he would not approach, so too did he not run. And it was a man that the light began to lick, of short hair and clanking armour. There at last the turning of a ray caught the emerald shard in his sallow face, and Ogwold saw that it was the apparition of Byron. The eyes of the child shot open.

The ogre's stomach pitched, and all that had suspended him vanished. He fell back and away, and the light darkness was stripped of that faint, seeking light which had given it form, such that it was whole, and just as when there had been only light, now there was only shadow. Then there were hard arms wrapped around his waist. A white flash opened his eyes. The silver walls of Zenidow rose up around him, and there above, slowly spinning on its axis, was the great sphere. Only moments must have expired since he had touched the changeful surface, for though he had all but fallen from the platform, his hand was still extended before him as when it had reached for the sphere. Behind him, quaking, split-legged and breathing hard, was Byron who had stopped his falling.

"By the gods you are strong for a Novare," Elts was saying to the mercenary.

"Or this one is light for a Nogofod," he grunted.

Sylna replaced her bow between her shoulders, and laughed a long tinkling laugh. It was refreshing in the tense majesty of their surroundings. "I wouldn't be surprised if he could lift Ogwold off the ground! Carrying that sword around at all hours of the day as he does."

Byron shoved Ogwold forward back into the middle of the walkway, and at once slumped over his knees. "I think not," he said, huffing and straightening up.

Ogwold stumbled, righted himself, and looked back up at the sphere. Then he turned and his face brought the laughter from them all. "I know how it can be woken," he said in a tone none before had heard from his lips. "It told me in a dream."

Sylna's eyebrows shot straight up. Byron squinted, righting himself and crossing his arms. Elts smiled, and said, "It is a mental thing, is it not? You were contacted?" She quickly went to the Alium, and before anyone could stop her, she placed her own bare hand against its surface, and closed her eyes. There was a short silence before she turned back. "Ah. Nothing for me, though it is an exhilarating thing to feel."

"That's part of it," said Ogwold. "All three of you played a different part." He then related the details of his vision. The others listened silently, and when he was done they stood for some time thinking.

Sylna was the first to speak. "This child is of course the Alium. Ogwold was the first to discover it, and so he gives us our vision. I am next by the logic of this vision, to attempt the wakening."

"It wouldn't listen to me," Ogwold said. "But you brought something out of it, a voice. Still, it seemed to me that Sylna understood its meaning as little as I. That's when Elts approached, and then something surely changed."

The Xol murmured. "Perhaps the song is merely the aura of some psychic language more discreet. A member of the Xol could more likely hear it."

"Then what is Byron in all of this?" Sylna cut in.

"He was the last piece," Ogwold said slowly. "When you and Elts brought the Alium to him, he resisted, but even then its eyes were opened."

"I don't know why that should be." Byron's eye shut in annoyance. "I'm only with you now by my oath to Ogwold."

"I believe him, you know," Ogwold said, turning to the others.

"As do I," said Elts. "What you have done for Zelor and I is already deserving of great trust."

Sylna frowned. Returning her gaze to the great sphere, she went and placed one slender, ringed finger against its changeful surface, then followed with the rest of her hand, closing her brown eyes. A few moments passed. There was only the endless drone in the enormous chamber. Sylna could feel the orb slowly rotating beneath her touch, but nothing came to her beyond the strange fluid sensation of its impossible material. She drew away and frowned curiously up at the thing.

"No vision?" Ogwold cocked his head.

Sylna laughed nervously. "Really it is incredible that you had such a contact just through touch. There is something different, I suppose, about you, Ogwold. It can't have gone so naturally for Nubes; he was gone away to Zenidow for many months; and anyhow, on his return, he told me there is only one path to the Alium's dreams, whenever I should come so close."

Ogwold gasped. "Through the Fabric!"

Elts agreed. "Meditation is the only way we mortals might approach an object so inscrutable. Sadly, I am dumb to the Fabric. If Ogwold's dream is a message from within, it is rather Sylna who might find the thread between us."

The witch nodded, stepping forward as she turned her hat nervously against her brow. "I shall try of course, though I cannot perceive the Fabric so easily. My practice requires time and silence."

Sylna unshouldered her bow and knelt before the immense sphere. Her spine was straight but relaxed, chin tilted downward. She closed her eyes, and there was a palpable stillness about her. Slowly she raised the slender white wood, drew back its silver string, and levelled the arrow of her soul. In the draw were tension and resolution both, at first contending one against the other, now finding that sudden equilibrium whose discreet source was her personal window unto the invisible world.

In the moment of total balance, a still hush radiated from her aim, pulsed over the curvature of the great orb and spun smoothly outward through the wide and quickly brightening walls of Zenidow. Where it passed, the high walls were opened, falling into a bottomless silver-white ocean so awesome and changeful in its geometry that the dimensions of ordinary reality were like the slightest froth upon its massive waves.

If even that most superficial foam was too brilliant, the raging walls of the chamber were so clamorously bright and violent in their folding as to blind the eye that lingers. But that evolving and scalding light was almost dim in contrast to the great radiant complexity of the hovering sphere itself—like an enormous all-seeing eye—in the midst of the living metal, as though the sun itself had been lowered into the room, so pure and wondrous that naught but light was in its seamless face.

Eyes hooded over the glare, Sylna attuned her other senses to the Fabric, feeling the gentle precision of her bow, and slowly grew accustomed to its greater glory in this space. The deathless light about her began to even, and in time she was able to look upon it and study its nature, marvelling at how idly Elts had spoken of perceiving such wonders already. Often she had wondered about that chief characteristic in the Xol which Nubes had so commonly described; to be born psychic, to awaken first in the light of the Fabric.

And just as Elts had said, though the transforming sameness of Zenidow's walls seemed to extend their weave out unto the lay of Altum beyond, the great sphere itself seemed wholly unconnected from its tapestry, for not a single thread extruded from its form. All around its circumference she searched, and up and out through the high walls beyond it, the deeps below it, but still it hung before her unattached. So it was that she too began to feel a solitude here, and turned her attention to her own threading, see how it connected to Zenidow, where she might have some link with the mountain. She saw now how thick were these cords between her and the platform upon which she sat, and looking to the company as well revealed that they were all but stitched into the very substance of the place, perhaps more cohesively and neatly than in any other place in the world. This, she thought, must account for their ability to manipulate the walls and open the doors to the heart of the place, but none of these uncountable threads strayed even near to the great orb itself.

And so she discovered it, looking down once more upon herself, as if it had been lying just before her nose, a silken line which led from her own heart almost invisibly out over the open chasm where no other slightest form of Fabric seemed to reach, disappearing into the core of the sphere. It was as if all her life she had followed this one cord all to Zenidow, and she wondered how in her meditations never she had seen it or distinguished it from the other lines which bound her to the world. Softly the bowstring twanged. In astral form Sylna sent forth the manifold of her consciousness in a silver needle streaming into the Alium.

At once the boundaries of its radiance encapsulated her, but there was no pain or increased brightness, so that—accustomed as she now was—she moved lucidly through a field of white. So endless and complete were its dimensions that she could not know whether yet she sped on to its nucleus, or if she had come to a halt there already, or if there was a centre at all, as though she had come upon an entire universe here removed in its physics from that she knew. Then she heard it. A sweet melody of one note, yet somehow rising and falling in tone. Just as the details of the surface of the orb were at once different and impossible to distinguish, the different sounds of this sweet, eternal voice were at once the same sound and many others. Everywhere in the endless white ether where Sylna now floated could this sound, these sounds be heard, so that coming from all places, and welling up within her, she was completely enthralled, and time ceased to be.

It was as Ogwold had described in his dream. Remembering that distant name, Sylna recalled herself. Though the song continued, she was able to distinguish her own soul from its great totality. Now she heard truly that the song was of one voice. Though there were many others, perhaps all voices, helixed and coded into that strand of pure harmony, it came as from one mouth, as from one being, and that being was Alium.

The music of the orb at once became apparent to Elts. It was as though it had always been sung to her, as if she were remembering it even, from a time lost. She listened carefully as the words flowed out over the room and through her blood, coming as from all directions while Sylna sat peacefully in meditation, enraptured in the astral world, while Ogwold and Byron watched her grow ever more attentive on some invisible thread of meaning to which they were not yet privy. Then Elts began to sing:

> *The Old King in a prison of flame waits,*
> *For what gods would oppose his Usurper.*
> *Three so loyal met to forge that rescue*
> *Long ago, but the black fleet's hunt was wise.*
> *Red eyes saw and darkness fell, yet godly*
> *Light struck the rebel forge, and so you lived.*
> *As All on high, the One, had changed their work*
> *Your makers raged against the Enemy,*
> *And cast you sleeping to the endless stars.*
> *Now listen, child—dream of your wakeners.*
>
> *First shall be Ogwold, last son of Caelare,*
> *Brother to Nogofod, spawn of the sea.*
> *Out of wonder comes he to you seeking*
> *Dreams of his own. Where once was a strong arm*
> *Comes loss; where once was a solitude comes*
> *Growth—for in you, he is reborn by touch.*
>
> *Next shall be Sylna, Ardua's heiress,*
> *Daughter of Primexcitum, doomed to fire.*
> *Stormcaller, she will send from Pivwood,*
> *Tall and ancient, the guiding tongues of light.*
> *As you were for her lost father fashioned,*
> *Only she can uplift your voice from sleep.*
>
> *Third shall be Elts, last daughter of Caelare,*
> *Scourge of an Empire in its mantle dressed.*
> *She summons the wind with borrowed magic,*
> *Yet of the Xol there are few so prescient.*
> *Though this place of rest she will seek in wrath,*
> *Her listening mind will be humblest and clear.*

Lastly, among them walks a mortal pure.
Byron—you will know him by his lonesome
Eye, green-stained in the nightmares of his foes.
So too will he cut down the one who would
Destroy you, but knows he not the true weight
Of his blood: the decision rests with him.

Sylna had returned to the surface of the Fabric with the first words of the song, and listened quietly with her bow resting across her lap until it was done. Ogwold sat heavily on the ground as his part of the music was deciphered. Byron's face was all shadow, his arms tensely crossed.

When Elts had finished she bowed her head, and her tails were posed in the aspect of thanks. "Such was the lullaby of the Alium," she said, and there was a long silence thereafter.

"But who is the singer?" Ogwold mused.

Byron smirked. "A fair question."

"Nubes must have heard and interpreted only pieces of it," Sylna muttered. "He knew that I was in it, and Ogwold..."

"But not us," Elts agreed. "Yet here we are."

"You are a child of Caelare," said Sylna to the sorceress with dignity. "As are you, Ogwold."

"But what about you!" Ogwold bellowed, hardly controlling the volume of his voice. "You are related to Primexcitum. He's the god of the gods! And he's your dad!"

"No, he cannot be my father. I already have one! And Primexcitum has been imprisoned for millennia." Sylna did not seem as shocked as she perhaps should have been, but still her eyes were wide with uncertainty. "I had a vision of his burning cell when I first came to Muewa, and discerned that I had some relation to him. If the song is accurate, I am at most a descendant far removed in blood." She stood and removed her hat, rotated it awkwardly in her hands. "But... that is not important. If these are our instructions, we must comprehend the stanza concerning Byron." She suddenly fitted the hat back to her head snugly and composed herself.

The mercenary grunted, unchanged in countenance. "Seems like all it said was that I'm not like you all, half god or whatever."

"Because you are mortal, you make the final decision..." Ogwold thought out loud. "It's just like Wygram said, about Primexcitum's Decree! He didn't think the gods should ever bother the mortals, and so mortals can make their own decisions. But clearly the gods are involved in our doings in some ways. Maybe this waking of the Alium is too big of a decision to make without mortal input." He turned gazing up at the vast sphere.

Sylna began now fully to pace back and forth. "Certainly I am reminded of that philosophy... Really the whole idea behind it is to make sure that there is free will for mortals as there is for gods."

Now Elts spoke up. "We must consider why Primexcitum made such a decree. He was inspired by his own maker, All, who promised not to interfere in his own life. But in the song, All seems to have done this very thing in completing the Alium. God broke Its word; but not quite yet, because the Alium is asleep. In fact, I believe All itself is in a way incarnated in this orb. If we waken it, we are breaking that primordial promise, we are bringing All into the universe All promised not to interfere with. Our own free will may be at stake, and certainly the free will of the gods as well."

"I see what you mean," said Sylna. "We may be standing in the very presence of the One incarnated."

"Sounds good to me," said Byron gruffly. "I have no issue with waking up this Alium. It's easy enough to recognize the ships of Duxmortul in the song as well. In that case, this thing was made to defeat the Shadow." Byron reached back and hefted Azanog onto his shoulder, grinning.

"You must be right!" Sylna gasped.

Elts' tails flicked. "Well I suppose it really is your decision, Byron. I won't stop you."

Ogwold's head swung speaker to speaker, his jaw loose. "Hold on a moment! We might lose our free will? And how do we know All is going to help anyone but the gods?"

"You're one to talk," Byron laughed. "You trust everyone you meet!"

"Perhaps the Alium is not exactly All itself, but a different spirit imbued." Now it was Elts who sat upon the platform, for she had fully accepted the mercenary was set in his mind, and the voice and the words of the song had moved her deeply.

Sylna, however, was still quite anxious, and could not keep still. "Even so, it is a power far beyond not only our own gods but the High Gods as well."

"If we're all going to die anyways, we've got nothing to lose," Byron said with sudden exuberance. "I doubt this marble can be harmed, so I'll use the key I know best," he grunted, stepping forward swiftly; then he swung out his sword into the living silver light.

The blade arced high through the air, and came crashing down through the side of the great orb. Ogwold, Sylna, and Elts shielded their eyes and staggered back from the exploding halo round the stoic mercenary. Torrents of light erupted about the path of his weapon's edge as it drove deep into the luminous, seething flesh, but Byron only gritted his teeth and began to laugh wildly as he pressed onward, advancing on his lean legs until he was swallowed up in radiance. Then there was a tremendous, brilliant flash of light, and all was dark.

Clean, earthy air rushed over Byron's face, and he blinked his eye, still emblazoned with the blinding face of the sphere. Slowly the flash faded and dispersed into multiple points of light, which were the stars, dusted across a cloudless navy firmament. All around were the black peaks of the high mountains, and to the east but the long, neon blue moon Xeléd cresting their craggy shoulders. The hilt of Azanog was still tightly crushed in his fist.

He was out in the crater, but sitting up he could see clear across to the other side, for the great mountain Zenidow had entirely vanished. In its place before him was an infinitely deep and dark pit, as though whatever once caused the vast caldera in the land had now sunk further down into the bowels of Altum.

Byron was seated upon a broad ledge some twenty meters from the abyss. Beside him was splayed the grey hulk of Ogwold, fast asleep, and behind them Sylna slumped against a smooth boulder. The witch started at the sound of his boots upon the rock, but the ogre required many a powerful shake before rolling over and yawning cavernously, blinking his eyes, and then leaping up with a holler as he took in the strange sight. His bellowing woke Elts, who they now saw nearer to the rim of the great hole.

Silently the company gathered at the edge, and stood in awe of its vacancy, peering into the endless dark. Way down in the deepest, purest black, the space seemed more empty and wondrous than even the spaces between the stars on a moonless night. But even as Ogwold was thinking so, he thought he saw a single such pinprick of light far away in the centre of the world, and it seemed now to be drawing closer and closer. Sylna spotted it next, then Elts, and Byron, but none spoke as it grew brighter and more lucid.

Suddenly and swift as an arrow it shot silently past their eyes and up into the night sky, arching across the coal-beds of stars and banking off along the crater's face. Slowly, gently hovering, it came to pause not unlike the little sphere which Ogwold had brought so far into the mountains, yet as it now approached them they saw it was not a sphere at all.

Floating towards them just above the rock was a being of amorphous shape, its texture and arrangement of parts slowly changing, as though it were a collection of silver and white liquids suspended in space. It swam through the air like an amoeba, then ceased to move when it was but a meter removed from the company, hovering as in observation.

Suddenly it condensed into a slim body no taller than an adolescent Novare, which sprouted silver limbs like little arms and legs. Between its nimble shoulders lastly formed rose a simple, oval head. Upon its seamless surface there opened wide and curious two large white eyes, and a soft, thin mouth.

"You were in my dream," said the silver child.

Grady Lynch grew up shooting hoops and telling stories. He loves all fiction, but there is no form of art so inspiring to him as the novel. *Alium* is his first contribution to that sphere. In even its most minor characters and smallest themes, it speaks to all those books and authors without whose spirits it could never have existed.

CPSIA information can be obtained
at www.ICGtesting.com
Printed in the USA
BVHW071545200922
647490BV00001B/42

9 781928 011798